DUNGEON LORD

ABOMINABLE CREATURES

HUGO HUESCA

PROLOGUE

The Lotian faced some of the most dangerous assassins the ancient kingdom of Akathun had ever birthed. They didn't like him. It was clear by the way their fingers twitched near the sheaths of their daggers they feared him. And fear could be more dangerous than hatred.

He knew full well that showing even the slightest hint of hesitation could end up with his throat slit and his body dumped unceremoniously into Undercity's canals. It'd resurface on some beach outside the city, bloated and half-eaten.

No one would miss him. His master, after all, did not tolerate failure.

The Lotian smiled and said, "Grand Master Gezved, you look awfully tense. There's no need to worry. You've my assurance, I'm here tonight as a friend."

The Akathunians reeled at the implicit threat: the suggestion that a lone man was dangerous enough to make the Grand Master of the Unseen Brotherhood be afraid despite being surrounded by a dozen of his best assassins. The Akathunians had ten thousand experience points pooled together in that room, and not a single one of them would help if they earned the wrath of the Lotian's master.

One of Gezved's brutes scowled and made a surreptitious sleight of hand when he thought the Lotian wasn't looking. From his sleeve, he produced a tiny metal cylinder that held a sharp steel wire Akathunians used to skillfully cut throats and sever limbs.

Without looking at the man, Master Gezved gestured for him to stand down. The Lotian's smile gained an inch.

"We're aware of your traditions, Malikar. 'He comes at night, bearing gifts...' No, I don't think Lotians either know or care about loyalty or friendship," Gezved said. "Since your arrival in Constantina, you've brought with you nothing but doom. Look at what Nicolai's revolutionaries brought on us after their demise. Weren't you their sponsor? The Inquisition roams the streets, forcing my men to hide in the shadows, and my splendid Brotherhood is relegated to doing business in the lowest slums just to stay away from the gaze of the griffins patrolling the skies. No, Lotian. I should have your throat cut and be rid of you!"

Ah. The honorable assassin. The Lotian fought off an almost overwhelming impulse to smirk with disdain. It was pathetic how people like Gezved believed pretending to care about unspoken rules, about honor and loyalty, would somehow redeem them from the terrible deeds they performed every day. Just ask the slaves the Akathunians kept in cages, languishing over their own dung, how they felt about Gezved's honor.

Then again, the Lotian wasn't here to make friends. He was here to deliver a message.

"You honor me, Grand Master, by comparing my humble self to that of the Boatman himself," he said. "But I am a mere mortal, stranded in this Murmur-forsaken country of Starevos with little to show for it. I have precious few friends in this city, and, like it or not, the Unseen Brotherhood could find a very profitable friendship if we were to sit down and talk without all this... uncivilized mistrust."

The tension in the room felt like a rope pulled to its limit, close to snapping. They were at the highest point of the Charcoal Tower, the Unseen Brotherhood's infamous headquarters. The room itself was shaped like a wedge, with ample open windows letting in the cool sea air, while the vaporous silky curtains flowed sensually behind the Akathunians, who were dressed in their black, tight tunics with open necks that revealed skin covered in tattoos.

There was nothing behind the Lotian but the closed door from where he'd come and the pair of windows to his sides. The floor was bare, revealing the silver engravings that formed a concentric magical circle with a powerful anti-magic field in place. It was a smart detail. The Akathunians excelled at physical confrontations —at ending fights before they even started. With an anti-magic effect in place, they robbed any possible attacker of their best advantage over the assassins.

"So many words, yet so little meaning. You love the sound of your own voice, don't you, Malikar?" the Grand Master asked. "Speak your piece and let us be done with this farce. After that, I'll decide what to do with you."

"How kind of you. Though it turns out, I've a gift for you with me," the Lotian said. "Nothing as trifling as a trinket, Grand Master. Something that a man with such a high Spirit rank may find more valuable. Indeed, I bring you the gift of prophecy."

A stunned silence spread through the Akathunians ranks like a plague. Then, after an instant, the laughter started. The Lotian let them have their moment, smiling himself, as if he were in on the joke.

"Prophecy!" Gezved exclaimed, smirking and looking over his shoulder at his subordinates. "Women's games, nothing more! A way to pass the time in the hot nights of Akathun while waiting for our return. Malikar, it's not the way of men to pierce the veil of time. Ours is the present. You may keep your prophecies, they're of no value to us."

"Ah, you misunderstand me again," the Lotian said, placing a hand on his chest to show his remorse. "My mistake, Grand Master. The warning I bring is not magical in nature—indeed, it's true that not even the most powerful Diviner can predict the future. If they were to try, Objectivity would erase them without fail. No. Only the Shadow Tarot can create images of what *may* be, and the Lady of Secrets won't part with her favorite Artifact. But even she knows far less than she thinks. My personal knowledge allows me to make predictions, based not on magic but from logic alone. This is how I can say I bring a prophecy. Because I know something the Unseen Brotherhood does not."

The smiles disappeared, much to the Lotian's pleasure.

"My patience runs thin, Lotian," said the Grand Master.

The Lotian nodded as if he were in a heated debate and his opponent had just made a decent point. "Have you looked from on high while a city burns to the ground with all its inhabitants trapped inside? At night, with the golden fire reaching up to the sky, it's truly a glorious view fit only for the gods themselves," the Lotian said. "There's a new player in town. Someone who is shaking up the balance of power in the city. They're the *real* reason the Inquisition has set up shop in Mullecias Heights. I know that the Thieves Guild likes to pretend that we're dealing with an ordinary smuggler, but the Brotherhood are more realistic, are you not? We've all seen the signs that a Dungeon Lord has infiltrated Constantina, and he cares little for the old ways."

At that, Gezved frowned. "What do *you* care about upholding the old ways? You're an agent of chaos. Your mere presence risks everything we've worked for since our arrival to this continent."

"Chaos invoked with a purpose is the tool a man of destiny may use to build a new world order, Grand Master. But if wielded by inexperienced hands whose only purpose is to enrich themselves and their own... then chaos becomes the true bringer of death," said the Lotian. "Here's my prophecy. Soon enough, Undercity shall burn. It may be too late to stop the pieces from falling off the board even if you were to kill the newcomer today. And when the fire comes and whatever is left of the Brotherhood stands over the ashes of your life's work, perhaps you'll be more eager to accept my master's gifts." The Lotian bent his knee. "That's all I've to say to you. Until we meet again, Grand Master."

The Akathunian's lips parted and turned into a grimace of anger. "You come into my house uninvited, speaking nonsense that can only be interpreted as vague threats against my people, and then you pretend we'll simply let you leave? I don't care who —or what—is this creature you call master, no one defies my Brotherhood and lives!"

At that, his brutes charged at the Lotian, swift like the wind, their legs propelling them forward much faster than a normal human could move without talent-enhancement. Some bared their daggers at the Lotian like beasts showing their fangs before the kill, and he could see the glint of the razor-wire between the hands of the rest. A few men remained behind and pulled small crossbows from behind their backs.

The Lotian had been expecting all this. With one hand, he reached for one knife he kept on his jacket and threw it at the Grand Master, watching the blade draw an arc as it soared through the air, aimed straight at Gezved's chest. The old man reacted a little too late—even *advanced reflexes* were useless if you activated them too slowly to do something—but one of his Assassins jumped into the knife's path at the last second. The Akathunian grunted when the knife pierced his chest, then collapsed, warm blood soaking his black tunic.

The rest of the Akathunians paused in doubt for a mere instant, torn between their objective and their sacred duty to protect their Grand Master. For the Lotian, this second of hesitation marked the difference between life and death.

The window to his right was the nearest. He turned his back to the Akathunians, ducking under the path of the crossbow bolts, and sprinted toward it as fast as he could. It was wide open. Without stopping, and without bothering to give even one more taunt to the Brotherhood, he jumped through—

And he was out into the open, frozen in the middle of the air for a fraction of a second while his momentum fought with the forces of gravity, but lost.

He dropped like a rock, with a volley of bolts soaring after him. His cloak fluttered like black succubus wings, and the twin moons beckoned him, two Queens in a kingdom of darkness and stars. Behind him, the Charcoal Tower was a blur, and the buildings of the city below rose to meet him. Far in the distance, he could see the district of Mullecias Heights, their lavish white streets shining gold under the lamplight.

Constantina was beautiful, and it would bring the Lotian much pleasure to watch it burn.

But in the meantime, it was good that his fall had brought him far enough away from the Unseen Brotherhood's anti-magic circle that he could cast a single, well-chosen spell.

"*Levitate!*" he exclaimed, canceling his meeting with the floor mere instants before it was too late to reschedule.

When the Akathunians reached the bottom of the tower and poured into the streets like angry shadows, the Lotian was nowhere to be found.

CHAPTER ONE

FALL OF THE REBELLION

A black sea of chitin surrounded the grassy hill. Fangs were piercing flesh, waves were crashing against one another, a conflagration of clicking mandibles filled the air with white noise. Ichor soaked the grass, pooling into the terrain, dyeing the silver strands of spiderweb that covered the landscape blue. Beyond and around the fighting mass of spiderlings, spider warriors clashed together, trying to run the other through with their horns while doing their best to avoid being speared in turn. Right behind the lines of clashing warriors, the princesses of both sides ordered their troops around the battlefield, trying to outmaneuver the enemy or goad them into making a mistake. In the distance, the figures of three Spider Queens lumbered behind the fight with the protection of their royal guard, looking for the right opportunity to join the fray.

Dungeon Lord Edward Wright, Master of the Haunt, stepped away from his forces and into the thick of the front-lines. At once, enemy spider warriors rushed him, hissing, fangs dripping poison through their clacking mandibles. Ed swung his spear and drew a long arc in front of them, forcing them to stop to avoid their front legs being cut through.

From the corner of his eye, Ed saw a horned spider jump at him, legs bent forward and her horn aimed right at his neck. He had been expecting it, as he knew the combat style of spider warriors well. Almost without thinking, he activated his *improved reflexes* talent and had the world slow down around him. The spider's path through the air became a placid lunge.

Ed planted both feet in the ground, hefted his lance with both hands above his head, and ran her through mid-air, driving the spear's tip through the connection between her torso and abdomen, causing blue goo and guts to fly everywhere. Ed gritted his teeth at the added weight. He pushed his knees upward and forced the dying spider skyward, almost as if he were hefting a bleeding flag into the sky. He turned around and used his back to bring the spider crashing down against one of her sisters, who had jumped just an instant after her. The impact rattled Ed's bones and strained his joints, but it was overshadowed by the grim satisfaction he felt at seeing both spiders crumple as if made from wet paper, their legs twitching as they rolled on the grass.

The effect of *improved reflexes* ended, leaving him with a barely noticeable strain on his body. The *vitality* potion he drank before the battle was still in effect, which meant he could take a couple risks with his talents.

At once, the rest of the horned spiders closed in, their mandibles and horns jabbing and thrusting toward him. Ed wore a breastplate and thick leather armor underneath, courtesy of Undercity's Thieves Guild. Thanks to his *pledge of armor*, he deflected the few spider's attacks that managed to reach him as if they had been pulled away by an invisible force.

And for each bite and horn thrust, Ed struck at them thrice as fiercely, gritting his teeth as particles of blue goo sprayed across his face. His spear was slick with blood, threatening his hold. His cloak was heavy with mud and gore, and it muffled all sounds coming from him, turning him into a silent killer in the middle of the chaotic battlefield.

Three horned spiders came to reinforce the group of five he was dealing with. Before they reached their allies, Ed speared one of the first group straight through her eye, steel breaking chitin with a terrible crunch. The other four rushed at him and he jumped away, trying to pull his spear free, but his grip slipped at the last instant.

A sharp spider leg left a long scratch on his chest-plate as he activated his *reflexes* again and jumped back, leaving his spear and reaching for his sword.

Alone, Ed was more than a match for these seven horned spiders. Still, he was only a mortal. If they overwhelmed him with their numbers…

But, of course, he had numbers of his own. That was the whole point of being a Dungeon Lord. As the spiders rushed him before he had a chance to draw his steel, magical purple crows flew past Ed, crackling as they did.

The crows smashed into the spider's faces, aiming at their eyes, and exploded into a shower of sparks and scorched exoskeletons. In an instant, eyes popped and hair caught fire. The spiders screamed in agony and scrambled. Ed drew his sword and dove through the confusion, hacking and slashing his way across the melee in an almost blind rage. More reinforcements flooded in, but now his own horned spiders fought alongside him, strands of web flying over his head in all directions as copies of himself appeared in different spots of the battle, drawing the attention of the rebels away from the real Dungeon Lord.

Ed grinned as one of his copies only a couple steps away was webbed and speared through by the horns of three horned spiders. They hissed in triumph and then in confusion as the illusion dissipated into uncountable raindrops. Their confusion didn't last long, though, because the real Ed jumped in and hacked the horn off the nearest spider.

He was about to deal the critter a killing blow when a tough, elvish-looking woman reached his side. She had powerful legs and muscles taut like steel chords.

"*Cleave!*" Marshal Kes bellowed, and her sword drew an impossibly accurate arc through the grouped-up horned spiders, striking each of them with equal force before moving on to the next. In a single instant, she had killed almost as many horned spiders as Ed had in the last several minutes of the fight.

"Hey!" he called, frowning. "I was dealing with those."

The former-mercenary-turned-minion snorted. "You're covered in sweat, Ed. Time for a breather." The Haunt's spiders streamed past them and forced the rebels away.

Now that she pointed it out, Ed realized he was soaked. He studied the front-line as the ebb of battle flowed away from him. "I can still go for a while longer."

"Maybe, but your casters are almost out of spells," Kes said. "Are you a foot-soldier or a general, my Lord?"

Ed clenched his jaw. His blood was running hot in his veins, clamoring for the thrill of battle and victory while his heart raced in his chest, demanding the broken corpses of his enemies to be laid on bloody piles at his feet.

His temper was getting the better of him again. That kind of attitude could get him killed.

"Very well," he said quietly. "Let's go. But if Clovis still won't make a move, I'm coming back."

Kes nodded and, without taking her sight away from the battle, signaled with her free arm.

"*Nimble feet!*" Alder called from somewhere far behind them. A frantic flute melody fought the noise of the battle. The music lifted a weight from Ed's shoulders, making it as if his body weighed nothing at all.

Ed and Kes ran back toward four approaching figures headed their way through the allied streams of horned spiders. Six hell chickens, feathers black like night were bound together by leather straps and ropes. Monster Hunter Kaga and Yumiya rode the two at the front, and the others were meant for Ed and his friends to use in their ride away from battle.

Technically, hell chickens were much more dangerous than horned spider warriors. Or, at least, the Haunt's strain were. They had more in common with a velociraptor than a real chicken, with claws capable of gutting a human in the blink of an eye and a beak hard enough to puncture chain-mail.

Ed and the Monster Hunters had tried to use the hell chickens in combat for months now, but it was harder than they originally thought. They were mean sons-of-bitches, and no matter how much the kaftar trained them, the creatures were just as likely to attack the Haunt's minions as they were its enemies.

This group was the more amicable of the bunch, which wasn't saying much. Thick sheets covered their beaks and claws, their gazes averted by black squares to keep them from seeing anything that would piss them off—which was pretty much everything.

For all that trouble, though, they made for fantastically agile mounts. Ed and Kes climbed on their respective hell chickens using quick, practiced motions while making sure the creatures never saw them at all. Soon enough, Lavy and Alder reached them as well and mounted up.

"Finally!" The young man exclaimed. His blond hair grew wild in all directions, with blue eyes constantly wandering into the clouds. "I'm out of spells already. That illusion combo is more magic-intensive than I thought."

"You have a sword, Alder," Kes reminded him. "You're decent enough with it, you know. You should use it more."

"Agreed," Lavy said. She was a pale young woman wearing clothes more appropriate for a ball than a fight. She had purple eyes that marked her Lotian heritage, and messy black hair in dire need of a brush. "It's improper for a man to cower while others do the fighting."

"Lavy, you were right next to me!" Alder pointed out. "And you know how to use a sword as well."

"Maybe, but I'm far more valuable as a spellcaster than as a mere warrior."

They rode away from the thick of the battle into a nearby hill that Ed had chosen days before for that exact purpose. Once there, he steadied his mount—the smell of spider ichor was making it hungry, and he had to pull hard at the reins to stop it from charging back onto the battlefield. In response, the creature craned its long, feathered neck and tried to snap at Ed, but the straps clenching its steel-sharp beak stopped it.

"Easy, Eyegouger," Ed said, patting the creature's neck.

Next to him, Marshal Kessih of the Haunt stood uneasily on her own mount. "Now that I stopped you from trying to solo the entire rebellion, I'll admit waiting here makes me uneasy too. Catching our breath while our forces fight in front of us, it doesn't feel right—even if they're just horned spiders." Her right hand hovered over the sheathed longsword hanging at her side. Her hand clasped the reins of her mount hard enough to whiten the knuckles of her three remaining fingers.

"It's all part of the plan, Kes," said Lavy, Head Witch of the Haunt. She was dressed in a pompous purple dress, made for her by the human inhabitants of the Haunt. It had brass buttons tightening the silk corset, which had been sewed to resemble a spider's web. Her thin cape was of a shiny black which, combined with her sickly pale complexion, gave her a mystical look she no doubt enhanced on purpose. A collar made of skull-shaped beads hung around her neck. The only mismatching parts of her apparel were her leather riding boots and thick leather gloves, meant to protect her fingers in case the straps around her mount's beak failed to keep it shut. Not that it'd make much of a difference against the huge serrated fangs that the hell chicken sported. "If Laurel is to secure the loyalty of the rebellion, we must deal with all the Queens at once," she said. "No use spending our energy dealing with mere warriors."

"And also you don't expose your neck to all those mandibles

before you run out of spells," came the response of the Bard Alder Loom, Chronicler of the Haunt.

"Alder, you were cowering at the rear!" Lavy repeated.

Ed squinted, keeping his eyes on the battlefield. "If you must bicker, do it quietly, you two. I'm trying to pay attention."

That earned him a disbelieving snort from Lavy. "No way. You mean to say you can tell what's going on? It's just spiders as far as the eye can see!"

Ed turned back to face a very confused Witch. "You mean you don't know the difference between our spiders and those of the rebellion?"

Lavy shrugged. "They are spiders, Ed," she said simply. "There's no difference, as far as I'm concerned."

"I have to admit, even for me it's hard to follow the course of the battle," Kes admitted.

"Well," Ed said, "let's see." He pointed at a melee between several spider warriors. "Look at their midsections. Laurel's brood has gray and black hair over their chitin, and they're usually leaner and smaller than the rest. Queen Pirene's are sturdier and their mandibles are fatter. You can see them by our flanks, reinforcing our warriors' charge. The ridges in the abdomen of Queen Bumelia's brood are serrated instead of interconnecting, which makes sense, given they're more aggressive. Those two princesses that are trying to rush the rebel Queens are Bumelia's." He pointed them out. The two princesses were trying to carve a path through the thick of Gloriosa's royal guard, with little success, their warriors slowly giving ground to the enemy. "They must retreat soon. The rebels will probably try to flood through the gap."

"Right," Kes said, frowning hard. "Laurel should reinforce them before the entire flank collapses. What is Bumelia thinking?" Queen Bumelia was nowhere to be seen, the same as Laurel and Pirene.

Ed gave her a grin, then went on. "Now, for the rebels. Queen

Cornelia and Queen Gloriosa are young regents—" Laurel had killed their mothers during the spring skirmishes "—so their brood is still growing. Cornelia's spiders are the ones with the red and brown hairs and the curved horns. Gloriosa's are impossible to miss—they're albinos. Finally, there's Queen Clovis. Her brood has emerald eyes. She's the one about to flood Bumelia's flank. Clovis is one tough lady—older than anyone here."

Spider Queen Clovis was the size of a warhorse, with mandibles that were strong enough to crush plate armor. Gray scars stood in place of three of her eyes, and the rest of her chitin was covered in deep scratches that were the horned-spider-equivalent of medals and trophies from past battles. She reminded Ed of Queen Amphiris, Laurel's predecessor. While Ed was speaking, the rebel Queen Clovis and her royal guard were tearing into Bumelia's princesses, routing their formation into disarray. Clovis attacked from one flank, using the royal guard of Gloriosa as an anvil—pushing the princesses against each other and forcing them to retreat. Clovis' spiders chased them, their mandibles severing legs and their webs catching on their enemies, slowing them down. Clovis herself closed in only when it was obvious there was little risk for herself, but her presence still meant a huge morale increase for the Rebellion, since she was now the first Queen in the thick of the fighting. As a result, the rebel spiders fought around her, pushing back Laurel's forces.

"Ed..." Kes started, her impassive martial stance faltering at what seemed to be the Haunt's first disastrous engagement. "Perhaps we ought to drop a few fireballs on them. Thin the ranks a bit."

"And risk having them disperse?" Ed said, shaking his head. "No way. We have them right where we want them."

"I mean, maybe we shouldn't be so close to the action," Lavy called from the rear, sounding nervous.

"Look at the spiderlings," Ed said, pointing at them. "You'll understand."

Laurel's spiderlings weren't behaving normally.

The ebb and flow of black chitin moved with an energy that resembled mercury when compared against the sluggish, honey-like waves of the rebels. Some were jumping in the air like fleas while others enveloped and overran their counterparts.

"No," said Lavy, "I really don't. Spiderlings look even *more* alike than adult horned spiders!"

"See, spiderlings never retreat from these kind of battles—if they do, the Queens would rather just kill the entire lot and replace them all," Ed explained. Horned spiders didn't care much for the survival of their offspring between larval stage and adulthood. "To get past them, the other spiderlings need to kill them all, which almost never happens—there isn't much of a difference in the number of spiderlings, or their strength, between broods. They're pretty much evenly matched. This is on purpose.

"A lone spiderling is useless against adult horned spiders, but if they engulf a spider warrior, it usually means a bad time for her. To protect themselves against enemy spiderlings, the broods use their own, which keeps both groups locked for the duration of a battle."

Lavy shook her head. "Okay, so I don't see how that stops us from becoming spider meal in a few minutes—"

"Our spiderlings fell into a couple of barrels of Andreena's Agility potion," Ed said.

As if responding to his words—but actually reacting to an order given by a nearby princess—the Haunt's spiderlings charged as one through the ranks of the rebels', overrunning them in seconds. In normal circumstances, spiderlings were evenly matched, so the extra ranks in Agility due to Andreena's brew meant a massive, completely overwhelming advantage. About half of the Haunt's numbers forced themselves past the wall of enemy spiderlings, and the remaining half rushed in to keep the rebels from pursuing.

The spiderlings ran and jumped through the files of warriors, headed straight for Clovis. The Queen saw them coming and ordered a retreat, but suddenly, the retreating warriors from Bumelia's brood weren't running for their lives anymore. They were back in the fray, forcing Clovis' royal guard against her, leaving little space to maneuver. A cluster of Pirene's princesses led a charge against both Clovis and Gloriosa, who was trying to break the sudden resistance from Bumelia's troops.

The enhanced spiderlings arrived straight into the midst of the mess and turned the chaotic center of the battlefield into an even more confusing affair. They launched themselves against enemy warriors and princesses and hung there for dear life. Their mandibles were too small to pierce through the adult chitin, but a covered spider couldn't fight as well—they barely could see—and many of them panicked and thrashed about, giving Laurel's forces an opening to run them through with their horns.

"See?" Ed said. "It's all under control."

"If you say so," Lavy muttered.

Kes placed a hand on Ed's shoulder. "Over there! The other two rebel Queens are rushing in."

Seeing Clovis' predicament, Gloriosa and Cornelia were leading an attempt to rescue their de facto leader. Laurel's forces near their charge retreated—the combined might of the three groups of royal guards were too strong—and allowed the Queens to reach Clovis. With three Queens now on the battlefield and none on the Haunt's side, the tides of battle changed directions. A brave group of spiderlings tried to cover Gloriosa's white face to threaten her eyes, but she shook her body like a wet dog and the little critters flew off.

"Finally," Ed said, watching the three furious Queens take control of the center. They and their retinues may have been surrounded by Haunt's troops, but this only meant it was a target-rich environment. "That's my cue. Kes, do you mind?"

The Marshall blinked, then caught the meaning of Ed's words.

She grabbed him from the neck of his leather armor and kept him steady.

"Thanks," Ed said. "Be back in just a minute. *Murmur's reach.*"

There came a flash and the stink of sulfur, and his soul left his body, taking the shape of a black cloud.

Ed swept above the battlefield. Being a disembodied spirit was an eerie experience. For the duration, all his physical attributes dropped to zero, leaving him only with his Mind, Spirit, and Charm. His eyesight and hearing were replaced by a radar-like sixth sense. Living creatures were bright shapes against the dimmer background of the forest, and a dark expanse with distant stars glimmering in the distance replaced the blue sky. In this form, he felt no exhaustion, nor hunger, nor thirst. There was a metaphysical, faint, inhuman coldness. As a spirit, all his emotions came muted, like they were sifted through a cloth, and the sensation of coldness intensified the longer he spent in the form, as did his emotional detachment. Thankfully, it all went back to normal as soon as he was back inside a body—either his or someone's else.

He wondered what would happen if he refused to find the body of a minion to posses, or didn't return to his own. Probably nothing good. Somewhere below the bright shapes of the three rebel Queens were surrounded by a tightly knit formation of lights.

He descended through the battlefield and went underground. Most of the creatures there were minions of his, directly or indirectly. Once he had selected a suitable body, there came an overpowering sensation of *suction,* and he shot inside like a leaf captured in a tornado.

A blink later, he was a spider warrior, with the physical attributes of his new, temporary body. He glanced around with his multiple eyes, which were shining with an eldritch green light, showering the cavern in threatening shadows and throwing menacing reflections on the chitin of the spiders that surrounded him.

Being a spider was just as hard to explain as trying to describe the color red to a blind man, and Ed had never produced an accurate portrayal, to Alder's disappointment. Walking on eight legs was as natural as walking on two. Eating fleas wasn't delicious, but it wasn't unpleasant either—it was akin to brushing your teeth at night. Producing spiderweb *was* pleasurable, but in an entirely glandular way.

"Ah, welcome, Lord Wraith," said Queen Laurel. She was hunched at the end of the cavern—which was barely enough to contain her bulk—next to her two subordinate queens, Bumelia and Pirene. These two stared at Ed with unbridled fear. *Murmur's reach,* the possession spell, was one of the better known powers of a Dungeon Lord—and one of the most feared.

"Queen Laurel," Ed greeted back. "Your enemies are right where you want them. Shall we?"

As a spider, Ed shared the creature's instincts without being bound by them. It was the mental equivalent of moving into a new apartment whose previous owner hadn't yet finished moving out.

Said previous owner was still present, somewhere in the basement, peeping through a doorknob and hoping that Ed wouldn't get her body grievously wounded—or worse—while he was at the helm. The waves of the spider's apprehension flooded him.

Don't worry, he sent back. *I'm only here for a few seconds.* He added an emanation of calmness to his thoughts, to better keep the spider at ease.

"We shall," Laurel said. "Have your drones do me the honors and I promise the battle will be over before you've had the chance to reach it."

Ed vaulted out of the spider warrior and flew out of the cavern toward the bright spot over a distant hill—his own body. This time, the path was straight, as if he was riding an arrow shot straight at his heart, with him having no control over it. He saw his body approach, and then, in a blink, he was himself again.

Air rushed into his lungs. While he was away, his brain kept all his base functions going, but coming back in still felt like breaching the surface of a lake after remaining underwater for long enough to black out.

The metaphysical cold dissipated. Kes released her grip on his back, and he steadied Eyegouger, careful not to expose any limbs to the angry hell chicken.

The ground a few paces away from the three rebel Queens collapsed inward, forming a coarse ramp from which a stream of angry horned spiders flowed out, led by Laurel and the other Queens, charging straight at the heart of the enemy resistance before Clovis had a chance to react.

Laurel clashed against Clovis with the strength of a landslide. Chitin splinters exploded in all directions. Legs broke, web flew everywhere, and the Queens hissed and roared like angry predators. Steam rose out of open wounds... and then Laurel broke out of Clovis' range, leaving the other Queen heavily wounded. Laurel allowed her royal guard to finish the job, which they did with exceptional enthusiasm, first dispatching Clovis' winded guards, and then beginning the slow process of webbing Clovis into immobility. The rebel Queen tried to fight, snapping at the warriors with frothing mandibles and brandishing her horn as if it were a sword. The warriors evaded her attacks, always keeping a safe distance as they let exhaustion and blood-loss take their toll on the massive Queen.

Around them, Bumelia and Pirene repeated that exact scene against their counterparts, while the Haunt's clusters finished breaking the rebels' ranks. Spider princesses ran for their lives while covered in Agility-enhanced spiderlings, and warriors pursued them with their horns aimed down toward their abdomens. Ed knew if a princess managed to escape she could morph into a Queen with enough resources and time, and eventually rebuild her cluster, so he made sure the eradication was absolute.

The battle was won with acceptable losses—for horned spider standards, that is. The forest was awash with bodies and the wounded, and it'd no doubt mean a feast for Hoia's carrion beasts. A few fat black birds already circled the clearing, eagerly awaiting their time to feast.

Ed shifted atop his mount and the sight left a sour taste in his mouth.

He was irked that Laurel had made good on her promise and ended the battle so quickly. Experience points were becoming harder and harder to come by the more troops he gained to fight his battles for him.

In any case, it was a resounding victory. The rebel Queens would join the Haunt under Laurel's direction, and the constant fighting for power between the different clusters of Hoia would stop.

Technically, by killing a few hundred spiders today, Ed and Laurel had saved thousands.

Goosebumps traveled down his back. That kind of thinking scared him. He sounded like an Inquisitor.

"HOIA IS YOURS, DUNGEON LORD." Queen Laurel bent her front legs in an approximation of a curtsy. A few angry scratches were visible around her body and mandibles. The horned spiders had formed two lines, with Ed's group on one side and Laurel, her princesses, and the captured rebel Queens at the other end. The surviving members of the rebel clusters had been encircled by the Haunt's troops, who were ready to pounce at them at the first sign of treachery—not that there was much to worry about. With their Queens at Laurel's mercy, and thus controlling access to the cluster's entire ancient memories, which were passed generation to generation of Queens by consuming the flesh of the previous ruler. Without the memories, any princess that tried to rebuild the cluster would be forced to start from the very beginning, with no memory of their enemies or tactics.

After he dismounted and handed the reins of Eyegouger to Kes, Ed studied the blank expressions of the prisoners. Their gazes were fixed on him as he strolled down the royal guard's formation, knowing well that the fate of their Queens—along with their own lives—hinged on Ed's will. And, judging from the resigned air with which the massed bodies held themselves, they had been surprisingly quick to accept their situation. It was clear that, somewhere in those ancient memories of theirs, they remembered having been "recruited" into a Dungeon Lord's minionship before. They knew what would come next.

Best to get it over with. Ed strolled alone among the ranks of immobile spiders. His footsteps made no sound as they struck the ground. His green cape swayed in the wind in perfect silence, which was its entire function—it was enchanted to support a *sneak* user by muting the clank of armor and footsteps.

"So, he arrives for his victory stroll," muttered Clovis, struggling to speak past a phlegmatic cough. Her black, beady eyes were fixated on Ed's, unbridled hatred emanating from her expression. The Dungeon Lord found himself glad that the Queen was almost entirely covered in spiderweb restraints. "A human. How shameful. For one of our own to be defeated by a mere meat-bag—" she attempted a sideway glance at Laurel "—I expected... more."

Ed ignored the old spider, since there was no point in trading insults with a defeated foe. Instead, he regarded the three former rebels at the same time. "You know who I am, and why I'm here," he told them. The air carried the smell of spilled spider guts. "Queen Laurel already made you the offer I'm extending now. You chose violence instead, and got it. There won't be a third chance."

He held the gaze of the three defeated Queens, trying to guess what their decisions would be and hoping that they'd choose the path that would save their lives. Gloriosa seemed uncertain. Her pink eyes were riddled with exhaustion and fear. Cornelia was unsure and scared, judging by the tremor in her back legs. Clovis, on the other hand...

"Curse you!" she bellowed, spitting bloody phlegm at his boots. "You overstep the boundaries of the Mantle, Dungeon Lord! It is one thing to bind my brood to a minionship pact with a stronger foe, yet entirely different to become the servant of one of my kind! I am a *Queen*, not a lowly spiderling!"

Ed's plan was to keep the different clusters of horned spiders in check by having the Queens would forge a pact of minionship with him, but as a condition of said pact, they'd become the direct underlings of Laurel. By doing this, he hoped to sidestep the brutal politics that spider-kind liked to play. Laurel wouldn't be able to betray him without losing control of her entire power-base, and the other Queens wouldn't dare break the pact for fear of having the entire combined might of the other clusters falling on them. In exchange, Laurel would make sure the others stopped devouring sapient creatures, a detail that the villages surrounding Hoia would certainly appreciate.

It was a win-win scenario. Except, of course, for the conquered Queens.

"If we were to renounce consuming sapient flesh," said Gloriosa in a low voice, as close to pleading as her dignity would allow, "it would greatly diminish our sources of food. My brood could not support its current numbers, and we'd have to make due with fewer warriors and princesses. And without the extra nourishment, my spiders would become weaker, sluggish—dumber, perhaps. We'd become shadows of our former selves!"

"As a member of a species whose flesh you like to consume, I can't tell you how sorry I am to hear that," Ed said dryly.

"You'd weaken your minions over senseless sentimentality?" asked Cornelia. "What kind of Dungeon Lord are you?"

"The kind that is about to run out of patience."

Gloriosa and Cornelia exchanged weary glances. "You're leaving us with few options," Gloriosa said. Ed repressed a smile. They'd fold. He could see it.

"Cowards," Clovis said. Perhaps she could see the same thing Ed did. "I am a Queen, you wet sack of meat! I shall die as one. I reject your pact." Her mandibles clacked in what would've been a dangerous smile in a human. "Are you brave enough to do the honors, Dungeon Lord? Or shall you keep relying on your minions?"

Ed raised an eyebrow at her. A nervous whispering spread among Laurel's court. He could imagine his friends' reactions at hearing Clovis' challenge. *It's clearly a trap. She will try to kill me when I get close enough.* It was suicide. Even if she succeeded, Ed's minions would make short work of her—

Except that, if he died, all his pacts would cease to exist. The three different clusters wouldn't be bound to him anymore, nor to his laws. Worse, if Laurel wasn't bound, would she respect Ed's wishes and protect the lives of his friends? He somehow doubted it. Kes, Lavy, and Alder would suddenly be surrounded by hundreds of angry spiders in the middle of a brutal civil war.

He had to give it to Queen Clovis, she was devious. She'd read his situation and identified one huge, glaring weakness in his command structure. One bite was all it would take for all he'd built to crumble to dust.

Not that he'd be there to see it.

"Lord Wraith." Queen Laurel approached him. "Let me handle her."

So she's aware of the risks, too.

Ed considered his options. He may have lacked Laurel's genetic memory, but his Mantle—the black organ that had replaced his heart when he'd become a Dungeon Lord—had its own kind of vestigial instinct regarding his position. He had some awareness of important and ancient traditions, such as allowing a defeated foe to give a last speech, or delivering

23

an execution himself when the prisoner was of high-enough rank.

Sure, he wasn't bound to those traditions—he'd defied them before. But traditions were important for a reason. Often, they were guidelines and advice passed down from the old generation to the new. In this case, if he acted like a coward in front of his entire host of horned spiders it would erode their loyalty.

He glanced at the sword he carried at his side. It was normal steel, non-magical, and definitely had not been designed to dispatch a creature the size of Clovis. When he'd killed Queen Amphiris—Laurel's mother—he'd done so at great risk to himself. *How long can I trust my luck before it fails?*

"My Lord..." Laurel began.

"Very well, Queen Clovis," Ed said. "I'll consider this your last request." In a way, despite it all, he admired her courage. *Had things gone differently, she'd have made a terrific addition to the Haunt.*

"Then come, little Lordling," Clovis said, her voice eager and inviting, oozing black hunger.

Laurel hissed. "It's too dangerous," she whispered, careful not to let her spiders hear. "Your weapon won't kill her fast enough to stop her from having a go at you, webbed or not. Remember how long it took my mother to die?"

Ed remembered. "Don't worry," he told her. "I won't be using my sword." As he stepped toward Clovis, he undid the straps of his left leather glove. Then he sidestepped around Clovis, searching for the right spot.

"Won't his Nefariousness face me as he delivers me into Eternal Night?" Clovis teased. "How disappointing." Her body shifted around her bounds, as if she was trying to keep Ed in her line of sight, although he suspected that she was testing the amount of freedom the webbing afforded her.

She'll wait for the right moment, Ed thought. Even restrained, the Queen was lethal. She could trample him under her legs, crush him under her body, cut him in half with her mandibles, or spear him with her horn. She was a killing machine, a living weapon.

Well, Ed had weapons of his own. He stood a stride away from the bound Queen and then removed his gauntlet.

The whispering among the spiders grew in intensity. His left hand was a naked black bone surrounded by superficial glistening streaks that resembled cracks. The spot at his wrist where his skin and muscle connected with the necromantic appendage was an angry pink scar charred in several places. He usually kept the whole thing under wraps—it didn't hurt, but the sight was unsettling. Even for him.

Especially for him.

"What are you doing back there, Dungeon Lord?" Clovis asked. From her position, she couldn't see Ed, but it was clear that the reaction of the other spiders had upset her.

Ed sighed, raising his skeletal hand up to his head and flexing its bones around. *This will be faster than a sword, and painless,* he told himself. *Like she's going to sleep.*

He clenched his jaw and walked forward, right next to Clovis' bulk, and gently placed his skeletal hand over the third leg on that side.

Several things happened at once. Raw, hot energy flowed into Ed's body, as if his hand was a hose connected to a massive power generator. His Evil Eye activated by itself, green light bursting forth. Clovis's Endurance—a massive eighteen—was reduced by a single rank. She roared in surprise and jerked forward, pushing the bindings to their limit. Despite her being almost covered in the stuff, Ed was thrown backward about a foot, and only remained upright by activating his *improved reflexes* talent and grabbing at the leg with all his strength.

He watched in slow motion as Clovis bent her body toward him as far as she could. She broke a leg in the process, and the snap came to Ed's enhanced perception as an explosion. Her mandibles opened and closed with blazing speed, her bared fangs

HUGO HUESCA

dripping with poison. Almost lazily, Ed took a half-step back without letting go of her leg.

The mandibles snapped shut around empty air in the spot where Ed's right arm had been an instant before. He ended the effect of his *improved reflexes* and time regained its normal speed. From his new position, he was well out of her reach.

"Treachery!" Clovis bellowed as Ed drained her Endurance of another rank. "Black magic! Abomination! Daughters, save me!"

"Oh, cousin," Laurel said, bobbing her head. "Black magic? He's a Dungeon Lord. What else did you expect?"

Behind Laurel, the defeated spiders watched in dead silence. Nobody stepped forward to save Queen Clovis, which matched what Ed knew of horned spiders. They hoped that Ed would allow one of the princesses access to Clovis' body in exchange for minionship, thus ensuring the lineage would not go extinct.

Raw energy kept flowing into Ed's body, and every ten seconds Clovis' Endurance was reduced by another rank. She struggled the entire time, but never managed another strike as threatening as the first. And with each rank shaved off her massive Endurance, she grew weaker.

All the minor aches from Ed's body went away, as if he'd just woken up. That was the problem with black magic. It felt *good* —almost overwhelmingly so. He was bristling with energy, trembling head and toe, all the muscles in his body twitching as if they were trying to burst free and run a marathon by themselves.

He activated his *improved reflexes* in rapid bursts, along with his *ancient lord* aura. He used both to do absolutely nothing—simply trying to burn the excess heat flowing into his body.

Even his brain was racing. He knew talents in the world of Ivalis ran using the body's natural fuel. Activating talents forced the body to emit waste heat.

Technically, he was spending as much energy as he siphoned in. He should have been able to do it all day, or as long as Clovis lasted. In reality, the experience was akin to trying to sprint at

26

maximum speed through a marathon while hooked up to a drip of coffee spiked in adrenaline, and he suspected that if a team of medics from Earth could've looked at what was going on inside his body, they would've run away screaming.

In the end, he had to take two brief rests to stop himself from overheating before Clovis' Endurance dropped to zero. Her struggles, though, ceased earlier. Ed only realized she was dead because the stream of incoming energy ceased. The faucet had run dry.

He let his hand drop to his side. A shimmering patina had appeared over the black bones, like transparent skin with the texture of a bubble's surface. Immediately, Ed's body began a quick return to normal—the stolen energy dissipating in the air around him in streaks of vapor-like currents. His clothes were swamped with sweat.

Next to him, Clovis lay unmoving, a Spider Queen killed by a Dungeon Lord's touch. Nobody else in the entire clearing uttered a single word until Ed straightened his back and headed for the other two remaining rebel Queens.

"So," Ed said, extending his black hand toward them. "What's it going to be?"

Gloriosa and Cornelia joined the Haunt with no further complaints.

ED'S DUTIES on the battlefield promptly ended after that. The spider lines dispersed, and they swiftly assigned the haul of prisoners to medical duty, trudging through the fields to find any spider whose wounds weren't fatal or incapacitating. Clovis' cluster set itself on sorting out the line of succession, which meant a death-match among the princesses and the troops loyal to them. The other clusters left them to it.

Kes and the others waited for him at the top of the hill. He waved at them and headed their way, eager to return to his dungeon. Blue ichor soaked his boots, his throat was dry, and there was a slight tremor in his hands that had nothing to do with exhaustion. He was prey of a strange, almost electrical mood. Every detail of the world around him came to him in perfect, inhuman precision. Even the faintest noise was enough to startle him. A small part of him wished there were some rebel spiders left for him to fight.

He shook his head. Laurel was nearby, ordering around a group of princesses from the conquered clusters. On a whim, Ed approached her.

"Lord Wraith," she greeted him. "What a spectacle you made of Clovis' execution. I'd heard the rumors about your condition, but I wasn't sure what to make of them." The group of princesses took a glance at him and hurried away, suddenly eager to accomplish whatever Laurel had ordered them.

"I'm not sure what to make of it, myself," Ed admitted.

"It's the proper way to deal with our enemies," she said. "In war, all advantages must be exploited."

Ed clasped the gauntlet of his left hand with his right. "If you say so." He studied the battlefield. The spiders on medical duty also executed any combatant, friend or foe, who was too far gone to recover. If their condition was uncertain, they were left on the battlefield. It was brutal. Inhumane. But these creatures *weren't* human. Did that make what had happened here acceptable? Perhaps. Death and brutality were the ways of the spiders. But... wouldn't that make him more akin to a horned spider than a human being?

Not that he was so sure of what qualified as "human," these days. Or if he still counted as one. His heart and his hand certainly weren't, anymore. Who knows what else might change in the days to come?

"I wanted to thank you," Laurel said. "You fulfilled your promise. The power of my cluster extends far beyond what we could've achieved by natural means. My memories will become a very interesting addition for my successor."

Ed wondered what a successor of his would think, were they able to trudge among his memories. Hell, what would anyone think? If Lisa or Mark could see him now, would they recognize the same man who'd worked with them in the Lasershark store? He didn't feel like he'd changed all that much. But here was a field littered with creatures who had died by his command. Wasn't that the power he'd so hungrily desired when Kharon had approached him the day it had all started? He swallowed with difficulty, realizing his throat had gone dry. There was an unnamed dread coiling in his chest, like a slumbering snake beginning to stir.

"I suspect we're not done adding memories for your successor, Empress Laurel," was all he could tell the spider.

Laurel beamed at that, giving her own meaning to his words. "Indeed," she said. "Oh, indeed."

CHAPTER TWO

ONCE AN INQUISITOR

T he green shine of the Dungeon Lord's eyes died slowly. He lay under a pool of his own blood, surrounded by the broken corpses of his minions, his back against his Seat, the stone surface of which had fractured under the might of the Heroes' offensive spells. The man that had so proudly stood against the magical onslaught was now but a human-shaped lump, nothing remaining of the dignity with which he had conducted himself until his messy end. Around the Seat, his dungeon walls and ceilings had melted somewhat. A few hours more and the entire construction would disappear altogether.

Gallio found the knowledge fitting. Like a moral added at the end of a children's tale.

Yet he could feel his throat clenching while he climbed the steps of the Seat Room toward the fallen figure.

It can't be, Gallio thought, when he was in front of the fallen Dungeon Lord. *It can't be him.*

He almost turned back. But he was an Inquisitor, and Inquisitors stared at the light of truth, even if it blinded them. So he reached for the hood and pulled it back just as the light abandoned the Dungeon Lord's eyes.

Gallio stared at the face of the dead man. And kept staring, his face a mask that could've been set in stone.

His companion reached his side atop the raised dais. She scowled at the corpse. "So, it isn't him."

"No," agreed Gallio. "Not this time, at least." This Dungeon Lord was someone he had never seen before—a Lotian called Jiraz. The man had smuggled himself into Starevos to face the Heroes, hoping to find his destiny. He had found it. Just not the one he'd expected.

A part of Gallio was relieved. What would he have done if the dead had been Edward Wright instead of the stranger? True, at least it meant that the otherworldly Dungeon Lord was still alive —which meant that so were Gallio's people. It also meant that Gallio and Wright could still stumble into each other. If that happened, the Inquisitor would be forced to break an oath to fulfill his duty to the Light. But in doing so, he'd condemn himself.

Whatever he did, he could not win.

"Good," said Alvedhra, still glaring hatefully at the dead Dungeon Lord. She knelt next to the corpse while drawing an enchanted silver dagger, which she used to sever the corpse's head from its body. It was standard Inquisitorial procedure—one could never be too careful with Murmur's favorites—and Gallio nodded. She had learned well, and not a single movement of hers was wasted. Some expert hacks, and the deed was done. She kept the head, grabbing it by the ash-covered hair.

"Any news about our mutual friend?" he asked her in a whisper, making sure the other members of the Militant Church inspecting the Seat Room weren't listening.

The Heroes were getting close to Undercity, some groups already prowling the countryside. If Edward Wright hadn't yet escaped from Starevos, it was but a question of time before the Heroes reached him and he shared the fate of all other Dungeon Lords before him.

Alvedhra shook her head while wiping the blood from the dagger with the corpse's cloak. "No. I've put out as many feelers as I dare to without alerting him, but other than the surge of necromantic energy in Hoia Forest last winter, there's been no clue. Not that the locals care." Her upper lip stiffened. "Most of my contacts write about Undercity's officers trying to put down a new smuggling group. Seems like the nobility is more concerned with their purses than the sanctity of their souls. I bet they'll change their tune when retribution comes, but by then it will be too late." Alvedhra spoke with the zealous intensity of the recently converted. Usually, they mellowed out with time. But she'd need her passion to steel herself for the trials that awaited the expedition.

Maybe it's a good sign, Gallio thought. *If Wright is keeping his head down—or better yet, he's gone altogether—there's a chance the Heroes may pass him by.*

And yet...

Gallio and Alvedhra walked down the steps of the dais, their red capes fluttering with the small breeze that came from the cracks in the dungeon. A small entourage of servants, men-at-arms, and clerks waited for them at the bottom.

"The Dungeon Lord is dead," Alvedhra announced, releasing the severed head from her grip and letting it roll away. "You may approach."

"My gratitude, Eminence," said Master Enrich. The grizzled Militant Church veteran went past the Inquisitors and climbed the steps using a silver-tipped cane to keep his balance, his famous metal wand hanging from the strap of his belt and swaying with each step. A pair of servants followed him, carrying the surgeon's tools that Enrich would use to extract the Dungeon Lord's heart. The so-called Mantle.

While Enrich set to his grim task, Gallio met with the other Inquisitors. Even with the Dungeon Lord dead, there was still work to be done: Survivors that had slipped the Heroes, supply caches yet hidden in the wilderness that an enterprising minion might use to re-start the holds of its former master, and treasure chambers waiting past the Seat Room, well-guarded and loaded with lethal traps.

Gallio was the senior Inquisitor present, so he was in charge. Which meant that if anything went wrong past this point, the fault would fall on him. Besides, there were still a few higher-ups who hadn't liked his return, and they were even now keeping an eye on him, eager to pounce at the slightest mistake.

It didn't worry him. Let the old whiners play their games of favorites and politics. He was here because his pledge to Alita demanded it. Nothing more, nothing less.

"There aren't as many batblin corpses as we expected from the scout reports," he told one sturdy Inquisitor named Oak. Oak was prideful and tall, and lacked an ounce of common sense in that thick head of his. In short, he was young. Just like Alvedhra. Just like Gallio had once been. "Send Rangers along with the Militants to reinforce the perimeter. If the batblins ran away before the battle, there'll be tracks all over the place. The critters aren't known for their discipline—specially when scared to death."

Inquisitor Oak nodded. "Yes, Eminence," he said.

Gallio nodded and turned to leave. As he did so, Gallio shifted his gaze up toward the shadowy arcs of the ceiling, which were covered in webs and dust. For the briefest instant, he could swear he saw something small and hairy shift near a corner. A rat, maybe? He was about to say something about it when a servant entered the chamber in a rush, his white tunic scraping at its hem against the dirty cobblestone floor.

"Eminence Gallio!" the servant called. "Cleric Zeki sent for you. He's searching for survivors under the dungeon, and our group located a hidden catacomb. Cleric Zeki says you should come at once! The Dungeon Lord's vampire survived the fight. The creature is locked in its own coffin, Eminence. Its fate is in your hands."

CHAPTER THREE

BACK TO THE HAUNT

The forest gave way to the Haunt's holdings long before they reached the dungeon itself. The first sign of civilization hidden among the forest was a pair of Scrambler Towers framing the entrance to Haunt-controlled territory. The Towers were octagonal stone pylons with a series of rune engravings covering every side and a spherical railway of brass magical systems crowning its top. Illusion enchantments disguised the Scramblers as a pair of decrepit trees with skeleton-thin branches, and a complex mesh of magical traps loaded with Mind compulsions were always on standby. If triggered, they launched an area-of-effect series of *minor orders* meant to cause any uninvited guests to go about their business elsewhere, and make them believe it had been their idea.

The brass sphere at the top was the most important part of the Tower, and a perceptive eye could see a faint shimmer on the surrounding air—the telltale clue of heavy magical activity. The sphere was a complex counter-spell system, focused on neutralizing Divination attempts. It hid the Haunt from most kinds of scrying, masking the magical emanations of the dungeon's ley lines.

When Ed had bought the Dungeon Upgrade: *Scrambler Tower*, the fully functional load-out had manifested itself in his mind, ready for use whenever he had the resources to build them. He could've left it at that, but curiosity had gotten the better of him, and with Lavy's help, he had studied the inner workings of the Scramblers.

The anti-Divination sphere was so complex that Lavy hadn't been able to even fathom how it worked—apparently there was Unholy magic involved—but the other parts turned out to be simple. The Haunt's ley lines powered the whole contraption. They only worked if set directly over one. The traps reloaded their spells this way, and the trigger mechanism was an *alarm* spell enchanted with *permanency*. A secondary *permanent* a*larm* would trigger a *message* spell to warn Ed if someone managed disbelieved the Scrambler's disguise, or pierced its anti-Divination field.

Ed would've loved to have a chat with the person or entity who had designed the Scramblers and trade ideas. If he focused on their schematics, he could "edit" them with his own alterations, but for the time being, he lacked the expertise to try.

Someday, I'll know your secrets, he thought, throwing the Scramblers one last lustful glance as his group left them behind. *Switch the anti-divination field for one that locates stuff... figure out a way to translate that data as coordinates and feed them to a* fireball trap *with an aiming mechanism, and we'll have automatic fireball turrets everywhere we want.* He needed to learn magical theory. So far, he had seen and used exclusively pre-made spells, but as soon as he figured out the source code needed to create those spells in the first place... well, he *was* a software designer.

Ivalis would soon learn the sheer destructive power of databases and SELECT * FROM spell functions.

"You're chuckling to yourself again," Alder warned him as they rode.

"Oh. Sorry."

"You should be," Lavy said. "Your evil laughter needs a lot of practice before it befits a Dungeon Lord of my status."

"Don't you mean *his* status?" Kes asked, lifting an eyebrow.

Lavy threw her hair back. "I'm the Haunt's Head Researcher. That's a status symbol in itself. For the Haunt, mind you."

They found the next sign of civilization about an hour after passing through the Scramblers. A group of four kids of varying ages lay under a tree, enjoying its shade while they ate raisin-like berries gathered from nearby bushes. The kids called to Ed and the others as they passed. Alder waved back at them.

"Their parents will be pissed when they catch them slacking off," Kes said with a grin after the kids were out of sight.

"It's a nice day," Ed said. "It'd be a waste if nobody got to enjoy it."

In any other circumstance, a group of kids playing deep in Starevosi woods would've been suicidal, but the Haunt's holdings were patrolled by horned spiders and batblins—and few critters dared venture into a Dungeon Lord lands, unless they intended to join him.

Ed threw a glance at a lone boulder near the grass road they were following. To a stranger, it was solid rock, but to Ed, it was hollow and had a wooden door. Several feet away, a small trail of violet vapor rose from a fist-sized hole in the ground and dispersed itself in the air.

The rock was the entrance to a small underground farm carved by Ed's drones. The kids' parents were probably inside— Ed activated his Evil Eye and confirmed that no *alarms* had been triggered within—working the fields. They were growing gray puffball, which was a mushroom-shaped tuber about the size of a batblin and native to the Netherworld, so they could grow underground. It tasted like a watery potato, but it was nutritious, and you could grind it into coarse flour to make a calorie-rich bread that lasted a while in storage.

Crops native of the Netherworld had quickly become staples

of the Haunt's diet. Most of them fed on Dark emanations the way a normal plant fed on sunlight. The problem was that Netherworld plants poisoned the soil and made it unsuitable for growing a normal plant for centuries, unless a powerful Cleric intervened and *cleansed* it. Growing the crops underground solved that problem, but there was still the issue of the gas.

Ed studied the vent that allowed the violet vapor to exit the underground farm. All the Netherworld plants exuded that vapor. It wasn't explosive, nor was it poisonous, and it had no visible side-effects. It smelled like taro tea. Andreena, the Haunt's Herbalist, thought it was the stuff the Netherworld's atmosphere was made of, and Ed was willing to bet his non-skeletal hand that ignoring that detail would bite him in the ass eventually. So all farmers, much to their annoyance, had to subject themselves to monthly health checks, just in case anything went sideways.

Not that anything had in the few months since Ed had built the farms.

At first, Ed had intended to have drones tend to the crops, but drones were dangerously incompetent with most tasks not related to a dungeon's creation and maintenance... although Ed sometimes wondered how much of that incompetence was feigned out of laziness. They were very skilled at sculpting rock, for example. That very week, a drone had carved a statue showing the process of horned spider reproduction in extravagant detail. Horned spider reproduction was best described not at all. Unwilling to let the statue terrify everyone in the Seat Room, he had sent it to terrify everyone in the Prison instead.

Since he couldn't use drones, he had gone to the villagers for help. Beforehand, he'd wracked his brain for incentives to get them on his side. Extra coin? Better housing? Free booze?

The reaction of the first former farmers he'd approached had been among his biggest culture shocks since his arrival at Ivalis.

"You mean we get to have our own land?" the couple had asked. "And you're only asking for a *tenth* of the crop in return?"

"Huh?" Ed had suddenly realized that his whole perspective on feudal-like social contracts was probably wrong.

All their lives, the farmers of Burrova had owed allegiance to Galtia, the capital of Starevos and where the headquarters of the local branch of the Militant Church was located. The tax collector would come right after harvest season was over and take half the crops. No farmers ever owned the land they worked, and after their death, their sons could consider themselves lucky if the farm wasn't reassigned to somebody the local authorities liked better. After paying the tax, the leftover crops were used to feed the farmers and their families until the next harvest. Whatever remained of that, which wasn't much, was sold to buy whatever they couldn't make themselves, such as shoes, a donkey, or buttons to repair a tattered vest.

"I mean, it's underground," Ed had warned them.

"Have you ever had to chase down a pack of scared goats after the fence breaks in the middle of a Starevosi storm?" they had retorted—perhaps with more curtsies and some "my Lord" sprinkled here and there, but that had been the gist of it.

Not only had most of the Haunt's villagers volunteered to tend the underground farms—they had considered it an incredible gift. In this world, everyone, from a lowly peasant to the mightiest king and all his armies, depended on a bountiful harvest to survive. Ed still wasn't sure what to make of the realization, but he had redoubled his efforts to make sure the Haunt was self-sufficient. The only things stopping him from covering the entire forest with underground farms were that the sheer space each farm required a lot of drones and a lot of time to dig—and he couldn't spare either—and that not all ground was suitable for digging, even with his Mantle's magic strengthening the caves against quakes.

"The plants exhale this mysterious gas," he had told the farmers. "Seems to be safe, but you know how those things go."

"A pack of werewolves ate my cousin and his entire family. The gas smells better than I do. We'll take our chances."

In the end, they had come to an agreement. One adult member of the family would become a minion of Ed. It was a necessity, to ensure that they wouldn't run away, and it also allowed Ed to make sure they were safe.

If the Haunt ever fell, and the Inquisition purged its minions, the non-pacted adult was to run away with the kids and hide in the nearest village. It wasn't a pretty prospect, but it was life, and it was better than the alternative.

Those words were quickly becoming a staple in Ed's inner monologue.

After leaving the farms behind, the group stopped in a grove to rest and let the hell chickens cool down. Ed summoned a group of drones to gather branches, and Kes started a quick fire using flint —she always traveled with it, along with a battered iron skillet she refused to give up.

They ate hell chicken sandwiches made with puffball bread and thick slices of cheese, and drank warm mead.

"You know? Last summer, we almost got killed by a mob of batblins," Lavy said, patting her belly after she finished. "Now, those critters do the fighting for us. If you ignore the Militant Church and their Heroes, I'd say we're doing great."

"Me too," said Alder. "I wish life could always be this easy." He sighed. "Beer and food, friends, an army of horned spiders. All the simple pleasures. Then again, a few months of that and I'd run out of things to chronicle."

Kes straightened and threw fistfuls of dirt at the fire. "I aspire to live a life that would give a Bard nothing to talk about." She winked at Alder, then tossed a chunk of hell chicken breast to her mount, Neckbreaker, who caught it in the air and devoured it whole.

The group crested a rocky cliff that was too steep for a normal horse, but that the hell chickens climbed with ease, their razor-sharp talons digging into the ground like it was Rolim's flesh. The Haunt's mainland was located inside a depression deep with vegetation at the outskirts of a mountain range that extended all the way up the Starevos coast and flanked Undercity on its other end.

When Ed had first arrived in Ivalis, this section of Hoia had been growing untamed and was rich with predators. Nowadays, the predators were of a different nature. Vast, growing circles of tree stumps broke the green evenness of the forest, with crude lumberyards slowly growing next to them like ticks getting fat off their prey. Gravel roads snaked through the terrain in all directions, getting swallowed in the distance. Faint smoke trails rose up to the sky.

The way to the dungeon led Ed and the others past the three growing batblin encampments, each built next to the other like orphans huddling together for warmth. They were protected by rough and shoddy palisades with only a few dozen sheds surrounding a bonfire, and dozens of batblins racing around, hauling materials, food, and weapons. From a distance, it was impossible to tell if they were playing, or working, or fighting each other. Ed suspected that they were putting on an air of business because their scouts had seen him approach.

Two of the encampments were fully enclosed by the wooden walls, with the third still being constructed. Ed's drones were working on the last third of the walls, dancing over cut logs piled in pyramids next to the construction site. The imp-like creatures weren't happy working with wood, but at least they were competent... enough. Their purple-and-pink tunics swayed with the evening breeze, and the crackle of the bonfire behind them gave the tunic's engraved Lasershark an almost-lifelike imitation of a swim. While Ed watched, purple tendrils of magic manifested around the drones and, directed by their dancing, ate a few of the logs before transforming them into stakes and ropes that snaked in the air and built themselves into the palisade.

"I swear that every time I look away, the batblins double their damn numbers," Lavy said, covering her eyes with her hand to glance up at the smoke rising from a dozen different bonfires. "Soon enough they'll outnumber everyone but the spiders."

Ed scratched his chin. It was true that the third encampment hadn't been there the night before. It wasn't even connected to the tunnel network yet. "Seems like Klek and Tulip are doing great at their recruiting gig." *How many clouds can the forest support?* He knew that batblin meat was—*had been*—an integral part of a horned spider's diet. The number of spiders in the forest suggested an equivalent number of prey, which meant there were more batblins hiding in the forest than one may think at first glance. Nowadays, Klek and his riders spent whole nights without returning to the Haunt, but they weren't close to finished finding all the clouds out there.

"I think they're growing their numbers the old-fashioned way," Alder pointed out. A pair of startled batblins scurried off inside the bushes when they saw the hell chickens approach.

"It's because no one is hunting them inside our domains," Kes said. "Batblins' main survival strategy is to out-breed their predators. Wetlands, in a couple of years we may have a problem in our hands. Netherworld crops or not, there's only so many creatures the land can support."

"That has an easy solution," Lavy said. "We'll just eat the batblins—there are enough of them to feed us." She snickered at the idea, but it was obvious she didn't mean it. Most of her research assistants inside the dungeon were batblins, and Klek was her regular sparring partner.

Kes and Ed exchanged glances. The Marshal's fears were well-founded. *The Haunt is growing fast. How long until we can't hide it anymore?* After all, even with the Scramblers, there were obvious signs of civilization that simply couldn't be hidden.

There had even been a faint trickle of villagers from neighboring lands, approaching the Haunt and asking to be let in. How they had learned about its existence in the first place wasn't hard to guess: not all the Burrova survivors were Ed's minions. So far, they'd eluded the Inquisition's investigations, but the arrival of newcomers was a signal that information was leaking.

Some nights, Ed couldn't sleep. One of these days, he'd wake to find out that the first team of Heroes had found their way into the Haunt. And once that happened... even if he defeated them, that'd only mean that the rest of the player-base of Ivalis Online would make a bee-line for his dungeon. He knew exactly how they would feel, in fact. The pride at being the first—and only—player to defeat a particularly troublesome Boss, along with frustration when he couldn't seal the deal and another team finished the quest before he could return to claim revenge.

If he had only known why those Bosses didn't respawn...

Lavy's words danced in Ed's mind. He had the numbers to put up a fight. He knew things about the Heroes that a normal Dungeon Lord didn't, and his grasp of Earth's technology and tactics was good enough that he could get it to work to his advantage if he used magic to plug those areas where he lacked expertise.

But he'd still take losses, no matter what. People would die defending the dungeon, and bodies would pile up as high as those bonfires.

Unless I find the way to turn the tables.

THE WRAITH'S HAUNT

Dungeon Lord Edward Wright.
Drones 55
Dominant Material Cave Rock

THREAT 65 - LOCAL - 35 Heiliges - Represents how aware the outside world is of the dungeon and how willing / able / ready they are to do something about it. A 100 indicates imminent destruction.

OFFENSE 3000 - A representation of the strength a dungeon's forces can muster during an attack (raid or invasion) outside the dungeon itself. It represents the experience they would award, as a group, if they were defeated (but not absorbed).

DEFENSE 4500 - The experience the population of a dungeon would award if they were to be defeated (but not absorbed) during the defense of said dungeon. It's multiplied by a percentage given by the dungeon's upgrades and defenses.

MAGIC GENERATED 100 - Measures the magic created by the Sacred Grounds that can be put to use in different endeavors or to power dungeon upgrades.

MAGIC CONSUMED 35 - Measures how much magic is consumed.

POPULATION

82 HUMANS (12 combatants)
    1 avian combatant
    324 batblins (61 batblin combatants)
    Spider Clusters: 1 Empress, 5 Queens, 23 princesses, 92 warriors, ? Spiderlings, ? Wounded.

. . .

AREAS

LIVING ZONES:
Living Quarters
Storage
Treasure Chamber
Caravan Camp
Mess Hall

MILITARY FACILITIES:
3 Batblin camps
1 Training Facility
5 Spider Dens
1 Kaftar Dojo
1 Prison

RESEARCH INSTALLATIONS:
1 Witchcraft Laboratory (Upgraded: Library, Runemaker Hall)
1 Herbalist Workshop (Upgraded: Medical Facility)
1 Taming Stable

SACRED GROUNDS:

- The Seat.

1 Light Altar
1 Dark Altar

PRODUCTION:

1 Forge
1 Brewery
5 Hell chicken Breeding Grounds
1 Kitchen
1 Mining Facility
Underground Farms
Stables

DEFENSE:
Heavy Dust traps.
Fake Floors.
Secret Passages.
Defensive Spears.
Batblin Sentries.
Spider Sentries.
Defensive Potions and Runes.

DUNGEON UPGRADES
Drone Permanency
Scrambler Towers

ED DISMISSED the prompt with a thought. The increase in power from the spider's conquest had completely offset the dent that Nicolai made in the Haunt's defenses months ago.

When compared with the batblin encampments, the kaftar camp was a veritable fortress. Pointed tents made out of leather and cotton were organized in circular patterns with watch-towers guarding its perimeter. A few young warriors practiced combat drills in a sanded field, handymen fixed broken tools under the shadow of their wooden sheds, and lumbermen teams delved into the forest under the protection of scouts armed with spears and long fang-like daggers. Kaftar clan-members marched at the edges of the camp, keeping their eyes on the woods despite the implied protection of Ed's creatures. Technically, the kaftar cackle wasn't in Ed's employ, they were more like allies of the Haunt. Only ten of its members—grown from the original five—had taken minionship with him, and two of those hurried to meet Ed's group as they passed alongside the camp.

"Greetings, Dungeon Lord," said Kaga as he pressed one arm to his chest in salutation. "I take that the spider rebellion has been quelled."

"Kaga, Yumiya," Ed nodded at them. "Everything went as planned. Thanks for the insights on the warring dynamics of horned spiders."

"Anytime," said Yumiya. She was Kaga's second-in-command and the Haunt's foremost expert in monsters—and how to kill them. Both kaftar were dressed in black armor made out of hardened spider chitin. They wore no shoes or gauntlets since the shape of their hands was too paw-like for that kind of protection. At one point, Kaga had tried to add the spider's horn as an ornamental weapon into the armor design, but he'd kept poking himself with it. "How did the Agility potion fare with the spiderlings?" Yumiya asked.

"Well enough," Ed said. "It did its job, but it didn't last as long as Andreena thought it would. It also only enhanced them by a couple of ranks instead of the usual three to four."

Yumiya grunted thoughtfully. "A spiderling's metabolism is always on overdrive, so it's no surprise it burns through the potion. Their size plays a part, too."

Ed nodded. Potions didn't scale well with critters, as they were crafted for humans. "Well, we're onto something here. It'll be worth it if we keep experimenting."

Yumiya interpreted that as an order and crossed her right arm across her chest. "I'll do as you ask, Dungeon Lord. But it may be quicker if you'd allow us to experiment on the spiderlings directly."

"Let's keep our mad science as friendly as we can, shall we?" Ed grinned at her.

While they talked, Kaga had approached the hell chicken mounts and was examining Kes' Neckbreaker with an inquisitive eye. The hell chicken had eye blinders in addition to the straps on its beaks, and the claws on its legs and wings had been sheathed with wool and leather.

"How did the mounts fare?" Kaga asked Kes, keeping a prudent distance from Neckbreaker's beak.

"Well, they behaved, more or less," Kes said. "At least this dung-for-brains didn't eat any of the fingers I've left." She tapped at Neckbreaker's feathers. "You managed to reduce their aggression, Kaga, but I'd say not enough for actual combat—there's no way they wouldn't turn on us the instant we took the straps away. And they lack the temperament, anyway. If one of our riders was wounded, not only would his mount turn against him, but all the others would as well."

The group stared at the hell chickens in silence. One of the advantages of being elite monster hunters was that Kaga and his team knew how to tame wild beasts, and they'd been working on the hell chickens—to some measure of success. The kaftar named each beast and were trying their best to transform them into warmounts. If they succeeded, the Haunt would have a great advantage over other dungeons: war horses were rare and expensive, but hell chickens were faster and far more murderous counterparts that were also very easy to grow.

It was risky, but with the Heroes trailing the borders of Hoia, the Haunt needed all the advantages it could get.

"They're less aggressive when well fed," Kaga mused. "But they'll still pounce on anyone the second they sense any weakness. I've never seen anything like it. To be honest, at this point taming these magnificent creatures is a personal mission of mine. If I could get the clan to raise a couple hundred of them…" He lowered his ears, lost in thought, probably thinking of bloodshed and warfare. "Ah, who knows what could happen," he added wistfully.

"To be honest," Ed said, "I like the new version better."

A month ago, Lavy had managed to fix Saint Claire and Tillman's Stupendous Hell Chicken Farm. The new kit had turned out smaller hell chickens, which were gray and lacked the aggression of their counterparts. But Ed had kept the existing design, as well as the farms already in place, because a population of murderous, easy-to-grow beasts could come in handy. A few hours after adding Lavy's design to the Haunt, he had received a letter from Saint Clarie and Tillman testily proclaiming that tampering with their devices voided the warranty.

"They're good climbers," Alder added, probably because he felt that Kes was being too harsh on her assessment. He patted his mount, Blood Fiend, who twisted its neck to throw Alder a murderous glance which the Bard ignored.

"Actually, that's true," Kes said, then shrugged. "But I honestly don't see how that helps us. Not counting Scar, we can't teach these assholes anything, and we can't trust them."

Lavy shook her head and dismounted. She stood right next to her mount, Scar, at a distance that would've prompted an attack from any other hell chicken. Scar merely pretended she wasn't there. "You only need to figure them out, is all. If they sense any weakness, they'll pounce, but they won't risk defying someone stronger than them. So… just don't have any weaknesses."

Scar kept its crimson eyes fixated away from Lavy. It took its name from the long line of cracked and burnt tissue that crossed its beak side to side. Since its first encounter with Lavy, Scar had been the only one of its species to show a willingness to listen during taming, but only to the Witch. It seemed, to Ed, that they had reached a kind of murderous understanding.

"Or be crazy enough that the damn shits buy your bluff," Kes muttered.

They all dismounted, and Kaga waved a group of young kaftars to take over the reins of the obsidian mounts. The kaftar tamers dragged them toward the stables next to the cackle's camp, bribing the chickens with bloody steaks and the Netherworld fungi that was the other half of their diet.

"Keep trying, so long as it's safe," Ed told the monster hunter. "They're too valuable not to. Maybe there's a way to fix the aggression problem, though. Perhaps we can alter Saint Claire's *tranquility* potion somewhat."

"Maybe," Kaga said. Potions were outside his area of expertise. He was a user, not a crafter. "But it has to be a change that doesn't take away their killer instinct. A fine line to tread, I'd say."

After the kaftar had taken their leave, Ed and the others strolled past the clan camp and the jagged outcrop under which the Haunt's dungeon was built came into sight. The boulders were shaped like broken edges rising defiantly up to the evening sky. Past them grew a sea of mountaintops, half-clouded by mist and snow, hiding the sea from view and casting the countryside in its shadow. The view dwarfed even Hoia, and it was Ed's constant reminder that, no matter how larger the Haunt grew, it was nothing but a tiny dot in a world that hadn't been crafted for human-sized creatures. Those mountains in the distance were the true owners of the world, slumbering titans that cared nothing for the games of the Light and the Dark.

The marketplace stood right under the skirt of the outcrop. It was tiny by all measures of size, both human and geological. The terrain was naked ground flattened by the daily stomping of dozens of feet, with several refurbished tents with straw roofs standing around the road that connected the dungeon to the kaftar camps. About a dozen villagers lounged inside the tents or walked around despite the late hour. Heorghe's wife, Ivona, was in the middle of a heated discussion with a middle-aged man named Bryne, who wore a black eye-patch emblazoned with a silver lasershark. By the looks of it, Bryne wanted to trade Ivona a small roll of blue cotton fabric in exchange for a pair of shears with brass handles, but she was out-haggling him with so much passion that it was a hair-breadth away from coming to blows.

When contrasted to the mountains above, the marketplace was tiny and inconsequential. But to Ed, who knew its history, it meant much more.

At first, the tents had been a temporary camp built to house the survivors of the attack on Burrova. The villagers had been forceful guests of the Haunt, prisoners in all but name, and thought of Ed and his minions as tyrants. That had all changed after Nicolai and his forces had stormed the Haunt and unleashed an undead abomination that had attempted to drain the life out of its inhabitants. Defeating Nicolai had almost cost Ed his life and the lives of his friends, but afterward, the villagers' hatred had evaporated, despite the deaths of several men and women during the fight. Now, most of them lived inside the dungeon where Ed could best protect them, but they still preferred to spend time outside. Day-to-day life in Ivalis was dictated by sunlight, after all.

Bryne sighed loudly and added two packs of waxed hemp to his pile, thus finally getting Ivona to accept the trade. A few of the villagers caught sight of Ed's party and waved at them, some of them bending their knees slightly or crossing their hand over their chest in the kaftar's way. Ed returned the wave awkwardly, wishing people would stop treating him like some kind of royal figure. It set a bad precedent, because a part of him liked it.

That part of himself was the reason that the Dark god Murmur had chosen him to become a Dungeon Lord in the first place, despite Ed's refusal to join his ranks. Murmur apparently hoped that, in the end, the allure of power would become too great as the corruption grew too entrenched to resist. Humans, to the Hungry One, were but the instrument with which he proved his philosophy. Even the most virtuous man in the world would fall if Murmur offered a deal he couldn't resist.

Ed… disagreed. But even he had to admit that some days were harder than others. And he was far from the most virtuous man in the world.

"Dungeon Lord," Bryne called, hurrying to meet Ed. "Marshal Kessih, Masters Lavina and Alder. I take that we triumphed against the rebellious spider scum?"

"Obviously," said Lavy with a prideful grin. "What else did you expect? Victory was inevitable with me leading the charge."

Bryne shot her a nervous smile. "Of course, Master Lavina, of course. Didn't mean to imply otherwise." Ed rolled his eyes. Most of the villagers were deathly afraid of Lavy because she spent a large portion of her time trying to raise the spirits of the dead to serve her. It was an image that the Witch was happy to indulge.

It's like she's trying to get burned at the stake.

"Lavy, you helped just as much as I did," Alder began, but the Witch pretended he was part of the scenery.

"Spread the word," she told Bryne. "Tell everyone of our victory. Celebrations are in order!"

Kes shot Ed a glance. "Are they?"

He shrugged. "Maybe they are. Victories should be celebrated." One never knew when they'd have to mourn defeats. On the other hand, he barely had time to sit down and relax these days. How could he, with the threat of Heroes looming over his Haunt like a scythe? "But you'll have to toast in my absence, because I'm changing clothes and heading for Undercity. Oscor and I are meeting with Karmich and the Guild."

"I'll go with you," Kes said.

Ed shook his head. If he let her, Kes would work day and night until she collapsed from exhaustion. "Take a breather, Kes. I'll ask Laurel to lend me her Royal Guard."

"Ah! A feast," said Alder, pretending not to have heard Ed. "A Bard's natural environment. What a perfect time to share my new verses with an eager public." He smiled broadly. A captive audience was to him what baby seals were to a shark.

"Sorry," Ed told him. "You know I need you in Undercity with me."

Alder looked crestfallen. "We're still pretending I'm the one calling the shots? I swear, Ed, everyone there already suspects who you are."

"Alder, you should know having a suspicion that you can ignore is very different than someone forcing you to confront it," Lavy said petulantly. She picked at her fingernails and grinned. "Don't worry, I'll have the batblins toast in your honor."

"Oh, great. That makes it so much better," Alder said sadly, but he made no more complaints.

"Thank you, my Lord," Bryne told Ed. "Your Cruelness is most gracious. But, with all due respect, we refuse to celebrate without you alongside us. We'll wait until you return, and then we'll feast. Otherwise, it wouldn't be a celebration at all."

"That… that's very nice of you to say, Bryne. Thank you," Ed said. Behind him, he could sense Alder trying to withhold a cheer. "I'll try to deal with these matters quickly and be back in a couple days at the most."

"One more thing, my Lord, with your permission," Bryne said, holding his hat in front of him. "Are there any news about the Heroes?" Bryne looked over his shoulder and bent his fingers in the shape of a ward against ill-fortune. "Word's been spreading," he said, lowering his voice to a whisper. "Other dungeons between Galtia and Undercity have been attacked. Bandits and renegade kaftar live in most of them. But my cousin says that another Dungeon Lord fell recently. He says the Heroes are coming closer by the day."

"I see," Ed said. He exchanged glances with his friends. Alder's smile had left his face, and Lavy was pale. They both knew firsthand the destructive capability of the inhuman creatures that the Militant Church used as their anti-Dungeon-Lord-weapon.

"Don't worry, Bryne. We aren't like other dungeons. When they come, we'll be ready."

Bryne faked a confident smile. "The Light shall rue the day it defied the Haunt!"

"Just don't let our friendly local priest hear that, or we'll never survive the sermon," Lavy urged the villager as they left him behind. Then, she asked, "So, what's our plan? We have a plan, right?"

"Oh, we do," Ed said, smiling broadly. "Do you know what a railroad is, Lavy?"

"No," The Witch raised her eyebrows and glanced at the others, who shrugged as well.

"Don't worry," Ed said. "You will."

THE ENTRANCE to the dungeon was disguised by illusions of solid rock. It led to a tunnel lit by magical torches containing glowing crystals instead of flame, which bathed the rock in soft purples and pinks. Rows of crude stone statues shaped like winged gargoyles twice the size of Ed lined each side. Their eyes were engraved diamonds, which shone under the torchlight and gave them a lifelike aura, as if they were following the Dungeon Lord as he went. The gargoyles were another creation of his drones as evidenced by the fact that his minions had had to add a woolen loincloth to everyone.

So far, the gargoyles were just statues, but Ed had known as soon as he had seen them that he'd animate them as soon as he found out the appropriate spell. If there wasn't one, he'd create it from scratch. *I only hope we can glue those loincloths in place.*

He thought of Ryan, his former boss at Lasershark, and imagined the expression he'd make if a naked gargoyle rushed at his character in the middle of a raid. *Maybe my drones are on to something.*

"There's the mad grinning again," Kes warned him.

They left the tunnel to arrive at the dungeon's main hall. Once, it had been a partially collapsed cave hiding a few rotting crates of provisions that Dungeon Lord Kael Arpadel had chosen to keep away from his main dungeon. One could barely find that cave, now. The jagged roof had been replaced by a polished dome built out of stone slabs covered with obsidian plating. Diamonds encrusted in the obsidian imitated Ivalian constellations. A silver chandelier hung from the dome's apex, with long arms surrounding its body and giving it a spherical shape meant to represent Ivalis' most famous moon, Camcanna. Regenerating candles burned at the upper end of each of the eight arms, and the black wax rained down to the marble floor, where it flowed through canals carved as the figure of a mighty Lasershark— much to Ed's dismay.

Braziers burned in brass stands along the circular walls, each shaped like an elongated skeletal arm. Tapestries covered the walls. Most of them showed, in the drone's crude needlework, the history of the dungeon since its creation. In one, Ed and Lavy faced the batblin band back when Ed had first arrived in Ivalis, with Alder cowering behind the duo. In another, Spider Queen Amphiris collapsed as the ground gave way under her and Ed charged her with his flaming sword. A different scene showed Inquisitor Gallio and Ed standing at opposite sides of the broken body of the mindbrood. Farther along was the scene of a huge bonfire, with a humanoid figure writhing among the flames.

Ed wasn't much of a fan of those tapestries. His favorites were the ones the artisans of Burrova were slowly adding to the bunch. They were normal pieces of art, the kind, he guessed, that might be found in the home of any Starevosi individual that could afford it. Flowers, coats-of-arms of famous kings, the ashen face of a mythical vampire, even a depiction of Oynnes, god of Commerce, handing a golden coin from the heavens down onto a starving crowd below.

The drones' artwork and the villagers' homey decorations

didn't mesh well at all. But Ed found it fitting. Life was built upon contrasts, even when they didn't pair well together. A home in perfect harmony was one where no one lived.

The dungeon was very far from perfect harmony.

Brewer batblins pushed small carts carrying beer barrels, trying to move through the same tunnels that the Kitchen batblins were using to haul food. Both teams wanted to enter the tunnel first, and neither were willing to yield. While Ed watched, one of them threw a pie, and then an all-out brawl started. Nearby Research batblins—Lavy's assistants—hurried away from the combat area and whispered among themselves in a way vaguely reminiscent of the Witch.

Villagers around the Lasershark engravings gossiped between themselves after a day of hard work. They were carpenters, traders and merchants, leather-workers, candle-makers, tailors, cobblers, and more. Ed knew most of their faces and some of their names. A few had been with the Haunt since Burrova, and others had arrived on their own, heeding the grapevine rumors of the Haunt's prosperity that seeded the neighboring villages. They had brought their trades with them as well as their families.

A group of elite Janitor batblins saw the battle between Brewer and Kitchen and hefted their mops and crowd-control sticks and dove valiantly into combat, their child-sized gambeson tunics deflecting beer mugs and fruitcake projectiles. The villagers began taking bets. So far, the ferocious Kitchen batblins were winning by circling their service carts and bunkering behind them, but the grizzled Janitors were storming the defenses, even after their leader had been knocked-out by a flying salsa jar.

Ed smiled, basking in the cacophony of cursing and thrown cutlery. The air smelled of lavender and thyme and burning incense. He took a moment to enjoy the warmth flowing up from the floor, which came from the furnace down below.

Ah, home at least, he thought happily.

Then he rained drones all over the brawl.

CHAPTER FOUR

SOLE SURVIVOR

High above the vaulted domes of Jiraz' dungeon, a batblin hung with most of his body glued to the center of a spiderweb. His weight pulled the fine silver lines taut. Instead of struggling, though, he remained as stiff as he could. An involuntary twitch from his fingertips would send waves of vibrations spreading through the strands like water filling up a labyrinth.

Many of his kind had found horrifying deaths when walking through a dark forest alone and wandering into the sticky trap of a horned spider eager to sink its claws into soft, delicious batblin flesh. And the horned spider that glanced at this lone batblin from her vantage point on the ceiling was a princess, a full station above the lowly warriors that preyed on his kind. To most batblins, it would've been a nightmarish situation.

But Klek Adventurers' Bane wasn't like most batblins. He paid no attention to the lurking mass of the horned princess. His eyes were closed, and his long, pointed ears were tense with focus.

"Don't move!" Tulip hissed, her mandibles clicking with irritation. "You must remain still, or the vibrations will scramble and become unreadable."

"*More* unreadable, you mean," Klek whispered, barely moving his lips. "It's a mess down below, and I can barely understand what's going on."

"There's not much to understand," Tulip said darkly. "It's a massacre, and if we escape soon, we'll be next!"

"Don't worry, Tulip. They can't see us," Klek assured her. Similar to him, she wasn't like most horned spiders. Tulip was small for a princess, exchanging brawn for speed and a healthy dose of common sense that some may call cowardice. To Klek, they were the same thing. Tulip's concerns were well founded. If the Inquisitors roaming Jiraz' dungeon looked up, there was a chance their gazes may pierce the shadowy corner that Klek and Tulip occupied. If that happened, Klek had no doubt about the outcome. His own common sense told him he was insane, risking himself like this on the off chance of finding something that Lord Ed could use against the Heroes who, day by day, neared the Haunt's territories. He tightened his jaw, willing himself to remain calm—a racing heart could be enough to set off the vibrations.

"This should be a job for a spiderling," Tulip complained after a moment of silence. "Unlike us, they are expendable."

"No one is expendable," Klek chided her, trying to keep the edge out of his voice. "Spiderlings ain't clever. That's why Lord Ed entrusted this quest to us. We cannot fail him!" He took another deep breath and focused on his *echolocation* talent, which allowed him to sense the world around him using sound bouncing off surfaces. It was an activated talent, with a small energy expenditure. Normally, using it required no concentration at all, but this wasn't a normal circumstance. "Now be quiet! They're moving already."

"Damn snack, thinking he can preach to me," Tulip mouthed to herself, yet loud enough for Klek to hear.

"Shhh!" he urged her.

Tulip shut up, leaving Klek's whole attention on the vibrations coming from the spiderweb. He listened, moving his ears around as he tried to build a mental map of the surrounding chambers.

There were about two dozen humanoids in the rooms below. Six of them were armored, their every step clanking loudly and making distinct vibrations that Klek quickly learned to distinguish. Inquisitors. They paced through stone corridors and tunnels and guarded the rest of the group as they stripped the dungeon and its former inhabitants of anything of value.

Metal rang against metal as trinkets, weapons, armor, and other assorted loot was thrown into carts and wheeled out of the dungeon to the surface, away from Klek's range of hearing. Dungeon Lord Jiraz had traveled to Starevos with a small fortune. Lord Edward's spiderlings had told him that Jiraz had built three other dungeons before this one, all of them annihilated by the same group of Heroes. Jiraz probably would've kept going for a while before running out of resources, but the Heroes had caught him before he'd added an escape route to this dungeon. Klek shook his head. Had Jiraz been a batblin, he would've known to never lift a finger without at least three different escape plans.

Jiraz' demise was both a blessing and a curse for the Haunt. His presence near Hoia had drawn several groups of Heroes away from Galtia where most of them stripped the swamps out of werewolf clans and searched the frozen mountaintops for the surviving vampire nobility of Starevos. With Jiraz gone, the Heroes would be starving for action. If they didn't find it soon, they might return to Galtia, but in the meantime, their presence was a danger to everyone not under the protection of Heiliges and its Militant Church. Lord Edward's plan was to study the Heroes and the Inquisitors from afar until he could figure out the way they worked, then hopefully uncover the way to defeat them.

Who created the Heroes? How do they work; and can we make our own? These had only been a few of the questions Lord Edward asked aloud during countless nights pacing in the War Room. He insisted that the Heroes didn't fit the world of Ivalis as he—or anyone else—

understood it. They were unnatural. Artificial. Made in that specific way for a specific reason. *If we can find out why, we can use it against them,* he said. *The first thing we must do to defeat a powerful enemy is to know the rules they follow. Find their limits, then exploit them.*

Klek wasn't a powerful warrior like Marshal Kes or Monster Hunter Kaga. Batblins were low on the food chain of a dungeon's minions, usually little more than arrow fodder. Expendable, just like spiderlings. But Lord Edward didn't see the world that way. He had given them a warm, safe home to hole up in winter, and found them a place in the dungeon's hierarchy. Batblins were the Haunt's backbone: messengers, cooks, and brewers. They assisted Andreena in potion-making and helped Heorghe work his forge. Most of the elite janitorial squad came from their ranks. The batblins of the Haunt were very different from what they'd been while surviving the unforgiving life of the forest being chased by humans, and spiders, and wolves alike. Klek himself differed greatly from the terrified batblin he'd been before the Haunt.

He was willing to do *anything* to avoid returning to those times.

The spiderweb registered the sound of footsteps approaching a nearby Inquisitor. Despite being unable to distinguish the man's features, Klek found the Inquisitor familiar, in the way a hound may recognize the mailman by their smell. Klek held his breathing. Below, voices took the shape of waves as they crashed against the hard stone surface around them. Instead of causing the waves to break and dissipate, the stone carried them, vibrating in a tiny way that would've been impossible to sense by normal human—or batblin—senses. Tulip's web, connected to the stone, picked the vibrations and transmitted them to Klek.

Using his *echolocation* to translate the garbled mess of information that the stone picked up was an interpretation of the talent that strained the limits of Objectivity's patience, and even then, Klek had to use all his focus to filter the vibrations of that conversation out from all the other background noise that came to him at the same time. It was like putting his head down a confluence and guessing which water came from which river by drinking as fast as possible.

"Eminence... survivor... passageway..." Rats scurrying through holes in the walls. People arguing. The clank of metal.

"—found?" Someone taking a piss in an isolated corridor. A sneeze. The rattle of a wheelbarrow.

"Coffin inside... dark magic..." The Inquisitor and his interloper headed down a damp tunnel where several other Inquisitors and their helpers surrounded a hollow box that rested above a raised marble dais. Klek strained to follow the conversation, but he was reaching the limits at which he could make sense of the vibrations.

The other Inquisitors paced around the dais. An angry buzzing traveled through the web. Klek had heard it before, in the Haunt's laboratory, where Lavy worked her magic.

"Jiraz' right hand..."

"The vampire."

The word captured Klek's interest. He redoubled his efforts.

"Destroy... it?"

There was a pause, while the leader considered his options. "No," he said. "Execution... Constantina. Rebels must see..."

Klek furrowed his brow. A pearl of sweat traveled down his nose and disrupted his mental picture. When he found the correct vibrations again, the familiar Inquisitor was ordering everyone around. He didn't seem disturbed. Someone brought a long chain and waited until the magic around the dais evaporated. Then they chained the box. *A coffin*, Klek thought. He heard the grunts and the strain as six people lowered the coffin down and heaved it on their shoulders. They carried it out, with the Inquisitors following.

Soon enough, they left the batblin's listening range. He sighed and relaxed his body, feeling as tired as if he'd run most of the day. His pelt was slick with sweat.

"You hear anything interesting?" Tulip asked.

Klek signaled at her to release him. Her legs and mandibles set to unravel her web with an instinctive dexterity that would've been the envy of any seamstress. "I think so, yes," he said, fighting off exhaustion. "The Heroes' that cleared the dungeon missed a minion."

"That's not unusual," Tulip said. "They miss many minions. Sometimes they don't even bother with the weakest ones, as if those were beneath their notice. The Inquisition hunts the survivors down after the Heroes have gone, makes sure there are none remaining."

"This is different," said Klek. "The minion was a vampire. Jiraz' second. The Inquisitor chose not to kill him, though. They're bringing the coffin to Undercity with the vampire trapped inside." He shivered. Even though vampires were nightmarish creatures that preyed on the weak and innocent, being trapped inside a box waiting for execution was too unnerving to consider. Batblins and tight spaces didn't mix.

Tulip finished freeing him from the web strands and helped him take hold of the small leather riding chair on her abdomen. Klek found himself upside-down, holding on by the strength of his legs and the straps he grabbed at with two hands. *Don't look down,* he reminded himself. Tulip had told him she was agile enough to catch him with her web if he fell, but it was not a possibility he was willing to test. He hurried to tie the straps around his waist, then secured his legs using a complicated system of metal belts and buckles.

"Vampires are difficult to kill," Tulip said while Klek worked. "There's a chance it may have fought the Heroes. He may know a thing or two about them."

Klek nodded. *Find someone who has seen them up close* was another of the tasks that Lord Edward had set for them. At first mention, it had sounded easy. Lavy and Alder had survived a Heroic attack, hadn't they?

After weeks of searching, Klek found out just how lucky Alder and Lavy had been.

Although some minions survived a dungeon raid, they were all non-combatants: skilled workers, servants, apprentices, slaves, maybe prisoners from enemy Dungeon Lords. If they weren't in the path that the Heroes followed to the Seat Room, there was a chance they could escape the eventual collapse of the dungeon. Evading the Inquisitors that would arrive in the area shortly thereafter was another story.

These Inquisitors had chosen to bring the vampire to Undercity instead of breaking the coffin down and exposing the creature inside to sunlight.

"We need to tell Lord Edward about this," Klek said aloud. "And fast. Hopefully before the coffin arrives inside the city."

"Anything for a chance to leave this death-trap," Tulip said. "Grab on tight, snack. It'd be a shame if you fell down and your splatter alerted everyone to my presence. And keep your eyes closed—I've no use for a dizzy rider."

Klek grimaced, then grabbed a hold of Tulip's horn and a fistful of leather straps just as the spider darted across the stonework and skittered down the wall toward the empty, dark tunnels of the dungeon. After a while, Klek judged they were close enough to the ground he could risk a look without losing his nerve. He took a quick peek and saw an unending line of broken, bloodied bodies left in the Heroes' wake. There were humans and elves and dwarfs and gnomes piled atop each other, kaftar with charred fur, giant blowflies torn to pieces, a naga spread across the full length of the corridor, minotaurs with black tongues out, frozen in a paroxysm of pain. In death, there was no difference between sapient creatures, monsters, and beast. They all ended up being just meat. Klek's stomach churned.

"I told you not to look, snack," Tulip chided him as he heaved and tried not to puke.

- *You've advanced a Dungeon Mission!* Infiltrate the ruins of Jiraz' dungeon.

DESCRIPTION: *A group of Heroes has defeated a neighboring Dungeon Lord, and the Inquisition is active in the ruins.*

Win Condition: Escape the ruins and inform the Haunt of your findings.

Reward: Experience, Recruitment chance (Vampire Lieutenant), Increased faction standing.

Bonus: Succeed without being discovered.

Defeat condition: You are detected, captured, or killed.

CHAPTER FIVE

THE GUILD

Ed's drones helped him and Alder get ready for the trip to Undercity in under two minutes. They brought four of the few horses the Haunt's stables fielded, along with all the provisions and assorted goods they used in their deals with the Thieves Guild. They also brought four cloth bundles set in pairs across two of the horses.

Alder glanced at them, and then did a double take when he saw one bundle shift awkwardly. "Ed, are those people in there?" the Bard asked.

"Yes," Ed said. "I was going to tell you about it. We'll finish a small side-quest while we're out in the city. They are the prisoners we kept from Nicolai's attack. I finally figured out a way to deal with them."

The bundle shook again, more frantically, as the young man inside found meaning in Ed's words, but the prisoners were up to their necks in horned spider paralyzing venom, and their attempts at freeing themselves were sporadic and far too feeble to ever succeed.

Alder gave him a worried look. "So... what are we going to do with them, exactly?"

"Well. I figured we should just let the sea do our dirty work for us," Ed said, and winked at the Bard. The bundles' shaking increased.

UNDERCITY'S HARBOR swayed with the current. The floating wooden platforms which extended all the way from the beach to the merchant ships were the Ivalian way of dealing with the effect that having two moons had on the sea currents. Ed stood right below a small trading ship called *the Strenuous*, with Oscor the dwarven smuggler next to him, and Karmich the Thief on his other side. Alder was a few strides behind, watching how the fishermen hauled Ed's cargo into the ship.

"You know," the Bard said loudly, as to be heard over the chatter of the harbor and the yells of the sailors as they worked. "When you said we were letting the sea do our job, I thought you meant something else."

They'd smuggled the captured prisoners all the way into the harbor with some help from Oscor's band. The bundles had gone to the bottom of a rug-maker's cart, and after a generous bribe to the guards convinced them to not look very hard at the cart's inventory, the merchant reached the harbor just in time.

"I figured the prisoners would think the same thing," Ed called back. "A bit of fear serves them right for trying to kill us, don't you agree?"

"So, what will happen to them, Master Edward?" asked Karmich pleasantly, while he munched on a sweet-roll he'd stolen from a bakery down the street.

"They get another chance at life, I suppose," Ed explained. "*The Strenuous* is headed all the way to Plekth, taking the long route to buy and sell spices in every port. Our rebel friends will become part of the crew and work to earn their living. Once they reach Plekth, they'll be free to go or remain as crew-members of *the Strenuous* if they so desire—just as long as they don't return to

Starevos, I don't care what they do. But I gave a letter to the captain for him to give the rebels when they reach Plekth. If they want to stay a while in the Old Continent, maybe our mutual friend won't mind taking them in as apprentices for her guild."

It had been hard to decide what to do with the prisoners. The Haunt couldn't just release them in Starevos, since they knew where the dungeon was located, but Ed wasn't comfortable with the idea of killing them. He'd finally landed on a compromise he was satisfied with. Sure, being forced away from their home country into a sailor's hard life wouldn't feel that way for them, but it was the best Ed could do.

Karmich considered his words. "She'll have to forgive them for almost killing her first. But knowing Kat, she has forgotten about their part in that adventure already. After all, she's terrible at holding grudges."

"Just what I was thinking," Ed said. Thinking of Katalyn gave him a pang of nostalgia in his chest, a feeling that was both pleasant and painful at the same time. The free-spirited Thief-turned-Rogue was a true adventurer, a woman born to chase after danger and adventure with nothing more than her wits and a confident smile. Although Ed and she had been together only for a short time, he still wasn't able to look at the sea without it reminding him of her.

Oscor bent his stout body over the edge of the platform, plugged one of his nostrils, and blew hard out of the other. "All right, enough with the sea. Water is meant to make strong booze, not to stand and gawk at." He tugged at his beard with one dirty hand. Behind them, Alder made a gagging noise barely muffled by his sleeve. "Time to talk shop, Master Mercenary."

The moment was gone. Ed gave the distant horizon one last look, then shook his head to clear his mind and nodded. "Let's talk shop then, Master Oscor. How about some drinks?"

. . .

The Galleon's Folly's cramped frame shook so hard from the carousing inside that a foreigner stuck there might have believed the earth was shaking. Inside, locals mixed with sailors in bouts of drinking competitions, boasting matches, and randomly sparked bouts of fist-fighting that ended as soon as they started, usually with the fighters forgetting all about it and scrambling to the bar for more social lubrication.

Ed's private table was set in the far corner of the tavern, giving him a straight view of the entrance and easy access to the secret back exit. Nearby, a bunch of local whores chatted up a group of sailors who, by the way they "discreetly" elbowed the others on the ribs, thought *they* were the ones getting lucky tonight. From what Ed knew of the Galleon's Folly locals, though, by the end of the night, the whores would walk out of some dark alley with their purses full, having done little to none of the job that made their profession famous. The sailors would probably scramble back to their ships in the morning, with one hell of a headache and more than a few bruises.

"Ah, life's good when business is blooming," Oscor said, pouring himself another glass of ale. He relaxed his back and patted his quickly engorging belly. Not all dwarves were barely functioning alcoholics, but not all dwarves were Oscor.

"I'll toast to that," Karmich said, eyeing the whores. He was probably calculating how many Vyfaras were in those sailors' pockets and wondering how to get a cut off the profits for himself.

Next to Ed, Alder smiled and nursed a cup of warm cider. Neither of them were drinking tonight. "So, how's the Guild dealing with the local... ah, administration, these days?"

"Same old, same old," Karmich said. "For the people in the know, there's always an angry man of justice with a big hammer looking down on the little guys trying to make a living. Whether the hammer is steel or silver makes no difference. We make do, just as always." He took a long swig of his tzuika and grimaced at its strength.

Ed rubbed his chin. It was true that life went on as usual inside Undercity, despite the implicit threat of the Militant Church, who kept a close eye on the comings and goings of the city. So far, the Inquisition had remained pretty much away from the daily lives of its inhabitants—their mission was to deal with the Dark, not with petty theft and smuggling. Technically, the only threat that Ed ought to fear, at least when talking about his business in the city, was from the King's tax officers. But he also knew that although the status-quo had a tendency to reassert itself, it also had weak points which could explode with catastrophic conse-quences if pressured.

What could happen if the Inquisition put their fingers on one of those?

"I'm glad you and yours are happy with our friendship, Karmich," Ed said aloud, to change the subject and to get to the point of the meeting. "But I reckon the only thing better than making a pile of money is making an even *bigger* pile. Perhaps it's time to get our little alliance to the next level."

Karmich finished his tzuika and bent forward, smiling. "Is that so, friend Edward? Please, tell me more."

"In fact, Oscor here is the one best suited to explain what we have in mind."

Oscor nodded. "A while ago, Master Edward and I had a long chat about my birthplace, back in the steel-topped Manslan Peaks. We talked about the songs the miners sang while heading into the bowels of the earth first thing in the morning, about the lazuli vaults where my ancestors are buried, and about the beautiful dwarven women with their braided beards as varied in color as opals. One particular thing caught our friend's imagination, though, when I told him the way our miners transport themselves and their cargo back to the surface. It's funny the things humans latch on. I'd rather talk of dwarven women and their jeweled hair for days on end, but to each their own." The dwarf shrugged, then went on, "Master Ed was quite taken with the concept of mining carts and the simple rail mechanisms we use to quickly move them from one end of a tunnel to the other. He had me describe in detail the inner workings of one and was so insistent that I was forced to draw him a Hogbus-be-damned sketch on a napkin. A few days later, his kaftar met with me for our weekly stock exchange, and they claimed Ed was now building a working prototype of one of our dwarven carts. A week after that, and the kaftar claimed they'd made the trip in a fraction of the time it usually took, thanks to Ed's machine."

"That's the kind of story that would get even the best Bard thrown out of a tavern for making too bold a claim," Karmich said. "But knowing just how resourceful our adventurer friends are, I'm inclined to believe it. I just wonder, what does that have to do with the Guild?"

"Think about it," Ed said. "Before, moving the stock from our headquarters to Undercity was a dangerous odyssey. Our kaftar friends, the Haga'Anashi clan, had to risk discovery by the King's officers with every trip—and that was before the Inquisition began patrolling the woods. All it took was a single day with bad luck and it would compromise our operation. Hell, even the time was an issue. Reaching Undercity took the Haga'Anashi most of the day, and they were never able to move as many barrels as we'd have liked to because the weight was prohibitive. We had bottle-necked our production. A single tunnel with one cart changed all that. Now the trip is safer than ever and at a fraction of the time."

He paused to allow his listeners to process his words, just like Alder had taught him to. "Imagine ten tunnels like that," Ed said after a bit. "I know that the Guild has more charters all over Starevos, and there are even rumors of a charter in Galtia itself—"

"Completely unfounded," Karmich said with a wink.

"My group could lay a system of tunnels that reaches most of Starevos in a couple years. If you help us with the expense, we can even protect those tunnels from incursions, as well as keep them hidden from the Militant Church. The sea may be guarded by the Heiligian fleet, and the Inquisition's griffins may patrol the sky, but the underground is mine. I won't deal in pixie dust or slaves, but there's a market for untaxed silk, spice, tobacco, and of course tzuika and ale. For a fee, you could use the tunnels to move your stock all over Starevos. No other Guild would even come close to competing with your prices. Summoning circles are expensive and unreliable, and Portals are even worse."

Unless you happened to be a Dungeon Lord with access to a ruby vein, of course. Ed lacked materials to set up a Portal network—even a single Portal was out of his reach for the moment—but even if he did, a Portal only allowed for a certain amount of mass to be transported through in a day before it ran out of energy.

The tunnels were the best possible solution. His drones had no limit—that he knew of—to how much earth they could chew. They could only work a certain distance away from him or a dungeon Seat, though, which was the reason he'd need a couple years to set up the network. His plan was to create many hidden, smaller dungeons using Scrambling Towers all over the country and have each of those protect a part of the tunnel system.

It'd take a solid amount of minions to man those dungeons, but Ed had an entire Spider Empire backing him up. He was sure he could figure things out.

"How promising," said Karmich. He turned back and raised a finger to Max, the bartender. "If what you're saying is true, and I've little doubt it is, Grand Master Bavus himself will want to know about it as soon as possible. There's good business to be had in those tunnels. Although..." He scratched the side of his nose and looked at the ceiling with feigned carelessness. "Our Grand Master may consider it... as someone who doesn't know Master Alder and yourself as well as I do... strange that you're able to just lay out the infrastructure of an almost country-wide digging operation in a couple years, instead of multiple decades. And the expense! Kingdoms could go bankrupt just by thinking of doing what you're proposing, Master Edward. Not that we don't trust you, of course. It's just that I'd like to offer Bavus a good reason not to jump to conclusions."

Ed smiled with just as much feigned disinterest as Karmich while matching the Thief's posture. It was a neat Charm trick that Alder had taught him. "See, I understand how that may appear suspicious. But our... corporation just hired a specialist spell-caster... ah, a Geomancer from... Plekth. Yes." Next to him, Alder winced and smacked his own forehead. Ed ignored it. Not everyone had Bluff as a main skill. "This Geomancer developed a magical breakthrough, allowing us to lay out the tunnels quickly and with little expense. So there's no need to worry about it." He even waved his hand like Alder sometimes did while powering through a weak part of a tale, as if trying to draw attention away from it. Ed hoped it was part of a Charm talent he had yet to learn.

Both Oscor and Karmich beamed and nodded repeatedly to show their agreement. "So a Wizard did it," said Karmich. "Makes perfect sense. *Perfect* sense, Master Edward. I'm sure Grand Master Bavus will be satisfied with this reasonable explanation. No need to even speak further of it. Wetlands, forget I even brought it up!"

A cute waitress with a knife strapped to her thigh brought the Thief his drink. He smiled at her and gestured for her to come sit on his lap. She smiled back and pointed at her knife. Karmich let the matter drop.

"Good to know we squared that up," Ed said. He had expected something like that. The Thieves Guild and Oscor's smuggling operation knew there was some... *strangeness* going on with Ed and Alder. It was impossible to hide things like their relationship with the Haga'Anashi kaftar or how they hid their operation so well from the tax officers. It added up. But the beautiful thing about dealing with Thieves, smugglers, and others of their ilk was that as long as there was some clear profit to be had from maintaining their relationship with mysterious adventurer Edward Wright—and a very risky element to thinking too hard about *what* exactly he was—then they'd pretty much be willing to overlook anything as long as Ed could come up with the right excuse.

Given that nearly everyone not Dark-aligned wasn't willing to deal with a Dungeon Lord, no matter how well intentioned he was, his relationship with the Guild was refreshing.

The Guild and the Haunt had a good thing going. With any luck, it could even last.

Life rarely works that way, though, a bleak part at the back of Ed's mind chimed in.

THE HAUNT CELEBRATED its victory against the spider rebellion the evening following Ed's return from Undercity. They all stepped into the Mess Hall at more or less the appropriate hour, wearing their best clothes. A year ago, that would've meant a not-so-dirty shirt or dress, but thanks to the seamstress' skills and the discrete trading with the neighboring villages, those of the Haunt had slowly rebuilt the possessions they'd lost during Burrova's destruction. Tonight, Ed saw many green capes, fashioned similarly to his own, as well as more than a couple purple dresses with tight corsets like the ones Lavy favored, and even a few brave men trying to wear the Haunt's emblem, the Lasershark, stitched to their expensive vests with varying degrees of success.

Ed wasn't a fan of the Lasershark, but so far he hadn't changed it, and at this point he suspected it was best if he resigned himself to it—the Haunted liked it, at least.

The Mess Hall was a great chamber in the middle of the dungeon. Ed had built it to fit most of the Haunt's inhabitants—although he was running out of space. The ceiling was a forest of stalagmites, some of which were as long as spears. Candlesticks and magical torches hung from them like exotic, luminous fruits. Silvery web swayed with the dungeon's airflow, like the breath of a slumbering titan. Horned spider princesses traversed the webs, hauling meat around and having an upside-down replica of the celebrations below.

He sat at the end of a long stone table that fit several dozen people. Batblins and kaftar and humans filled several other similar tables that occupied most of the Mess Hall's center. Drones ran through the corridors left among the rows of wooden chairs, acting as impromptu waiters. It was a job they absolutely despised, and drones often found passive-aggressive—emphasis on aggressive—ways to protest jobs they hated, so Ed only used them this way during special occasions.

"The situation, as I was saying yesterday," mumbled Governor Brett while he chewed, "is terribly grim. The Haunt's expenses are hugely demanding, and we cannot depend on our... er... aggressive commerce forever. Undercity's Treasury is hunting for us, I hear, and no matter how good the ruffians that our Murderousness employs are at evading it, the Treasury always sinks its teeth in its prey! You can trust me, I'd know!" He barked a mirthless laugh for emphasis, sending flecks of food flying everywhere. "We need to institute tributary laws at the Haunt, soon, or we could face disaster," he announced, brandishing a finger at Kes. "Of course, given I'm somewhat of a legal expert myself, I'd be in charge of drafting our constitution. For the benefit of the Haunt."

Kes was staring daggers at the man. "In case you haven't noticed, we are in a war for survival against the Inquisition itself. We cannot waste time on bureaucracy—it'd only slow us down." She stabbed her steak with ravenous enthusiasm. The main dish involved smoked ham bathed in a sauce made of a sweet yellow berry, the taste of which was reminiscent of fermented pineapple, though it was poisonous if you ate too much. "The Haunt can't demand taxes from its inhabitants—not yet. It has no economy, they have no coin to pay us with, and we can build everything we need from scratch, anyway. Or have you forgotten that his 'Murderousness' can create real estate by hollowing out the rock under our feet?"

Ed took a long sip out of his tankard of ale. He had no interest in politics, and the mere phrase "institute tributary laws" made him want to yawn. The ale probably had a hand in that, too. No, better to let Kes and Brett duke it out.

He shifted his attention away. Forgemaster Heorghe was eating what—judging from the growing pile of bones on the plate in front of him—had been an entire gray hell chicken a few minutes ago. The blacksmith was drinking straight from a bottle of tzuika as he went, and judging from the annoyed look of his wife, Ivona, and the already empty bottle near his current one, drones would have to carry him to his chambers in a few hours. A shame, because otherwise Ed and Heorghe could've had a chat about the Haunt's engineering projects, which was always a welcomed way to pass an evening.

Close to Heorghe was Priest Zachary, who was sipping a greenish soup sprinkled with nuts. Most of his attention was in an argument against the batblin Drusb, the Haunt's main cloudmaster. Judging from the trail of soup dripping from Zachary's chin, the discussion was getting heated.

"Preposterous, preposterous!" Zachary bellowed. "Hogbus never won that bet, he cheated Oynnes when he disguised himself as a horned bear!"

Drusb waved Hogbus' holy symbol at the priest. The symbol was an old stick with bells and colored pebbles hanging from it, and a pewter bear-shaped medallion at the center. "Silly human, you know nothing! There is no such thing as a horned bear! Hogbus outsmarted dumb Light god fair-and-square, not his fault Oynnes forgot that wood elves can talk to animals!"

"Don't wave that thing my way!" Zachary waved his own holy symbol at the batblin, a fist-sized coin of solid gold with a hollow center.

The conversation failed to captured Ed, especially since he wasn't on speaking terms with most of the Ivalian gods. Murmur was an asshole, Alita was an asshole who also wanted him dead, and Hogbus, from what he'd heard, suffered from the divine equivalent of fleas. That left Oynnes as the Haunt's patron. He was a giant gold digger, but at least he was willing to accept Zachary's offerings without looking too hard into their origin.

On the other side of the table, near the fireplace, Alder sat on a suede sofa and played a mellow tune on his lute to aid the digestion of the dozen sleepy children that were his audience. The Bard had his flute and harp next to him, so Ed judged that Alder intended to milk the attention for all it was worth.

"Something troubling you?" Lavy asked. She plopped into the seat next to him and set her plate down on the table. She had skipped the main course and gone straight to the dessert: marzipan cakes bathed in hot jam and sprinkled with dried fruits.

"Was it so obvious?" Ed asked while Lavy nibbled a cake.

"You've barely touched your food," she pointed out.

Ed glanced at the small pile of empty plates around him, then raised an eyebrow at her.

"I meant that you only ate enough to survive Kes' training tomorrow," clarified the Witch.

"Oh. Makes sense."

Lavy snatched up a glass of tzuika from the tray of an annoyed drone that was passing by them. "It isn't healthy, you know, to spend your time worrying about that over which you have no control. It's terrible for your skin, and it will age you before your time. As someone who barely cares about things, I'm the perfect counter-example." She pinched her cheek. "See? Not caring works."

Ed snorted. "My skin will have to handle it." He scratched his chin. "Klek and Tulip have been gone for almost a week. It's the longest they've been away, and their task is risky."

Lavy crossed her hands. "They're fine. Neither of them are

prone to take risks lightly… and with Klek's luck, anyway, it's likely he'll return having soloed the Inquisition. We'll have to add Hero-Destroyer to his list of titles."

"I believe that," Ed said with a low chuckle. Then, he shook his head. "I just hate having to wait. Even if it is for a reason, it makes me feel too much like a typical Boss at the end of a raid, just hanging out in his cave until the Heroes arrive."

They paused while Lavy chewed a cake. Next to another table, a group of men and women talked over Alder's melodies, exchanging rough jokes and laughing at those too drunk to stand.

"You should try to join them," Lavy suggested. "It's not fair you don't get to celebrate the Haunt's victory along with everyone else."

"Look more carefully," Ed suggested. He waved at the revelers, like a Bard ending an illusion spell. The laughter from the circle came with an edge of forced bravado. The mothers' eyes kept darting toward their children, as if worrying that a hungry horned spider would drop from the ceiling to carry them away. The men carried daggers and hunting knifes at their waists, like Kes, Ed, and the kaftars did. To Ed, that was the most telling sign, because he knew the reason he was always armed.

They expected an attack at any time and hoped to be as ready for it as they could.

"I gave them a victory against an enemy created by my own choices."

"You're describing war itself, Ed," Lavy said. "These people are no strangers to suffering, so they take whatever cause there is for celebration. They'll even cheer if our spiders defeat a bunch of other spiders. But I also know you well enough to understand that the life you led back on Earth wasn't much like ours." She gazed at the biscuit she held between her fingers as if divining some profound truth from it. "To us Ivalians, see, this is the way it has always been. A monster may end them tomorrow. Or a fire. Or a zealous Inquisitor. They may get drafted as arrow fodder. Maybe their dungeon falls to an invading army. There's always sickness, or famine, or flood. They may run into bandits while traveling, or encounter wild animals." She looked like she could go on, but changed her mind. "What I mean is, the Heroes are just another name added to a long tally. They aren't your fault, just like what happened to Kael wasn't your fault. It's just the way it is. Our friends may act terrified when I call on the spirits of the dead, but death is as normal to them as it is to me."

Ed could almost feel the caress of the tongues of flame dancing in the fireplace as they cast their shadow upon his face. The airflow made the shadows flicker on the floor tiles like lurking ghosts. He appreciated Lavy's attempt at cheering him up, and he knew she was right. But she had misread the reason for his bad mood. It wasn't guilt. It wasn't the weight of responsibility. But how best could he put it into words?

He almost wanted to let the conversation end there, but he thought it over. Closing himself off to his friends would be a mistake. A weakness he couldn't afford.

"Do you remember the terms of the bet I made with Kharon when I became a Dungeon Lord?" he asked without taking his gaze from the fire.

He had told her the story not long after they first met, back when the Haunt was but a cave with some rugs thrown in. "The Boatman bet that power is the shackle of man. He believes that the only thing required to make you serve the will of Murmur was to receive the Mantle," she said. "It's the Dark doctrine, you know? I had to know a bit of it, even though I hated it, as an apprentice for Warlock Chasan. The Mantle takes its name from an old Lotian saying. 'The only difference between a King or a Tyrant is the color of the cape.'" She grasped a corner of her violet dress in her fist. "It's a load of dung, Ed. These clothes may be the dress of a Witch, but if Alder wears them, he won't become Lavina. We are who we are, no matter what."

A few years ago, he would've agreed with her in an instant. *The thing is, Kharon wasn't talking about clothes. The mantle we wear is the power we wield,* Ed thought.

The lives of everyone in the Haunt hinged on him. If they thrived, it'd be thanks to everyone's efforts pulled together. If they died, though? His fault alone.

That was a Dungeon Lord's Mantle.

It was no wonder that every other Dungeon Lord he'd heard about was crazy.

CHAPTER SIX

BOOTCAMP

"Spears are simple," Kes told her audience. She had one such spear resting vertically next to her, the iron point aimed at the Training Ground's ceiling. "They build your strength, and your stance, and teach you good habits. Master the spear and you'll have the foundations for the sword and most other martial weapons."

The Training Grounds bristled with activity. A group of disheveled batblins ran circuits around the chamber, cursing and wheezing as they went, their tiny legs pumping up and down, their furry behinds shaking like that of a chicken. It would've been comical had Kes not been in charge of shaping their sorry asses into proper combat-ready shape.

"To start, you'll learn the basic stances, and we'll progress from there. All you need to know today is that spear-fighting is built around thrusting at three specific areas: the face, throat, and gut." She demonstrated with three quick attacks against a training dummy. The recruits stared in awe.

Kes wanted to scream. Despite drinking enough water to drown a kid, the hangover threatened to split her head open side to side. *What the hell do the Brewers put in the booze?* She didn't want to know. Actually, she hoped she'd never find out.

No matter how bad she felt, she couldn't let it show, not even for a tiny second. The nine sorry men and women that would become the backbone of the Haunt's garrison were as hungover as she was, and they'd take any sign of weakness as an excuse to complain. *Humans.* One would think having an Endurance average of 10 would mean they were tougher than an Avian teenager, but if Kes had learned anything in her life, it was that no matter the species, boots would find an excuse to complain about anything.

This current batch was green. They were greener than grass on a bright summer day after a hearty rain. Volunteers, the lot of them, so she'd to give them props for their courage, although she suspected that none had known what they were signing on for. *Isn't it like that always?* There were only nine volunteers, but that was almost as many as Burrova guardsmen, and taking the batblins into account, the Haunt's armed forces were about as numerous as that of a small town's. After Nicolai's attack on the Haunt, most of the villagers had been happy to let the fighting fall in Kes' hands, as well as Ed and his army of spiders, so even nine human recruits to take care of protecting the Haunt was huge. Even so, at first they'd serve as a sort of community watch, only taking arms if needed and working their normal jobs otherwise. Costel, for example, was a baker. Young Ivan was a butcher, and Old Ivan was a drunk whose brothers had "volunteered" him for guard duty after one too many mornings having to drag his ass home.

"With a spear, you want to stab. That's how you kill an enemy. You'll still learn to swipe and chop, but understand for now that it works differently than with a bladed weapon." She demonstrated a brutal chop that mashed the side of the iron tip against the dummy's temple. Against a human, it would've meant a broken skull. "You want to crush, rather than cut." The recruits nodded almost in unison. Kes could've bet her nonexistent retirement fund that they hadn't understood a word. It didn't matter. She'd *make* them understand.

"This is an underhand hold." Once again, she demonstrated. "Rear hand goes here, above the spear. Now you do it." The boots hurried to imitate her with their training spears.

Their ages ranged from fifteen to thirty, except for the only woman, Costel, a stocky forty-year-old widow who wanted to be a guard because, as she had told Kes, she wanted to know what it felt to kill someone. Her husband had choked to death in his sleep under mysterious circumstances. Costel was Kes' most promising recruit.

She did a passable underhand hold. "When can we practice against real people?" she asked Kes.

"When I'm sure you won't kill each other by accident." Kes tried not to add any emphasis on the word "accident." "Even with training weapons, a mistake can maim or kill. We'll wait on practice combat until you're better trained, and until your gambesons are finished. Padded armor can turn a caved-in skull into a mere contusion, so don't dismiss it because it isn't steel." Since Heorghe was up to his eyebrows with work, he'd offloaded the gambeson' job on the seamstresses, who had only a vague idea of what the process entailed. It would take a while until they managed a passing armor, but they'd get there.

Costel grunted and said nothing more, but she occasionally stole hungry glances at the dueling ring, from which the sound of metallic clashes emanated.

Young Ivan was the second to get the right form after Kes corrected a couple mistakes. While she went to instruct Old Ivan, Young Ivan tried to snap his spear at a forty-five degree angle, and smashed his foot with the butt of the spear. He hopped around on one leg while the others mocked him.

Green. A bit greener than that and maybe she could sell them in the market as produce.

Kes corrected their holds again, then had them spend the next few hours entering and leaving what the Cardinal Command called the basic defensive stance of spear-fighting. She followed along, giving them pointers and fixing common mistakes. It was hard work, and it was excruciating while hungover. But a part of her was ecstatic. It'd been so long since she'd revisited the Cardinal fighting style that it was like catching up with an old friend she hadn't seen in years.

"Sir—Ma'am—my hand is bleeding. Is it supposed to do that?" asked Yemal, a twenty-something male with five children and one more on the way.

"No, Yemal, you're holding your spear wrong." She grabbed his wrists and showed him the right way. Again. "Don't worry. Eventually you'll get calluses in the right spots."

Yemal sighed. "My hands will end up being only calluses, then."

"Just think of how weak in the knees your wife will be when you turn up transformed into a mighty warrior," Old Ivan egged him.

"She said that if I get killed and I leave her alone with the kids, she'll bed my brother," Yemal said. "She hasn't talked to me since I signed up," he added.

"Why would you volunteer, then?" someone asked from the back.

"I have a pregnant wife and five children. This is the most peaceful morning I've had in years."

Green! With the money from the produce sale, Kes could buy a club and some nails, which surely would make for a more effective defense system than these humans.

I seem to recall a boot that complained as much as them, Sergeant Ria told her from the back of her mind. *Hell, didn't you cry during your first night at camp?*

Fuck off, Sarge, Kes thought. *You weren't there for that part.* She knew that the voice of her old, grumpy sergeant was only a trick of her imagination, a product of too many blows to the head mixed with the trauma of losing her wings. It still beat having to relive Ria's eventual fate over and over again, as well as the fate of the rest of her squad. And some days, anyway, Kes welcomed the company of someone who *got it,* even if it was a ghost, or insanity, or whatever. *What would you have done in my place, anyway?*

Ria would've been brutal the first weeks, to cull the weak and force the ones who stayed to bond over their hatred for the sergeant. Then, slowly, as they improved and become real fighters, she'd have allowed them to earn her "begrudging" respect, as if they'd forced her hand by sheer effort instead of it being the entire point all along. That had created a different kind of bond between the unit and Ria, which eventually expanded into a fiery loyalty to the Cardinal Command and the values it represented.

It was a tried-and-true method at creating warriors. But Kes couldn't use it. She didn't have an unending tide of new recruits to fill the ranks of the ones who broke. These nine were all she had. If she pushed them too hard, fewer would join next time. But if she pushed them too little, they would become a danger to themselves at best, and mean bullies at worst.

Maybe she could inspire them some other way. Kes bit her lip and followed Costel's gaze. Most the boots were stealing glances at the dueling grounds. *I can use this,* she thought.

"Five-minute-break, everyone," she announced. Before they had a chance to relax, she added, "Come with me. There's something you must see."

She led them toward the dueling grounds like a mother duck guiding a line of sweaty, tired ducklings. When she stopped a few paces away from the stake circle, the boots bunched up behind her.

"These are two of my best students," she told the group. "They've been training for a little over three seasons, following the same program you'll go through. If you apply yourselves, you'll be as skilled as they. Perhaps you could even surpass them."

In the ring, Ed and Alder exchanged parries and ripostes

repeatedly using dull-edged longswords. They'd changed much since they'd first started training. While they still had a long way to go, the changes in their bodies already showed. Alder's lanky frame was being shaped into an athletic build, and the warm lines of his face were now framed by a powerful jaw. He appeared less like a Bard every day, which was a stark contrast to Ed, who looked more and more like a Dungeon Lord with each passing season. The gaunt and tall young man Kes had first met had become a trim, broad-shouldered warrior with callused hands and unruly black hair reaching his shoulders. He was gaining pounds of muscle along with each Endurance and Brawn rank, and even his stride became more grounded as time went on, as if Ivalis itself warmed to his presence. To Kes, it seemed as if there was a sort of promise in the way Ed was growing—as if, if she focused, she could see past him and gaze into the future, into the Dungeon Lord he would become once he fully eased into his role.

And you're helping him become that man. You're pouring into him all you know, all that pain and life have taught you along the way, Kes thought. *Once his training is over, Lord Wraith shall have a part of him that is Kessih of Greene as well as the part that is Edward Wright.* The idea was both exhilarating and terrifying at once. This was the hidden power of mentors—the way they became immortal and achieved true mastery. *Will he add my voice to my teachings when he thinks of them, the way Ria's voice lives inside me to this day?*

Kes' throat had gone dry. She forced herself back into reality, and away from those thoughts. Peering into the future could be too much for a mortal, even if it were the nebulous, uncertain future of *could be* and *may be.*

No, best to live life one day at a time. Today, Ed and Alder were still her trainees, and the gods knew she had a lot of road yet to walk with them. Their stances needed work. A parry there was too slow. The riposte would've crushed Alder's wrist in a real fight. It comforted her. Things were as they should be. She wasn't ready for immortality just yet.

One of the rookies behind Kes took a sharp breath and whistled. "Me, fighting like a Dungeon Lord? Kes, you're talking nonsense. Are you still drunk?"

Ah, Kes thought. *Yes.* There was a reason she'd come here. She gave the rookie her best challenging smile and eased herself back into her mantle of mentor. "Fighting is a skill, Rasvan, not a magical power. You can see Alder and Lord Edward's character sheet as well as you can see mine. If you raise your *melee* skill as high as theirs, what makes you think you cannot fight as well?"

The boots stood still as they focused on Ed's character sheet. Kes followed suit, although by now she'd come to know the stats of most of the Haunt's inhabitants by heart. She started with Alder.

ALDER LOOM

Species: Human
Total Exp: 270
Unused Exp: 0
Claims: Bardic School of Elaitra - Journeyman.

ATTRIBUTES

Brawn: 10
Agility: 9
Endurance: 10
Mind: 10
Spirit: 9 (+1 Minion of Dungeon Lord Edward Wright)= 10
Charm: 13 (+1 Minion of Dungeon Lord Edward Wright)= 14

SKILLS

. . .

KNOWLEDGE (BARDSHIP): *Improved (I)* - Pertains to the owner's knowledge of a specialized, secret topic. This skill allows access to the Bardic subdomain's utterances.

BARDIC PERFORMANCE: Basic (IX) - Represents the Bard's capacity for performing under the pressure of an audience without penalization to the bard's magic.

-Basic status allows the Bard to suffer no penalty to performing an utterance in the presence of a crowd if there's no danger involved.

-If danger is involved, each extra rank of Basic allows the Bard faster utterance casting and lessens the risk of disruption if they suffer damage or are attacked.

SURVIVAL: *Basic (VII)* - Represents the owner's capability to survive when far from civilization. Basic ranks imply they can survive in a non-lethal environment and situations. They can build a basic campsite, know that some berries are dangerous, how to start a fire, and so on.

MELEE: *Basic (III)* - Measures the user's progress in physical combat. It opens up melee-related talents as well as advanced martial skill specializations.

Talents

BARDIC UTTERANCES: *Basic (IV)* - Allows the bard to use utterances, the magical variant of the Illusion and Control hybrid subdomain: Bardic.

-Basic ranks allow the bard to perform any basic utterance that they know and have practiced enough.

-Allowed utterances: 4 basic per day + 1 basic utterance due to Dungeon Allegiance.

ENERGY DRAIN: Active. Varies per utterance.

SPELLCASTING: *Basic (II) - Domains: Illusion(Mind). Forbidden: Rend -* Represents the owner's magical ability.

-Basic status allows the caster to use and learn all basic related spells of their domain. Extra ranks improve each individual spell's characteristics, such as range or damage.

-Allowed spells: 2 basic per day + 1 basic spell due to Dungeon Allegiance

EMPATHY: *Basic -* Allows the owner to sense emotions in humanoid creatures familiar to the owner.

-Basic status lets the owner sense strong emotions that their targets are not actively trying to hide.

ENERGY DRAIN: Active. Low.

DUNGEON MINION - DUNGEON MINION. The owner is a minion under the command of a Dungeon Lord. The Minion receives bonuses according to the Lord's power and is recognized by the Dungeon Lord's dungeon as an allowed entity (unless otherwise specified).

RESIST SICKNESS: *Basic -* Allows its owner to resist disease and sickness.

-Basic status allows the owner to resist non-magical sickness as if they had Endurance of 15 and were in optimal conditions (clean, well-fed, rested).

IMPROVED DODGE - ALLOWS the owner to perform, up to the limits of their own body, the correct set of movements to avoid being hit by a non-magical attack as long as the owner sees it coming.

ENERGY DRAIN: Activated. Moderate.

UTTERANCE LIST

Nimble Feet - Creates an area of effect around the Bard that allows them and their friends to retreat as if they possessed an Agility of 15. This effect ends if the users enter combat.
Duration: 5 minutes.

BARDIC IMAGES - As long as the Bard is playing his instrument, five illusory copies of himself are created on the battlefield. They are indistinguishable from the real one, and will do their best to keep attention away from the Bard. If the Bard uses Bardic Images along with a Spellcasting slot, he can change the form of the copies to another person, but they will behave as normal illusions and have to be directly controlled.

DAZZLING DISPLAY - Any creature with direct line of sight to the performing Bard is stunned by the Utterance and feels compelled to pay its full attention to the Bard. The creature can attempt to resist the effect by contesting its Charm, Mind, or Spirit against the Bard's Charm. This effect ends if the creature is attacked.

Duration: 3 seconds.

SPELL LIST
Minor Illusion, Arcane Flare.

ALDER WAS CREATING AN INTERESTING BUILD. A focus on illusions was something Kes' had seen only a few Bards go for, so she had little frame of reference. As far as she knew, most illusions were resisted by either the Mind attribute or the Spirit, but Alder was certain that he could eventually purchase Bard-exclusive talents to force his targets to use Charm against his own Charm, and that was where he was focusing. Ever since he'd begun practicing his songs and performances again, he'd gained two new utterances, which he used defensively. Kes approved of that choice. Only shock troops spec'd into full aggression. Everyone who valued their own hides tried to make themselves as hard to hit as possible.

On the other hand, she wished she could convince the Bard to go for more physical talents other than his new *improved dodge*. The reason was that magical talents weren't always at hand. An enemy spellcaster could use an anti-magic field, or buff their own attributes to resist Alder's illusions. Physical talents were more reliable and much cheaper than magical ones.

At least Ed hasn't made his choice yet. The Dungeon Lord could still resist the siren's call of magic and go for the more sensible approach. Ed liked to hoard his experience points until his skills were high enough to show him a more flexible list of options. He'd bought an expensive *improved metabolism* because he had realized that some Dungeon Lord's talents couldn't be shut down, like his *pledge of armor*, and was saving the rest of his points until he raised his *Dungeon Engineering* skill to Improved.

This plan, however, Kes wasn't so sure she approved of.

HUGO HUESCA

Improved metabolism implied that Ed planned on picking more always-on talents, which was a dangerous line to tread. Too much strain to his body and the chances that he'd keel over dead in his thirties skyrocketed, no matter how powerful he became by then.

She focused on Ed until his character sheet appeared in avian glyphs in front of her.

EDWARD WRIGHT

Species: Human
Total Exp: 460
Unused Exp: 107
Claims: Lordship.

ATTRIBUTES
Brawn: 12
Agility: 11
Endurance: 13
Mind: 13
Spirit: 14 (+1 Dungeon Lord mantle)= 15
Charm: 13 (+1 Dungeon Lord mantle)= 14

SKILLS

ATHLETICS: Basic (VI) - The owner has trained his body to perform continuous physical activity without penalties to their Endurance. For a while.

-Basic ranks allows them to realize mild energy-consuming tasks (non-combat) such as running or swimming without tiring. Unlocks stamina-related talents.

. . .

MELEE: Basic (VI) - Measures the user's progress in physical combat. It opens up melee-related talents as well as advanced martial skill specializations.

DUNGEON ENGINEERING: Improved (VII) - This skill represents the user's knowledge of magical constructs pertaining to dungeon-craft. As it improves, it allows for new rooms and traps, as well as adds to the Dungeon Lord Mantle capacity of storing the user's own blueprints.

COMBAT CASTING: Basic (V) - Pertains to the speed and efficiency of spells cast during combat or life-threatening situations.
   -Basic status allows the caster to use spells every 20 seconds - 1 second per extra rank. The caster must say the spell names aloud and perform the appropriate hand gestures.

LEADERSHIP: Basic (VIII) - Reflects the owner's capacity of inspiring and managing his troops and minions. For a Dungeon Lord, improving this skill adds to the bonus he and his minions receive.

Talents

EVIL EYE - ALLOWS THE DUNGEON LORD TO see the Objectivity of any creature or item. If the target of his gaze possesses a strong Spirit (or related Attribute or Skill) they may hide their information if the Lord's own Spirit is not strong enough.

ENERGY DRAIN: Active. Very Low.

. . .

HUGO HUESCA

Dungeon Lord Mantle - The mantle is the heart of the Dungeon Lord and represents the dark pact made in exchange for power.

-It allows the Dungeon Lord access to the Dungeon Lord status and powers, as defined by the Dungeon Screen.

-It allows the Dungeon Lord to create and control dungeons, as per the limitations of his Dungeon Screen.

Energy Drain: None.

Improved Reflexes - Allows the owner to experience increased reaction time for a small burst of time.

-Basic status elevates his reaction speed to a degree dictated by the owner's Agility, for a duration of 3 seconds per use.

Improved Metabolism - Reduces the energy costs of all talents by 25% - the caloric requirements of the user are increased by the same amount.

Energy Drain: Activated. High.

Resist Sickness: Basic - Allows the owner to resist disease and sickness.

-Basic status allows the owner to resist non-magical sickness as if they had Endurance of 15 and were in optimal conditions (clean, well-fed, rested).

Spellcasting: Basic (IV) - Domains: general. Forbidden: Healing - Represents the owner's magical ability.

-Basic status allows the caster to use and learn all basic related spells of their domain. Extra ranks improve each individual spell's characteristics, such as range or damage.

-Efficient status grants the owner 1 extra basic spell.

-Allowed spells: 1 basic per day + 1 basic spell due to Dungeon Lordship

ENERGY DRAIN: Active. Varies per Spell.

ANCIENT LORD AURA - The owner creates an aura around him that enhances allied beings inside its area of effect. Affected beings can use the Dungeon Lord's Spirit as their own while this aura is active. Their physical attributes are also enhanced +1 while this aura is active. If the creature is a minion of the Dungeon Lord, they are immune to fear while affected by the aura.

Duration: 1 minute.

ENERGY DRAIN: Activated. Moderate.

PLEDGE OF ARMOR - Any armor that the Dungeon Lord wears is considered magical, as if it had a minor *protection* enchantment. This bonus stacks with any *protection* enchantment the armor may have, or any other similar defensive enchantment. Magical armor can deflect spells of similar power-category, as well as normal weaponry.

Restriction: Selecting this talent locks out the Pledge of Bloodshed advancement option.

ENERGY DRAIN: Passive.

Spell List

Minor Order - Command. The caster forces a target creature to follow a simple order as long as said order is not immediately against the creature's moral code or presents a threat to its life.

ELDRITCH EDGE - ENCHANTMENT. The caster adds a magical flame to the edge of a weapon. This flame makes the weapon magical for the duration, allowing it to bypass weak magical defenses and mundane ones.

Duration: 1 minute per Spellcraft rank.

MURMUR'S REACH - COMMAND (Mantle) - The caster possesses a minion located in the same dungeon as the caster. The caster's body is left defenseless during this time.

Duration: Ten minutes per Spellcraft rank.

OLD IVAN SNORTED after he was done reading the character sheets. "Dungeon Lords are magical up to their balls, Kes. Us normals can't compare. We're going along with this guard thing because it's a bad idea to tell a Dungeon Lord to take his idea and shove it, but c'mon. Don't dare tell us that guards will ever be anything more than arrow-fodder."

"Oh. I see." Kes caressed her chin as if deep in thought. She glanced at her two pupils, then at Old Ivan. "Well, if you say so. Since you seem to be more observant than me... Ivan, can you tell me what kind of magic are Alder and Ed using?"

"Well..."

Oblivious to the discussion, Alder closed in on Ed. The Bard held his sword over his right shoulder, grasping it with both hands. He and Ed circled each other for a brief instant before Alder lunged forward and launched a diagonal cut aimed at Ed's chest. The Dungeon Lord adjusted his stance and parried in such a way that he stopped Alder's blade outright. Ed advanced, keeping his edge on Alder's, trying to divert the Bard's sword away from his own body while aiming the tip of his blade at Alder's neck. Alder faded backward and to the side and brought his sword back to a neutral stance. Ed did the same, but at the last instant threw a blindingly fast vertical slash. Alder reacted by instinct and hefted his sword at an angle to catch Ed's. Right as the blades met, Alder stepped forward and used the impact to make his blade bounce aside, spring around Ed's blade, and trace a horizontal arc aimed at the Dungeon Lord's helmet. Ed chased the attack, bending his whole body away while bringing his own sword down atop Alder's, but he wasn't fast enough and the Bard's sword struck his arm just as his own tapped Alder's shoulder.

They both stepped back, acknowledging the strikes. After a couple seconds to regain their breaths, they went at it again, this time with Ed being the aggressor.

At no point did they use spells or talents. Kes studied their movements with a neutral expression. She couldn't avoid a surge of pride at seeing how far they'd improved. It seemed to her that only yesterday she'd been forced to watch them stumble. After months and months of daily training, they knew all the basic stances and how to use them to develop a chain of attacks or parries as needed. They knew how to use their legs to power a strike, and their instincts were slowly getting to the point where they'd know if an incoming attack was worth parrying with, say, both hands instead of one.

They weren't anywhere close to perfect, and Kes' trained eye picked a dozen tiny openings and errors in their stance that she'd have to drill out of them soon, before they became bad habits. Their reaction times lacked the years and years of experience that would take thinking out of the equation, and their attacks and feints were loudly announced by their body language and positioning. In a fair fight against an expert, they'd lose. But to an untrained eye, the chain of attacks, defenses, and counter-attacks was nothing short of impressive.

Which was the entire point of Kes' bringing the boots to watch.

"Well, maybe they aren't using magic *right now*," said Old Ivan as he crossed his arms. "But just look at his talents, Kes! Lord Edward can't even turn off that magical armor of his. That's not the kind of talent we'll ever have access to. No matter how fair our Dungeon Lord practices, he simply isn't as easy to hit as a normal human being!" He turned his head, looking to see if the rest of the boots agreed with him. Most of them either did so openly or were nodding to themselves.

Kes knew she had them. "So, normal human beings aren't as good warriors as magical ones?"

"Yeah," said Old Ivan. "That's the ugly truth."

"Well, how lucky you are that none of you are normal humans anymore," Kes said. She let her audience digest her words—perhaps she'd spent too much time around Alder—then spoke again right as Old Ivan opened his mouth. "Let's take a look at your own talents, shall we, Ivan?" She used her instructor voice, so the rest of the boots followed her example.

- Ivan Ardine of the Haunt, human. Exp: 40. Unused: 0 Brawn: 11, Agility: 8, Endurance: 12, Mind: 7, Spirit: 6, Charm: 7. Skills: Brawling: Basic III, Craft(leatherworking): Basic X. Talents: Resist Disease, Steady Hands, Dungeon Minion.

"QUIT YOUR DAMN STARING," Old Ivan said. Among Burrova's villagers, it wasn't exactly polite to stare at another person's sheet without good reason. It made people nervous. "What's your point, Kes? I'm an honest man, there's nothing unseemly in my stats."

"Look at that *dungeon minion* talent," Kes told him. The man blinked in confusion. "It's right there on your sheet—or have you forgotten about it already? I hope not after you had to recite that dreadfully long pact condition."

The boots winced. Ed's infamous pact conditions were marked in the Throne Room. Any person wishing to become a member of the Haunt had to recite them in their entirety, and that was no easy feat. Ed called them the Haunt's Terms of Service, but he refused to explain why.

"What about it?" Old Ivan asked.

"It's clearly magical," Kes explained. "It improves your attributes and would add extra spells to your daily limit if you had *spellcasting*. That means there's magic inside you, whether or not you know how to use it. It connects you to the surrounding dungeon, and to our Dungeon Lord. And didn't you say that they are magical up to their balls? Half of that magic is focused on improving the dungeon and its minions." Kes was now addressing the entire group. "As Lord Edward unlocks more talents, his minions also grow in power. Remember Klek and Tulip? The two of them could take on all of you, and they're only a batblin and a spider," she said. "Listen. Bards have a concept called the IC line that talks about adventurers and normal people. Adventurers take a lot of risks, so they rake in hundreds of experience points. So far, you've taken few risks, and that has been the smarter choice. But with my training, and the Mantle's magic, you can take bigger chances and survive. Imagine what you'll become with enough experience points and enough training. Guard duty would only be the beginning."

"What does the 'IC' stand for?" someone asked.

"Don't worry about it," Kes said, waving her hand. She realized she had their full attention. A part of her understood why Alder acted the way he acted. Motivation was a powerful tool. And perhaps all drill sergeants needed to love the spotlight, in order to do what they did best.

"Think, people. Imagine going to sleep without being terrified of some creature breaking into your home and devouring your family. For once, the monsters under the bed may be scared of *you*. Sure, you'll never be invincible. No mortal is. But you'll at least have a fighting chance! That's how Lord Edward feels every day. Imagine charging at a Spider Queen and winning. Forget the riches and the magic. You know what real power is? It's knowing that, no matter how stacked the odds are against you, you'll always have a fighting chance." Kes left out the darker side of that implication, because they didn't need to know—not yet. Ed's Mantle had been bought over a pact with the Dark god Murmur. The Dungeon Lord's minions, by the nature of their pact with him, benefited from Ed's power, but also shared the risk that they could be corrupted by it as well. Whatever became of Ed in the years to come, the Haunt and its inhabitants would follow.

Costel had a greedy glint in her eyes. "That's a pretty picture you paint, Kes."

"Bah! Even if she's right, minions are still arrow-fodder," Rasvan pointed out. He and Old Ivan shared a nod.

"You're right, most Dungeon Lords use their minions that way," Kes said. "*Most* Dungeon Lords are now dead. Look behind me. Would someone planning to hide behind his minions come to train here, morning after morning, for hours on end? The Haunt has survived this long, Rasvan, because we don't do what got others killed. And that's the final lesson I'll teach you today. The Haunt, this thing we're building, is more than a structure carved out of rock and ley lines. It's more than a dungeon, as well. The Haunt is something that will *last*, and you're a part of it. But it's a responsibility too. I know you don't understand, yet. You volunteered for personal reasons, after all. It's all right. Someday, it'll make sense. In the meantime, keep thinking I've gone a little insane. What I want from you is to pretend that you get it. I need you to yell 'Yes sir!' and then come back tomorrow to learn the best ways to disembowel any son of a bitch that dares threaten your home!"

"Yes, sir!" her nine boots yelled in unison. Kes flicked away a strand of hazelnut hair caked in sweat. *Where the hell did that come from?*

There are two ways to train a mule, Ria told her. *Carrot and stick. I liked to use the stick. You're waving the promise of a carrot at them and hoping they're hungry. But be careful, boot. Here, in the basement of your mind, it looks like you believe your own words more than you'd like to admit. That's dandy for a draftee, but very dangerous for a professional soldier.*

Fuck off, Sarge. The Minion talent gives one extra rank to Charm. *Demagoguery. That's all it is.* "Class dismissed," she said aloud.

She watched them leave. They were sweaty and barely able to stand, and they stole curious glances her way when they thought she wasn't looking. Young Ivan pointed to his temple and swirled his finger, Rasvan laughed, Costel sneered.

"Green," Kes whispered.

- Your Drill Sergeant skill has increased by one rank. Upon reaching Advanced status, your students will be able to purchase Improved-ranked military talents you teach them even if they don't fulfill the skill requirements.

CHAPTER SEVEN

TIME TO STRIKE BACK

E d woke to a dull noise in the dark. Still in the throes of his dream, he tossed the covers of his bed aside and grabbed the crystal vial he kept on a stand. A feeling of cold doom crept up his arm like an infection.

"Oh," he said. "It's just you." He returned the holy water vial to the stand, and the doom evaporated.

The old drone regarded him with eyes as big and round as dishes. Half his imp-like face was covered in coarse white whiskers, and the rest was wrinkled. "Pfft," the drone told him, showing Ed the tip of a snake-like tongue.

"Someone's at the door?" Ed almost went back to sleep. To be honest with himself, he'd half expected a different visitor. But the Boatman had kept his promise—he hadn't returned since their last encounter, and that had been months ago. Ed should have considered that a victory, but Kharon's absence made him nervous. "One second."

He jumped out of the bed and waved his hand in front of the magical torch by the wall. It turned on and bathed the bedchamber in warm purple light. The floor tiles were warm thanks to the Haunt's heating system. Ed hurried to a dressed stand while the drone watched with a judgmental frown at his sluggishness.

At first, Ed hadn't even considered keeping a drone inside his chambers while he slept. He had enough *alarms* spells in place, anyway, and drones weren't exactly quiet and respectful of people's rest. Kes had convinced him to try it by pointing out that *alarms* could be dispelled, and a drone at least could scream if someone entered the room uninvited. *It's just the smart thing to do,* she had told him. *What happens to the rest of us if you choke on a grape when no one is around?*

He threw on a comfy green tunic and slipped into his Thieves Guild boots while tightening the Guild's utility belt around his waist. "Have them come in," he told the drone after making sure the wrappings covering his left hand were in place. The old creature scoffed and disappeared into the antechamber. For the life of him, Ed couldn't guess at what rules governed the age and physical features of a drone. For all he knew, it was completely random. This one had already been like this when he'd summoned it for the first time. It was as if the creature had been born to be a butler.

The door to his chambers opened, and he heard unsteady footsteps. Ed hurried to the antechamber, waving magical torches on as he went along. The purple light illuminated a ragged batblin dressed in a doublet with the Haunt's Lasershark sewn by its lapel. He was holding a scruffy hat in his hands, turning it around nervously.

"My Lord," the batblin squeaked. "Terribly sorry for waking you up, my Lord, but you said to do it if it was important—" Ed frowned. It bothered him that the batblin could be afraid of angering him simply for following his orders. "Terribly sorry!" the batblin exclaimed, seeing Ed's expression.

Ed noted the critter's split ear and the burnt patch of fur poking out of the doublet's neck. "Drusb, is it not? Don't be afraid, you only followed my instructions. Tell me, what happened?"

"Klek and Tulip, sir," Drusb said. Ed's heart froze mid-beat. "They've returned, sir, and are asking for you. I told them you were sleeping, but they insisted. Said you'd want to hear their report *at once.*"

Ed let out the breath he had been holding. *They're alive.* For a resourceful batblin like Klek, a scouting job wasn't as dangerous as it was for others, but there was always the chance that something could go wrong. "I'll meet them in the War Room," he said. "And wake the others, have them catch up with us there."

He hurried to grab his green cape from the hanger next to the door while Drusb grimaced and looked back at the darkness of the corridor outside. "Even the Witch? She is... cranky when woken, sir. Scary."

Ed was already out into the corridor, hurrying for the stairs. "You're right, send a few drones first, just in case she wakes up with a mood."

Drusb gulped, then his footsteps receded as he rushed for the other chambers.

THE FIREPLACE CRACKLED in the War Room, the flames waving under the supernatural light of the torches. Feverish concentration permeated the air. Ed hunched over a parchment map of Constantina and its surroundings, studying a pair of red pins set between Hoia and the ruins of Burrova. The map was spread on a mahogany table reinforced with bronze and carved with grotesque figures at the legs and edges. Klek had climbed atop the table and was carefully pinpointing the exact location of Jiraz' dungeon, while Tulip hung from the ceiling by a strand of web.

"Where's Lavy?" Alder said, forcing down a yawn. He was reclined on a mahogany chair which had a back taller than anyone present and a skull engraved at its top. "She's the only one missing." Kes had her back against one tapestry that adorned the walls, while Kaga sat on the floor next to the fireplace, enjoying the warmth on his bare back.

There was the faint noise of a commotion upstairs. Ed vaguely sensed that a few of his drones had been unsummoned. "She just woke up," he said.

A few minutes later, the two drones by the doors pushed them open, and a disheveled Witch strolled into the room. "Fine, fine, I'm here. This better be important, my beauty sleep is ruined." She rubbed her eyes with her sleeve and took notice of everyone in the room. "Klek? When did you come back?"

"Just now, barely completed my quest in time," Klek told her.

Klek looked very different from the malnourished batblin that had originally joined Ed and the others. A kaftar-made serrated dagger hung from a black sheath at his side, and his fur was shiny and thick. He was bulkier than Drusb now and approaching his tenth rank in Endurance. Ed could've sworn the batblin had even grown an inch or two. Kes' training, paired with a healthy diet, had done wonders for Klek. And he was much more confident nowadays. "You don't need beauty sleep, Lavy," he told her.

Lavy half-snorted and waved her arm at him. "You flatterer. It won't help you if you ruined my sleep for nothing, mind you." She plopped down on the nearest chair.

"Thank you all for coming," Ed said. "Time is short, though, so... Kes, you mind?"

The Marshal stepped forward, the very image of martial gravitas. "I'll be brief. The Haunt's survival in Starevos caught the attention of a minor group of Lotian Dungeon Lords down on their luck. They came here testing their fortunes and have been waging a campaign against the Inquisition's Heroes for a few months—with little success. Their idiocy bought us some breathing space, and a chance at finding the Heroes' weakness. The Haunt's command—"

"That's us," whispered Alder, smiling while elbowing Kaga. "I'm a commander now."

"—the Haunt's command," Kes went on, "gave our agents Klek and Tulip the Quest: Find a witness of Heroic attack. They've been keeping an eye on the activity of Dungeon Lord Jiraz in the region, at great risk to themselves. They completed their quest today. Jiraz is gone, but one of his underlings survived the destruction of the dungeon." She rummaged through the table, found a parchment, and held it up for everyone to see. It was the drawing of a coffin that matched Klek's vague description. "We believe it to be a vampire. Although we don't have intelligence reports to confirm it, we suspect he was Jiraz' second-in-command, and fought the Heroes along with his Dungeon Lord in the final battle. After his body was destroyed he returned to his coffin to regenerate, where he was captured by the Inquisition, which arrived after the Heroes left the area."

"Sorry for butting in, Kes," Alder said, "but I thought vampires turned to dust after being destroyed."

Lavy clapped with delight. "A Nightshade vampire! I have always wanted to meet one." She stood and grabbed the coffin drawing from Kes' hands. "Nightshade is a vampire breed native to Lotia, so it's no surprise that Alder hasn't heard of them. They're much cooler than those lame Heiligian Marauders, and more passionate than those dry Starevosi Oldbloods."

"You sure sound like you know a lot about those guys, despite never having met one," Alder told her.

"Well, yes. I've read a lot about them." Lavy's lip trembled and her cheeks turned bright red. "In research tomes, I mean. For research."

"*Right.*"

The Witch hurried to change the subject. "Nightshades are the most resilient vampires around. An ancient one is almost impossible to kill—they just keep coming back. Somewhere along their progression tree they can unlock a talent that allows them to turn to mist if they're slain, and they return to their coffin instead of dying. I think it's called *mist heart* or something like that—"

"Sort of like a lich's phylactery?" Ed asked. That would be a useful talent to have, although having to protect a coffin was much harder than hiding a small trinket. "Interesting." He made a mental note of asking Lavy the specifics of the other vampire breeds later.

"I'm more familiar with Oldbloods," Kaga shared. "A distant branch of my family used to hunt them, a long time ago. Vampire hunters! Those were the days..."

"Thanks for the intel, Lavy," Kes said, snatching back control of the conversation. "Jiraz' vampire is in the hands of the Inquisition. They're bringing his coffin to Undercity to execute him, probably as a show of force—to intimidate the rebellion."

Heiliges had conquered Starevos more than a decade ago, and small rebel groups still sprang up here and there. Nicolai's group had been one of those. It was all part of a complicated plan by Murmur to buy his favored kingdom, Lotia, enough time to rebuild its army so it could challenge Heiliges' supremacy again. Ed knew that the presence of Lotian Dungeon Lords in Starevos meant that Murmur's plan was working.

"I want that vampire," Ed said. "The chance that he knows something about the Heroes we don't is too big to pass up."

Alder gave him an alarmed look. "You want us to attack an Inquisitorial convoy? That's suicide!"

"The losses will be substantial," Kaga agreed. "But if the Dungeon Lord orders us to fight, my kaftar will honor our pact with him."

"Me too," said Klek. "I ain't afraid."

"You should be," Tulip admonished. "But as Queen Laurel's representative in this meeting, I can assure you the horned spiders shall uphold our pact with Lord Wraith."

"Thanks, everyone," Ed said. He couldn't help but feel touched at their loyalty. "But we are not going to fight them. We will steal that damn coffin right out from under their noses." He straightened his back and held the gaze of everyone in the room. "This stalemate has gone on long enough, people. I love turtling inside my base as much as anyone, but every Dungeon Lord that tried that before is dead. The Heroes respawn, we don't. The Haunt cannot hide forever, and I don't know about you, but I'm tired of being on the defensive."

He had another reason for wanting to take that coffin. Back on Earth, Ed had been part of the ranks of gamers that the Militant Church used to hunt Dungeon Lords. He had a perspective that no other Dungeon Lord had, but he'd never seen the Heroes in the flesh. After he gathered enough information about them, he knew he could put the mystery together. He could figure out how to *win.*

"Wetlands, Ed, you're serious," Lavy muttered. She smoothed a wrinkle in her tunic. "No one here is *that* good at stealth... perhaps if we send word to Karmich and the Thieves Guild? We can have a team waiting for the Inquisitors when they enter Undercity."

"That won't work," Kes said. "Klek and Tulip left for the Haunt as soon as the Inquisitors headed for Undercity." She pointed to the location of Jiraz' dungeon on the map and traced the route through the forest until it reached the Haunt. "Unlike spiders and batblins, horses aren't good at nighttime riding, so the Inquisitors are camping somewhere around here—" she traced a circle with her finger over an area of a secondary road that led to Undercity "—and will arrive at the main road early in the morning. Now, if I were in charge of the convoy, I'd have an escort team ready to meet me in the main road to reinforce my approach. Catching them after they enter the main road is out of the question. Attempting the steal in Undercity is even worse. If we're doing this, it has to be tonight."

"Wetlands," Lavy said, more to herself than anyone else. "I guess we're doing this."

"Don't worry," Ed assured her. "I have a plan. We have an hour to set everything up. Kaga, gather your team and the hell chicken mounts. Alder, wake Heorghe and Andreena and have them come here. Lavy, get some rest, you're going to raise the dead tonight. Klek, Tulip, tell the raiders it's time for their first mission. Kes, you're with me."

Part of him was exultant. Despite the late hour, he was wide awake. Finally, he had the chance he had been waiting for.

His friends accepted his instructions and hurried to set them in motion. His chest beamed with pride. They were no longer a terrified bunch with no idea what they were doing. Despite all the horror of the mindbrood, and all the pain that Nicolai had caused, those experiences had taught them all something important. They could defend themselves and win. They could strike back. Hell, they could even punch first.

Ed's eyes flashed green as he focused on the link between himself and his minions. This power was an extension of the way the Mantle worked, a neat little detail he had discovered after raising his dungeon skills high enough. He brought up an empty sheet and focused his will to add blazing green letters to it. When he was done, he sent the new sheet out through the connection created by the pact between Dungeon Lord and minion.

An announcement appeared in front of him. It was based on his handiwork, but the finer details, like the Bonuses and the Rewards, came from some unknown source. He knew that every minion was seeing the same screen. It read:

- *A new Dungeon Mission is active!* Raid the Inquisitorial Convoy *(Time sensitive)*.

Description: A group of Inquisitors is traveling to Undercity with a coffin containing a vampire that witnessed the Heroes in action.
Win Condition: Deliver the coffin safely into the Haunt.
Reward: Experience, Recruitment chance (Vampire Lieutenant), Plunder Wagons.
Bonus: Succeed without killing anybody.

Bonus: Keep your presence hidden from the Inquisitors.

Defeat condition: The coffin is destroyed; the convoy reaches the main road; the Haunt's agents are killed or captured.

"So THIS IS one of those quest things that has everyone so excited?" Andreena asked as she turned the phantasmal screen around her hand. "Interesting. I never would've guessed that the fastest way to get someone to do what you want is to call it a quest. Perhaps I'll task my apprentices with Quests instead of odd jobs."

Ed grinned. "Go ahead. I have yet to hear someone complain about a stuffed Quest List." The Herbalist had arrived shortly after Alder and the others left the War Room. Despite the late hour, she seemed as cheerful as always—she was used to people waking her up in the middle of the night. Her curly hair was gathered in a messy bun, and she was dressed in a function-over-form brown dress and an old woolen jacket. She had locks of strange plants hanging from her belt, the way an artisan may carry a hammer, as well as a tin flask filled with her personal brew.

"I bet it won't be the same unless it's a Dungeon Lord's quest," said Heorghe, suppressing a yawn. He was dressed only in his trousers, boots, and a furred coat that looked suspiciously like a bear pelt. "Gives it legitimacy, you know."

Governor Brett coughed. He was wearing woolen pajamas. "Am I correct in assuming I can share the rewards of this quest without actually entering combat? No offense intended, your Fiendishness, but I doubt I'd make a useful warrior," he said as he patted his belly and gave Ed a meaningful look.

So far, Ed had only issued a few personal Quests here and there. The kaftars had "Find a way to tame hell chicken mounts" as a quest, for example. It was the first time he had issued a dungeon-sized quest, so in a way, he was treading new ground. "I think that everyone who chips in gets a share of the rewards. At least, that's how it's worked before."

"Excellent." Brett's eyes glinted with greed. "Then, how may I be of service, Lord Edward?"

"If we succeed, we're gonna have a vampire inside the Haunt," Ed said. "I don't know if he'll want to work with us—or if we'll want to work with him—so we need to make sure security is up to par. Get a hold of Zachary and figure out ways we can protect the place in case the vampire tries to escape—traps, spells, guard protocols, containment rooms. Anything you can think of, and don't worry about coming up with a silly idea. We'll figure out what is feasible and what isn't when we return."

"I understand," Brett said. "This task shall be accomplished to your utmost satisfaction, my Lord, you can count on it. I'll come up with clever new policies that not even an elder vampire could outsmart." He saluted Ed and stood up to leave. On his way out, he reached for a tray by the table and grabbed a clay mug filled with a warm, bitter tea Andreena had brewed to invigorate them for the night.

Ed bit his lip. Brett, despite his... personality, was a fairly competent Governor, if one ignored his tendency to fatten his own pockets on the down-low. He'd come up with a good idea or two. Ed would have wanted to do it himself, but there was no time.

"There goes his Pompousness," Heorghe said after the Governor had left. "I wonder how he'll try to sneak himself into extra authority this time."

"The same way he always does," Kes said, looking up from the pile of parchments with checklists, map sketches, and theory-crafting about the Inquisitors' talent choices. "He'll want to create a committee and name himself president."

"I expect more creativity from him," Ed said. He turned to Heorghe. "So... it looks like we'll need to test our railway out a bit earlier."

Heorghe closed his eyes as if Ed had punched him in the gut. "I was hoping you wouldn't say that, Ed. I hate showing off a project before it's ready."

"Sorry, I know. I wouldn't ask if it weren't important."

"Of course. I hope you have a way of slowing down the cart, since I haven't added the brakes yet."

Kes looked up from her papers again. "Railway?" she asked.

"Dungeon Project: Underground Railway," Heorghe explained. "The railway is a method of transporting goods between the Haunt and Undercity without having to rely on horses. Ed thought of it and asked our dwarf friend Oscor to help with the schematics. Seems like dwarfs have been using railways in their mines for a long time."

A good chunk of the Haunt's income came from smuggling booze and other items into Undercity, but the logistics of moving the product to the city was a pain. The horned spiders absolutely refused to be used as beasts of burden, horses had a hard time traversing Hoia's hidden roads, and it took a while for Ed's drones to push the carts around. When it was completed, a railway between Hoia and Undercity would solve that problem.

Ed also planned to exploit it as much as he could. Beginning tonight.

"How does that help us now?" Kes wondered.

"We need to get the coffin away from the Inquisition's reach," Ed told her. "Hauling it on our backs and hopping away won't work, so the railway is our best shot." It would be dangerous. For the plan to work, Ed's group would need to raise hell to distract the Inquisitors.

A lot could go wrong, which made getting the plan right from the get-go even more important. Ed could see Kes thinking it over. Recently, before she and Ed had had time to know each other, the avian would have refused to take such a risk. That was how a mercenary survived—by choosing when to turn tail and fuck off. "Very well," was all the Marshal said tonight, before going back to her papers.

"I'll need to scan the prototype," Ed told Heorghe, "to add it to my Evil Eye's list of dungeon rooms."

"Of course. I'll assemble it as fast as I can," the Blacksmith said, then he rose. "You really should figure out a way to slow down the cart, though."

As he headed to leave, Kes handled him a long parchment. "Give this to the forge helpers, have someone read it to them. It's a list of all the supplies we'll need. Have them sent to the middle of the market, and we'll handle it from there."

"Got it, Kes." The drones opened the door for the Blacksmith and closed it after he'd left.

Ed sipped Andreena's tea to clear his mind. It was bitter and herbal-ish—nothing at all like coffee, which was a shame. Next on the list was... he shifted in his seat to face Andreena.

"You want potions," the Herbalist said.

"I want potions," Ed confirmed. "What do we have in store?"

"*Vitality* potions have the longest shelf-life, so there are three barrels ready. *Agility* potions take a while to make, but we have a barrel left-over from the spiderlings. I have a few bottles of *Staunch* elixir, it helps stop blood-loss." She gave him a quick rundown of the rest. Water-breathing draughts, Cold-resistance flasks, and the rest were basic medical supplies and stimulants.

"We'll take all the *Staunches*, and have your assistants fill flasks with *Vitality* for everyone," Ed said. "Also, prepare some raw meat infused with *Agility* and... and this tea, for good measure," he said as he held up his mug. "Hell, now that I think of it, can you mix it with our *Vitality* too?"

"You're just begging to have your heart explode out of your chest at thirty, aren't you?" Andreena said, pursing her lips. "Well, not my place to tell a grown man how he should treat his kidneys. Or liver. Or pancreas. You want a potion combo, you'll get a potion combo. Just don't drink more than the dose I'll put in the flasks or, you know." She pointed at Ed's chest and made a bursting motion.

114

"I'll sign you a waiver if you want," Ed told the Herbalist with a nervous chuckle. He was sure she was exaggerating the heart-explosion part. *Right?*

"Won't be necessary." Andreena jumped to her feet and rubbed her hands together. "I'll have your potions delivered at the market in half an hour, Ed."

"Thanks, Andreena."

After she left, the only ones remaining were he and Kes. The sand in the hourglass on a corner of the table was about half done. "Time to put on our weapons and armor," Ed told the Marshal.

"Have the drones bring them here," she said. She held her stack of papers in front of Ed. "Let's go back over the plan, Ed. There won't be any do-overs once we piss off the Inquisitors. So, start from the beginning."

Ed glanced at the avian handwriting, some kind of cuneiform language he couldn't understand. "Very well. The plan goes off in stages. First, I'll need time to create a temporary dungeon…"

THE MARKET BRISTLED with nervous energy. The night was cloudy, with the moon nowhere to be seen. Had he been superstitious, he'd have thought it a good omen. It'd be easy to hide his forces in the dark—most of them had some variant of night-vision. The Spider Riders had their *echolocation*, and the kaftar had an acute sense of smell. If all else failed, Ed's drones could see in total darkness and would guide anyone who got lost.

Eyegouger and the rest of the mounts were tied to a pole at the end of the market, being watched by a nervous young kaftar. The hell chickens squeaked from their half-open beaks, and their red eyes followed Ed's movements. A line had formed in front of Kes and Lavy, who had appropriated a couple of wooden stalls to set up shop and distribute runes, bows, and ammunition with the help of a group of batblins. The spider warriors rested by a corner while their batblin riders fumbled to strap their chairs and stirrups to the spiders' torsos. Kaga's Monster Hunters were giving their weapons one last look-over before the trip. Their shaggy tails wagged, and their cackles pierced the night like the war-cry of anxious predators.

Ed glanced at the sky again. The speed at which the Haunt had mobilized was nothing short of astounding. It was as if the entire population shared the nervous energy that had been nestling inside himself the last couple of months. Eager to spring to action, so when the time had arrived, it would find them ready.

"Tonight's gonna go straight into my chronicle, you know," Alder said as he caught sight of Ed and strolled over. The Bard had changed his colorful attire for the black leather armor of the Thieves Guild, with a sturdy brown shirt underneath and his duelist longsword hanging from a tight belt. Ed was dressed in the same way, with his green cape hugging his shoulders and swaying with the breeze.

"Is that so? You should let me have a look someday," Ed said, only half-jokingly. Alder's "A Most Impartial Chronicle of the Haunt and its Rise to Power" was the Bard's self-proclaimed masterpiece. According to him, once it was finished it'd tell the entire history of the Haunt since its beginnings, from the perspective of an eye-witness: himself. As far as Alder knew, no other modern Bard had attempted such a feat, mostly because Dungeon Lords, as a rule of thumb, reacted poorly to anything short of devoted adulation. Ed, though, already suspected that Heiligian historians wouldn't consider him worthy of praise, so he figured he may as well trust Alder to tell an impartial-*ish* version of their lives. Perhaps someone out there, a long time from now, would find them. Perhaps they'd even believe a word or two.

"No way," Alder said, grinning. "Friendships get strained when one part sees what the other thinks of them."

Ed mirrored the Bard's smile. "I'm sure you're overreacting. If it's the Haunt's honest chronicle, then I have nothing to fear." It was a conversation they'd had a couple times already, and it had become sort of an inside joke between them.

"It's the honest part that people have an issue with. They all say they have nothing to hide, but when the truth disagrees with them, suddenly their critique is expressed by hanging the Bard and setting him on fire unless he changes his tune. That's why Elaitra stopped bothering with chronicling Dungeon Lords a long time ago. Being impartial is very hard with a noose around your neck and smoke tickling your toes."

"Perhaps some Dungeon Lords had a noose around their necks too," Ed said. "Maybe we haven't heard of them only because it's Heiligian Bards sharing their stories."

Alder scratched his chin. "I've often wondered why Lotia has no Bards of their own. Every one I know is an Elaitra student."

"You want me to give you a quest to investigate more?" Ed told him. "Could be interesting to find out why."

"How about we finish this one, first? It looks like our brave troops are almost ready."

"Right." Ed passed a hand through his hair and took a deep breath of chilly air. He was less troubled now, his hands steadier, as if his mind had needed a bit of a distraction to fully focus on tonight's mission. Talking with Alder had that effect on him. The Bard lived his life with his head in the clouds, and often a short visit was relaxing.

He headed for the middle of the market. Almost everyone was ready and accounted for. Most eyes fell on him, as if they expected him to say something. His throat had gone dry. "I won't lie and say that tonight will be easy." A couple of the batblin riders close to Klek exchanged worried glances. *Great start, asshole, just tell them you're afraid of everything, and their mothers are going to be brutally fucking murdered.* He fought back the impulse to back down and let Kes handle the speech. "But we are ready for this. We've trained, and we've got the element of surprise on our side. Stick to the plan and all will be well." Klek cheered, and a few batblins imitated him. The spiders were silent—speeches were not their thing at all. One of the Monster Hunters cracked his knuckles and patted Lavy on the back, almost sending the Witch sprawling. *At least I can count on the kaftar to keep the morale high,* Ed thought. As long as they knew they got to fight *something,* the kaftar were happy.

Alder stepped up next to Ed right as he was about to order everyone to move out. "Remember, people! Tonight, you represent the Haunt. Your victory is *its* victory as your defeat would be its shame. Fight bravely, oh warriors! Our Dungeon Lord will be right in the thick of battle with us, so make sure that when he turns your way, all he sees is a proud minion of the Haunt. And if you find yourself giving in to fear, just think of all the experience points we're sure to rake in!" He drew his sword and hefted it upward, as if to stab the sky. To Ed's surprise, the kaftar and Kes imitated the gesture. Lavy and the batblins watched on, looking as confused as he felt.

"Nice speech," Ed whispered at Alder. "Where did it come from?"

The Bard sighed with satisfaction. "The Canticle of Dawn, by Melchiades. '*Numerios the Pure addresses his troops*' closing verse, paraphrased, abridged." He chuckled to himself as he walked away.

Kes had everyone take their places in the marching formation. Dungeon commanders were at the center, with the kaftars as rearguard. Spider-riders were in the front, flanked by Laurel's spider warriors, with spiderling scouts already tracking the Inquisitors' camp.

As Ed hurried to his spot in the middle of the formation, next to Kes and Lavy, he saw movement from the corner of his eye. Heorghe hurried out of the dungeon's entrance. A group of four Forge batblins chased after him, carrying together some kind of wooden display.

"One moment!" Heorghe called as he reached Ed's group.

Sweat drenched his forehead. "Sorry for the delay, was too sleepy earlier to realize you may want this." His assistants caught up to him, and he gestured at Ed to approach as he flicked the brass latch of the display and pushed the top open to reveal its contents. "Finished it last week, I did. Brett wanted to make a big show of giving it to you, but I figured you'd appreciate it more right now."

Several plate armor parts rested on a violet pillow. A shiver ran through Ed's spine. He'd almost forgotten all about it. The last time he'd seen that steel, it had been a charred mess taken from the remains of Nicolai while Ed's drones fanned the flames. Heorghe, perhaps acting out a Starevosi Blacksmith's own ancient traditions, had transformed the steel of Ed's fallen enemy into an armor fitting of a Dungeon Lord.

The result went beyond Ed's expectations. The breastplate was one large piece of metal etched with Gothic patterns that combined flowery geometric shapes with open-mawed skulls and thorny roots. The etchings were silver and glinted under the light of the torches, but the rest of the armor was black as night, with waves of softer darks undulating across its surface, as if invisible flames engulfed the armor. Ed found it both beautiful and cruel. A gift and a warning.

"There wasn't enough salvageable steel left to make a full plate set," Heorghe explained over Ed's shoulder as he took in the details of the rest of the armor. "But we can add those extra pieces later."

The helmet was a singular, visor-less piece with an opening shaped like a "Y" that left the eyes, nose, and mouth exposed. Its lines were sharp and angular, resembling the threatening frown of some imposing giant. One gauntlet had spiderweb etching across its surface, and the hand had been shaped as a vaguely spider-like head, with steel points at the knuckles resembling fangs. The other was ridged, bent, and interconnected, taking the shape of one big skeletal arm and hand. The greaves matched the gauntlets.

"This is incredible," Ed whispered. "You outdid yourself, Heorghe."

"That I did, that I did. But I cannot take all the credit. Most of those etchings aren't mine, your drones added them as soon as I finished the breastplate—but don't worry, I looked and there ain't a single obscenity... that I could find. I had no idea they could work metal, to be honest, so it took me by surprise."

"Neither did I," Ed said. He brushed the artwork with his hand. Even his inexpert fingers could sense the quality of Heorghe's craftsmanship. "Is it enchanted?"

"Not yet, but it can be. You'll need to hire an expert, though, because that's beyond my talent-tree. In the meantime, your *pledge of armor* works, right?"

Ed grabbed the helmet with both hands and lifted it, feeling its weight. Almost absently, he summoned a group of drones to help him don the armor. "Thank you, Heorghe. I'm in your debt," he said as the drones grabbed the armor and eased Ed into it.

"Ah, just stay alive out there," the Blacksmith said with a proud little smile. "I'll go back to sleep, so you all make sure to be back when I wake up."

Glad to try, Ed thought.

"Finally," said Lavy as the drones hurried to tighten the straps of Ed's greaves while he slipped back into his cape and worked the leather fasteners. "It was about time you donned a proper Dungeon Lord outfit."

Like Lavy, most of his retinue stared at the new armor. Ed could hear the whispers. What were they saying? Perhaps he looked ridiculous in the damn thing. Alita's tits, he was a programmer, not some kind of feudal warlord.

Is that still true, though? He caught Kes' gaze. The avian had a pensive frown on her face. When she realized Ed was looking her way, she turned away and whispered something to herself. "Seems like Lord Wraith found his armor. They grow so fast, eh, Ria?" it sounded like she said. Ed couldn't make sense of it.

"What's so important about proper attire?" Alder asked Lavy.

"Well, we couldn't have him running around wearing the same rags as a common Thief," Lavy said petulantly. "Might give people the wrong idea."

"The wrong idea?" Alder lifted an eyebrow. He was wearing those exact Thief rags. So was she, at that—no use for pretty dresses out in the middle of a battle.

"Oh, yes," Lavy said, ignoring Alder's tone. "It could've made people think that Dungeon Lord Edward Wright was only a mere mortal—a human who dies just as easily as any other."

"But I *do* die as easily as any other," Ed pointed out.

"That's why it is the wrong idea," Lavy said. "There's no need for them to know that."

Ed barked a laugh, set his hood over his head, and turned on his Evil Eye. "You know what? You may be right," he told the Witch. The eldritch light bathed the armor and made the flames ebb and flow, creating the illusion that he was some nightmarish monster lurking in the dark.

When the Haunt's forces left to intercept the Inquisitors, a Dungeon Lord that looked the part led them.

CHAPTER EIGHT

BLACK MAGIC INCOMING

Gallio woke in the candle firelight of his tent to the overbearing suspicion that something dreadful was headed his way.

For an instant, he lingered between nightmare and wakefulness, unsure of which was which, as if his cramped travel tent that smelled of garlic and old incense were too good to be true—as if the only possible reality had to be those dark tunnels of his dream, expanding forever, carrying unending hordes of red-eyed creatures with oily carapaces and razor-sharp teeth toward the unsuspecting village of Burrova. Gallio still thought he could hear the lingering ring of the Dungeon Lord's laughter as his creatures burst forth from the skulls of Ioan and Vasil and Kes and Alvedhra. His skin shivered with the phantom pain of fangs piercing him all around, and his body shook as he struggled against a dozen inhuman arms holding him down while the Dungeon Lord skittered to a stop in front of him and extended his dozen arms to allow a sea of insects to slither out of his body and crawl their way toward Gallio and inside him, where they began to feed—

His hand fumbled around until he found the small brass flask next to his bedroll. He took deep breaths and emptied his mind until the memory of the nightmare faded until all that remained was the beating of his heart and the chirping of insects outside. Then he took a long drink of his tea, allowing the milky liquid to sweep down his throat. According to the priest that made it for him, the concoction was supposed to keep the nightmares at bay, but for the effect it had—or lack of it—Gallio suspected that the priest was pocketing his quarter-Aureuses instead. Gallio furrowed his brow. Deception among the members of the Militant Church carried a heavy penalty, but it wasn't as if Gallio could report the priest or punish him in any way. After all, he couldn't explain his dreams to the Inquisition without telling them of the battle of Burrova, of the mindbrood, and of Ioan and the Dungeon Lord Edward Wright.

The penalty for hiding a mindbrood's existence from the Inquisition was harsher and more thorough than deception, but that wasn't what worried Gallio. Even if the mindbrood was long dead, even if all danger had been extinguished as Burrova burned, the Inquisition would still drown the entire region in flames to protect the rest of the world from the slightest risk of infection. Brutal, without a doubt. Also, without a doubt in his mind, the right thing to do. Sephar's Bane had almost destroyed civilization. Any measure was justified, no matter how cruel, as long as it ensured that the Bane would never come again.

What was a lone village when weighed against civilization's survival?

But Burrova's mindbrood had been a fluke, merely the fruit of a lone egg bought by Ioan's treachery. The Ranger had planned to force the Inquisition to torch the region to justify a rebellion against Heiligian rule in Starevos. Gallio couldn't murder the people he'd lived among and grown to love because of a lone man's madness. That was his secret sin.

The Militant dogma warned against cultivating too much empathy, because the Militant Church's sacred duty was to do the things that no one else dared to, no matter how necessary. Even if it meant fostering resentment among the common folk, the good of the majority was more important.

Gallio knew this. It had been drilled into the core of his soul since he'd first set foot on a Militant Temple, just one scrawny kid among thousands of new arrivals, all volunteered by their noble families vying for the honor of having their child pass the harsh trials that would welcome them into Heiliges' finest. What would his House think of him tonight? Gallio had lost contact with them after his exile into Starevos. Even now that Alita had accepted him back into her ranks, he hadn't sent even a single letter, and neither had they. Perhaps, because deep down, he knew that broken honor could be mended, but the scars never faded.

These dreams are Alita's punishment for my weakness, Gallio surmised. He set the flask away from him with a frown of contempt. He often thought that his nightmares carried a kind of poetic justice. After all, Alita's blessing upon her Inquisitors protected their minds from breaking under the horrors of carnage and tragedy, but Gallio hadn't been an Inquisitor for most of the battle of Burrova, and thus, the things he'd seen there would always be with him when he closed his eyes. *I'll accept the Goddess' punishment as it comes, without trying to ease my way out.* He swore to himself he'd never touch the concoction again. In fact, he ought to pour it on the ground. It didn't even work, anyway.

He reached for it, still frowning, but his hand stopped when his fingertips brushed the brass cylinder. Gallio sighed and left the flask there, knowing full well that he'd drink from it again the next night. This wasn't the first time he'd danced this dance.

Disgusted with himself, he unzipped his tent and crawled out, letting the night cool the sweat soaking his shirt.

THE CAMP WAS QUIET, the light of the fire in the middle and the torches across its perimeter fighting to keep the absolute darkness of a night without a moon at bay.

The Inquisitors slept in individual tents separated from the non-combatants, set up in a line between the forest and the river bend that protected the campsite's rear. The air was heavy with humidity, and clouds of insects rose from the otherwise quiet, murky waters of the river. Gallio glanced back, squinting through the torchlight, trying to peer into the dark outside.

Rivers could be dangerous in Starevos, where the hidden currents were the least of their secrets. Scaly beasts and other horrors lurked under the waters, invisible to all but the keenest eye, ready to jump out at an unsuspecting traveler and draw them under to their watery doom. Ioan and Alvedhra had always warned him and the villagers to avoid rivers after dark—it was only common sense. But the Inquisition had their own kind of common sense, and using a river bend to set up camp had tactical advantages that greatly offset the risks. For one, many powerful Dark creatures hated running water, including Oldbloods and Dungeon Lords, and that alone turned the brown waters into a blessing in disguise.

At the camp's center, by the fire, stood one big tent—Master Enrich's—overseeing the caravan carts, which were heavy with the loot taken from Jiraz' vaults. Next to those were the horses, tired from the day's intense pace toward Constantina, and past them was the stake circle that surrounded the improvised tents that safe-guarded the coffin containing the Inquisition's prisoner. An Inquisitor guarded each cart. One Inquisitor glanced at Gallio with sleep-starved eyes. Gallio shrugged with sympathy, still remembering the times when guard duty would fall on him.

Gallio headed out the opposite direction, toward the line of trees and past the camp's limits, where the three lookouts guarded the camp from any danger that might come from the forest. Cleric Zeki saluted him lazily as he passed and made no comment. The Cleric didn't like Gallio much, and he barely bothered to hide it.

The Cleric was immersed in the Inquisition's politics, but was too old to climb its ladder, which over time had translated into a bitterness unseemly of a man of his powers. Still, Zeki took his duty as seriously as anyone else. His pair of *hawk guardians* flew in circles over the camp, two lone golden stars shining above. At the first sight of trouble, the magic hawks would warn the camp about any incoming evil far better than any *alarm*. Furthermore, Zeki's *divine circle of respite* protected the area around the camp from black magic's means of incursion. The glow of its runes bathed the Cleric in light.

The camp was as safe as it could be, not even counting the dozen Inquisitors ready to *smite* their way out of any trouble. And yet Gallio couldn't shake that feeling of danger away. The effects of his nightmare still lingered.

He left Cleric Zeki and kept going until he reached the *circle of respite's* outer limit, only a few paces away from the forest-line. There, a small fire crackled before a figure sitting on a log. She was covered in a heavy blanket, with a silver-infused longsword resting across her lap, and an ivory bow next to her, along with a quiver full with swan-feathered arrows.

"Up already? You still have a few hours left before your shift," Alvedhra greeted him as he sat next to her and allowed the fire to seep into his bones.

"Couldn't sleep," he told her. "I don't need much, anyway. You'll understand when you're my age."

The former Ranger grinned. "Don't start that dung with me. I've wood elf blood from my mother's side. At your age, I'll be just as fresh as I am today." She flicked a strand of her cropped hair away from her heart-shaped face. Her ears were indeed slightly pointy, although that could mean nothing. Many Starevosi claimed to have elven blood somewhere on their family tree. Some believed that the few extra years of youth increased their marriage prospects. For others, it was mere vanity.

"If you say so," Gallio told her, returning the grin. "Anything new in the front lines?"

"Not at all," Alvedhra said sadly. "A few overgrown rats and a curious wolf pack that sniffed around before fucking off. Alita's mercy, I *almost* wish bandits would try their luck on us. The Light knows I could use the extra points." She focused and summoned her character sheet. "There are so many talents I need to rework my build..."

Gallio winced in sympathy. Alvedhra's predicament was the reason most Inquisitors began their training from a very young age, as some divine talents turned normal ones redundant, wasting the experience invested in them.

It was extremely hard to alter one's character sheet after buying a talent, but the Light could do things with its divine experience points that mere mortals couldn't. One such thing was to buy special talents for their favored devotees, which was the reason all new Inquisitors gained the same starting package of *smite* and *pledge of the faithful* without paying for them—it was Alita herself who bought the talents, a trivial investment of experience for one such as her. *Smite* turned *power attack* obsolete —*smite* did its job much better, and with the added benefit of royally ruining the day of any Dark-aligned creature struck by it. *Pledge of the faithful* was a huge catch-all concentration of life-improvement talents like *resist disease, resist poison, improved metabolism, enhanced endurance,* along with a few others. Despite the advantages, divine talents had a few weaknesses. Unlike their physical counterparts, they were magical, and thus could be rendered inert by anti-magic fields. And, if the Inquisitor were to fall out of Alita's grace, the goddess could simply take the talents away and regain the invested experience points—like Gallio himself knew very well.

Thus, while it was possible for an Inquisitor to become extremely powerful by increasing his stance in Alita's eyes without ever spending a single point, it was also possible he could lose it all in one day, if he were to displease the goddess.

Not that any self-respecting Inquisitor should ever worry about that possibility. Those without sin had nothing to fear at all. Gallio realized he had a sour taste in his mouth. *Keep going like this and you'll end up as bitter as Zeki.*

"Patience," he advised the former Ranger. "You'll gather enough experience points, in time. And you can always devote yourself further to Alita's service and hope the goddess increases your powers herself. Then you'll be stronger than the average Inquisitor—sadly not all your Ranger talents have a divine equivalent."

Alvedhra clasped the arrowhead she kept on a string around her neck. "The problem is, I don't have that kind of time. My revenge has to come now, or Enrich's Heroes shall deliver it for me. And praying for Alita's blessing seems plain wrong, you know? The matter between me and Kessih of Greene is personal. It would be selfish of me to involve the Light."

Gallio bit his lip as silence extended between them. Alvedhra hadn't been there for the battle of Burrova. But she had seen the ruins, and she remembered Edward Wright's deception while they battled Queen Amphiris in Hoia, along with Ioan and Vasil. She knew nothing of the mindbrood or Ioan's true nature, so she blamed the village's destruction and all the mindbrood's killings on the Dungeon Lord, and on the avian who had betrayed her to join him. Worst of all, Gallio couldn't explain what had happened —not without damning her and himself and all the village's survivors. As the Ranger's zeal grew with every passing day, Gallio's hope that she'd come to understand his reasons—and the reasons of Kes—diminished further and further.

He suddenly felt very alone. Alvedhra had been one of his first friends back when he had arrived in Starevos, and nowadays she was his only reminder of the years he'd spent as Sheriff. And yet, the distance between them grew, with her being none the wiser.

"Alvedhra... I..." He searched his heart for answers, trying to find the courage to tell her something that would lift the burden off her shoulders. Perhaps, even, the truth. Shouldn't he trust her? She was an adult, and his apprentice, and certainly had a right to know. If only he were strong enough. "There's something I haven't—"

She grew silent, her entire body tense. "Shh," she urged him, raising a hand his way. "Listen."

Gallio could hear nothing, except the sounds of the forest and the faint current of the river against the rocks. His hand reached for his longsword anyway, and he eased an inch of steel out of his scabbard. He felt very naked without his armor, laying forgotten inside his tent. "What is it?"

"The silence," Alvedhra whispered. "The birds grew quiet. And I swear I can see mist in the distance... but at this time of the year? But it can't be. The *alarms,* and Zeki's spells..."

"Trust your instincts," Gallio said. "You're a Ranger. Those skills are part of you, and will always be. Use them in the service of the Light."

The Ranger swallowed and reached for her sword. "Then I'd say we're under attack," she said gruffly. "There's black magic incoming."

It was as if her words had frozen the air in his lungs.

As he gathered air to raise the alarm, one of Zeki's *hawks* dove like a falling star toward the forest and exploded in a circle of light that surrounded the treetops only a few hundred paces away.

All around camp, the shrill sound of the *alarms* went off. Gallio could see Zeki's stunned face as he squinted at the light of his own spell pointing unerringly at the direction danger emerged from.

"To me, Cleric!" Gallio ordered, his voice charged with authority. In a fight, there was no time for personal likes or dislikes, and both he and Zeki knew it. The old Cleric grabbed his spiked mace and rushed toward Gallio and Alvedhra, his long gray whiskers shaking as he ran.

Inquisitors poured out of their tents in varying degrees of undress. Gallio noted with disapproval that most hadn't had the presence of mind to grab a breastplate or a helmet. Then again, neither had he. *Victory has turned us complacent,* he thought.

"What's going on?" Zeki asked as he reached Gallio. Like Alvedhra and the third lookout, Zeki wore a breastplate and a helmet over his thick gambeson tunic. Protocol dictated full armor for lookouts at all times through their shifts, but in practice it was too cumbersome and most Inquisitors turned a blind eye to the rule.

"We're about to find out," Gallio said. It was incredible the way adrenaline cleared the mind. All his worries were gone, carried away by the wind. All his fears, gone. Only what was to come mattered. "Ready your buffs, cast at my signal. *Golden stone carapace* on me, *avenging grace* on Alvedhra, and prepare a salvo of *holy bolts* on my signal."

"Got it."

"Alvedhra, switch to arrows, ready an *explosive* one." At that moment, Hector, the third lookout, reached them. He was a young Heiligian blond, whose beard needed a trim. "You're to come at the front with me, kid."

"Yes, sir!" Hector said, his yell piercing the night like a bolt.

Tendrils of mist spread out of the woods as the night grew colder and the light of the torches seemed to falter. *Here we go,* Gallio thought, just as the first figures rushed out of the mist and through the underbrush. Eerie screams filled the air.

The creatures floated inches above the ground, their arms extended toward Gallio and the others. Their bodies were gray and transparent with hair floating as if underwater, with their open mouths and eyes resembling dark graves.

"Specters," Zeki uttered, stating the obvious.

"Specters!" Hector brandished his spear, and took several steps forward. "Abominations! Blemishes in Alita's eye! I shall *smite* you all!" The tip of his lance burst in a white light as if having grown suddenly forge-hot.

"Get back here, you idiot!" Gallio reached for the kid's shoul-

131

ders and shoved him hard. "Let them come to us, that's what the *circle of respite* is for!" Hector turned with flared nostrils and showing his teeth, but stood his ground. *Good. Wouldn't want the kid flogged for insubordination.*

Letting the undead reach them was the best option, and not only because it gave time for the rest of the men to catch up. As long as the circle's magic stood unbroken, the specters would have a hard time breaking the invisible barrier that protected the camp. And when they did, they'd fight severely weakened.

"How many?" Gallio asked at Alvedhra, who had the keenest eye of the bunch.

She turned her head like a hawk, ready to draw her bowstring and launch an *explosive arrow* at a moment's notice. "Just five. Shouldn't be a problem."

Gallio raised an eyebrow. *Just five?* That few specters wouldn't give pause for a single Inquisitor.

Then a shimmering skeletal hand came out of the ground midway between the specters and the lookouts' fire. The hand floated up, grasping at the empty air as if pulling the rest of its body by an invisible rope. A skull followed it with blazing green pinpricks of flame burning in empty eye cavities, along with a tattered shroud that swayed in the nonexistent breeze.

"WRAITH!" someone screamed.

Gallio frowned. *Is this the same wraith that appeared in Hoia? The Diviners told us it had been destroyed.* A voice in the back of his head told him that there was something that didn't add up with that wraith. It looked *wrong.* But why?

The undead abomination stood at its full height and regarded the Inquisitor with its terrible smile as its five specters rushed forward. And then it charged... to the side, away from the lookouts. Toward the back section of the camp. The one filled with non-combatants.

"Oh, dunghill," Gallio muttered. All hell broke loose.

CHAPTER NINE

DESPICABLE HEROICS

The light from the magical hawk engulfed the forest.

"How long until they figure it out?" Kes asked. She was covering her eyes with her forearm, protecting her sight from the sourceless daylight. It was fading, quickly, but its blinding surge had ruined the group's night vision. The kaftars had still not recovered—their eyes were more sensitive, and the spell had stunned them.

"Probably not long enough," Ed said, squinting past the line of trees toward the camp, which was still hidden by the light's after-effect. He was surprised by how well the simple spell had worked on him. When it had gone off like a giant firecracker out of nowhere, he'd been sure the Inquisitors had launched an artillery shell his way. The light had stunned him and sent him sprawling down as if the surge had gone off inside his own brain.

Dungeon Lords are vulnerable to the Light's spells, he reminded himself. *Better not be hit by one again.* Back in the Haunt, he and his minions had pooled their knowledge about the spells and talents the Inquisitors would have at their disposal, and had been sure that none possessed a combat spell that worked at such long range. Since they were all still alive and unhurt, the spell hadn't been meant for combat. Ed guessed that it was an *alarm* variant on steroids—not only warning the Inquisitors of incoming danger, but also briefly stunning said danger and pinpointing its location.

He knew that no plan survived contact with the enemy, but seeing how close they'd come to damnation chilled him to the bone. Thankfully, neither Alder nor Lavy shared the Dungeon Lord's vulnerability, because otherwise the entire plan may have gone to hell.

The Witch knelt with her hands oozing black and purple energy which flowed around her. She was already hard at work raising the second wave of specters, which was probably a good idea, since the Inquisitors would make short work of the first five.

Lavy's spell was called *summon specters*, and she had learned it on her own by sheer enthusiastic research. Unlike necromancy, which worked only with flesh and bone, her Witchcraft could summon the spirits of the dead, lay curses, and perform a bit of scrying. It was the swiss army knife of black magic.

"Rise, my beauties," Ed could hear her whisper. "Heed my calling and spread terror among the living!" Maniacal rapture contorted her face. "Yes!" she exclaimed as five new silhouettes took shape among the mist. "Yes! Rise!"

Nothing about that incantation was part of the spell, Ed told himself. She was only doing it out of love for her trade. Admirable, yet a bit concerning.

Close to Lavy, Alder held his flute to his lips and played a quick, eerie melody filled with jarring shifts in rhythm and tune. The surrounding air rippled with spent magic, his eyes were closed, and sweat poured across his forehead. The Bard was earning his weight in gold, because his part in Ed's plan involved using almost all his magical arsenal at once. First, he had cast *minor illusion* to create a facsimile of Torst near Lavy's specters, and then had used his bardic utterance *bardic images* to create five copies of the original wraith illusion. In total, the combo ate two spells and one utterance, but the result was worth it. *Bardic images* created five *indistinguishable* copies of the original target. They were easily dispelled, but a powerful Spirit rank wouldn't reveal them as a fake. Furthermore, these images were smarter than an illusion. They moved around on their own—designed to pull aggro away from the caster by tricking his enemies into thinking each image was the real version.

As long as Alder kept the magic of his melody going, those five images would do their best to trick the Inquisitors into thinking each was the original wraith illusion…

Probably best that we don't overuse the combo, Ed thought. Objectivity probably wouldn't like the concept of illusions copying illusions to deny the enemy a Spirit contest. He wished he knew of a way to *test* the limits to which Objectivity would let him go. Instead, the way the magic of Ivalis worked was a sort of honor system. He could bend the interpretation of the spells and talents' descriptions, but if he tried to break them, or went too far, he'd simply be deleted out of existence—no take-backs or do-overs.

Magic and the scientific method, it seemed, didn't like each other.

"He can't keep going forever," Kes warned him. The light had faded enough by now that Ed could see the first image of the wraith fly around the Inquisitorial encampment, dodging bolts of light, arrows, and javelins as best it could. One lucky bolt made contact and caused it to dissipate into magical raindrops.

"Whoops," Alder said, stopping his melody for an instant. He took a deep breath and resumed playing. Another of his images flew out, bellowing dramatic threats in its otherworldly voice.

"Lavy? More undead, please," Ed said. He activated his Evil Eye. Technically, they were standing above a single-chamber dungeon he'd created as soon as they arrived—in fact, it had been that action which had prompted the blinding spell to fall down on them.

As long as they were in the same dungeon, Ed could sense all his minions in a vague way, as if he had a dungeon-sense that brought that awareness inside his head, along with other nifty details such as the right spots to build a cave, and what to break in order to collapse one.

"The riders are waiting," he went on. "But the drones can't dig into the camp as long as the area is contested." When Heroes, Inquisitors, or other powerful foes consciously controlled an area, it greatly hindered his attempts at creating a new dungeon there or expanding through tunnels, but it also established a clear limit to his dungeon-sense, as a sort of magical ownership keeping him at bay. Not all of his enemies possessed this talent, but most of the magic users did.

Instinctively, he knew that contesting an area was as simple as getting a group of living creatures in there. In other words, the easiest way to take a controlled territory was to get a couple of his minions there to throw the previous occupants out.

Luckily for him, his Spider Empire had a lot of living creatures.

"Second image is down!" Alder announced. His cheeks were reddening from the effort of keeping the utterance up. "I think their leader is on to it!"

Ed glanced up at the second *hawk*-like spell that still encircled the sky above. As he watched, the hawk dove at full speed in the opposite direction of the fight—toward the river. The shine that followed claimed the attention of most of the Inquisitors not fighting shades or wraith images. The dome of light turned the murky waters of the river into crystal for an instant and revealed dozens and dozens of horned spiders swimming in complete silence toward the camp.

Screams ran as the Inquisitors bellowed orders and split their forces to deal with the new threat. An instant afterward, Ed's dungeon-sense informed him that the camp was currently contested.

His Evil Eye blazed as he relayed his will to the drones underneath him.

. . .

"*SMITE!*" Gallio's sword turned into brilliant molten gold and struck the approaching shade with terrible intensity. The creature turned into grains of white light with such violence that it forced back the other two undead monsters. They hissed at him, but the golden sand-like armor summoned by Zeki's *holy carapace* protected the Inquisitor from the specters' *drain endurance* trait.

An arrow hit one of them and the creature exploded. Hector handled the last one with three furious thrusts of his silver-infused spear, which bypassed the undead's resistance to non-magical attacks and destroyed it.

"Zeki!" Gallio called as he readied himself—several more specters were headed his way from the forest. "What the hell is that wraith doing?"

"No idea!" came Zeki's answer as the Cleric shot a *holy bolt* at the flying creature. The wraith dodged with a speed and agility that, Gallio was sure, was impossible. *Has it gone sentient?* A sentient wraith was a very rare and dangerous phenomenon, the product of an almost impossible mix of circumstances. But wouldn't a sentient wraith know it was suicide to attack the Inquisition directly? It wasn't as if the undead monster was doing much—so far, it was content to do flying passes at the camp, screaming incoherently at everyone in sight.

One lucky enchanted arrow struck it and the wraith disappeared in a shower of mist—just like that, gone like a common specter. Before Gallio had time to close his mouth, the wraith reappeared, cackling like a mad kaftar.

Gallio had the sudden certainty that he was being tricked.

Then the second *hawk guardian* descended with a fury into the river. Gallio turned to the surge of light and stared at a horde of chitinous creatures half-submerged inside the black, mirror-like water. *Chitin.* His nightmare was back at the forefront of his thoughts all of a sudden, and his soul froze in cold horror at the prospect of facing an army of mindbroods. He almost dropped his sword and ran.

Instead, he sprinted over to Alvedhra, trusting Hector and Zeki to handle the remaining specters. "Can horned spiders swim?" he asked the Ranger.

Alvedhra looked him over like he'd gone insane. "What? Of course they can, they're arachnids..." She shot another specter, then followed his gaze. "Oh. *Oh.* Fuck!"

The first spider warriors had left the river and were charging at a group of bewildered Inquisitors. Each spider had their backs completely covered in spiderlings, which rushed out onto the battlefield as soon as their adult counterparts touched the ground. Gallio had never seen horned spiders use transport tactics before. As he watched, the spiderlings overran the surprised Inquisitors by the shore before they had time to use their crowd-control talents. In a blink, the spider warriors had them immobilized in strands of web.

The cold fear in Gallio's soul was taken over by a terrible, smoldering certainty. He knew the person responsible for this attack. *And those spiders are definitely contesting the circle of respite.* Hoping beyond hope, he turned to Zeki. "Your spell?"

The Cleric shook his head before returning his attention toward the wraith—he brought it down with another bolt, and the creature disappeared. This time it didn't return. *An illusion?* But his Spirit ranks should have resisted it...

It was no matter. "They're mixing illusions along with their minions, be careful!"

Damn it! There was no time to lose. With a Dungeon Lord involved, it was impossible to hold a zone without heavy-duty magic. Gallio had seen Edward Wright fight before. "Alvedhra, you're in charge," he told her. "This is a Dungeon Lord attack, so I must make sure Master Enrich knows to summon the Heroes."

Alvedhra knew him well enough to read his face, even in the middle of battle. "Ah," was all she said, her expression inscrutable.

Gallio clenched his teeth. *Damn it all!* "Don't do anything stupid. The camp needs you to hold the line." He wished he could tell her something more, make sure she'd listen to his commands, but the Inquisition needed the Heroes *right now.* Still cursing, he turned and ran toward Master Enrich's tent. He could see the spider warriors skittering in the dark. They destroyed all lanterns as they went, and somehow one had drowned the fire by throwing mud at it. Here and there, blazes of light shone as Inquisitors *smote* the critters down, but more always took their place. A Wizard tried to cast *daylight,* but as soon as he did, spiderlings rushed toward him and the man disappeared under a wave of black chitin. The spell fizzled out, and even his struggle was hidden from view.

Priests and servants ran among the battle, adding to the confusion. People were tangled up in bundles of web, hidden beneath the wheels of the carts, and trying to help the Inquisitors by throwing pots and rocks at the spiders—which hindered the Inquisitors more.

It was a mess. *Wright must've sent an entire cluster against us.* Had it not been for the distraction of that wraith, they'd have easily pushed back the horned spiders…

He reached a battle between two Inquisitors and two spider warriors. The men were powerful and well trained, but they were Heiligians with zero experience fighting horned spiders. One Inquisitor was already tied up in webbing, and the other's movements were sluggish from the paralyzing venom. "*Smite!*" Gallio rushed in as the spiders readied to finish the job, thrusting his sword at the nearest creature's mouth, between the mandibles. His golden blade crushed the spider's mandibles and roasted its brain. Smoke poured out of the critter's eyes as it screamed in agony, blue ichor flowing out of its mouth. The surviving creature roared and jumped at him, but Gallio was ready—he stepped sideways while freeing his sword and flicked his wrist to launch a blindingly fast swipe that cut the spider's two front legs down.

The spider warrior collapsed and fought for balance, trying to stab his horn in Gallio's general direction to keep him away. It was useless—his sword had a longer range. He put the beast out of its misery. When he was done, chunks of grayish spider gore covered his sword and his shirt.

"You two, come with me," he told the stunned Inquisitors. Why were they looking at him like that? Killing a pair of horned spider warriors wasn't all that impressive. He helped the first man cut himself free of the webbing, though he lacked an antidote to help the other. The kid would have to trust his *pledge of the faithful* to cleanse the venom from his system.

The three of them fought their way to the camp's center, where the fighting was heaviest and the grass was covered by writhing men-sized bumps of webbing. A team of three Inquisitors on the offensive was a force to be reckoned with. Legs and mandibles slid away from Gallio's golden carapace armor, and his divine-enhanced sword broke through chitin as if it weren't even there. The spiders retreated when he and the others neared, choosing to give ground instead of dying senselessly. *Just as well.* "Hold here!" Gallio told the other two as they reached Master Enrich's tent.

Gallio flapped open the entrance. Master Enrich stood in front of an overturned table, with the corpse of a horned spider warrior laying on its back, legs still twitching. Enrich's iron wand was in his hand, smoking from the tip. That wand possessed strange, powerful destructive magic. A curious weapon, unlike anything else in Ivalis except perhaps some dwarven machines. No one was really sure where Enrich had gotten his from. "Gallio," the man called as he saw the Inquisitor. "What the hell is going on?"

"A Dungeon Lord is attacking," Gallio said. "I believe the one responsible for Hoia's wraith is behind this. The attack may be retribution for Jiraz' death, so he may look to capture you, or he may be after our loot and the vampire's coffin. I'm certain we can beat the minions back, but we don't have enough men to ensure he fails at all his possible objectives. We need the Heroes."

Enrich waved a shaking hand at the stand by his bedroll, toward the strange, boxy device he used to manipulate the Heroes. "I've already sent a quest request," he explained. "No one has answered yet, though. Few people are connected to the server—it's late at night back home. Let me update the request..." He hurried out from under the table and rushed for the device. With his back bent, his fingers flew, seemingly at random, smashing a series of buttons on the device's lower section. "The chance to loot a Dungeon Lord is sure to attract somebody, no matter the hour—"

"You do that," Gallio said. He had no time to listen to the man prattle on. "I must go, the battle is far from over." Looking out of the tent, he could see that two brave Inquisitors had reached their war horses and had maneuvered right next to the riverbank. They stabbed at the spider warriors with long spears, pushing them away from the river and deep into the camp, which was more and more in Inquisitorial control.

"You cannot leave me alone!" Enrich exclaimed, his eyes opening wide with panic. "I'm almost out of ammunition!"

Gallio raised an eyebrow. "I won't leave you unguarded." He stepped out of the tent and nodded at his small group. "Keep an eye on him. Make sure nothing comes close."

The men nodded, and Gallio hurried for the river where the two riders were keeping dozens of spiders at bay. With the horses' extra height, the spiders couldn't reach the riders. One critter launched a strand of web at the legs of a horse, but its rider calmly intercepted the shot with his spear. He waved his weapon around, shaking it free of most of the webbing, then charged at the spider and ran it through with a *smite*-empowered strike.

If we can keep the spiders away from the river, they won't have anywhere to retreat to. They can't run into the forest without first going through us. And Gallio certainly would make sure that didn't happen. Destroying the entire cluster would surely weaken Wright's forces. *Perhaps that will force him back into hiding.* Gallio smiled. Here he was, hoping against hope that this wouldn't end in tragedy.

He reached the horses, which were tied to posts next to the carts. The nearby bushes shook with the breeze. Seven or eight non-combatants hid nearby, watched over by a few young Inquisitors. A servant girl gave Gallio a hopeful look, her fingers crossed in front of her chest as if in prayer.

"Don't worry. Those beloved by the Light have nothing to fear," he recited, almost mechanically. He hurried for the nearest horse and jumped on. Riding bareback was another thing that Ioan and Alvedhra had taught him, but *fighting* without proper stirrups was another thing entirely. His plan was to use the horse to traverse the battlefield, then dismount and reinforce the riders contesting the river while on foot.

One rider used a *cleave* variant to swipe his spear across the line of spider warriors, severing fangs and legs in one fluid motion. The golden light of divine talents going off lit the scene like thunder-strikes. The man straightened his back and roared a challenge as the horned critters were forced away from his spear. He looked like a hero straight out of myth, framed against the river while his features were lit by his defensive buffs. A proper servant of the Light. Proud and unbeatable.

The river exploded behind him and a huge black shape the size of a war horse fell over both rider and horse, its extremities extended hungrily like the fingers of a titan's hand breaking the water. The rider barely had time to turn and scream a curse as the Spider Queen fell over him like a shroud. His terrified horse tried to both jump and dash at the same time, and only managed to propel the Inquisitor down into the mud, which saved his life. The spider's legs closed around the panicking horse, and in a second the animal had disappeared, along with the spider, under the surface of the water.

It had happened in the blink of an eye. Gallio, along with the rest of the non-combatants, had watched it all happen.

The Inquisitor exchanged a glance with his horse. It was probably the adrenaline, but Gallio could've sworn there was a flash of intelligence in the beast's eye as it gave him a look impossible to mistake. It said, "Guess that good old Thumper wasn't all that beloved by the Light, eh?"

It's going to be a long night. The second rider was, quite understandably, hurrying away from the river, while the first former rider scrambled away into the bushes, covered in mud.

Gallio made a quick decision. "Push them into the river!" he ordered to anyone who would hear as he rode parallel toward the waters. "Force them away from the tents!" It'd probably be better for morale if his men thought the spiders were leaving because the Inquisitors forced them to, instead of that being the critters' plan all along.

To add to his increasing lists of problems, he realized that Alvedhra and the other lookouts were gone.

"HE's SEEN US!" Vogkord mumbled with horror. "We must run, quick!"

In front of them, hidden by the foliage of the bushes, Inquisitor Gallio paced around the battlefield. He looked fearsome in his summoned armor, even if it was fading already. It only drew attention to the spider's remains that littered his body and sword. The batblins' mounts clicked their mandibles and shifted in place, eager to challenge the Inquisitor and prove themselves fitter than their fallen brethren.

"Hold," Klek told both Vogkord and the spider warriors. "If he'd spotted us, we'd be dead already." Or perhaps not. He'd met Gallio, once, a long time ago. He didn't seem to Klek like a cruel man. But Sheriff Gallio and Inquisitor Gallio could very well be different persons entirely, even if they shared a body. Just like

Klek Spider-rider was a very different batblin than Klek the half-starved.

The group waited, tension filling the space among them. There were five batblins and a spider warrior for each. Klek had hand-selected all members of his squadron for their bravery and discipline—which wasn't saying much given his starting pool of volunteers, but he worked with what he had. No one moved, and Gallio gave no signs of having seen them.

Something was happening by the river. Gallio rode away, shouting angrily, to Klek's relief.

"Good call," Tulip whispered at him. "Now, if my brave snack-leader could figure a way to get all those big snacks away from our objective?" She was referring to the pack of scared humans that were huddled close to the loot carts as well as the guards protecting both them and the coffin that was Klek's riders' main goal.

"We should smack them!" exclaimed Strodzark, waving his lanky arms in what he probably thought was a threatening manner. "*Pack tactics* makes us invincible—it's they who should be scared of Strodzark!"

"Oh, dear," said Saffron, Strodzark's spider. "Someone calm him down before he does something stupid. Please?"

"No fighting," Klek said. "We're here for the coffin, that's all." Besides, he very much doubted that the ten of them could handle the guards without casualties, even if they overpowered three alert Inquisitors. No, the situation called for a more careful solution.

Strodzark let out a nasal whine and crossed his arms.

"Tulip, we need a distraction," Klek said. "Can you get the spiderlings to help?"

"Ah, certainly," Tulip purred. She bent her legs and clicked and clacked at the grass, using the particular spider language that all warriors learned in their youth.

The horned spiders bloodthirsty nature was still alien to most batblins. It was the hardest part about getting the rider units to work. Klek and Tulip had bonded during the Haunt's defense. They had fought together and knew that they could trust one another. The others hadn't had the time to build a similar link. They worked together on Lord Edward and Klek's wishes, but nothing else.

Perhaps that would change tonight.

The wait didn't last long. Klek's *echolocation* gave him an excellent view as the first guard scratched his back, distractedly at first, and then with increasing alarm. Another guard gave him a confused glance one second before realizing spiderlings were crawling all over their bodies. He screamed as he dusted the spiders off in a rage, but more took their place. Soon, both men were dancing, trying to keep more spiders from climbing on. An instant later, the remaining guard and the unarmed humans followed suit.

One lanky man in a tattered tunic even broke and ran away, flapping his arms and yelling in horror for help. In the distance, fireball runes went off and off, over and over.

"Now is our chance," Klek said. "Quick, while they're distracted."

The riders and their mounts snuck out of the bushes and headed for the cover of the carts, using the wheels to hide themselves from view—not that anyone was looking their way anymore. Screams filled the night. Near the river, the Inquisitors slowly pushed the warriors toward the river.

Klek undid the knots tying the tarp that hid the cart's contents and pushed the heavy fabric away to reveal cramped boxes and rolls of fabric, packs of weaponry tied together, ornamental pieces of armor, and wooden boxes engraved with precious gemstones.

"Get anything valuable, but leave the heavy trinkets," Tulip ordered while the rest of the batblins rummaged through all the carts.

"How do we know what is valuable and what isn't?" Lily asked, her mandibles clacking shyly. "All these human baubles look the same."

"You leave that to me," Horm told her as the batblin pocketed a silver locket. "You find anything shiny and I'll hold on to it for you!"

Working together, the group piled the valuables over a tarp they spread on the ground. Klek gestured at Tulip to get her attention. "We need to secure the coffin."

"Lead the way, my brave snack." Both spider and rider hurried for the coffin's tent. The guards were only a few paces away—one was rolling on the ground, and the other had torn his clothes away and frantically passed his hands back and forth across his body. He was covered in red, angry little bites.

"It's a miracle they can still stand," Tulip muttered. "That much poison could paralyze even a bear."

The coffin lay in wait inside the tent, secured by heavy silver chains. It was a black old box that must've been an impressive piece of artwork a long time ago. The paint had faded, leaving naked wood on its edges. Hollow spaces where gemstones had been engraved stared at Klek like empty eye-sockets. A silver family crest marked the oak lid.

Klek could've sworn that the temperature in the tent was colder than outside. He nervously reached the coffin, walking over several salt magical circles as he did so.

"We just tripped three *alarms*," Tulip warned him. "Those guards will be pissed once they have the presence of mind to realize we're here."

"Hopefully we'll be gone by then."

Tulip webbed the coffin. Klek split his attention between watching her work and keeping an eye on the confusion outside.

"What now?" Tulip asked once she was done.

"Now, we wait for Lord Edward's drones."

Klek waved over at the riders outside—their spiders had webbed the tarp like Tulip had done with the coffin. Together, the eight critters dragged the bundle to the tent by pulling on the ropes, grabbing only the sections of web that the spiders had taught them wouldn't stick.

Once the ten of them were reunited inside the tent, they stood around, nervously looking at Klek, as if it was his fault the drones hadn't arrived yet.

"They'll be here at any moment," he assured them. Outside, the guards had dealt with the spiderlings and were nursing their wounds. Farther out, half of the spider warriors had entered the river. Gallio was nowhere to be found.

"They're abandoning us!" Vogkord wailed, rubbing his hands together. "Don't you see, Klek? We've lost the river! The spiders are retreating, so Lord Edward will leave us here!"

Strodzark and Horm exchanged nervous glances.

"Calm down, idiot," Rose told her rider. "You're making too much noise. People will hear!"

"She's right, keep quiet," sighed Saffron. "And my sisters are not running away—they're retreating on purpose."

"You want Vogkord to think that!" Vogkord pointed an accusing finger at the spiders. "So Vogkord gets killed instead of you."

Klek realized he was losing control of the situation. He opened his mouth, but Tulip spoke over him. "Keep talking and I'll web your mouth shut. How are we supposed to get *you* killed instead of us if we're right here with you, you dumb little—"

"The Heroes are here," Lily whispered, her voice quivering.

Klek's blood froze in his veins. The others kept arguing for a beat, then silence spread among them in a flash.

"What did you say?" Strodzark asked.

Klek crossed the tent and reached Lily, who was stealing glances through a hole in the fabric.

A summoning circle had appeared out of nowhere, red and gold lines of fire forming runes in midair, shining like angry stars, but hovering only ten or so feet above the ground. The magic lines gyrated slowly while people cheered. The grass at the bottom was charred and smoking, and three humanoid figures stood in eerie calm at its center.

One was a female elf wearing a white tunic under silver armor, another was a male dwarf covered head to toe in heavy plate, and the last wore black leather armor and hid their face under a black cloak. They were armed with a mace, a tower shield and an axe, and two curved swords, respectively.

Their eyes lit up with red light as their bodies jerked to a measure of life. Klek caught sight of blank-like features in a skin not unlike porcelain. The Heroes moved.

Next to Klek, Lily shivered. He couldn't blame her. They were low-level critters caught in a Heroic path. It wasn't hard to guess what happened next.

"That's it," Vogkord said quietly. "We're doomed."

This time, no one had any desire to contradict him.

THE HEROES CARVED a path of destruction through the ranks of the remaining spider warriors.

"You've got to be kidding me," Ed said quietly, as his minions ran for the river or were destroyed. "I know those guys."

"What?" Lavy asked. Sweat covered her forehead, and she was completely out of spells. "You mean the Heroes that are annihilating our forces?"

Ed nodded. There was no mistaking them. The group had always liked to play the same roster of characters—even if they died, they simply made them again. "The dwarf is a Guardian called Shadow Zero. Mark Thompson plays him. The elf Cleric is Layla Moonshine, played by Lisa Anders. The Rogue is Rylan Silverblade. My former employer runs him. They are my old party."

Alder whistled. "They're incredible." Ed's former group moved with mechanic precision, dealing with pockets of spider resistance one at a time. Lisa's Cleric's fast cleansings kept their movements unhindered by web while the Rogue disappeared into the shadows and reappeared an instant later to *sneak attack* Pirene's princesses and royal guard. Mark's Guardian ran through the battlefield with the grace of a boulder, drawing aggro as attacks bounced off his meteoric plate armor.

It was so different watching them from afar. They looked nothing like the outdated graphics of Ivalis Online.

A chill ran through his back. *All this time that's what people watched when I ran with my party.* That's what Kael Arpadel had faced. Unfeeling humanoid creatures built for killing, culling living beings without mercy or hesitation. He focused on his drones and the tunnel they were digging. They were so close to Klek and the riders... but the Heroes' path was right in their way. He willed his drones to speed up, his urgency flowing like electricity between the mental link with them. They were already going as fast as they could, though.

"Isn't that too much of a coincidence?" Kes asked, rubbing her chin. "It has to be some kind of trick. All the Heroes around, and you run into your old party?"

Ed shrugged. "IO's player-base was already low when I arrived in this world." For all the procedurally generated content, IO had many failings that other games in the genre lacked. Spotty servers, buggy advancement, a bitch of a difficulty curve, a non-existent tutorial, and many others. Its players, like Ed, had stayed because they enjoyed the plot and the small—but dedicated—community that had grown around the obscure game. "Most people played in Heiliges. We knew it as the Light Kingdom, though. The four of us liked to play in Starevos because it was the least populated area, so we had more experience points to ourselves. I guess they never left."

This was bound to happen, Ed thought. It was as if he was caught in the middle of a train-wreck, his old life colliding with the new.

"Can you... just tell them that it's you?" Alder asked. "Let them know what happened, get them to help?"

"Yeah... That will not work." Ed and Ryan, his ex-boss at Lasershark, hadn't left on the best of terms, mostly because Ed had smashed the other guy's face into his own desk before quitting the job. On one hand, Ryan had had it coming. On the other, Ed doubted the face-bashing had helped Ryan see the error of his ways. Perhaps if he could separate Mark and Lisa he could talk to them. Not that it'd do much to help. "First of all, they'll probably attack us on sight without reading our chat. Even if they listen, the Militant Church controls the interface. There's nothing stopping their sys-admin from simply changing the text to a copy-pasted evil speech—"

A thought tore across his brain like an arrow. *How many did I kill while they were begging for mercy?* His throat dried in his mouth.

"So we're right where we started," Lavy said with a heavy sigh. Nearby, an owl screamed into the night.

Kes drew her sword and readied her shield. "Not exactly, Lavy. Get behind me, we got incoming."

A surge of adrenaline buried Ed's worries in some vault in his head—he'd deal with them later. He drew his sword and readied himself to activate his talents. Alder did the same, hurrying to his side, with Kes guarding the other. The four of them were alone in the clearing.

Somewhere in the foliage behind them, Eyegouger and the other mounts bawked angrily. The owl screamed again, three short warnings.

"We're running out of time," Kes said.

A woman came from the tree-line in front of them.

How did she get so close without anyone hearing her? Even the warnings had come with barely seconds of leeway.

This mystery, at least, was solved when the Inquisitor strolled into view, her bow drawn and an explosive arrow nocked. A Ranger, skilled in tracking and moving silently through the forest.

Ed had fought with this particular Ranger before, a long time ago. Alvedhra had changed since then. Her face was fuller, and she had more muscle in her body. An extra couple ranks of Endurance and one of Brawn, probably. Her hair was cropped short, her heart-shaped face shared the tan of a full-blooded Starevosi, and her high-cheekbones and sharp chin could've made her Ioan or Nicolai's cousin.

"Oh, time's certainly ran out for you," said Alvedhra, flashing a smile full of teeth.

"THEY'RE COMING THIS WAY. I'm sure we can take them," said Strodzark, not really sounding that sure of himself.

"Let them come," said Rose through an angry hiss. "I'm ready."

Tulip turned to her sister with a click of mandibles that was the spider equivalent of an eye roll. "Then you deal with them, dear." She faced Klek, who was in the middle of the tent, staring at the floor with a distant expression. "Snack, we need to leave while we still can. The drones aren't coming. Perhaps we can sneak out through into the forest if we're very lucky, but staying here is not an option."

Vogkord nodded. "She's right, Klek. We've no chance against them."

"We can't leave," Klek muttered. "The Haunt is counting on us."

"The Haunt doesn't pay us enough to die for it!" Horm exclaimed.

Klek turned his small hands into fists. "They'll be here," he said, with a finality to his voice that admitted no further discussion. "I know it."

Outside, the sound of battle was fading. It was a strange paradox: the Heroes had unleashed a cacophony to the battlefield that had quickly turned into a deathly silence. They made no noise. No war-cries. They didn't even call out their spells.

It's like they're barely paying attention to us while they kill us.

"Klek," Tulip said. "Guards are approaching. If we don't leave now, we're dead."

"Look," Klek said. "Anyone that wants to leave can do it. But every minion that fought outside is gone or dead. This is the safest spot in the entire camp, so make your call."

"Hogbus save us," said Vogkord sadly. "I knew I should have listened to my mate."

A strong breeze reached the tent and made the entrance flap and flutter. Despite himself, Klek jumped like everyone else. Someone squealed.

The ground above Klek's feet began to shake. Acting by reflex, Klek jumped away barely in time. The ground collapsed and became a ramp as it fell with a heavy *thud.* A dirty drone in a purple-and-pink tunic stood atop it. It had a yellow mining hat with a shard of magical torch at its front. It regarded the stunned riders and their mounts with a disapproving look, then gestured at the cart behind him, which was connected to the stone floor by a strange iron line that extended beyond Klek's view.

With a dignity that befitted the Adventurer Slayer, Klek patted himself clean of most dust—with little success. "Right," he said. "What are you waiting for?" he told his crew. "Get to work! Secure the loot to the cart so we can do what we do best."

One by one, the crew overcame their surprise. The spiders pulled the coffin and the bag of loot toward the cart, while the riders secured it. Outside, it was quiet enough that Klek could make out the sound of voices heading their way.

Tulip reached his side while the others worked. "Turns out you were right again. Tell me, brave snack, what is it that we do best?"

Klek gave her his best confident smile. "Running for our lives. We have no equal at that."

The horned spider chuckled darkly.

· · ·

"ALITA'S TITS," Alder whispered. He turned to Kes, his eyes wide. "That's Alvedhra!"

"I can see that," Kes said, sharply. She was pale, the muscles in her arms taut with tension. "Alvedhra. What are you doing here?" she asked the Ranger. "And what the hell have you done to your character sheet?"

Ed activated his Evil Eye and stole a quick glance.

- Alvedhra, human Inquisitor. Exp: 275. Unused: 15 Brawn: 12, Agility: 13, Endurance: 12, Spirit: 12, Mind: 12, Charm: 12. Skills: Archery: Improved IV, Tracking: Improved I, Religion: Basic VII. Talents: Explosive Arrow, Smite, Pass Without Trace, Pact of the Faithful.

The Ranger's talents were all over the place. *She's become an Inquisitor?* Last time Ed had seen the Ranger, she'd suffered an allergic reaction to spider venom in the middle of a battle against Queen Amphiris. Kes had saved the Ranger by making a pact with what she thought was an evil Dungeon Lord who had tricked them into trusting him.

With time, as they had gotten to know each other, Kes had come around. Now she was one of his most trusted friends.

Alvedhra, though… she hadn't been there for that part. Only for the betrayal.

"I could ask you the same damn thing, *minion*." Alvedhra gave the word such a dark emphasis that Kes involuntarily took a step back. The Inquisitor turned to Ed. "So this is what you really look like, Dungeon Lord. The armor and cape suits you better than your scrawny adventurer disguise, I'll admit. Your pet batblin is missing, though. Yes. How different things are. And my, that's such a huge experience gain you're sporting, Kes. I wonder how many innocents you had to kill for it."

"You have no idea what you're talking about," Kes said.

"Is that so? Correct me where I'm wrong, then. You became a

Dungeon Lord's minion and helped him raze Burrova and kill Ioan and all the others. Last winter, you and he tried to release a sentient wraith into Constantina... but failed. So you rallied more Dungeon Lords into Starevos, then built a base here. And now you're raiding the goddamn Militant Church!"

"Oh, come the fuck on," Lavy muttered. She was inching for the bushes toward Scar and the other hell chickens.

Alder frowned and lowered his sword. "At least you got two of those right, Al."

Kes glared at him. "Alder, *don't*." She glanced back near Ed and raised her fist without making eye contact. "I deal with her on my own, understand?"

"Got it," Ed said, trying to appear nonchalant. Klek and the riders were running for their lives inside the tunnel while the drones collapsed it as they passed. *We really don't have time for this.*

"I hope you're better at 'dealing with me' than you were at securing this clearing," Alvedhra told her. Everything about her demeanor just oozed fury. "It was trivial to sneak here undetected. And now I've got your Dungeon Lord surrounded, Kes. It's over. A single gesture and he dies. Your reign of terror ends tonight, and by Alita's grace, it'll be by my hand."

"Are you even listening..." Kes shook her head and didn't finish her sentence. Her hands clenched her sword so tightly her knuckles were white. "Look, we didn't summon the wraith—we *killed* it. And I don't know what Gallio told you, but we didn't burn Burrova. Ioan did, and we stopped him."

Alvedhra loosed her arrow. Ed's eyes flashed green, and the arrow exploded midair in a puff of smoke. Lavy yelped and jumped back a step. No one else acknowledged the attack—Kes didn't even blink.

"I'll kill you for speaking like that of Ioan," Alvedhra said. "He was a hero, and he died defending the village from a Dungeon Lord's attack, like you should have done. You say that's a lie. Am I wrong in saying you're his minion, then? Do you deny it?"

Kes shook her head. "No. I don't deny it."

Ed wanted to clutch his head and scream his frustration away. Kes *couldn't* tell her the whole truth! Because doing so would be admitting the mindbrood's existence—to an Inquisitor, at that—and then Hoia, Undercity, and every village in the vicinity would get purged by holy fire. He had stumbled into a situation that could be resolved by all parties involved calming down, drinking tea, and talking for a while. But they *couldn't* do it!

And Kes knew it.

"So, the one truth you can't twist is the one you own, yet you expect me to believe all the others you can't prove." She grabbed a small metal piece she carried on a necklace. An arrowhead. "I found this in Burrova's ashes. It's Ioan's. When you're gone, I'll bury you with it, so he can find you in the afterlife. We'll him decide if you're worth forgiving."

"Go fuck yourself," Kes said quietly. "Your new friends are no saints, you know. If you want someone to blame, it's them. They go killing anyone who won't bend the knee to Alita, and when we *dare* defend ourselves, you scream to the heavens as if we were the ones burning entire villages down."

Alvedhra let go of her necklace and nocked another arrow. "The Militant Church gave me a home after I lost mine. They nursed me to health. They gave me purpose, taught me how to hone my hatred into a weapon of good so that I could stop massacres like those from ever happening again." She paused, and her face was distant for a second. "I won't fail them, Kes. There's only one thing I need to know—one thing I keep asking myself. Because, you see, I thought I knew you, that you weren't one to fall for the sweet lies of a servant of the Dark. What did he offer you in the first place? Was it riches? Women? Your homeland taking you back?" Alvedhra shook her head, although Kes' expression didn't change. "No. Tempting, but not enough to fuel such a betrayal. It has to be something deeper. The true wish of your heart." For an instant, Ed's gaze met with the Inquisitor. He didn't like what he saw there. "He offered your wings back, didn't he? He told you he'd make you fly again, and then you sold your soul and did everything he asked of you—like the good whore you are."

Kes drew a breath as if someone had stabbed her. Ed knew that Alvedhra had unearthed Kes' greatest pain—something very intimate that Kes had shared with her in a way she hadn't with him or anyone else. Alvedhra had paid back Kes' perceived betrayal in the same coin.

The Marshal raised her head. She just looked... tired. Very much so. The vivid image of a person with no more fucks to give.

She sighed and said, "Okay." Then she raised her shield, aimed the tip of her sword at the Inquisitor's neck, and advanced.

"Now!" Alvedhra said immediately, entering a defensive stance. "Get them, now!" She stared at the trees.

Kes stopped and looked around, her shield covering her face.

Nothing happened.

Alvedhra cursed in Starevosi and drew her bowstring. "*Explosive—*" Something red-feathered struck her neck. Her arrow went wide and disappeared into the underbrush. The Inquisitor blinked and reached for a small bamboo shaft protruding from her neck. She blinked again as she removed it to reveal a small syringe attached to the shaft. "What?" she repeated.

The surrounding trees shook, and five tall kaftar jumped down from the branches above. The spotted furs under their leather armor shook with the breeze. "Bet you didn't see that one coming," Kaga said, barking a laugh. "Not such a good infiltrator, after all, am I right?"

"Right you are, boss," Yumiya said, flashing a grin of yellowed canines.

"Kaftar!" Alvedhra reached for another arrow, but her hand missed its mark somehow. "What have you done to my men?" She seemed to have trouble standing.

"Sleeping draught," Kaga said, pretending he didn't see Kes' furious scowl. "They're having such sweet dreams, you should join them."

"A poison? Ignorant barbarian, I'm an Inquisitor. My faith shall burn through your silly juice in an instant."

"Sure." Kaga shrugged. "But that draught is my great-uncle's personal recipe. He used to hunt were-alligators all over the misty swamps of the distant south, near the Wetland frontier." The kaftar had a nostalgic glint to his eye. "Those were the days. That draught would put any were-gator to sleep, force them to revert back to normal. If your faith can burn through it, maybe people should pray to *you* instead of the Light, young lady." As he spoke, he and Yumiya calmly strolled for the Inquisitor, with the remaining kaftar hanging back outside the clearing.

Alvedhra's entire body was tense with raw effort as she forced herself forward on willpower alone, step by step. "Blasphemous, ignorant fool. You won't stop me from having my revenge." With a trembling hand, she grabbed an arrow and nocked it. She took aim at Kes. Ed readied himself to *reflex* a drone her way. "I am Alita's hand on this cursed earth. Through my arrow, her will... be done!"

She released her grip with a guttural war cry. Her bow shot from her hands into a very surprised drone. Alvedhra studied the arrow that she was still holding, raised an eyebrow, and then collapsed into Yumiya's waiting arms. The Monster Hunter deposited the Inquisitor on the ground with a careful motion.

"Another victory for great-uncle Shigo," Kaga declared off-handedly. "That man was an artist." He took the weapons away from Alvedhra's snoring body with practiced ease.

Kes reached him, her face flush with anger. "I told you I'd deal with her on my own!" she told the kaftar.

Kaga bared his teeth and pulled back his ears like a puppy rebuked, but only for an instant. "My apologies, Kes, I must've missed that order while we were dealing with the Inquisitor's two friends. In truth, she should never have come this far, but those two made so much noise it's no wonder we missed her approach." By his side, Yumiya nodded.

Ed squinted, unsure if he had read the kaftar right. *Is he actually angry because Alvedhra managed to sneak past him?* Somehow, she had done so in a way that also missed the kaftar's presence entirely.

Tonight, two expert infiltrators had passed by each other without either being aware of the other.

If Murmur is watching this, he must think mortals' lives are a black comedy, Ed thought.

Kes rolled her eyes at the kaftars. She gave Alvedhra one last sad look, then straightened her back and returned to Ed's side. "There'll be more, Ed, and they'll bring those Heroes with them. We need to leave right the fuck now."

There were no more spiders in the camp, and Ed could see men and women moving in a flurry of activity. He wasn't sure if they were coming this way yet, but they *would*.

"I'll go get Scar," said Lavy, who had kept a healthy distance from the action since running out of spells. "By the way, Kaga, I've an ex in a dungeon somewhere I'd like you and your great-uncle to meet."

"You point and I'll dart," Kaga said cheerfully, hiding his blow-pipe within the folds of his armor.

At that moment, a section of the ground in front of Ed gave way with a rumble, collapsing in a way that created a ramp for the creatures below. There followed the unmistakable crash of a wooden cart stopping the old-fashioned way against a wall of dirt. Ed took a step back as the dust settled. A sweaty batblin emerged, almost completely covered in grime.

"Lord Edward!" Klek exclaimed, his eyes wide and his ears pulled flat against his head in fear. "The Heroes are on their way, we must run—" the batblin caught a glance of the clearing "— what happened here?"

"Family reunion," Ed said quietly. Behind Klek, the spider

warriors were pulling the remains of a heavy-laded cart through the ramp. They seemed cranky. "Let me help you guys with that," he said, reaching for one of the web strands. At least the cart seemed in condition to move, but he realized that the lid of the web-covered coffin had gotten cracked slightly during the impact. *I hope that Lavy didn't exaggerate the vampire's resilience,* Ed thought. If the coffin worked anything like a cocoon, the creature inside wouldn't be able to survive even that small amount of damage. But there was nothing Ed could do about it, except cross his fingers.

A batblin with dark fur and a pointy nose peeked from the cart's tarp at Alvedhra's sleeping body. "Ooh, shiny!" he cooed. "Come, Lily, let's hold on to those trinkets!" He gave Ed a guilty grin. "For the Haunt, of course."

THEY HAULED the coffin that had started all this mess atop the cart. The family crest drawn on its lid was some mythical creature with many barbed heads and a huge body. Possibly a hairy variant of a hydra. *I hope you're worth it, vampire.* It'd be a shame to have to kill the monster inside after going to all this trouble for it.

Kaga jumped atop the cart and grabbed at the reins. He convinced the hell chickens to move by a combination of threats, pull of the reins, screams, and pleads. Scar turned his long neck at one point and snapped at the kaftar, but Lavy clicked her tongue and the mount froze in place. One by one, the hell chickens moved, dragging the cart along with them. Slowly, as they tested the limits of their strength, they gained speed. Kaga guided them. When they left the underbrush behind, they began to gallop. Ed took a deep breath and ran after them.

He wasn't even winded when one of the Monster Hunters reached his side. "Dungeon Lord, we're being chased," the kaftar told him. "A single rider is ahead of all the rest by several minutes.

It seems like he knows the forest better than the other Inquisitors. He'll catch up unless we intercept him. Shall we take care of it?"

Ed thought it over. An Inquisitor that knew the forest better than the others, and with Alvedhra in the same group. It wasn't hard to do the math. "I think that's an old friend."

He wasn't keen on meeting Gallio—the man certainly wouldn't be happy about tonight. But if Ed didn't, Gallio would overtake the cart and probably try to stop them. Then it'd come to violence, and one of them would likely die.

Gallio wasn't a bad man. Ed had seen him risk his life during the attack on Burrova. They'd fought side by side—that had to count for something. Perhaps, he owed the Inquisitor an explanation.

"I'll go with you," he told the kaftar. "Alder, you've two utterances left, right? Let's *nimble feet* to speed things along." He quickly organized the travel. Kes, Lavy, and Klek would stay behind to guard the cart. Ed and Alder would take Kaga's kaftars and either catch up or meet them back at the Haunt.

"Be careful," Kes told him. She didn't insist on coming along, which said volumes about her state of mind.

It wasn't long until they met with Gallio—all Ed had to do was slow down to a stroll and soon enough the sounds of a horse's gallop through the undergrowth reached his ears. The Dungeon Lord waited with the kaftars and Alder guarding his sides.

Gallio came into view seconds later, riding bareback atop a chocolate gelding. He had changed little since last time they met. Tanned and short, with a strong build and pale blond hair now kept down to a stubble. A fever burned in his eyes, and his shirt was wet with grime. And his character sheet had his attributes a couple ranks higher.

When he saw Ed, he urged his horse forward. "That's the second time you leave Alvedhra behind in that state," he told Ed matter-of-factly.

"That's far enough, Gallio," Ed said, raising an arm. He'd seen the Inquisitor's *sunwave* in action once, and once had been enough to know it was better to stay out of its radius. "She'll be fine, the draught only put her to sleep. It's better than what she intended to do to Kes, in any case."

"Of course." Gallio closed his eyes and sighed. "You've gone too far, Edward. Attacking the Inquisition, stealing our prisoner? I knew this would happen. You went from a well-intentioned young man into a Dungeon Lord bold enough to oppose the Light's will directly."

"Well, perhaps if the Light hadn't filled the countryside with murderous... I don't even know what to call those things, but they sure as hell aren't Heroes... then maybe we wouldn't be forced to defend ourselves!" Despite himself, Ed felt anger bubble in his blood. He attempted to keep his temper in check, but dealing with the Inquisition was like trying to reason with a bully who kept hitting you and then ran screaming to an adult the second you hit back.

Gallio shook his head. "That's not how it works. *You* chose to become a Dungeon Lord. By that decision, you became the Dark's servant. You are an enemy combatant in the middle of a war zone. You can die or you can surrender, but you can't ask that we leave you alone. And don't give me that look. I know full well you aren't as innocent as you claim. Or have you forgotten the wraith you tried to raise to sentience?"

Alder smacked his forehead. "Here we go again."

"Gallio. You, of all people, should know that things are more than what they look like," Ed said.

"And yet, most of the time, they end up being exactly what they insist they aren't."

"We KILLED that wraith while the Inquisition twiddled their thumbs!" Ed's eyes flashed green for an instant. He clenched his teeth and repressed the outburst. "Ioan wasn't acting alone, Gallio. Whoever gave him the Bane's egg wanted that wraith out there spreading chaos. I've prisoners that can tell you the same. Their leader, the real culprit, had dealings with a rich Lotian spellcaster. That's about as much as they know, but it means that whoever was behind Burrova's attack is still out there! We can't waste time fighting among ourselves, we need to be looking for *him!*"

The Inquisitor's expression was inscrutable. Discreetly, a kaftar nudged Ed's shoulder. They'd wasted too much time already. It was time to end the negotiations—one way or the other.

And it seemed that Gallio had reached the same conclusion. "You can get a prisoner to swear on anything you want. I know this." He raised his sword in challenge. "But if what you're saying is true, then come with me willingly. We tried it your way before, and it led us nowhere. It's time to trust the Light. It's harsh, but only because it must be. Come with me and tell this story to the Inquisition, Edward. Submit to Alita's judgment."

"Have you gone nuts?" Alder asked. "You're asking him to go die horribly!"

"No. I'm giving him the chance to redeem himself."

"Enough," Ed said. He spoke in a whisper that dripped cold anger. "We're leaving now, Gallio. I advise you don't try to follow. The Haunt will take care of the Lotian. I just thought you ought to know." He nodded to Alder. The Bard fumbled for his flute and lifted it to his lips.

"*Nimble feet!*"

Gallio scowled and aimed his sword at Ed. "I'm afraid I cannot let you leave. I'm a sworn Inquisitor, Edward. Last time we met, I told you it'd be this way. My duty is to apprehend you or die trying. And no offense, but you don't have enough minions with you to stop me."

Ed's kaftar raised their fanged scimitars and blowpipes and barked a challenge. "We'll see about that!" one of them exclaimed.

Gallio charged.

Ed's eyes burned green as he turned his anger into raw will. He still had all his spells, and his chat with the former Burrova's

Sheriff had left him itching to use them. His body tingled with magic as he poured his power into a *minor order*. *"Stand,"* he said, his voice charged with Mind-altering power.

It all happened too fast to see. Triumph shone in Gallio's grin —Ed had tried to use *minor order* on a seasoned Inquisitor who was all but immune to that kind of magic. Raw surprise replaced the Inquisitor's grin as his horse rose on its hind legs suddenly, its eyes as confused as Gallio's.

Ed watched as Alita's warrior smacked the ground butt-first. Terrified, his horse hurried away. To his credit, Gallio was already surging to his feet, unbridled rage marring his face.

"And that's our cue," Alder said. "Now hurry up, you don't want me entering combat and ending *nimble's* effect."

"Indeed," Ed told the Bard. As one, they indulged in one of the Dark's greatest tradition: the honorable tactical retreat.

With Alder's music powering their legs, they quickly put some distance between them and the Inquisitor.

Ed was beginning to think they'd gotten away with it when he heard the scream.

"You cannot run from fate, Edward! *SUNWAVE!*"

We're safe. We're well out of range, Ed's brain instantly announced, as he activated both *improved reflexes* and his aura to squeeze a few extra inches out of his stride.

Behind him, day replaced the night for a single instant. He had been right. He kept running, with the kaftars and Alder screaming for their lives as they went.

Then the heat reached him.

It took him entirely by surprise. His left hand began to heat up under his gauntlet. Nothing worse than a sunburn, at first. But the sensation grew. And grew. In seconds, Ed's entire hand was burning as if white hot—without the relief of nerve death. In an instant, it was as if the sun itself was shooting up his veins and into his heart, burning all the way. It was like being cooked alive.

Ed screamed and fell, his mind and body unable to handle the sudden, absolute, overbearing agony.

The pain reached its zenith. Ed blacked out.

- You have gained **25** experience for leading a successful raid.
- Your attributes have increased. Spirit +1.
- Your skills have increased: Athletics +1. Leadership +2. Your aura's energy expenditure has been reduced.
- There are new talent advancement options for you.
- There are new Dungeon Upgrades available for research.
- You have a **Condition**: Curse: Weakness to Holy magic.

CHAPTER TEN

CUSTOMER SATISFACTION

H azy neon light bathed the store. A long time ago, there had been a smoke machine, but it was broken now. Probably for the best. Smoke machines and delicate computer parts didn't mix in the slightest, but good luck convincing corporate of that. A snazzy vaporwave playlist came from the speakers, and the acrid smell of tobacco traveled through the unending rows of electronics like an invisible cloud.

The playlist was Lisa's. It was very much her aesthetic, and bringing it to work with her was a way to help forget that her life was only $7.25 hourly above slavery. The tobacco smell was Miss Olesinska's, and it was probably her aesthetic too. All of Miss Olesinska's many layers of clothing smelled of tobacco, her remaining teeth were stained yellow, and her tongue was one shade away from black. She was eighty-nine years old, and had driven herself to the Lasershark store carrying her Dell Dimension XPS R400 in the backseat, cables trailing behind like snakes. Time had yellowed the white case, just like it had done its owner.

"The Facebook is slow, I worry it may have the virus. My grandson is a computer guy, but he told me to bring it to you this time, dear. Better safe than sorry, he said, so here I am," Miss

Olesinska was saying as Lisa hooked the Dimension to the oldest monitor around and booted it up. After the BIOS was done running, Windows 95's cloudy sky greeted her. It was a logo she hadn't seen in a long time.

This computer is older than me, Lisa realized. She was in the presence of history itself.

"He's such a handsome young man, my grandson. I should introduce you two, you know? He's a hard worker, graduated first of his class last year—how old are you again, honey?—doesn't matter, meet him anyway." Miss Olesinska kept on like that, listing off the heroic deeds of her grandson.

Lisa opened the explorer and found the problem. A host of search bars inundated the screen, leaving only a few sad lines of space available for any actual exploring. Half of those bars belonged companies that no longer existed. *Sweet dreams, you bastards,* Lisa thought. It was like stumbling into bloatware's version of an elephant graveyard. Killing them would be a cyber-archaeologist nightmare, like stomping on a fossil. Perhaps she could figure out a way to transplant them into a virtual environment so they could live on. It'd be like having her own retro malware retirement home. The exact kind of meaningless gesture that gave her pleasure.

"Can you fix it?"

"Don't you worry," she told Miss Olesinska. "Here at Lasershark we thrive on customer satisfaction. We take care of the problem one hundred percent of the time or you get your money back, guaranteed." What she really wanted to say was, *Don't you worry, my fair lady. I shall guard this elder artifact with my life.* Then again, corporate didn't like it when someone deviated from the standard speech.

"I'm glad to hear that," Miss Olesinska said, all kindness and smiles. She paid Lisa and promised one last time to introduce Lisa to her grandson.

Lisa watched her walk very slowly to her car and fumble for

the keys for about five minutes. Miss Olesinska drove off in a way that begot both awe and horror. Lisa unhooked the R400 and carried it into the back, which lacked the store's carefully constructed image. The walls were plain white, flaking in spots, and the lighting came from cheap bulbs. There was a water cooler in a corner. The cooling feature was turned off to skim cents off the power bill.

Mark sat in front of an IKEA table strewn with disassembled computer parts. He was eating a sandwich and gestured a greeting at Lisa as she came by and searched the table for enough space to set down her beautiful charge.

"Holy balls, is that what I think it is?" Mark managed through a mouthful of sandwich.

"Yup. Kneel, Guardian, for you stand in front of ancient royalty. This baby rocks a Pentium II killing machine and hasn't seen a USB port before."

Mark set his sandwich away. He bent over the case and took a long sniff. "Ah, old plastic and a hint of cigarettes. They don't make them like this anymore," he said. "Do you think it can run Doom?"

"Bitch, it can run the shit out of Doom," Lisa said, crossing her arms.

"I think the valiant Cleric of Aucrath misunderstands. I already know it runs it. My question was an attempt to introduce the *real* issue. Are we going to install Doom on this old computer and play it after work? And yes, we could play it on any other computer, probably including the fridge's. But this is the authentic experience, Lisa."

"*Ah,*" said Lisa. She grinned. "Interesting." She sucked at first-person shooters, but so did Mark, and a chance like this was scarce. Most of the old computers that came into the store were non-functional, after all.

Someone behind her gave a shy cough. Lisa turned—Mark and she were supposed to be the only ones at the back. The owner of the cough was a kid sitting on a plastic chair, right next to the water cooler. He was somewhere between sixteen and eighteen years old and had brown hair, a dollar haircut, faded jeans, battered sneakers, and a carefully ironed dress shirt. A yellow folder rested on his lap, and he gripped it compulsively with both hands.

"Who are you?" Lisa asked. Because she was surprised at having missed the kid, the question came out harsher than she'd intended. He shifted in his seat, uncomfortable.

"He's here for the job posting," Mark explained.

"Yeah," the kid said, looking down.

Lisa turned to Mark. "So, Ryan's finally getting around to replacing Ed?" She didn't even remember how long it had been since she and Mark had carried the workload of three by themselves at no extra pay. *Any time now*, Ryan would say whenever someone dared bring up the issue. *And get back to work, it isn't break time!*

Mark showed her his open hands. "Don't think it's by the goodness of his heart. I hear corporate is coming by in a few weeks, and he needs the opening filled to fit the guidelines."

"I see," Lisa said.

Ryan's office was upstairs. The faint afterglow of his new monitor shone through the windows. A heavy electronic locket guarded the aluminum door. Lisa knew she should be happy her workload would ease up soon, but she couldn't avoid a frown that drew deep lines across her forehead. Her sister, Diana, liked to tell her she shouldn't frown like that because it'd give her wrinkles in a few years.

She strolled toward the kid and extended a friendly hand. "Hi, I'm Lisa, and this one over here is Mark."

"Omar." The kid accepted the handshake with a sweaty palm.

"Omar, how did you find about the store?" she asked.

He got a white A4 sheet out from his folder. "There was an ad with an URL in Woodside's cafeteria." Woodside was the local community college. "It brought me here." Lisa grabbed the A4 and saw that Omar had printed the job listing from the Lasershark page.

Now that's something I haven't seen in a long time. It hadn't changed since she'd used it herself.

She realized that she wanted to warn the kid, despite her common sense telling her she should let the matter drop. After all, something had to pay the bills. And what could she tell him, anyway? That the listing was grossly exaggerated?

"We have a young, fun, dynamic environment," Lisa read aloud. *That means you'll be working long hours, the foosball table is broken, and that the pay is shit.* Omar nodded.

It wasn't as if she hadn't looked for another job. She had, many times, and found none that could count as an improvement in any meaningful way.

"Kick-ass salesman," she went on. *That means you'll get run to the ground with unpaid overtime.*

At first it hadn't been so bad. Retail sucked, but it sucked for everyone, and Lasershark had originally been just a temporary gig —just until she could put her degree to work. She had come to Lasershark knowing fuck-all about computers, but she had bonded with Mark and Ed—and a few others who weren't around anymore—over shared hobbies, and they'd given her a hand whenever she had been lost. Nowadays she found that she liked computers more than she liked people.

"Dynamic workplace." *Ryan changes his mind faster than a revolver door spins.*

"You'll be treated as family, not an employee!" *Oh boy. I don't know where to begin with this one.*

She set the page down. Omar was still nodding. It broke her heart.

"Look," she began, but then trailed off.

"Lisa." Mark warned her, reading something in her face.

"You're a gamer, Omar?" she asked. Of course he was. "What

about RPGs?" He shared that he was an MMO player, had cut his teeth in WoW just like Ed and Mark. He'd fit just right in, and that was the problem. "Cool. So. You know how people joke online about being only an NPC in their real lives? You know, a non-player character?" *Well, in Lasershark, we're not really joking,* she wanted to say, but then heard footsteps coming down the stairs from the office. She shut up.

Ryan was dressed in a tailored Armani suit with a Zelda t-shirt underneath. His blond hair was slick and drawn back, and his nose was even more perfect after the cosmetic surgery. "Ah, if it isn't the newest addition to our family." He extended Omar a handshake, but got too close to the kid as he scrambled up to his feet, forcing Omar to lean back against the wall with his legs bent over the chair as he shook Ryan's hand.

Omar's face reddened, but Ryan gave no sign of noticing. He stood back a little. Lisa's lower lip twitched in a repressed scowl.

Such a tiny gesture, so easy to chalk up to an honest mistake. Hell, Omar probably thought it had been his own awkwardness getting in the way. The tiny gestures added up, though, and they all advanced the same goal: Ryan making sure he was the greatest person in the room and that everyone else knew it.

He probably had read about that power move in one of the books he kept in his office.

"Nice meeting you, sir," Omar said.

"None of that. Ryan will do." He smiled beatifically and flashed Lisa a sideways glance. He'd probably be a fantastic boss for the new hire for a while, at least until he got bored of the charade.

"Thank you, sir. Ryan."

"So, I heard you talking with Lisa about WoW? I'm a bit of a gamer myself, you know," he confided. *I'm just like you*, Ryan's demeanor suggested. As long as I like you, I'm just like you. "In fact, we've a little gaming group here in Lasershark. Mark, Lisa, and I have this game, Ivalis Online. We like to kick the shit in it on the weekends. Maybe you should join us. No pressure, of course," he said. He patted Omar on the shoulder like a benevolent king giving a subject the chance to prove himself in court.

Not for the first time, Lisa wondered what it'd be like to disappear. To just grab whatever she could carry on her back and go. Nine out of ten missing persons were lying dead in a ditch somewhere. She'd read the statistic a while ago, on some e-rag or another. Perhaps the stats were wrong.

Perhaps she loathed herself enough to trust the roll of the dice.

"Well, thank you, Ryan, sir. Sounds great. I hope I don't suck too bad," Omar was saying.

"Ah, don't you worry about that. Everyone is a noob at the start, right? No sweat, the group is very newbie-friendly—that's the way I like it. Right, guys?" Ryan smiled again.

Yesterday, while they were grinding randomized quests, the group had fought a cluster of horned spiders to protect a camp of Ivalis Online's good guys from some random Boss' machinations. They'd earned a nice Story Quest for their effort, despite initially low exp and item yield. It was part of IO's charm. All quests had a chance to lead to a dungeon or a final Boss battle if you kept at it. Even the small ones. That hadn't stopped Ryan from calling her a dumb cow for forgetting she could use the spell *thunderstorm* to force the Spider Queen out of the river. She didn't consider herself a terrible player, but it was hard to think with someone judging your every move and calling out even the tiniest mistake.

Could she complain about the cow comment? Sure, but the HR lady was Ryan's aunt, and Lisa had an overdue rent payment. She doubted the dice would roll in her favor.

"Sure, Ryan," was all she said in the end.

"All right," Ryan said. "Well, Omar, why don't you pass by HR to get the last boring minor details worked out? Lisa, Mark, you ought to get back out front, though, you know how clients have a goldfish's attention span!" He chuckled.

As she left, Lisa thought about that e-rag and its missing persons stats. Sometimes, late at night, right before falling asleep, when darkness lovingly embraced her consciousness, she wondered about that last one person out of ten.

The one that made it.

She wished she could dream of herself in that person's place. But she never did.

Instead, she dreamt of a never-ending dungeon topped by a burnt-out sky where colossal creatures preyed on each other above the fiery clouds, and of the cackling of mad gods across impossibly vast distances. Those nights, she'd wake up covered in sweat, and every time she'd swear the nightmare had followed her to the waking world—that the inhuman creatures with black beady eyes stood past the feet of her bed and beckoned her closer with a smile full of teeth.

But when she blinked, they were always gone.

CHAPTER ELEVEN

DARK PATRON WANTED

E d sat at the head of a large wooden table set under the shade of a gnarly tree. Teapots, mugs, and other utensils were cluttered in front of him. Exotic clothes of all shapes and colors covered the chairs, as if their wearers had suddenly vanished and left them behind. The world had a pastel color palette, and the sky above was pink with fluffy blue clouds the texture of cotton candy.

A fat caterpillar rested on the other end of the table, smoking from a pipe that left purple rings after each exhalation.

Ed looked down and realized he was wearing a blue sundress.

"Absolutely not," he said, raising an eyebrow. The sundress' fabric extended and changed shape as if responding to his will, and he was now wearing a patched-up suit a size too big for him, thick black boots, and a gigantic top-hat that bobbled above his head like a skyscraper.

"A shame," said a floating smile right past his left shoulder. "Blue suited you better, I'd say." The smile had too many teeth, and a hint of a black worm-like tongue.

"I was wondering when you'd appear," Ed said. He sighed and

poured himself some tea from the chinaware. Since he was here, he may as well make himself comfortable. "Weren't you supposed to stay away from me? I liked our previous understanding, Kharon." He took a sip of his tea, but was disappointed to find it had no taste despite its appetizing caramel color.

The floating smile rippled and waved through the wind, danced past Ed's shoulders, and spiraled to a stop right above the nearest chair. A face white as snow materialized around the smile, followed by the rest of the body. The Boatman was a tall fellow, rail-thin, with arms and legs that extended like branches. He had no lips, no nose, and no ears—only a pair of beady black eyes that mocked everything and everyone he set his gaze upon. He was wearing a purple coat fashioned out of a fat cat's pelt, with a rabbit scarf knotted around his neck.

"Don't pretend like you didn't miss me," said Kharon. His sing-song tone masked a faint buzzing that came from his throat every time he opened his mouth.

Ed reached for his own head, ready for the splitting ache that accompanied Kharon's presence, but it didn't come.

"I'm not actually here, dear Edward. That's why our agreement still stands. After all, this is only a dream." Kharon extended his arms as if making some dramatic revelation.

Ed raised his feet and rested them over the table. He forced himself to relax and deny Kharon the satisfaction of making him squirm. "So you can enter dreams, too?"

Kharon smiled. His attire transformed into a black-and-red-striped t-shirt and gloves outfitted with razor-sharp knives. "There's no realm too distant for the reach of Murmur's Boatman, Edward." He flicked his finger-knives in playful menace. "Careful. If you die in real life, you may die in the dream!"

"You're spending too much time on Earth," Ed told him. "It's rubbing off on you."

"Well, I could tell you the same about Ivalis. You've gone

native, friend Edward. Look at you, all dolled up into a mighty Dungeon Lord. Fresh out of his first clash with the Inquisition, even. And you almost made it out without a scratch. Impressive. Murmur is pleased with your progress." Kharon used one of his blade-fingers to clean a dirty fingernail. "And when Father Dearest is pleased, so am I."

"And I don't care," Ed said. After all his encounters with the human-shaped aberration that was Murmur's envoy, Ed had found that the best way to deal with Kharon was to force himself into almost apathy. Otherwise, he risked losing himself into abject terror just by considering the impossibly vast differences in power between a human mortal and the Dark demigod. "What happened back there? Gallio's *sunwave* was out of range, but I blacked out anyway." He shuddered at the memory of the burning pain.

Kharon switched back into his cat costume. "Straight to the point, like always." He served himself some tasteless tea. Since he lacked lips, he poured the drink straight into his open maw. "Let's talk about magic, since your time is oh-so-valuable. Are you familiar with that game Earth kids play, the one where you enslave mythical creatures and have them crush your enemies for you? Those creatures are vulnerable to their counter elements. Well, Light and Dark magic work kinda like that. Dark magic is all about flexibility and creative interpretations of its effects. Light is a heavy-hitter. Powerful, and to the point."

"Makes sense," Ed said. "But it doesn't explain why Gallio's *sunwave* hurt me without even reaching me."

"As a Dark-aligned creature, you're vulnerable to the Light's combat spells. But you're not just any Dark creature, no. You're a Dungeon Lord, the ultimate agent of the Dark's will upon the world. It would cheapen Murmur's name if any brave farmer and a plucky princess could one-shot a Dungeon Lord with a single *smite.* So, your Mantle comes with some built-in optimizations, defenses to bridge the Light's combat advantage. Dungeon Lords are still vulnerable to *smites* and *sunwaves* and so on, but not as much as, say, a wraith. *But,*" he said, waving a finger. "But, something happened the night you got that hand of yours, Edward. One accidental interaction between opposing types of magic. Contact with the wraith imprinted some of its characteristics on you, like your *drain endurance* touch power, and it opened a spectral talent-tree that the living shouldn't have access to. It also added the spectral weakness to Holy spells onto your character sheet. Like with that game from Earth, your sheet has two different types now, and both of them are vulnerable to Light magic."

Ed winced and stared at his black skeletal hand. "So, you're saying I'm half-ghost now? Last time I checked, I can't phase through solid walls or create specters at will."

Kharon shook his head. "Think of the specter sub-type as a smudge on your character sheet. It happened by accident and it's not optimized. It was sheer luck you got anything useful out of it at all. If you want those spectral talents, you can invest experience points in them, like always... but I don't know what that will do to your body, or your mind. The undead and the living don't mix, obviously, and much less in the same body. It could very well kill you if you aren't careful."

"How about if I cut off the damn thing?"

"Then you'd just be down a hand. The accident changed your sheet, Edward. Those bones are only a symptom, not the disease."

"Great." Ed massaged his temple. "Okay, I can tell you're not done yet." Best to get all the bad news at once.

Kharon smiled beatifically. "That's the spirit. And you're right. More bad news. Remember your Mantle defenses that Murmur so lovingly built for you? They're gone. All of them. Alita's divine bolt charred them away. If you're keeping count, that makes you thrice as vulnerable to Holy magic as a normal Dungeon Lord, so congratulations, you're the current world record holder. The prize is that in your current state, even a glance from a *sunwave* is enough to utterly destroy you, no matter how many defensive buffs and enchantments you stack. That's why the heat from Gallio's attack sent you straight into unconsciousness. I doubt he knew it'd happen. He probably only wanted to scare you and make you dismiss your auras—you made him fall off his horse, after all."

"*Shit,*" Ed said. The Haunt had just challenged the Militant Church. This was a disaster. If the Inquisition found out about it, they could bring him down with a snap of their fingers. "Does anyone else know about it?" he asked.

"No. But Gallio saw you going down, so he'll know something is up. I'd say you're in a race against time, Edward. Eventually, even if Gallio doesn't put two and two together, someone else will."

Okay, keep calm, Ed thought. Magic had brought him into this mess, it was reasonable to think magic could get him out. In fact... he stared at Kharon and narrowed his eyes. The Boatman never did things out of the goodness of his nonexistent heart. If he had snuck into Ed's delirious mind to explain all of this, it was because he was planning something.

The Boatman smiled. "Come on, give me some credit. I have been nothing but helpful since we began our friendship. Is it that hard to believe I only want to give you a hand?" He chuckled. "My 'plan' is simply to give you some advice. What divine magic messed up, divine magic can fix. You need a Dark patron, Edward. You know what I'm talking about. Like the deal you have with that Oynnes fellow, but with your good friend Kharon instead." He pursed his lip-less mouth in a mock pout. "In fact, I admit that the Dark is a bit offended that you haven't given us half the attention you're giving Oynnes. A sacrifice here and there could do wonders for your standing, you know? Boons, special talents, more nifty spells like *Murmur's reach.* I know you have a Dark altar already set up and everything, you would only need to start using it."

Ed raised an eyebrow and said nothing.

"It's a sweet deal," Kharon said. "Who better to be your patron than your best buddy? I'd give you all the cool stuff. How about creating Portals at will once per day? Kings would kill to have my patronage. Hell, the sacrifices wouldn't even have to be virgins, I'm pretty open-minded." He crossed his arms and stared proudly at Ed. "What do you say?"

The Dungeon Lord lowered his teacup on the table. He tapped the wooden surface as if pondering Kharon's offer. "You know, before I worked in IT, I had a brief stint in sales," Ed said. "I remember this trick they taught at induction. Upselling, they called it. Turns out, it's easier for a person to make several small purchases than one big one, even if the total of the smaller purchases ends up adding up to more. That's because the human mind has a hard time keeping track of many small investments, and once we're agreeing to one, it's easy to say yes to a couple add-ons here and there. Do you want fries with that? How about tire insurance for your new car? Like that." Ed pointed a finger at Kharon. "I think I've got you figured out, Kharon. You're Murmur's salesman, aren't you?"

"I've been called many things," Kharon said, with a big grin on his face. "But that one is a first."

"To start with, you offer your mark one great deal. 'Become a Dungeon Lord, travel to a new world, there's no commitment to the Dark, don't worry. You are free,' you say. Then, once your target agrees, you begin the upsell. 'Is the Inquisition giving you trouble? Try this new spell.' 'Hey, since you're doing so well, how about you pray to me in exchange for some extra power?' And since the commitments you ask are so small, and the benefits so big, people don't realize how much you're actually influencing them until it's too late, and they don't recognize themselves anymore. That's you, Kharon. That's what you do. Do you deny it?"

The Dungeon Lord held the gaze of the Boatman. Neither was smiling. The dream had, at some point, lost its friendly coloring. The foliage and the sky seemed faded, somehow, as if the cute paint was flaking and you could see the brick underneath.

"You know," Kharon whispered. "Many would kill to have me as their patron."

"Well, go ask them instead," Ed said.

Kharon extended a hand, and with a deliberate movement swept the chinaware off the table. Ed stiffened his back and reached under the table for the missing weight of his sword.

The Boatman's grin was full of teeth, and something oily and dangerous shifted behind his eyes. "There was a time," he muttered, "when I walked among the mortals like the tornado passes through a city of glass. Entire civilizations raised immense temples in my honor hoping I wouldn't pay them a second visit. They waged wars to obtain enough sacrifices to appease my wrath, and the lines of prisoners extended beyond the horizon. My priests worked day and night with their obsidian knives. The currents of blood that ran through the steps of my temples dwarfed those of the sea. You'd do well to pay me some respect, Dungeon Lord, just in case there comes a time when I walk the walk once again."

The Boatman let his words linger in the air for an instant, and then set a hand on the table and rose to his full inhuman stature. "Anyway, nice catching up, Ed. If you change your mind, just say so and we'll talk like adults. If not... well, any other patron will do, as long as you get one. Even a glancing *smite* would be enough to turn you into a vegetable in your current state." He chuckled and allowed the aura of raw menace around him to ease up a little. "That would be a shame, wouldn't it?"

Ed unclenched his jaw and watched as the Boatman turned

transparent and slowly disappeared until only his smile was left—and then even that vanished.

The Dungeon Lord was left alone in his dream, and he could feel the waking world coming to claim him. His heart raced in his chest. He stared at the gray sky.

For a second there, he'd seen the *real* Kharon, not the quirky persona the Boatman liked to put on.

"Good to know I get on his nerves too," Ed told himself.

CHAPTER TWELVE

POWER GAMING

E d knew he was awake because his body ached all over, his head spun, and the air smelled of wet batblin. A fuzzy shape obstructed his vision. He groaned.

"He's awake!" a voice exclaimed. "Quick, give him some space."

A shame. Without Kharon, the lucid dream had been almost nice. Peaceful, even. He wondered if he still had time to go back if only for a few minutes.

Don't you dare, he told himself. *You've too much work to waste time on sleep.* The Inquisition wouldn't vanquish itself, after all. He groaned again and blinked until his blurry vision steadied. Klek's big puppy eyes stared at him.

"I knew you'd wake up," the batblin told him, moving back so that Ed could sit.

Ed grinned at him. "I'm becoming superb at getting hit. Shame there isn't a skill for it." Klek's unwavering faith in him always cheered him up.

He was back in his room, naked from the waist up, his legs covered by the bedsheets. Someone had spread a nasty green unguent on his chest. Around him, the silver magical circles glinted softly.

"Actually, there is," Andreena told him. The Herbalist stood next to the bed. She had covered Ed's nightstand with a tray full of assorted herbs, a steaming teacup, and a mortar filled with more green unguent. "It's called *first aid,* and if you keep waking me in the middle of the night to use it, I'll have it maxed in a couple more years."

"Well, I'm always glad to help a master of the arts."

She pushed the cup onto Ed's hands. "Drink this, just in case you've got a concussion." It smelled of peppermint, but was bitter and grassy. Ed wished that Andreena would, at least once, add a spoonful of honey to her creations.

As he drank, Lavy, Alder, and Kes entered the room. They had been waiting nearby, judging from the time it took them to arrive. They had changed out of their armor into their usual attire, and other than Alder's shoulder sporting a bandage, they seemed unhurt.

"So, we won," Ed told them with a small smile. It seemed like a safe assumption to make.

"I knew it was a mistake to let you go," Kes told him grimly. "Dealing with Gallio on your own was an unnecessary risk, Ed. We almost lost you."

Alder coughed. "He wasn't alone. I was there, and so were the Monster Hunters." He nodded to Ed. "After you went down, the kaftar carried you back to the caravan. I provided them with Bardic support as we ran, of course."

"What the hell happened back there?" Lavy asked. "Alder told us Gallio's *sunwave* missed, but then you screamed and went unconscious anyway. Were you hit by some other spell?"

Ed explained his dream and Kharon's visit between sips of tea. Kes paced around the room, a frown deepening in her face as she heard the bad news about Ed's massive weakness to Light magic. Klek sat by the door, a spear in his hand, as if he feared that the Inquisition might come knocking to finish the job.

"Kharon's visits always get us in trouble," Lavy said when Ed was finished with his tale. "And now he wants to be your patron? What an *asshole*."

Alder glanced nervously at the shadowy corners of the ceiling. The Witch rolled her eyes at him, then went on, "Ed, I know a bit about Dark patrons. Warlocks like Chasan take their powers from them, and that's how they can cast more than just a few spells per day. Don't let the name fool you—it is just another form of servitude. If you were to accept Kharon's offer, he'd be able to order you around. Give you quests, demand sacrifices and loot, and whatever magic he gave you in exchange he could take away at any moment." She puffed her chest. "Witches and Wizards may have fewer spells per day, but at least the magic comes from *us*. As a fellow spellcaster, tell me you won't accept that offer!"

"Don't worry," Ed assured her. "I'd rather get *sunwaved* again rather than work with him. But that doesn't mean I'll refuse the patron idea entirely. Just to hedge my bets," he assured her, seeing her face redden. "Perhaps a small alliance of convenience, like the one we have with Oynnes. There has to be some Dark demigod or spirit or something that is *not* an asshole. We two are living proof that not all the Dark-aligned are like Kharon."

Lavy pursed her lips, but let the matter drop, which suited Ed just fine, because he still didn't know what had happened with the rest of the group after he'd blacked out. He asked his friends about it.

Alder filled him in on the small details. Ed had slept all morning, with Andreena assuring everyone he was actually asleep and not in a coma or something. Then Kes took over with the recounting of how they'd escaped in the first place.

"It was close," Kes told him. "Alder and the kaftar returned with you in tow not five minutes after you all left, Ed. It happened very, very fast. We threw you in the cart and ran like hell, knowing that the Inquisitors could easily follow our tracks all the way back home if we messed up." She kept pacing around the room as she spoke. "I feared that with you unconscious, the drones wouldn't listen to our commands. We'd have been doomed, then, because we couldn't wake you up no matter how hard we tried. The drones guided us to the tunnels near Burrova, though, just as planned. I think they knew how dire the situation was. We used the tunnels to change directions, and then collapsed them when we were out. I doubt they'll find our trail again, but they know we are nearby. It's only a matter of time before the Heroes come knocking."

Ed nodded. "Then we better hope that our gambit pays off. How's the coffin?"

Lavy and Kes exchanged glances. Ed felt a knot of apprehension form in his stomach. "We have no way to know," Lavy said at last. "We left it in a room near Zachary's chapel. The lid is cracked, but nothing leaked out, and there are no signs that the vampire inside is, well, permanently dead. We didn't dare look inside, just in case we jiggled loose something important. Governor Brett and Zachary secured the room in case the vampire tries to escape. You should take a look, I think Brett earned his keep this time."

"Got it," Ed told her. He pushed the bedsheets away and stood. Andreena gave him a disapproving look, but didn't stop him as he reached for a shirt, his belt, and his weapons and ordered his drones to help him don his armor. "You think the vampire will appear tonight?" he asked the Witch.

"Only one way to know," she said.

"Then let's put the rest of the day to good use," Ed said. He flashed his Evil Eye and took notice of the rewards for the battle against the Inquisitors. "I've quite a few unused experience points now, walk with me while I read the new talent descriptions."

Andreena took her leave. "Well, there's a batblin with a sprained ankle I must check up on. It's one of yours, Klek, so you should pay him a visit later, I'm sure he'd appreciate it. Ed, come see me immediately if you're feeling dizzy. Or if you feel anything out of the ordinary. I've no experience dealing with magical aftereffects, so I can't promise you won't sprout a donkey tail all of a sudden."

"Do you guys mind waiting for me in the War Room?" Ed asked his friends as he summoned a group of drones and ordered them to help him don his armor.

"Sure," Alder said with a fake shrug. With the Bard's high Charm, it was no surprise that he suspected Ed was planning something. "Klek, Lavy, why don't you come with me?"

"What, did you suddenly forget the way down the stairs—" Lavy shut up when he caught Alder's meaningful stare. "Ah, what the hell, sure."

Klek looked at the both of them as they hurried out of the room, then followed the pair. Kes frowned and headed for the door.

"Actually," Ed said as the drones helped him throw the gambeson tunic over his head, "do you mind staying behind, Kes? I wanted to talk to you about something."

The Marshal bit her lip as if she were considering refusing his request. In the end, her martial sense triumphed, so she put on a neutral expression and closed the door. "Yes?"

Ed took a deep breath, unsure of how to begin. "It's about what happened back there in the Inquisition camp. With Alvedhra."

"Look. Ed. We don't have to do this," Kes said sharply. "No offense, but you're a human from another world, and I'm an avian. We don't have enough common ground to have a chat about my feelings, and neither of us are even very good at it."

"Maybe," Ed said. The drones, unaware or unable to under-stand the situation, barked gibberish at each other as they latched his greaves' straps behind his leg. "Still, you are my friend, and even if I'm not an old, wise Dungeon Lord that knows exactly what to say, I'm still here for you. If there's anything you want to say, well, I can listen."

Kes rubbed her eyes with one tired hand full of scars and only three fingers. "Ah. I guess you're right. Sorry about the attitude.

It's just that the gods keep shoveling dung into this giant heap and one day you realize it's about to topple above your head... I mean, in other words, there's too much shit going on. That's the thing you say, right? 'Shit.' " The avian used her leg to push a chair her way and took a seat near the bed.

"Shit's the right word," Ed said. "It's a bit more versatile than 'dung,' actually. You can use it to say a lot of things. 'Shit's downright fucked,' 'that shit was incredible,' 'shit just hit the fan.' "

"Is that literal? People in your world like to hit their admirers with dung?"

"Only on social media and in High School," Ed said.

"I see. It sounds like Volantian politicians to me."

Kes and Ed chuckled, both well aware that the other had no idea what they were talking about.

"In her place, I would've done the same thing," Kes blurted out. "Ever since we're hatchlings we're taught to mistrust the pacts of Dungeon Lords. We learn about how devious and cruel they are, and that no matter what, trusting one leads to corruption and death. I cannot blame Al, no matter how much I'd like to. Back when we made our pact, I thought I was going to die. It's hard to explain. I didn't know the real you, I only knew the tales about your... kind. It took me some time to realize that tales sometimes are just tales. But without the minionship pact ensuring that we couldn't trick each other, I don't think I would've ever trusted you."

"Fair enough," Ed said. "From what I understand, mistrusting a Dungeon Lord is probably the smart thing to do. But I disagree about you not trusting me without the pact. With enough time, we would've realized we are on the same side. I believe that to be true to the very core of my being, Kes. Perhaps Alvedhra will come to realize it as well."

Kes shook her head and grinned mirthlessly. "Ah, bother. See what I told you? I suck at talking about feelings. I've misled you without meaning to. I'm over Al, Ed. I've been through break-ups before, I'm not a hatchling anymore. When it's over it's over, and life's pile of dung is always growing whether you're done digging out of the most recent landslide or not, so you may as well enjoy it while you have fresh air. And, hell… There are things you can't take back after you say them, even if you don't mean them, and Al crossed a line back there. If the gods somehow become merciful, perhaps in the future she and I may come to amicable terms, but that's pretty much it. She's not what I'm concerned about."

"Oh." Ed blinked. What could he say to that? "I'm sorry." That would have to do.

"When we made our pact, I thought I was going to die," Kes repeated, this time giving an edge of intensity to her words. She bent forward on her chair. "Don't you see? In a way, that's what I wanted, Ed." She frowned, her gaze lost in some distant memory. "All my life I've wanted to end injustice. To stop people from suffering. When I was a hatchling, I'd see the bigger kids picking on the smaller ones and my blood would just *boil*. I got into so many fights the elders thought I simply loved violence. And maybe I do. Who knows? Maybe justice is just the lie I tell myself so I can stab as many people as I want, but if it is, I sure wish it at least felt better."

She rested her eyes on her sheathed sword, studying it intently, as if looking for some deep truth inside. "My urge to fight never went away as I aged, so I joined the Cardinal Command. I believed it was the right thing to do. I was stronger and bigger than most avians, and there was a war going on. So, I volunteered. I still remember what I told my mother when she heard the news. I'd fight so others wouldn't have to. And I'd be the best at it, damn it, so the minotaurs would have to think twice about coming after our people. I arrived at the Cardinal Command's boot-camp and I found myself surrounded by people just like me. Scared, nervous, excited. *Green*. And then Ria and the others forged us into finely tuned weapons. Together, we were invincible. We would uphold justice with our wings and our spears. Then the fighting began and all that plummeted straight into the ground."

Ed's throat knotted up all of a sudden.

"Avians' only advantage against a minotaur are our wings," Kes explained. "They are bigger and stronger than us, and they can saddle their bodies with energy-demanding talents because of their insane Endurance. No matter how well trained or how many hundreds of experience points you have, if you fight a minotaur head on, you'll die. So we fight them in waves, from afar. Our army tries to break their ranks by raining projectiles and area-of-effect spells on them, and they hold on with defensive magic, nets, and ballistas. Most battles, neither army breaks and we go back to camp and repeat it all the next day. But if, say, the minotaur flank fails at blocking a volley of spells and they lose cohesion, then our squads dive in." She demonstrated by plunging her hand down through an imaginary air current and then lifting back up, at right at the last moment. "We use enchanted spears we call steel talons —a long, weighted shafts with a barbed tip—and fly almost straight down at max speed. The minotaur archers try to guess our flight pattern and shoot us, and sometimes they get lucky. An arrow from a bow strong enough to resist the pull of a Brawn 25 arm can turn half-a-dozen avians into mincemeat before anyone realizes what just happened. If the arrows don't kill you and you aimed your path well, there's this instant where you have a minotaur right below you and you have all the momentum of your plunge, so you spear them with your steel talon right as you pull back up. Mind you, this only works because we enchant our wings, otherwise we'd just splat on the ground. If you don't miss the strike, the steel talon's magic will fight the enchantments of the minotaur's armor—which is a very thick piece of plate. If the steel talon wins, it will probably penetrate the armor out of sheer momentum. Then the barbed tip will do its job, and the minotaur will bleed out in seconds, prey to his own blood pressure and lack of oxygen. That's their weakness, you see." She winced for an instant and drew a horizontal line with her hand. "*Our* weakness, on the other hand... right after spearing our target, there's this window of time when we must fly low, parallel to the ground, where we're open to counterattack with only our side-weapons to defend ourselves. It only lasts about five seconds before we can regain altitude, but it feels like hours. I lost most of my friends that way. Torn to pieces by axes or dragged down by weighted nets. The lucky ones had time to cut their own throats before the minotaurs captured them."

Perhaps Kes had more of Alder in her than she realized, because without intending to, she'd sown an image in Ed's mind, like a wide painting of an unnamed battle. He saw a scorched mountain pass overlooking a glistening green sea, with rows upon rows of armored giants like humanoid tanks holding axes as big as a man's torso. He watched figures breaking through a field of clouds like falling stars, these elven amazons wearing copper and flowing tunics, holding talons several times their size. He heard their war cries as they dove through the incoming minotaur arrows, the projectiles tearing holes through the span of their white wings, culling their numbers. He saw the fury in their faces painted gold by the sunset and crimson by the blood of their fellow warriors. He felt in his bones the reverberation of the impact as they reached the lowest point of their dive together, then blood and dust bursting up into the air. Bodies collapsed with minotaur and avian rolling brutally on the ground, dead on impact, crumpled wings stained with mud and guts, and the survivors frantically pulling up as the axes and arrows pursued them and, sometimes, struck the avians out of the sky and pulled them back to earth while their hands futilely reached for the sun as it rose farther and farther from their reach.

One avian that made it out had Kes' features. She was looking over her shoulder as she flew up and up among the survivors, her face contorted in pain as she saw what she was leaving behind, broken and bloodied on the ground below.

"They told us how dangerous the dive was," Kes said. "And also how crucial to victory it was, because without the dive, our armies had no way of reaching the minotaur command to assassinate it. With enough training, we could make it out alive, they told us. It was a lie. Training had nothing to do with who lived or who died. It was luck. Either you got targeted or you didn't." She steadied herself. "I thought I could protect them. I was wrong. The war lasted a long time, and somehow I lived long enough to stumble my way into a promotion, but deep down I knew that I had failed. But I *kept* trying. I don't know why. Maybe I am just too stubborn, or maybe I just love violence deep down. When my squad got killed, I thought it was over. One last defeat. Apparently some god is entertained by my failures, though, because I survived, although my wings were broken beyond repair and had to be amputated. They exiled me like a carrion avian and I came to Starevos swearing I'd never fight again, but it turns out I don't know anything else *but* fighting. After a month in Undercity without a single coin in my pocket, it was either taking up the sword again, or the whorehouse."

Ed winced.

Kes went on, "I came to Burrova and stayed. The Rangers and the Sheriff needed an extra pair of hands, and I had the experience. At least a village only a few hours away from a port city should be easy enough to protect, right? We know how that went... And then I met *you*. A Dungeon Lord, bringing death and calamity to my village. You were about to kidnap Alvedhra, remember? At least, that's how it looked. Then I saw my chance to do something truly good. If I exchanged myself for her, I'd redeem myself. The girl would live, and I would die because I'd have refused to work with you, and then I'd have finally *won*." She raised her hands and then let them fall limp to her sides. "And then I got to know you and the others better, and... everything became so confusing."

"That's... good, isn't it? Surely things aren't so bad now," Ed said. At once, he wished he had a few more ranks in Charm so he could've thought of something more helpful to say.

"Ed. I love the Haunt," Kes said. "In a way, it reminds me of home, while at the same time being entirely different. I love the way our people strut around trying to act Dark because that's what they're supposed to do, but they only have Alder's tales as examples, so they're terrible at it. I love the way our batblins and horned spiders puff their chests with martial dignity because *you* expect them to act that way. You think they're more than forest critters, and so they *are*. I love waking up in the morning and realizing our community is bigger than it was the night before. That's dangerous, Ed. Loving something means you either get to see it die, or it gets to see *you* die. And the gods know the Haunt has its fair share of danger. Seeing the way the Inquisitors think of us, how cheap our life is to them... I don't know. It's the same way I would've acted in their place, so I can't help but wonder if seeing all this—" she drew a wide arc with her arms "—be destroyed is exactly what I deserve. Perhaps that's why the gods are preserving me, and why I keep surviving things that should have killed me long ago."

It was strange, hearing herself open up to him in this way. Kes had been, by far, the most closed-up of Ed's friends. A tough warrior who kept her feelings in check. For her to speak to him so freely... it was a level of trust that Ed hoped he could someday be worthy of.

At the very least, today, he could take her fears and concerns seriously. He wasn't sure what help he could be to her—their lives were just so... different. But she had trusted him, and she deserved for him to at least try his best. So he focused.

"Did you... are you using *improved reflexes?*" Kes asked after a while, raising an incredulous eyebrow and staring at the tension in Ed's face.

Ed ended the talent. "I needed time to think about what you said. It's a lot to take in." He massaged his neck. "Look, I can't lie to you and tell you things will be all right, because shit may hit the fan at any time and we both know it. But I also think you're underestimating your own victories. I think they vastly overshadow the defeats."

"Ed," Kes said kindly, "I'm not sure that 'not dying so far' counts as a victory."

"But that's exactly it," Ed pointed out. "It is a victory when your enemy is death itself. Every day—no, every second you are alive is a victory. Death only gets to defeat us *once,* and then it pretends all those millions of times *we* won don't count. Well, they count to me, and I know that deep down they also count to you. Death is a sore loser, Kes, but we don't have to be. Justice is not something that we define by the way we die. A good friend once told me I didn't get to decide if I was a good or bad person. It's those who we help or hurt who set the score. So go ask the people of Burrova —the people of the Haunt—if they think you've protected them. If you've upheld justice. If you've done your best. And, forgive me if I overstep, but I could bet my life that your old squad thinks you have, because you think the world of them and I'm sure they felt the same way about you. And I'm sure we—Alder, Klek, Lavy, and the others—cannot ever replace what you've lost, but we can be right there with you when it's time to fight again, because I don't think you're the kind of person that ever surrenders, and there's a lot of wrongs to be righted. Perhaps it was luck that has kept you alive so far, but you get to decide *why.* And I think you know that."

There was a heavy pause while the two mulled over their words. Ed flicked a pearl of sweat away from his forehead. He could feel the cool dungeon air calming his heartbeat.

"It's a shame you never met my old squad. I think would've liked them," Kes said. "We were all horrible at speaking of what was going on inside, but they were like you. So full of defiance, they honestly made you think we could go against the gods themselves and win." She tapped the side of her nose, then gave him a genuine smile, the kind that erased ten years of hardship from her face and let the idealistic avian girl she'd been a long time ago shine through in all her radiant beauty, if only for an instant, before the grizzled survivor returned. "Now I'm all nostalgic. You know what? Sometimes, people with high Charm may say beautiful things that make you feel all fuzzy inside, but once they leave, all that stuff vanishes. Words are air—except worse, because you cannot soar on them. But when warriors speak their truth? When we raise our fists and rage against the heavens? That's real. That's our soul." She stood up, groaning as she did so. "Thanks for hearing me out, Ed. I don't remember the last time I talked about my life, if at all. I didn't expect it, but I guess you were right. Speaking about it helped."

Ed smiled, unsure if he'd actually done anything right. Kes had done it herself. All he'd done was trust she would. "Sure. Any time."

By now, the drones had long finished fitting the armor. He stepped up and the two of them headed for the door.

"A word of warning, though," Kes said, only half-jokingly. "I may be a bit testy for a while. I'm still fucking angry, after all. Feel free to call me out if I take it out on you guys."

"We'll handle it," Ed said. "What else are friends for?"

Kes grinned. "For one, they're very useful at drawing aggro," she said.

THE LIST of Ed's available talents had grown since the last time he looked, thanks to Kes' training and his own increasing expertise as a Dungeon Lord. The options now dwarfed the rather rigid character builds he'd worked with in Ivalis Online.

He had a drone bring him a coal stick and used an empty section of wall to do some quick calculations.

"What about *power attack*?" Kes suggested. "That's a fighter's cornerstone talent, and I'd sleep a lot easier knowing you had it in your arsenal."

"He needs more arcane power to throw around," Lavy said. "Since we still haven't found spellbooks so we can learn new formulas, he should get all the magical talents he can use as a Dungeon Lord."

"How about more defenses like his *pledge of armor?*" asked Klek. "Perhaps with the right defenses in place, we need not worry about those nasty, shiny attacks."

Alder shook his head. "If Ed stacks too many always-on talents like the *pledge,* the strain on his body could kill him. Many famous heroes met their untimely demise that way, you know. *Power strike* could work because it's an activated effect, the same as his Evil Eye. My own build is going to focus on activated talents, for example, so I can get a wide variety without worrying about my heart exploding at thirty-five."

"All those are all good suggestions," Ed said. "I agree with the three of you, actually. Here, look at my favorite options." He focused and made a conscious effort to share his talent sheet with his friends.

POWER STRIKE (30 experience) - The user adds +1 to his Brawn attribute when making an attack with a melee weapon.

Energy Drain: Activated. Moderate.

DUNGEON VISION (20 experience) - The Dungeon Lord can watch any location in an owned dungeon he's currently inside as if he were present there. The location must be uncontested.

Energy Drain: None.

HYPNOTIC EVIL EYE (40 experience) - The Dungeon Lord's Evil Eye is upgraded with an activated Gaze attack. Hypnotic Evil Eye forces the target into locking stares with the Dungeon Lord for a minute unless they resist a Mind contest. On a failure, the target can't avert their gaze and is vulnerable to Mind spells and illusions cast by the Dungeon Lord.

Energy Drain: Active. Low.

Choosing this upgrade disables the Veil Piercing Evil Eye upgrade tree.

VEIL PIERCING EVIL EYE (30 experience) - The Dungeon Lord's Evil Eye is upgraded with a constant effect. The Evil Eye can now detect invisibility and similar forms of concealment and has an advantage at piercing illusions and magical misdirection. Veil Piercing cannot affect Legendary-ranked magic or higher.

Energy Drain: Constant. Very Low.

Choosing this upgrade disables the Hypnotic Evil Eye upgrade tree.

PLEDGE OF BURNING ARMOR (60 experience) - The Dungeon Lord's Pledge of Armor is upgraded with new effects. As an activated effect, he can surround his armor in magical fire similar to the effects of the spell Eldritch Edge. This wall of fire won't damage the Dungeon Lord or his minions. In addition, the Dungeon Lord can now resist the effects of non-magical heat, as if he possessed the Resist Elements talent.

Energy Drain: Moderate while activated, very low otherwise.

PLEDGE OF MUTED ARMOR (40 experience) - The Dungeon Lord's Pledge of Armor is upgraded with new effects. Upon falling unconscious or being otherwise impaired, a team of four rescue drones is generated around his person. The rescue drones will stop at nothing to drag the Dungeon Lord to the nearest safe place, but they lack defensive capabilities. In addition, the Dungeon Lord can hide his armor's magical output at no extra energy cost.

Energy Drain: Constant. Very Low.

Choosing this upgrade disables the Pledge of Burning Armor upgrade tree.

ELDER LORD AURA (80 experience) - The Dungeon Lord's Ancient Lord aura is upgraded with new effects. He and the minions in the area of effect are now resistant to Holy magical sources. His minions are immune to mind-control magic, and all the attribute bonuses they receive from Ancient Lord aura are increased by one extra rank.

Energy Drain. Activated. High.

WRAITH STEP (50 experience) - The Dungeon Lord gains the ability to instantly transport himself to any uncontested location of a dungeon he owns and is currently inside. All the items he wears on his person are transported as well.

Energy Drain: Activated. Moderate.

BANSHEE SHRIEK (50 experience) - The Dungeon Lord gains a scream attack. Any creature within hearing range must immediately pass an Endurance contest. If they fail, they become frightened and unable to cast spells. Any creature with a Fortitude rank lower than five is instantly killed instead.

Energy Drain: Activated. High.

· · ·

ADVANCED SPELLCASTING *(60 experience)* - Improves the Spellcasting talent, allowing the user to cast Advanced-ranked spells.

-The user starts with one advanced spell per day besides his basic ones.

-Upgrading to this talent slows down improvement of the basic version.

Lavy whistled when she was done reading. Since Objectivity governed everyone in Ivalis, talking about experience and talent choices was a globally shared hobby. "Remember when our hardest choice was between *resist disease* or *resist poison?*"

"This is only the curated version," Ed said with a hint of pride. "I left out all the *endure elements* to save time."

"That's what a rigorous training regimen will do for you," Kes said. "Now that you're reaping the benefits, I'll drive you even harder, Dungeon Lord."

"I can see those talents aren't cheap," Alder mused. "Our talent choices are already improving, so the point cost will keep increasing from now on. How many points does the average Dungeon Lord earn? Even the most adventurous Bard taps out before a thousand or so."

"Lord Kael had about two thousand when he died," Lavy said. "He was strong, but he wasn't the most powerful Dungeon Lord ever to walk the earth... so maybe three thousand as the upper limit?"

Kes nodded. "Adventurers and mercenaries cap out near two thousand, I'd say. If they live long enough to reach that level, they're aging and slowing down and they've kingdoms and armies that do the fighting for them, so even if they wanted to, they would have no reason to leave their castles. Their combat skills and physical attributes slowly fade, but that's just how life goes. It happens to everyone... unless you're a lich, I guess."

Ed scratched his chin. "Heroes don't have that problem. When I played IO, we racked up tens of thousands of points in only a few days." In hindsight, the ease with which his character had thrown around spells bewildered him—he had about six daily spells as a Dungeon Lord, and that was after months of grinding. "That means I need to make every talent count if I'm to go against them."

"Not alone," Klek reminded him.

"Of course," Ed said. He gave the batblin a thumbs-up. "I'm counting on you, man. You have any suggestions for me?"

Klek told him to get the talents that would make him seem bigger and meaner, so everyone would leave the Haunt alone. Ed didn't have a rebuttal for that—the logic was flawless.

He had a hundred and thirty experience points to allocate. It would be a considerable increase in power, so he wasn't making the choices lightly. But it also meant he couldn't buy all the talents he wanted—not all at once, at least.

"The aura upgrade seems powerful," Kes said. "Resistance to magic is something most warriors would give an arm for. It's expensive, though—it'll leave you space for *power strike* and perhaps the dungeon vision." She scratched her chin. "Not that I look forward to not having any privacy."

Lavy cursed under her breath. "Just great. I hadn't thought of that."

Ed raised an eyebrow. "If I get the talent, I'd obviously respect people's privacy. It'd just let me react faster in case an *alarm* triggers."

"Sure," Lavy said, narrowing her eyes. "Like an *alarm* that triggers when the ladies' baths are in use. Don't you think I'm not on to your plan, Dungeon Lord."

Ed decided to ignore the comment. "What about you, Alder?"

"Well, *I* would combo the *vision* with that *wraith step* talent to instantly arrive at the baths when that alarm triggers—"

"I mean, what talents would you get?"

"Ah. In that case, I'd want to get both the Evil Eye upgrades. I've heard of a couple Dungeon Lords that devoted themselves to maxing out theirs, and they could do pretty impressive things. For instance, Lord Khalfair—Numerios' archenemy—could turn his enemies into stone *and* animate the stones to fight for him. He had this amazing garden decorated with his defeated foes where he and Numerios had their final battle..." Alder sighed nostalgically. "I wrote a dissertation on that tale back in Elaitra. Anyway, if I had to choose... *Hypnotic Evil Eye* would combo nicely with my illusions, but you don't use those. The burning armor one, then, if only because I'd look incredible playing my music while on fire."

"I can't believe you'd invest in a sixty-point talent just because of vanity," Lavy said. "I'm glad that Ed is more mature than that."

Actually, he's right. Strolling around while casually on fire would be great. Ed was sure he had once fought a final Boss with that talent while playing Ivalis Online. If he was right, then the *Burning Armor* upgrade path involved some sort of damage reflection and increased elemental resistances. It had made for an interesting fight... but was it the best path for Ed's build? Some gamers, like his friend Mark, ignored armor's stats and went for the coolest-looking item. There was allure in that approach, but it was anathema to Ed's power-gaming ways.

"If I could set myself on fire and not burn," Klek mused, almost to himself, "I could sleep anywhere in the forest, and no wolf would try to eat me..."

Ed coughed politely and decided to change the subject. "And you, Lavy?"

"You know magic is simply superior. *Advanced spellcasting*, obviously. In fact, I'm picking it up soon, myself. I want to improve my specters—as they are, they're little more than fodder for the Inquisitors, and to make them a threat I need access to advanced hex rituals. I'd also get that *banshee shriek* talent, because getting swarmed by assholes with heavy sticks is a Witch's nightmare. I'd combo it with an Endurance-draining spell, which fits my build, and hopefully they'd all die in a single cast." She smiled dreamily. "With any luck, their bodies would all strike the floor at the same time."

Alder took a step away from the Witch.

Ed considered his options. The biggest issue was that he didn't have enough experience to buy all the talents he wanted outright. So, he'd have to prioritize. Which ones did he need *right now?* "I'll have to take *pledge of muted armor,*" he said. "The drone effect would've been very useful after Gallio's attack, and hiding the magical output lets me blend in better in Undercity." It was a shame to lose out on the cool burning effect, but following the *muted* path adhered better to his character build. He wasn't supposed to draw aggro to himself, since all an enemy needed to do to destroy the Haunt was to kill him. Covering himself in magical fire would just paint a huge big target on his back, begging for a volley of *fireball* runes. "I wish I could take the aura, but it's simply too expensive, and with such a high energy drain I doubt I could keep it running for long enough. I'll leave that upgrade for later and go for *advanced spellcasting* instead, along with *veil piercing Evil Eye.*"

"Just so you know, going the advanced route will slow down your basic spell grinding," Lavy pointed out. "That's why I'm waiting a bit before buying it."

"I plan to wait a bit as well," Ed said. "But not too much. *Advanced* will let me pick two spells without a spellbook, right? Those could really come in handy."

"So, no *power strike,*" said Kes. "Well, it's your funeral. Don't complain when someone sticks you inside an anti-magic field and you have nothing to hit them with."

"Ah, luckily for me, I've a Marshal who can hold her ground in that case," Ed told her with a grin. "Don't worry, I'll take *power strike* eventually, along with *wraith step* and *dungeon vision.* They all fit my build, and since they're activated, they won't strain my body." He planned to get the aura upgrade, but first he'd need to raise both his Endurance and his *leadership* skill, which had the side-effect of reducing the aura's energy cost.

With that said, he bought the *veil piercing* and the *pledge of muted armor* upgrades, leaving him with just enough experience points to buy *advanced spellcasting* once he was done grinding basic spells.

He nodded with satisfaction as his character sheet updated itself to reflect the upgrades. He had a vague physical awareness that he was now stronger than he'd been an instant ago. The sensation was like waking from a good night's sleep and finding his favorite breakfast already waiting for him.

He decided to try the improved Evil Eye right now. He turned it on, feeling the familiar heat spread across his face as the eldritch green flames drew shadows across the walls. "Any difference?"

"I think…" Lavy said, squinting at him. "If you look carefully, there's a sort of blue sparkling at the end of the flames. Nothing too dramatic, so I would've missed it if I hadn't looked for it."

"Sparks, then." Ed turned off his Evil Eye, feeling a bit dejected. Magical talents could sometimes have very dramatic effects, and others you wouldn't know they were there without reading the character sheet. *Guess not all Dungeon Lords can go into combat covered in magical flames.* Perhaps, if he *really* wanted to, Alder and he could figure a way to imitate the effect using illusions…

Ah, but that would be vanity, he thought sadly.

"Well, do you *see* anything different?" Kes asked. "Any hidden enchantments, maybe?"

Klek turned around as if expecting an unseen attack. His ears gyrated like radar dishes, ready to follow any suspicious sound.

Ed took a careful look around. "No, I don't think so. Everything looks normal to me, but that doesn't mean we're safe. The upgrade doesn't detect Legendary magic or higher."

"If there is a Legendary illusion or mind-control effect in place," Kes told him, "we're screwed anyway, whether or not we could see it."

"That's reassuring," said Alder. He didn't look very reassured. "I've a bit of experience saved up, too, so I'll run it your way later, guys. I'm wondering just how far I can push my own illusion magic. I want to make it a part of my performances, you know? Like some kind of… special effect, like the ones in that vision I had."

To Ed's surprise, the chapel was in use when he and his friends entered. Two dozen villagers dressed in their best suits either sat respectfully in the rough wooden benches or chatted among themselves near the back. More than a few of them wore shoddy necklaces with bits of silver, and sometimes an entire head of garlic.

Ed raised an eyebrow. He had built the chapel as a mean to get holy water and blessed weapons. As far as he was aware, the villagers from Burrova prayed to neutral local deities, like Hogbus, and spirits in charge of fertility and harvest and death. Oynnes, a Light-aligned god of commerce, shouldn't have gotten any attention from them. Yet here they were.

Unable to ignore his curiosity, he stopped near the entrance. The magical torches were set to a low glow, and incense burned in a brass lamp set over the altar at the end. A female batblin wearing a white dress stood next to the altar and played a few notes on a lute. Some villagers had their eyes closed and their hands crossed as if in prayer, while others knelt over small baskets set in lines before the altar. The baskets' insides glinted in the low light. Ed squinted and realized they were filled with coins. Aureus cents of bronze and steel, Vyfara cents with a tiny gemstone fragment engraved, but mostly the dull, multi-colored rings of small-denomination Balts, the local currency before Heiliges conquered Starevos.

Ed and Lavy exchanged an alarmed glance. *Did we start this?* he mouthed at her. The chapel was dedicated to Oynnes. The god of commerce. The villagers had lost their places of worship in Burrova's destruction, so now they had taken to this one instead.

Lavy bit her lip and raised her shoulders. *Maybe,* she mouthed back.

It was another cultural difference that marked Ed as a stranger from another world. Back on Earth, religion was a complex matter that involved tradition, culture, laws, family, and individual consideration. Ivalis was similar... except that the gods answered the prayers and were *aggressively* interested in getting people's worship. Even better if they stole their enemies' worshipers.

On one hand, the average Ivalian farmer family could influence the local weather during harvest by performing the adequate sacrifices. On the other hand, however, they could just as well get kidnapped and sacrificed by crazed cultists who wanted to convince their multi-tentacled deity not to eat *them* for that night's dessert.

Ed wasn't sure which world had the best system.

A group of four by the back caught sight of him and his companions and their chat halted. Ed recognized a few of them as they approached. Bryne was there, his eye-patch making him instantly recognizable. He had showered today, which was an improvement. Darla was next to him—she was the local gossip, a woman with both the attitude and odor of curled milk. The other two were recent additions to the Haunt, a candle-maker and a hatter that had left their towns to join their families in the Haunt. They'd both taken minionship recently.

"Dungeon Lord, what a pleasure to see you out and triumphant," Darla half-sang. She had a garlic medallion dangling from her neck. Next to Ed, Kes stared daggers at the woman. "It was said on the grapevine that you had fallen during the raid— that a terrible spell had cursed you to an unending sleep, and that the curse could only be broken by true love's kiss. Hell, there was a line of brave damsels about to form, eager to save our handsome, *unmarried* Dungeon Lord. I'm happily married myself, of course, but I would've gladly sent my daughters to do their duty for the Haunt."

Ed's eye twitched. "Well, I'm glad to put those rumors at rest." He didn't mind the teasing as he knew—hoped, actually—that most of it wasn't serious, but he wasn't yet used to rebuking it gracefully from his position as their Dungeon Lord.

"Ah, don't mind her," Bryne said. "She started those rumors herself, I reckon." He grasped his bonnet in both hands, nervously. "We didn't mean to bother you or your companions, Lord Edward. We just wanted to say we're glad the quest came out right, is all. Everyone saw the Quest Screen update itself with our victory against those accursed Inquisitors, but we had no news beyond that... I figured I could get the kaftars drunk later tonight and make them spill the beans, but until then we came here to thank Oynnes for his part in the Haunt's success."

"Sharing the news *is* my job," Alder said, full of hurt feelings. "I was getting to it! Making sure the tale is properly glorious takes time, you know."

Ed massaged his chin. "Thanks for worrying, Bryne," he said. The man perked up at the mention of his name, which surprised Ed. Did that small gesture really mean that much? "I'm sure that between Alder and the kaftar's version of the tale, you'll hear all about it soon enough. In the meantime... do you mind answering a small question? What exactly are you praying for when you come here?"

"Oh, I thought you already knew, given that you gave us the chapel in the first place. We kinda figured you meant for us to use it, and to be honest, it was a good call." The villager seemed eager to help. It was strange how things changed. Not long ago, Bryne had tried to lead a small rebellion to escape the Haunt. "Oynnes is an easy fellow to understand, my Lord. He likes the good stuff. Gold, I reckon, but any cold, hard coin will do in a pinch. The bigger the favor, the more he wants. So we barter with him. For a few cents, he helped Long Lurk here—" he pointed at the hatter next to him, a man who looked the part of his nickname "—find his favorite hammer. It appeared inside one of those baskets, just like that. I gave him three Balts, and in exchange he made one of my cows recover from the runs. Things like that. Oynnes enjoys when we make money, so we can give him a part. Kind of like Brett's taxes in Burrova, only Oynnes is actually useful."

"I see," Ed said. From that perspective, the practice seemed harmless enough… although he wondered what would happen if the villagers began bribing Oynnes to mess with their business rivals, and then those answered in kind. A divine-enhanced price war couldn't end well at all. And there were also the Starevosi deities to worry about. "Won't your previous deities get mad that you're now praying to a Light god?" he asked Bryne.

"I reckon they will," said Bryne, smiling from ear to ear. "Serves them right. The lazy rascals didn't help much while our livelihood burned to ash, so a bit of pressure is exactly what they need to step their act up. I'll bet you a red Balt that during this year's Spriveska they'll be all cozy and charming. Perhaps even Hogbus' avatar will stop by for appearance's sake."

Thanks to his Mantle's sixth sense, Ed knew that standing there with his mouth wide open would be an unseemly thing for a Dungeon Lord, so he caught himself in time. Barely. A god's avatar showing up for a small community's Spriveska? Bryne *had* to be exaggerating.

He was about to ask, but Darla spoke first. "Speaking of the Spriveska," she said eagerly. "There'll be one this year, right? I don't mean to offend! The grapevine, is all, they wonder… seeing that you come from another world, they wonder if you'll really care for our festivals and traditions. Obviously, I told them all to pound dung with that attitude—" Ed noted how she didn't mention at any point who "they" were "—but still, people are wondering. They would listen to me better if I could tell them my reassurances came straight from your mouth, my Lord."

Ed didn't need his Mantle to know the only possible response to that kind of set-up. "Of course there'll be a Spriveska this year," he said, with a tone of incredulity that earned him a pride-filled glance from Alder. "I'd never even dream of not having one." *I'm appalled that I even have to say it aloud,* his quasi-offended tone said.

He hadn't the faintest idea what a Spriveska was.

The villagers exchanged bright smiles. "I'll let everyone know," chirped Darla. "The entire Haunt shall know I was right!"

Ed nodded and inwardly wondered just how much trouble had his mouth gotten him into. He made a mental note to ask Kes later what the hell was he supposed to do. The Marshal's face was inscrutable... although he could swear she had been repressing laughter just before he looked.

It's probably my imagination, he hoped.

Time to change topics. "Bryne," he said aloud, putting on a serious expression, "let me get this straight. You guys are playing an incredibly dangerous game of setting deity against deity, just to force them to give you better stuff when the Spriveska arrives?"

Bryne saw his face and his smile dropped, but then Ed clasped the man's shoulder. "Good man! That's a very proper attitude for a Haunt citizen. No, really, I mean it. When the world and the gods want to play games with us, the Haunt plays back, and we play for keeps. Remember that." Ed winked at the villagers and took his leave.

As he walked off, he heard Bryne mutter to himself, "A Haunt citizen," with his voice full of amazement.

Kes matched his pace. "Ed?" she whispered at him. "Are you trying to transform the Haunt's entire population into danger-loving rule-abusers like you? Because that's what you'll get if you keep praising their silly little games like that."

Ed's smile grew an inch. "See," he told his friend, "I was thinking that my mouth probably already got me into a bit of trouble with that Spriveska comment, and you know what people say. In for a penny..."

He tossed a quarter-Aureus into one of the baskets.

13

CHAPTER THIRTEEN

FRIENDLY NEGOTIATIONS

There was a small door to the right of the altar that led to a passageway that split in three. One path went to Zachary's private quarters, another to the cemetery, and the last one to a grim, humid chamber with a low vaulted ceiling and naked slabs of granite as floor that served as a chamber to prepare the corpses for burial. Today, the black tables strewn across the chamber were thankfully empty, except for the one with old coffin, set straight into the middle of the room. Zachary and Governor Brett watched it under the protection of three of Kaga's kaftar, armed to the teeth with rows of silver-tipped stakes and vials of holy water.

"Ah, Lord Edward," said Zachary as Ed and the others approached. "Glad to see the grapevine was wrong about your injury. I knew that a devoted follower of the Light like you, even though unjustly exiled from the flock, couldn't possibly have fallen prey to a Holy attack." He puffed his chest up and gave Brett a slanted "I-told-you-so" look. The Governor, and one of the kaftar, rolled their eyes when Zachary wasn't looking.

The fact that an "unjustly exiled member of the Light's flock" had been the one directly striking at the Inquisition this time around never seemed to cross Zachary's mind. It was interesting, the lengths that people could go to maintain their personal world-view, so long as it was convenient for them to have it.

Ed wondered if there was a way for him to know when he did the same thing. But wasn't that, by definition, impossible?

"Well, thanks for the vote of confidence, Zachary," he said aloud. "I'm eager to see what you did to protect us from our... guest. Lavy here told me that you and Governor Brett outdid yourselves."

Now it was Brett's turn to puff out his chest. "Master Lavina would be right, if I may say so myself." He made an ample gesture toward the coffin with his arm, like a chef presenting a perfect dish. "Right this way, Lord Edward, Master Kessih, Master Alder, Master Lavina."

He guided them in a way that resembled a proud museum guide, with Zachary tagging along—looking vaguely resentful at Brett hogging the spotlight. "The crux of the quest that Lord Edward wisely entrusted to us was dual in nature. How to protect ourselves from our guest and keep him from escaping, while at the same time protecting it from true destruction. Our solution was, I hope, both clever and simple."

Brett pointed at the floor around the table, which had a magical circle drawn with a mixture of silver dust, salt, and a tar-like substance to make it stick to the slabs of rock. He then pointed at the ceiling where a similar circle was drawn exactly above the first. Ed nodded in approval—the two circles were similar to the ones in his room. The Haunt was getting good at making them.

"This is to keep the creature out," said Brett. "A simple measure. Even a child could've thought of it—" Zachary raised an offended eyebrow at that "—what makes it truly clever is the fact that almost every section of this chamber has been heavily sanctified, except the area inside the circle. The kaftar wanted us to warn you about it, but obviously their fear was misplaced, since you're clearly unhurt and the rumors were wrong, anyway."

Ah, shit. Ed almost expected to burst into holy flames right then and there, like a cartoon coyote that stepped into thin air but only fell when he remembered how gravity worked. He opened his mouth to speak, but someone had already beat him to it.

"Brett," Kes said with a dangerously sweet voice. "You forgot to mention this when you showed us the room." Her smile was full of teeth. "It's true that Lord Edward wasn't hurt, but keeping the information to yourself was not your call to make. In the future, *please* inform me—the head of Security, remember?—of all potentially dangerous adjustments you make, especially if there's magic involved."

Brett paled at the rebuke. "I mean, I didn't—we didn't—"

"Actually, it's the Head Researcher who should be informed of any dangerous magic," Lavy pointed out, calmly picking a fingernail.

"Both of us, then," Kes said.

"Make it three," Alder said. "I'd like to be close enough to see the fireworks go off once someone messes up."

"Klek will probably want to know as well," Lavy said while Brett stammered apologies. "If only because the crazy little guy would try to slap the holy flames off Ed if it came to it."

Ed took a deep breath. He suspected that he knew the reason why so many Dungeon Lords had unavoidably gone raving mad after a few decades.

"Look," he said. "It was a mistake. It happens. No harm was done, just simply be more careful next time." Besides, the blessings had came from Oynnes, and the greedy deity was friendly to anyone willing to barter with him. Hell, respecting one's own business arrangements was one of Oynnes' core tenets for his faithful. Surely Ed was safe from him. Or as safe as he could expect to be, at least.

"Your Brutalness is most kind," Brett said, bowing.

Ed pointed at the coffin. "What other measures are in place?"

"We made sure the people are well protected in case of an escape, unlikely as it is. All our guards were equipped with Monster Hunter silver-tipped stakes, and the captains got a vial of holy water. In addition, we've fashioned necklaces with a bit of silver in them, and everyone that enters the chapel must wear one. It's a small layer of protection that will hinder the vampire's feeding. Just a way to buy time for our forces to capture him while he's weak." Brett raised both eyebrows as if surprised by his own cleverness. "The villagers took over the idea and made their own necklaces, though, using garlic and other small charms that may or may not slow the creature down. It's hard to distinguish between real magic and local superstition, even for me after all the years I've spent among them."

Lavy shook her head. "It won't slow him down that much, I think, but it's better than nothing."

Before Brett could go on, Zachary stepped in and cut him off with a wave. "Ah, I'm best equipped to explain the next problem we solved. You see, Lord Edward, my blessings and the circle will force the vampire to remain around his coffin—as well as nullify most of his powers—but there was still one we had to deal with. Some vampires can enthrall with a gaze, not unlike a more powerful version of the *minor order* spell, and in most bardic tales about them they're able to use said power to force a captor to break the circle or their bindings."

"I'm not sure if Oldbloods are actually the ones with that power," Lavy said. "It gets confusing, and sometimes the... research tomes seem to forget which type the protagonist is and mix their powers and weaknesses around. But Brett's right, if they have it: they like to use their hypnosis to enthrall the attractive young priestess guarding the circle... but as it turns out, vampiric Mind magic doesn't affect their destined soulmates..." Lavy trailed off, her cheeks turning pink. "I mean, those with a very strong Spirit."

Alder narrowed his eyes. "I'd love to have a look at those research tomes of yours, Lavy."

"Alas, they were all lost forever in one of Kael's dungeons," the Witch quickly blurted out.

"*Right.*"

Zachary took a white handkerchief from his tunic and cleaned a bit of sweat from his scalp. "To combat their gaze, we fashioned this." He rummaged through his pockets and brought out a circular piece of glass tied to a rough wooden handle. The glass' surface seemed covered in dust and Ed realized it was silver. "Anyone interrogating the creature is to hold this lens at face-level. The glass is blessed and doused in holy water for good measure. It should... in theory... protect the wearer from the hypnotic gaze."

Kes stepped forward, staring at the lens with critical eye. "Okay, I admit I'm not the best versed in magical matters... but how, exactly, is a bit of glass supposed to stop someone from being hypnotized?"

Everyone turned to stare at Lavy.

"Oh." She tossed her hair back, looking for a second like a fawn staring in wonder at the quickly growing shadow of a gryphon on the surrounding grass. "Well, I approved it because it makes sense —in theory. Almost all kinds of offensive magic need to establish a connection between the caster and his target, after all. In other words, to pierce someone with an *ice bolt* you need to aim and actually hit them with the damn thing, you can't simply have the wounds appear on their body—enough spellcasters tried to get away with *that* in the good old days and were instantly gobbled up by Objectivity." She raised her eyebrow a fraction of an inch at Ed in a gesture that he could only interpret as *so don't even think of it.* "Gaze attacks—and perhaps even Ed's Evil Eye if you *really* want me to get theoretical—must have a way of creating that connection, even if we cannot see it. Like... some sort of invisible ray."

"That... sounds quite plausible, actually," Ed said.

For someone who was mostly self-taught, Lavy was capable of some impressive academic feats. She had learned her *raise specter* spell on her own, for example, just by stubbornly throwing herself at the problem until it gave in and spilled its secrets. It was interesting, though, seeing her doubt herself when speaking about something she was quite talented at, when she was so confident at pretty much everything else.

She's probably knows enough to realize how much information she's missing, Ed thought.

"That's how Numerios defeated Lord Khalfair," Alder said. "He held a magical mirror against Khalfair's gaze—the Dungeon Lord was immune to his own magic, but his minions weren't."

Ed nodded. Alder's example was anecdotal, but the Dungeon Lord was sure they could test Lavy's hypothesis by playing with mirrors in her laboratory. "You know what? I think we've just gotten a small Magical Research quest here," he said aloud.

"Oh, I love those," Lavy said, clapping with delight.

With an effort of will and a flash of Evil Eye, Ed gave Lavy her own personal quest.

Lavy's eyes glinted with greed at the rewards. She was in the process of showing Alder the screen when Kes stepped hard on the floor to get everyone's attention.

"Sorry to interrupt your very interesting discussion about ways to goad the Objectivity into destroying you," she said, "but the sun is setting, and you're having this chat right in front of a vampire's coffin."

Alder winced. "Right. We got a bit carried away," the Bard said.

Ed turned to Zachary and Brett, who waited next to the silent kaftar guards at a safe distance from the coffin. "Thank you for your help. You both did very well."

Zachary bowed, and then raised a surprised eyebrow as he read something in his character sheet. "Will you look at that," he said. "We were part of a side-quest for the Haunt's Raid."

"Twenty experience points," Brett boasted. "Not bad for a day's work."

When the two left the chamber, they looked very pleased with themselves.

ONCE ZACHARY and Brett had closed the door behind them, Kes strolled to the Monster Hunters, her back straight and tense like a steel bar.

"Have everyone leave the chapel," she told them, "and have a drone bar it from outside. Return here when you're done, but first make the announcement: The Haunt is now on violet alert. All *alarm* spells and traps are now activated. All our citizens must remain in the company of at least another citizen and within screaming distance of a guard patrol. Until I give the all-clear, anyone who forgets the password when asked for it by a guard captain is to be detained for their own safety and put under watch until Master Lavina or Lord Edward can confirm their identity. Anyone *not* a guard captain asking for the password is to be detained and watched. A guard captain *not* asking for the password using the specific wording we rehearsed is to be detained and watched." Her instructions kept droning on and on until even Ed lost track of Kes' paranoid security measures.

The kaftar listened with perfect discipline. "Yes, Marshal," they said once she was done. They saluted her by crossing an arm to their chest, then turned and saluted Ed the same way before leaving the room.

"Satisfied?" Ed asked.

"Not by a long shot, but I cannot burden the Haunt with anything further until they're better trained," the Marshal said. "Better that they pay attention to the basics than mangle proper security measures."

"Basic?" Alder asked. "You call that *basic?* You didn't even tell us the passwords. If Ed steps out of this chamber, I think he would be detained and watched!"

"Well, of course I would be," Ed said. "Violet alert means there is risk of subversion, sabotage, impersonation, and or infiltration. It's designed to deal, as a worst-case scenario, with a shape-changer loose inside the dungeon. If I were to step out of this room before the all-clear signal is given, it could mean I'm being impersonated or enthralled."

"Ah, Alita's tits, you're encouraging her!" Alder exclaimed. Then, he glanced nervously at the floor. "I mean, by Oynnes' bountiful grace..." he mumbled.

"Of course I encourage her," Ed said, trying to repress his grin. "That's her job, Alder."

"But... If someone is controlling you, couldn't he have you give the all-clear, anyway?" Alder asked.

"Indeed," Kes said. "That's why no one who knows the all-clear signal can handle the prisoner directly. We'll leave the room and let someone else who doesn't know the signal take over. Normally, a trained professional would do it, but we don't have one, so we had to improvise."

"But you never told *me* the signal!" Alder exclaimed. Then he winced as realization settled in. "Oh, no."

"Sorry, man," Ed told him. "I need to ask the vampire some questions about the Heroes, so... I may need to hang on inside your mind for a bit while Kes guards my body in the chapel. Don't worry, I'll leave you in full control. I'll only be listening and telling you what questions to ask. Think of it as your own personal adviser hanging out inside your head." Back on Earth, people paid good money for that kind of remote support.

Alder had the kind of face that couldn't hide his true emotions unless he was actively playing a part. He glanced down, bit his lip, fidgeted with his hands, and said, "No way. No way in hell I'll be vampire bait. There's nothing you can to do convince me, so just forget about it."

. . .

"I JUST WANT to make it officially known that this sets a bad precedent for Bards everywhere," Alder said quietly. He stood alone in the middle of the chamber, only a few feet away from the coffin and the magical circle that was the only thing protecting him from the creature hidden inside. "What we're *supposed* to do is watch from afar, preserving events for posterity. Not as a juicy vampire midnight snack."

Ed's voice came straight from inside Alder's head. *You don't care about impersonating me with the Thieves Guild.*

"That's different," Alder said. Speaking to Ed felt vaguely like speaking to himself, in an entirely concerning way. "I can use that to flirt with all the sexy, leather-clad Thieves of the Guild, which is a sacred Bardic duty. A hard job, often dangerous, that I must uphold nevertheless."

Ed's amusement flashed down Alder's body much like it had been his own, mingling with Alder's wounded pride. In fact, if they weren't careful, thoughts and emotions could mix, making it hard to figure out where it had come from. Alder thought of it like being in a very cramped sauna back-to-back with another man, both trying their best to keep their privacy to themselves.

It's not so bad, the Dungeon Lord told him. *If your mind is a house, I'm in the basement right now, looking out through a window. As long as I don't pry inside a drawer or a broom closet, I won't stumble across your private diary or anything like that.*

"That's actually good to know," Alder said.

Of course, there was no way for me not to see that garden filled with nude statues of Heorghe's daughters. I wonder what he'd have to say about it.

"Ah, go on, make fun of the poor Bard," Alder said, frowning. Then he raised an eyebrow. "There isn't... You wouldn't tell Heorghe, anyway, would you?" He chuckled aloud because Ed was chuckling in the basement. Alder wondered how long it would take to go insane if they kept going like this.

He distractedly caressed the silver bits of his new shiny necklace. The smell of garlic rose to his nostrils. He wasn't unarmed—quite the opposite, in fact. He carried his sword, his flute, a bag with Lavy's runes, and a pair of blessed silver-tipped stakes that the kaftar had given him. And Kes was in the next room, with a cadre of Monster Hunters ready to spring into action should anything happen.

Of course, a vampire could rip his throat out before anyone had time to react at all.

Don't think about that! he chided himself. "How much longer do we have to wait?" he asked aloud. Technically, he could just think at Ed and it would be faster, but Alder felt more comfortable this way.

Not much longer. It's dark outside. If our vampire wasn't destroyed when we damaged the coffin, we should meet him soon.

And as if the creature had heard Ed's thoughts, the light of all the magical torches in the room dimmed. A rush of cold air, almost freezing, seeped through Alder's clothing. It reminded him of Nicolai's wraith. He shivered, but not because of the cold.

A hollow knock came from inside the coffin; and the heavy wooden lid began to creak open.

"Here we go," Alder said with a small voice. Along with his fear came a rush of furious clarity. It was easy for Alder to tell that he wasn't the source of this sensation. His fear screamed at him to run away as fast as possible from the monster. Ed's instincts, on the other hand, clamored like the clarion's call for the pointed sword at Alder's side, in case he needed to tear the vampire's throat before it had the chance to attack.

So this is what it feels like to be a Dungeon Lord, Alder mused. Even when in danger, a Dungeon Lord was a predator. Never prey.

The vampire probably felt the same way.

Focus, Ed thought at him. *It's coming.* Alder reached for his sword and slid an inch of steel out of the scabbard.

Another crack came from the lid's iron hinges, and the slab rose an inch away from the coffin. A dirty mist flowed out of the dark interior and poured into the stone floor and up onto the chamber like a spectral waterfall. Slowly, the lid rose another inch.

Alder had the strange sensation that the creature was having a hard time dealing with the lid's weight. But that was impossible. Lavy had been very clear that Nightshades were inhumanly strong. And besides, why would a vampire sleep in a coffin it could barely get out of?

More likely, the undead monster was toying with him—lulling him into a false sense of security, perhaps. He drew his sword another inch, and noted that the mist remained contained inside the limits of the magical circle. That, at least, was encouraging.

An air of humidity and old dust fought for dominance with the smell of garlic in Alder's nostrils. A humanoid silhouette half-emerged and half-materialized from inside the coffin, obscured by the mist, as an invisible current siphoned the mist into the coffin, as if swallowed by a gigantic lung.

Alder raised the lens that Zachary had fashioned and held it right in front of him. He kept his gaze focused on the slightly distorted vision of the glass.

"Ah, is it you, Jiraz?" asked a woman's raspy voice. "I'm not going to lie, darling, I thought we were goners this time. May Murmur damn the Militant Church!" There was a sharp movement from inside the mist, like a head turning sharply. "Wait... You are not Jiraz."

Long, curly hair flowed in the nonexistent breeze, golden like a sunshine but without its warmth. Alder caught glimpses of gray, wax-like skin pulled tight over sharp bones, and of a black funeral dress that could've been worn by a Lotian noble a hundred years ago, but was now ragged and with sleeves half-eaten by moths. A black sash hugged a slender waist, and a small, elegant hat full with flowery laces covered the golden curls that framed the scowling face of the corpse.

"Who dares breach the sanctity of my tomb?" the vampire asked, still half-hidden by the mist. "Know that you've forsaken your blood for this transgression, mortal!" Her voice was raspy, faint, and dreadful, like a whisper in a graveyard.

Something about the challenge and threat in her voice awoke an instinctive fury inside Ed that burned in Alder's mind like the explosion of a *fireball*, as if his bones and his veins were white hot with violent, Dark magical power, and before the Bard could even realize what was going on inside his body, he was standing as tall as he could, his back straight like an iron rod and lips curled in a regal scowl.

"*I dare*," he exclaimed, Ed speaking through him with a Dungeon Lord's authority. Green heat shone out of Alder's eyes for an instant, showering the vampire in light and shadow.

The creature growled like a beast and stepped back, her arms spread in an animalistic fashion to protect the coffin behind her. "Dungeon Lord!" Her fangs gleamed under the afterglow of the Evil Eye, pearly white and sharp like needles.

Alder was acutely aware that he was caught between two powerful beings of the Dark squaring up—recognizing and sizing each other up all at once, like a pair of bucks crossing antlers in Elaitra's forests, or two Bards exchanging drunken quips in a tavern.

Except that these two were much more dangerous than a drunken Bard or a horny deer. Alder wondered if it was a good moment to cast *nimble feet* and make himself scarce. And then the mist cleared, and a fact that had been nagging at a small part of his brain was now in full display, and the part of his brain that was too distracted by fear couldn't ignore it anymore.

Uh, Ed thought, confusion smacking the teeth out of his anger as he saw through Alder's eyes.

"Uh," Alder agreed. He blinked and scratched his chin. "Ain't that something," he said.

The vampire frowned with indignation, as if she couldn't believe that Alder and Ed had dared break the Dark tension between them. "What's the matter?" she asked in her archaic wording. Then her frown deepened. Her red eyes traveled down Alder's body, all the way to his feet, and then upwards, all the way up into his eyes. She had to throw her head back for that. A look of dismay replaced the frown. "Dungeon Lord, are you, perhaps, possessing the body of a giant to confront me?"

"I'm afraid not," Alder told the creature, who was in the shape of a ten-year-old dead girl.

The vampire sighed and turned to her coffin. She passed her small hand across the cracked web on the center of the lid.

"Dunghill," she hissed.

The vampire's name was Jarlen. She had been Lord Jiraz' right hand for about a year, but at some point before that she'd also served under his grandfather's reign. Alder managed to convince her that she wasn't directly in danger, for now. He told her she had been "rescued" from the Inquisition by Dungeon Lord Edward Wright, and that an offer of minionship may be on the table if she behaved. That didn't put her at ease, but at least it got her to stop snarling.

"So, Jiraz didn't survive the raid," she said when Alder was done explaining. She flicked a golden lock away from her face. "Well. Serves him right. I told him that leaving the Netherworld for this awful country was a bad idea."

"Wasn't he, like... your mate or something?" Alder asked, unable to stop himself. Her callousness had taken him by surprise.

Jarlen gave him a dismissive glance and scoffed. "And?" she asked. There was no emotion in those dead eyes. No grief, no regret. Perhaps a hint of rage, but Alder's *empathy* talent easily let him know that most of that rage was directed at him and Ed, because they were keeping her captive. No, Jiraz' was dead, and that meant he was no longer of any use to her, so he may as well never have existed.

Alder shuddered.

I don't like her either, Ed told him. *But remember why we're doing this.*

The Bard went ahead with his questioning. After all, the faster he got it done with, the faster he'd be able to leave the chamber. It was too cold, anyway.

Jarlen's memories of the Heroes' attack were fuzzy. She recalled that the Rogue had separated from the other Heroes and had tried to sneak into Jiraz' Throne Room while the others dealt with a shock detachment of naga spellcasters. Jarlen had taken command of Jiraz' personal guard and had ambushed the Rogue while he dealt with a trapped section of the dungeon and fought off a bunch of acid slimes. Jarlen had been sure that her ploy had worked—the Rogue had been overwhelmed, at first, but then the Heroic Cleric had broken ranks and headed to rescue the Rogue while the Warrior kept the naga occupied. Jarlen had felt the burning pain of a holy spell striking against her back, and then the Rogue's scimitars had flashed across her neck—after that, everything had gone dark. Her *heart of mist* talent had taken over, instantly turning incorporeal and flying straight back to her coffin.

"And what about your... condition?" Alder asked. He gestured at her current size with his free hand, careful not to drop the lens away from his face.

"It must've been the fault of those damned Inquisitors!" Jarlen said through a snarl. "They cracked my coffin, so mist must've poured out before my body had a chance to regenerate. It'll take years before I'm back to normal! By the Dark, I swear that when I get my hands on them, I'll drink them dry and then bathe in their innards while they're still live and writhing!"

Alder swallowed. "Yeah. It must've been them. Screw those guys." The effect of her diminished form only added to her creepiness. She lacked even a tiny ounce of a child's innocence. She looked exactly like a small animated corpse dressed up with doll's clothes, but her facial expression was adult and cruel, and her lips parted a bit too much over her mouth, as if the skin was too tight to fit her skull.

Don't let her intimidate you, Ed told him. *She's the one who should be scared.* But Alder could feel through their shared connection that Ed was unnerved as well, and he was trying to reassure himself as much as Alder. *Ask her about the Heroes. In general, I mean. We need to know if she and Jiraz had faced them before. What are they?*

Alder doubted she'd cooperate without first negotiating a minionship pact, but he asked her anyway. The vampire's golden eyebrows rose an inch, then she chuckled mirthlessly. Alder noted the way her eyes turned distant—calculating. Using his *empathy* talent to read her emptiness was almost as telling as if there had been something there the first place. "I know who you are," she said at last. "Lord Wraith, is it not? The Netherworld is hot with gossip about you, your Lowness. The first otherworldly Dungeon Lord. Summoning you was a move stolen straight from the Light's playbook. Some think it's a shameful display of desperation to bring a stranger to deal with our problems. They'd rather you to go back whence you came. I'm not so sure, myself." She narrowed her eyes to slits. "How did you survive here? When Jiraz and I came to Starevos, we tried to contact you—forge an alliance, yet you refused to answer. Why?"

Because you're murderous lunatics, Ed thought.

"We're the ones asking the questions," Alder said.

"I was more than twice your age before I became a vampire," Jarlen told Alder. "I know all the tricks, kid. I want proof you won't destroy me afterward. I want a pact."

Ed had already discussed with him what to say if she asked for a pact. "Best I can do is a temporal offer," Alder said. "We shall speak the truth to each other, and will respect the spirit of the pact as well as the letter. For the duration, we won't harm you, and you won't harm us. No escape attempts, either."

The vampire's face was a gray mask. Again, Alder detected no emotions other than the constant undercurrent of anger. He had the eerie sensation that his *empathy* had misread her the first time around. She was angry because he was warm and alive, and she was cold and dead, and she wanted to take what he had and drink it all into her. "I see," she intoned. "Interesting offer." She shuffled closer to the lines of the magical circle. "But then again, why bother with all this wariness, Lord Wraith? As creatures of the Dark, we're kindred spirits. We should be talking as equals, eager to join forces against the Militant Church. Just have your vessel break this flimsy circle. *Step over its boundary, my darling, and we can have ourselves a merry chat.*"

An enticing, pale purple light shone out of her eyes as she spoke that last sentence. Alder could see the beam through the dirty lens. Its light was diffused, filtered somewhat by the enchantments in the glass, but the Bard could now see how shoddy its craftsmanship had been—the magic unraveled as Jarlen's magic punched through with ease, to Alder's horror.

Jarlen's words seemed coated in honey as they reached his ears. They echoed inside his head, warm and lovely like the lullabies his mother sang to him when he was a baby in the cradle.

Alder?

Nothing in the world would be more lovely than following Jarlen's gentle suggestion. And she was right, anyway. Why would they distrust a potential ally as powerful as her? She could do so much for the Haunt. If only they showed her the tiniest bit of confidence...

Alder, don't listen to her!

Alder took a step toward the circle. Jarlen's eyes widened with anticipation, a smirk drawing on her face as her hands extended to embrace him warmly as soon as he was over the boundary, and he was almost there, his feet hovering an inch behind the limit of the circle, with all his weight set to finish that step—

And he was yanked out of his body by a black roaring cloud inside his head, violently shoved into some backward basement inside his own mind. As soon as he'd lost control of his body, his common sense had returned, as fast as he'd hit the basement's floorboards. He was horrified with himself, and at what had been about to happen.

He watched through two distant holes of light—almost in slow motion—as his leg passed the boundary of the magical circle, carried by his own body's forward momentum. What he'd thought of as a small step had been practically a leap. Alder saw how the little undead monster hissed with pleasure and hunger and flung herself at the Dungeon Lord—at Alder—as fast as a blink, her claws aimed straight at his eyes.

Alder screamed as the shadow of the vampire covered his face.

And he saw how Ed used the very same weight of the leap to drive himself forward in one single fluid motion, then punched Jarlen straight in the mouth.

JARLEN'S tiny frame flew backward and smashed against the table of her coffin with a sharp crack, looking more confused than hurt. Ed almost thought that the coffin would fall on her, and he felt compelled to let it. But the thing didn't move at all, which in hindsight made sense. He didn't have superhuman strength, after all, and the vampire didn't weigh enough to shake the table much.

Ed stepped away from the circle and threw a quick glance behind him, just as Kes flung the door open, sword drawn. "Keep back," he told her. "It's under control."

"Like hell it is," the Marshal snapped. Klek was right behind her, dual-wielding a pair of stakes that looked like miniature spears in his small hands. Ed realized that the batblin and the vampire were about the same size.

The vampire cursed in ancient Lotian. Ed could've bet that she was insulting Alita's genitals in luxurious detail. "In my true form, I would've torn that arm out of its socket," she said matter-of-factly. "Even cursed, I'm stronger than this vessel you inhabit, Lord Wraith." She *almost* sounded like a child whining, but that inhuman face left no room for doubt.

Ed waved his friends away—he wasn't willing to risk them getting hypnotized, since he didn't know how fast Jarlen could spam the damn ability. Alder and he were the safest ones in the room, anyway—if Alder failed a mental test, Ed had a chance to pass it himself, which had been exactly what had happened.

"You may be a rank stronger," Ed told Jarlen, "but you still are a fraction of his weight." His hand—Alder's, actually—pulsated painfully after the strike, and perhaps there was a cracked knuckle somewhere, and even then Ed had only pushed the vampire away. Jarlen wasn't hurt at all, despite him having struck her as hard as he could.

Near the door, Kes stared daggers in the general direction of the magical circle. Ed waved at her again. *It's fine,* he told her with a look. Klek looked confused. He made small stabbing motions with his stakes, giving Ed a meaningful glance. "I'll let you know if it comes to that," Ed reassured him. Reluctantly, Klek lowered his stakes. The Marshal and the Spider Rider left the chamber and closed the door behind them.

Jarlen cursed again, then straightened, and seemed to calm herself in the blink of an eye. "Well. I had to try it. It almost worked, though," she said.

"I should kill you for that," Ed told her, trying to mirror her calmness. She unnerved him much more than he'd like Alder to know. A dead body, gray and cold, yet still animated and able to move with a fluidity and grace that rivaled that of any living being. It was unnatural. Orders of magnitude worse than a zombie. Almost as bad as a wraith. Perhaps he ought to leave and collapse the ceiling on her and her coffin, then set the splinters on fire afterward, for good measure. Let her try to survive *that*.

But he had risked his life and the lives of his friends to get the creature to the Haunt. He couldn't just let that effort go to waste.

"For what, trying to defend myself against an obvious trick?" Jarlen told him. "A temporal pact! What a joke. There were no guarantees you'd let me go when you were done questioning me. And you don't seem that enthused about my services, Lord Wraith, which is frankly baffling, given the incredible powers I could set at your disposal. Maybe you desired a demonstration of my capabilities. Was I right? Are you satisfied with my little demonstration? The *hypnotic gaze* is only a small taste of what I can do, of the ruin I can bring upon your enemies."

"And little good it did you against the Heroes," Ed said pointedly. "No, Jarlen, you have it wrong. A prisoner gets no say in the terms of their imprisonment. My temporal pact gives you no guarantees I won't kill you, but I can simply kill you without it, anyway. What you're getting is one single chance to prove your worth, on my terms." He raised three fingers. "First, you'll show me your character sheet. No more surprises. Second, you'll tell me all you know about the Heroes. How to fight them. How to kill them. What are they made of, when did they appear? All of it. And last, you'll tell me of all the ugly deeds you've done as a vampire, so I can know what to expect of you." *And to know if I should kill you outright, if you turn out to be as monstrous as you appear,* he thought. "Do all that, and then we can talk about minionship."

Jarlen's eyes seemed like two embers of fury in her tiny dead face framed by golden curtains. "At least you speak your mind, Dungeon Lord. But you're ignoring one small detail. I'm worth nothing to you if I'm destroyed. On the contrary, I've friends in the Netherworld willing to pay a nifty price for my release. I doubt you'll simply get rid of me if I refuse to speak." She crossed her arms and smiled at him. "Leave me imprisoned if you wish. I wonder how long it'll take for you to come back, begging to take me in, while the Militant Church pounds at your doors."

Ed made his hand into a frustrated fist. She was right. He couldn't just kill her outright, not without figuring out what she knew. And he was on a literal deadline—every day, the Heroes' attention neared Hoia, and the Scramblers wouldn't keep them away indefinitely.

But was he willing to let what was very possibly a psychopathic mass murderer—or worse—into the Haunt, just because he had a use for her? Wasn't that exactly what the Lotian Dungeon Lords did—recruit inhuman monsters that were willing to go to lengths any decent being would outright refuse?

Call her out, Alder thought at him.

I can't, Ed thought back, sharing all his doubts through their mental connection. *If she stands her ground afterward, I'll lose all leverage if I don't follow through.*

The Bard performed the disembodied equivalent of shaking his head no. *Trust me on this one, Ed. This is what I'm good at. You called her a psychopath. I think I know what you mean by that—you're saying she cares for nothing and no one. Except, you're wrong on one thing. She cares about herself. This will work. Trust me.*

Ed took a deep breath and made his choice. "Well, sad to see this was all a waste of time," he said aloud. He didn't need to fake the twinge of annoyance in his words. Without looking at Jarlen, he snapped his fingers and two drones appeared in front of him with small puffs of smoke. "Our negotiations with our guest failed before they began," he announced. "Gather firewood and collapse all exits. I want this chamber burnt to a crisp come daylight."

The vampire huffed, "Bah!" and smacked her dry blue lips.

The two drones snapped to attention and threw malicious glares at the magical circle as they talked among themselves in their unintelligible language. Ed turned to leave. For a moment, the only sound in the room came from the drones' chatter and his boots clanking against the stone floor. *Fuck it,* he thought as he walked away. *There are other Dungeon Lords around, perhaps they'll cooperate.*

He was reaching for the heavy reinforced door when he heard the vampire stomp on the ground. "Wait!" she exclaimed, a twinge of desperation in her voice.

Ed grabbed the handle and pushed the door open. Light from the hallway's torches flooded the chamber.

"Lord Wraith, wait!" the twinge carried a pinch of hysteria now. "It was all a mistake, I was just testing your mettle—"

Ed stepped out of the chamber, barring the door hard enough for the vampire to hear it.

Ed let his drones pile firewood around the magical circle for an hour, with the vampire's cries bouncing around the rocks of the dungeon. In the meantime, he returned to his own body back in Zachary's quarters—which the priest had helpfully vacated. The batblin cooks brought a cart with dinner for him and his friends while they rested and let their nerves settle.

It had been a long night. Ed was sure that, if he closed his eyes, he could see the glow from Gallio's *sunwave* coming his way, and could almost feel the heat prickling his skin.

He nibbled on some buttered toast and downed it with long gulps of goat milk, which was creamy and slightly sweeter than cow milk. He handed Klek a honey jar, into which the batblin's snout disappeared for several minutes.

Outside, in the mortuary, Jarlen kicked and screamed as the drones piled wood around her.

Kes munched on fistful after fistful of nuts and talked about what she'd do to Zachary and Brett for giving them a faulty lens.

Jarlen pleaded and smacked herself against the invisible barrier of the magical circle, the distinct crackle of energy reaching Ed's ears as clear as day.

Lavy sat in a corner, unwilling to get anywhere near Zachary's unkempt bed. She seemed to be in a terrible mood, and only spoke once, to make sure everyone knew that Nightshades were supposed to be better than the one in the mortuary, and that Jarlen was probably a mistake of some kind, and perhaps they could try to enter the Netherworld and try to recruit another one? *Preferably an adult male,* was the unspoken sentence on her lips. She crossed her arms and pouted. Everyone else shifted uncomfortably and tried their best to think about *anything* other than the Witch's tastes, except for Klek, who was too busy with his jar of honey to pay attention, anyway.

Alder ate little and drank much, his hands shaking a bit. The experience of almost having been siphoned dry had clearly rattled him, but the Bard recovered surprisingly fast—it wasn't his first brush with death. Soon enough, he was regaling everyone with the tale of his front-row experience to how Ed had punched an undead toddler so hard it vaulted into the air and *almost* landed back into its coffin. Alder looked more than a little tempted to alter his tale a bit in later retellings and add that last little detail in.

"All right," Ed said, after everyone was full and had rested a bit. He could sense his drones piling firewood past the hallway. Jarlen had stopped shouting and was now sitting atop her coffin, brooding. It was the small hours of the night, somewhere between one and three AM back in the world that had working clocks. "I think that's enough of a timeout for her to get the point."

HE HAD a single horned spider enter the mortuary. Her name was Saffron, one of Klek's own. Ed hitched a ride inside her mind just in case, using another casting of *Murmur's reach,* but this proved unnecessary.

Jarlen accepted Ed's temporal pact as soon as the offer left Saffron's mandibles.

14

CHAPTER FOURTEEN

THE INQUISITOR'S DILEMMA

The mid-afternoon sunlight streamed into the hall, breaking into a myriad beams as it came into contact with the fractal crystal panels that composed the ceiling and bathing everything with a dance of rainbow dots. The light shone on the Examiners' silver-padded shoulders, the marble table in front, the plate armor of the Inquisitors guarding the exit, the sober plants that hung from clay vases up the walls, and straight into Inquisitor Gallio's eyes.

Gallio squinted and fought back the need to cover his face.

Symbolism like that wouldn't escape the Examiners—the forlorn Inquisitor, blinded by the Light and turning his back from it. It was the reason they'd chosen to conduct the examination at this time of day, with the sun at their backs.

That was very much the Examiners' modus operandi. Why trust the Goddess to provide meaning when it was faster to manufacture it?

"Remind me, Inquisitor, how many men were under your command?" prodded Examiner Harmon, his minotaur-size bent over the tiny carved chair to an almost comical effect.

"Thirty Inquisitors, Eminence, not counting the Church's personnel led by Master Enrich," Gallio said.

Examiner Harmon was sixty-something human male, with a long, braided mane of gray hair falling over his shoulder and hiding the long scar that snaked through his neck and cheek—a trophy from the Starevosi campaign. Harmon was a war hero, a by-the-rulebook kind of man, someone who would have a kid whipped senseless if the child dared pocket an apple from a market stand. He let no sin go unpunished, which in turn made him the perfect Examiner, and it also gave him a chip on his shoulder against Gallio, the black sheep who had returned to the flock after, famously, refusing to follow a direct command from a superior Inquisitor.

"And you still allowed yourself to be defeated by a bunch of spiderlings?" asked Harmon. Gallio could imagine the frown in the man's tanned forehead, but he couldn't see it—the sunlight turned Harmon into a burning silhouette, impossible to gaze at, almost as if he were Alita's unrelenting truth made flesh.

Which was probably the entire point.

Gallio tried not to grind his teeth. "It was a Dungeon Lord's ambush, Eminence," he said. "And we defeated it. A total victory, with no losses for our side and only a few wounded. On the other hand, the Dungeon Lord lost most of the horned spider cluster, and was almost killed during the encounter." He didn't mention that it had been his own *sunwave* which had dropped Edward Wright, although Gallio was still unsure of how that was possible. He could've misjudged the distance through the confusion of the moment, but has sure Edward should have been safe.

"Is that what you call a total victory?" asked a woman's voice, barely bothering to hide the derision in her voice. Gallio turned to the bony silhouette next to Harmon's, that of Examiner Bartheny. "You kill a bunch of horned spiders—not exactly a difficult feat for a devoted servant of the Light—yet you fail to strike any blow of consequence. The cluster's Queen got away, and so did the

Dungeon Lord. And they even managed to escape with the assets from Jiraz' dungeon. *Hardly* what I'd call a victory."

Gallio blinked and took a deep breath to steady his temper. He probably failed an internal Spirit test, because he could sense his blood boil. "With all due respect, Eminence, we did all we could with the resources at hand. I had to make the call between protecting our non-combatants—which included Master Enrich himself—or protecting the Heroes' *plunder*. Perhaps we should consult the scripture to see what Alita would think of my decision, although I do think that 'protecting the innocent' ranks pretty highly in her mind."

"You forget your place, Inquisitor," Bartheny said venomously. "You are the one under examination, not us, nor our knowledge of the sacred tenets."

Bartheny was Harmon's second-in-command, although not officially, since the Examiners were supposed to be three equals. She was tall, thin, and severe, all sharp lines and disapproving eyes. She was King Varon's aunt-in-law, and this alone ensured that she'd make Archbishop before long, if she played her cards right. Pacifying Starevos would greatly hasted her advancement.

"Examiner Bartheny is correct," said Examiner Hatter, the third and last member of that day's ugly meeting. Hatter was a portly red-headed elf with just a dash of gnomish blood somewhere in his family tree. The combination gave him an affinity to magic, and he was an accomplished Wizard by his own right. He had a big, round nose and bright gnome-pink eyes that shone with arcane power. He also stank of stale wine and moldy cheese, and was probably drunk up to his ears if only because "Examiner Bartheny is correct" seemed to be the only words he could utter for the duration of the meeting.

Bartheny shot an openly hostile glance at Hatter, then went on. "And, since you so helpfully brought up the sacred tenets, Inquisitor Gallio, let me remind you that 'root out evil anywhere it takes hold' is Alita's main commandment to her devoted. 'Protect the innocent' is a fine and proper moral aspiration, but it's a subordinate tenet, since the only sure way to protect the innocent is to destroy evil forever, no matter how difficult or costly. This is, quite possibly, the most important lesson an Inquisitor may learn."

"A lesson which you failed," said Examiner Harmon, rattling his fingers on the long marble table. "Even when the Militant Church kindly sent you to Starevos as a chance for you to come to this realization on your own."

Gallio straightened his back. "Eminences, with all due respect—"

"You keep saying that," snapped Barthen. "Apparently you think it replaces showing some respect."

"With all *due* respect," Gallio repeated through a clenched jaw, "our detachment was under-manned since the start. We've been walking blindly through Dungeon Lord lands for months on end, with no aerial support, barely any runes, and shoddy magical weaponry. This ambush, or something like it, was bound to happen. As such, I believe it was payback for Jiraz' defeat. We were lucky it wasn't worse."

He couldn't avoid the resentment coming through his voice. It had been Harmon's call to send Gallio's detachment without even a single griffin.

This was the reason Gallio was happy to remain a lowly field agent of the Inquisition, while the Examiners, Bishops, and Archbishops played at their games. Politics muddled what should have been simple: Destroy evil. Protect the innocent. Kill the Dark's servants.

But it was also the reason the Examiners could toy with him like he was a straw doll in the hands of a child.

Or like Murmur toying with a stranger from another world.

"Enough," said Examiner Harmon, his cruel eyes barely visible under the great bulk of his face. "We've heard enough. You came here to make yourself responsible for your mistakes, like befitting someone of your rank, *Inquisitor.*" Harmon's scar turned a shade of purple. "And because of that, the Examiner Heads of the Inquisition dictate that you should be stripped of command, until—and if—you prove yourself worthy."

Gallio lowered his head. He'd seen the decision coming for a while now—Harmon had only been looking for an excuse, and eventually he would find one. But still, the demotion hurt. It was like suddenly being stripped of his clothes and cast out into the cold. It reminded him of his exile, and the way the other Inquisitors had looked at him when he'd boarded the ship that brought him to Starevos—no longer important enough for the Inquisition to spare the cost of having him step through a Portal.

He wondered if the guards behind him would look at him the same way those others had, back in Heiliges.

Probably not, he decided. After all, this time, he was still an Inquisitor. He could still cast a *sunwave,* a feat that only a chosen few could perform, regardless of their ranking. It was Alita herself that decided who held her blessing, not Harmon or any Archbishop, no matter how much they'd love to think they did.

He let himself drop to one knee and saluted the Examiners. "As you command. I shall face this punishment and learn this lesson you've set for me." He held Harmon's gaze, letting him know he wasn't defeated.

"We are not done yet," said Bartheny, clicking her tongue. She nodded to the guards behind Gallio, and one of them hurried outside. "Command of the Hoia Inquiry is to pass under a new Inquisitor, one appointed by us. You'll remain his service and follow his orders with the respect due to a superior officer. You're on thin ice, Inquisitor Gallio. One more failure, and I doubt Alita herself will welcome you back into the fold."

Examiner Hatter sighed, then gave a wet burp and massaged his belly. "She's right, you know," he told Gallio with a sad nod. Bartheny's eyes widened with disgust. It looked like she had been close enough to Hatter to *taste* that burp.

Gallio decided that maybe he liked Hatter, after all.

The clanking of metal alerted Gallio of the guard's return. Inquisitor Oak—the stiff, tall kid under Gallio's command—followed the man.

Oak gave Gallio an ashamed nod. Gallio returned it, albeit confusedly. What was Oak doing here?

"Inquisitor Oak is, as of now, the new commander of the Hoia Inquiry," announced Examiner Harmon, as if he was emitting a divine verdict from his tall chair.

Gallio's mouth parted in disbelief. "Oak?" he asked, almost as if speaking to himself. "But he's too young! He will only get himself killed—"

Oak's ashamed expression turned sour, his cheeks flushing. "I'm as capable as any, I assure you."

Gallio cursed inwardly. Through his carelessness, he'd lost what little goodwill Oak had had for him. "You don't understand —" he began, trying to fix his mistake. *They want to set you up,* he thought desperately. *You have never faced a Dungeon Lord before, you don't know what that's like.*

"Our decision is final," said Harmon.

"Unless you wish to hang up your sword and return to Heiliges," Bartheny said. "We could have a merchant ship ready for you this very night, ready for free passage back home." She smiled with fake kindness, like she'd made him an offer too good for him.

Gallio's insides twisted with anger. "That won't be necessary, Eminence," he told her. He looked straight at the silhouettes of the three—Harmon's bulk, Bartheny's rigid posture, and Hatter's ample chin resting on a bored fist. "Am I free to go?"

Harmon waved at the door with a careless gesture. "You are dismissed. Inquisitor Oak, remain with us for a bit longer, if you please. We must discuss your new responsibilities."

Gallio saluted, although no one was looking at him any longer, as if he'd dropped from reality after they were done with him.

And, in a way, for people like them, he truly *had* disappeared. He had been a small, unseemly stain in their orderly organization, so they'd simply reached down and flicked him away like one might a fly.

He missed Burrova.

It was a lonely walk, out into the open exterior corridor over the mansion's garden, then down a long spiral staircase with burnished brass handrails. The steps were made of beautiful white stone infused with black veins and flecks of silver. Stepping out the stairs into the garden was like coming down from the Argent Plane into primal Ivalis below just as it was before the Light came and issued order and warmth into wildlife in the times before the Age of Myths.

Gallio had once walked among the gardens of Cildel, the royal stronghold, back when he'd taken the Inquisitor's oath for the first time. The Pledging was a special occasion, a yearly event where the Militant Church presented its best acolytes to the King and the good people of Heiliges, so that they could learn the faces of their future protectors. King Varen himself had cast his golden sword over Gallio's shoulder and given him his blessing, his steel-gray eyes shining silver under the Heiligian blue skies. Gallio could recall many details about that day: five-year-old Prince Varon hiding in his mother's skirts and chewing thoughtfully on a wooden toy, the soft whispering of the fountains mixing with the song of the garden's cicadas, and the pride in his own chest threatening to burst out like a balloon.

Becoming an Inquisitor had been his lifelong dream. The Militant Church took on many children, but few were suited to take the Oath. Those who were worthy became the people's protectors, defenders of the Light, a bulwark against the encroaching darkness that threatened to drown good and beauty everywhere.

Gallio wasn't sure when the Harmons and the Barthenys of the Inquisition had drowned his childhood ideals with their scheming and plotting, but it had been long before his exile.

Today, he recalled something else about that day. When compared with Cildel's ordered rows of carefully trimmed flowery mead—its orchards with their golden and red apples, and its dovecotes of white pigeons—this mansion's garden was as wild and shoddy as a kaftar's cottage.

Apparently, the gardeners of Mullecias Street had a fundamental disagreement with those of Cildel about what made up a tasteful trim, because every noble house and mansion preferred this unkempt style. The Starevosi nobility's architecture was rough on the outside, naked stone and iron fences contrasted against an opulent interior, with open stone corridors surrounding a jungle of a garden. Wild Plekthian cushions tall enough to hide a lion fought for sunlight against pink caladiums and palm trees from distant shores of places whose names Gallio knew only from Bardic tales.

On Mullecias Street, seemingly the only function of gardeners was to ensure the plants didn't kill each other or poison the soil. According to Alvedhra, who knew more of plants and soil than he ever would, Constantina's air was so salty that the fact the nobility and the merchants managed to maintain any kind of exotic gardens at all was proof enough of their riches.

Gallio suspected there was something to be gleaned from the contrast between these two gardens he'd encountered at very different times in his life, and his mixed feelings about his role as an Inquisitor.

But he wasn't in the mood for deep realizations. What he really wanted was to go back in time, find Ioan, Kes, and Alvedhra and go achieve the fabled *advanced drunkenness* status that Marya insisted her brew could deliver like no other in all of Ivalis.

Marya's tavern had burned to the ground, just like his former life.

Gallio found his last remaining friend waiting for him by the garden's fish pond. Alvedhra was wearing her civilian outfit—a white cotton shirt buttoned up to her neck, with long sleeves that hid her wrists, linen pants, and sandals. Her eyes were bloodshot, and her step unsure. Despite the Clerics clearing away her poison, whatever those kaftar had used to put her down had struck her like a mace to the head. Even days after the ambush, she was still showing the aftereffects.

"You look like dung," Alvedhra told him as he approached. "If you need some sleep, I found a concoction that works like a charm. You should try it." She grinned, and for an instant she was back to being the freckled Ranger apprentice under Ioan's tutelage, madly stricken with the broody avian mercenary that had arrived in Burrova looking for work.

"I may take you up on that," Gallio said.

Alvedhra was tossing bread from a cloth bag into the pond, to the delight of a school of dish-shaped, rainbow colored fish. Gallio stepped next to her and watched the fish fight amongst themselves for every tiny piece.

"The Examination didn't go well, did it," Alvedhra said after a while.

"And where did you get that impression?" Gallio asked.

"For starters, you keep looking at my fish like you want to *sunwave* them."

Gallio blinked, then brandished a stern finger at her. "Don't be silly. The *sunwave* is meant only for the enemies of the Light. Although—" he narrowed his eyes at the pond "—those fish *do* seem a bit suspicious. I wonder if they've paid their tithes lately."

Alvedhra barked a laugh. "Just say the word and I'll go gather firewood for the pyre." She tossed a handful of bread at the fish, then pocketed the bag and turned to Gallio. "So. What happened?"

"Well, it turns out I'm no longer your superior officer."

He told her the rest in broad strokes, trying to keep his personal feelings about the Examiners out of it—she was still his apprentice, after all. By the end, not even years of martial discipline could keep his shoulders from slumping a bit.

"There has to be a mistake," Alvedhra said after he was done.

"The ambush clearly wasn't your fault. Why would the Examiners act like that?" She stroked her chin and pursed her lips in frustration. "We're all on the same side."

Gallio shook his head. "That's the problem. An Examiner is really an Inquisitor's Inquisitor. They're technically outside our order, but since they only answer to the Archbishops, they're free to do as they wish."

The Militant Church's hierarchy was relatively straightforward. It had three branches. The "Church" dealt with the congregation of the Light, the teaching of the holy tenets, and the spread of the religion across Ivalis. The "Militant" part meant that, in cases of war, it was the duty of the Church to summon and lead the armies of Heiliges. And finally there was the "Inquisition" whose sworn mission was to look deep into the hearts of men and destroy the evil they found there, one way or the other, in order to stop the corruption of the Dark from taking over the world.

The leaders of the Militant Church were, in descending order of importance, Alita herself, her seven holy consorts, her Holy Avatar—which hadn't incarnated in centuries—and then the minor Light gods in an awkward sort of "revered elder" position. After the divine came the mortal leaders. The King was first... in theory. Then, at the same level of authority were the Archbishops, leading the Militant Church on the day to day, the Supreme Inquisitors, and the Knight Generals who commanded the Heiligian army.

The Examiners were Inquisitors, but their duty was to ensure the integrity of the Inquisition itself, and to protect it from Dark corruption. They didn't answer to the Supreme Inquisitors, but to the Archbishops, and were hand-selected from their positions in the other two branches. Harmon, for example, had been a Knight Captain, then a member of the Royal Guard before his summon, and Bartheny had been a Bishop.

"Then you should write to the Archbishops," Alvedhra said.

"Present your case to them. They're the best of us, aren't they? Surely they'll see that the Examiners got a bit… overzealous."

Gallio grinned mirthlessly. It was strange seeing how someone as grizzled and street-smart as Alvedhra could be so naïve in some matters. But could he blame her? He had trained her in the ways of the Light. She saw the Militant Church as how it should be, instead of how it actually was.

Who was in the wrong? Despite her age, Alvedhra had succeeded the trails of the Inquisition, her training as a Ranger speeding her along the initiation and basic training, and her devotion earning her the favor of Alita herself. Perhaps she'd be casting *sunwaves* before long.

It was clear that the Light rewarded devotion. The only question left was why Gallio himself was worthy of the *sunwave*.

"Let's consider this a test of my faith," Gallio said. "If Alita's design provides for me being a leader, then it shall be so. In the meantime, we should focus on keeping Oak alive."

Alvedhra nodded, relieved.

They walked together through the garden, letting the aroma of flowers and wet grass relax their bodies and minds. There was no stench of fish in any home of Mullecias Street.

"There's one more thing we need to discuss," Gallio said after a while. "But first, let's drop the Inquisitor mantle for a while, Alvedhra. Let's speak as friends."

Alvedhra read his intentions instantly. "Gallio—"

"Kes," Gallio said. Alvedhra winced as if someone had brandished a knife in her face. "We haven't talked about what happened since the Clerics cleansed you."

"To be honest, I came searching for you to talk about something else. I was hoping you'd forget about this," Alvedhra said honestly.

"Really?"

"Well, I know it was foolish. That's why I called it 'hope.' "

They reached a small bird fountain made of granite. There was

239

a sculpture atop the fountain, representing some Starevosi pagan god. Possibly a spirit of Harvest, judging by the size of its breasts, but there was no way of knowing—the head was missing, probably smashed by some overzealous Inquisitor.

Alvedhra spoke first. "I'm sorry for leaving on my own during the battle. I let my temper get the better of me, and it forced you to rush in without reinforcements. I could've gotten you killed."

"Look, if I had an Aureus for every time I lost my temper and did something stupid, Oynnes himself would have turned me into his Avatar long ago." That got Alvedhra to smile and roll her eyes, which had been the point. "I'm worried about *you*, Al, not about your tactical mistakes. Seeing Kes like this, out of nowhere, must've been hard."

It was for me, Gallio thought, recalling his encounter with Ed. The Dungeon Lord had changed from a young man—almost a kid, really—into a barely recognizable warrior. With his face hidden by his helmet and that cape masking his proportions, it may have been any Dungeon Lord in that forest. But the voice had left no room for doubts.

"That's my point, I guess," Alvedhra said. She strolled to the bird fountain and rummaged through her pockets until she found a second bag, this one full of birdseed, which she used to restock the fountain's brass plate. Gallio wondered if she just carried bags of seed with her all day. "I shouldn't have lost my temper. What happened to Kes... I've fought with myself so long over it, you know? At first, I didn't want to believe it. It had to be some kind of mistake. A ruse. I figured Kes would kill the Dungeon Lord when she had the chance, then she'd hide somewhere. Can I tell you a secret? If she had—killed the Dungeon Lord, I mean—I wouldn't have chased her. I know that destroying the minions of the Dark is our duty and all... but..." She shrugged and made her hands into fists, visibly fighting tears. "Goddamn it."

Gallio shuffled next to his friend and hugged her. Dealing with... displays of emotion other than zealous rage wasn't something they taught kids in the convent which meant that the way most Inquisitors dealt with emotions was by repressing them for decades until something cracked and they heard voices or screaming in their sleep. "There, there," he said lamely.

Alvedhra hid her face underneath her hands and took a deep breath. Then she brushed her cropped hair away from her forehead—a reflex from when it had been longer. "There, there?" A very tiny grin curled on her lip. "Really?"

"Don't judge. Charm is my lowest stat."

Her grin grew a quarter of an inch. Gallio nodded with satisfaction. Humor was the multi-purpose weapon of the emotionally stunted, and he brandished it as fiercely as he would a sword if his back were against the wall.

"That person we found in the forest wasn't Kes," Alvedhra said quietly, out of nowhere. She crossed her arms and glanced at the blue sky. "I know that now. Denial, anger, blaming myself... all those are parts of grieving, like the Priests say. I was mourning her loss, because she *died* when she pacted with a Dungeon Lord, even if her body is still there, acting and speaking like she would've. Do you understand?" When she faced Gallio, there was a glint of vengeful fire in her eye. "There are so many tales of evil creatures taking the shape of the ones we love and pretending to be them. Changelings. Sephar's Bane. High elves switching human children for their own. I decided that a Dungeon Lord's pact is much the same thing. If you don't reject the Dark, it consumes you. Kes is gone. And if I wish to avenge her, I must destroy the Lord that took her. Perhaps then, if I free her soul, Alita will allow her entrance into the afterlife." The intensity in her eyes quieted slowly, like the embers of a fireplace, leaving only a tired Ranger. She slumped. "Does that make any sense?"

I don't know, Gallio thought. *I don't know!* Were Inquisitors supposed to be this full of doubts? Had the heroes of old—the ones of flesh and blood—always wondered if the step they took was the right one? It couldn't be. Nothing would ever get done if good people were as unsure of themselves as Gallio was. Dungeon Lords would crush them easily, since Dungeon Lords never faltered.

The last time that Gallio's faith had swayed, people had died, and he'd lost Alita's favor.

He knew the answer Alvedhra expected. The one he *should* give. Of course she was right. Evil should be burned from the world. Whatever Alvedhra told herself as a motivation would do.

But... but Gallio also knew that Alita wasn't famous for her mercy. "Cruel Golden Bitch" was one of the many nicknames the Lotians had for her, and they—may the Light forgive him— weren't entirely wrong. She was unforgiving because she *had* to be, of course. Giving an inch to the Dark, allowing doubt and fear to stay her hand, would mean losing Ivalis to eternal night.

Even if Alvedhra killed Edward Wright and released Kes' soul to receive Alita's judgment... Gallio had little doubt what the sentence would be.

And if I tell her that, what will it achieve? She still has her duty. What did the tenets say about white lies? He was sure that speaking the truth had to be somewhere in there.

"I don't know if it makes sense," Gallio told her, hating himself for his cowardice. "I'm but a mortal, and cannot speak for the Goddess. I can only do my duty as best as I can."

"My duty. Right." Gallio could see her holding onto his words like a drowning woman to a log. "You are right, of course. I shall do my duty above all else. Thank you, Gallio. I needed to hear that. Here, there's something you need to see."

There is something wrong *with this,* Gallio thought as Alvedhra rummaged through her pockets again. There was something he had missed. Some meaning he'd mangled. He'd done something *wrong,* even if he'd aligned with the tenets. How could that even be?

But Alvedhra was already moving forward, drawing confidence from Gallio's hollow assurances. She produced a small wooden tube and showed it to him. "Remember this?"

It was the dart that the kaftar had used to put her to sleep.

"Nasty concoction," Gallio said, while wondering on the inside what that had to do with anything. "You kept it?"

"More like it hitched a ride on my neck while I was being dragged to safety," she explained. "As a Ranger, I was taught that if you're bitten by a snake, you should try to capture that snake and bring it with you to a healer." She held the dart between her fingertips and raised it above her head. "I think that, in my dazed state, I thought this was somehow like being bitten by a snake, so I held on to it."

"Was it any use to the Clerics?"

"No," Alvedhra said with a dismissive wave. "Not at all. But after I had time to clear my mind, I realized I recognize it."

Gallio titled his head as he processed Alvedhra's words. "Recognize it?"

"I'm a Ranger," she said simply. "This is my country, and I spent most of my life around these lands. Kaftar clans are nomadic, but they move in cycles. This clan, I've met them twice before." She gestured at Gallio to grab the dart. "See those markings over there? Vaguely resembling crossed scimitars if there's good light. It's the symbol of the Haga'Anashi. It means 'Raventop's Grudge' in Heiligian, which is what I called them—way easier to pronounce, if you ask me."

"What does their name mean?"

"Beats me. Most likely werewolves ate their grandparents because they're mean Monster Hunters, and they're damn good at it. Cities and villagers hire them to clear rotface infestations, or acid blobs breeding in dank cellars, perhaps find some rabid pixies down a well. There are rumors, though, that they work for Dungeon Lords too. They help them collect monsters for their defenses, their experiments, or their personal collections. I guess the rumors were right, this time."

Gallio nodded, studying the crisscrossed, serrated slashes that were the symbol of the Grudge. "It seems that way, yes. Do you think they recognized you?"

Alvedhra shook her head no. "First time I met them, I was a kid. They came to Burrova and got rid of a nasty group of harpies that had been eating the livestock—"

"Harpies? I'd no idea there were harpies around Constantina."

"There aren't any now." Alvedhra retrieved the dart and pocketed it. "Second time, I was an apprentice Ranger. Our master brought Cousin Ioan and I to the Haga'Anashi campsite. A Dungeon Lord had died in the marshes near our territories; a couple cockatrices escaped from his dungeon, and it was nearing their mating season. They were too dangerous to hunt alone, so our master hired a squad of Monster Hunters to find them and deal with them before they could multiply and ruin the local ecology."

They sound very useful, those kaftar, Gallio thought. It was the sort of duty an Inquisitor should do if they hadn't been all so occupied dealing with their own infighting.

"Their chieftain was Kagelshire—or something like that. Judging from the spotting on his fur, I would bet my bow the kaftar that dosed me was Kagelshire's son or nephew," Alvedhra said. "You know what that means?"

"It means the clan won't be too far from Wright's dungeon," Gallio said. He could feel his eyes go wide. Alvedhra was right. This was big—the sort of thing they should bring to their superiors immediately. If they got a lead on Wright's main dungeon, they could deal with him in a single blow. With one well-targeted spell to disable any Portals, and Wright's story may come to an end.

Gallio's blood froze in his veins. Yes, Wright's story would end, but so would the story of all the Burrova's villagers he'd saved because of Ioan's betrayal. *Only if he didn't send them away,* Gallio thought, desperately. *He promised he'd free them in the neighboring villages.*

But he knew how much a Dungeon Lord word's was worth, didn't he? How could he have been so foolish? There was no doubt in his mind that Wright had kept as many innocent villagers as possible in his dungeon, a safety net to prevent Gallio from prying too hard.

Not that it'd change a thing. When they first met, Gallio was but a Sheriff. Today, he was an Inquisitor. His duty was perfectly clear. Wasn't that what he'd told Alvedhra only an instant ago?

He'd played himself.

"Alita, have mercy on my soul," he pleaded in a whisper.

"What did you say?" Alvedhra asked.

It was eerie—to think that the death of so many could be decided in the middle of a garden full of life.

"Let's hope that Inquisitor Oak is up to the task," Gallio said. He walked away all of a sudden, forcing Alvedhra to jog to catch up with him. He was eager to get to a place with hard floor under his boots.

Suddenly, he couldn't stand the sight of the garden.

CHAPTER FIFTEEN

Jarlen

JARLEN OF THE HIDDEN CATACOMBS

S pecies: Elf Nightshade
  Essence: (73 years since conversion)

ATTRIBUTES
  Brawn: 18 (-6 for Cursed Form)
  Agility: 17 (-6 for Cursed Form)
  Endurance: 18 (-6 for Cursed Form)
  Mind: 13
  Spirit: 10
  Charm: 8

SKILLS

. . .

Combat Casting: Advanced (II) - Pertains to the speed and efficiency of spells cast during combat or life-threatening situations.

-Basic status allows the caster to use spells as quickly as their body can sustain. The caster must perform the appropriate hand gestures.

Melee: Basic (IV) - Temporal skill, can become trained or be improved to open the brawling branch.

Stalking: Improved (III) - Stealth-tree branch. The owner knows how to move without being detected.

Knowledge (Anatomy): Improved (IV)

Knowledge (Ancient History - Lotian): Improved (VII)

Candlemaking: Basic (IX)

Taxidermy: Advanced (V)

Leadership: Basic (VI)

...

Essence Talents

. . .

NIGHTSHADE

HEART of the Mist

VAMPIRIC ENDURANCE

VAMPIRIC REGENERATION

HYPNOTIC GAZE

COMPEL CRITTERS

BLOOD POTENCY

MIST SHAPE

CREATURE of the Night

ENHANCED THRALL

...

. . .

WHILE STUDYING Jarlen's character sheet, Ed couldn't help feeling like an archaeologist looking at an ancient parchment recently unearthed. Even the format of the sheet looked outdated, and the list of skills she'd picked up somewhere along the way was too big to list, even if undead learned skills at a very reduced rate.

The interrogation was interrupted by the incoming sunrise, at which point Jarlen was forced to go back to her coffin. Ed and the others left her there and spent the day sorting out the loot they'd earned from the pillage of the Inquisition wagons. After that, Kes ran so many security drills in the early morning that everyone had their nerves on edge by supper, enough so that a woman jumped under a table when a batblin dropped a spoon next to her seat. Priest Zachary made bank selling polished brass trinkets he'd crafted earlier that day to the nervous Haunt citizens, swearing the charms were anointed by Oynnes and that they'd protect them against vampire bites and hypnosis. When Lavy heard about it, she confiscated both the trinkets and the profit.

Ed went to sleep early, right after supper, and had his drone butler wake him up before midnight. He met with his friends at the entrance of the mortuary, and together they headed inside to finish the interrogation.

Jarlen was already waiting for them, sitting on her coffin, her legs dangling from its edge. She looked emaciated and, as she spoke, wouldn't stop staring at Alder's neck, much to the Bard's dismay.

The vampire had been fifty-something when she was alive— the elven equivalent of her mid-thirties. She'd been a vampire for longer than that, and in total she was almost a hundred and a half years old.

She'd lived in Lotia while it was still a kingdom not unlike Heiliges, but when it had been ruled by the cadre of the Dungeon Lords of old. She had lived through the revolution that became, after years of bloodshed and chaos, the seeds of modern Lotia: a group of warring city-states which barely tolerated one another if they weren't openly fighting amongst themselves, all of them tied to the Netherworld and the worship of Murmur. The modern Lotian Dungeon Lords lived in the no-man's land between the cities, fighting everyone—themselves most of all, but also the cities' armies, and roving bands of Heroes that the Inquisition summoned, at great cost for themselves, straight into Lotian territories.

Ed himself had played the "Evil Empire" expansion of Ivalis Online. It had been the first-ever DLC, right after the main story-line, which involved cleansing the "Light Kingdom" of all Dungeon Lord presence. In the expansion, Ed had scoured the rainy Lotian hilltops and marshes one Boss at the time, racking up EXP by the thousands, hordes of monsters dying at the heels of his Wizard as he launched endless blizzards of magical damnation at them. He'd left empty dungeons in his wake, destroyed Nether-world detachments, and routed marauding mercenaries from the city states. It was eerie to realize that, even before his arrival, he'd been an unaware player in Ivalis' current state of affairs.

Hearing Jarlen speak arose in Ed a kind of hunger not unlike the one the vampire held for human blood. For a long time, he'd been painfully aware of how large his gaps in knowledge about his new world were. His access to history books was limited, and Starevos' records were mainly focused on its own history, most of which was oral, not written. The majority of those few books had been lost, anyway, after Heiliges had invaded the country and implanted a steel-clad hold on Starevosi libraries, most of which were in Galtia, the capital, whose palace was currently occupied by a Heiligian princeling.

Ed had had to buy a few black-market books through the Thieves Guild. The fat tomes had been written by Elaitran chron-iclers and were stocked in the Haunt's library between Lavy's Witchcraft tomes and a few scrolls on monster biology that Kaga's clan had lent the Haunt. The Elaitran books were biased toward Heiliges and the Militant Church, but Ed hoped to unearth the truth by contrasting them against Jarlen's eyewitness account, and maybe find a sliver of truth in the middle.

Don't think of her as a member of the Haunt just yet, he told himself. He had little doubts that Jarlen was a monstrous creature, but the question was, was she the kind of monster that could be contained—like the horned spiders? If she wasn't, she'd have to go, no matter how useful she was.

"Tell me about the Heroes," he said.

A heavy tension filled the air. Klek bent forward, his bat ears straightened in rapt attention. Jarlen squinted and pursed her lips.

"As you wish," she said simply. "It all began fifteen years ago, around 834 in the Old Calendar, during the reign of King Varen the Fair in Heiliges and Count Bastavar in the Free City of Yhin. 834 was a good year. Plenty of easy prey with potent blood to increase your *essence.* I served under Dungeon Lord Jiraz the Old. Back then, the most recent Jiraz was but an apprentice learning to create drones and carve holes in caves." Her eyes glazed over as if remembering a particularly nice trip to the beach. "Archlord Everbleed hid in his tower, behaving as if the times of the ancient Lordship hadn't died with the fall of Sephar. Saint Claire and Tillman, meanwhile, plugged their ears and pretended their coffers hadn't dried up decades ago bankrolling the fight against Bastavar and his revolution—which was *not* a good time at all to be a vampire, let me tell you... There was always a risk you'd wake up and find that your mortal thralls had listened to too much propaganda during the daylight hours and now you had a stake through your heart and your butler was building a pyre around you... But I digress. Year 834. Old Jiraz fought the marauding armies of the Militant Church all around the Western Lotian frontier, while the Arpadel dynasty brought the fighting to Heiligian shores, and the Dungeon Twins—Heines and Vaines—roamed like a tornado past the black shores of Vros, leaving devastation in their wake. It was experience points and essence all around. You wouldn't believe how much fun I had. The rivers were awash with blood, and mud, and bodies, and Necromancers could go for a stroll and stumble into a pile of bones as tall as their head, ready for raising. Such a great time to be undead."

Ed's mind raced as Jarlen spoke, trying to assemble important facts that she was merely throwing around in passing. As an afterthought, he summoned a drone by a corner and ordered him to transmute pen and parchment to take notes for later. There was a timeline to follow here, but history class had been one of his weaknesses back on Earth, and Jarlen wasn't making it easy—she was so old that she digressed constantly and changed decades in the middle of important points. He attempted to ground her words. First, there'd been the ancient Lordship, which had lasted an indeterminate amount of time and had ended with Sephar's Bane, which had caused the Inquisition to reform into its current, bloodthirsty form. Long after that, a revolution had ravaged Lotia, and Bastavar had kicked the last Archlord into a tower somewhere. Lotia had split into free city-states, and then Heiliges invaded, and the Dungeon Lords invaded them *back*, but by the sounds of it, war between both countries was the normal state of affairs. Lavy and Alder had been about ten years old, Kes had been a soldier in the Cardinal Command, and Klek hadn't been born yet. Ed himself had been in High School, an angry orphan living with his relatives and deciding between joining the military for the benefits or drowning in debt to study computer science.

"No one paid much attention to the first Hero," Jarlen went on. "The Militant Church sent it against Lady Golsa, who destroyed it with little effort and thought nothing of it. There wasn't much to tell. After all, every spellcaster and their mother were trying to develop new tools to kill their enemies at a distance. I prefer up close and personal, myself. But then a second Hero came knocking at Golsa's doors, and a new one after that, and then they came in groups, and *then* people began paying attention. Minions of different Dungeon Lords talk among themselves, see—mostly to keep an eye on working conditions, and experience points earned per year, and salaries and things like that. Eventually, everyone in the Netherworld knew about Golsa's situation.

"It was a joking matter, at first. Golsa destroyed the Heroes over and over again, and the Militant Church spent more gold building them than she did fighting them. Heroes were little more than expensive golems, and every Aureus wasted on them was an Aureus that wasn't going to sponsor *real* adventurers or Inquisitors. Golsa outfitted her Throne Rooms and Main Halls with the destroyed constructs and showed it to her friends at parties, bragging about how she'd defeated each specific instance, not unlike a kaftar big-game hunter. She made everyone *jealous*. But not for long. Each iteration of the Heroes had some new improvement, and in hindsight, the Militant Church chose their first target *perfectly*. Golsa lacked Vaine's military genius, or the Arpadels' bravery, or Euric's insane Charm build. Golsa began losing ground more and more with each battle. The Heroes now carried an assortment of runes and could activate them by themselves, which no golem before them could have done, and they wielded enchanted weapons and armor designed for sentient hands—on top of layers upon layers of enchantments on their own bodies. Golsa lost minions in droves, some to the Heroes, but most because they saw the writing on the wall, ended their pacts, and snuck off to the nearest Netherworld Portal to find some new Dungeon Lord. Allies of Golsa aided her at first, but the Heroes never stopped coming, and eventually she ran out of good will. She lost her outposts first, then her resource dungeons, then her inner dungeons, and then she took refuge in the Netherworld. I think the old crone is still hiding there."

The drone scribbled as fast as it could, its pointed tongue protruding from its lips. Alder looked at its writings, shook his head, and took the parchment and pen away from it, then began writing himself, scratching and amending at the same time he followed Jarlen's tale.

"So, they didn't kill Golsa?" Lavy asked. She massaged her

chin. "My mentor, Warlock Chasan, mentioned her once or twice —he was one of the minions that left her when things grew dire. He always wondered what wound up happening to her."

"I'm glad to help put that mystery to rest," Jarlen told her, giving a fake smile. "After Golsa, the Militant Church sent Heroes against other Dungeon Lords, and her tale was repeated over and over again. It didn't matter how smart, or strong, or rich a Lord was, the damn constructs *just kept coming*. Most Lords simply escaped into the Netherworld like Golsa had done, but eventually the Heroes developed a spell that could neutralize a nearby Portal. Thank Murmur, the spell still has a low success rate, but luck doesn't last forever." She drew an imaginary line in the air with a long yellow nail. "When the first Dungeon Lord fell, hunted inside his own dungeon like a rabbit, things got out of control. A new version of the Heroes appeared, with capabilities far beyond the previous iterations'. This new Hero needs no runes to cast spells. Even worse, they are able to grow in power, much like a living being can gain experience points. Many Dungeon Lords met their demise while trying to distract the Heroes by creating disposable dungeons to keep them occupied, only to have the Heroes grow into unstoppable killing engines. I believe this was the fate of the last of the Arpadels."

Ed gave Lavy a concerned gaze. His friend's expression was distant. "Yes, it was," she told the vampire. "Glad to put that mystery to rest."

Jarlen nodded, unaware or uncaring of the Witch's turmoil.

"Enough with the history lesson," Kes said. "How do you put them down?"

"Like you would any other golem, I guess," Jarlen said with a shrug. "You can inflict overwhelming damage that renders them useless, or bypass their magical defenses and melt their inner workings. Anti-magic circles leave them unable to cast spells, and powerful magical afflictions—like fear, blindness, and silences— can affect them much like any living creature, but not for long.

Thing is, they're much more resilient than any mortal. And even if you deal with them, a new Heroic batch will come, and there are less minions this time around, so even if you win..." She drew a downward spiral with her hand to underline her words.

"All spells can be countered," Lavy said, raising an eyebrow. "How come no one has captured a Hero, cut it open, and figured out how it works?"

"Do you think no one else has thought of that, little Witch?" Jarlen snapped at her. "Of course we've tried. The damn things either teleport away or *explode* when they're beaten! By Murmur, they off themselves even if you freeze one with ice magic! Some Dungeon Lords dug into Golsa's ruins and found some of her early captured Heroes—they didn't explode back then. They were just golems, nothing special about those, except that they had expensive remote-controlling enchantments installed. No. The newer versions are something else, but we cannot force rubble to share its secrets!" Jarlen bared her fangs in frustration.

Ed ignored the vampire's outburst. Something in her description had set his imagination off, and now he could barely pay any attention to her. She'd said something before, something about him, the first time they'd met, but her exact words had eluded him. He felt as if he were standing next to one huge realization, like a detective that passes next to the unrevealed killer and tenses up, his instincts picking something up but not yet *knowing*.

"You told us that they could grow," he told the vampire. "Do you know how?"

"Oh, most minions have seen it in action, even if they don't live long enough to tell the tale. Of course, I'm the exception. When a modern Hero destroys a Throne Room, something *interesting* happens. Don't worry, Lord Wraith, I fear you'll know what I'm talking about very soon. The entire dungeon melts as if made of a Nightshade's mist. Afterward, the Hero becomes much stronger, as do their weapons and armor. It seems as if they feed on the dungeon, somehow, although I don't know how that is possible, and if any remaining Dungeon Lord knows the procedure, they've kept it to themselves." She smoothed a crease in her black dress and turned to Ed. "You now know about as much as I do, Lord Wraith. To end my story, Jiraz the Young killed Jiraz the Old and came to Starevos, following the rumors of an otherworldly Dungeon Lord, a weapon designed by Murmur as an answer to the Inquisition's constructs. I believe Jiraz half-hoped, half-feared, that you would be an artificial creature not unlike the Heroes. I don't know how he would've felt about the truth. If you allow me to be honest, I don't see any powers or skills you may have that will allow you to succeed where every other Lord has failed."

I really wish I had one, Ed thought. In many of his favorite games, the player character had a power that set them well beyond the level of their enemies, allowing them to tear through unending hordes of mooks. Life, though, didn't work that way. Ed already had powers that set him well apart from the rest of humanity—those of an "ordinary" Dungeon Lord. Those powers hadn't been enough in the past. Ed's duty was to protect those under his care, and then when raw magical power wasn't enough, he'd have to fill the gaps with ingenuity and determination.

And right then, he remembered Jarlen's words. *The otherworldly Dungeon Lord. A move taken straight from the Light's playbook.* Associations flared in his mind like fireworks, one after the other. The Heroes self-destructing when defeated, the mechanism to feed on a dungeon. Golems controlled from afar. His suspicions grew upon realization after realization and became certainty.

He gave Jarlen a slanted grin. "Back where I come from, knowledge is power, and you've already told me something that I don't think many Dungeon Lords know."

"Yes? And what's that?" Jarlen asked, tilting her head like a predator sniffing the air for signs of danger.

"The Militant Church didn't create the Heroes," Ed said. "Someone from my world did." Next to him, Alder inhaled sharply, and his pen scratched a line on the parchment. "Thanks, Jarlen. You've given us much to think about. I'd say that's enough for one night. Tomorrow, we'll talk about your fate."

LATER THAT NIGHT, Ed and his friends sat in the War Room, their faces heavy with sleep. Amphiris' leg cast long shadows across the table, which was strewn with untouched snacks.

"Are you sure?" Kes asked Ed, while he glanced at Alder's notes.

"Almost," Ed said. "It only makes sense. The way she spoke about it, Alita has been summoning people from other worlds before Murmur brought me to Ivalis." He looked at Alder for confirmation, but the Bard shrugged apologetically.

"The Militant Church doesn't tell Elaitra all their plans," Alder explained. "Even if they did, I wasn't far enough in my training to be worth the trust of such a secret. There *are* mentions of strange adventurers brought from distant lands to serve the Light in the war against the ancient Lordship, but those records are ancient, Ed, and 'distant land' may have simply meant another continent, like Plekth."

Ed nodded. "What about you, Lavy? Did Kael or Heines ever mention anything about their grandfathers fighting strangers?"

"Their grandfathers?" Lavy chuckled softly. "I think both Alder and that vampire bitch failed to explain the expanse of time we're talking about when we speak of 'ye olden days,' Ed. Simply put, the creation of the first Dungeon Lord is Year 0 in the Old Calendar."

"Oh," Ed said. "What year are we in, again?"

"850."

Ed thought of his timeline. *I'm going to need more parchment,* he realized in dismay. "I see," he said. "But there are other details that point at someone from Earth being behind the Heroes." He scratched his hair, trying once again to speak of terms like data security protocols and digital rights management, that had no easy counterpart in a world where magic had kept an industrial revolution from happening. Then Ed realized that maybe there *was* a counterpart after all. "Okay, tell me, what happens when a Wizard wants to sell a new spell? There has to be a way to stop someone from buying the spellbook, then copying it for free and spreading it around, right?"

It was a bit of a leap to think that Ivalis had an equivalent of a patent office, but Ed already knew that there were a few spells that everyone could learn, like *ice bolt* or *fireball,* and others that could only be obtained by studying the appropriate spellbook.

Lavy rested her back against the wall. "You're thinking of meta-magic," she said. "Extremely advanced theory. Meta-mages are specialists that spend most of their lives studying the science of casting spells that modify other spells. When, say, Wizard Bob develops a *fireball* variant, he brings his spell-notes to a meta-mage, who will imbue the notes with a custom meta-spell. Thanks to this, Bob's notes cannot be copied or reproduced without his permission, and cannot even be comprehended unless you bought the notes from Bob himself or an approved spell-shop. If you do buy *Bob's fireball,* then you can understand the spell and cast it, but you cannot teach it to others—unless you buy more copies, of course."

Ed's fingertips tingled with excitement, even the ones of his skeletal hands. At last, he'd found something where he held the undeniable home advantage, a situation where he wasn't racing after the knowledge that everyone else in Ivalis already had. DRM was something he knew well—he'd earned the damn degree that proved it.

"And you can dispel those meta-spells, can't you?" he asked.

"If you manage to get a hold of the same mage or one who's more powerful," Lavy said, "but it's usually cheaper to just buy the spell-note. If you don't have the money, there are seedy parts of the Netherworld that deals in unprotected notes that are cheaper.

These spells are lesser-quality imitations of the original, but if you have a keen eye, you can sometimes find a spell that works just as well as the expensive version. My own *crow familiar* is one of those."

"This is all very interesting," Kes said dryly. "But I fail to see what it has to do with the Heroes, Ed."

Ed nodded gratefully at Lavy before turning back to Kes. "See, we have the same meta-magic in my world. We call it DRM, but we use it for software... software is like a spell-note that isn't magical, and works only as information. I know the Heroes' creator came from Earth, because there people have also tried to add meta-magical protection to advanced military weapons."

"What, like enchanting a sword to prevent anyone from making a similar one?" Kes asked, raising an eyebrow. "How would you even enforce such a thing? The Cardinal Command has its secrets, like our flight formations, but it's not like we could treat *knowledge itself* as a spell and add meta-magic to it. I don't need to be a Witch to know Objectivity would eat anyone who tried."

"She's right," Lavy said.

"Well, Earth has no Objectivity," Ed pointed out. "There's also no magic, so people have to get creative." He remembered his first meeting with Kharon, back when the Boatman had told him that Murmur had summoned Ed because people from Earth had a different perspective than the people from Ivalis. "A guy from Earth that wants to stop Dungeon Lords from capturing his Heroes and studying them won't think about something as Ivalian as meta-magic. He'll just enchant his designs to blow up if they fall into enemy hands. Problem solved."

He watched as understanding lit his friends' faces. "Heroes are protected in the way a person from Earth would choose, instead of an Ivalian spellcaster," Lavy said.

"So, the Inquisition has their own Lord Ed?" Klek asked quietly.

"I... guess that's one way to put it," Ed said. "More like, they have an Ed with fifteen plus years of a head start, with all the resources of the Militant Church at his disposal, and who probably was in the military before being summoned."

"Wetlands, we're fucked," Lavy said, suddenly having gone pale. "This explains so much..."

"Trust me, it could've been worse," Ed told her, and he meant it. "We should be glad the Light was so... naïve when they summoned him. They probably used a spell that looked for a powerful war-mage, and it got them the closest thing, a military software developer. Had they known what to look for..." Ed shuddered. If the Light had summoned a biologist, or a nuclear physicist... a bio-engineered plague or a fucking nuke were bad enough on Earth, but if they were mixed with magic... the consequences could be cataclysmic. He wondered if Objectivity could save Ivalis from becoming a molten, radioactive ball.

Hell, the Dark was very lucky that this mysterious developer had *only* sent Heroes after it. Ed himself had already come up with several ideas about mixing magic with basic programming principles. With fifteen years and a country's resources at his disposal...

How come the Light hasn't steamrolled Murmur already? Ed thought. There was something there that didn't make sense.

Whatever the reason, he decided the Haunt couldn't possibly bank on this streak of good luck to continue. "I hate to say this, but we need to talk to the Lotian Dungeon Lords, and quick."

"Ah, I'm not looking forward to that," Lavy said. "Most of the Lotians are murderous bastards that sacrifice people to increase their power. I know there are less bloodthirsty Dungeon Lords hiding all over the world—Kael's minions got notice of them dying all the time. Perhaps we could talk to them instead?"

"I'd like that, too," Ed told her. "But one way or the other, all Dungeon Lords step into the Netherworld eventually. That's where we go next."

"Then you're in luck," Lavy said after a crestfallen sigh.

"Jarlen's our best bet to reach one of the few civilized parts of the Netherworld."

"Jarlen," Kes said wearily. "It was about time we discussed what to do with her."

Ed nodded. Deciding what to do with the vampire would be crucial. "What do you all think?"

"I don't like her," Klek said, shivering. "The way she looks at us —wolves look at batblins the same way before they pounce. I don't think we can be safe with her around. She may eat us in our sleep."

"That's what pact magic is for," Ed pointed out. "In fact, binding Jarlen with a pact may be the safest bet for everyone, not only the Haunt."

"The *safest* bet would be to kill her," Kes said, patting her silver-tipped stake. "She's a bloodthirsty monster who wouldn't give much thought to devouring us if she were in our place."

"Yes, I know that," Ed said. "But we could say the same about the horned spiders, and yet here we are, working with them."

Lavy raised an eyebrow. "Surely you don't think a vampire and a horned spider are even close to being the same thing. I don't get it, Ed. Back there, in the mortuary, you were all up for killing her at the first sign of trouble."

"And a few days ago, you were all up for a Nightshade in the Haunt," Ed told her, waving with his hand and grinning slightly. "Look. It's true I don't like her—I doubt anyone here does, actually—but she's our prisoner. I can't kill her because I dislike her, that'd be a Rylan Silverblade move."

"Who?" Alder asked.

Ed shook his head. "It's just some asshole. Never mind. My point is, we should think this through. Not for her, but for ourselves."

His friends mulled over his words, although begrudgingly.

"I guess we could use her knowledge," Alder said. "I mean, she's as biased as she claims Bards are, but still. She's like a walking history book."

"Forget her knowledge," Lavy said. "She knows how to enter the Netherworld, remember? She was a Dungeon Lord's second-in-command. We can use her to create a Portal to one of the main cities. And we *need* the Netherworld, Ed. You cannot go around with that weaknesses to Light magic or you'll become a charred husk the second some Cleric sneezes your way."

"Thanks for the mental image," Ed told the Witch. But she was right. The problem with the Netherworld was that it was a pretty big place, from what he'd heard. He could make a Portal right then, since he had the materials and the gold. But he lacked coordinates, and without them, the Portal could send them *anywhere* in the Netherworld, and the demonic monsters that roamed there would make a mere vampire blush. After all, the Netherworld-based Saint Claire & Tillman thought of hell chickens as *snacks*.

It's the kind of place where it's better to bring a guide, Ed thought.

Kes grimaced, while she distractedly toyed with her stake. "If we see her *only* as a tool for the Haunt, her powers could be a nice addition. An undead can't be mind-controlled through normal means, or put to sleep, or poisoned... she could plug several weaknesses we have." Something cruel glinted in her eye. "The Inquisition will take her presence as more proof that we're evil—not that they needed proof before." It was clear that she was thinking of Alvedhra. "Screw it, if we're to be guilty, we may as well commit the crime."

Ed gave her a worried look. Of the others, only Alder seemed to notice the Marshal's inner turmoil. The Bard bit his lip and turned to Kes, but Klek spoke up:

"If there's going to be a wolf in the Haunt," the batblin said, "it should be shackled. Our spiders are loyal to their pack, like batblins. We have common ground. Jarlen has no pack. So she needs a shackle she cannot break."

They kept the discussion going for a while. Eventually, they circled back to the same points and realized they were getting tired.

Their next course of action was clear. After securing Jarlen, they'd go to the Netherworld and investigate. Then Ed would figure out a way to capture a Hero, bypass the self-destruct mechanism, and see just *what* was the construct was made of that allowed it to absorb the strength of a dungeon and act as a living creature.

Ed massaged his legs, trying to ease circulation back into them. Studying a Hero would, hopefully, show him its weaknesses. But that was only part of it. Ed didn't care about eradicating the Heroes. After all, most Dungeon Lords were murderous, self-admitted tyrants that delved in human sacrifice. Perhaps the Inquisition and them deserved each other.

We leave them to their war, Ed thought, *as long as they leave us alone.*

But there was also the unknown person from Earth who had created the Heroes in the first place. Ed knew, beyond a shadow of a doubt, that he needed to find that person. He needed to show him, make him *understand*, that the Light was as extreme in its methods as the Dark.

Ed bit his lip and realized he'd been holding his breath. *Who the hell are you?* How long had that person—the first Hero, in a way—been out there? What lies had the Inquisition made him believe?

The desire to speak to that Summoned Hero was overwhelming. Perhaps, together they'd be strong enough to oppose the mad gods that ruled Ivalis with an iron fist.

How's that for a win condition? Ed thought.

"Before we leave," Klek said, jerking Ed out of his daydream. "I'm curious. What happened before the Old Calendar started? There had to be something before the Lordship. *Had* to. Right? The world wasn't just a blank canvas until the first Dungeon Lord came along." For some reason, there was an eagerness in Klek's

eyes that made Ed think the answer may have been more important to the batblin than he let on.

Lavy patted Klek on the shoulder. "Same old, little guy, same
old. People being born, then growing, eating, fucking, dying, and
killing each other since the dawn of time. The only difference
was, back then they did it with weaker weapons. Probably made
of bronze, I'd say. Stone, before that."

Klek looked down. Alder chuckled and said, "That's one
cynical way to talk about the past, Lavy. Don't mind her, Klek.
Some people just don't have the right temperament to study
history. They get stuck in the ugly parts and fail to see the pretty
sunsets. Before the Lordship was the Age of Myths, my friend—an
epoch without equal, that us Bards can only dream about. It was a
time of legends, of Titans and Dragon Kings, and of the clash
between them that altered the shape of continents."

Ed blinked, then stared at Alder, eyes round like dishes,
wondering if he'd just heard what he thought he had. By the looks
of it, Klek was as stunned as he was.

Meanwhile, Lavy stared daggers at Alder. "Don't act like those
ancient Heiligian folk tales have any basis in reality, Alder. You
will only confuse Klek. And let me tell you where you can stick
your pretty sunsets—"

Klek turned to Ed, smiling broadly. "Did you hear that?" he
asked quietly. "*Dragons,* Lord Ed. Can you imagine that?"

"Yes," Ed said, smiling back. Somehow, it was relaxing to know
that no matter how important and world-breaking seemed the
events that involved him and his Haunt, they were still a mere blip
in the scroll of history.

NOT LONG AFTER, Ed and the others faced the vampire. This time,
Ed explained the terms of his pact offer to Jarlen. She listened,
growing more and more discomfited with each demand. Ed spoke
for a long time.

Then Jarlen couldn't take it any longer. "Would you have me starve?" she interrupted, raising her voice. "I've dealt with strict terms to a pact before, Dungeon Lord, but yours are *incomprehensibly* tyrannical. If you were asking me not to feed on humans in your dungeons' surroundings, I'd understand—perhaps you need those humans for some scheme. But to not feed on *anyone, anywhere?*"

Ed forced himself to ignore the unease the vampire gave him. "Actually, you can't feed on any *sentient* species," he corrected her, adding emphasis to "sentient" because she'd used the word "human," instead. In Heiligian—which was the language that had magically replaced Ed's English when he'd arrived on Ivalis—the word "human" could mean either "human" *or* "any sentient species," like elf, dwarf, gnome, naga, kaftar, batblin, and a long etcetera. In his time in Ivalis, Ed had come to notice a few small other details like that, leftovers that the language-replacing spell had failed to correct.

Normally, it earned him little more than a funny look when he said something in a strange phrasing. But, in this case, Ed was absolutely certain that Jarlen had said "human" because she hoped to weasel her way into a more permissible diet.

"I can't sustain myself on animals alone!" Jarlen exclaimed, raising her hands in disbelief.

"You can't, or you don't *want* to?" Ed prodded.

"Look, animal blood may keep me alive—" She rolled her eyes at Alder's reaction to her phrasing "—but I can't increase my essence with it! I can't earn experience points like a mortal; I need to drink the blood of mortals to grow in power. If I go too long without it, my essence will drain away. I'll eventually become as weak as a newly awakened Nightshade, and what use will I be then?"

"So, drinking sentient blood is how you earn experience," Ed said. He massaged his chin and sighed. "Okay. Do you need to drink it from the living?"

Ed was sure that at some point he'd gone insane without realizing it. He was casually suggesting defacing the dead because it was much better than exsanguinating someone poor sod.

"Only if it's still warm," Jarlen said. "Otherwise it does nothing. Perhaps… five to ten minutes since the heart stopped beating."

I can work with this, Ed thought. "Let's compromise, then. You can drink the blood of any fallen enemy of the Haunt."

Jarlen's expression brightened. "That's much better, Lord Wraith—"

"You can't, however," Ed went on, "kill an enemy solely to feed on them. You need a very good cause to kill someone—if they won't surrender, or if they're too dangerous."

"So now a Dungeon Lord has terms of engagement, like the damned Cardinal Command?" Jarlen asked, her face souring again. "By Murmur's non-existent compassion—what has the world come to?"

Ed turned to Kes. "How reasonable are the Cardinal Command's terms of engagement?"

Kes tilted her hand a couple times in the universal gesture for "eh, good enough, I guess."

"Good enough for me. Jarlen, you'll follow the Cardinal Command's terms of engagement to see who you are allowed to kill."

Jarlen rolled her eyes upward and launched into a long string of Lotian cursing.

"I hope that isn't directed at me," Ed told her.

"I was praying to Murmur," Jarlen said when she was done. She cleaned a pinkish stream of saliva on her chin with her dress. "I was begging him to torture Jiraz' soul for convincing me to come to this stupid country only to die and leave me in your hands."

"Fair enough."

From what Ed had heard of the distant Volantis Enclave, they were more reasonable than Heiliges or Lotia. Using their army's rules would do, at least until the Haunt drafted its own.

"At least I'll be able to hunt minotaurs," Jarlen said, thoughtfully.

Kes perked up at that. "Of course. You can kill as many of those bloodthirsty fuckers as you—"

"Actually," Ed hurried to say, "with minotaurs, you are to do what I—no, what Klek would do in your shoes."

"Why me?" Klek asked, surprised at hearing his name.

Because you may be the best of us, Ed thought. But he only smiled and shrugged.

"Why?" Jarlen asked, her voice seeping with frustration. "If only I could understand your reasons... Why do you care about what I do in some random city a hundred miles from here? Those people would sell you to the Inquisition in a heartbeat, Lord Wraith. To pretend to care about your subjects is mere politics. You need their goodwill to rule without distractions, true, but you gain nothing from this. Nothing at all."

Ed opened his mouth, then thought better of it. He had been about to go into a long tirade about basic human decency, but what was the point? Jarlen didn't care at all about that. In fact, she'd only lose respect for him as a Dungeon Lord if she thought he cared. No. To keep her under control, she needed to know he had a Dungeon Lord's reasons.

"You say that a Dungeon Lord may protect those living in his territories—to keep them pacified," Ed told the vampire. "What about those living in lands he will control in the future? Wouldn't he wish to keep those people pacified, too, so that when the time comes his rise to power is as smooth as possible?"

Jarlen mulled this over. "Interesting," she said. "Perhaps it even makes sense. I've heard of conniving Dungeon Lords who would Charm their way into power rather than rely on Brawn. And where would your ambitions lead you, Lord Wraith? What are the frontiers you are planning for your Haunt? Will you be satisfied with Hoia and its surrounding villages? Maybe you're vying for Undercity itself, as well as its lands. What about Galtia with its belt of mountains? Maybe the frontiers of your future domains extend even further beyond, well past Starevos itself? Maybe Lotia should be worried about your ambitions. Maybe even Heiliges. I hear the weather there is nice—for mortals."

Ed held the vampire's gaze. *Where will your ambitions lead you?* he asked himself.

He wanted to face the Light and the Dark, force them to back away.

No, that's too simple, too far away from you. What do you really *want?*

He wanted Gallio to realize he didn't need the approval of the Inquisition to do good. He wanted Alvedhra to realize that evil could fester anywhere, even in those donning golden armors and silver tunics. He wanted to show Ivalis that the Light and the Dark were the names that two warring groups of mad, god-like beings had given themselves—nothing more, nothing less. But more than that, he wanted to prove to Murmur, and Kharon—and to himself more than any—that he could achieve everything without becoming Rylan Silverblade and all he'd come to represent in Ed's mind. Even if it meant that Ed would risk becoming someone *much* worse.

Simply put, when Ed looked deep inside himself, he found that this conflict was at the very core of his soul.

It was who he was.

"All those frontiers sound nice," Ed told Jarlen. "To start with, at least." Because right then and there, he'd decided that he'd welcome in anyone who would share his vision, anyone who rebelled against becoming the plaything of Alita and Murmur, anyone tired of the games of the Light and the Dark. Right now, the Haunt was but a tiny hideout in the heart of a hostile country-side. But it was also more today than it had been before, back when Alder and Klek and Lavy and him were hiding in caves, barely surviving being eaten by spiderlings.

Tomorrow, the Haunt would be *more*. And one day, perhaps, if they all were strong enough and dedicated enough and had an enormous amount of luck... then the Haunt would become strong enough to take on the Light and the Dark and win.

It was a fight worth fighting.

Ed realized that he was smiling, and that he'd closed his hand into a resolute fist. He also realized that everyone in the mortuary was eyeing him strangely. It took him several seconds to understand why.

He'd come across this discovery about himself—about his life's goal—when looking into the abyss of Jarlen's eyes, but no one else had heard his reasoning.

Ed's heart desire was: *I wish to save this world.*

But what he'd *said*, instead, had been: *I wish to rule this world.*

Two similar phrases, but with entirely different meanings. And which was more real? Ed knew that, sometimes, the brain could deceive even itself in its rush to justify its selfish desires as righteous, and that the truth may show when the mind got careless.

Which was the goal, and which the justification? Would he rule the world in order to save it, or would he save it only because he wished to rule it?

It was as if the cold hand of a wraith—or his own black hand, for that matter—had reached through his chest to grip his heart.

He'd faced creatures that would have given nightmares to the bravest of men. He'd bested the mindbrood, and the Spider Queen, and the Wraith, but he had never *understood* Murmur's gambit until now. He'd never stopped to consider the chance that he had never had a chance of winning the gamble, because he'd lost it before it even began.

Because, perhaps, the most abominable creature of them all wasn't a Dungeon Lord after all. When "human" could mean many things, all Dungeon Lords were humans, and that would mean that monsters were born and not made.

"Ah," Jarlen sighed. It seemed as if someone had lifted a heavy weight from her back. "Finally. I was wondering when would the Haunt's Dungeon Lord show his true self." She gave him a smile more frightening than any of her previous threats and posturing —for this was a smile of genuine happiness. "I salute you, Lord Edward Wraith. I am Nightshade Jarlen of the Haunt. At your service."

And with those words, the pact was forged.

CHAPTER SIXTEEN

CHARACTER CREATION

Lisa rummaged through the rows of cardboard boxes and plastic bags while doing her best to ignore the rats' squeaks coming from behind the plaster walls of the storage area.

"It should be here, somewhere," she told Omar.

The new hire sported a brand-new Lasershark purple-and-pink vest, with the eponymous shark smiling at the center. His curly hair was pulled back into a tight bun and held together by a copious amount of gel. It was his third day on the job, and so far he'd done tolerably well.

"Mister Ryan was so kind lending me a laptop," Omar said.

Lisa fought back the urge to roll her eyes. "Sure," she said. *Where is that damn thing?* She was sure she'd left it somewhere nearby... Perhaps past the stack of busted motherboards?

"I mean, it's so cool, right?" Omar went on. "I never would've thought I'd get paid to play games on the job. It's the dream, isn't it?"

"Sure is." She dug through a pile of faulty power supply units. The laptop wasn't there, either.

In the end, it wasn't Omar's fault that he wasn't able to read social cues, although that did little to comfort her. She could just tell him directly and be done with it, but that would mean having a long chat with Ryan—and or his aunt—and where would that leave her?

Playing games on the job wasn't as cool as Omar hoped. First, the store still had to run, so Mark was doing the job of three people right now. Second, Lisa knew she'd need to stay for several extra hours to finish inventory, and she knew Ryan's thoughts on overtime: it was the kind of word a *team player* shouldn't even keep in their vocabulary.

Third, she was sure Ryan only wanted Omar to get the hang of Ivalis Online before the weekend so Ryan wouldn't have to teach the newbie the ropes on his own.

The laptop was half-buried under a small mountain of black trash bags full of useless CDs that offered free anti-viruses, free email accounts, and free trials of some corporate slide-show or spreadsheet processor.

"Here you go," Lisa said as she dusted the surface of the bulky thing with the back of her hand. The laptop was old and technically the property of the store, but its previous user had added a bit of personality to it with a couple stickers, one of a scantly clad elven Wizard from a popular MMORPG, and another of a giant hulk of a demon that was the final Boss in the same game.

Omar grabbed the laptop almost reverently. Lisa found the charging cable inside one of the plastic bags and handed it to him as well, then stood and massaged her legs.

"Hopefully it still works," she said as they exited the storage area into a dusty hallway with naked wooden walls decorated only with plastic-wrapped A4 sheets printed with memos and motivational messages from HR. An intermittently working light-bulb hung from a cable on the ceiling, and a cockroach's shadow skittered on the floorboards.

They reached the back of the store and cleared a space on the table near the water cooler. Omar grabbed an old mouse, then connected the laptop to an outlet. While it booted up, Lisa took a quick peek at the front—Mark seemed to be doing okay. At least the store wasn't on fire, which was all anyone had a right to expect. They made eye contact across the phone case rows. Lisa gave him a grimace, and Mark gestured up at Ryan's office and mouthed something foul before hurrying to the register.

"What's the password?" Omar asked when she returned.

She sat next to the kid, who tensed up at her closeness and glanced at her out of the corner of his eye. Lisa pretended not to notice and turned her chair to an angle to put a bit more distance between them, playing it off as getting a better look at the screen. "Let's see," she said. "System04. All lowercase, a zero before the four, no spaces."

Omar typed the password under the username, which was "Ed. W."

It was a small miracle that Ryan hadn't tossed the damn laptop away. After Ed's mysterious disappearance, Ryan had searched his workstation in case it hid any clue as to Ed's whereabouts, but despite Ryan's hopes it turned out that life didn't work like a mystery movie. The laptop only contained work-related data, Ed's work email, Ivalis Online, and a pair of flash games that Ryan used as further evidence of Ed's malicious incompetence. Lisa recalled Ryan's disappointed frown with a small smile of her own. *What did you expect to find, a terabyte of scandalous porn, his new address, and a written confession? Every one of your employees is computer literate, dude.*

The desktop took several painful minutes to load, then it showed a black background and a sparse spread of icons. Omar took a few seconds to find IO's pixel-art icon on the screen, and double-clicked it with an eager grin.

"I've reading up on this game," he told Lisa while the .exe loaded. "I wanted to download it into my own PC, but there's no official download link anywhere, only cracked single-player versions."

"Yeah, we've talked about it on the forums," Lisa said. Despite it all, she couldn't stay away from a bit of game-related gossip. "Apparently the devs stopped answering mails or calls without explanation and took down their site a few years ago. No one knows why; the game has a rabid fan-base, so they would've bought anything new the devs launched."

After a black loading screen, the words PANTHEON appeared in golden letters, along with an audio file, like the metallic sound of drawing a sharp sword in a movie.

"These are the devs?" Omar asked.

"That's right. Weird bunch, you know? Ed and Mark loved them because they were so quirky, but I think that's the reason the game never took off in the first place. They added dozens of limitations that made no sense, all in the name of immersion, but they made the game unplayable unless you're *really* trying to get into it."

"To be honest, I'm even more curious now."

"You'll see what I mean."

After the PANTHEON screen came the usual legalese, a warning that the game wasn't appropriate for children, and a disclaimer that the devs weren't responsible for the shit players did to each other while in-game. Then came a pixelated introductory video about the single-player campaign's main character fighting hordes of bad guys while a narrator rambled on in the background about justice and destiny. The CGI had aged terribly, but Lisa found that it only added to the game's charm.

When the video was done, a start screen took its place, with the Good Kingdom's castle in the background, besieged by hordes of the Evil Empire. On the right side of the screen appeared a list in a medieval typeset:

- Campaign
- Ivalis Online
- Options

- Forums
- Account
- Exit

OMAR CLICKED ON IVALIS ONLINE, which filled the left side of the screen with another menu. It was divided into four rectangles which had a character portrait in each of them, with bars showing their names, stats, levels, and hours played. Each character was a different level. The one on the right, an elven Wizard, was the strongest and had the longest playtime, and the one on the left was a rookie Warrior with only a few hours played.

"On a fresh account," Lisa explained, "you can only have one character at the time. Apparently, Pantheon wanted us to prove we were worthy of the responsibility to keep more characters, so we have to unlock more slots by killing Bosses and the like."

"I've played games that do that," Omar pointed out. "Nothing weird about it."

Lisa grinned. "It's in the way they frame the reward. Think about it. Most games IO's age pretend the players *are* the characters, to maintain immersion. Player characters are the ones killing the baddies and finding the loot. But IO rewards the players *themselves* and keeps talking at them the entire time. If you have a careless play style and keep killing your characters, the game scolds *you*, and may take features away in punishment. There are even a few guys who got banned from the multiplayer version because they died too much."

"Okay, now that's strange," Omar said. "Not even EA does that."

"It pissed off some of the fan-base, but most only shrugged and told the angry ones to get good."

Omar snorted. "Sounds about right."

"So, let's get you started on the campaign first, okay?" Lisa said. "It's an extended tutorial. After you're done, you can delete the two weakest characters and make your own."

Omar left the Ivalis Online menu and hovered over the Campaign, showed a New Game and Continue options. "Are you sure this guy won't get pissed I'm messing with his account?" He tapped at the laptop's stickers.

"Well… he hasn't logged on in a while, so he's probably moved on by now," Lisa said, trying to keep her voice level. She had always wondered how well Lasershark's security cameras could pick up audio, because Ryan had the tendency to show up at exactly the worst times. "To be honest, Ed's a touchy subject around here. I wouldn't mention him if I were you."

"I heard bits of gossip here and there," Omar went on, oblivious to Lisa's discomfort. "He's the guy who lost it, isn't he? The one who attacked Mister Ryan and ran away from the police. Crazy fucker, am I right?"

Lisa glanced at the corner where she knew the security camera lurked. "Sure," she said. "Whatever."

Technically, Ryan's story was right. Ed had lost it, no question about it. She had been raised to find violence unacceptable under any circumstance. Still… Lisa couldn't shake the feeling that Ryan had pruned his version until it showed only one side of the tale. He hadn't mentioned the constant verbal abuse, for example.

Still… did that justify smashing someone's face against a desk?

Lisa felt a pang of guilt on her chest, and she shook her head to clear it. She'd spent a year barely thinking about Ed and his assertive "I quit, Ryan" delivery. But Omar couldn't help but bring it up over and over, and she was sure it was awakening Ryan's old grudges. Lisa would've very much preferred he didn't, primarily because before he'd made a target out of Ed, he'd focused his nastiness on *her*.

Her hand gripped her jeans. *Yes, that's the real problem, isn't it?* she thought, angry at herself.

Not even Omar could miss the meaning of a "whatever," so he

shrugged and returned his attention to the screen, which was fine by her.

Clicking on the New Game option prompted two "are you sure?" text-boxes, and then a new video began. It told the story of the Good Kingdom, a peaceful and prosperous land that had lived in harmony for generations, which had earned them the jealousy of the Evil Empire—

"Evil Empire?" Omar asked, looking at the screen as if someone was pranking him. "Good Kingdom? Who the hell came up with these names?"

"I think it's supposed to be tongue in cheek and self-aware of the tropes," Lisa said, getting defensive like any gamer who finds her favorite game being even slightly criticized. "Anyway, the story is mostly an excuse to kill shit, and Pantheon's mechanics are way ahead of their time, so who cares if their campaign abuses all the fantasy clichés around—"

"Okay, okay, I get it," said Omar, raising his open palms in surrender. "Tongue in cheek it is."

The Evil Empire had sent a terrible curse called the Culling upon the Good Kingdom. During the Culling, the Evil Empire's agents had killed thousands of the Good Kingdom's people, burned their cities, and salted their fields. The Wise King Varen suffered nobly for weeks while the Evil armies grew in strength and prepared for the final strike, until a brave young man heard the call of destiny, grabbed his sword, and bravely set to rally the forces of Good into a desperate attack to retaliate against the Culling and bring the fight into the Evil Empire's lands. Along with his three plucky companions, of course.

At that point in the video, the screen zoomed from the Hero's village into his home, bypassed the straw roof, and showed his silhouette sleeping in bed as one of his companions ran into his room, bellowing for him to wake up, since he was already late to his meeting with the village elders.

The Hero rose, and a character creation menu deftly replaced the cut-scene with no obvious loading screen.

"Neat," said Omar.

"Not bad for a fifteen-year-old game, right?" Lisa asked proudly.

"So, what's the story about?"

"Without spoiling much? You assemble your squad, fight a couple minor bad guys terrorizing the Good Kingdom, level up, then travel to the Evil Empire to confront the Big Bad—Zailos, or something like that." She left out the tragic betrayal at the mid-point of the campaign, or the bittersweet ending with the Player Character's heroic sacrifice.

"Okay. Seems pretty straightforward."

"The multiplayer takes place after the campaign," Lisa went on. "You're supposed to help the Good Kingdom finish off the baddies. The main goal is to hunt down this Everbleed guy—he's in the campaign as well, starts as a minor boss, but takes over when you deal with the Big Bad."

The character creation let Omar play with the Hero's name, stats, class, and appearance. The placeholder name was "Dasius," which Omar replaced—in a dashing display of creativity—with "Omar." He then began changing Dasius' appearance into his own likeness.

Lisa knew some people could spend more time customizing their characters than actually playing the game, so she went for a drink of water, then checked on Mark again.

He was talking to a customer dressed in an expensive black suit, a tall man partially hidden by a signboard displaying the newest overpriced ethernet cable. Mark kept throwing quizzical glances at the back, then nodding, but he seemed to be doing fine. The rest of the store was empty, which was a bit strange, but Lisa chalked it up to the rest of the crew timing their break. As long as they came back soon, Ryan wouldn't notice. Probably.

That's how you survive, isn't it? she told herself, breaking her train of thought. *You keep your head down, make yourself small, and hope your problems don't notice you. The only reason you're stuck here is because there's a fight waiting for you, yet you refuse to fight it.*

It all had started, well, like in Omar's case. She had been a new hire, and Ryan had seemed like the dream boss. Attractive, charming, and relaxed. If Lisa hadn't been dating a tattoo artist a couple blocks away... Goosebumps traveled down her back. *That's one hell of a bullet dodged,* she thought.

Ryan had flirted playfully with her at the beginning, nothing serious, just friendly banter—or so she'd thought. She'd made it clear she wasn't available, but wasn't too insistent over it. Later, her younger sister had told her that had been a mistake and that she should have been sterner, that guys like Ryan used even the slightest opening to stick their foot in the door and act pissed when you tried to close it.

Lisa and her sister had argued quite a lot over that analysis. Lisa believed that it was insane to try to control everyone's interpretations of her every action—it wasn't fair, or even possible. Her sister seemed to pull it off without effort though. Diana had just graduated and had already landed a rockstar internship in a promising marketing start-up, thanks to her make-up tutorial vlog with three million followers. She was also the kind of person that claimed that her pay-to-win smartphone energy-timer game made her hardcore into gaming.

In the end, Lisa had rejected Ryan's advances, and he hadn't taken nicely to it. His personality had taken a total u-turn, going from charming and straight into "you're an ugly cow" territory, and he then proceeded to make her life a living hell while she unsuccessfully looked for another job. Then Ed had come along, a lanky nerd who had, for some reason or another, redirected Ryan's attention and ire to himself.

And here you are again, she thought, *hoping that someone else takes the fall instead of your sorry ass. When will you learn to fight your own fights, Liz?*

The room had turned a strange shade of white. Surprised, Lisa propped herself against the wall and took deep, steadying breaths.

"Are you okay?" Omar asked, looking up from his laptop. "You're looking a bit pale."

"S-sure," Lisa stammered, barely paying any attention to him. Her head was pulsating something fierce, sending red jolts of pain through her nervous system in the rhythm of a heartbeat.

On a whim, she turned to the register, half-expecting to see an unearthly creature smiling at her beneath a signboard. But Mark was alone, and the bell by door at the front chimed as someone closed it. Mark turned to her with a quizzical expression. He had a black letter in his hand.

Was someone singing in the distance? Lisa shook her head again and fought the urge to clasp her forehead. "Actually, do you have any aspirin?" she asked Omar.

The air reeked of pungent chemicals and rotten fruit.

"No," Omar said. "But I could call Mister Ryan and ask—"

"Forget it," Lisa said, waving her hand. "It was nothing." She forced herself to straighten her back and fake a smile. "I bit my tongue, that's all."

Before Omar had a chance to reply, she strolled out toward the front, acting as if nothing was wrong. Mark saw her and waved her over.

"Hey, Liz. You wouldn't believe what just happened," he told her with an uncertain grin.

"Funny you mention that," she said, but Mark wasn't listening. He held the black letter in front of her.

"This is for you," he said. "From a head-hunting company, or something like that. The dude just left and wasn't very clear, but it seems like you got a job offer."

LISA GRABBED the letter without thinking. Her mind had gone blank with surprise. As her headache receded, the feeling of incoming doom that had almost overwhelmed her went away as well. She'd almost expected Mark to tell her that her house had burned down. A letter from a headhunter company was completely out of left field. She wasn't even aware her resumé was still out there, or that anyone was looking at it.

"Weird, isn't it? I told him you were working in the back, but he said the timing wasn't right and just left."

Lisa scrutinized the card. It had her full name and address on it, and the sender put simply "Mr. K. Posseur. Head-hunter."

"Yeah, it's pretty strange," she said, eyeing Mr. Posseur's handwriting with distrust. If it was a joke, it'd be a cruel one, which was exactly the kind of humor that Ryan favored most.

"Well, even if it is, there's nothing lost by looking, right?" Mark told her. He shrugged. Mark was a good guy and a solid friend, but his attention span could use a few extra skill ranks. "So, what do you think about the new guy? Will he be ready to do some questing soon?"

Lisa glanced back. The glow of the laptop reflected on Omar's glasses while his hands danced across the keyboard and mouse. "Perhaps some low-level jobs until he's done with the campaign. We could get him to main Ed's Wizard, but there's no chance in hell he won't fuck up until he figures out what he's doing."

If Omar led them to a party wipe, Ryan would show him his true colors fast enough, which would only add to Lisa's guilt about hiding behind the new hire. In a messed-up way, helping the new kid do well was a way for Lisa to redeem herself.

"I doubt our brave leader will have the patience to stick with low-level quests," Mark pointed out. He then raised an eyebrow while glancing at a point past Lisa's shoulder. "Oh, speaking of. Time to go look busy by that corner over there, I guess."

Ryan came down the stairs of his office and stopped a few feet away from Omar. The two of them chatted amiably for a while. Ryan seemed very pleased with himself for some reason, which only added to Lisa's growing worry about the letter being a prank from him. But Ryan barely looked her way. Instead, he clapped Omar in the back and pointed at the front door. Omar smiled, closed the laptop, and grabbed his jacket.

Lisa frowned and headed back, wondering if Ryan had finally lost it. "What's going on?" she asked.

"Oh, Lisa, there you are," Ryan said. "I was just telling our friend Omar here he could take the day off and practice his skills. It's a slow day, after all, no need to kid ourselves. I'm sure that between Mark, you, and me we can keep the store running no problem. Just don't make a habit out of gaming on the job, okay?" This last part he said to Omar, winking as he did.

"Sure, boss, you've got it," Omar said, grinning knowingly while, at the same time, completely missing the point. It reminded Lisa of a lamb heading happily to the slaughterhouse, thinking it was about to be fed.

After the kid had left, Lisa turned to Ryan. "Only us three? Where's the rest of the crew?" she asked.

"Ah, I told them to take the day off as well." Ryan's grin grew a few inches, and Lisa had the glaring suspicion that she'd just fallen straight into some kind of trap. "After all, it isn't fair that they have to work hard all day while others get to sit on their ass neglecting their duties and playing video-games, don't you think?"

What else do you expect people to sit on instead of their ass? Lisa thought. But that kind of attitude was Diana's domain, not hers. What she said, instead, was, "But you told Omar he could! Why punish him for something you told him to do?"

Ryan brandished an admonishing finger. "What makes you think I was speaking about him?" he asked, smiling cruelly. "No, I was talking about *you*, Lisa. Who gave you the right to sit around while others pick up your slack, I wonder? That's always been your problem, you know—I mean, other than being too plain. It's your personality. People can just tell you think you're better than us."

If he'd sprouted wings and a beak, Lisa would've been about as dumbfounded as she was now. She could only but stare at him in disbelief and mumble a miserable, "What?"

"At this rate, I'll be forced to note your lack of team-spirit in this month's performance review." What little extra over minimum wage Lisa earned was set as a bonus for "good performance" that Lasershark corporate delivered monthly. In other words, Ryan had decided to dock her wage on a whim. "Lucky for you, I'm an amazing boss. I'm probably too permissive, but I'll reconsider your review if you close the store on your own this weekend. You think you can manage that without screwing up?"

At that moment, Lisa realized several things. The first was that it was the beginning of summer. The second was that Ryan was dressed for going out. The third was that he'd set her up only because he wanted to bail for the weekend without admitting it.

She could feel the texture of the black letter under her fingertips. Even the paper felt expensive and exclusive. It was the kind of letter that Ryan would receive, not her. Her hand gripped the paper a bit too tightly, as if clutching to a lifeline as she drowned in the ocean.

"I'll do my best," she said blankly, as she marched for the broom closet. "Have a nice trip," she called over her shoulder. Her words carried just a hint of mockery. Her attitude surprised even herself. Perhaps she had more of Diana in her than she'd like to admit.

"You better," Ryan said. "And watch that attitude, Lisa. Hot girls can get away with that, but it just makes you look like an ass. All right?"

Lisa opened the closet and buried her face inside so he wouldn't see her roll her eyes. "Fucking asshole," she whispered. Was that the best he could come up with?

ON FIRST GLANCE, the letter didn't seem to be one of Ryan's jokes —which was all the better, because Lisa was sure she'd have gone murderously insane if it were. On the other hand, there was no guarantee it wasn't some kind of idiotic—or even dangerous —scam.

Whatever it was, it definitely wasn't a conventional job offer.

DEAR LISA.

DO YOU FIND YOURSELF STUCK? Has your life turned stale?

We can offer you hope.

How would you like to have an entire world at the grasp of your fingertips?

This is a new chance to get things right.

To get the respect you deserve.

All this can be yours if you prove yourself worthy of working with us.

You have a glowing recommendation, and we only need proof that you've got what it takes to excel in a highly competitive environment.

We'll be watching you with great interest.

YOURS,

Mr. K. Posseur,

The Dark.

THERE WERE NO DIRECTIONS, and no number or email for her to contact. There was no mention of what she was supposed to do. Not even pyramid schemes were this cheeky.

Lisa re-read those few lines repeatedly, her confusion growing by the second. What kind of job offer was that? *We'll be watching you?* That sounded more like a threat than anything else. She shuddered and hid the letter in the pocket of her apron as she carried the cleaning instruments out of the closet.

We can offer you hope.

For a while now, she realized, she'd given up on hope—she'd even stopped looking for a new job. The worst part about the deranged letter was the implication that they were, indeed, giving her hope despite her desperate attempts to quench it.

And what kind of company named itself The Dark, anyway?

CHAPTER SEVENTEEN

BRANCHING ENDINGS

L avy's laboratory was a two-story circular chamber covered in shadows and cobwebs, filled to the brim with strange devices and dusty pieces of furniture. Ed and Klek navigated through a maze-like series of shelves and bookcases that rose up to the ceiling. Leathery tomes loomed above Ed as he went, and small animal skulls hung in groups of three from the ceiling, with tiny fragments of magical torches burning from inside and setting the empty sockets ablaze with menacing fire.

Klek took one look at Lavy's decorations and shivered. "Scary ladies live in scary homes," he muttered to himself. Near a corner, a centipede as long and thick as a human arm skittered out of sight.

"At this point," Ed told the Spider Rider, "I'm sure that she does it because her Witch apparel gives bonuses to her Hex magic."

"Is that true?" Klek asked, his eyes widening.

Ed shrugged apologetically. "It would explain a lot of things."

They found Lavy sitting on a cramped workbench partially hidden by a stack of parchment rolls, several menacing brass contraptions, and a mercurial magic ball as big as her head. She was resting her head between her arms and didn't acknowledge their presence. Next to her arms on the table was a huge human skull, which was missing several teeth and was cracked in several places.

"Lavy?" Ed asked.

Lavy sniffed and jerked to her feet, her hands crackling with sparks of Hex energy. "Dunghill!" she exclaimed, blinking several times as the energy dissipated. "Ed! Didn't anyone tell you to knock? You scared me."

Ed and Klek exchanged a confused glance. Lavy looked like hell. Her hair was a frizzy, tangled mess, her eyes were sunken, and oily liquids stained her purple dress.

"The batblins said you had something to show us," Ed told the Witch. "Perhaps we should come by later?"

Lavy blinked again. "Ah. Of course. I called for you." She gave them one of her famous Lavy grins. "You'll want to take a look at this. Lavina's amazing genius triumphs once again!" She rested a hand over the cracked skull and bent forward, smiling like a madwoman. "Remember the Lenses quest? I've made huge progress on it. There is now a working prototype."

Klek looked at Lavy, then at the skull. "Is that... is that the prototype?" he asked.

"Oh, this? No, little guy, this is a personal project of mine." She patted the skull distractedly, with something akin to fondness in her expression. "It's a trophy, like Ed's in the War Room. It belonged to a guy named Rolim. He was a very strong son of a bitch, built like a minotaur. I want to raise his spirit and put it inside a golem, to see if that could somehow improve the golem's physical stats."

If anything, Klek seemed more confused. Lavy pursed her lips and straightened her back. "The prototype. Right. Follow me, guys, and prepare to be amazed."

She led them past a huge stone oven embedded in the wall, which was surrounded with iron shelves and tables strewn with pots filled with clay dust and crystal vials full of bubbling liquids.

Near a corner, a huge crystal dish hung from the ceiling by a pair of thick ropes. It was as big as Ed's torso, and it seemed to be engraved on the inside with an array of fine brass and copper lines that vaguely reminded Ed of circuitry.

Lavy stood proudly next to the dish and beamed. "Isn't it amazing? I did it myself. I mean, with a bit of help from drone transmutation, of course."

Ed walked closer to the dish to study the engravings. Upon closer inspection, he was sure the shapes traced by the connections between the lines reminded him of the glyphs often found in a rune. "Lavy, this is great work, but... when did you find the time?"

"Well, a Witch has her ways," Lavy said. Ed was sure he saw a faint twitch in her left eyelid.

"When was the last time you slept, scary lady?" Klek asked her, his ears straightened with concern.

Lavy grimaced. "Three minutes ago! Not that you should care. The Haunt cannot afford to lose eight hours of my mind every night!"

"Didn't you say once that not sleeping makes people age faster?" Klek asked.

"Well..." she said, then pursed her lips. "You want to see what the damn thing does or not?"

"Just—just promise us you'll take a nap afterward, okay? Don't push yourself too hard," Ed told her.

The Witch made a vague, non-committal gesture with her arm, and then rummaged through the ribbons of her dress until she found a small trinket. She held it up for Ed and Klek to see. It was Zachary's looking glass—the one that had failed to stop Jarlen's hypnotic gaze. "Warlock Chasan once told me that, with spellcraft, you can learn more by studying someone's mistakes than from their successes. Well. More like, he mumbled it to himself while he worked, and I happened to be in the room." She frowned. "So, the first step of my quest was to ask myself, why did

291

this lens fail? Simple: Zachary and Brett are not spellcasters." She raised one finger. "Sure, Zachary can *cast* a few spells, because he's a Priest, but that's not the same thing. A spellcaster is a trained specialist that knows the theory of magic. There's a world of difference between using something and knowing how it works. In this case, Zachary simply assumed that by piling a bunch of minor divine blessings on a glass, it would be enough to counter Jarlen's spell. That's a common misunderstanding of magical theory, so of course it instantly unraveled when tested. It would be like throwing a splash of water and a piece of ham into a pot and hoping for stew."

Ed decided not to point out that she hadn't voiced any complaints about Zachary's experiments, either. He knew that Lavy's self-esteem was more fragile than she let on, so he let small details like that pass... as long as she wasn't a dick about it, like she'd been when they first met.

"You need fire to make a stew. The ingredients need to meld together, or you'll create a useless mess," Lavy went on, gesturing with her fingers over Zachary's trinket like a Chef working on a dish. "Same thing with spellcraft. To create an enchanted object, it isn't enough to just throw a spell on top and call it a day. You need the fire that melds the magic and the object." She pointed at the brass lines inside her giant version of the lens. "I made these using the *engrave rune* talent. You're looking at an enlarged version of the inside of a rune, actually. The reason it had to be so big, well, it's because *engrave rune* is designed to work with runic stone, not with glass. But I'm sure I can make smaller versions with more practice."

She traced the path of one brass line with her fingertip. "A rune is created by mixing *engrave rune* with the spell you want to use to charge the rune. *Engrave* lets you design the artificial ley lines, and the spell both shapes the lines and powers them with enough magical charge to use the spell. In this, craft imitates life, because the body of a magic user works in much the same way. All living creatures have a system of biological ley lines inside ourselves—some Clerics believe this is our soul. Pouring experience points into the *spellcasting* talent allows these ley lines to develop, to grow in complexity so we can, in turn, cast more complex spells—what we call Basic types, and later Improved, Advanced, Heroic, and so on. To power each spell, the ley lines use the body's internal magic supply, which replenishes every day as long as you're well-fed and well-rested. This supply is limited by your size and your species, of course, which is why we can cast only one or two spells when we start our training. It only grows when upgrading your talent past the Basic type, *but* with practice we can teach our body to be more efficient in its use of our supply, so we can cast more spells with the same amount of energy. That's what increasing the spellcasting *skill* does." She finished her explanation and crossed her arms, looking proud.

She has a right to be, Ed thought. She was a world ahead of the apprentice she'd been when they'd first met, both of them confused and barely understanding what was going on around them. It was amazing to see the speed at which she was learning, now that she had the right tools and a nurturing environment for her self-esteem to develop.

Almost immediately, he realized as well that she—and Alder and Kes and the rest of the Haunt—had done the exact same thing for him, with no one realizing it.

"Still with me?" Lavy asked.

Klek glanced at his belly, then at the giant dish, as if expecting to find the ley lines growing out of him like vines. He nodded dubiously.

"Sure, Lavy," Ed said. "And thanks for the lesson. You've taught me a lot today."

She beamed at him. "I was worried I was talking too much." She patted her dish again. "So, how about a little practical test? The dish is engraved with a specific counter for your *minor order* spell, Ed. Since the ley lines are built as a countermeasure, they need no charge, but they only work on that specific spell. Let's give it a try, all right?"

Before either of them could raise any objections, Lavy had already ushered them into place. Klek stood with his back to the wall, staring nervously at Ed past the softly swaying crystal of the glass between them. The dish's surface slightly distorted the batblin's figure.

"This should be pretty straightforward," Lavy advised. "Ed, simply cast *minor order* on Klek. Klek, if my lens works, you shouldn't even have to pass a Spirit test, so just... stand there and look pretty."

Klek's snout trembled with worry, but then he steeled himself, and the Adventurer Slayer replaced the scared batblin. "Do your worst, Lord Ed," he said.

Ed gave him a thumbs up. "All right, then. Here I go." His Evil Eye blazed green as he focused his will to cast *minor order*. "*Jump!*" he ordered, his voice booming.

The air around the dish rippled, like a stone breaking the surface of a lake. Klek tensed. For an instant, a green gleam danced through the glass like a reflection from a candle, and then it was gone. Nothing happened.

"Did you pass a Spirit test?" Lavy asked the batblin. Ed shook his head at the same time Klek did. There had been no clash of wills at all. "Yes! It worked! Damn, I can't believe we didn't blow up—" She began to cackle, caught herself, then said, "I mean, *of course* it worked. I knew it would. This just proves it, is all."

Klek raised an eyebrow and shuffled away from the dish.

"Well done, Lavy." Ed patted the Witch on the shoulder and walked closer to the copper array. He set his normal hand on the surface of the glass. It was warm, but cooling. He did the same with his skeletal hand, though he found nothing out of the ordinary. He'd hoped that the dish could "store" the charge of his spell, like a rune or a battery, but he suspected the Haunt's research wasn't anywhere close to that yet.

"Sadly, it's too large to use against magical gazes," Lavy said, full of fake humility. "But I was thinking we could use the design to improve the Scrambler Towers? Divination is outside my area of expertise, though, so we may have to find a Diviner to help."

"Great idea," Ed said. "We'll see if we can hire someone through the Thieves Guild." It would have to be someone who didn't ask too many questions about having to work on a very obvious Dark design, though, but it shouldn't be much of a problem. It was incredible what people failed to notice if the pay warranted it.

He turned to face Lavy. "If you think of any other way we can use the dish, let me know. And if you manage to solve the size problem, I was thinking we could add them to the helmet's eye slits. Make the glass thicker." Hell, if she improved the design enough, they could add a whole load of improvements to the Haunt's helmets. Telescopic and night vision, illusion-piercing, magic detection... At the very least, it would save those of the Haunt a couple dozen experience points in talents.

Lavy's grin widened. "I like the way you think. I'll let you know if I come up with anything. In the meantime, I've got a few shiny new experience points to throw around."

- *A Research Mission has progressed! Lens Technology.*

Reward: Technology (Improved Scrambler Towers) Requires further research. Further research may also reveal other applications.

A new technological path is available: Lens Technology (Miniaturization).

Progress through this path to unlock Design: Smart Helmets.

IT WAS A WELL-KNOWN fact among Ivalian spellcasters that increasing your body's magical abilities using experience points had a peculiar interaction with your mind. Bardic repositories were full with reports of Wizards and Warlocks buying an improved Spellcasting talent and experiencing the distant past, other worlds, planes, or even branching time-lines for a brief minute while the ley lines of their bodies expanded.

The visions were confusing and rarely had any useful meaning, despite constant attempts by Diviners to use them in prophecy and scrying. Nevertheless, attempts in the other direction—to shelve the visions into a "curious but useless" category—also failed because of the few occasions when they actually worked.

For example, Alder had told Ed of the Wizard apprentice who discovered he was the last heir of a long-thought-lost royal family through his very first vision, or of the Diviner who had found the location of a buried ancient city through his Advanced Spellcasting vision.

The problem with this kind of "useful" visions was that there was no way to distinguish them from their random counterparts, and the "long-lost heir of the throne" is a common claim among usurpers who need an excuse to stage a coup. In the case of the Diviner and his lost city, it was his Guild who led the expedition to uncover it, only after following a completely unrelated lead, long after the original Diviner had died in utter poverty and ignominy after all his peers ridiculed him for trusting a random magical hunch instead of their dusty scrolls.

The Wizard apprentice had been executed for trying to stage a coup against the kingdom regent, and it was only posthumously that his vision was confirmed by a couple pesky Bards who uncovered a damning piece of evidence buried by the regent himself. The adventurers hired by those Bards as protection led a very quick, yet bloody revolution that ended with their leader executing the regent and replacing him. Sadly, it turns out that violent murder-hobos don't make for competent civil servants, and the little kingdom soon found itself in yet another peasant revolt, only this time Heiliges, its neighbor, saw a chance for an easy annexation and took it. The Heiligian army marched down the little kingdom's palace finding only token resistance, and the King executed everyone involved—and their mothers for good measure—and that was the end of that mess.

This is all to say that, among the spellcasting community, random magical visions from no clear source were considered more trouble than they're worth.

When Ed found himself standing in the middle of a black lake surrounded by a colossal man-made cavern, he set to learn as little as possible from this particular vision, lest it come to bite him in the ass later on.

The lake extended until it reached a raised stone platform in the distance. The walls at both sides of the lake fed the waters with a constant stream coming through rusty grated outlets, and Ed could almost feel the current raging beneath his feet. He was standing on the water without gravity complaining, so at first he'd thought he was simply standing atop a shallow puddle.

Then he saw the shapes far, far below, constantly changing size as they swam up and down, their figures only vaguely reminiscent of fish and even then, only of their worst qualities.

As a Dungeon Lord, Ed had an instinctual fear of running water only a hairbreadth away from a full-blown aquaphobia. His powers were fueled by the ley lines of the ground, of warm soil and cold rock, and in the middle of a lake he was about as magical as a naked batblin facing a wolf.

So he hurried as fast as he could toward the only source of solid ground that he could see—the platform several hundred meters away. He tried not to wonder what would happen if the spell that kept him walking over the water suddenly ended, and if the creatures lurking underneath would care much for details like, "You can't eat someone that's technically not here at all."

Tall brass braziers at his sides lit as he went, bathing his shoulders in a kind of ultraviolet light that would've been at home in a rave back on Earth. An open tent rose in the middle of the platform, dominated by a pyramid of emerald green cushions as big as Ed, each embroidered with golden scales, bells, silk knots, and silver whistles. Lavish tables full of exotic fruits and curated meats surrounded the cushion pyramid, with one small stone table right in front of the pyramid.

Languishing behind the stone table was a woman half-buried in the pile of cushions, with her raven-black hair cascading over her naked torso like a curtain of night. Even at a distance Ed could tell she was beautiful beyond description, in a way that could draw the breath from a man or make Bards fall weeping to their knees. As he approached, she smiled lazily, grabbed a grape the size of an Aureus, and took a bite in a way that was at the same time enticing and innocent. Ed caught a glimpse of her breasts rising up with every deep breath, and could feel his throat drying, even in a vision.

He distrusted her immediately.

Even so, there was nowhere else to go, and he strolled almost placidly in the rhythm of a dream until he reached the platform's feet. Then he climbed a small series of steps and was face to face with the mysterious woman. Her eyes were ink-black, and her irises seemed to swirl as if containing stormy clouds, the implication of thunder only faintly hidden by her full red lips.

Ed stopped in front of her, finding himself unable to speak. This didn't worry him—it was just a vision, after all, and one could rarely interact with a dream. He could only wait until his mind got used to the increased magical influx, then he'd wake up in his room, his shiny new Improved Spellcasting talent ready to greet him with two spells for his choosing.

"Lord Wraith," the woman greeted him with a musical voice. "At long last. I was wondering for how much longer would my brother keep me from meeting such an... enthralling experiment."

She bent forward in a way that made Ed glad he didn't have a physical body at the moment, and gestured for him to sit on a small seat in front of her stone table. He did as she asked, still unable to control his movements. "You may address me as Regent Korghiran, or My Lady of Secrets, if you prefer."

Ed stared at her, unable to speak or move.

Korghiran made a tall flourish with her hand, as if greeting a crowd, and a deck of golden cards appeared between her fingers out of nowhere. The deck looked heavy and metallic, with sharp edges bolted to a mercurial back that seemed to weave in the very pattern of Korghiran's eyes. With a careless smile, she shuffled the deck several times, making cards fly between her hands, then dance atop the table and jump, disappear, and reappear in Ed's hands only to return to her grasp a second later.

"The Shadow Tarot," she revealed, as she finished her shuffle and set the deck on the center of the table, right between her and Ed. "The perfect instrument to woo an ambitious young Dungeon Lord in the prime of his life. It brings the gift of knowledge, my dear. Of a very secret and guarded kind, too."

With a dexterous wave, she spread the deck in a perfect arc across the table. "Prophecy," she whispered. "A magic far beyond the ken of mortal Diviners, and even beyond most Demon Regents of the Netherworld. But between you and me, Lord Wraith? It's more useful as a bit of dining entertainment between friends, the perfect excuse to get to know each other. You shall see what I mean."

She pointed at the cards. "Pick six cards, form a triangle with three, and an inverted one with the rest, right behind the first. Go on, don't be shy."

Ed did as she asked. He selected his cards after a bit of hesitation, then ordered them in a sort of rhombus' spread.

Korghiran smiled and slid the first three cards back to her side of the table. "This set represents three possible futures where you fail to achieve your goals, Lord Wraith." She turned the cards on their backs to reveal swirling windows with tiny human-shaped drawings coming in and out of frame. "Regardless of what many mortals may believe, the future is not set in stone. It is fluid, like a

Nightshade's mist seeping through the cracks of stone, or the branches of a river carving new paths through the centuries. The Shadow Tarot is a tool to understand the present, Lord Wraith. So gaze into the cards, and behold the consequences of your actions."

If he'd had control of his body, Ed would've refused, but this vision left him no room for choice. He bent forward and stared deep into the cards, and the view seemed to react to his attention and panned into a closer view.

The card showed him a sunny day with no clouds, the view to the shining blue sky partially obscured by a rough wooden contraption fitted with iron restraints. A man knelt in the frame, his back painfully bent toward the floor, and was bound by his wrists and neck to the device, his face obscured by dirty patches of black hair.

"A common fate among Dungeon Lords," Korghiran pointed out. "Captured by the Inquisition and summarily executed." The image shifted enough to reveal the man's face, and Ed stared at his own deformed visage. His throat tightened as he caught sight of the web of angry scars obscuring most of his features, the purple bloated skin, and the red, empty eye-sockets burned away with fire irons.

Korghiran waved her hands at the image as if goading it into showing more. "In this future, you refused to use lethal force against the Inquisition, arguing that they had good intentions—although misguided. It is a courtesy our Heiligian friends won't extend to us. The Inquisition poured through your dungeons, slaughtered all your minions, and captured you. At least your conscience is clean, isn't it? Although you don't seem particularly at ease with your situation, at least from this vantage perspective. Would you agree?"

The Ed in the card screamed in terror and tried to wiggle free of his restraints as the executioner entered into the frame. The real Ed recognized the man, despite the ceremonial white tunic and armor and the golden spurs hanging from his chest. Gallio didn't seem particularly happy with the situation, either, but at least he had his eyes. They stared blankly at nothing in particular as he swung the sword at the beaten Dungeon Lord's neck. There was a spray of red, and the head rolled out of sight. Some other Inquisitor came to remove the body and began the bloody process of tearing the black heart out of its chest.

The vision went dark. "The only way to remove this branch of possibility from your tree is to take refuge into the Netherworld, Lord Wraith," Korghiran said, amused. "A few Dungeon Lords have accepted our offers, and they live comfortable lives, albeit with no further delusions of world domination. Does that interest you? Many Regents would take you in if you're willing to pay their price."

The next card showed a paved street surrounded by gigantic towers of steel and crystal. It took Ed a couple seconds to realize he was starting at a city block from Earth. A disgruntled hobo stood on a wooden stool and screamed at the passing crowd, which did its best not to notice him. His nose was red with drink, his eyes injected with yellow and disease, but Ed could recognize himself even through the overgrown beard and hair.

"Ah, this is one I haven't seen before," Korghiran said, with evident pleasure. "It seems that you displeased Murmur in this future, Dungeon Lord. A bad idea, and that's an understatement. The Dark Father is patient with those who amuse him, but even his patience has a limit—and he can have quite the temper, once he gets going... I wonder what you did to earn his ire, though. This version of you seems to believe Murmur will invade your home plane."

Crazy homeless Ed was holding a cardboard sign. "He Comes," it said. "The End is Near! We Must Fight, Before it's too Late! Trust No One!" It seemed to be the source of Korghiran's assumption that Murmur had decided to invade Earth, and the real Ed saw no reason to believe otherwise. His card counterpart was trying to raise the alarm, rally the troops, and prepare some kind of defense. Obviously, people had thought him insane.

On the other hand, judging by the stains of indeterminate origin on his shirt and the half-empty bottle by his feet, perhaps future Ed *had* gone a bit crazy.

"It seems you didn't take well to being expelled from Ivalis," Korghiran said. "That's something for that Bard of yours to mull over, I'd say. Most heroes in the olden tales return to their homes after their quest is done, their adventure having changed them for the better, readying them to transform their villages in return. In your case, though... your Haunt *is* your home. It makes you wonder if you'd fit better the role of antagonist rather than of the spunky hero in Alder's chronicle, don't you agree?"

She laughed merrily at her own joke. Ed disliked her more and more by the minute. There was something deeply *cruel* about her that reminded him of Kharon, although the two couldn't have been more different, physically.

The third card showed only a black screen. Ed and Korghiran stared at it for a while, but it didn't change. Korghiran frowned and waved her hands at it, with no results. She raised one perfectly trimmed eyebrow. "A faulty card. Even an artifact of power such as the Shadow Tarot needs a tune-up every century or so, or this happens. My apologies, Lord Wraith. At least it's nothing to worry about. Let's say that in this branch, Objectivity erases you out of the tapestry of time after earning its ire one too many times. Boring, yet possible nonetheless."

Ed had to agree with the Regent on that.

She stacked the three cards back into the main deck of the Shadow Tarot and turned her attention to the remaining three.

"Are you feeling a little gloomy, Dungeon Lord? Watching yourself be executed or go insane can be demoralizing. But look here. In these three futures, you are triumphant! I saved them for last to erase the sour taste of your bad endings. Observe..."

The first image revealed a place deep underground, panning through a never-ending maze of passageways and empty cracked halls ravaged by a terrible battle fought long ago. Skeletons in rusty armor lay in heaps, their hands still clutching their broken weapons. The scene was lit by a magical gray-green light coming from a tall human figure roaming through the halls, passing through wall and stone as if they weren't there. This creature was covered by a tattered cloak that had been green in another lifetime, but which dried blood, gore, and murk had turned into a brownish black.

A wraith, Ed thought. The undead seemed unaware of everything, even itself. Something told Ed that it had been wandering like this, aimlessly, for years and years.

Then the creature turned back, as if to gaze directly at Ed, and Ed saw the faint, translucent layer of skin that surrounded the creature's charred skeleton, the same spectral features of Ed's cursed left hand.

"Behold, the Wraith Lord roaming his Haunt," Korghiran said. "Isn't he impressive? In this future, you *do* move past your gripes over using lethal force against the Inquisition—after your friends and allies are killed in a raid that you barely survive. To protect what remains of your home, you abuse Objectivity to its very limits, rake in thousands of experience points, and use your game knowledge to design a character sheet unlike anything modern Ivalis has seen. The Wraith Lord isn't fully undead, nor is he Dungeon Lord, nor human, yet is somehow greater than the three. His power may indeed rival that of some Demon Regents— just don't tell them I said that. Ha!" She tapped the card with a fingertip. "And look! The Wraith Lord rains doom upon those that defy him."

As she spoke, the Wraith Lord walked through a wall and came to a giant hall where a group of adventurers waited for him. They weren't the inhuman Heroes of the Inquisition, but real elves, humans, and dwarfs. Flesh and bone. They were armed to the teeth, but their faces seemed emaciated, ashen, and hopeless, as if they'd been roaming the Haunt for a long time.

Just how big is that place? Ed thought.

The Wraith Lord attacked without hesitation. The adventurers defended themselves—or tried to, at least. What followed could only be called a fight by the most lax definitions.

With a flick of his wrist, the Wraith Lord sent a river of gray fire that engulfed a stout dwarven Knight, ate at his defensive enchantments, and reduced him to a burned crisp all in the span of seconds. The other adventurers threw *fireballs* and advanced magic that Ed didn't recognize, but the spells died in the air long before they reached the Wraith Lord.

Another snap of the wrist, and the room itself came alive. Pillars of stone became as flexible as snakes and fell over the elven Cleric, the floor grew mouth and fangs and swallowed the Thief, and statues charged at the remaining warriors. One of them, a gnome girl, lost her nerve as her companions died around her, and she dropped her scepter and ran away, backing herself onto a corner in her panic. Dozens of spectral hands came out of the wall without warning, restrained her, and dragged her screaming and kicking into the stone, where she disappeared without a trace.

After the third flick of his wrist, there were no adventurers alive. The air in the hall had been transmuted into acid.

The Wraith Lord floated away as if nothing had happened while his dungeon corroded the corpses into nothingness.

"Isn't it inspiring? Don't you wish you could do *that* to your enemies *right now?*" Korghiran asked.

Ed was torn. Sure, the appeal of that kind of power was obvious. But the brutality... and the Wraith Lord didn't seem to possess a human mind or emotion anymore; he didn't even appear to be *aware* he had been fighting those adventurers. He simply soared through those empty stone halls, cold and alone, killing everyone who dared invade, as the centuries passed by.

How is that a victory? Ed thought. Whatever the Wraith Lord was, it wasn't Edward Wright.

Korghiran set the card away and selected the second one. "Ah, another promising branch. It seems that you're an ambitious fellow, Dungeon Lord. The ancients would've approved... before their own ambitions led to their downfall. But never mind that. This card is my favorite so far. The Unearthly Tyrant."

The man in the card donned a suit of black plate armor that covered him head to toe. Ed recognized the design as his own, albeit heavily upgraded. Gemstones as big as a fist were engraved in the chest plate and helmet, rubies and emeralds glinting over the polished sheen of the steel. His black coat was fit for a king, made with the pelts of mythical beasts and sewn with arcane silver patterns. The sword at his waist could've slain a giant, it was impossibly heavy and imposing, but the enchantments in future Ed's armor seemed to be able to handle the weight with ease.

This branch's Ed sat on a regal throne near an open window that showed a view of a city down below and a distant mountain pass beyond it. A castle, then, instead of a dungeon. And the throne room wasn't empty, but filled with sycophants and nobles dressed in rich garments. Some faces seemed vaguely familiar. Ed saw a few Akathunians in the crowd, as well as a minotaur with a web of blue tattoos covering his body. He spotted demons with purple or red hides and long, leathery wings, and vampires wearing white silk stained with crusty blood. There were Necromancers in their black tunics, as well as naga witches, and giant balloon-like monsters that floated lazily among the throne room. Kaftar guards protected future Ed's flanks, and a pair of old Wizards whispered advice in his ear.

"In this branch, you play smarter against your enemies. Instead of pursuing revenge and sheer destructive power, you become a political figurehead. With a little help from the Netherworld and a little training, you learn how to use your pact magic—the most dangerous tool of a Dungeon Lord—to subvert the ruling class of

Starevos. Instead of relying on dungeons and a few minions against the Heroes, you throw armies at them, bankrolled by Lotian coffers. After expelling the Militant Church from Starevos, it's the natural next step to take the throne. To maintain your power-base and popular support, you surround yourself with expert minions from Lotia and the Netherworld, and they teach you many things. And power comes with its own rewards. Observe. Here is the Unearthly Tyrant partaking of the spoils of the most recent war against his neighbors."

The scene changed, and an open vault with a shallow pool at its center replaced the throne room. The air was vaporous, like in a spa, with an exotic garden surrounding the pool. Silk drapes hung from ropes in rows all over the room and swayed with the breeze. Women danced between the drapes, their skins gently caressing the silk, their naked feet skirting over the paved floor. There were dozens of them, dressed only in their jewelry and scant garments that left nothing to the imagination. Long, thin golden chains shackled their necks and ankles.

Ed saw himself relaxing in the pool while young women massaged his shoulders and fed him fruit from clay bowls. This older Ed was pale and thin, with trimmed long hair and a goatee. He seemed to enjoy himself.

The real Ed couldn't take his gaze away from those golden chains. The smiles across the girls' faces was obviously forced, but the Tyrant seemed not to notice or care.

What the hell is he doing? Ed thought.

"You don't look so happy, Dungeon Lord," Korghiran said. "It's a bit late to pretend you're one of those chaste Heiligian heroes that your Bard loves to harp about, don't you think?

"Perhaps, at first, the Unearthly Tyrant had his reservations— just like you do. But armies need their supply lines. Akathunian slavers provided an inexpensive option, freeing your treasury for important uses like paying your minions and maintaining your power-base, or to keep the Starevosi from starving. Isn't that more important than what happens to a few slaves? Most of them are enemy soldiers, anyway. Without slaves, your kingdom would crumble, and thousands would perish. The women in your harem have it the best, really. They're pampered and cared after by your servants so they may serve you well in turn. Would you rather they take their chances on the streets below your palace? I bet they'd rather be a Tyrant's concubine than a sailor's whore, wouldn't you agree?"

Korghiran laughed, and Ed's blood boiled in his veins. That was one future that would never come to pass. The Shadow Tarot and Korghiran could go stick that card wherever it fit them best.

"Don't worry, Dungeon Lord. Your Netherworld minions will make you see reason, I'm sure," Korghiran said, amusement dancing in her expression. "One last future, will you? And then you're free to go. Let's take a look. Oh. What do we have here..."

The last card showed Ed in his Haunt, surrounded by his friends. Kes and Lavy, Alder and Klek, and many others. There were no golden chains anywhere in sight. They looked happy and healthy. Older. Ed didn't need to look at their character sheets to know that everyone there had at least a thousand experience points under their belts, and they were loaded with magical gear and artifacts of power.

It was the first of the futures that hadn't ended up worrying Ed. This seemed to displease Korghiran, who waved her hands over the card a couple of times until the scene changed.

Future Ed was sitting in a strange dungeon room loaded with bulky metal devices and glass screens hanging from the ceiling.

It can't be, Ed thought. Computers. Those things were crude computers. He saw vacuum tubes crackling with magical energy and electricity, bulbs transmuting themselves in different shapes as they processed data, long copper cables transmitting spells in and out of the room while the glass monitors displayed vast arrays of information and commands.

Two others were in the computer room along with future Ed.

The first one was a short, muscular man with strong shoulders and a light blond beard. He manned one steel and wood keyboard with a bit of difficulty.

Gallio, Ed thought. What was he doing in the middle of a dungeon? The Inquisitor didn't appear a captive. He was smiling and joking around with Ed and the third person in the room. This other man was a scrawny red-head with bad posture that sat cross-legged in his chair as his fingers flew along his own keyboard. He was dressed in a silk white shirt and black trousers, all in the style of Earth. He even had crude glasses.

Ed had never seen him before, but something about the red-head was vaguely familiar—although thinking too hard about it made Ed dizzy.

Future Ed pushed a switch and a sub-routine activated. The card changed views several times to show the cables crackling with magical energy through several internal tunnels until they arrived at a colossal open chamber with a tower at its center, raising past the ceiling and into the night sky. The tower activated and came to life, engines roaring and wheels turning. A crystal at its top lit up, as well as several interlocking magical circles on the floor and walls. Several glass coffins surrounding the tower powered on a series of runes drawn across their surface, and the surrounding air became oily and wavy.

"This is something that you don't see every day," Korghiran said. She tapped on the card with disapproval. "If most Demon Regents saw you working with an Inquisitor, even as just a possible future, they'd slay you where you stand. Although I admit, I'm curious. It's a terrible habit of mine. So let's dig deeper."

Back in the vision, the scene changed again with dizzying speed, until it settled on an entirely new place. A small dungeon was carved into the face of a mountain, decorated in a foreign manner that Ed didn't recognize. A Dungeon Lord with blazing red eyes sat in his Throne Room and dared a group of adventurers to move forward. The adventurers advanced, faces grim and weapons drawn, right as several Heroes dressed in black and white teleported to the middle of the room.

The Heroes attacked minions and adventurers alike with inhuman efficiency. Ed realized they were disabling everyone in the room without killing them. A few Heroes fell to traps or spells, but the instant they were downed they teleported away, and fresh reinforcements took their place. In a few seconds, they'd taken captive both the adventurers and the Dungeon Lord, shackled them with anti-spellcasting handcuffs, and Portaled out, leaving only a few very stunned and roughed-up minions, who stared dumbfounded at the space the Heroes had just vacated.

Ed realized he was just as dumbfounded as those minions.

The scene returned to future Ed's computer room, where he was celebrating with the other two.

In this future, Ed realized, there was no Inquisition. Not only had he defeated it, he'd replaced their cruel version of the Heroes with a new and improved one, using knowledge from both Earth and Ivalis. These new Heroes could stop any attack on the Haunt without risking the lives of anyone, and they could secure the Haunt's territories against any foe. They'd make the other Dungeon Lords—even the Militant Church—play nice.

They could bring peace.

He could bring peace to Ivalis. Not only could he side-step Murmur's wager, but destroy it. There was a chance, no matter how small it was, that Ed could achieve a decisive win against the Dark and the Light. This card was proof of it.

Korghiran snapped the card from the table and returned it to the Shadow Tarot. "We've seen enough for one vision, Lord Wraith. Before I return you to the material plane, let me give you a word of caution. Gazing into the future is dangerous. Striving too hard for a vision to come true may prevent it from happening altogether. It may fail anyway. You could fall down a flight of stairs tomorrow and die, and then all your cards would come up blank."

She waved him away, and Ed stood up at once. Even then, although he couldn't speak, she seemed to sense the question in his mind.

Why are you showing me all this?

"Because the best way to achieve a future you desire is to ally yourself with powerful friends," Korghiran told him with a sweet little smile. Behind her, the pyramid of cushions stirred, and she stood a few inches above the table. "And there's no friendship better for a Dungeon Lord than that of a Regent of the Netherworld."

She rose well past the height of a normal human being. The cushions rolled out as if the chamber was quaking, to reveal a sinuous serpent torso that extended for meters and meters until it fused seamlessly with Korghiran's waist. "Come to me, Dungeon Lord Wraith. Come to the Netherworld and ask for an audience with the Lady of Secrets. We'll see about forging a future that satisfies us both."

And with that, Ed was dragged away from the towering naga and back into his own body.

CHAPTER EIGHTEEN

BOUNDARIES

"That's one hell of a vision," Alder said once Ed finished telling his story.

He'd awakened in the real world a few hours before, his body already tingling with the power of his *improved spellcasting*. But before he'd ever chosen his two new spells, he'd called for his friends and gathered them into the War Room.

"You're telling me," Ed said. He was too excited to sit down, so he paced around the room like a threatened animal. "Was it even real?" he asked.

Lavy took a deep, steadying breath and threw a loose strand of hair away from her eyes. "Did you know of the Demon Regent Korghiran? Perhaps you heard about her and it influenced the vision."

"I'm pretty sure I didn't."

"In that case... she's real, I can at least tell you that. I've only heard about her in passing, but the naga spellcasters in Kael's dungeon worshiped her something fierce. They call her the Lady of Secrets because, well, she hoards them. She rewards those that tell her something she doesn't know, and the reward grows with the information's value. Her Warlocks are nosy assholes, for obvious reasons—Illusionists and Diviners, mostly. Chasan didn't like them—they always tried to steal his spell formulas."

"So, it happened," Ed said, scratching his chin.

"Not necessarily," Alder pointed out. "Visions can be tricky like that. They may show you things that are only *partially* correct--if that makes any sense. Hell, this vision where you saw your futures may have itself been a vision of a possible future, and that was why you couldn't speak or move."

Klek clutched his head. "This is making me dizzy."

"Same," Ed said. "It seems the only way to make sure is to go into the Netherworld and ask this Demon lady herself."

Kes frowned. "I don't like it. It's an obvious set-up. She showed you several futures, but only one *good* one. All others are dungeon-a-pie. Wraith Lord? Unearthly Tyrant? There's no way you're heading down either of those paths, Ed, not with us around."

Alder gave her a nervous smile. "Alita's tits, Kes, you don't tempt fate like that."

"I've seen too many friends with a bright future ahead of them get split in half by a minotaur's axe for me to give a flying fuck about fate's designs," Kes said sharply. She bit her lip and made a visible effort to calm down. "What I mean to say is… Korghiran wants to manipulate you, Ed. She wants you to come to her for help so you can get those *kemputers* of yours, but she'll use you to forge whatever future *she* wants instead."

Ed's jaw was clenched shut so hard he was getting a headache. He hadn't told his friends about the most unsavory details regarding the Wraith Lord or the Tyrant.

And why should I? They'll never happen, I'll make sure of it. And now I'm forewarned. Hadn't Korghiran said that the Shadow Tarot only showed the path his current and past decisions had set up for him? That meant he only had to make choices that led him to that third good future. *The only future that counts is the one I'll create.*

The alternative was just too terrifying to contemplate.

"Mortals can be so melodramatic sometimes," a voice said

amusedly, her words echoing as if coming from a great distance.

Ed's hand automatically grabbed his sword's handle and pulled an inch of steel out of its scabbard as he turned around toward the source of the sound. Klek and Kes did the same with their own weapons while Alder and Lavy jumped in their seats and stared in alarm at the purplish mist that seeped into the room through the crack of the door.

THE MIST LAUGHED and coalesced into a small human frame. Locks of hair so blond it was almost white appeared from the mist, followed by a burial dress, and a pair of long fangs like daggers. "Seriously, look at you," Jarlen said. "All grim and concerned about a bit of friendly Netherworldly politics."

"Nightshade. What do you want?" Kes asked, her hand still resting on her sword. "I don't recall you being invited to our meetings."

"I'm Dungeon Lord Wraith's most powerful minion," Jarlen said matter-of-factly. "Of course I should be here. If a *batblin* can attend... But never mind that. I was merely looking for Lord Wraith to inform him the materials are ready to create the Haunt's first Portal. It was a good thing I overheard your conversation, though, before a bunch of clueless mortals could confuse my Dungeon Lord about the way the world really works."

Lavy sniffed in indignation. "What the hell do you mean?" Her fingers twitched in the way they always did while she was preparing to cast a spell.

"Lavy," Ed warned her. The Witch lowered her arms, but didn't relax.

"*Of course* Regent Korghiran wishes to use you," Jarlen explained, ignoring Lavy as if she wasn't there. "She's a Regent, you're a Dungeon Lord. She uses you, you use her. It's just like in politics, or mating. Where did you think Dungeon Lords get their most powerful minions, from a board in a tavern? No. You go to the Netherworld, vie to earn the interest of a Regent, and find if there's something they desire that you can give them. In turn, they'll grant you minions and magical gear. It's not complicated."

"That's one ugly worldview, Jarlen," Alder told her, shaking his head.

"I see it how it is," Jarlen replied. "You've an advantage, Lord Wraith. Korghiran came to you, so that means you have something she wants. Use it. If you play your hand right, that's a golden chance to improve your standing that many other Dungeon Lords would kill for. For starters, you may find a sponsor willing to fix your weakness to Holy magic, in exchange for only one small, tiny favor."

Ed tapped his forehead with his finger. She was making one hell of a good argument. *Too* good, almost. But if she had some ulterior motive, wouldn't the minionship pact protect him from it?

"You care a lot about Lord Ed's trip to this Demon Lady," Klek said, voicing Ed's own concerns. "Why?"

Jarlen smiled. "Because if our Dungeon Lord thrives, I thrive. The way to succeed is to ally yourself to a powerful being, and there are few more powerful than Regent Korghiran. Perhaps your ambitions cloud your judgment, Lord Wraith. If you think you can score a better sponsor... there are ways. When the other Regents find out the Lady of Secrets is interested in you, they'll want to uncover why. Information is power, after all. You can use this, if you don't mind pissing off an insanely powerful demigod."

"I'm trying not to make a habit out of that," Ed said.

"So you don't deny it, vampire," Lavy said. "You want to use Ed so he can improve your lot for you."

"Isn't that exactly what you're doing, *Head Researcher?*" Jarlen asked mockingly, only now acknowledging Lavy's presence. "I can only fathom what a dungeon digger with *basic spellcasting* had to do to get into a prominent position in Lord Wraith's court."

The tension in the room turned sharp. Ed could see Lavy's

cheeks turning a bright pink as she stammered her way through a retort.

Ed didn't need Alder's Charm to know that Jarlen had found a sore point in Lavy's self-esteem and jabbed at it. A long time ago, Ed and Lavy had shared a bed. It had only happened once, during a time when the both were emotionally vulnerable and wondering if they'd live through the week. After that, they'd decided they worked better as friends.

Lavy had earned her position herself, by being there since the beginning, working day and night to make the Haunt something more than a glorified hole in the ground with a stone chair in the middle. She had no reason to mind Jarlen's words.

But does she know that? Ed wondered. Here was the Haunt, growing in size and power with every passing day, and now Ed had earned the interest of the same Regents that Kael Arpadel had allied himself with while Lavy and Alder were only apprentices.

And along came Jarlen, a newcomer, a creature who packed enough punch to fight everyone in the room—Ed included—and perhaps come out on top. It was little wonder that someone could feel inadequate in her presence. And perhaps a small part of Lavy *did* wonder if that night had influenced Ed's decision to name her Head Researcher.

The worst part was that he could even understand Jarlen's point of view. She was capable, experienced, and powerful, and yet she was being ignored in favor of others a tenth of her age.

Ah, shit. Reassuring people was Alder's specialty, not his. The problem was, he didn't have the patience to navigate the situation with anything resembling grace. Although... he had seen the hurt in Lavy's face, and he wasn't in the mood for a graceful approach.

Kes strolled toward Jarlen, but Ed beat her to the punch and stopped her with a firm palm on her arm. He faced the vampire instead, towering above her in a way that almost made him believe he was about to scold a ten-year-old instead of a murderous undead psychopath.

"Enough," he said, trying his best to keep a level head and failing, as evidenced by the green sparks flaring from his eyes. "You're not only insulting a trusted lieutenant, you're also insulting *me*. Your attitude is unacceptable, Jarlen of the Haunt. If you desire a better position, you can start by treating everyone in this room as if they were me—fuck it, make that every *single one of my minions.*"

Jarlen's eyes narrowed in fury. The way she looked at him was animalistic, the kind of rage that precluded guts being spilled on the floor. "Would you shame me—" she began.

Ed was too pissed to care about her pouting, vampire or not. "Shut up. You claim to be my best minion? Well, these *mortals* here fought a mindbrood alongside me, and they did it with two basic spells, a sword, a wooden stick, and a flute. Yes, Klek was there too! Where were you then, Jarlen? Where were you when we defeated a wraith and an invasion at the same time? Lavy was there, fighting and killing people with twice her experience points. Hell, you weren't exactly helpful when *we* saved *you* from the Inquisition!"

"That's not fair!" Jarlen snarled.

"These are my friends, Jarlen, I don't deny that," Ed went on, slowly replacing his anger with a firm sternness that a father may have used to correct a bratty kid. At least, that's what he hoped he was doing. "They're also my seconds-in-command for a reason. They've been with me since the beginning, and each one of them has put as much of themselves into the Haunt as I have. Insult them and you're insulting what the Haunt represents—and that won't help your standing with me, because I fucking *love* this Haunt. Do you want status? Then the smart thing to do would be to prove your worth. It may or may not be fair, but that's how you get *my* respect, Jarlen. Do you understand?"

A part of Ed wondered what would happen if the vampire laughed in his face and broke the minionship pact. Then they'd both be out of luck, because the Haunt needed Jarlen to enter the Netherworld safely, and she needed them to survive in Starevos.

But it was hard for him to expect a hundred-year-old vampire to see him as an authority figure for the same reason he would've hated Ryan's ten-year-old hypothetical manager.

On the other hand, he was a Dungeon Lord, and she was her minion, and in the end that out-weighed everything else. Jarlen backed down, shoulders slumped. "Yes. You've made your point, Lord Wraith," she said begrudgingly.

"Good," Ed said. "Then I think there's an apology you need to give."

Jarlen lifted an eyebrow in a way that made Ed wonder if he'd pushed too far. Then she turned to Lavy and forced a smile that, on her cold, dead, tiny face, looked like something out of a nightmare. "My sincere apologies, Head Researcher. It seems that my temper got the best of me. It won't happen again."

Judging from Lavy's expression right there, Ed was certain she wasn't about to be a gracious winner, so he threw her a glance that said, "Don't make me start on you *too*." Thankfully, she caught his look in time and clenched her mouth shut at the same instant she forced out a tight smile for Jarlen.

"Apology accepted," the Witch said. "Let's just start over, all right?"

"That would be much appreciated, Head Researcher," Jarlen said.

The tension in the room diminished, but not entirely. It was as if Ed had plugged a gas leak with a bit of gum and good intentions. The patch would hold for a while, but if he didn't find a better solution eventually, the results wouldn't be pretty.

His thoughts were interrupted when Alder clapped enthusiastically. "I'm so glad we're all friends now," he said. "How about we get to creating that door to Hell itself so we can buy some new spells and equipment? I've been waiting months for this trip, you know."

- Your skills have increased: Leadership +1. Your aura's energy expenditure has been reduced.

ED PLACED the Portal in a heavily trapped chamber far below the bowels of the Haunt. He and the others walked down a tight, damp tunnel that branched up to other two different tunnels on the way up, both of them looking identical to the real one. Either of those would lead an invading party straight to a reinforced door and a trapped lock with a sign hanging above, saying, "Welcome to the Haunt. We hope you have a great time." The doors led to one of the Haunt's several hell chicken farms, where Ed had asked Kaga to put their biggest, meanest, hungriest hell chickens. If the invading party survived, they'd cross the farm only to realize that the door on the other side of the farm was merely bolted to naked stone.

As they went down the tunnel, Ed summoned his Evil Eye and read the status update that showed him his options for his two new spells.

INVOKE THE STORM - This spell creates a black cloud with a radius of 5 feet (+1 feet per Improved Spellcasting skill rank to a maximum of 15) above your chosen area. After several seconds determined by your Combat Casting skill (starting at 10, reduced by each Improved rank to a minimum of 2), lightning strikes every creature under the cloud. This lightning kills any creature with an Endurance below 8, and severely damages everyone else. Survivors must bypass an Endurance test to avoid temporary paralysis, and will receive a penalty to their Agility instead.

Dungeon Message - This spell allows you to send a 140—character message to any minion of the caster located anywhere on the same plane as the casting Dungeon Lord. The message is sent through the link between minion and Dungeon Lord, and as such, cannot be replicated by others. (Warning: this does not stop a minion with a very low Mind score from being tricked by non-magical means.)

Fireball - The caster launches a sphere of concentrated explosive energy toward the general direction of the target. Accuracy is improved by the user's Combat Casting.

Rune of Protection - The caster engraves an almost invisible rune on any surface. This rune lasts 1 year (plus 1 year for every Combat Casting skill rank). If a creature with a Mind score above 5 that is not the caster sees the rune, it triggers a small explosion and forces the creature (if still alive) to bypass an Endurance test or be rendered unconscious for five minutes.

If this spell is cast by a Dungeon Lord, they can choose to make any minions unable to activate *or* be affected by the rune.

Stone Pillar - The Dungeon Lord targets an area of solid ground of 5 feet radius which, after 3 seconds, bursts upwards in the shape of a stone column, rising to 20 feet or until it reaches a ceiling. This effect is limited by the availability of material in the chosen area and cannot be used to create matter out of nothing.

If the Dungeon Lord has an Improved Combat casting above 5, the channeling time is reduced to 2 seconds.

Engorge Vermin - A creature under the command of the Dungeon Lord is engorged up to the size of an adult wolf. Any creature larger than an adult wolf is not affected by the spell.

Warning: Attempts to exploit this spell are notorious for earning the attention of Objectivity with more regularity than other Improved-ranking spells for unknown reasons. Exploit at your own risk.

Invisibility - The caster and everything they are wearing are rendered invisible for 1 minute (+1 for every Improved Spell-casting skill rank). They are also blind for the duration of the spell unless possessing non-natural means of sight. They can still be detected by creatures that don't rely on sight to target their prey.

"Dungeon Lords get so many good choices for free," said Lavy at about the same time Ed was done reading. She was glancing over his shoulder at the ethereal words floating in front of him with a gleam of jealousy in her eyes that she didn't even bother to hide. "At least you don't have any Witchcraft or Necromantic spells in there or I admit I'd be pissed."

Jarlen looked back and took a few seconds to read the sheet as well. "That's because the free spells are constrained by the Dungeon Lord's skill ranks at the moment of upgrading *spellcasting*. Some even postpone their advancement for years until they grind out very obscure skills so they can get secret spells for free that would otherwise be almost impossible to find."

"Do you have any examples?" Ed asked her. As a gamer, he salivated at the chance of obtaining some ultra-secret, bragging-rights spell that no one else had.

"Sadly, it's not the kind of thing that Dungeon Lords share with their minions," Jarlen said. "I know that your *Murmur's reach* is reasonably rare, if that helps. It's a quest reward that Murmur or his Regents give to a Dungeon Lord that performed a useful service for the Dark. Regent Faranghis has one such reward. *Shadow tentacles*, an Improved-ranked spell with many uses, both in combat and recreation. Care to guess a few of its uses?"

"I'd rather not," Lavy said. "I know what Faranghis is Regent of."

No one dared inquire any further.

Just as the silence was getting rather heavy, Klek said, "*Engorge vermin* sounds nice. If Tulip and I were the size of a wolf, we could fight so much better."

"No way you qualify as a vermin," Ed said.

"I wouldn't mind being a vermin if that meant I get to be as big as a wolf," Klek said hopefully.

Kes raised an eyebrow. "Even without a single rank in spell-casting I could bet my ass that trying that stunt gets you Objectified instantly."

The batblin seemed crestfallen. "Perhaps there's another spell that buffs you, bud," Ed assured him. "If there is, I'll get it as soon as I can. Deal?" Klek nodded with enthusiasm.

"*Engorge vermin* seems like such a useless spell," Lavy said. "You can only use them on thunder wasps and acid oozes and the like? It should be a basic spell—there's no way it's as strong as *fireball*! Why does Objectivity even care that people abuse it?"

"I'm not sure that Objectivity cares about anything at all," Alder mused. "It's a set of rules that regulates the use of magic, the way I understand it. No feelings involved."

"The way *I* see it," Lavy said, "it's probably a divine asshole like Alita or Murmur. Probably one that hates magic-users and wants to make our life a living hell. It'd be nice to, for once, interpret a spell with an iffy description without having to look over my shoulder and wonder if I'm gonna get erased from existence."

Every spell-caster in the tunnel—Ed, Alder, and even Jarlen—nodded in solidarity.

"Well, in *engorge's* case I see why Objectivity activates easily," Ed said. "Without the warning, I'd have instantly picked it. Bend the description a bit and it's a killing machine."

"I really hope you aren't about to make a terrible sex joke," Alder said. "Because that's my job—*ow!* Hey!" He gave Lavy an offended glance as he held his soon to be bruised ribs.

Ed shook his head while Kes rolled her eyes and masked her chuckles with a cough. "Say there's someone powerful you want to kill," Ed said. "Like... another Nicolai. First, I'd *Murmur's reach* a spiderling, and I'd carefully skitter into his nostril or ear while he's distracted. Then I'd end *Murmur's reach* and cast *engorge vermin* on the spiderling. I'm pretty sure you can't regenerate from *that*."

Jarlen gave him an appreciative nod. "That's brutal, Lord Wraith."

"Also messy," Lavy pointed out. "I'd rather destroy my enemies with beautiful, *elegant* witchcraft."

"So, although I like the spell, it's probably best not to tempt Objectivity. There's no way I'd be able to resist playing around with it," Ed said. "What about the others?"

"No idea," Alder said happily. "I just want to congratulate you on upgrading your Spirit, because when I met you, you would've gotten the spell immediately and already tried to raise an army of trained, giant fleas."

Ed grinned. "Well, fuck you too. Also, that's not a bad idea at all."

"*Message*," Kes said. "Get *dungeon message*. I don't care what else you do, get that one."

"You're kidding, right?" Lavy said. "*Message* is *definitely* a bloated basic spell. You're saying that a hundred and forty words is worth a damn Improved spell slot? No way, not with *Fireball* around! You can't say anything of use in so few words, anyway. Perhaps if the spell had *twice* as many letters allowed *and* you'd already gotten all other Improved spells beforehand."

"Actually," Ed pointed out, "it says 'characters,' not words. So 'Lavy' is already four characters."

"That's way worse!"

Kes shrugged. "It's the middle of the battle, everything is chaos and confusion, and your reserve shock cavalry Captain gets a voice straight into her brain saying, 'Left flank is being overrun. Reinforce immediately,' then proceeds to save the entire battle with a single, well-timed charge. This Dungeon Lord version of *message* cannot be intercepted, decoded, or compromised—for just an Improved spell slot? Sounds like a huge bargain to me. There are a few generals in the Cardinal Command who would sell their firstborn for it."

"Uh," Alder said, scratching his chin. "That's a great point, Kes. It's just... *message* is so boring..."

"I think I'm with Kes on this one," Ed said. "I bet that every general and their mothers use dozens—if not hundreds—of *message* runes in every battle. Boring or not, it's too useful to ignore." Thankfully, he already had a bit of practice working around the 140-character-limit.

"I feared you'd say that," Lavy said. "What about the other spell?"

"Get *stone pillar*," Jarlen said. "Don't bother choosing the most useful spell. *Stone pillar* and *dungeon message* are both very hard to find. *Pillar* is mostly for dwarven Power Levelers and Dungeon Lords, and *dungeon message* is for Dungeon Lords only. In the future, you should choose all your spells this way, Lord Wraith, and have your Head Researcher buy the other spells in the Netherworld and teach them to you. Teaching spells will also increase her own skills, so it's an easy way to train your spellcasters."

Lavy cleared her throat nervously. "Of course. I knew that."

"Of course, Head Researcher. I'm but humbly helping you save your breath for much more important matters—those worthy of your time."

Alder and Ed exchanged a glance, and Ed wondered just how high Jarlen's brown-nosing skill was. At least her trying this route was much better than her former attitude.

It's jarring, though, seeing how fast she changed her personality when she realized she couldn't get rid of Lavy the other way, Ed thought. He had to remember that both personalities belonged to the same actress playing different roles. Jarlen would do or say anything to further her stance in the Haunt, and it was Ed's job as a Dungeon Lord to make sure that the best way for her to grow in power was also the most beneficial one for the Haunt and its inhabitants.

I will need to grind more Charm, he thought as he selected the two new spells and the information about how to cast them flowed into his brain with a pleasant tingle. He decided to ask Alder for help when they had some free time, although he dreaded to think of the possible ways the Bard could train him.

CREATING a Portal wasn't as simple as just creating the room using Mantle magic. To start, it required a Dungeon Upgrade with a cost of one hundred Vyfaras, which wasn't too much of a hit now that half of Undercity's cutthroats were drinking the Haunt's brew, but the actual materials were also hard to find. At Ed's command, rows of drones came in and out of the chamber carrying stacks of metal ingots easily taller than their heads.

The drones didn't seem bothered by the fact that they were nonchalantly hauling several times their weight, although a drone was pretty much useless in a fight and far weaker than any other minion around, excluding spiderlings. When something was directly related to dungeon-building, the drones' magic seemed to boost them way beyond their normal limits.

Along with the drones, a small contingent of minions slowly arrived, all geared up and ready to go. They'd be Ed's escort during his time in the Netherworld. Although arriving in a Regency was safer than Portaling into a random zone of the Netherworld, there was still the risk of a rival Dungeon Lord—or any other type of Dark creature, really—seeing an opening and trying to test their luck.

Kaga, Yumiya, and the other seven Monster Hunters led the group. They were dressed in their best garments, with colorful tunics and clean weapons and armor. One of the trip's objectives was to find a martial instructor for the kaftar, of an art in which they weren't already experts themselves.

Klek and Tulip led their Spider Riders, with the batblins doing their best not to look terrified and failing spectacularly. Their spiders tried to keep them in line, with varying degrees of success.

Kes' group of trained guards were there too. Technically, they weren't supposed to leave the dungeon, but she wanted for them to gain experience—the normal kind—and perhaps build up their confidence. The group had trained for a few months now, and looked slightly better than they had when they'd first volunteered, although Ed hoped they wouldn't have to test their skills in a fight.

Finally, six horned spider warriors which had been loaned to Ed from the cluster empire's royal guards rounded up the detachment.

With Lavy and Jarlen as damage dealers and Alder buffing everyone's stats, the group wasn't shoddy at all. A veteran Dungeon Lord with thousands of experience points would still steam-roll them, but it was impossible to prepare for every danger. At some point, Ed had to cross his fingers and hope for the best.

The ingots slowly grew in several piles in front of the chamber's walls. Three out of four ingots were cold iron, the rest silver. Cold iron, according to Jarlen, was a metal that was naturally found in the Netherworld and was crafted in Ivalis by infusing normal iron with a mineral found in soil poisoned by Netherworldly crops. This mineral was wet and oily and, when distilled, looked like something taken out of the lung of a horned spider. It smelled like that, too. Ed's best guess was that it was a concentrated residue of the dark emanations.

Heorghe had needed several attempts at getting the proportions of mineral and iron just right, but once he'd gotten the hang of it, he insisted it was relatively simple to make. Beside using it to build Portals, cold iron was needed in item enchanting and ring-making. Cold iron was cheaper and faster than following the Heiligian way—which involved lots of silver and gold—but the items crafted with it were vulnerable to Holy magic.

After the cold iron and the silver, the drones brought a small coffer with rough rubies from the treasury. Rubies were extremely illegal in all Heiligian-controlled territories, with squads of Treasury Diviners constantly tracking any smuggling attempt. This strained the crown's coffers, but it was a necessary expense to stop Dungeon Lords from creating a vast networks of Portals that would make them almost impossible to catch.

So, with no rubies in Undercity's black markets, the Haunt had had to rely on the drones' natural instinct of finding mineral veins to slowly build up its supply. The problem was, even with the drones' magical senses, Starevos simply lacked a high enough concentration of rubies for Ed to make many Portals.

Right now, he could afford this one and, with luck, a second one in a few weeks.

According to Jarlen, Lotia was the happy owner of the two of the three main ruby mines in Ivalis. Lotia traded part of these rubies to the Netherworld in exchange for gold and favors. In the Netherworld, the rubies were hoarded by the Regents and used as payment to their favored Dungeon Lords. These Lotian rubies were, of course, enchanted against Heiligian scrying the same way Vyfaras were.

The gemstone trading was only a part of the complex, inter-locked economy that pulled the Netherworld and Lotia into a sort of mutually beneficial relationship. Jarlen's unvoiced implication had been that Ed himself ought to benefit from it, with the help of a suitable sponsor.

Ed grabbed one ruby from his hard-earned pile of gems and studied it, shifting it so it caught the light of the torches from several angles. *It seems that quite a few people have been trying to nudge me toward the Netherworld Regents lately. Kharon, Korghiran, even Jarlen.* In his experience, there were no such thing as coinci-dences when dealing with the Dark's machinations. If everyone insisted on him finding a Dark sponsor, it was because Murmur, directly or indirectly and for unknown reasons, wanted him to do it.

He hid the ruby in a fist and sighed. His first reaction would've been to flatly refuse to go, like a child rebelling against a parent just for disobedience's sake. The problem was, it was more complicated than that. If he never stepped into the Netherworld, he'd stunt his growth as a Dungeon Lord. He'd never gain access to most spells, specialist minions, room layouts, traps, enchanted items, and so on. He'd be easy prey to the Inquisition and Heroes, and it'd be flat-out idiotic to have a go at them without help.

The help, though, would come from pretty unsavory characters. If the Regents and Kharon were related, Ed doubted they were nice people at all. And the Lotian Dungeon Lords weren't exactly care-bears. Slavery, human sacrifices, murder, and debauchery were the favorite hobbies of the other Dungeon Lords. Lavy had told him that not *every* single one of the Lotians were assholes, but those that weren't didn't have many friends, weren't as strong, and had fairly low life expectancies.

In an ideal world, Ed would be able to find those Dungeon Lords and build his own faction. The plan was to test the waters first, before making a ruckus that would direct the Lotians' attention to himself.

Having his mind set on his objectives and the reasons he was pursuing them was his best shot at avoiding Murmur's manipulation. And Ed knew exactly what he wanted. He wanted to find out who had created the Heroes—that man he'd seen along with Gallio and himself in the Shadow Tarot—and Ed wanted to explain his side of the story to him.

It was clear now that the Heroes had been created by someone summoned from Earth. Someone who knew his computers, and who had used the Inquisition's resources to design the Heroes. He'd tested them against the Lotian Dungeon Lords over and over, improved them, ironed out their flaws, and then streamlined them.

For some reason, he'd also decided that it was best to leave their control to gamers from Earth instead of training the Inquisitors in their use. Ed could make a few guesses as to why—if it was hard for some middle-aged people to use a computer, what those people from a magical realm who had never even seen a keyboard in their lives?

Knowing this gave him hope. Someone from Earth—a programmer like him—would be willing to hear him out, because he would lack the years of indoctrination that the Militant Church instilled upon its Inquisitors. And if Ed and him were to join forces... the result could be amazing. Dungeon Lord magic improving the Heroes would, without a doubt, shake Ivalis' power balance to its core. Ed had a chance to change the world for the better, and he wasn't the kind of person to sit on his ass and let the opportunity slip away.

For better or for worse.

He only needed to find that person from Earth and let him know Ed existed. And what better way to start than by making a bit of noise?

He tossed the ruby into the pile. "Okay, everyone, step back," he said as he cleared his mind of worries. "Materials can go flying around during room transmutation, so be careful. I don't want any to get wounded before we enter the Portal."

After the last batblin was at a safe distance, Ed activated his Evil Eye and found the nearest ley line—a faint undercurrent of raw magical power flowing through the earth like blood through veins. He then summoned a list of his available room designs, which appeared in the same bright green lettering as his character sheet. He navigated through it: Barracks, Hell Chicken Farms (Black and Gray), Scrambling Towers, walls, traps, Quarters, Storages, Vampire Den, Crypts, Prison, Torture Chamber (this one was unused), Training Hall, Libraries, Kaftar Dens, Batblin Quarters, and Kitchens.

Once he'd found the Portal design, he super-imposed it on the empty chamber and focused his will to imprint the design on the stone. At once, his drones set to work. They chirped with excitement and began their eerie dances across the room. Through his improved Evil Eye, Ed could follow the transmutation with a degree of detail he hadn't been able to before.

The ley line flared as if reacting to the drones' dance. Slowly, a small fork in the river of energy extended toward the chamber and connected itself to it. At once, an almost invisible flood of raw power poured with high speed into the room—something that Ed hadn't seen before. The intensity took him by surprise and he took a step back, which earned him a couple confused stares from his minions. It appeared he was the only one seeing it.

The magical energy prickled his skin and made his tongue tingle, but it didn't seem to be harmful. The drones' dance grew in intensity and the current took the shape of a spiral in the middle of the room, like an invisible tornado. The energy condensed at the drones' command, and tendrils became tongues of black smoke that reached for the materials strewn across the room like eager fingers. The mist resembled the emanations from the Netherworldly plants. It carried metal, wood, and gemstones around the room like they weighed nothing, and poured itself into them.

The materials began to change. They melted together, glowing bright with eldritch energy, changing shape and size before being propelled into place by the mist.

Chandeliers sprouted from the floor like plant stalls, already complete with burning candles. The floor by the center shook and trembled, and a raised circular dais grew from three steps. Liquid metal poured itself in an arc at the center of the dais, slowly casting itself into the shape of a circle's perimeter, big enough to reach the ceiling and with a metal base to steady it. Steel cables extended from the walls and connected themselves to the Portal, as runes etched themselves on its surface, forming a complex web. Ed raised an eyebrow. There was something familiar about the shape of the Portal, but he couldn't quite put his finger on it yet. A dozen rubies etched themselves onto the Portal, and the mist seemed to be finished with it. A metal control panel sprouted a few feet past the dais. A carpet unfurled out of thin air and violently covered the floor, only barely giving everyone time to step over it. Finally, the mist disappeared as the drones' dance reached its end. The ley line and its smaller fork flared one last time, and then returned to normal—although Ed was sure there was a tiny reduction in its size and flow, which was now being used to power the room.

Once their job was done, the drones began adding details and decorations to the room, half of them by transmuting left-over materials directly, and the rest by running out of the chamber, only to return eerily fast carrying objects from storage, like tapestries and small busts. Ed noted that a couple of the busts and the statues hadn't been made by drones, but by the Haunted citizens.

The drones would work for days on end, getting the feel of the Portal room just right. It was the first impression any newcomer would get of the dungeon, and it was important for it to be just right. Friendlies should feel awed and impressed, and rivals should be properly intimidated.

As the drones fitted a couple black-flame braziers on the hands of six stone knights set on the sides of the carpet that extended from the Portal to the entrance, Ed realized why the Portal's concentric rings looked familiar.

"Does every Portal look like that?" he asked aloud.

"I don't think so," Lavy said. "Kael's was carved with the Arpadel coat-of-arms, and Heines' was like a wolf's open mouth."

"The Head Researcher is correct, Lord Wraith," Jarlen said graciously. "Why do you ask?"

"Don't worry about it," Ed said with a dismissive wave. If the dungeon designs were influenced by the Dungeon Lord's mind, it was no wonder that Ed's Portal resembled a damned Stargate.

Even the control panel was familiar, although the runes were Ivalian. Jarlen strolled behind it, then inspected it until she was confident enough to try a couple shifts on its command wheel. "I know the location of three territories, Lord Wraith—Xovia, Raaga, and Bregor. They were Dungeon Lord Jiraz' favored hunting grounds. Raaga is too dangerous for your current power. On the other hand, Bregor would be a waste of your time, since it's mostly visited by beginning Dungeon Lords who wish to gather oozes and dagger wasps. Xovia is a nice middle-ground. There's a hub of trade at its core, surrounded by wildlands filled with useful monsters to populate a dungeon. I humbly suggest we head there first."

Ed looked at Kes. "What do you think?"

"It sounds reasonable," Kes said. "Except the wildland part. I'd like to stay away from those, if we can help it."

"Xovia it is," Ed said.

"As you wish," the vampire said.

She input a series of commands on the wheel, then pushed it down firmly. The air around the Portal flowed with magical energy. Instinctively, Ed and the others took a step back as the rings of the Portal shifted and the rubies glowed a bright crimson. A distant hum vibrated through the chamber, filling everyone's ears, as reality inside the Portal's rings was torn open with a red flash.

Behind Ed, one of the kaftar barked an impressed laugh. Instead of the stone wall, the space was now replaced by a slab floor strewn with rubble and grime, a cracked wall with burnt-out torches, and the howl of the wind through a distant passageway. The air was tinted crimson, and carried the smell of sulfur.

Ed checked his weapons and pushed his cape back, making sure he had easy access to his sword's handle in case something awful was waiting at the other end of the Portal.

"We'll go first," Klek announced suddenly. Next to him, Tulip gave him a worried snap of her mandibles, and the Spider Riders shifted nervously in their saddles.

"Thank you, Klek, but I think the honor should be mine this

time," Ed said, grinning with a confidence he didn't feel. "I can't let you hoard all the experience points, now, can I?"

Although the rational course of action would've been to send the kaftar or the spider guard first, Ed knew how important it was that his minions—his people—knew he was willing to take the same risks they'd face. But, even beyond that, on a visceral level, he simply wasn't willing to let Klek risk his life for him in such a way. Rational or not, when faced with the dark unknown, Ed needed to be the one leading the charge.

"Be careful," Kes said. "We'll be right behind you." She patted him on the shoulder as if she could read his thoughts.

Jarlen groaned. "There's no need to be so... melodramatic, my Lord. This watchtower was built by Jiraz' grandfather and should still be protected from incursions by Jiraz' mercenaries for a month or two per their contract. I know these men, and I'll convince them to let us through without issue. We'll be perfectly safe, I assure you."

There was a poignant silence after that, only broken by the dull thud of Alder smacking his forehead with his palm.

"Right," Ed said. He quietly drew his sword and made sure his helmet was properly fitted.

He strolled into the unknown, the weight of his armor feeling like a comfortable promise of protection against any danger. As his foot crossed the Portal, he couldn't help but remember that first Portal he'd stepped through, a long time ago, when Kharon had sent him into a dilapidated cave in time to save a Witch and a Bard from a rabble of angry batblins. Thinking of the Boatman reminded him how there were dangers in Ivalis against which no enchanted armor could stand. As he crossed the boundary of the Netherworld, he felt as vulnerable as he'd been on that first day in a strange new world.

His intuition turned out to be right. Not five seconds after stepping into Jiraz' watchtower, Ed was already covered in blood.

CHAPTER NINETEEN

RIDING THE CINDERPEDE

I t happened in the silence between heartbeats. Ed saw a rush of movement bouldering toward him, a heavy club hefted above a scaly gray head, and his body reacted before his mind could. He lifted his longsword, both hands above his left shoulder and the steel tip aimed chest-high, as he took a heavy step forward and readied his knees.

The impact surprised him as much as it did the creature. He felt resistance as his steel encountered flesh, and then there was wet, sickening pressure as the sword bit past skin and muscle. Ed found himself face to face with a very confused, bald humanoid creature, with a head like a huge battered potato—only uglier. It had flat, rotten teeth and tiny eyes almost hidden by an over-grown forehead.

Ogre, Ed's brain helpfully provided instead of something less useful, like a battle-plan.

Both ogre and Dungeon Lord examined the foot of steel protruding from the ogre's belly. Ed had aimed as high as his own chest, which meant—

With a furious, pained grunt, the ogre rose to his full height—two heads taller than Ed—with foam bubbling from his oversized mouth. With one burly hand, the creature raised his club again, and with the other he reached for Ed's sword.

The Dungeon Lord reacted, once again, with training honed into instinct through sheer repetition. He pulled back with all his strength, ripping his blade out of the body with a burst of blood and steaming meat, then used the motion to power a downward slash that stamped a terrible wound into the ogre's shoulder, right next to its neck. A fountain of blood sprayed upward, then the ogre's club thundered against Ed's side and crashed him into the ground like a rag-doll.

There was a flash of light. Ed sprang to his feet, still holding his sword. *That hit just broke all your ribs,* he told himself. *Probably also collapsed a lung.* He wondered if Andreena's herbs could heal one of those.

He took a deep breath and regained his stance. Strangely enough, he could breathe just fine. More than that, unless the adrenaline was masking his wounds, he was barely bruised at all.

Right. Magic armor. It seemed like the *pledge of armor* talent was worth its weight in gold.

The ogre wasn't faring as well. He was holding his innards in with one hand, and his other arm was slick with blood pouring from the wound on his shoulder.

Since nothing was charging at him at the moment, Ed took a chance to gaze at the chamber he was within. He saw an uneven, obsidian-like floor with stalagmites growing several feet upward. Five more ogres were frozen in surprise around a shoddy camp built out of rocks and twigs, with their even shoddier weapons laying next to them. All wore dirty loincloths, but the females had tits like huge, hairy tents of skin flapping down to their bellies, which Ed was sure was a sight that would come back to haunt him as soon as he tried to sleep.

He glanced back at the ogre that had attacked him. He was probably a sentinel, left to guard the Portal's entrance. The

Dungeon Lord smiled. "I don't know if you can understand me, but I'm giving you one last chance to surrend—"

Then the Portal behind him flared to life with several bursts of sulfur and red light, and many things happened at once, the end result of which were several dead ogres.

A dozen magical purple crows flapped over the ogres' heads, pecking at them as Alder's magical clones ran around looking confused. The horned spiders surrounded Ed while Kes sprang next to his side and thrust the tip of her sword into the wounded ogre's eye without saying a word. Klek and his riders charged through the ogres' midst while they were distracted by the illusions and the crows, and webbed their weapons away from their reach right as Kaga and his Monster Hunters rushed into the fray and slashed at necks and tendons with their scimitars, cackling like madmen as they went through their bloody work.

It was a massacre.

Only one lonely ogre reacted fast enough to do anything at all, and she ran away through a shadowy exit with a broken door laying at one side. A burst of thick mist snaked through the air after her. Both were out of view when the ogres' screaming began —and then ended.

Ed and his minions stared at each other through ragged breaths. Ed realized everyone there was as surprised as he was. The battle hadn't even lasted half a minute. He had lacked the time to activate his *improved reflexes* or think about casting a spell. Hell, to think of it, if it weren't for Kes' training, the ogre would've clonked him on the head and probably permanently wounded him before anyone had time to help. It was a sobering idea, and a great motivation to not slack off during the next sparring session.

Kes shuffled next to him, her sword still at the ready. "Told you I'd be right behind you," she said.

Ed nodded. "You stole my kill, though."

"Bah, I'm sure there's a wraith somewhere for you to attempt to solo."

Behind him, Kes' new recruits shuffled forward, their spears shaking in their hands. They looked incredibly out of place in the middle of the carnage. One of them poked at Ed's dead ogre with her spear, seemingly disappointed.

After them came Lavy and Alder. "What were those things?" Alder asked. "I didn't even had time to study their character sheets."

"Ogres," Ed said. It was strange to know something about Ivalis that the Bard didn't. "A few Dungeon Lords used them in Ivalis Online. At higher levels, they can cast spells and wear armor. These had weapons fashioned out of bone and rotten wood, though. They don't strike me as minions of anyone."

"So much for 'We'll be perfectly safe,'" Lavy muttered. She smoothed a non-existent crease in her dress. "At least you had me backing everyone up. Where's Jarlen, by the way?"

The vampire returned through the exit where the ogre and the mist had left. Her burial dress was slick with greasy blood and bits of meat, as was half her face. She walked happily through the dead ogres and their ravaged camp site. A few of the Monster Hunters reached for their weapons when she passed them.

"Anyone called for me, my dears?" Jarlen sang. Her belly was bloated like a balloon, and her cheeks had a cozy pink color to them. She belched wetly, and one of Kes' recruits heaved as if trying not to puke.

Ed barely passed an Endurance test to not follow suit. *Whoever said that vampires were sexy should have a long chat with Jarlen,* he thought.

"Lavy's right," Kes said, strolling angrily at the vampire. "You told us the entrance would be protected." She jabbed the stump of her index finger at Jarlen. "Did you lead us into a trap, vampire?"

"How in Murmur's name could I have? I'm a minion!" Jarlen snapped, then she visibly withheld herself. "Beg your pardon, Marshal Kessih, this was my mistake. I thought the mercenaries hired by Dungeon Lord Jiraz would honor their contracts until their time ran out. I was obviously wrong about their loyalty."

"Obviously," Kes said, but her animosity had run out. She gestured at the rest of Ed's entourage. "Everyone, take your positions! We don't know if there's any more of those minotaur droppings waiting in ambush. If anyone's hurt, say so now."

No one was. The group hurried to heed her call, except for one batblin who was busy looting a dead ogre. His spider dragged him back to the other riders before Kes had time to single him out, however.

"What do you know about them?" Ed asked Jarlen, pointing at the corpses. For his kill, he'd gotten ten experience points, but the batblins and the kaftar had earned far more than that.

"As you said—ogres," Jarlen prattled on, clearly happy to change the subject away from her mistake. "Natives of the Netherworld, technically a minor form of demon, like imps—or drones. The word is, they were created by Regent Volkhan, Lord of Strife, to use as disposable shock troops in the Age of Myths. Afterward, they sort of... spread around. They're very hard to get rid of, like batblins. This lot here was a group of young ones, they must've been looking for refuge from a bigger threat and found the watchtower empty. They're not very smart, but have a primitive understanding of combat. Killing is basically the only thing they're good at."

Ed felt a pang of guilt. Young ogres, hiding from the dangers of the Netherworld, and he'd slain them without a single chance at surrender. *On the other hand, they* did *attack first.* His empathy could only extend so far, and although it pained him to admit it, the fact that they were butt-ugly helped a lot to dehumanize them.

"I see. Anything else?" he asked.

"They're brutes, but breed enough of them and you may get a natural spellcaster once in a while. Otherwise, fatten them up, get a dozen to gain enough experience points, have them buy defensive talents, and clad them in the heaviest armor you can find.

Natural siege-breakers. Have them charge at any structure—or, well... anything smaller than a city, really—and they'll tear it apart. Not particularly useful against Heroes, at least in small numbers. Then again, nothing is."

"Noted," Ed said. "How many do we need to start... ah... to grow them in the Haunt?"

Jarlen shrugged. "I lack expertise in that area, Lord Wraith. Two, perhaps?"

"I'm sure it doesn't work that way," Ed said, cringing inwardly. Inbreeding probably wouldn't help the poor fucks' looks.

"Your orders, Dungeon Lord?" Kes said, using her formal tone.

This is real, Ed thought. Since he was the one calling the shots, the lives of everyone here were his responsibility. *Wetlands, when did* that *happen?* "Like you said, we don't know if there are more of them, so we secure the place," he told Kes. "If there's any remaining ogres, try to capture them instead. Don't risk yourselves for it, though."

Kes nodded, then began barking orders. "Monster Hunters, you're on trap-finding duty, good luck. Use the spiderlings to stay in touch. Klek, you and Tulip use that *echolocation* trick of yours and pinpoint anything that moves that isn't us. Spider Guard, you know what to do—nothing gets near to our Dungeon Lord. Casters—that includes you, Jarlen—we assist the Hunters in putting our new ogres to sleep. Haunted guards... you stay here and protect the Portal. If we come back running and screaming for our lives, you have my permission to do the same." She clapped several times to hurry them. "All right, everyone got it? Then hop to it, earn those experience points!"

Seeing them spring to action and work in unison awoke in Ed something akin to pride. The idea that they *hadn't* been fighting together as a unit for years was almost unbelievable. It made him proud to be part of the reason they were working together. Batblins, humans, kaftar, spiders, avian, even a vampire now. They formed the Haunt. *His* Haunt.

The idea made him so elated that he almost didn't care that every single one of them would be stealing his kills.

In the end, there weren't even that many kills to steal. Klek and Tulip reported only three remaining ogres, who were scattered through the watchtower's upper level as sentinels. They'd heard the ruckus below and had been waiting in ambush behind a barreled door. There were other creatures around, critters and beast-like demons, but they'd run away the second Ed's forces got near them.

That was disappointing. Monsters were supposed to go *toward* the adventurers, not away from them. But it made sense, as Ed had to remind himself. After all, he wasn't an adventurer. He was a Dungeon Lord, and his group was technically a raiding party more than an adventuring group. Hell, they were a few dozen members away from being a warband. Of course anything with a Mind above five would run at the sight of them.

- Ogre. Exp: 200. Brawn: 18, Agility: 10, Spirit: 8, Mind: 4, Charm: 4, Endurance: 16. Skills: Melee: Improved V, Survival: Basic V. Talents: Armored Hide, Magical Resistance (Basic).

Once the Monster Hunters cleared the first level of traps, Ed's party set to dealing with the ambush. Since the upper level's floor was built out of wood, Ed had them take position in a ring beneath the ogres above. The spiders drew a huge web net dangling from the ceiling, the kaftar prepared their sleeping darts, and the rest raised a couple of Lavy's runes, just in case. That done, Ed summoned a group of drones and had them collapse a section of the ceiling.

Seconds after they began to chomp came a crack like thunder, and dust and broken wooden boards cascaded down into the

HUGO HUESCA

webbing below, followed by a short stream of rotten furniture and three extremely surprised ogres.

The kaftar shot a volley of darts and, while the ogres struggled against the webbing, the horned spiders skittered around them and bit them over and over with their paralysis-inducing fangs. It took several tricky seconds before the ogres stopped struggling, but even the highest Endurance couldn't resist a high-enough dosage.

"We're way over-trained for this," Kaga pointed out while a group of horned spiders dragged the webbed, unconscious ogres through the Portal a few minutes later. "I was hoping the Netherworld would be a better test of my skills."

"Don't you worry, kaftar," Jarlen told him. "There's plenty of challenges left for you."

"Two males and one female," Lavy said, scratching the side of her head. "It's probably not enough to set up a self-sustaining ogre farm."

Ed sent a couple drones along with the captured ogres, with instructions on how to adapt a couple free cells of the Haunt's jail to contain the creatures until he got back. "We'll get more later. These three will help our Monster Hunters learn how to train them." He turned to Jarlen. "Do you know how Jiraz secured the minionship of non-intelligent creatures?"

"There's three ways that I know of, Lord Wraith," said Jarlen. "First is, you don't bother. Grab a couple monsters like acid oozes and toss them into a chamber you want to defend for cheap, throw them some rusty iron a few times a month, then forget about it. Your drones will try to take care of their other necessities on their own if your skills are high enough. Second, you use a Mantle spell—*Shackle Mind*, I believe. It works only on beings with a natural Mind of three or below. Any affected creature won't attack you or yours, but it's an effect a clever adventurer can disrupt. Third way, you can build a special... enticement room. Man it with a couple succubi and they'll happily convince

340

almost anyone to become your minion." She gave him a cruel grin. "Best thing is, you can find the room design, the succubi, and the spell right here in Xovia. Shall I make the arrangements?"

"I'm not interested in torture chambers," Ed said, attempting to keep his voice level. "But thanks for the information."

Jarlen made a small curtsy to mask the disappointment in her expression.

After that, Klek led the team to the areas where the watchtower's marble walls had fractures and holes that monsters could use to get inside. They hurried to plug those with webbing and stone, which was only a temporary measure, but would hopefully dissuade anything nasty from taking a bite out of the Haunt guards while the others weren't there.

Ed noted that his drones had a much harder time working on the white stone than back on Ivalis. The obsidian-like surface of the ground they couldn't manipulate at all—their bites simply bounced off and did no damage. He filed this discovery in the back of his mind and readied himself to leave the watchtower.

Jiraz' mercenaries hadn't bothered to close the entrance after them. The chains lay like dead, rusted snakes in knots among the floor, and the six-foot-tall doors swung back and forth with the thick, Netherworldly wind. Past the entrance came the first view Ed had had of the Netherworld since his arrival in Ivalis.

The sky was crimson red and engulfed by angry, coal-black storm clouds, chains of thunder shining through. The air was heavy with dust and buffeted hard against Ed's face, forcing him to raise a hand to protect his eyes. The ground was the same obsidian mixture of stone and crystal, and it extended in jagged breaks and crests as far as the eye could see. It was all sharp edges and smooth surfaces that made it easy to lose one's footing in an instant. The landscape was black with little or no vegetation, but it sloped downward in several parts, as if Ed and the others were standing atop one of the fingers of the hand of some gargantuan titan from the Age of Myths. The slopes extended so far below that Ed couldn't see what was at the end, other than more black clouds like the ones on the sky.

For all he knew, the Xovia landmass floated in the middle of more sky, completely disregarding the laws of physics. Or they were walking atop some kind of Netherworldly volcano. Both explanations left Ed with a bitter taste in his mouth, alongside the eerie sensation that the world itself was dangerous and could leash against him at any time.

"Is this some kind of desert?" Ed asked, searching for the plants and vegetations he was currently cultivating in his underground farms.

"Not at all," Jarlen said happily. "On the contrary, Xovia is considered a very fertile land, highly sought after by other Regents."

"Yeah, I can tell," Alder said. "I'm almost drowning in all this greenery." He swatted away a non-existent branch.

"I think that Master Alder is vastly underestimating the true size of the Netherworld," Jarlen pointed out. "There's a reason why Portal travel is a must, even with all its difficulties and dangers, instead of more mundane means. In any case, Jiraz did have some clout, even in the end, and our current location is fairly close to the Citadel—about a day's journey, I'd say." She pointed at a tiny section of the horizon where something like a gray button contrasted against the jagged obsidian world—although it may have been a trick of the light. "Unless the Regent chooses to give us a lift, that is."

Klek gave the vampire a sideway glance. "But no one knows we're here..."

Jarlen smiled mischievously and said nothing. It was at about that time Ed realized the ground was trembling.

If seen from far above, say, while mounted on a griffin, the beast that emerged from the fracture line closest to the watchtower may have looked like a dotted caterpillar with hundreds of yellow legs allowing it to climb through the obsidian slope and into the ground above, its antennae twitching with an air of perpetual curiosity.

Seeing it from the height of a normal human being, like Ed did, was another thing. It was as if someone had mistaken the proportions of a train with that of a house, elongated it a couple dozen times, and then mounted the thing onto an impossible series of yellow hydraulic legs. The antennae were easily the width of his arm and had spiked ends like a pair of morning-stars. The head was a wedge of armored chitin the color of rusty steel dotted with multicolored rings of greens and oranges, and the mouth was a—thank the gods—toothless cavern that opened slightly as if to taste the fresh air.

"Cinderpede!" Kaga exclaimed, his voice walking a fine line between amazement and hysterics. "And it's coming right at us!"

Several hundred meters separated the giant creature from Ed's party, but it was clear it was headed their way, and it was surprisingly fast for a being of that size. At once, half the group drew runes or bows, and the other half took a couple discrete steps back toward the watchtower—and the Portal. Yumiya, Kaga's second, drew her blowpipe, gazed at it, whined, and pocketed it again.

"Stand down, everyone," Jarlen said. "Xovia's Regent has sent a welcome fitting for a Dungeon Lord. The cinderpede is the best way to span the distance to the Citadel. You have my word it's perfectly safe. As long as no one pokes it with a sharp stick, that is."

Lavy turned to her, hands crackling with the purple energy of a barely contained spell. "You knew about this?"

"Why, could it be that the Head Researcher hasn't ever seen a cinderpede?" the vampire asked without losing her grin.

Ed sighed and carefully used his gauntlet to brush away a pearl of sweat from his forehead. *I should have seen this coming,* he chided himself. The advance of the cinderpede would've been majestic if it hadn't been headed straight their way. He noted idly that even the batblins had taken a cue from him and Kes and remained relatively calm, not counting the many shuffling quietly toward the watchtower—with Alder among them.

"It's fine," Ed told the Witch. "Jarlen only got away with it because she genuinely believes we're not in any danger."

"Danger? I'd never!" Jarlen exclaimed. "I'm only doing my job —helping the Haunt!"

Kes turned to Ed. "What's going on?" she asked him, quietly.

Ed shook his head. Like in most things, it made sense in retrospective. The way Jarlen had become so helpful once she'd realized Ed wished to head to the Netherworld, the way she'd discreetly convinced them to go to Xovia instead of anywhere else…

He faced the vampire and told her, "How long have you been working for Korghiran?"

The vampire patted her distended belly and smiled beatifically with that dead face of hers. "Ah, a lady should never reveal her secrets."

HOURS LATER, while sitting comfortably on an embroidered silk cushion inside Kistog's tent, Ed could almost forget that he was riding atop a damned giant centipede.

Almost.

The tent itself was a work of art. It was fashioned out of a warm red and gold fabric with one wooden column sustaining the arches of the ceiling. The carpet hid the chitin of the cinderpede from view, and if it weren't for the constant, rhythmic movement of its legs, it would've been like riding a luxury train car. His minions rode under conditions only slightly less luxurious—the tents were smaller and more cramped, and lacked the incense and all the silver cutlery Kistog had lying around. Still, Ed couldn't help but feel vulnerable without Kes, Alder, Klek, and Lavy covering his back.

Kistog himself lay placidly under a stream of cushions in much the same way his master had been when Ed met the Regent of Xovia. The naga flicked his snake tail and used the edge with surprising dexterity to throw a couple more incense sticks to the brazier burning over a golden tray close to him.

"We've been waiting for your arrival ever since our dutiful associate informed us you'd grace us with your presence," he half-purred at Ed. The naga was dressed in an ample green tunic embroidered in smoky floral patterns, and his chiseled arms were covered in golden brands that marked him as the property of Korghiran herself. He moved and talked with a snobbish affectation, and it was clear he took great pains to avoid prolonging the "sss" in his speech—and he almost succeeded.

Ed gave Jarlen a dubious look. The vampire was half-asleep from her feast on ogre blood, with a very satisfied expression on her face. "The Lady of Secrets indeed. Korghiran could've sent an invitation instead of going through all this trouble, you know."

Jarlen chuckled and licked one finger marred with crusted blood. "Lord Wraith, you're the only Dungeon Lord I've ever met that dislikes gifts."

"Nothing is ever free," Ed told her. Although, he had to admit she had a point.

Jarlen had been a servant of Korghiran long before she'd ever become a minion of Jiraz the Elder. Apparently, it was a given that most of a Dungeon Lord's "elite" demonic minions came from their relationship with one Regent or another. Technically, vampires and naga weren't demons, but Korghiran was in the business of collecting skilled individuals with juicy bits of knowledge. Having lived as long as she had, Jarlen fit the bill perfectly.

When she'd heard about Ed's vision with the Regent, the vampire had understood her master's wishes and nudged Ed's path to converge with the Regent's. Since Korghiran had no *current* ill intentions toward the Dungeon Lord, Jarlen's minionship pact had allowed her to act as she had. Yes, technically, Ed had nothing to complain about. In reality, though…

The Mantle's pacts can be gamed too, he thought. He'd always acted on the assumption that pacts were air-tight. Jarlen had easily danced across its limits. Who knew what other ways there were to exploit the rules?

Ed had been avoiding other Dungeon Lords for far too long. There were tricks that he didn't know, and for a while there, he'd come to believe he was the only one around who dared to push Objectivity's buttons a bit. From the looks of it, the Demon Regents of the Netherworld had been at it for thousands of years.

"In this case," Kistog said, easing his way back into the conversation, "it's as close as it gets. Regent Korghiran has put this cinderpede at your disposal for traveling to the Citadel at your leisure. Her name is Ilma. You'll find that she's not only a regal way to move around, but also a fine way of avoiding the… nuisances of travel by foot. The Netherworld can be a dangerous place even for the mightiest Dungeon Lord, if caught unaware."

"So I hear," Ed said. "And in the meantime, I guess you'll make me an offer too good to pass up, right?" He glanced outside the small window of the tent.

The never-ending storm swirled across the vast red sky, and the fractured landscape crested in the distance. He saw the first hint of vegetation then, a huge mushroom-shaped tree growing right at the edge of an obsidian slope, with roots reaching down to the emptiness below. Thanks to Ilma's height, Ed could see that the tree's crown was rich with gray puffball. The tubers apparently grew inside the tree, with only their gray tops visible, but the violet smoke flowing upward was unmistakable. Tiny red and brown figures buzzed angrily around the puffball farm, wielding farming instruments.

Kistog calmly reached for a silver tray with tea utensils and poured out two cups of a steaming, unknown brew. He made no motion to serve Jarlen anything, and she didn't give signs of caring. Ed ignored the cup the naga set in front of him, but Kistog drank from his own without a care. "It seemss I was misinformed, Lord Wraith. Have you had experience with the Demon Regents after all? You appear to be familiar with their ways."

"A relative of Korghiran, maybe," Ed said, thinking of Kharon. "I'm not sure." He sighed, and then squared his shoulders. "Enough with the cryptic one-liners, Kistog. If we keep this up we'll reach the Citadel before saying what we want to say. What does she want? Your master, I mean."

Kistog's cup clinked against the china dish as he set it down with a practiced, fluid motion. "Why, what all Regents want with promising Dungeon Lords. She'd like to offer you a quest, and the chance to be rewarded handsomely if you succeed." He smiled in a way that befit his sixteen ranks in Charm, but the gesture was marred by the naga's bifurcated tongue flicking the air in a fraction of a second.

"No offense, but I've my hands full with Quests at the moment," Ed said. "Some days, it looks like I get them faster than I can finish them."

"That's the sign of a Dungeon Lord on the rise. But don't worry, this is not a quest that you need to fulfill right now. Indeed, the next Endeavor won't begin until next year."

"Endeavor?"

Kistog and Jarlen exchanged knowing glances. Jarlen winked at the naga. "Truly, this must be the first time you've entered the Netherworld if you haven't yet heard about Evangeline Tillman's inheritance, Lord Wraith," Kistog said. "Allow me to explain. Saint Claire and Tillman was one of the Netherworld's most famous corporations, a joint venture between the famous Dungeon Lord Saint Claire and the renowned Witch Evangeline Tillman. Together, they created a juggernaut of industry that pushed the boundary of sscientific and magical research. Banking, sspellcraft, weaponry, creature design, even farming and etiquette training. Saint Claire and Tillman put it all together and packaged it neatly together for the young, enterprising Dungeon Lord. This was the corporation's claim to fame. For almost a hundred years, Saint Claire and Tillman single-handedly fueled the Lotian war-engine againsst Heiliges, and since they're exclusively located in the Netherworld, there was nothing the Militant Church could do about it."

Jarlen sighed with nostalgia. "The good old days. I remember them as if it had all happened yesterday. A newly Mantled Dungeon Lord could simply pact with a Regent, ask for a small loan, and have Saint Claire and Tillman set him up with everything he needed. Spells, designs, weapons, monsters—all but experience points. He'd only need to point at a neighboring city and start the pillaging." She shook her head, lost in her memories.

"I won't bore you with the history lesson," Kistog said. "Today, Saint Claire and Tillman is gone. Evangeline and Lord Saint Claire are long dead, and the fabled Board of Advisers is long dismantled. The Standard Factory is but a phantom operation, maintained only by golems and self-sustained security systems blindly following the last instructions they got decades ago, powered on by ever-dwindling magical reserves. Inside the Factory's grounds are hidden treasures beyond measure, but that's irrelevant. The Factory *itself* is the prize, Lord Wraith, and in the handsss of a smart Dungeon Lord, its value soars beyond the treasury of Heiliges and Lotia added together. The Standard Factory contains all the magical systems used by Saint Claire and Tillman to equip Dungeon Lords. The asssembly lines, the monster customization facilities, the enchanted weaponry stock, even their altered crops are sstored there. Imagine what a ssingle Dungeon Lord could do with it. He'd become as powerful as a Regent, almost, with the reach and influence of a King. Think of the possibilities!" The naga's black tongue slithered up and down in excitement.

Ed raised an eyebrow. "All that sounds very nice. What does it have to do with me? I'm not sure how the Netherworld deals with inheritance, but where I come from, fortune is either given to the closest descendants of the owners or the assets are claimed by the government. I'm pretty sure a random Dungeon Lord can't just step inside the Factory and claim it for himself. Otherwise, someone like Alaric Everbleed would've done it already. Or one of the Regents, for that matter."

Jarlen smiled lazily. "If it were only so simple."

"Indeed, indeed," Kistog said. "Lord Wraith, all of Saint Claire and Tillman's descendants, those singled out in the wills, at least, died under surprising yet totally natural circumstances. These things happen all the time, you see. Terrible, terrible luck." Ed's eyebrow rose another inch, which Kistog seemingly took as a clue to explain further. "One was terribly depresssed. He grabbed a crosssbow and shot himself twice in the back of the head. We do not understand how he managed to reload the second time, but it was truly a testament to his commitment. Another one mistook a vitality potion for a deadly acid that had been, due to a terrible miscommunication, labeled the exact same as the potion. Another one accidentally ran a dozen times straight into the knife of an Akathunian ambassador—"

"I get it," Ed said. "No living descendants. Why won't the Regents claim it?"

"Evangeline and Saint Claire were a... peculiar pair," Kistog said. "A bit paranoid, in their later years, one could say. They believed some Regents were jealous of their amassed wealth, so they built the Standard Factory in the heart of Raaga—a hotly contessted territory with no Regent. If any Regent were to claim the Factory for himself, he'd start a war that the Netherworld cannot afford, given the trying times we live in. Furthermore, all the other Regents would ally against him and surely end him, since no Regent is strong enough to fight all others at once."

"Not that they haven't tried to sneak their way inside many times," Jarlen pointed out. "They forge their alliances and go to their secret meetings, but the nature of a demon always betrays them. They simply cannot work together for anything important without backstabbing one another."

Kistog looked away, nervously. "That's your opinion, Jarlen, not mine." He rubbed the bands on his arms. "Lord Wraith, the only way the Regents can access the secrets of Saint Claire and Tillman without setting the Netherworld aflame is to follow the rules. That is, to respect the wishes of Evangeline Tillman, as stated in the last point of her will." He took a deep breath and quoted, " 'In the event that all my living descendants would succumb to untimely deaths under mysterious circumstances, all my properties and holdings are to go to the first Dungeon Lord to come in possession of the Standard Factory's bill of ownership, which is located in my office's desk. Good luck.' "

Ed blinked. "Really? But that only makes Dungeon Lords kill one another instead of Regents," he said.

"That was the point, I think," Kistog said. "Tillman was a famous ssponsor of the Lordship, but she was an idealist. She dreamt of a world where Dungeon Lords and Regents could set their differences aside and work together for the common good of the Dark and what really matters—the extermination of the Light and all its followers. A nice ssentiment, but also impossible. Like Jarlen here has said... nature has a way of asserting itself."

Ed shook his head in disbelief. He'd been in the Netherworld for only a couple hours and was already overwhelmed with the sheer... moral dissonance that their inhabitants spouted with no visible self-awareness. *It's as if they're trying to be as evil as possible on purpose,* he mused. He wished Alder was here. The Bard always acted as if his head was in the clouds, but his insight into human nature went beyond Ed's. Perhaps he could make sense of this mummer's farce.

Although, and he hated to admit it to his very core, the idea of the Standard Factory had him tempted. At the very least, he was willing to hear the rest of what Kistog had to say.

"Go on," he told the naga.

"The Endeavor is Tillman's postmortem attempt at achieving her dream. A yearly contest to which all Dungeon Lordss may attend. They and a small selection of minions enter the grounds of the Standard Factory and try to reach Tillman's office. We suppose her plan was to force Dungeon Lords to work together and reach an arrangement and share the Factory among themselves. So far, everyone has either retreated, or succumbed to the Factory's defenses, or been backstabbed by their peers. Word on the street is, we *need* a winner. We cannot afford to lose Dungeon Lords to one another as well as the Heroes. It's unsustainable. So Regent Korghiran has magnanimously taken matters into her own hands and help a worthy Dungeon Lord win the contest. One pure of heart, brave, with no ties to the Netherworld to corrupt him, so he may achieve Tillman's dream—"

"Oh, go fuck yourself," Ed said quietly.

Kistog's tongue flickered in disbelief. "I beg your pardon, Lord Wraith?"

"Do you think I'm a dreamy farm-boy who wants to avenge his father? You were doing so well until you tried to take me for an idiot," Ed said. Next to him, Jarlen looked as if she were barely containing a fit of laughter. "Tell me what Korghiran really wants."

"Your Evilness! I assure you, everything I said is the utmost truth!" Kistog was the very image of an affronted snake-man. His tail tensed with hurt pride, as if the very idea that Ed thought him dishonest wounded him to the core.

Ed could feel the anger bubbling through his veins. He could stand someone lying to him. But if there was something that made him lose his temper in a second, it was people treating him like an idiot. "Either you tell me what she really wants, or you can walk the rest of the way on foot to explain to her why you failed to recruit me."

His words hung in the air like a sword for a second. Kistog rose slightly from the cushions, his mouth partially open to reveal a pair of fangs dripping oily poison. "Would you threaten to throw me out of my own cinderpede, Lord Wraith?"

At this point in his life, Ed had been threatened by creatures so powerful and terrifying that the sight of the angry naga was like seeing a child throwing a tantrum. He leaned back on the cushions to relieve the weight of his armor and spread his arms without a care in the world. "It's *my* cinderpede, Kistog. And no, I wouldn't throw you out of Ilma. My vampire would," he said.

The naga's brow contorted with fury. He opened his mouth, then closed it and stared blankly at Jarlen, who was smiling broadly from ear to ear.

"Sorry, Kissy," she said. "Minion duty. No hard feelings, right, dear?"

Ed could almost see the gears turning in Kistog's mind. The naga sat down.

"Smart Kissy," Jarlen said.

"The truth?" Kistog said sourly. "Every Regent wantsss a piece of the pie. Since that bitch Tillman left no way for the Regents to claim the Factory without starting a war, they have lowered themselves to working through Dungeon Lords. Every single man and woman with a Mantle beating inside their chest that steps into the Netherworld gets an offer. Regent Korghiran got a small group of Dungeon Lords to work together, and by that I mean they *hopefully* won't attack each other as soon as they meet. She wants you in her side. The rule is, the team reaches Tillman's office and then they sort out who gets what. The Regent doesn't care about the specifics so long as one of her team gets the bill of ownership."

Now that's better. With the cards over the table, Ed could tell that Korghiran's offer was even more dangerous than it looked at first glance. If every other Regent was pulling their weight and forcing the Dungeon Lords under their influence to work together, allying with one Regent over another could earn the anger of other Dungeon Lords well before the Endeavor began.

I've somehow stumbled head first into a Faction quest-line, Ed thought, scratching his chin.

In an RPG, a Faction quest-line made you choose between different opposing groups to advance the story. Completing Quests for one group increased your status and standing in that faction, but increasing it too much usually angered the other factions and made you lose out on their Quests and rewards. Ed wasn't a fan of those type of Quests because he hated going in blindly, knowing that no matter what he did, he'd miss out on content and items. Ivalis Online lacked that kind of game mechanic—it was a good old murder-fest, simple and to the point. Obviously, real life wasn't as charming.

"Thanks for being clear," Ed told the naga. "There's only one more thing. Why would Korghiran bother? I assume she wants a bite out of Saint Claire and Tillman's property."

Kistog grimaced and twirled a lock of greenish hair. "It would be of little use to you," he said. "The Lady Regent wants Tillman's spellbooks, logs, and patents. The knowledge locked away in the Standard Factory's vaults interest her greatly. The Factory itself is of no use to her." He frowned and raised a warning finger at Ed. "And don't try to cheat her. You'll find that Regent Korghiran can be quite reasonable, but she's also happy to kill a Dungeon Lord that stands in the way of her curiosity."

"Noted," Ed said. It was as fair a deal as he could expect. The naga had vastly understated the value of Tillman's intellectual property—probably on purpose—but Ed's many jobs before coming to Ivalis had taught him that information was much more valuable than plain old hardware. It was very possible that Tillman's intellectual property was worth many times more than the Standard Factory.

And *yet.*

"I'll consider it," Ed told Kistog. "But not today. Like I told you before, my hands are full."

"Of course, of course, Lord Wraith." Now the naga relaxed his shoulders and smiled. "Regent Korghiran understands that you'll need time to deal with your business in Ivalis. She only asks that you give her preference when you're approached by other Regents—"

"Actually," Ed said, grinning like a Ranger watching a rabbit nibble on the bait of his trap, "I'd be happy to give her offer priority. But there are a couple things another Regent may offer that could—" *What would Alder say in my place?* "—persuade me to evaluate their offer."

He was absolutely sure that he and Kistog had entered some kind of Charm contest. Ed hoped that his 14 ranks would be enough. The naga had 14 as well, though, given that he was the Netherworld's equivalent of a recruiter.

"Is that so? And what would those things be?" Kistog asked slowly.

Ed took a deep breath. *Here goes nothing.* "I want to free my dungeon from the danger of Heroic invasion once and for all, and I need access to all the resources I can get. Gear, spells, manpower, even disposable monsters to throw around. I'm doing a bit of research as well, on the whereabouts of a Dungeon Lady named Golsa. If she's still alive, she and I are due for a long chat. Finally, I'd like to know if Korghiran has heard of a person from a world called Earth having been summoned to fight for the Light... probably not long before the first Heroes started showing up."

"Only a year as a Dungeon Lord and already making a ruckuss," Kistog muttered, more to himself than to Ed. "I wonder how long it'll be before you bite off more than you can chew, Lord Wraith." He waved his hand at Jarlen, who had bent forward in a way that was at the same time both perfectly innocent and utterly threatening. "Never mind that. Regent Korghiran has allowed you to pretty much roam freely around the Citadel. You'll have access to our vendors and sspecialists, although ssecuring their loyalties is up to you. She's even willing to grant you a line of credit, as long as you use it wisely. On the second and third demands...

that's a bit more difficult. I've never heard about Earth before, but nevertheless, I'm only the Lady's servant. I'll mention it to her. But I can already predict that she'll demand a bit more of a reason to trust you with her secrets on the matter of Lady Golsa. *Perhaps* the Lady of Secrets knows about Lady Golsa's fate. Perhapss she'll need to cash in a few favors. It'll be much easier if she's in the right mood, if you catch my meaning."

"I do," Ed said. It was the Faction quest-line all over again. To get the information he wanted, he'd have to increase his standing with Korghiran's faction. Perhaps he ought to get it over with and make it into an official quest for the Haunt.

At least we're making progress, he told himself. *Not bad for our first foray into the Netherworld.* He had only had to informally ally himself with one of Kharon's siblings and, perhaps, earn the animosity of who knew how many others, including potentially the Boatman himself.

And he knew very well that Kistog hadn't shared all of Korghiran's plans. By now, he'd had enough dealings with the Dark to know it never revealed its true intentions until it was too late. But it was nice to have a Regent from the Netherworld try to manipulate him into doing her bidding instead of having to deal with the envoy of Murmur himself. It was a refreshing change of pace, and since he had absolutely no intentions of playing by Korghiran's rules at all, he decided he couldn't hold it against her, either.

"I'll consider your offer, and in the meantime, I accept your master's gifts in the name of the Haunt." Ed stood up, his armor clinking as he did, and Jarlen hurried to follow suit.

Kistog's triumphant smile faltered. "Where are you going, Lord Wraith? We haven't arrived at the Citadel yet. Pleassse, sit down. Let's celebrate the beginning of a beautiful friendship."

"We're not friends, naga. My friends are back there," he said, pointing back over his shoulder, "and I mean to join them. Thanks for the tea."

He was almost to the tent's door when he heard the shuffling of the rugs as the naga slithered his way. "Wait, Lord Wraith," Kistog called. "Just one last thing. My master told me to give you this. Sshe said you'd know why."

The naga handed him a sturdy card with a metallic edge and a familiar scene playing out on its face, with three men working at the keyboards of a Control Room. "The Shadow Tarot is going to be missing a card if I keep this," Ed pointed out.

"It wouldn't be an Artifact of Power if it couldn't replace a losst card," was all Kistog said.

Ed glanced at the card again, and all it implied. A part of him wanted to throw it back in Kistog's face and have Jarlen make good on Ed's defenestration threat. But it was as if the three men in the image were looking straight at him. Smiling, hopeful, confident. Ed sighed and pocketed the card as he left.

20

CHAPTER TWENTY

NETHERWORLD

A stream of imps flew well above Ed's head, over the high stone rooftops and the sharp walls of Xovia Citadel and into the spiral bee-hive that was the Regent's Palace, which rose well past any other building in its surroundings and almost challenged the skyscrapers on Earth.

"Alright, everyone, we're here," Ed told his minions, who fanned out in a half-circle in front of him and forced the crowd to part in their wake. A couple minotaurs gave them angry glances—which Kes returned a hundredfold—but no one dared mess with a Dungeon Lord and his minions, which was a welcome change of pace, and more so because some of the Netherworld's inhabitants seemed like the kind of beings you wouldn't want to meet in a dark alley at the end of the night. Or a well-lit alley in the middle of the night. Or a perfectly open street in the middle of the day. "Let's make the best of it."

"What's the plan, Lord Ed?" Klek asked. He and his Spider Riders surrounded the couple of small coffers full of Vyfaras that Ed had brought from the Haunt. Hopefully, with Korghiran's line of credit backing them up, they wouldn't need to spend much from their own funds.

357

The Citadel itself spit in the face of anything resembling reasonable laws of physics. It rose above the fractured landscape beneath it, growing around the Palace like bulbs extending from a sturdy plant stem. The Citadel walls were more like a partial cocoon protecting it from aerial incursion, with massive orange runes enveloping the city in an invisible aura meant to stop most magical means of invasion, as well as divination.

To reach the Market Bulbs sector, Ed's group had had to climb through the bottom of Korghiran's palace first—which seemed to mostly consist of gigantic staircases—and then through the main bridge. It was a small miracle he had lost no one along the way.

"We've figured out quite a bit regarding the Heroes in the last few months," Ed said. "We've seen them in action, watched how the Inquisition uses them, and learned their history. I think it's time we investigate how they work. Closely. I mean for us to capture one."

That simple statement earned him a couple of incredulous stares. "You do remember that they explode in your face if you try to imprison them, right?" Lavy whispered to him.

"That's why it's so important," Ed explained. "No one has done it because the Inquisition has gone to great pains to make their capture impossible. But we know things that no Ivalian native does."

"You mean, that the Heroes' creator came from your world," Alder said. "At least, that's what you think."

Ed's eyes flicked left and right, past the crowd of inhuman inhabitants and sellers. He and his minions stood in the middle of the street of one of the Citadel's Market Bulbs. The thick bridge that connected it to the bottom of Korghiran's palace grew like a stone tongue out in the horizon. Several lesser bridges connected the bulb with its neighbors, and the shade of its wall covered the street in a partial twilight only broken by the fragile light coming from hundreds of paper lamps eerily floating several feet above the ground, following some kind of mystical current flowing all through the city, giving the impression that the sky was enveloped by dancing red stars.

"It's true," Ed said. He could almost feel the weight of the Shadow Tarot's card hidden inside his pocket. "And until he or she shows up, there are a few things I want to try. And I'm going to need everyone's help."

The stares turned into excited whispering. "What do you need us to do, Lord Ed?" Klek asked.

Ed grinned. "Well, to start, we are going to build an enticing fake dungeon—one that the Inquisition won't be able to resist sending its Heroes against." He paced in front of his minions as he pointed at each different group. "Jarlen, you know people here, don't you? I want you to recruit me some minions. Find me the worst of the worst. People that no one will miss, but those who are dumb enough to take a dangerous mission."

"You want disposable minions," Jarlen said, sounding bored. "It's nothing out of the ordinary. Shouldn't be a problem."

"Kaga," Ed went on. "You and your Monster Hunters will find the biggest, meanest monsters we can keep under control. No need to set up breeding camps for each type, but if the price's good, remember that we're on Korghiran's tab, so don't worry about running up the numbers."

"We'll find creatures that put the fear of the Haunt into the heart of our enemies," Kaga said with a salute.

"And go with Jarlen when you've got a bit of free time," Ed said. "I haven't forgotten about my promise. I owe you a martial artist mentor, and it's about time we square that debt. Take one gold chest with you, and if you happen to meet someone that grabs your interest, feel free to bribe him into coming back with us."

The Monster Hunters cackled excitedly as Yumiya grabbed a coffer.

"Next. Lavy." Ed stepped in front of the Witch. "Go on a spell shopping spree. Be responsible, though."

"Oh, yes. *Finally.*" The glint in Lavy's eyes was the same as those of a kid whose parents told him there'd be Christmas every week that year.

"Come back with a Diviner, though," he advised her. "As well as someone who knows how to work enchantments into traps. I've got a couple ideas for your dish design and our Scrambling Towers. It's pretty important."

"Got it. Spend our fortune on spellbooks, hire a Diviner and an Enchanter." She rubbed her hands. "Can I leave already?"

Ed nodded, then continued on, stopping in front of Klek. "Klek, you and your Spider Riders will find us some trap-makers. The Thieves Guild's already helping us with normal trap-making, so we want to get someone that specializes in magical traps. I don't know how to explain the kind of trap I'm looking for, so here's my best description. It has many small, interchangeable parts that the creator can swap in and out. The idea is to get the trap-maker to teach us how to integrate magical traps into the normal workings of the Haunt, if that makes any sense."

Klek scratched his hairy chin. "We won't fail you, Lord Ed."

"Batblins are excellent at laying traps. Good choice using us for this important mission, Lord Wraith," Tulip said.

Ed nodded, then headed for Kes and Alder, who were waiting patiently for him. "The three of us will head into the nearest inn and crunch some numbers. Kes will deal with strategy, Alder will tackle psychology, and then the three of us will put it together. Also, I could use a drink," he admitted. "Actually, everyone's free to join us when you're done with your tasks. Drinks are on the Regent."

That earned him a few complicit laughs and a bout of clapping from Yumiya. Ed took a deep breath. Behind his helmet, sweat turned his hair slick and glued it to his forehead. The Netherworld was boiling hot. "Okay, everyone. Let's get to it!"

His minions spread through the bazaar, mixing with the local demonic population.

As soon as she found herself alone, the first thing Jarlen did was to head straight for the Citadel's prisons and kill a man.

She bribed the guards to look the other way and disable the magical defenses for ten minutes while she misted her way through the door slit of a prisoner's cell. The prisoner had once been a favored minstrel in Korghiran's court, but had fallen out of favor when caught stealing a silver chandelier inside his jacket.

Despite the weeks of imprisonment, the minstrel still looked somewhat healthy under the layer of grime and dried shit. It wasn't kindness on the guards' part—on the contrary. A man lasted longer under torture if they kept his Endurance up.

So she was doing him a favor, actually. But the minstrel didn't bother thanking her—he was too busy screeching in terror in a puddle of his own urine. At least he didn't try to pray to Alita as the vampire fell upon him and tore his throat out with her fangs. She giggled and danced as the blood sprayed across her face like rain, and she drank straight from the torn jugular like an open faucet. She wasn't even that thirsty, but a healthy human's blood tasted like sweet nectar compared to that greasy ogre mess.

Later, she'd have to burn her dress and buy a new one, but it had been worth it. She memorized the guards' faces, because she knew she'd have to make quite a few visits to the Netherworld in the following years, and she had no intention of surviving on animal blood like Lord Wraith intended her to.

It's probably some kind of test, she told herself, although with little conviction. Some Dungeon Lords were very... peculiar. They made up the strangest tests for their minions, expecting nonsensical answers. Depending on the Dungeon Lord, failing their tests could have lethal consequences. It wasn't fair, but that didn't bother Jarlen. She had enough experience dealing with Dungeon

Lords to make sure that another minion would take the test first. After that, it would be easy to figure out what kind of response the Dungeon Lord wanted.

So far, Dungeon Lord Wraith hadn't abused the minionship pact to punish a faltering minion, but it was only a matter of time. And one way or the other, Jarlen would figure him out.

She stopped by her favorite seamstress, a fat gorgon that used her hair tendrils to speed up her work. When Jarlen left the store, she was wearing a dress fashioned in a style that had been all the rage in the Netherworld only a few decades ago—a fitted black piece with a high neckline, long open sleeves, a laced corset, and a multi-layered skirt decorated with multiple bows. Had she been back in her normal form, that of a beautiful corpse in her mid-thirties, she would've gone with something more modern, perhaps black leather and brass tracks, but in the meantime she knew that the classics never really went out of style.

She also got a black umbrella to protect her skin. Technically, since the Netherworld lacked real sunlight and was bound by perpetual twilight, she was in no risk of burning to a crisp if she stayed out too long, but the brightness bothered her eyes and, if she wasn't careful, could mess with the internal magic that protected her body from decay, as well as give her face an ugly green tint that would be a bitch to regenerate.

Now it was time for business. The first official stop of the day was to pay a visit to the local Dark temple. It was a black mass that occupied an entire bulb of the Citadel, its walls filled with ample open windows and murder-holes so the winged inhabitants of the Netherworld could happily come and go. The eerie chanting from the slaves reached her ears long before she entered the temple.

After wandering around the torture chambers—which were purely recreational—and through the garden of skulls, she caught sight of a priest she'd had dealings with in the past. The once supple and strong naga was now old and brittle, his shiny green scales turned milky white from time and the strenuous life as a Dark priest.

He didn't recognize her in her diminished form, but she quickly refreshed his memory by whispering a few choice words in his ear while he preached to a group of would-be-Warlocks about the virtues of the Dark. The priest immediately shut up and glanced at her with wild, fearful eyes.

"Yes, darling. It's me," Jarlen said, laughing at the naga's bewilderment. "How about you tell your students to piss off and come have a chat by the skull garden?"

The old priest began to pretend he didn't remember the favor he owed her, but Jarlen made sure to mention, several times, her position as a minion of a Dungeon Lord with the Regent's favor, and soon enough the priest was all pleasant smiles and empathetic nods as she gave him a long list of demons and assorted Dark entities she'd need to populate Lord Wraith's new dungeon.

"The imps and the junkers shouldn't be a problem," the naga told her, wringing his hands nervously. "Sadly, I can't help you with the rest of the list. No, really, Jarlen, I'm serious. Even if the temple *could* summon a Devil Knight to fight for you, the truth is, Dungeon Lord Edward Wright has performed no act of Dark piety at all since his investiture. Despite Murmur's good will, Wright hasn't sacrificed a single prisoner and hasn't paid tribute to the Dark, nor has he contacted our temples or priests. By Murmur, the most he's done is erect a single unholy altar in our name, and not once has he prayed there—or even made a demand for more power. How are we supposed to help him out when he refuses to play by the rules?"

Jarlen rolled her eyes. "I'm sure Lord Wraith has his reasons. Are you really going to give up so soon, Qaail? What a shame. Almost as shameful as your reputation will be if what we did back in Efir reached the Archpriest's ears."

The priest's eyes widened in fear. "Please, Jarlen, understand! Even if I were to draw the magical circle, light the black candles, and sign the incantations, anything stronger than a junker would refuse to help you. Worse, the Devil Knight would probably kill all of you just for bothering him! If you really need the Dark's help, have your master perform the rites, and then we can talk. But before that point, my hands are tied," he said.

"Very well. I'll let this stand. This time," Jarlen said. She made a mental note to bring the matter up with Lord Wraith once the time was right. "But I still need something bigger than a junker for our grand finale. Come on, Qaail. There must be *something* you can do to help."

The old priest sighed and rubbed his arms. "Maybe there is something," he mumbled. "You didn't hear this from me, but remember the Corpse Architect that disappeared after the shameful zombie accident a few years ago? Word in the temple is, he's back in the Citadel. Perhaps you should have a word with him. I think he has refused to work with any Dungeon Lord since the... accident, but if you're persuading enough, who knows?"

Jarlen's tight lips drew into a cruel smile. "Tell me more," she said.

BROOM STREET WAS a Witch's dream come true. It was a long, sinuous road parallel to Grimmoire Boulevard, its buildings cramped against each other like twisted trees fighting for sunlight. Shoddy rooftops loomed over Lavy and her retinue as they explored the mysterious shops that lined the paved limestone road.

Half the locales in Broom Street lacked a name or any identifying sign—they were little more than huts with glass displays showing totems, dried animal parts, pelts, skulls of endangered monsters, and brass cages for golden snakes and rats with far too many pairs of eyes. The owners were dirty men or women from distant Heiligian hills with no name, or shaggy clansmen from the swamps that surrounded the mountains in the Lotian countryside. They were strange fellows with undecipherable customs, just as eager to bless you or curse you if you looked at them the wrong way—or any way at all.

The other half of the street was where true danger lay: Fancy storefronts with glass doors lined with bronze, names like Eradium's Bazaar, Botanica Magica, or Cures and Curses hanging from elaborate signs next to their displays. An untrained apprentice could easily think that Eradium's Bazaar was the safest store to shop for her master's new tunic, instead of that suspicious muddy hut with an old gnome hag who kept scowling in the apprentice's direction and spitting on the ground. The apprentice would spend a small fortune on an ermine tunic lined with cendal, enchanted with *flight*, only to discover when her master wore it that the tunic was actually a transmuted cursewing—a kind of bloodsucking, flying, sheet-like monster native of Raaga. The cursewing would wrap around the very surprised master and take off, thus teaching the apprentice a valuable lesson in reading the fine print of an item's description.

If the apprentice went back to Broom Street, she'd discover that Eradium's Bazaar had disappeared overnight, leaving behind an entirely different—but just as threateningly unthreatening —shop.

In short, Lavy found that Broom Street was the best place in the world to buy the sort of spectacular spells needed to do any kind of decent research.

A lesser Witch may have gone mad with the power of having a near-unlimited credit line backed by the Regent of Xovia, but Lavina Odessa Trevil of the Haunt was a consummated professional, with a will of steel and an iron-clad restraint that made her the perfect woman for the job. The last few hours, she'd resisted the allure of the cursed artifacts and exotic garments from distant lands and focused exclusively on the mission at hand.

Of course, to buy the spells and magical items that Ed wanted and that she needed for her Laboratory, she first *needed* to earn the respect of the shopkeepers—if they mistook her for an apprentice they may attempt to con her. So she had *had* to buy a beautiful scarlet cloak lined with miniver, as well as a golden brocade vest with a skulls-and-flowers pattern. Obviously she couldn't strut around wearing dirty shoes with her new clothes, so she was forced to buy a new set of ivory satin shoes with a rhinestone buckle and lace trim.

Since she wasn't a credulous apprentice, she hired a pair of ogre thugs to shake the shopkeepers around a bit to make sure nothing in her new wardrobe was actually a cinderpede in disguise. This proved wise—the first set of shoes turned out to be cursed, and would've forced her to dance until passing out had she worn them. After her ogres finished presenting a formal complaint in Lavy's name, the shopkeeper's assistant had offered the Witch plenty of apologies and discounts while the shopkeeper was carried off to the nearest Priest.

The discounts were so good that it would've been a disservice to the Haunt to let them go, so Lavy had been *obligated* to buy half the inventory. By the time she left the store, she had so many bags that the ogres couldn't carry them all, so once again she was in the distasteful position of having to rent a carriage. It was self-evident, though, that moving by carriage in a crowded street was very hard without a pair of lackeys to part the crowd for you, so Lavy was forced to call upon Korghiran's credit once more, sure that she was acting strictly in the Haunt's best interest.

"Out of the way!" exclaimed her golden-haired lackeys as they cartwheeled and danced across the middle of the street, the pair of undead horses that pulled Lavy's carriage only a few steps behind. "Make way for the beautiful and talented Lavina the Witch! Out of the way!"

Safe from the jealous glances of the rabble in the road, Lavy relaxed in her comfortable seat as the carriage made way through Broom Street. She was surrounded by piles of parchment and rows upon rows of boxes filled only with the most necessary pieces of magical gear.

She glanced out the window. "I like that store," she told Jakesh —her naga shopping assistant. "What do you know about it?"

The storefront that Lavy was pointing at was of grim black wood, with an ebony sign proclaiming in silver lettering, "Welcome to Clarence Coldren's Wondrous Runes and Relics Shop." It had no display, and the interior was hidden from view by a black curtain hanging behind the glass door.

Jakesh frowned and adjusted his brass spectacles. "Clarence Coldren? I've never heard of that name. How strange, I could've sworn this storefront was empty in the morning." The naga's tail shifted nervously.

"Excellent," said Lavy. She rapped on the wooden panel in front of her with her ivory cane. "Driver, you may wait for us here."

At a signal from the driver, the lackeys hurried to open the door for Lavy, then threw a rug on the street before helping her down, so she wouldn't have to sully her new shoes. In doing this, she was merely protecting the assets of the Haunt.

She waited on the street, surrounded by her servants, for her ogres to catch up with her on foot. As she waited, half a dozen halflings with shaved heads and dressed in ragged togas headed her way. Lavy's lackeys stopped them before coming too close.

"Excuse us, madam," a halfling told her, "we're looking for our master. He... ah, gets into all sorts of trouble when he drinks, and hasn't shown up in days—"

At that moment, the ogres arrived. "No talking with Master Lavina," one of the brutes said, and the two of them ushered the halflings away.

Lavy shrugged and went inside Wondrous Runes and Relics.

The walls were surrounded with rows of packages and assorted items that reached the ceiling, with tables full of trinkets and gadgets, and magical braziers that wavered with a non-existent breeze. A bald man with an oversized head and three azure eyes walked out from behind the counter and headed toward the Witch. His skin had a vaporous texture to it, as if he somehow was in two places at once.

"Ah, welcome, welcome to my humble store! I am Clarence Coldren, at your service!" He shuffled toward Lavy, his head bobbling with every step. "What can I do for you, my fair lady? Allow old Coldren to fulfill the true desire of your heart! Perhaps you desire to level your beauty like warriors upgrade their battle talents?" With one hand, he rummaged through the nearest pile of trinkets and pulled one of them out, seemingly at random. It was a simple silver-leaf circlet. "Behold! With the circlet of Princess Parastar, you can become the very likeness of an eternal elven maid! It can be yours at the fair price of ten Vyfaras..." He waggled the circlet at Lavy.

The Witch grinned, took the circlet, and handed it over to Jakesh.

The naga examined it with a critical eye, then shook his head. "This circlet would've enchanted your ears to grow pointy and set you under a compulsion to think you're eternally young every time you wear it."

"What?" Clarence Coldren smiled nervously. "Where did you get that idea...?" He stepped back as Lavy's ogres strolled his way, patting their batons against their huge hands.

"I'll take it," Lavy said. "Toss it with the others, Jakesh."

"An excellent choice!" Coldren said, keeping a careful eye on the ogres.

The naga grimaced. "But, Madame Lavina, that's a cursed item! You cannot possibly think to use it—"

"Of course not," Lavy said. "Ha, a circlet to make me more

beautiful?" She scoffed at the idea. "Why, that's like spitting into a river to make its waters wetter."

"Then... what use could you have for it?" Jakesh asked.

"Simple. When I return to my Laboratory, I shall take it apart and discover its inner workings. What better way to learn curses than to study cursed items themselves? It's much cheaper than searching for expensive scrolls, in any case—and I'll train my skills in the process," Lavy explained. Then, she grinned and turned to face the shopkeeper. "But since the circlet *is* cursed, I'll give you only one Vyfara, Master Coldren. Is that alright with you?"

"A Vyfara!" Coldren exclaimed. "I wouldn't break even with that amount!"

Lavy shrugged. "Well, if you don't take it, I'm afraid my associates here will certainly break *something* of yours. You did try to curse me, after all."

With a slow and deliberate movement, one of her ogres swiped the trinkets off one table. The noise of broken glass and crumpled wood drowned Coldren's protests.

The second ogre strolled to the rows by the back.

"Fine!" Coldren exclaimed, his three eyes wide with fear. "A Vyfara is alright."

"Perfect," Lavy said. She walked among the shelves with an appraising eye, with Jakesh and the shopkeeper hurrying to match her pace. "What else do you have for me?"

Coldren bit his lip and reached for one shelf, this time without his previous cockiness. "Well... I have this batblin paw. It grants the user three wishes—"

"Throw it in the pile. That's another Vyfara for you," Lavy said. Her grin grew several inches wider at the shopkeeper's expression. "What else do you have for me?"

Broom Street was a Witch's dream come true.

· · ·

Ed watched while the line in front of his table grew as people all across the Citadel heard that the Haunt was on the lookout for new minions.

The Dungeon Lord sipped his drink and relaxed as Alder, who had the highest Charm of the bunch, handled the interviews.

"My patron grants me experience points according to how many innocent souls I sacrifice to them," said the elven Warlock currently facing Kes, Alder, and Ed. "If I'm to work with you, I need to take into account the amount of experience points I am to earn. Tell me, how many innocent prisoners do you capture in any given year, and how many of those would I be allocated for blood sacrifices?"

Alder turned to Ed, who was making a slashing motion with his hand across his neck. The Bard turned to the Warlock and smiled politely. "Thanks for passing by. We'll call you if anything comes up."

After the Warlock came the leader of a roving band of were-wolves. He wanted money and prey to hunt, which could be arranged, but the hairy man bowed out when he heard where the Haunt was located. "Undercity's a damn honey trap," he said gruffly. "The Heiligian Navy won't let anyone escape by sea, and the Inquisitors of Galtia will hunt anyone down that tries to escape the other way around. Sorry, Dungeon Lord, it's too risky. I would make for a lousy mercenary if I chose to fight a campaign with poor exit strategies."

Kes sighed as the werewolves left.

A pair of naga Clerics walked out when they realized Ed wasn't willing to install a blood fountain in their quarters so they could perform their rituals.

"Does the Dark *really* make their Clerics use blood fountains for their rituals?" Ed asked, fighting the urge to pull at his hair in frustration.

"Actually," Alder said, "I think that was an excuse. According to my *empathy* talent, the Clerics had mentally checked out when we told them how much we could pay them."

Kes frowned. "Don't we have Korghiran's credit?"

"Only for a couple days," Ed said. "Salaries are on our tab, and we can't strain the cash flow from the brewing business—if we invest too much on minions that are only useful for fighting we won't be able to expand our business. It's the old Real-Time-Strategy conundrum. We have to choose between early-game aggression or a strong late-game economy."

"You lost me," Alder admitted.

"I mean, we need to keep our expenses in check so we can hire a merchant ship in the future and sell our booze all over Starevos." On the street outside, a pair of assholes kept screaming at the crowd to get out of the way of a black carriage pulled by undead horses.

Alder, who seemingly was incapable of listening to business talk for more than a second, turned distractedly to the carriage past the window. "Someday we'll have that kind of money."

"I don't know," Kes said. "Even if we did, what kind of asshole drives a carriage through a crowded street?"

Ed's plan was to hire minions that had specialties other than killing people, so that the Haunt wouldn't go broke trying to bankroll an army it couldn't sustain. Sadly, that weeded out a good chunk out of the current prospects.

Still, Alder hired a group of artisan trap-makers led by a gnome inventor that had been exiled from his community because of his profound lack of respect for basic safety protocols. Half of his shiny blue hair was missing, burnt off by an explosion a long time ago. He was willing to work on the cheap, as long as he could remain in Xovia, which was alright with Ed.

After the trap-makers they ran into some trouble, because the remaining minions demanded higher wages when they heard that they'd be headed to Undercity. Like the werewolves, most people knew it was too risky to have a couple Portals be all that kept them safe in case shit hit the fan.

"We cannot pay that at the moment," Alder told a golden succubus dressed in a white tunic. "But you could marry me, and then you'd have half my stuff—okay, see you around, then!" He waved at her as she flew out in a huff. "She's totally into me," he told Kes.

"Our budget is a bit tight, but think of the experience—" he attempted, but the Akathunian Poisoner—also an accomplished chef—left without letting him finish.

Little by little, the line of prospects thinned.

"—sure, work will be hard and possibly lethal, but think of the sense of pride and accomplishment you'll get—"

Outside, a group of bald halflings were handing out pamphlets with the drawing of a missing person on them, but everyone continued walking, not paying any them any mind.

"Think about your future work offers!" Alder exclaimed, more than a little desperate. Hours later, there was only one prospect left—a floating blue pufferfish who sounded young, although Ed didn't know enough about floating pufferfish biology to make a guess at his age.

"I do! All the time," the pufferfish said nervously. "Master Alder, Lord Wright, I really need the job. No Dungeon Lords are willing to hire an untested Diviner because of the risk of angering Objectivity, but the Xovian School of Advanced Divination won't teach someone without five years of field experience."

"Risk of angering Objectivity?" Alder muttered, giving the pufferfish a worried sideways glance. "No one told me about that."

"There's nothing to be concerned about," the pufferfish hurried to say. "I'm very careful, I swear! In any case, I specialize in enchantments—making crystal balls, for example. Scrying is what's truly dangerous!"

Ed, Kes, and Alder exchanged a knowing glance. They could use a Diviner who specialized in enchanting to help Lavy with her dish research. The Dungeon Lord massaged his chin. There had to be a way to convince the pufferfish to work with lousy pay and in constant mortal danger...

"I don't know," Ed said, as inspiration struck. "You look quite young, and the Haunt gets a lot of applicants."

Kes raised an eyebrow, but Alder caught on and played along. "There are at least a dozen Diviners who would like to work for us," he told the pufferfish. Technically, it wasn't a lie. There *were* a dozen diviners who would like to work for the Haunt—*if* the Haunt could pay them more, and *if* they didn't have to travel to Starevos.

"But... I'll work harder than anyone else!" the pufferfish said desperately.

Ed felt a pang of guilt for toying with the Diviner's feelings, but he had to play with the hand he'd been dealt. "Look," he said. "Understand that if we hire you—and I'm not saying we will—we won't be able to pay you as much as a full-fledged minion, since you haven't completed your training."

The pufferfish nodded with enthusiasm. "I understand! My Xovian School degree will make up for that... once I get it."

Only if the student loans don't drown you first, kid, Ed thought, shivering at the memories. He decided that if the pufferfish handled himself well enough, he'd get a raise as soon as the Haunt could afford it.

"Screw it," the Dungeon Lord said, turning to Alder. "Let's give the kid a chance."

Alder smiled. "You're hired."

THERE ARE features of a city that were ever-present, regardless if the city was a corrupt port under Heiligian occupation or a Citadel from what could be argued was the Ivalian version of Hell itself.

Taverns were one such fixture.

This tavern was one of the seediest places in the Citadel. The Innocent Slime Girl's Pub was populated by exiled minotaurs with no home in Ivalis and no options other than coming to the Netherworld to survive, nagas that had been rejected for the priesthood or Korghiran's service, and assorted humanoids not fit for taking the minionship.

It was also currently occupied by a group of kaftar Monster Hunters. One of them, Yumiya, was standing next to the door with a carefully maintained disinterested air. She regarded Jarlen's approach with a raised eyebrow and a hint of a snarl.

"Vampire," the kaftar said. "Get your business done elsewhere. We're busy here."

There was a crash of a nearby window as some lowlife was thrown clear through. "It looks that way," Jarlen said. "But my business is inside, sadly. Aren't you supposed to be working?"

"We are holding auditions for our next teacher," Yumiya explained.

Jarlen raised an eyebrow. "It looks to me like you're starting tavern brawls all over the Citadel."

"The best way to find the greatest warrior in a city is to fight everyone in it."

"Of course." Jarlen's smile became a bit strained. "Do as you wish, I won't get in your way." She shouldered past the Monster Hunter, trusting that Lord Wraith's pact of minionship would prevent the both of them from coming to blows. "Here, hold my umbrella," she told Yumiya.

The tavern brawl was reaching its climax. Most of the furniture had been torn to shreds, the floor was littered with battered nobodies gasping for air, and a kaftar was standing on a table and howling like a madman as he fought off a couple Akathunians with a table leg. Jarlen's height—or her lack of it—came to her advantage. She walked through the chaos with no one taking notice of her.

The bar was empty, save for a sullen man in a black suit

hunched over in the corner, and a shell-shocked bartender who was cleaning a glass tankard with a dirty rag.

"You're missing the show," Jarlen told the man as she sat next to him and gestured at the bartender.

"Aren't you too young for alcohol?" the man asked while the bartender poured some tepid ale in the tankard, then slid it over the table straight at Jarlen, who caught it without a second glance.

She passed the tankard to the man. "For you. You look like you need it." He ignored the gesture, his gaze lost somewhere in the distant land of memories. Behind them, someone flew through the air and crashed against the floor a few feet away from the fireplace. "I've been looking everywhere for you, Doctor Frederick."

"I'm not for hire, vampire. Not anymore."

Jarlen frowned. Had she not wanted something from him, she would've torn his throat out for speaking to her as if they were equals. She opened her mouth to respond, but paused as a tan halfling wearing some kind of brown tunic climbed atop the chair next to them.

"Terribly sorry, Missy, terribly sorry. Are either of you going to drink that?" the halfling asked. Without waiting for an answer, he grabbed Frederick's tankard and took several long gulps. "Sorry, sorry, don't mind me, I'm just passing by." A kaftar jumped him from the back, and the halfling absentmindedly smashed his tankard against the Monster Hunter's forehead, spewing ale everywhere. "Alright, then. Nice meeting ya!" The halfling charged back into the fray, kicking and punching like a small tornado, which was a small marvel seeing that he was so drunk he could barely stand.

"Anyway," Jarlen said. "Yes, I've heard you refuse to perform the work that made you famous, good doctor, and that the Regent herself can't make you reconsider. A shame, really. Good will doesn't last forever."

"Let me take a look at you." Doctor Frederick glanced at her for the first time. "Nightshade, less than two centuries old. Not your first botched regeneration, either. Recently fed. A fine undead specimen, yes. In a different time… no, in another life-time, I could've crafted beautiful art out of your flesh. But those days are long gone." He shook his head. "You don't understand, vampire. You cannot fathom the pain that lurks in my soul, tearing at me from the inside." He showed her his open palms. "These are the hands of an artist, but that same art killed my wife. The love of my life. How can I accept the song of scalpel and gauze when every time I close my eyes I see the fire—"

"Excuse me, I think there's been some kind of error," Jarlen said. "You mistook me for someone who cares."

The doctor shut up. Behind them, the drunk halfling gave a howl, and shortly after Kaga sailed though the air past the bar, only inches away from Jarlen. The kaftar disappeared behind the bartender, who did his best to ignore this. There came the crash of broken glass, and then Kaga reappeared, pelt disheveled and covered in pieces of bottles, a wild look in his eyes.

"Get me that halfling!" he bellowed as he jumped back into the fight. "We don't leave the Netherworld without him!"

"As I was saying," Jarlen said. "I don't care about your back-story. I'm building a quick dungeon, and I need something big and angry to put at the end. Something that won't die the instant the Heroes look its way. Since you aren't working at the moment, money must be tight, right? There must be some creature you've stashed away somewhere that you can exchange for *this*." She set a heavy bag full of Vyfaras on the table. "It's enough to pay for quite a few months of moping around looking like an idiot."

Doctor Frederick clenched his jaw, but his eyes remained on the bag. He glanced doubtfully at the bartender.

"Your tab is running quite high, sir," the bartender reminded him.

The doctor sighed. "I may have a little something," he told Jarlen.

· · ·

THE HAUNT'S PORTAL CHAMBER buzzed with activity as, a few days after their departure, the expedition returned with their hands full of loot and empty coin purses. Following the strict security measures established by Marshal Kes, the Portal was guarded by two rows of horned spider warriors and a team of elite Janitorial batblins going through a checklist as, one by one, the minions stepped out of the Portal.

"One Bard, human," said Strit, as Alder reached the batblin's spot in the checkpoint. Strit checked his wooden tablet. There was a parchment with a list in it. Since he didn't know how to write or read, someone had helpfully drawn the faces of the expedition for him. He found Alder's visage as a rosy-cheeked male with blond hair, and scratched it. "Move along, citizen," he said, waving the Bard in.

"A Witch, human." Strit marked a scratch through a drawing of girl's face with a pointy hat on her head. "Go on." Lavy was followed by a group of drones carrying bags and bags of loot, of all shapes and sizes. Strit could swear he saw a batblin paw jutting out of a box at some point. Once the drones were done piling the bounty against a corner of the room, they headed back into the Portal.

After Lavy came Costel and her guard team. Strit frowned and turned to his second-in-command, Janitor Thuddle. "What number comes before five?"

Thuddle showed Strit the extended palm of his right hand, along with a single finger from the left. "This many."

Strit nodded knowingly and scratched every human face in his list that wore a bucket helmet. "Don't get yourselves in any trouble, now," he admonished the humans as they stepped past him.

Then the kaftar Monster Hunters arrived, and both Strit and Thuddle exchanged worried glances. What in Hogbus' name were they supposed to do if there were more drawings than fingers on their hands? "Uh," Strit said, thinking fast. "Is your group complete?" he asked Kaga. The kaftar leader looked a bit worse for the wear, with a black eye and a bloody nose, but he seemed otherwise cheerful. "Anyone missing that we should know about?"

"Not at all!" Kaga said, patting the batblin on the back.

"Very well, uh… move along, then, but we'll keep a close eye on you," Strit said. As the kaftar marched past, he made a show of scratching their faces one by one. Then he stopped, frowned, and turned to Thuddle once more. "Thuddle, do you know if kaftar younglings are hairless?"

Thuddle examined the half-sized, hairless humanoid that stumbled around with the kaftar group, the figure wincing at all the sharp lights and clutching his head as if he were afraid it'd fall off of his neck. "Yes," Thuddle said. "I reckon that's just an ugly baby kaftar."

"Are you sure?" Strit asked. Thuddle had a reputation for making things up instead of admitting he had no idea what he was talking about. "He looks quite hungover to me."

"Well, of course," Thuddle said, hands on his hips with an air of superiority. "Kaftar start drinking young so they stop getting hangovers when they're adults. It's like that story where the Shaman injected himself with a bit of spider venom, with a bit more every day, until he was completely immune."

Strit scratched his belly. "That makes sense."

Then it was time to account for the host of horned spiders, and soon enough he'd forgotten all about the kaftar.

Hours later, by the time Strit and Thuddle were almost done, they saw the armored figure of the Dungeon Lord emerge from the Portal. He, the Marshal, and the vampire Jarlen were directing the drones as the creatures pulled on some chains. Strit watched in awe as a wagon slowly emerged from the Portal, carrying a cage so big it barely fit through the Portal.

Some sort of creature lay inside the cage, a powerful snout framing a pair of red, shiny eyes carrying the glint of a predator. It had long horns that could impale a row of batblins without much effort. Strit saw powerful muscles at rest, stitched together as if they came from many different animals.

"What is that?" he asked, instinctively taking a few steps back. He hoped the Janitors wouldn't have to deal with an escaped… whatever that thing was.

Jarlen smiled and patted the iron bars of the cage. "This," she said. "Is our Boss fight."

CHAPTER TWENTY-ONE

TEST DUNGEON

The fragile light of the scented candles arranged on her window's ledge mixed with the pale blue shine of Lisa's computer monitor. She was in her pajamas, chomping on a cookie with one hand and working through Ivalis Online's character selection screen with the other.

She was home alone—her sister had gone out again, to meet with those marketing hotshots at the club. Before leaving all dolled up, Diana had suggested that Lisa could still meet up with them, if she hurried to toss on some makeup and borrowed a dress from Diana's closet. Both of them knew it was an empty if well-intentioned offer. Lisa wasn't a nightlife kind of gal; the music was too loud and the smoke turned her hair into a mess. Besides, why would she be out dealing with the advances of drunk assholes when she could be saving some virtual world or another?

"Ah, keep telling yourself that's why," she said through a sarcastic chuckle. "Let's pretend it isn't because of the crippling social anxiety."

She cracked her knuckles and selected one of her Clerics, a test character that she wouldn't mind losing while the new kid learned the ropes.

The screen powered through a loading screen and then flashed white as the music of the Light's temple began to play. Soon, Lisa glanced at her Cleric from the typical top-down perspective of most isometric RPGs. The pixelated graphics showed a checkered black-and-white floorboard and an ample vault with carved statues of the Light gods lining the walls. About a dozen other Player Characters came and went to and from the Portal built above a raised dais surrounded by golden candles, right above a huge painting of Alita, first among the gods.

The goddess was clad in golden armor that covered her body in many layers of protection and made it seemingly impossible for her to raise her shoulders. Her white hair escaped from the back of her helmet and cascaded down her pauldrons like a snowstorm. She held Aucrath, the goddess-turned-spear, in both her hands as Alita challenged the forces of the Dark, implied by the painter by a black smudge by the corner of the landscape, right where Alita was aiming Aucrath's tip.

Mark arrived a few minutes after Lisa, using a low-level Fighter to test the waters, although armed with a high-level axe borrowed from his main account.

"I hope you don't mind losing it if shit goes sideways," Lisa told her friend once they were done connecting through Teamspeak.

"Yesterday I got a new one, so it'll be okay, I hope," Mark said. "So, how's your Saturday night going so far, Liz?" The unmistakable sound of a soda can being popped open came through the speakers.

"Same as yours, asshole," Lisa said.

"Ah, well. I was just wondering if you'd be off to some mysterious new high-roller job after getting that headhunter's letter, you know."

Lisa's smile faltered. "Actually, I haven't talked to them at all."

The other Player Characters flowed around Lisa and Mark, who remained like motionless, pixelated statues as they chatted.

"Really? Perhaps you've become attached to our magnificent Lasershark empire?" Mark asked.

"That's not it," Lisa said. "It's just... there's something iffy about that calling card." In fact, she'd kept it at the very end of the bottom drawer of her desk ever since she arrived home with it, and had refused to look at it twice. Something about the way Mark had described the man who'd left her that card gave her goosebumps.

"I see," Mark said thoughtfully. "Perhaps it's for the best. One can never be too sure when you're going to go for an interview and discover a familiar black couch right next to the interviewer's desk. *Although...* starring in one of those videos pays better than minimum wage, right? Perhaps it *is* your big shot after all."

A few seconds later, Omar logged in.

"Sorry?" the new kid asked, caught right in the middle of Lisa's choice words for Mark.

"Not you," she said through Mark's chuckles. She clicked on Omar's character and confirmed it was one of Ed's test Wizards, a mid-level one he carried around to check out new game areas. "How was the campaign, you finished it already?"

"Sure," Omar said. "Way too short and trope-y, but I liked it. The final battle reminded me of Final Fantasy VI because the last bad guy kept changing shapes."

This prompted a brief but passionate discussion about which Final Fantasy game had been the best one. Ryan arrived during Mark's passionate speech about Cloud and Sephiroth's secret relationship. When the "Rylan Silverblade" name on the friend list turned green, both Mark and Lisa shut up as if caught by the effects of a *mute* spell.

"Ah, good," Ryan's smug voice came from Lisa's headphones, sounding slurred. "Everyone's here. Saves me the trouble of herding cats." He laughed to himself.

Is he drunk? Lisa thought, frowning. It *was* a Saturday night, and Ryan was rich. Sometimes, she wondered what would prompt a guy like him to spend his weekends forcing people he didn't even like to play with him, when it was clear he had time to have a social life, if he chose to.

"Hey, Boss," said Omar. "What are we going to kill tonight?"

You don't have to lick his boots at every chance. One on one, she thought that Omar was okay. But his constant need to earn Ryan's approval was getting on her nerves. A few more days like that and she guessed she'd try to avoid the two of them altogether.

"Well," Ryan said, drawing the word a lot longer than it needed be. "I just got a notification on my phone. Remember that Undercity storyline that hadn't moved along in months? Apparently there's a new dungeon that just popped up."

"Finally!" Omar said. Lisa was fairly certain he had no idea what Ryan was talking about.

"Yup. I reckon if we hurry through the Portal, we'll be the first to take a bite out of that sweet XP," Ryan went on. "Most other assholes in the forums are grinding in the far North, I think. Fighting a werewolf insurrection or something lame like that."

"Werewolves aren't lame," Mark complained quietly through a private chat with Lisa.

"I mean..." she said. "They are *everywhere* in Starevos. There's no way to grind for items without aggroing like five clans at once."

Despite it all, she was interested in Undercity's storyline. It was clear from out little information had trickled out in the last few months that the payoff to it would be something big.

"Screw werewolves," Omar said, agreeing with Ryan.

"Alright, then," he said. Rylan Silverblade III headed for the Portal, followed by Ed's former Wizard. "Enough chitchat. All of you losers ready? Remember, new guy, stay behind me and do everything I say. You'll be fine."

They found the dungeon not long after leaving the second Portal, the one that threw them out of the temple and into the city of Constantina, where they used the Light-provided vendors to stock up on healing potions and new weapons for their characters. Ivalis Online featured a weapon-degradation system, which was strange given the other game-play features it lacked, but by now every remaining player had accepted that Pantheon did pretty much anything they liked and ignored most feedback.

The other thing that Pantheon hadn't added was an active compass, which always made finding the Quests and dungeons a pain in the ass, but the community had learned to make do by sharing coordinates and landmarks. In this case, the dungeon's entrance was hidden behind a waterfall that led to a pristine river with a nasty current hiding underneath.

"Isn't there a secret exit we can use instead?" Omar asked, while the other three discussed how they'd bypass the river to reach the curtain of water.

"That's not how it works," said Mark patiently. "If we knew where the secret entrance was, we'd be using that one instead and *this* would be the secret exit." His stout dwarf character kept a safe distance from the river. With his heavy plate armor, he'd sink like a rock and end up teleported back into the temple, a hefty gold coin fee automatically deducted from his inventory. "Besides, if you take too long to attack, sometimes they just collapse the entire dungeon and move the minions elsewhere."

"How annoying," Omar muttered. "I wonder what the developers thought when adding that feature."

"It's probably for realism," said Lisa. "But never mind that. Your character specs in ice magic, right?"

"Yeah, I think so."

Lisa suggested they use the Wizard's magic to freeze a path into the waterfall. "There's one Wizard daily, *sleet dragon breath*, that freezes everything in a straight line. It should have enough range, hopefully."

"What a waste of time," Ryan said with a dismissive snort. "We haven't even started looting and you're already wasting a daily? Whatever. I'll wait for you inside. Last one in gets to be the loot mule!" His Rogue climbed up the wet, moss-covered scarp like it was nothing, and disappeared under the waterfall in mere seconds, a feat that none of the rest of the team could imitate, since Lisa's Cleric had Spirit as her main attribute, and the Wizard obviously used Mind. Agility simply wasn't their thing.

Mark opened a private chat again. "What an idiot," he said. "If something kills him without us, he'll probably blame us. Again."

"Then we better hurry," Lisa said, sighing. She returned to the party chat and said, "Well, let's not keep the man waiting. Omar?"

"Ah, sure," said the new kid.

Sleet dragon breath raised a small fogbank as it struck the water and left a jagged ice road for them to use. Omar went first, then Lisa, and Mark at the end. After the dwarf had jumped into and past the waterfall, the path cracked and collapsed.

Rylan Silverblade waited for them at the end of a small natural cavern, filled with eroded stone covered by moss and lichen so thick that Lisa could almost smell it. There was a heavy iron door in front of Rylan, with an engraved monster instead of knob.

"Is that a shark?" Mark wondered. It was way too pixelated to tell, but the creature seemed to have a siege weapon mounted on its back.

"Probably a new type of monster," Lisa said. "We better hurry inside. An underwater fight would be terrible with half of us in heavy armor."

"Just shock them with thunder magic," Ryan said as his Rogue worked through the lock and disabled a pair of pretty obvious dart traps. A pit trap, which couldn't be disabled, was marked on everyone's screen once the Rogue identified it.

"Mark, get this open," Ryan ordered, stepping back as the heavy lock fell with a thud.

"Aye aye, Captain." Mark jumped over the pit trap and charged the door with a bull-rush tackle. The impact threw the iron doors wide open with the deafening clang of metal hitting metal. "Hey guys!" Mark called, taunting the dark corridor that opened to receive them. "We're home!"

As a response, a stream of imps flew out of the shadows as spiderlings flooded the walls and ceilings and headed for them.

The imps were annoying, but Lisa had enough experience dealing with them. They weren't dangerous in small numbers, and they were barely intelligent, but they knew basic combat—they ignored Mark's Fighter and Rylan Silverblade and headed straight for the casters, wielding those cruel tridents of theirs as their obscene songs came through the speakers of her computer.

"We need crowd control against the spiderlings," Lisa advised Omar while her hands flew over her keyboard's hotkeys and activated a couple of macros. Her Cleric was the team's one man army against all things undead and demonic. Had she been running her main character, she would've used a *mass banishment* that would've sent the nasty critters back to Hell in a single strike.

Instead, her mid-level character activated a *circle of protection* to keep herself from getting swarmed, then enchanted her mace with a *holy smite* spell that made it glow like a blinding star, searing the darkness in its wake and turning several imps to smoke and ash with every swing.

A few steps in front of her, Mark set his tower shield on the floor and activated his *challenge,* an aura that forced any enemy passing him by to either attack him or suffer heavy penalties to their Spirit attribute. His axe wasn't the best weapon to deal with swarms, but his Endurance was so high that his health points barely registered a tickle as the spiderlings covered his body with bites.

"I can do this all day," Mark said while his character picked spiderlings off and crushed them under the weight of his boots.

"We don't have all night, Mark, I've got a life," Ryan said as he retreated past the dwarf's shield. The Rogue was a glass cannon meant for infiltration, scouting, and dealing massive damage to singular, elite enemies. And when Ryan wasn't the absolute best at everything, he got mad. "Hurry up and kill these stupid critters, new guy. Quick!"

"Sure, sure," Omar said nervously. "What should I use? You're all in my *fireball* area of effect!"

"No *fireballs* in an enclosed corridor!" exclaimed Lisa, Mark, and even Ryan in unison.

"Omar, Ed had a minor spell for dealing with weak swarms somewhere in his hotkeys," Lisa hurried to say. "Something to do with a fog. It shouldn't hurt us much, but it's lethal for the spiders." She swung her mace again, destroying three imps that were trying to strike her character in the back—as if she couldn't see them perfectly with the top-down view of the screen.

Although, they wouldn't know that, she told herself as Omar unleashed a freezing fog that engulfed the corridor for thirty seconds. Lisa's HP went down by about a tenth of a percent. When the fog cleared, it revealed a corridor littered with the twitching bodies of the spiderlings.

"Finally," Ryan muttered.

Lisa dispatched the last set of imps and laid down a *mark of healing* spell that recovered the party's lost HP over the course of a minute.

After that, they hurried down the corridor, with Rylan Silverblade at the lead, scouting for traps under the cover of shadows. This dungeon had a low ceiling. According to the Quest-log, the leader was using it to smuggle drugs and cursed items into Constantina—not that anyone besides her bothered to read the quest's descriptions.

It was marked as a medium-threat kind of dungeon, which meant the Boss at the end wouldn't try to implement some of the nasty tricks the high-threat dungeons liked to pull, like collapsing the entire thing over their heads, or flooding the corridors, or simply picking up shop and running away before they could engage in battle. It was because of these tricks that many players avoided the high-level dungeons like the plague, but Lisa enjoyed the challenge, and didn't mind spending a week or two chasing after a tricky Boss all over the map, because she knew that once she caught up with him, the victory was even more rewarding.

"There's some shit-tier critters up ahead," Ryan warned them. "Past that locked door. *Now* would be a good time for a *fireball*, actually. Mark, get it open so the new guy can have his time to shine, alright?"

"How nice of you, Boss," Mark said as his dwarf bull-rushed the chamber's iron door.

The chamber seemed to be a staging area for transporting the merchandise around. Lisa saw a couple disassembled carts strewn about next to iron-ringed barrels, with a small stream of water splitting the room in two. It was guarded by what seemed to be man-sized carnivorous plants, not that she had enough time to look before Omar waltzed in and unleashed a *fireball* rune that killed everything in sight.

LISA and the others worked their way through the dungeon over the course of two hours. Some of the traps were quite devious, and Ryan wasn't able to spot them all. The acid ooze that dropped from the ceiling and engulfed Mark when he stepped on a pressure plate had been especially annoying, because the dwarf lacked the Agility to get out, and although Lisa and Omar freed him before his HP reached critical levels, he lost most of his armor and weapons due to corrosion.

"Hah! What an idiot," Ryan said while Mark burned health potions to withstand the lingering damage of the acid. Then the Rogue stepped on another pressure plate and the floor collapsed, leading him down a long chute that ended in another acid ooze.

"Whoever built this dungeon has a thing for oozes," Lisa commented, ten minutes and many potions later, once they'd managed to get Ryan out.

"Remind you of someone?" asked Mark through a private chat so Ryan wouldn't hear.

"I'm just saying."

"No one built anything," Ryan muttered. Lisa didn't need to see him to know from his tone that he was fuming already. "Most dungeons are randomly generated, so this is all just shit luck and shit skill. Omar, *please,* next time you see an ooze freeze it with your damn ice, that's how you kill them as fast as possible!"

"What about a *fireball?*" Omar asked timidly.

"Do you want dozens of tiny angry oozes? Because that's what you get if you use fire against one… did you even read the wiki?"

"All right, guys, get ready. More junkers up ahead," Lisa said, more to get Ryan's attention away from Omar than because junkers ought to worry them.

Junkers, according to the database, were low-ranking demons above imps and below everything else. The Bosses summoned them from Hell itself to do their bidding. They were hunchbacked humanoids with a long set of claws instead of fingers, blind and deaf and butt-ugly. They detected prey through movement and smell, and if ignored could quickly take out a spellcaster, so the responsibility rested mostly on Ryan and Mark to keep them far away and manageable, which they did while Lisa and Omar blasted them to pieces using *ice bolts* and *smites* repeatedly.

They were neck deep in dead junkers when they realized they'd stumbled across the Boss Room, and only because they saw the tiny stone Seat hidden behind a giant cobweb.

In most normal dungeons, the Boss Room was the most important and luxurious single chamber around. It was the one with the Seat, the heart of the dungeon which, when destroyed, disabled most magical traps and the Portal. In this case, though, the Boss room was tiny, secluded, and partially flooded by a crack on the walls that let the water from the river above in. Cobwebs covered almost every inch, so much so that even the junkers got trapped sometimes. Ryan spent more time hacking the silver strands to pieces than actually fighting at all, and judging by his cursing, he was getting tired of it real quick.

"There's the Seat!" Lisa exclaimed. "Quick, someone take it out—"

Of course, the Boss appeared right before they could make their move. The wall next to them exploded out of nowhere, and a creature so big it barely fit in the chamber rushed at them, long and terrible horns aimed their way and blazing red eyes shining through the darkness. Its skin was black and bulging with muscle, with precise stitching holding together the separate body parts, some of which had clearly been taken from different creatures.

Lisa yelped and barely had time to set a couple wards of protection against physical damage up before the giant undead bull smashed against Omar—the Wizard's health halving with the collision—gored him straight through, and kept going. The bull smashed against the next wall and continued on, disappearing into the shadows while Omar's HP kept dropping.

"What the fuck," Ryan bellowed. "Move, you idiot!"

"I can't!" Omar exclaimed through the sound of frantic keystrokes. "It stunned me!"

"It didn't even say its speech," Mark whispered.

The Boss fight was on—Lisa could tell by the change in music. She jumped after the Boss, already preparing a healing spell.

The bull had finally stopped in the middle of an entirely new room. The creature seemed to be grappling Omar down on purpose, right in the middle of an anti-magic circle, its field encapsulating both Boss and Hero like a translucent bubble.

What the hell? Lisa thought. That was one hell of a nasty combo. Anti-magic fields countered spellcasters *hard,* and worse yet, dying inside one caused a final death, in which the player not only lost the character but all its loot. Final deaths were represented in game-play by a fierce explosion.

"Get the hell out of there, you idiot!" Ryan exclaimed.

"I can't, my spells aren't working!" Omar exclaimed, almost in hysterics.

Lisa tried to use a *healing command,* but the anti-magic field dissipated the spell like it was nothing. For a bunch of smugglers, the creators of the dungeon had invested some serious gold in this trap. *There are no creators,* Lisa reminded herself. *It's supposed to be all randomly generated.*

Since magic wasn't working, she had her cleric draw her mace and charge at the giant bull.

It turned out to be one of the most resistant undead she'd ever fought. Her mace, usually a perfect weapon against undead, simply wasn't heavy enough to deal with the bull's enhanced body. Its Endurance was ridiculous, somewhere in the upper twenties.

"Get. Off. Him!" Lisa saw how the last dredges of Omar's HP drained away. She tried to strike at the monster's head, but the creature kicked at her almost without noticing her, and the Cleric flew away from the Circle and into the wall's rubble.

"Do I have to do everything around here?" Ryan muttered as he and Mark entered the circle and rained blows upon the bull. This time, with the dwarf's axe taking chunks out of grayish meat away with each strike, and Rylan Silverblade's curved daggers tearing open tendon and joint, Lisa dared to hope that they'd be able to kill it in time.

Then the bull lifted the Wizard with one terrible bellow and smashed him back down again with all of its weight behind, several tons of bone and muscle. The Wizard's remaining HP vanished and Lisa could swear for an instant that she could see the pixelated body split—

The explosion was so strong that, for a second, Lisa believed her computer screen was shaking for real. Pieces of debris fell from the ceiling and a cloud of dust obscured her top-down view, not that she was looking—instead, all her attention was on downing health potions and casting recovery spells.

The dust cleared after a few seconds to reveal the silhouette of the bull, its skull picked clean of skin by the force of the explosion, and the many wounds it had sustained clear on its undead body. It glanced stupidly at the broken magical circle, and then at Lisa's Cleric. The monster raised a hoof and struck the ground.

"Oh, no you don't," said Ryan as his Rogue emerged from the dust at half-health. "Now it's *my* turn. Mark, set a goddamn flank for me, right now!"

The dwarf rushed at the bull with his battered tower shield lifted high, striking at the creature with it while releasing a *taunt* shout at the same time.

Rylan Silverblade unleashed his combo.

That was the thing with Rogue characters. They were hardly useful against hordes, but against a single opponent they really shone. And if there was something that Ryan loved, it was being in the spotlight.

First, he unleashed a *shadow strike* straight from the front, both blades glowing purple as the Rogue flashed and disappeared before the bull had a chance to make a move, only to reappear a second later behind the boss. A smoking criss-cross slash appeared on the bull's flank.

The boss tried to face the Rogue, but the *taunt* from Mark beat its Spirit and forced it to try to stomp the Fighter down while Rylan unleashed a *sneak attack flurry* from the back, purple light erupting from each strike. The Rogue then activated a *shadow step* followed by an *eviscerate*. Rylan disappeared in a puff of smoke and reappeared right atop the bull's neck as his curved daggers glowed red. The bull tried to dodge out of the way, but its bulk made it too slow—the Rogue fell upon its flank as his weapons swung down at the same time with magically enhanced strength. There was a sound of flesh tearing and bone cracking and the creature's head rolled on the floor, the light of its eyes slowly fading away.

Rylan Silverblade did a cartwheel and landed just before the bull's corpse had time to fall.

"Damn," Omar said. "You almost soloed the thing."

"There. That's how you do it," Ryan said. Then, under his breath, "Bunch of fucking noobs, really. I don't know why I waste my time with you."

With the Boss dead, destroying the Seat was a trivial matter. Lisa did the honors with her mace. The dungeon slowly collapsed around them, the experience points slowly tricking in through a status bar on a corner of the screen as they ran out. The way Ivalis Online worked, they'd get the gold coins they'd earned from the wreckage a few hours after the fact, sent straight to their inventory by the Church.

That was how playing Ivalis Online worked. It was a very strange game, and Lisa couldn't help but wonder about it. For a decade-old software, sometimes it could be quite realistic. Other times, it made no sense whatsoever.

Outside, back in the real world, it had gotten late. Diana would likely be home soon, drunk out of her mind, and hopefully alone. But in the meantime, the room was freezing and dark, as if the candlelight wasn't enough to fight off the strange, sudden fear that threatened to overwhelm Lisa.

With one trembling hand, she flicked on the light switch.

BACK IN THE War Room of the Haunt, Ed and Lavy studied the wreckage from the dungeon's final room using a crystal ball.

"Sorry about your dungeon, Lord Wright," said the ball's owner, a floating blue pufferfish with spikes protruding from its tough hide. Diviner Pholk was an abnatir, a kind of demonic inhabitant from the Netherworld. Pholk was young and timid and had spent most of his life studying. Ed was the first Dungeon Lord the abnatir worked for, and Pholk was visibly excited.

Ed couldn't help but think of him as "the intern."

"It's quite alright," Ed said. "It did what it was supposed to do.

Still, please send a *message* to Klek and Kaga to get more acid oozes whenever they've got some free time."

"Are the oozes part of your master plan?" Pholk asked, his giant black eyes bulging with amazement.

"Not really. I just really like them." Ed shrugged and then tapped the crystal ball as if dealing with an old TV and trying to improve the reception. "Did you find the beam?"

"It was as you said, Lord Wright," said the intern. "Using Master Lavina's crystal and my personal detection spell, I was able to pinpoint a beam spell connected to each Hero. The spell is too advanced for me to figure out much about it, but it seems to be some kind of complex mixture of effects. Instructions and conditions, along with status updates and confirmations. Whatever it is, it involves many schools of spellcraft." He said this with unmistakable admiration in his voice. "I'd give anything to talk with the person who designed it."

Likewise, Ed thought.

"How did you know?" Lavy asked Ed. "About the beam."

"I didn't. Not exactly, at least," Ed explained. "But there *had* to be some way the players control the Heroes from Earth, as well as a very good reason why the Inquisition is using gamers instead of trained Inquisitors to man them. You taught me that all spells need to connect with their target, so I figured there was some kind of magic involved and took the gamble."

"But golems do not need an external set of instructions," Pholk said. "That's what the Heroes are, right? Some kind of advanced construct?"

"Yes and no," Ed said. "They are a kind of golem with no autonomy, controlled by a third party through that signal. When the anti-magic field interrupted my old Wizard's control signal, and it suffered enough internal damage, an internal enchantment activated a self-destruct sequence." It wasn't terribly complicated to set up. A couple *fireball* runes, then a simple *status* mechanism hooked up to an *alarm* to trigger the runes.

The Head Researcher rubber her sleep-deprived eyes. "The control signal also triggers the teleport, then? No wonder it's Heroic-ranked. Only a few Heiligian Wizards are powerful enough to set up that kind of mechanism." She bit her lip and picked at her fingernails. "It's a double set of security measures— that's why all Dungeon Lords had so much trouble with it. If they interrupt the signal, the internal self-destruct triggers. If they disable the self-destruct the signal teleports the Hero away."

"Exactly," Ed said. "So far, we know for certain three things about the Heroes that the Dark does not: the signal, the self-destruct, and the power source."

"The power source, Lord Wright?" asked the intern.

"It's the thing the Hero construct uses to increase its own ley lines," Lavy explained. "From the looks of it, they do it by directly stealing a dungeon's energy output when they destroy the Seat. That's not a thing a normal golem is able to do. I'd say that if we were to open up a Hero, we'd find some kind of device related to a Dungeon Lord."

Pholk deflated a bit. "An artifact in each Hero?! But there are hundreds of Heroes! Not even Heiliges has that kind of fortune..." The intern shuddered. "If they did, we'd be doomed."

"Let's not get ahead of ourselves, then," Ed said. "We can learn more about the power supply by catching us a Hero and opening it up."

Lavy regarded him with a concerned glint in her eye. "And can you—us, I mean, can we do it? We just saw what happened when we tried to handle the double safety measures."

Ed massaged the stiffness in the back of his neck. "We can. Maybe. But the only way I can think of will be terribly dangerous."

"Of course it will," Lavy said. She placed a hand on Ed's shoulder, a surprisingly tender gesture, coming from her. "But we're going to do it anyway, aren't we?"

"Oh, yes." Ed grinned at her. "The good news is, if we get away with it... I think we just found a way to counter the Heroes. It won't be a perfect solution, but it's going to shift the odds in our favor."

Pholk ballooned in surprise. "Is that true, Lord Wraith? Have you finally ended the Heroes' advantage against the Dark?"

Ed shook his head and did his best to fight off an Alder-like urge to be mysterious until the very end. He lost. "Not exactly, Diviner Pholk. It'd be more accurate to say that Lavy was the one who did it."

Now it was Lavy's turn to stare at him with wide-open eyes. "What are you talking about? Me?"

"All this time, it's been right in front of us," Ed explained. "The dish you created? The towers we're building? That's our starting point. We don't need advanced Scramblers. We need to build the Haunt a couple Signal Jamming Towers." He paused for effect, then went on to say, "And then we build them all across Starevos."

2 2

CHAPTER TWENTY-TWO

HUNTING MONSTERS

The crowd in the Waterside Market flowed through the streets like an angry river about to flood—yet somehow it never did. Fights started and ended, cut-purses made off with their loot or were mauled by angry sailors, and homeless men with glazed, pixie-dust eyes stared straight ahead while begging for coin. No one stopped to enjoy the scenery—there was not much to enjoy anyway, and a bit of sight-seeing would mark you as a tourist, and thus a target, to the street rats that littered the alleys and shadowy corners. The air was hot and damp and stank of rotten fish and horse dung. The streets were paved with mud, drug stands and brothels sprouting to the sides like weeds.

In such a place as Constantina's Waterside Market, few paid much attention to a pair of kaftar running errands. Kaftar were common enough in Undercity, but that wasn't saying much. Despite non-humans being rare in Starevos, Undercity saw more intelligent species in a day than other Starevosi cities did in a lifetime.

Minotaurs, slime people, satyrs, and centaurs, even the occasional triton defying the mighty tide to trade ashore.

Few had seen a griffin up close, though. Griffins were Heiligian.

In a way, Gallio knew he should have been shocked by the rampant degeneracy going on around him. From his vantage point near the corner of the street, he saw a group of ruffians, none older than twelve, pushing an elderly Witch Doctor to the ground and stealing his purse as he screamed bloody murder their way. The kids ran off as fast as they could while the man sprung to his feet and cast a shoddy, black-market version of *arcane familiar*, which sent a pair of fanged, red, flying fish soaring through the air until they struck the back of one kid and sent him careening face-first into the mud, smoke pouring from the charred skin of his back.

Next to Gallio, Alvedhra tensed. He put a calming hand on her shoulder. "Easy there. Let the Watch handle it." He nodded at the rag-tag group of men that sauntered over to the fallen kid. They carried heavy sticks and round iron helmets that looked like inverted soup dishes. Once they reached the kid, who didn't look in any shape to move, they used their sticks to make damn sure.

"They are little more than thugs themselves," Alvedhra pointed out, doing her best to act nonchalant. Half the Watch dragged the unconscious kid away while the other half kept the merchant from charging at the boy, laughing as they did so.

"They *are* hired thugs," Gallio muttered. "Most of the professional guards were pulled into Mullecias Heights a few days ago. These bullies with sticks are the best the Waterfront can afford."

"The Militant Church is strong enough to protect itself," said Alvedhra. "And shouldn't we be the ones stopping them, anyway? We know that most criminals hang in these lower districts. Why can't we raid their hideouts and capture them all in one swoop? I'm sure the Light can't abide by us turning a blind eye to what goes here."

Gallio shook his head while keeping an eye on the pair of kaftar that pretended to mull over a fruit stand half a block away.

"The Inquisitor's role is to defeat the Dark. Petty crime is not our job." He gave a surreptitious nod at Cleric Zeki and Inquisitor Hector, who were watching the kaftar from the other end of the street. They returned the nod—all was good on their end as well. "Besides, you cannot imprison water between your fists. Water does what water does—it flows out. If we were to raid the Waterside like you suggest, the criminals would do what they do—they'd scram. Sure, we could catch quite a few of them, but the others would avoid the Waterside from that point on. They'd become much harder to keep an eye on, and they'd spread out their bases and operations to honest, hard-working districts."

Alvedhra let out a sharp whistle. "Are you saying we let crime run rampant by the Waterside to keep Mullecias Heights from being bothered?"

"I'm saying that anyone who steps into the Waterside knows what they're getting into," Gallio said without looking at her. "Now focus, Alvedhra." He pointed with his nose at the distant kaftar, who had left the fruit stand while Gallio was speaking. "They're on the move."

The Inquisitors left their posts and followed. Gallio could feel the sweat soaking his civilian clothes, and moving without the familiar weight of his sword felt wrong, as if he'd walked out the door of his quarters that morning without wearing trousers. Additionally, the shirt's cut was too loose and exposed. It felt like being naked. He much preferred his coarse Inquisitorial gambeson, the comfortable weight of his armor pressing over it.

He waded through the crowd with a casual stroll. He kept his head down and his brow furrowed as if he had somewhere urgent to go and wasn't the mood for trouble. It still didn't stop a pair of pickpockets, working in tandem, from trying their luck at his bag. He reached down and caught someone's hand near his belt. He broke it without looking at the man's face, whose whines grew weaker and weaker as Gallio walked away.

People left him alone after that.

The kaftar were far too short for Gallio to make them out among the crowd, but Zeki's shaved head was unmistakable, with an array of white scars drawing maps among the sunburnt skin. Gallio followed Zeki and Hector, matching their pace as to keep the unseen kaftar between the two groups.

The chase had lasted all morning and most of the afternoon. It had begun outside the city's walls, near the jagged hills of the farm-land, so close to the neighboring villages that Gallio's heart had raced for hours in his chest. Thankfully, the two kaftar hadn't met with any villager; they'd simply checked their surroundings, and then went into an underground storage camouflaged by carefully placed underbrush.

Gallio and the others, following Oak's orders, had crept up to the storage, disabled the *alarm* spells, and discovered a rough, drone-made cavern with a few left-over sacks of grain. Judging by the smell, the storage had been filled with ale or beer, and it had been recently emptied. Further exploring had revealed a tight tunnel lit by magical torches, with railway tracks set over the ground. Alvedhra had found signs of recent kaftar presence—hair and their rotten-meat scent—all over the place.

After a brief chat, the team had decided the tracks were like a dwarven mining system used to move people and ore across the vast underground distances of the mountains. Zeki had used a mapping spell to determine that the tunnel led straight to Undercity. They could've raced after the kaftar and captured them right then, but that would've only netted the Inquisition two underlings who probably knew little useful information about the Dungeon Lord and the extent of his infestation among the locals.

Still, Oak had been of the mind that Master Enrich should send the Heroes right then and there to burn the Haga'Anashi campsite to the ground.

Gallio had dissuaded him. They needed the Haga'Anashi for a little longer. If the Inquisition could map Lord Wright's presence, dungeons, and activities, they could *extricate* him in one strike that minimized innocent loss of life, and even catch him off guard—away from any Portal that may allow him to run and fight another day.

So they'd come to Undercity well away from the tunnel, and had tracked the two kaftar by inquiring among the local informers and homeless population, who were always willing to divulge information if you knew how to entice them to talk. Finding the kaftar again had taken hours, but eventually word came that two Haga'Anashi were headed for the Waterfront.

At some point, the kaftar had offloaded their booze cargo and ditched their cart, which meant they had had inside help among the city's locals. This spelled bad news for everyone. It lowered the chances that innocent life would be spared in the crossfire. Gallio hoped to Alita's mercy that those yet unknown helpers merely aided the Haga'Anashi in smuggling black-market booze and did not understand that the kaftar were working with a Dungeon Lord. *Perhaps* that could spare them.

But he didn't like their chances. With any luck, the taverns that bought the booze could be spared, but still... it was Oak's call. And if there was even a tiny chance that Wright had doused the booze with anything, the death-toll would rise to everyone who had patronized those taverns... No. The thought was too terrible to contemplate.

It was in Alita's hands now. The only thing Gallio and the others could do was keep finding out as much as they could. Information would save innocent lives, so he planned to sleep as little as possible over the following days, relying on his Inquisitor's talents to keep him going. They were in a race against time, after all, because the longer they waited the more likely the risk that Wright would try something nasty.

Even though the clan would be spared for a little while longer, there was no saving these two. The Inquisition needed to move fast, and the pair could give them names and locations.

Not even the Heiligian population knew this side of the

Inquisitorial calling. Most of the tracking was done without much magic, and that was the trick. Dungeon Lords loved to counter the Church's Diviners, but most of them forgot to cover their physical tracks. The Bards enjoyed to harp about battles and fire, about hard justice and necessary sacrifice, but in reality, most of Gallio's career had been spent on the road or on the streets, chasing at some lead or some suspect, always gathering information, and only rarely getting into a fight.

Sometimes he thought that, with the advent of Heroes, the Inquisitors were slowly being relegated to scouting jobs. Find the Dungeon Lord's lair, locate his secondary Portals, and then send the Heroes to do the dirty work.

It wasn't exactly true, though. Dungeon Lords were the Dark's main weapon against the Light, but not the only one. Gallio's work involved chasing away at hidden cultists among the common folk, tracking down the source of undead infestations, finding and destroying Necromancer's cabals, and so on—a never-ending list. It was as if, for every Dark follower he killed, two more took their place. And it wasn't only the Lotians doing it. No one was free from the danger of Murmur's corruption. A Heiligian who had fallen upon hard times was only one desperate pact away from a road to the Mantle or to Necromancy, for example.

Kaftar, though, had a way of ending up on the wrong side of the law more often than elves or dwarves. It was in their nature to look for trouble, in Gallio's opinion. This particular clan, the Haga'Anashi, was always eager for a fight—more so than their cousins. The Militant Church had ignored their antics for a while thanks to the useful services they lent to the Starevosi, but Gallio was sure that it was a state of affairs due for a change very soon. The Inquisition now had evidence of the Haga'Anashi aiding a Dungeon Lord.

These two kaftar would find that out soon enough. They had stopped, so Gallio did the same. Alvedhra and him scanned the crowd, searching for whatever it was the kaftar waited for. A pair of Akathunians hidden by their dark cloaks led a line of a dozen slaves in the middle of the street, with hired mercenaries forcing the crowd to part. One of the slaves, a male naga, gave Alvedhra a pleading look as they passed. His face was so covered in bruises it was hard to make out his features, but the red head and the tribal tattoos on his arms told Gallio the naga had come from Plekth. That naga was a long way from home.

And so was he.

Gallio closed his hand into a fist. What part of, 'If you deal with the Dark's envoys, the Inquisition will burn you alive,' was so hard to understand? And yet people did it anyway, and they had the gall to beg for mercy when inevitably caught, and then the Inquisitors would hear their screams when they closed their eyes for years and years, up to the point where their conscience couldn't stand it any longer and, against all orders, they'd forgive the life of a young orphan captured among the minions of some minor Dungeon Lord in the middle of nowhere, a kid who had only accepted the pact under threat of torture. How could Alita possibly demand the Inquisitors to take such an innocent life? Hadn't the kid suffered enough?

So they would let the kid go in secret, and then it would turn out that the Dungeon Lord had wanted to increase the strength of his minions so he'd infected them all with werewolf's saliva. The Inquisitors would only find this out come full moon, when the kid transformed into a murderous beast that would go through a bloody rampage in the Church's hospital, killing and maiming dozens until put down by the very same Inquisitors that had spared him the first time.

Those Inquisitors would then be forced to face the extent of their sins—of their failure. They'd look at the broken remains of the people killed by the werewolf, and they'd weep as they brought peace to the few survivors, who were now infected by the beast's saliva. All those innocent lives lost because they hadn't been brave enough to do what the Light required them to do. Most of them had taken their own lives afterward.

One of the survivors would be sent into exile, his faith broken and his honor lost. He would be shipped off to Starevos, where at least he would do some good. He'd find jobs as a mercenary and then as a Sheriff among the local population, and he'd slowly rebuild whatever could be salvaged of his faith and his conscience.

And then, just as he thought he could find a measure of peace, the Sheriff would stumble onto the path of another innocent, this one a young man from another world who had been tricked by the Dark to forge a pact with conditions he couldn't possibly comprehend.

It was as if history repeated itself. The stream of innocents to feed the Dark's hunger was never-ending.

The Sheriff had renewed his vow to the Light, because he was needed once more, and there was no one else to answer the call. And as sometimes happens with those who lose their faith and then find it again, it came back stronger, and the light of the *sunwave*—the mark of Alita's chosen—shone on Starevosi land by his hand.

He was unworthy. What Alita was saving him for, he didn't know. At the time, he'd thought himself so clever. He'd found a way to save everyone. By sparing the life of the Dungeon Lord, he'd saved the people he'd lived amongst. What evil could Edward Wright do? He would either resist the temptation of power and remain hidden all his life, or he'd quickly be defeated by the Heroes, like Kael Arpadel before him, and hundreds of Dungeon Lords before both of them.

Gallio had never expected Wright to resist. He'd never expected him to fight back. And he'd never expected him to *thrive*.

It was no wonder that the Militant Church's tenets demanded for the Inquisitor to lay down his conscience and allow Alita to deliver judgment instead, even when the sentence was terrible and inhumane.

Inhumane, Gallio thought. *It makes sense.*

How could a mere mortal like him hope to stand against Evil when mercy itself was Murmur's tool? Only the Light's cold justice could hope to stand against such an abominable being.

And now Gallio could only but wonder, as he and Alvedhra neared the dark alley where the kaftar had disappeared into, if he'd once again been tricked by the Dark. If, by saving a few lives, he'd condemned thousands more.

ACCORDING TO ALVEDHRA, the kaftar were excellent trackers in their own right, but all their training focused on monsters and beasts. They had little experience with the trappings of men, and even less experience maneuvering through a city such as Undercity. To their noses, the smell of fifty thousand inhabitants of Undercity must've been as overwhelming as the constant flash of thunders in a pitch-black night.

And she was right. The two kaftar only saw the Inquisitors' approach when it was already too late. They froze for an entire second, their ears rigid like a surprised dog's, their mouths open and their tongues partially hanging out.

The two hooded humans they were meeting with, however, reacted instantly. Right as Gallio was saying, "Stop, in the name of —" they were already drawing their daggers and readying themselves to lunge. Alvedhra aimed an *icebolt* rune while screaming at them to drop their weapons, but before she could fire, one of the humans grabbed something from one of the many pockets of his belt and snapped his fingers. There was a spark as he threw a small pellet to the floor, and then a cloud of thick smoke engulfed the alley.

"Don't kill them!" Gallio reminded Alvedhra, while drawing his own dagger and entering a defensive stance. He tried to peer through the smoke, but it was no use. His eyes watered, and he had to blink furiously to clear his vision.

Somewhere in front of him, Cleric Zeki screamed, *"Stormwind!"* and a violent air current slapped Gallio's cheeks while trying to throw him to the ground. Only his swordsman's balance steadied him, and the fact that Zeki knew he and Alvedhra were in the spell's line of fire. He caught Alvedhra's flailing arm, then pushed forward as the smoke dissipated in seconds, flushed out of the alley as fast as a sailor's wages in a whorehouse.

Two seconds had passed since the Inquisitors entered the alley from both sides. The kaftar were still too stunned to react—they'd drawn their scimitars, of course, but that would help them precious little. The cloaked humans, though, were gone.

How? Gallio stole a glance upward, at the rooftops of the dilapidated buildings walling the alley. They'd made no sound as they climbed, and their speed implied they carried special gear with them, maybe even enchanted. "Thieves Guild," he said, putting two and two together. "Oh. Dunghill."

"Wright's infestation runs deeper than we thought," Alvedhra said, half-growling.

The kaftar stood back to back, each one facing one end of the alleyway.

"That's a bad idea," Gallio warned them. "Haven't you realized what you're up against? Look at my character sheet."

"I don't see how we have many options left. We may as well give it a shot," one of the Haga'Anashi said, his voice surprisingly calm, given the circumstances. Gallio had to give it to them, the Monster Hunters had poise.

The wind buffeted the alley, making the kaftars' pelt sway in all directions. Zeki and Hector closed in from their end, and Alvedhra did the same. Gallio remained where he stood.

There would be no fight. The Inquisition couldn't afford to fight fairly when dealing with Dungeon Lords.

The wind became angry, and a sort of pressure pushed against Gallio's ears. The kaftar noticed it then, the shadow masking the moon, rapidly growing. An eagle shrieked, very close and growing even closer.

Someone screamed in surprise as a winged beast with the body of a lion landed gracefully atop the rooftop of the nearest building with such violence that it sent slivers of clay flying in all directions like shrapnel. Its beak was curved, designed to dig deep and tear the meat out of its prey, and its golden eyes surrounded by white feathers were focused on the kaftar below. A man in full Inquisitorial garb was riding the lion's back.

"So," said Inquisitor Oak, glowing sword in one hand and the reins in the other, "do you still feel like giving it a shot?"

CHAPTER TWENTY-THREE

DUNGEON UPGRADES

Setting up the fake dungeon had strained the Haunt's coffers even with Korghiran's line of credit. It had earned Ed no tangible benefit—no loot or new talent choices—but it had provided him a marginal amount of experience points, which was a welcome surprise. Apparently, defending and losing a dungeon was enough, according to Objectivity, to increase the dungeon owner's experience.

Ed stepped away from the table in the War Room, which was strewn with Lavy's new spellbooks, and faced his friends. "I guess it's finally time to buy *dungeon vision*. It's simply going to be too useful at defending the Haunt for me to pass up."

Lavy and Kes exchanged weary glances. "So, it looks like there's no dissuading you. Would you mind waiting until I come back before buying it, though?" Lavy asked. With a sigh, she stepped up and headed out the door.

"Wait, where are you going?" Alder asked.

"To take one last bath without wondering if someone's looking over my shoulder," the Witch replied, then left.

Kes trimmed her fingernails with a dagger while Alder chuckled to himself.

"Thanks for the vote of confidence," Ed muttered, rolling his eyes.

"Actually," Kes said, dropping the dagger on the table and standing up. "I'll be right back as well." She left without saying anything else.

"Women, am I right?" Alder asked, munching on a piece of cheese. He smiled innocently at Ed. "Always so distrustful."

"It's all right, Alder, you can go," Ed told the Bard.

"Oh, thank Murmur," Alder said as he jumped up and hurried out the door. "Sorry, Ed!"

Ed shook his head and sighed. Then he realized he wasn't alone in the room. "How about you, Klek?" he asked the Spider Rider.

Klek looked at him with big, round, confused eyes. "I don't understand what the big deal is," he said. "Baths! The water is cold and makes my fur feel weird. Soap stings my eyes. Why would you want to peep on baths?"

The Dungeon Lord eased himself back into his chair and considered this. "No idea, buddy. People are weird, is all."

Klek reached for a small bowl filled with insects and fruit and plopped on a chair next to Ed. "They are. They really are," the batblin said, deep in thought.

About two hours later, the Dungeon Lord and the Spider Rider reunited with their freshened-up friends. "All right, let's get it over with," Lavy said, sighing in defeat.

Ed shot her a small smile and activated his Evil Eye. A few seconds later, he bought the *dungeon vision* talent using his stored points along with the ones he'd gotten from losing the test dungeon.

Instantly, he felt the tiny change in his body, like a small twinkle rolling alongside his veins. It was as if he could feel his magical ley lines increasing in complexity. Along with the talent came the instinctual knowledge of how to activate it, which he did while standing up. This proved to be a mistake.

412

As soon as he activated the *dungeon vision,* a flurry of overwhelming sensations reached him through his Evil Eye. It was as if his eyeballs had suddenly flown out toward the ceiling in a second while still remaining attached to his skull. Suddenly, he could see the War Room from a top-down perspective—all the papers over the table, his friends' confused stances, their heads aimed his way, and his own body clutching the table as if he was a sailor holding onto a ship's railing for dear life in the middle of a storm.

He was still aware of his own body and could move normally —it only was his vision that had shifted. As a reflex, he tried to stand and gather his bearings. Instead of the view adjusting with his movement, it remained in the same position. Vertigo rushed in, and he fell to the floor face first, scrambling confusedly like a blind man while at the same time watching himself do it.

"So that went well," Kes said, helping him up.

Ed rubbed a sore spot on his knee as he deactivated the *vision* and everything returned to normal. "I wasn't ready," he said. "It's one hell of an experience."

"So that's why Lord Kael always sat down in his Seat before using it for a while," Lavy said. "I always wondered about that. Changing how your own senses work isn't so easy after all, right?" There was a hint of hope there, as if she were hoping *dungeon vision* wouldn't become part of Ed's repertoire of frequent talents after all.

Ed shrugged and gave her a guilty grin. "Actually… it was quite a familiar sensation. It's hard to explain. But it's not the first time I've seen this talent. On the contrary, it's like meeting an old friend."

He activated the talent again, but this time he was ready for it. He watched himself from his vantage point. Carefully, he stood up, easing his body into the different situation.

"How could you already be familiar with it?" Alder asked. "You said that Earth lacks any magic."

413

"Through a computer screen," Ed explained. *"Dungeon vision feels almost exactly like an isometric camera view. That means from the top down at a slight angle. Hell, I wonder if I can move it around—ah, there!"* It wasn't hard to visualize the controls shifting the imaginary camera around, and that was exactly how Ed thought of the talent—like a videogame's camera. Once he was able to finish the comparison, he quickly became used to it, and it stuck in his mind.

The camera brought him away from the room, bypassing wall and ceiling as if they weren't there. Outside, by the Kitchens, the Janitor batblins fought a small war against a baby acid ooze that had escaped from Kaga's breeding facilities underground. So far, the Janitors had managed to keep the acid of the ooze in check by covering it in flour, much to the cooks' chagrin. Then the Janitors chased the monster around, trying to catch it with a cast-iron pot. The problem was, the smaller the ooze, the faster it could move, and although most oozes were barely smart enough to feed themselves, this one had instinct enough to move away from the screeching batblins that kept throwing handfuls of flour its way. As the Janitors ran after it, they passed by a halfling wearing a tattered tunic, an individual that Ed had never seen around before. He was clutching his head and looking around, looking as if he had no idea where the hell he was. He seemed extremely hungover.

"Everything is business as usual in the Kitchens," Ed announced, back in the War Room.

He went down several levels. Jarlen's coffin was in the middle of her crypt, closed, with the vampire sleeping inside until the day cleared. On a whim, Ed tried to look inside, but the camera couldn't get pass the wooden lid. That meant there was a limit to the camera's knowledge.

It's probably for the best, he thought.

"What are you looking at now?" Lavy asked him.

"I'm just looking around your room," Ed lied. "It really needs some tidying up, you know."

Someone smacked him hard on the shoulder. Ed chuckled and ended the talent.

"Defending the Haunt will be much easier if I learn to master this ability," Ed said. "Not bad for a couple dozen experience points."

"It isn't supposed to be a powerful upgrade," Lavy said, pouting and crossing her arms. "I don't think you should overuse it. Kael—no, any Dungeon Lord I know of—just sat on their Seats, brooded a bit, and made sure their minions weren't messing anything up in their dungeon. Unless the place was under attack, of course."

So that's how most Bosses in Ivalis Online always knew where we were at all times, Ed thought. "Well, sorry to disappoint you, but I'll exploit any advantage I can get over the other Dungeon Lords. Murmur knows I'll need it." Especially if, a year from now, he was to face them in Tillman's Endeavor, a prospect he was still mulling over.

In the meantime, it was best to start practicing. "Kes?" he asked. "Would you mind designing a special training regimen for me? I'll try to spar while using the top-down view."

Kes raised an eyebrow. "Are you sure, Ed? A minute ago, you couldn't stand while using it."

"I'm pretty sure, yes. Do your worst."

A mischievous smile drew across the Marshal's lips. "Ah, my favorite words. Well, if you're sure... come with me, Lord Wraith. Let's test out your new toy."

Ed's good spirits faltered a bit. Kes had looked very enthusiastic as she left the room. *I mean, I did ask her...* he thought. But the way she whistled to herself gave him goosebumps.

"Now you've done it," Alder whispered. "Let's go, Lavy. We can't miss this. I'll need to witness it so I can accurately reproduce it in the Haunt Chronicles."

"That's one hell of a good idea, my dear Bard," Lavy said.

Ed's lips twitched a bit. "Fantastic." Not only did his friends get to see him make an ass of himself, future generations probably would, too.

A DAY LATER, the Dungeon Lord walked down the corridors and passageways of the Haunt, the cold underground air mixing with the warmth coming from walls and floor alike and becoming a pleasant breeze against his cheeks. He pulled up the neck of his tunic and patted his wild black hair away from his eyes as he swayed his way like a drunk man through a spinning corridor.

Kes' training had been rough. Although he had nearly a lifetime of gaming experience with the top-down view, it was another thing entirely to have his own body-and all his other senses—react to his input directly, instead of a character through a keyboard or controller like he was used to. But he was making progress, and to speed things up, he was using the *dungeon vision* to keep watch on himself at all times.

He'd only stumbled against the walls twice in the last hour.

Almost without making a conscious effort to do so, he moved the "camera" away from himself and down the rest of the corridor until he could see his destination. Heorghe had finished his work at the forge and was in the middle of guiding his batblin assistants to clean their workplace and ready things up for tomorrow. Near a corner, his younger daughter played with a small, hairy puppy that yipped silently at her.

Ed changed his viewpoint to hover right above himself and reached the forge after a few steps.

"Lord Wright. I was wondering when you'd stop by and visit," called Heorghe as soon as the blacksmith saw him. The batblins stopped working and glanced at them, doing their best to pretend not to eavesdrop. "Shame about what happened with your new dungeon. I heard all about it. A fine attempt, though."

"It did what it was supposed to do," Ed said. He ended his

dungeon vision effect, since it was getting awkward, but the dizzying change of point-of-view almost made him trip on his own feet. He recovered at the last second and pretended as if nothing had happened. "But thanks for the sympathy. In fact, that's why I'm here."

Heorghe looked slightly disappointed. "So, not because of the mine-carts. Too bad. I wanted to show you our new brake system."

"Later, my friend. Work comes before fun."

"I guess it does. How can my forge best serve you, Ed?" Heorghe asked, drawing near. "Can I interest you, perhaps, in a new set of eyeglasses? Word is, people have seen you stumble around like a blind batblin all over the Training Center."

"Real funny, Heorghe."

The two walked together, away from the prying ears of the batblins, while the broad-shouldered Forgemaster laughed under his breath.

"So?" he asked as they reached a secluded corner of the forge.

Ed handed him his sword. "Have you ever gone to the Netherworld?"

The man cocked his head. "Are you telling me to go to Hell, Ed?"

"Well... yes. But it's for work," Ed explained. "Think of it as a business trip. I need you to enchant my gear. Sword and armor, to start. Also, I need you to look into finding a cheap way to mass produce enchantments for our armory."

"The second part is easier said than done," Heorghe said. "If you make it into a quest, I'll see what I can do, but it's going to take time. Your gear, on the other hand, that I can do quickly enough. What type of effect are you wanting for your sword?" He hefted Ed's blade around, testing its balance and weight. "Perhaps a *vorpal* enchantment, so your enemies lose their heads when they fight you? The problem is, that kind of magic is out of our budget.

We could do *ice, thunder, fire…* you know, the basics. Or do you want something a bit fancier?"

Ed shook his head. "Actually, I need a specific kind of enchantment. Make that sword into an *anti-magic* weapon."

The smith looked bewildered. "*Anti-magic?* Are you sure, Ed? Swords are not the usual choice for an *anti-magic* field. I don't think there's enough space for the runes and the magical circle, and in any case, it'd be even more expensive than the *vorpal* enchantment." Heorghe tapped the sword's blade, as if to highlight his argument. "Besides, you're a magic-user as well. An *anti-magic* field would do more damage than good to you."

"That's not what I had in mind," Ed said. "I don't need the sword to project a field—I only need it to disable the enchantment of anything it pierces or cuts, if that makes any sense. It should be easier to make than an entire anti-magic field, right?"

Heorghe scratched his beard. "Yes. In theory. It's still a strange petition, but you seem to have something in mind for it. In any case, as the Forgemaster, it's my duty to make sure you realize that running someone through with your sword usually makes disabling their enchantments redundant, right?"

Ed smiled. "Most of the time. But yes, I do have something in mind." Something insanely dangerous that might end up with him eating a couple *fireballs* at point blank range, or worse. But it was better than not having a plan at all.

"Then I'll do as you say, Ed. I trust your judgment," Heorghe said. "What about your armor? Some strange request for it as well? Perhaps I can enchant it to break down at the first sign of danger, to keep your enemies confused."

"Thanks, but let's keep it simple. Add the best *magical armor* we can afford to it," Ed said. "Maybe something that can tank a *fireball* at close range, if we combo it with my *pledge of armor.*"

"So you do have expensive taste after all. It won't come cheap, but I agree with your choice. The Haunt needs you alive if we're going to keep hanging out with horned spiders and vampires."

The blacksmith waved for a couple batblins to come closer. "I'll have my apprentices go fetch your armor and I'll head into the Netherworld as soon as possible."

Ed thanked the man and sent a *message* to Kes to prepare a squadron to keep Heorghe safe. Then he activated his Evil Eye and created an Upgrade quest so Heorghe could get experience points for designing a way to mass enchant the Haunt's gear.

That done, the Dungeon Lord returned to his top-down view of the dungeon, found his next stop, and headed out of the forge while the batblins ran in all directions, scrambling to prepare for their trip.

THE SEAMSTRESS HAD their own workshop inside the Haunt, a couple chambers with materials, looms, and assorted tools for them to practice their trade. It was the first time Ed had stepped inside the workshop since creating it. Tapestries-in-progress hung from wooden hooks, with rows of bundles of cloth strewn in a chaotic mixture of color and material by the walls. The spin of the wheels mixed with the cacophony of gossip and singing as batblins and drones entered in and out, carrying cloth or finished dresses and other garments.

Ed strolled past the dresses and tunics on display and reached the middle of a circle of women from all ages who were working and chatting among themselves. He stood there awkwardly for a few seconds until one of them raised her eyes and saw him. She yelped and jumped to her feet, probably ruining the sleeve she had been working on.

"Dungeon Lord!" she exclaimed. The surrounding chatter died, making Ed quite literally the center of attention. "What a pleasant, albeit unexpected surprise," the seamstress went on. "The only member of your court that visits us with any frequency is Chronicler Alder."

"What can we do to help you, your Maliciousness?" another

seamstress asked. "Are you interested in a new tunic, perhaps?" She strolled around Ed in a playful, flirty way. "Black, perhaps, so it matches your eyes? We can get you some silver thread—that should do justice to someone of your station, my Lord."

"Or perhaps are you interested in us, Dungeon Lord?" a third woman asked, batting her eyelashes. The others laughed and cheered her on.

Ed had spent enough time around the Starevosi to know there was no winning this war while he was so outnumbered, so he gave her his best innocent smile and decided to play dumb, while trying to remember her name. "Thank you, Viorica. Perhaps another time. Right now, I need all of you to help me with an experiment." He gave them the small package he was carrying with him.

"Ah, a gift!" Viorica said. She hurried to open it while the others huddled around her to take a better look.

Inside, the package appeared to be a rough, very coarse sort of cotton-like fabric, gray and dirty-looking.

"What is this?" asked one of them, passing the fabric around her fingers. "It's so ugly. Did you shear a batblin, my Lord?"

"Rodika! Don't be rude!" Viorica exclaimed. Then she touched the fabric, looking both confused and disappointed at the same time. "But I do admit I have no idea what you wish for us to do with this, my Lord."

"It's thread made from spiderweb," Ed explained. At once, Viorica removed her hand as if she had been touching acid without realizing it. "Back on my native world, people discovered that you could use spider-silk to craft a very lightweight armor that is also useful against impacts. The problem was, since Earth's spiders are much smaller than horned spiders, creating a single vest is very expensive. So I figured, the Haunt needs a way to keep our minions safe... and we seem to have more than enough spiderweb to make into silk. So why not try it?" Hopefully, a spider-silk vest would be tough enough to withstand an arrow, yet lighter and less conspicuous than gambeson or plate.

The seamstress considered this, more than a few of them with a disbelieving, almost disgusted look to their faces.

"I'd rather not touch something that came from a horned spider's behind," Rodika said, frowning. "It's so... unsanitary." A few others nodded their approval.

"Come on, ladies," Viorica chided them. "Our Dungeon Lord came to us asking for a personal favor. It's our responsibility to the Haunt to do our best, no matter what the favor is," she said with another suggestive glance Ed's way. "How else are our brave warriors supposed to head into combat against the dreaded Light without knowing we're here, safely waiting for their triumphant return and doing our best to protect them?"

"You've spent way too much time with that Bard, Viorica," the third seamstress told her. But she regarded the spider-silk fabric with less obvious animosity. "Look, just keep those spiders away from me and I'll try to help out."

"That's the spirit, Narcisa," Viorica told her friend.

"How did you make this first batch?" Rodika asked Ed.

"Well, I transmuted it into thread using spiderweb," Ed explained. "I figured that there's some kind of procedure for making it into useful fabric, but I've got no idea what that may be. This was my second-best option."

Rodika shook her head and lifted a strand of gray thread. "A fine idea, my Lord, but I'm afraid it won't work. This thread lacks the quality we need to make it into a vest meant for combat. It'd fall apart. See?" She pulled the thread with little force, and it immediately broke.

"We'll have to conduct many tests," Narcisa said, but smiled at her own words. "Just like Master Lavina. It sounds fun, actually. Perhaps you could make it into a quest, my Lord? Reasonable people like us don't run around hitting monsters with heavy sticks, so experience points are scarce."

Ed nodded, happy that the seamstress were now in his side. It'd take time, but hopefully the next time an ogre clubbed him he wouldn't even get a bruise. And if the vests saved even one life, the effort would be well worth it.

Ed sat alone in his dimly lit quarters, enjoying a quick dinner while his drone butler hung by a corner and glared at him.

"Come sit if you want," Ed offered the drone. It was a chat they'd had many times. The drone's response was always the same, a half-assed curtsy followed by an obscene gesture when he thought Ed wasn't looking.

"Suit yourself," Ed said, chuckling. He wondered how close the drones were to imps, in nature, and where the hell they came from. He suspected it was one of those things where the truth was best kept under wraps.

He was eating with the door to his back. When it opened, he didn't bother to turn around. "Kaga, Andreena. I was expecting you." He smiled to himself. He'd been dying to say that line since he saw them leave Andreena's potion labs.

"Ah, yes. The vision thing," Andreena said as Ed turned to face them. "Thanks for reminding me I need to cover the ceiling with clothes if I want to take a bath."

"I—I don't think that's how it works," Ed said. "But thanks for the vote of confidence."

The herbalist shrugged. "Eh. I'm old enough to be your mother, so I probably have nothing to worry about. The Head Researcher, on the other hand—"

"So what do you guys want to talk with me about?" Ed asked in a hurry.

Kaga, who had spent the length of the conversation chuckling to himself, stepped forward. He was holding a small vial in one hand, and he set it on the table in front of Ed. It was filled with a sort of brownish-yellowish liquid. "We've made a small breakthrough in the hell chicken project," the Monster Hunter explained. "We figured you may want to hear about it."

Ed glanced at the Monster Hunter, and then at the Herbalist. "What's in the vial?" he finally asked. Something about the way Andreena smiled made him dread the answer.

"Before I tell you," the Herbalist said, "let Kaga here explain what he found out about our very own giant, murderous chickens from Hell, all right?"

"What's in the vial—"

"It always interested me," Kaga started, "how the hell chickens are pretty much willing to murder everything—including each other—no matter the size or the threat. Pretty much only Lavy managed to earn the respect of one of them, and we haven't been able to replicate her results. *But,*" he said, raising a finger, "they still live in small groups. They don't eat their offspring—not that often, at least. There must be a way for them to regulate their aggression, right? In fact, there may be several ways. This vial over here is the result of me putting that theory to the test. Do you know what pheromones are? My clan learned about them from a Witch Doctor who was also an expert in an almost extinct style of martial arts. Pheromones are a creature's way of telling friend from foe, and hell chickens work the same way. This vial is full with pheromones."

Ed grimaced as he uncorked it. It smelled like it looked. Rancid and disgusting.

"It's urine, isn't it?" he asked, hurrying to cork it again. His butler hurried to grab a couple incense sticks and light them to mask the smell that threatened to fill the room.

"Oh yes it is," Andreena said, her grin growing a few inches. "It's urine gathered from a female hell chicken a few hours before she laid a fertilized egg. I turned it into a very potent concoction that will last a couple days."

"Oh," Ed said. He blinked as he realized what he was hearing. "Wait a second. How the hell did you manage to get... this?"

"Let's not talk about it," was all Kaga said about it, with the distant look in his eyes of a man who has seen and done terrible things. "In short, anyone that douses himself with the pheromones won't be attacked by the hell chicken mounts. So far, it's been the only way my Monster Hunters have made any advancements in the mounts' training."

Ed and the butler exchanged terrified glances. "So we need to cover ourselves in hell chicken urine if we want to be safe from them."

"Safe is a... strong word," Kaga said slowly. "I mean, as long as there are no nearby male mounts who are in heat... Now that I think of it, it's mating season, so you probably don't want to get near the breeding pens if you're doused in pheromones." The kaftar snatched the vial away.

Andreena lost it at that, and began to laugh big, booming cackles while she hugged her belly.

Ed looked at the vial and shivered.

LAVY AND PHOLK were huddled in front of the Head Researcher's worktable, which was covered in strange tools, shears, engraving knifes, and other instruments, as well as a new dish like the first one the Witch had made.

Ed saw them long before entering the Research Laboratory, using his *dungeon vision*. When he reached them, the both of them turned to greet him. Lavy looked like hell—even paler than usual and with deep bags under her eyes.

"Ed!" she called. "Come take a look at this. We've made so much progress!"

The dish had its outer edge covered in tiny runic engravings, which came together to form an array of interlocking magical circles. It vaguely reminded Ed of circuitry.

"It looks finished," he said, touching the glass surface with his finger. It was cold to the touch, with no visible signal of its purpose or design. It was strange to think that such a fragile creation could tip the balance of power between Dungeon Lords and Heroes if properly utilized.

"Only a few details to fine tune," Lavy said. "We still need to test it, obviously, and figure a way to modify a Scrambler Tower to work with it. We'll need to abuse Objectivity a bit to create the effects we require, as well." She placed a hand on the spellbook on her lap. "Thankfully, I bought all the spells we'll need already."

Ed nodded. He was eager to start learning new spells with Lavy, but he'd had so little free time in the last couple of days... not for the first time, he wondered how days could pass by so quickly. If he weren't sure it wasn't the case, he could've sworn that Ivalian time happened faster than Earth's, where his 9-to-5 work shift at Lasershark could pass by so slowly that he'd wonder if time hadn't actually frozen.

I guess it's different when you're having fun... and fighting for your life and the lives of everyone you care about, he thought.

"Lord Wright, thank you for the opportunity of working on this project," Pholk said eagerly. "It's the chance of a lifetime, truly. For me to be a part of something this big, it's a dream come true. I cannot wait until we start massacring the Heiligians after crushing their damn Heroes for the last time!" he declared, puffing up with pride and battle-lust.

Ed gave the intern an uncomfortable grin. Sometimes, he forgot that the new minions weren't exactly the best of people. It was easy to forget, really. They acted so normal most of the time. Until they didn't.

"The only problem I see," the Dungeon Lord said, "is that we'll have to test it the hard way, in combat against a Heroic team. We'll need to hurry and create new disposable dungeons for our experiments, but that's no problem."

"Give it a month," Lavy told him. "Then the Inquisition won't even know what hit them." She smiled, almost as fiercely as the abnatir.

That was when the doors to the lab sprang open and Kaga rushed in. The kaftar had a maddened glint in his eye, and his tongue had lolled out from exhaustion. From the look of it, he'd sprinted all the way from the Haga'Anashi camp to here without stopping.

At once, Ed knew that something had gone terribly wrong.

CHAPTER TWENTY-FOUR

JUDGEMENT

G allio had a long, sleepless night where his mind took his body hostage and almost drowned it in a sea of vague guilt, where he swore he could hear the kaftars' screams all the way from the underground prisons of the mansion, many feet below his cramped quarters. The shadows of the branches scraping his window took the shapes of iron comb, plier, and thumbscrew, and the screech of the wind through the crack of his door was like a drill going through his ears.

Still, when he blinked and the moonless night gave way to a gray morning, he wasn't at all surprised by the heavy footsteps coming to the front of his quarters. In a way, it was as if he'd been expecting them all his life. It wasn't the first time the Inquisition had come for one of their own.

He had enough time to dress with a clean linen shirt, trousers, belt, and shoes, when the pounding against his door began, growing more demanding by the second.

"Inquisitor Gallio!" called a man. "The Examiners demand your presence *at once!*" His tone left little doubt that the meeting was not optional.

Gallio's trusted sword waited in its sheath by his bedside. It was clean, maintained in perfect condition, with a perfectly balanced weight to it. He reached for it and tied it to his belt as the pounding grew louder.

"Coming!" Gallio exclaimed.

For a brief instant, his gaze wavered between the door and his sword. He drew an inch of pale blue steel.

He knew he could take whoever was behind that door. If he really wanted to, he could clear a path all the way to the griffin stables and be well on his way to Galtia—or wherever—before the Examiners even thought of organizing a search party. After all, there was not a single other Inquisitor who could bring forth a *sunwave* in all of Starevos.

He even dared fantasize that he could land his griffin near Hoia Forest where, without a doubt, a grim-faced mercenary with black hair would welcome him into the small community growing out of carved rock and survivors like himself. Perhaps Gallio would get a reticent welcome to that place, but eventually people would forgive him. After all, he'd fought and lived among the community's inhabitants for years. Some of them were like little brothers to him.

Maybe even Alvedhra would come along. She looked up to him. She'd listen, maybe. And then it'd be just like the old times. Kes, Al, and him.

"It's too late for that, old fool," he told himself, chuckling sadly through his clenched jaw. He re-sheathed his sword and opened the door. *Best to face the music with some dignity*, he thought.

The Inquisitor they'd sent for him was little more than a young boy, fresh-faced with pockmark scars still red in his cheeks. Neither him nor the other two Inquisitors behind the boy could've stopped him, if he'd really wanted to run.

Instead, he pushed his hands forward and allowed the kid to cuff him with iron restraints. Each chain-link was engraved with tiny runes, to stop him from casting spells or using most magical talents.

"What am I accused of?" Gallio asked as his escort hurried him along the white corridors of the mansion. He kept his head straight and didn't bother looking at the other Inquisitors and members of the Militant Church, but he could hear their whispering as he marched down the mansion.

"Quiet," the boy told him. Gallio rolled his eyes. The griffin stables were on the floor below. He could smell the manure, like hot peppers mixed with wet earth. It'd only take a shove and a very brief scuffle... the three men were so close to him that him being in cuffs wouldn't make enough of a difference.

Instead, he walked with them until they reached the mahogany doors of the Examiners' courtroom. The kid stiffened his back and gave Gallio one last dirty look before knocking on the door and stepping away.

Gallio stepped inside the shadowy courtroom, whose windows had been covered by linen drapes. The three Examiners sat in their elevated chairs, only their frames visible in the dark. Harmon's broad-shouldered figure was in the middle, with tall and slender Bartheny to his right, and plump Hatter to the left.

The doors closed behind Gallio, the three Inquisitors taking their spots behind him, their hands resting on the pommels of their swords.

"Inquisitor," called Bartheny's stern voice. "Do you know why you're here?" A tiny strip of pale sunlight had evaded the drapes and fallen right over the woman's eyes. She gave no sign of noticing—her entire focus was on him.

Gallio held her gaze, and thought, *screw it*. "No, your Eminence. Although I suspect you're about to tell me."

"Speak to us in that tone again and I'll have you quartered," Harmon said with terrible calm.

"My apologies."

"The kaftar scum you so kindly helped capture has yielded to the interrogators," Bartheny went on, as if nothing had happened. "We've found that Constantina's lowlife elements are

429

guilty of aiding a Dungeon Lord for more than a year. Since only the Heiligian Navy is standing between Dungeon Lord Wraith's escape from Starevos by sea, we shall take immediate action."

It was as if someone had frozen his chest solid and then run him through with a heated iron. When Gallio spoke, his voice came raspy and distant, barely recognizable as his own. "And you needed me in handcuffs to tell me this?"

Harmon rose to his feet, sending his wooden chair flying backward. "You know what you did, traitorous scum!" Tiny flecks of saliva flew out of his mouth.

Gallio could've bet his life's savings that the former warrior was about to have him executed. But then came a tiny voice, almost out of nowhere, with only one word. "Allegedly," said Examiner Hatter, with one hand on his belly and the other flexing his fingers in the unmistakable tell of a magic-user preparing to cast a spell—if need arose.

Harmon's gaze drilled into Hatter's unflinching face. The fat man smiled kindly, and to Gallio's surprise, Harmon seemed to deflate. "Allegedly. Indeed, Examiner," he said, picking up his chair and sitting back down.

"The prisoners implied that Lord Wraith's dungeon is manned by survivors from Burrova," said Bartheny. "This contradicts the story you told the Militant Church upon your return, before being welcomed back into the service." Her lip curled as if she were gazing at a pile of dung. "Given the time you spent among the Starevosi while not in direct supervision of the Light, us Examiners have agreed there's enough risk that you may have skirted the fine letters of your renewed vows to protect your friends. We shall confirm or deny this theory by sifting through the corpses left in the Heroes' wake after they deal with Dungeon Lord Wraith. If guilty, you shall be executed. If not, your current status shall be returned to you with our *sincere* apologies." She held her hands as if in prayer. "In the meantime, you are off the case, Inquisitor. You are to wait in the prisons while we deal with Undercity's... infection."

Hatter rubbed his belly and sighed. "I'm sure you'll hate to miss all the fun," he said sarcastically.

"You're dismissed," said Examiner Harmon, gesturing at the guards to take Gallio away. "Get him out of my sight."

Gallio had dreaded this day would come. And now that he was living the nightmare, he found himself free from all emotion, as if a huge weight had been lifted off his shoulder. For the first time in so long, he had nothing left to fear, because the worst had already come to pass. As the Inquisitors reached for him and dragged him away, he realized it was as if he could see the scene play out from far away, like a god or a spirit floating above it all, observing.

He shook the Inquisitors free and stepped back toward the Examiners. "You know," he told them, fearless, like a Dungeon Lord giving his last speech as his dungeon was being raided and his last Portal was being collapsed. "This thing you plan to do to Undercity. You realize it'll only legitimize him, don't you?" He could see Harmon's wide-open eyes as the Examiner's fury washed all over him. It didn't faze him. "There's no going back after you do this. He'll see you as monsters, and so will the Starevosi. Everything they'll do to us they'll believe is justified, because of this. You'll create the abominable creature the Inquisition fears, Examiners, and it'll stop at nothing until we're broken and expelled from its kingdom."

Someone punched him from the back, right above the kidneys. Gallio bent over and heaved, and an arm locked around his neck. He couldn't breathe, and could barely speak, as the pressure and blood went to his head. Even then, he forced himself to look up, at Harmon and Bartheny and Hatter, to make sure they understood the gravity of the judgment they were about to pass.

How could the powerful be so blind? Perhaps those high chairs stopped them from seeing the wheels of history turn as it came to pass.

For the first time in his life, Gallio believed that the mighty and powerful weren't the drivers of history as the Bards and themselves made it out to be. No, they were history's tools, marbles smashing against one another from the powerful currents of destiny. It was as if, in one terrible, crystal-clear moment, he could see the gates of all possible futures thrown open. He saw armies of monsters marching against the armies of the Militant Church, he saw landscapes being littered by dungeons extending all across the horizon, and he saw hordes of mutated horned spiders flowing out of tunnels and drowning young Inquisitors—like the kid choking him right now—under the sheer weight of their numbers.

It wasn't magic. He hadn't suddenly bypassed Objectivity and unlocked the gift of prophecy.

It was just common sense.

And these three idiots just didn't have it.

"Don't worry, Inquisitor," said Harmon with a hint of mockery as punches began to rain down on Gallio. "The creature you speak of won't live for very long. No one ever does, against the Light's Heroes."

Gallio spat blood on the cold hard floor and looked up, although this time he only saw blurry movement as the world danced around him. His ears rang, and his throat burned as if on fire. "Then strike at Lord Wraith with all we've got," he managed to say with a raspy mess of a voice that was barely audible. "Use everything. Call all Heroes in Enrich's arsenal, all griffin riders, all Inquisitors. Summon reinforcements from Galtia. Spare no rune. Maybe then you'll have a chance at stopping what you started before it gains enough momentum."

"Don't tell us how to do our job, Inquisitor," said Examiner Bartheny, while Hatter looked sadly at Gallio's condition. "We're not the ones who screwed up. You are. Enjoy your cell."

Someone struck him hard in the head with a sword's pommel, and then it was darkness.

．．．

"I REALLY THINK you should come with us this time," Diana told Lisa, looking at her sister through the reflection of the vanity mirror while Diana brushed her hair. "There's this guy, Anton, who just broke up with his girlfriend. Poor thing. He's a production assistant or something. Anyway, we're gonna hit up the club with the guys tonight. Why miss it? There's nothing wrong with having a bit of fun."

Lisa grimaced. She hadn't slept well for the last week. Her nightmares kept waking her up. Right now, she would've drowned a rabbit if would satisfy whatever fictional creature lurking in her nightmares.

"Diana, that's not my scene," she told her sister. Perhaps tonight would be the night. "I don't know any of those people."

"Well, you'll never know them if you stay here all weekend," Diana replied. For an instant, Lisa saw a hint of concern glinting in her sister's eyes. "Before, it wasn't an issue, you know? You were having fun, playing with your... online friends, I guess. But now? I can tell you need a change of pace. I'm worried about you, Sis."

Lisa sighed. Perhaps her sister wasn't wrong. Lately, thanks to Ryan and her shit-hole job, she'd even stopped enjoying her own hobbies. Perhaps that was why she couldn't sleep. It was her mind's way of telling her something was wrong.

Maybe she'd need to do something crazy, like taking the offer the black calling card had made her. Why not? People went on adventures all the time.

Or perhaps she could do something less likely to end with her in a basement somewhere. Diana had fun and had a job that she enjoyed. "You know what?" Lisa started. "Maybe—" Her phone buzzed with a notification, followed at once with another one.

"You were saying?"

"Just one second." The notification was from Ivalis Online, an alert about a World Event that had just started, about some Lord Wraith Big Bad Guy who had invaded Undercity. Lisa smiled. Urban warfare wasn't that common in RPGs.

The other notification was from Mark. It only said, "Dude!"

"Well?" Diana demanded, now slightly annoyed.

Lisa shrugged. "Sorry, Di. Maybe next time." She avoided looking at her sister, so she wouldn't have to see the disappointment across Diana's face.

"Whatever," Diana said quietly. She grabbed her coat, a fluffy thing that looked like a deflated, giant rabbit. "Don't wait up for me!" She headed for the door.

"I never do!" Lisa shot back with a small grin.

She threw on her favorite hoodie and headed toward the fridge to prepare some snacks. It'd be a long night. With any luck, Ryan would even have some rich-guy thing to do and wouldn't show up.

Perhaps it would be like the old times.

SUNLIGHT POURED through the bars of the cell, falling straight on Gallio's eyes, forcing him to come to his senses. He grimaced in pain and squinted.

How the hell does Bartheny pull it off? He huddled in a corner and sat, hugging his body, aching all over. He didn't need a mirror to know he was a mess. The metallic taste of blood marred his mouth, his face was swollen and raw, and one of his eyes was closed shut. Even breathing was painful. He probably had a cracked rib.

"Assholes," he mouthed, massaging his sore throat. Slowly, his brain reassembled his scrambled memories of the last few hours. First, the beating. Before that, the Examiners. How Hatter had confronted the other two, in a small but obvious way. How Bartheny and Harmon had almost had Gallio executed.

And finally, what they were about to do to Undercity. He gave the window another glance, wondering if he'd be able to see the slums as the Heroes rampaged through.

"Some friends you have," said a low, raspy voice coming from behind Gallio's wall. The Inquisitor jumped in surprise and almost kneed himself in the face. "At least they treat their buddies just as bad as their enemies." The unseen man cackled softly in a way only someone with a snout could do.

"You're the Haga'Anashi we captured," Gallio said quietly, easing himself back down.

"Guilty. Thanks for that, by the way."

The Inquisitor didn't answer. He sat in silence, wallowing in his misery.

Eventually, the kaftar rapped on the wall. "Hey. You still there?"

"No, I headed off to Elaitra for a quick breakfast," said Gallio, grinding his teeth and clutching his head.

"Bring me some when you come back, will you?" Again, the kaftar cackled quietly, immediately followed by rasping wheezes of pain. "Listen, man. I don't know you. I don't even know why you're here. Probably because you're an asshole, but you're the best I can get. Your Light friends won't kill one of their own, right? Hear me out on this. They're about to do something terrible. Something from which there's no coming back. You need to stop it. Warn someone. Anyone. Lord Wraith. Perhaps he has the resources to save the city."

Gallio shook his head, then remembered the kaftar couldn't see him. "I'm afraid it's too late for that. And not a single Dungeon Lord has been able to hold off the Heroes for long. Even if he somehow survived an attack of this magnitude... Undercity's still doomed."

"The entire city? Or just the part that your people don't like?" asked the kaftar. "Yes. I bet you anything that after it's all done and over, Mullecias Heights and the other rich districts will be all that's left standing, not even a scratch on them."

"Perhaps." Gallio said. "Even if it is true, we're done. The Inquisition won't wait long. They're probably mobilizing the griffins as we speak, to pave the way for the Heroes. The gates are already blocked. There's a procedure. Please, stop talking to me. I cannot do a thing for you."

The kaftar chuckled one last, sad time. "Ah. But you have helped me already. You agreed with me. A part of you knows the Inquisition is not this high-and-mighty moral guardian it claims to be."

"So what?" Gallio said, clutching his head. "Why do you care?"

"Are you not an Inquisitor?" the kaftar said. Something in his voice changed as if the pain had eased up a bit. As if a kind of hungry eagerness had replaced it. "You just broke one of the most important tenets, did you not? 'Submit to the will of the Militant Church from the bottom of your heart.' " Gallio blinked in surprise and opened up his character sheet, despite knowing perfectly that nothing had changed. The sheet confirmed it. He hadn't fallen from Alita's grace. "It makes you think, doesn't it? That there's something more to your character sheet than what they've told you? That's one mighty *sunwave* you're able to cast, Inquisitor Gallio."

"What do you mean?" Gallio asked. "Who are you?"

No answer came. Outside, footsteps approached.

"Kaftar!" Gallio called. "Explain yourself. Now!"

The only response was the hard screech of the rusty door to the jail cell being pushed open. Two people strolled inside, the first one fully suited for combat—Alvedhra and Examiner Hatter.

Alvedhra met Gallio's gaze as the man stumbled to his feet, almost without realizing they were there. "Who are you talking to?" the woman asked, a look of concern in her eyes.

"The kaftar in the next cell," Gallio said calmly.

Alvedhra and Examiner Hatter exchanged glances.

"You're the only person in these cells," she said. "The Haga'Anashi both died during the interrogation last night."

. . .

EXAMINER HATTER HANDED Gallio a vial filled with a red liquid. "Here, drink this," he told him.

"What is it?" Gallio asked, eyeing the liquid with suspicion.

"It isn't poisoned, if that's what you're wondering," Hatter said, taking a small sip himself. "See? It's a healing potion, prepared by Cleric Zeki."

"Zeki hates me."

"And yet he's a member of the Militant Church who adheres to the tenets and believes in my orders with all his heart," Hatter replied. "He made the potion to the best of his ability."

Gallio drank the potion. It tasted of cinnamon, fresh strawberries, and childhood dreams. A pleasant sensation traveled down his throat and spread through his body. He guessed it felt like being hugged by a loving mother—not that he'd know. The pain lessened, enough for him to breathe easier and stand up without hobbling.

"Alita's mercy, they did a number on you," Alvedhra said. She threw Hatter a reproachful glance.

"Don't look at me like that," said the Examiner kindly. "I wasn't the one who shook off three guards only so he could mouth off to an Examiner."

"What are you doing here?" Gallio asked them both.

Alvedhra placed a gentle hand over the bars. "I heard what happened, came as soon as I could. Inquisitor Oak gave me some time before we have to leave for the slums. Even if you two have had your differences, we're still a team." She then nodded at Hatter. "On my way, I found his Eminence. He insisted that he was on our side."

Examiner Hatter nodded curtly. Behind the Examiner facade, Gallio saw a short, tired man who ate too many sweets for breakfast and drank too much. "Your loyalty is not in question, Inquisitor. After all, Alita granted you the *sunwave* during the battle for

Burrova. To question her judgment is to go against everything we hold sacred."

"And yet, here we are," Gallio said, crossing his arms. "What's really going on, Hatter?"

Alvedhra winced at Gallio's lack of manners, but the Examiner gave it no mind. He only sighed tiredly and shook his head. "Politics, Gallio. Same old. Same as always since the world began to turn." He looked over his shoulder. *"Greater circle of silence,"* he whispered, his hands glowing a pale blue as magic spread across the room. He cast a small string of spells to ensure their privacy. When he was done, Gallio suspected that only a demigod would've been able to bypass the protections. "Tell me, Inquisitor, how many others do you know that can use the *sunwave?*"

"What kind of question is that?" Gallio asked, frowning. "Many. All members of the Golden Circle. Inquisitor Errin of the King's Royal Guard. Examiner Harmon, even. And surely many others, out in the field, keeping a low profile."

Hatter waved a finger like a sausage. "Errin is a boaster. He claims to be able to use it, but hasn't fought in the field in years. I even doubt he has cast a single *smite* during that time. And I know from personal experience that Harmon, although an extremely powerful warrior and a real war hero, cannot cast a *sunwave.*"

"So what? That still leaves hundreds of Inquisitors—"

"There's only one man alive who has used the power Alita bestows on her champions. He's standing in front of me," Harmon said gravely. "No one else. Not the Golden Circle, not the war champions with thousands of experience points. Just a cynical ex-Inquisitor returned to the flock through mostly suspect circumstances, one who's so plagued by doubts about his faith even a blind bat like Bartheny can see it. That's it. The Militant Church has kept it under wraps. Not even King Varon knows. To maintain secrecy, the Examiners decided to allow any claims of being able to use the *sunwave* to stand unchallenged."

A flurry of emotions drowned Gallio's rational mind. "No way.

That's impossible." The *sunwave* was like a badge of honor for an Inquisitor, the equivalent in an army of the highest award that could be given to any soldier. It was impossible that, in all the Militant Church, a miscreant like him was the only one worthy of it.

Alvedhra looked at each of them with wild eyes. "But why treat him like this, then? He's a hero. A real hero, flesh and blood. He should be a symbol for us to rally to. Why would Examiner Harmon almost try to kill him?"

"Like I said, because of politics," Hatter responded gravely. "You're the wrong kind of symbol, Gallio. If the truth about you got out, we could send the wrong message to the world. Worse, we could send the wrong message to the Heiligian nobility. It's their pockets that sponsor the Starevosi campaign, after all."

Gallio raised an eyebrow. He was a man of action. A fighter. He understood as much of coin and politics as a spiderling did. "I don't follow, Hatter," he said.

The Examiner lifted a finger. "The Starevosi campaign is a royal mess. The King's coffers are almost dry, and the nobility is tired of paying for what is, in their opinion, a bad business venture. Financing the Heroes is already expensive. Having them active in three different countries—Lotia, Heiliges, and Starevos—is the crown's biggest financial drain. At the beginning of the campaign, both the King and the nobles hoped to use the Starevosi war tax to pay for the Heroes we need to protect our lands and to keep Lotia weak. But that has been a massive failure, Inquisitor. The war ravaged Starevos—they have little left to survive. Their nobility is in shambles, and the royal family has disappeared, taking what little was left of their fortune with them. So, our own nobility wishes to cut ties and leave. Take the Heroes out of here and focus on our homeland and our ancient enemy. King Varon, on the other hand, wants to find a way to remove the power the nobility has in his court. He hates to depend on their good will and their fortunes, and Starevos was his big shot. He's not willing to walk away. He's raising taxes and increasing the Militant Church's presence. This in turn angers the Starevosi and ensures they cannot afford to pay the tax anyway, so they rebel all over the country... which forces King Varon to raise the Inquisition's presence, and the expense grows with each Hero running around..." He made a circular motion with his hand. "Do you see where this is going, Inquisitor? What happens when a thriving Dungeon Lord is added to the mix? What happens when *you* step in?"

"I..." Gallio rubbed his temple with a pained frown. "A Dungeon Lord corrupting a city would force the Militant Church to stay in Starevos, no matter the expense. We cannot allow the Dark to get a foothold anywhere else. My presence... if what you're saying is true..." He shrugged. "What side is the Inquisition on? The King or the nobles?"

Alvedhra shook her head, looking as confused as Gallio felt. "The Militant Church is in the side of the Light. We don't take political stances. It's on the tenets."

"Well," said Hatter, rubbing his neck and looking contrite. "Perhaps what's true for the whole doesn't necessarily apply to the individual. Even if our organization stays away from court intrigue, our men and women come from children of both noble and humble births. That complicates things. King Varon is beloved by the common folk. Most of the noble Inquisitors still, although they'd never admit it, cling to notions of their blood making them better than their brothers and sisters. In other words—"

"Everyone's taking sides," Gallio said.

What was more jarring was that this had been going on for a long time, and yet he'd never heard of it. Thinking back, the distance he'd felt from his fellow Inquisitors—even those who were in the same rank as him gained a new meaning—he'd thought they avoided him because he was the black sheep. But maybe they wished to keep him out of the loop on purpose.

Examiner Hatter nodded sadly. "The Examiners are doing their best to prevent the Inquisition from infighting, Gallio. Despite thc way they've treated you, I believe Harmon and Bartheny have the best intentions. See, you are a powder keg. A fallen Inquisitor who found his faith again, then returned to the flock with Alita's blessing. There's power in symbolism, Gallio, and the symbolism about your tale can be quite powerful if used by the wrong hands. Both sides would love to get you on their side. Those that want to leave would claim that your powers mean that Alita trusts the Starevosi to protect themselves—maybe by creating a local branch of the Inquisition. Those that want to stay would say that your power means the Light considers it our duty to protect the country," he said. "And now, with Lord Wraith's presence in Undercity, the situation is even more volatile. Both sides are at each other's throats. Examiner Harmon and Bartheny needed to deal with the problem quickly and succinctly—no matter the cost—before someone does something they'll regret. Remember, if we fight among ourselves we're easy prey for the Dark. And even I fear what could happen if you're added into this mess."

"You beat him and threw him in prison because you don't want him to go out there and fight for the Light?" Alvedhra said, raising her eyebrows, her tone a mix of disbelief and righteous anger. "All because the King needs more *money?*"

Gallio eyed her with worry. She hadn't realized some of the implications of Hatter's tale. Heiliges had invaded Starevos more out of monetary concerns than of good intentions. She was the first Starevosi Inquisitor. No matter her feelings on the matter, once she'd had time to sort them out, she was as involved in this internal conflict as Gallio was, whether or not they both wanted it.

After all, Hatter had told them *both* his story. Gallio doubted that had been by accident.

"My apologies," Hatter said, sounding like he meant it. "It's hard to realize that our leaders are as human as we are. We mostly spend our time running damage control, just as confused about what's truly going on as everyone else."

"Why are you telling us this?" Gallio asked. He narrowed his eyes. "What side are you on, Examiner?"

The man sighed. "I'm an orphan, born and raised in the Militant Church. All my life. It's all I know." He straightened his back and his stance gained an air of strength and intensity, and for a second there, Gallio could see the reason why Hatter was an Examiner. He was more than he looked. "I told you my reasons so you could understand. So you would remain here out of your own free will because it's the right thing to do. Also, so you make up your mind. If you wish to take a side, I'll consider it Alita's will. But…" He and Gallio locked gazes. "While the fight is going on, I'll be creating a summoning circle to Galtia. I'd like you to come with me, once this is over. Something is *wrong* with the Inquisition, Gallio. The *sunwave* is the warning sign. This inner conflict is distracting the other two Examiners, but it's our duty to *examine* our wrongs and right them. There's even a risk that this mess is by design. By whom, or even how, I cannot tell. But together, we could get to the bottom of it."

So, there it was. At least things made some kind of sense, even if Hatter's explanation had created more questions than answers. Gallio looked outside, through the small barred window of the prison. Towers of smoke rose from the ports, marring the view of the crystal blue sea. The sky above was turning crimson, and the twin moons were but two slices of light, orange and green, like the smiles of twin gods observing the slaughter and accepting it as sacrifice.

He could only hope that not too many innocents were caught in the crossfire. That, somehow, Enrich was skilled enough to get the Heroes to target only the criminals. But that was vain hope, come from his knowing that he was as guilty as any other Inquisitor. In their pride, both Edward Wright and himself, thinking they could outsmart the Light, had only made things worse.

But, if the gods were fair, why punish people that had done nothing wrong? Why not punish him instead?

Unless it's not the gods who are doing it, Gallio thought. For the first time, he considered that him having the only *sunwave* of modern times could have some kind of meaning other than it being some sort of mistake.

"I'll do it," he said.

"Very well," said Hatter placidly. He eased his way back to the door. "I'll prepare the circle at once. Whenever we're ready, I'll send my men to free you. I'm sure Harmon will be too busy to find out about our... escapade, until it's too late. And then I'll convince him it was the best move." He faced Alvedhra and told her, "You're welcome to come with us, Inquisitor. This concerns you as well."

Alvedhra's expression was unreadable. Gallio had known her for many years, and still he couldn't fathom what was going on in the Ranger's mind. "I'll stay. For now," she said. "Inquisitor Oak is waiting for me. Regardless of the reasons of the Examiners, there's still a Dungeon Lord running rampant across a Starevosi city, and it's my sworn duty to purge the Dark." She clenched her hand into a fist. "I won't allow what happened in Burrova to happen again."

There was determination in the way she stood then, one hand on her sword hilt and gaze distant and determined.

You're not ready, Gallio thought. But he also knew there was nothing he could say to dissuade her. This was her path. Her very own personal quest. "Good luck, Inquisitor," he told her. "May the Light guide your path."

Master and apprentice faced one another, both fearing it may be the last time they saw the other. "And yours as well," Alvedhra whispered.

And then Gallio was alone again with his thoughts while Undercity burned behind him.

THE HOUSE HAD many rooms and many floors, and it was big and quiet in the way only a nearly empty house could be. A lone young man sat in front of his high-end desktop PC, wading through clickbait YouTube videos and meaningless social media drivel. It was a Friday night.

But he was only deluding himself, and he knew it. His gaze wandered across his room, at the consoles he'd stacked on shelves along with pretty much every game rated higher than an eight in the last few decades. His own Steam library wouldn't even fit in the room. He'd need a lifetime to play all that content, and yet he was bored.

There were many types of gamers. Most played for fun. Others, like Ryan, didn't even like gaming all that much. It was only that, in the end, they'd rather be anyone else but themselves.

If Ryan had too much peace and quiet, he'd have to listen to the things his brain had to say about him. *And nobody wants that*, he thought as he looked for another video.

When his phone buzzed with a message, he reached for it almost instantly, dreading that it'd be a notification for a spam email. In an ideal world, that cute doctor he'd met while traveling with his so-called friends would finally be returning his messages, but he'd learned not to get his hopes up. Girls were usually too stupid to realize what a great catch he was.

This time was no different. It was an Ivalis Online notification, sent in big bold letters, announcing a World Event.

- Undercity's Corruption! World Event. The city of Constantina in the distant kingdom of Starevos has been infiltrated by a terrible cult led by a powerful Boss. The only way to save the Good-abiding citizens is to delve straight into the corrupted parts of the city and fight in an epic battle against the hordes of cultists and minions of Lord Wraith before it's too late. Don't miss this thrilling urban warfare experience—come join the resistance against the evil Lord Wraith!

- Difficulty Level: High. Rewards: Very High.

Ryan sighed and deleted the notification. A World Event was a special type of quest where most players in a game could participate. In fact, it was usually too demanding for a single party—or even a big clan—to clear on their own. World Events moved the storyline forward in most online RPGs, and no player worth their salt would ever miss one for their favorite game. And the loot usually involved unique items that weren't available elsewhere.

Still, he'd have to deal with Lisa, Mark, and that other guy—whatever his name was—for several hours, and he wasn't sure he was up for it. Not only they were mediocre players who barely listened to him, Lisa was growing more and more nasty with him with every passing week. Sometimes he wondered why the hell she didn't quit at the store, but she was obviously not good enough to get any other job. He certainly wouldn't fire her and have to pay her unemployment wage, but the fact that plain Lisa dared act like she was somehow better than him was getting on his nerves. If only he could figure out a way to force her to do more cleaning overtime, she'd leave on her own. It was for her own good, of course. He only wanted what was best for people. That was why it was so unfair he had to spend the night alone in his room with only himself for company.

Lisa and that Edward asshole had been tight once. Ryan wasn't an idiot, he knew that his gaming "friends" spent more time talking on private channels among each other than with him. Who knew what Eddy had told Lisa before he'd gone insane and run away from the police? Hell, perhaps she was helping him hide.

For a minute, he ran wild with the idea of following her to her apartment, where Eddy would be hiding in fear, smelly and living like a hobo, wallowing in his own filth. Ryan would burst in like a shining paladin and extract his revenge on the man while the bitch bawled in a corner.

Ryan closed the tab of the children-falling-over compilation and looked at the ceiling. It was a cold night, which made his nose itch uncomfortably in a way he couldn't ever scratch. It'd been like that since that sociopath had smashed his face against his own desk.

I'd give anything for a chance to teach him a lesson, Ryan thought bitterly.

The world was shit and the gods could blow him.

He opened the Ivalis Online launcher. Mark and Lisa were already online—like he'd said, no gamer would miss a World Event of their favorite game if they could help it. Ryan smiled bitterly to himself—they hadn't even bothered to call him.

Well, he certainly wasn't about to let them have all the fun. He logged in with his highest-level character, Rylan Silverblade the First.

CHAPTER TWENTY-FIVE

JUSTIFIED USE OF VIOLENCE

The War Room was so cramped that the drones had had to take the table outside to make enough space for everyone. Ed stood with his back against the wall, wearing his recently enchanted armor over padded black gambeson. The faint glow of his armor's runes, hidden beneath the folds of the armor, gave an eerie appearance to his body. Over his head, the leg of Queen Amphiris was like a scythe about to fall on the unsuspecting public. He felt cold, despite the heated walls, in a way that his cloak could do nothing to change.

He took a quick tally of everyone in the room, flicking between normal and *dungeon vision* without even thinking about it. Kaga and his kaftar could barely keep themselves from jumping around—the news of their friends' capture had rattled them to the core. Klek was chatting with Drusb and a Rider named Vogkord, trying to keep them calm without much success. Zachary and Andreena were arguing by a corner, with Brett pretending that his knees weren't shaking. Heorghe and his wife, Ivona, exchanged gloomy glances and kept to themselves. Jarlen was sleeping in her coffin, and would be until sundown. Five horned spiders—one for each of Laurel Empire's clusters—hung from silvery threads on the ceiling. Alder and Lavy were to one side of Ed, and Kes on the other.

Did we cause this? he was thinking. *Is this blood on our hands?*

"It has to be some kind of mistake," Zachary was telling Andreena. "The Militant Church are the good guys. They don't go around killing innocents, they save them from the Dark!"

"They also decide who is innocent and who isn't," Andreena told the Priest. "And right now, we're public enemy number one. Remember?"

"Still! We must talk to them—explain our point of view. Oynnes agrees with us, we cannot be all that bad!" Zachary passed his hands over his shiny bald head, his jaw trembling beneath his beard. "A mistake. That's all it is. Someone misinformed Lord Wraith about the gravity of the situation. The Militant Church will jail the kaftar, perhaps chase after the Thieves Guild, have the King's officers close a couple taverns. That's all!"

"Oh, you poor old fool," Andreena said, placing a placating hand on the man's arm. "We both know that's not true."

Ed had never seen Zachary look so dejected. "We're supposed to be the good guys," he mumbled. "I only wanted... to help." He hid his face behind his tunic's sleeve.

The rest of the chatter followed along those lines, although Zachary was the only one willing to give the Inquisition the benefit of the doubt. Ed let them go on for a couple minutes, even though he knew they were there to hear him speak.

He did it because he was thinking frantically, setting aside everything that wasn't helpful to deal with the problem—he thought of Undercity's situation as "the problem" because it was the only way to keep calm enough to be rational. He ignored his feelings of guilt, and the fear that he could be about to lose everyone he cared for. There were only three questions that mattered:

What do I have? What do I need? And, lastly, how can I use what I have to get what I need?

Only that was worth thinking about. He could deal with his emotions later when there weren't any lives at stake.

He had the Monster Hunters. A few surviving monsters from the test dungeon. The Hell Chickens. Lavy's research. Laurel's Spider Empire, although it was still low in numbers because of the infighting. He had the Spider Riders, Diviner Pholk, and Jarlen, and his friends. He had the Haunt, so strong and yet so fragile, every life a precious resource he couldn't afford to lose. And he had himself, willing to do anything to stop "the problem" from happening.

Someone tugged on his sleeve, bringing him out of his reverie. It was Lavy, concern glinting in her purple eyes. "Ed," she began in a whisper. "You realize this is not only your fault, right? You need not fight alone."

Ed blinked. Since when could she read his thoughts?

"I've seen that look before," she explained, still whispering. "When you fought Nicolai. This time is different. You know that, don't you? If we are to win this fight, you must be something more than an angry Dungeon Lord. And we must become something more than minions."

"Lavy, I'm afraid I don't understand—"

At that moment, Governor Brett spoke up. "Your Eldritchness, are the rumors true, then? Has the Inquisition declared war on the Haunt?" Ed realized that the other conversations had died off, and that all eyes were on him. Despite his own confusion, it was his duty as their leader to explain the situation to them.

He threw Lavy one last confused glance, and then stepped forward. The others were assembled in a wedge in front of him, like a General rallying his officers before a civil war.

"A few days ago, we lost contact with our Haga'Anashi agents in Undercity," Ed announced. "We've reasons to believe the Militant Church were the ones behind it—our friends in the Thieves Guild confirmed it." He fought off the urge to pace around the room, fully aware of the need to present himself as calm and collected. "Through the spiderling grapevine we've confirmed sightings of heavy Inquisitorial activity inside and outside the city, as well as all nearby Heroic teams heading toward the city. The Thieves Guild is in contact with us through *message,* and they just confirmed that all the city gates have been closed off. We know what that means." He didn't need to add the rest—*it's Burrova all over again.* Back then, Ranger Ioan had decided to purge the village. Today, the Inquisition would do the cleansing. And tens of thousands of people would pay with their lives.

Chatter spread through his minions. He heard exclamations of fear, and anger, and disbelief.

"They'll never stop," someone said. "They'll never stop hunting us."

"I have family in the city!"

"You were supposed to stop this!"

"Hogbus, have mercy…"

Klek was so small compared to the others that people barely realized he was making his way through the crowd. Still, he kept at it, pushing and shoving until the others caught on and let him through. "So," the Adventurer's Bane said once he was at the front. "What's the plan, Lord Ed?" He didn't appear the least bit afraid, except for a slight tremor in his knees that only Ed noticed. "How do we win?"

"We cannot survive against the Heroes!" Brett snarled, his lip trembling.

Klek turned to the Governor with such fierceness that the man, who was several times his size, stepped back in surprise. "If you think that, then sit back and watch me! I'll be the *first!*"

Ed and the batblin looked at one another. Faintly, Ed nodded. *Thank you, Klek.* "He's right," he said aloud. "Undercity's fate concerns all of us. One way or the other, we put them in this situation. And I don't know about you, but I won't be able to sleep ever again if I let this happen without doing a thing to stop it. That's not the Haunt's way. It's not *my* way."

The chatter died down to a vague buzzing, and then faded to tense silence. Ed held the gaze of everyone in the room. Finally, it was Heorghc who spoke first. "Fine. Other than letting Klek loose in Mullecias Heights and having him solo the entire Inquisition, what do you need me to do?" he asked.

Ed grinned. "I'm going to need that enchanted sword, Forgemaster. And make sure all my warriors have the best armor and weapons available to us. Favor speed over everything else, though." He shifted his gaze across the room. "Here's the plan. We will head to Undercity, and we're going to build a dungeon inside Nicolai's catacombs. After, we'll evacuate the slums. Then we're going to build one hell of a special Tower, and we're going to send every damn Hero back to their masters. And once that's done..." His Evil Eye blazed with intense green fury, bathing the stone in terrible firelight. "Then we shall make it so those *monsters* that call themselves the good guys won't get to hurt us ever again."

CHAPTER TWENTY-SIX

WESTERN GATE

Mature hell chickens weren't in heat as often as the younger ones. This was crucial, and the very reason Alder and Lavy watched nervously in the middle of the forest, about half a mile away from the Haunt, as Ed's drones finished the preparations for their part in Undercity's defense.

Blood Fiend and Scar, their hell chicken mounts, eyed the pair as best as their eye slits allowed. Lavy had dabbed a bit of an old handkerchief in Kaga's... concoction—she refused to think further about it—then pocketed it. It had worked like a charm, reducing the mounts' aggression from "Every breath you take fills me with hatred" to "I'll kill you later, when I've got some free time."

"Are you sure about this?" Alder asked, eyeing the waiting drones nervously.

The drones waited for their command, standing above a pile of rocks about Lavy's height. One of them smiled mischievously at Lavy, as if it knew what she'd have to do soon enough.

"Of course I am not," she muttered. "I'd rather be *anywhere* else, Alder, including back in Heines' dungeon." She flexed her fingers to prepare them for spellcasting if the need arose. "But our friends

—ah, our coworkers—are counting on us, and if we fail people may die. That would be terrible for my reputation. We cannot allow it."

Alder grimaced. "At least if we stumble and they catch up with us, no one will be left to tell the story of how we died. That'd be one tale I'd rather not pass into posterity."

"Great, asshole, thanks for reminding me," Lavy said, shuddering. Behind them, she was almost sure she could see piles of smoke coming from Undercity. At this distance that could only mean the entire city was at risk.

Ed was there, as well as Kes, and Klek, and everyone else. When night came, even that bitch Jarlen would head over and do her best.

Lavy was terrified out of her wits. But the Haunt lacked the disposable numbers to oppose the Heroes... with *one* exception. And someone had to bring it to them before it was too late. "Let's get it over with," she said quietly.

Pale-faced, Alder summoned five illusions of himself and doused them with two entire vials of Kaga's concoction. Lavy pinched her nose. The smell was despicable. Next to her, Scar craned its neck in confusion at the illusions.

Before she could change her mind, Lavy mounted up onto Scar, and Alder did the same with Blood Fiend. Both hell chickens exchanged confused glances as their tiny prehistoric brains tried and failed to process the terrible series of events that were about to happen.

At Lavy's signal, the drones collapsed the pile of stones, creating a slanted tunnel below that it created a ramp up. The wind blew the concoction's aroma into the tunnel, which connected with one of the Haunt's hell chicken breeding grounds.

Almost at once, the ground trembled.

Scar craned its neck as far as it could and glanced at Lavy with one wide-open red eye.

She bent forward and pulled the reigns in Undercity's direction as Alder's illusions began to move. "Run," she urged it. "By all the gods, run!"

She didn't need to tell it twice.

"Nimble feet!" Alder exclaimed somewhere behind her as the two hell chickens jumped over root and fallen tree trunk in a desperate dash toward the city, with a veritable stampede of horny hell chickens following close behind, crushing everything under their step. *"Nimble-fucking-feet!"*

THE WESTERN INQUISITORIAL TEAM was one of the many squads deployed over the last few hours. Their mission was simple—nothing goes in and no one goes out until the Heroes are done with Undercity.

WIT consisted of a dozen Inquisitors and twenty Militant soldiers. It was led by Inquisitor Dismas, a veteran who had held the rank of Captain during the Starevosi war. He was a rugged man in his early thirties, trained for battle from a very young age. Dismas and the men under his command had been all hand-selected by Examiner Harmon himself, because WIT held a crucial position in the Inquisition's strategy.

Dungeon Lord Wraith's area of influence, after all, was known to involve Hoia Forest and the neighboring regions. If Lord Wraith was to make an appearance, he'd need to pass through WIT first, not that Dismas was very worried about the possibility.

He had encountered his fair share of Dungeon Lords and knew them to be a practical bunch. Wraith wouldn't risk his forces against the sheer Heroic manpower gathering outside and inside the city, with more and more Heroic parties being summoned by the second. Despite Wraith's growing power in the region, only a few Dungeon Lords of old would've been able to go toe to toe with the volume of Heroes that would be roaming the city in a couple hours.

This was the Inquisitions' trump card, and the reason they

held captured cities with only a couple hundred specialist warriors and not thousands of soldiers.

Still, Dismas looked up at the columns of smoke rising to the bleeding red sky, and at the tiny white sparks that danced through them in the distance—magic *hawks*, scouting the skies, ready to pinpoint the location of any enemy inside or outside the city. Even farther up, he thought he could see the silhouettes of the griffin riders as they glided through the clouds, but it could've been a trick of the eye. The air was tepid, and everyone was soaked in their own sweat under their armor. Most Inquisitors wore red leather under their plate, and leather was terrible for heat. Worst of all, there was no breeze to ease the temperature.

"I don't like this," Inquisitor Tius said, somewhere behind him.

Dismas regarded with a cold expression. "Would you doubt the piousness of our duty, Inquisitor?" It was one thing was to complain about the heat, but another entirely to break the tenets.

The man frowned. "No, Eminence. I'm talking about our position." He gestured at the surrounding terrain, the distant trees and underbrush, the plain rocky outcrops that circled the city walls, and at the iron gate looming behind them. "We're too exposed. Even with our *circles of respite* denying the enemy as much terrain as we can, we cannot surround the city with the amount of clerics we've under our command."

It was a common complaint from the newer Inquisitors, wet behind the ears, with little to no *real* combat experience. Dismas knew that if the Examiners could've had a choice in the matter, there would've been enough Clerics in Starevos to surround the country itself with *circles of respite* and more. But only a few recruits had the fortitude of Spirit to become divine spellcasters, and every Cleric that was sent to Starevos was a Cleric taken away from Heiliges—where even nowadays, new dungeons sprouting up here and there was not an uncommon sight.

He cleaned sweat from his face with a cloth, glancing down as he did so. A slight breeze made the yellowish grass tremble slightly, but did nothing to relieve him. He paid it no mind. He'd fought in worse conditions.

Hell, the fact that Undercity's Inquisitorial detachment had any Clerics or griffins at all was a testament to the city's importance as a strategic port, because sure as shit it wasn't kept around for its ugly sights or the ruffians that seemed to comprise its entire population.

"We've enough forces to do our duty," Dismas said. "Otherwise, the Examiners wouldn't have sent us here. And we do have the advantage. If he's coming, Lord Wraith must do so over clear terrain, with no place to hide for miles. Even if he brings an overwhelming number of minions, we'll have enough time to see him coming, *message* for reinforcements, and mount a resistance right in front of the gates until the Heroes arrive and crush him." After all, Heroes were the undisputed champions of direct combat, and few teams working in unison could make short work of hundreds of elite minions.

Dismas wasn't as sure of himself as he showed Inquisitor Tius. He'd fought against Dungeon Lords before. He knew they were a tricky bunch. Honorless, cruel, barely above the monsters they employed, in both morals and appearance.

If Lord Wraith managed to get a hold of five or six Devil Knights, for example… things could get ugly. And he couldn't forget that most Dungeon Lords' favored terrain wasn't aboveground, either. Technically, the Inquisitorial presence, as well as all the *circles* running everywhere in and outside the city, made the surrounding terrain contested, and thus impossibly slow for a Dungeon Lord's drone to build a tunnel within.

Unless, he thought, frowning at the glint of the sun in his eye and spitting something brownish on the dry grass, which the breeze was somehow making shake more and more despite Dismas being unable to feel the wind. A lone pebble rolled down a dirt slope. Dismas' eyes widened. *Unless those tunnels are already here…*

By the time the ground in front of him exploded upward in a shower of rock and dirt, Inquisitor Dismas already had his sword in his hand, had cast *smite* on it, and was in the process of barking orders to his team to rally around him. Then a horned spider the size of a warhorse charged like a boulder through the cloud of dust and ran him through with a horn like a lance.

Dismas tasted blood as pain emanated from his ruptured belly and through his body like red heat. The world around him spun with terrible violence as the Spider Queen flicked her head with a roar, shaking him off her horn and sending him arcing through the air in a shower of his blood and guts.

After hitting the ground, the Inquisitor clung to consciousness for long enough to see the horde of horned spider and kaftar engulf his WIT as it struggled to fight its way toward their fallen leader.

And then it was darkness.

THE BATTLE for the Western Gate was quick and brutal, only the start to what was sure to be a bloody night.

Ed, Kes, and Kaga stormed out of the tunnels just after the clusters of Bumelia and Cornelia, the former being the one who took down the Inquisitors' leader in one fell swoop.

This time, there were no speeches, no demands of surrender, no taunts exchanged between former allies. There were about thirty members of the Militant Church out in the field, and they were dangerous. Not as dangerous as Heroes, but enough for the Haunt to bring its numbers to bear before the Clerics had time to layer buffs on the Inquisitors or the soldiers could pull aggro away from them.

Ed rushed the field, sword in hand shining eldritch green, while his enchanted armor deflected bolts and arrows left and right. The battlefield was a scene of carnage. Horned spiders and Inquisitors clashed left and right, with strings of web soaring the air along with arrows and magic spells headed in opposite directions. In any other context, it would've almost been beautiful. But right under the lightshow and the explosions, people were dying.

For only a brief instant did Ed doubt—when he saw Queen Bumelia bite a female Cleric of about Lavy's age in half. Then he saw the smoke and heard the distant screams of the innocent people dying inside the city.

When the Cleric's friends tore through Bumelia's royal guard and fell upon the Queen, spearing her over and over as devastating magic tore through her chitin, Ed roared and dove into battle.

The entire Haga'Anashi clan followed behind, scores of Monster Hunters just like Kaga's elite heading into battle brandishing exotic weapons, some of which Ed had never seen before. A few rode on strange mounts from exotic places, but the majority were infantry meant for infiltration and indirect combat. They wore light armor, if any—leather and hardened wood, with chain-mail here and there for Kaga's close family, including his father, Kagelshire, a broad kaftar with a gray snout covered by a web of pink scars which marred his fur.

The Inquisitors that killed Bumelia saw him coming and realized who he was at once, thanks to the furious Evil Eye that he wasn't able to keep in check as adrenaline burned in his veins. One of them, a spellcaster, began a *holy bolt* that was cut short by a long, nasty dart protruding from his throat. The man gagged, and his eyes rolled over his head as he collapsed. The second one died when Kaga's throwing knife pierced his eye. The third one managed to dodge most of the volley of darts and knives—he had a buff up, a golden carapace that protected him from the rest of the projectiles.

Ed fell over him without thinking, his mind a blank canvas of violence and fury. His sword clashed against the Inquisitor's, who jumped back to regain his footing and attempted to enter a dueling stance while barking, *"Smite!"* Just as the white energy shone through his blade, Ed tackled the man, catching his forearm as both rolled in the mud. Ed drained the Inquisitor's Endurance using his black hand, and the man screamed in surprise and dropped his sword, which lost its enchantment as soon as contact with the caster was lost.

It was strange. All of Kes' training about techniques and stances, but in the middle of battle all of that theory just… faded away. Ed relied on his instinct to fight, and violence had always come naturally to him. He pushed the man onto the ground and struck the Inquisitor's forehead with the sword pommel as hard as he could. There was a sickening crunch of bone giving way, and the Inquisitor's forehead cracked back like an egg shell.

Just like that. Dead. This time, he didn't even know the man's name. That was the second man Ed had killed. And he knew it wouldn't be the last.

Two Militant soldiers rushed Ed while far more tried to wade past the horned spiders and the Haga'Anashi to reach him. He had to concede it to the Inquisition—they knew their win conditions. So far, his minions had kept him safe from any *fireball*, but it was best to keep moving.

And the best direction was *forward*. Toward the city where his people were dying.

He rushed the soldiers, who raised their spears his way. Ed was only vaguely aware of Kes running alongside him, and then past him, wielding sword and round shield. The Marshal angled her shield just as she entered the reach of the first soldier's spear. The man threw a lightning-fast strike forward, but Kes deflected it with her shield and then struck at the shaft with her sword, hard, throwing it into the ground and making the man stumble forward and lose his balance.

The second soldier was already closing in on her. Ed activated his *improved reflexes,* and the world slowed down as he jumped right next to the spear's path. He caught the wooden shaft with his black hand and pushed it away from Kes while continuing forward. He saw the terrified soldier's expression as he found himself face to face with the Dungeon Lord, as well as the way the man's eyes widened in surprise as Ed pushed his flaming green sword into his gut. A terrible black smoke escaped from the wound, and the soldier's lips trembled before Ed wrenched the weapon out. The Militant fell, clutching his belly and screaming in silence.

When Ed turned, Kes had cut down her soldier. "The Gate is ours!" she screamed through the cacophony of the battle.

"Not yet it isn't!" Ed shouted back. Around them, *magical hawks* fell everywhere in blinding flashes that would be visible from the vantage points all over the city, and the few Inquisitors who had avoided capture or defeat were sending desperate *messages* while his spiders tried to finish webbing and paralyzed them.

At best, the Haunt had only a precious few minutes to enter the city before the griffin riders and the Heroes fell on them.

Ed knew that a direct confrontation with dozens—maybe hundreds—of Heroes would inevitably end with him losing. The Haunt's only hope of victory lay in avoiding fights as much as possible, but they also needed to save as many lives as they could.

Looking down, he realized that his hands, armor, and cloak were soaked in blood that wasn't his. With trembling fingers, he touched the pocket of his gambeson above his chest, where he kept the Shadow Tarot card that showed him a bright possible future. He took a deep breath that felt like fire in his lungs.

"Stick to the plan," Ed told Kes. Around them, packs of his drones ran across the battlefield as the individual skirmishes died down. The drones picked up the wounded from both sides and dragged them back into the network of tunnels, where Andreena and her team of batblins waited, ready to administer life-saving aid. "The only way to evacuate the civilians is through the tunnels, but my drones cannot build with so many Inquisitors contesting the city. You're in charge, Kes. We're more familiar with the slums than the Inquisition, and the horned spiders know how to keep a low profile. Hide in the city, contest whatever you can, let my drones expand our network. Avoid the Heroes, and wait for Alder and Lavy to arrive before we begin the next step."

Kes nodded curtly. "What about you, Ed? Are you still set on your path?" She regarded him with concern. "You're going into the viper's nest. It may be far more dangerous than out in the city. We cannot afford to lose you."

"We cannot afford for me not to go," Ed said. It was common knowledge that the Inquisition was based in Mullecias Heights. An event of this magnitude would require whoever was controlling the Heroes' Quests to keep a close eye on things. There was a huge chance that if Ed went to the district, he could find the third person shown in the Shadow Tarot—the programmer from Earth. The creator of the Heroes.

If only Ed could make that person see his point of view—if he could convince him to stop the bloodbath... perhaps Ed wouldn't have to kill again.

He didn't dare to imagine what the consequences of failure would be. He needed this to happen, more than anything. His body burned with the urgency to end the fight. The victory condition was clear, and he was ready to die to achieve it.

Undercity was a shit-hole. It was filled with some of the worst scum Ivalis had to offer, not counting the Netherworld. Murderers, slavers, cutthroats, mercenaries, pirates, smugglers, and vandals. Its biggest industry was probably the whorehouses. It was easy to think that nothing of value would be lost if it followed Burrova's fate.

But Ed had lived among them. He'd seen bravery among Thieves, and loyalty, and even kindness. He'd seen the way the moons shone on the calm sea above the harbor, and he'd also seen the dawn painting the mountains gold and red across the horizon. The people from Undercity had welcomed him in with open arms, passing no judgment. A reject among rejects. Undercity was the Haunt's older sister, who had been through some rough times, but was pulling together.

Ed loved this city.

Right then and there, covered in Inquisitorial blood, he decided they would only pull him away over his cold, dead body.

To his surprise, Kes pressed the issue no further. "Very well," she said, clutching his forearm firmly. "Mullecias will be vulnerable. The Inquisition needs most of their manpower to keep the city on lock-down. They'll never expect an attack. Use surprise to your favor, do what you need to do, and get out quickly." She pulled him forward, so both warriors stood face to face. "Don't die, Ed."

Ed smiled fiercely and grasped her forearm back. "Sure. Take care as well. Try not to lose any more fingers."

With that, he left to find the Haga'Anashi and Queen Laurel, and Kes and the rest of the Haunt stormed the gates, the drones quickly chomping through the uncontested iron.

THE HAUNT'S troops entered Undercity through the Western Gate, finding only token amounts of resistance as they delved further toward the slums, where the battle was raging. A couple griffin riders took potshots at them from above, but Kaga's Monster Hunters shot volleys of *crow familiar* runes at them, forcing the Inquisitors to retreat.

Perhaps Alvedhra was there, circling the city, watching the carnage.

Kes shook her head to clear it.

It was Burrova all over again. Adrenaline pumped through Kes' veins, turning the world into a hyper-real canvas where everything seemed to happen in slow motion, and rational thinking was difficult, like swimming through honey. The flames that engulfed the buildings along the canal had an eerie, otherworldly calmness to them, and even the screams faded after a while, as her brain deemed them not directly worrisome. She saw families running down the streets, and groups doing their best to organize a resistance—Thieves, Akathunians, Necromancers, Witch Doctors, and many more. Undercity wasn't without teeth… but the Inquisition was adept at breaking those.

Kes had a warrior's mentality, her body reacting to the danger around her, emptying her mind of anything that would distract her from the only two reactions that ever truly mattered—fight or flight.

Had she been a mere foot-soldier, she would've welcomed the hyper-awareness. But she was in command. Again.

How did that happen? Last time, she'd gotten her entire squad killed. And now here she was, leading brave men and critters to their doom. What had she ever done to deserve that kind of responsibility?

Get a grip, Ria told her, coming to Kes once again, as the sergeant did whenever she was needed. *Every second counts. If you wish for your men to survive, the best way is to achieve your objectives as fast as you can.*

Kes swallowed and fought for a second with the tightness in her throat. And then even the beat of her heart seemed to fade away as discipline replaced animal instinct. "Alright, everyone, we've got a job to do. Queen Laurel, you and your spiders are on area-denial duty. Get every civilian from here all the way to the slums to safety—we need to clear a path for Lavy and Alder, they're counting on us. If a family is hiding inside a building, secure all entrances with web as best as you can."

Queen Laurel—*No, it's Empress now,* Kes thought—moved forward, her huge black bulk like a shadow in front of the darkening sky. Somehow, she was now bigger than her mother had ever been, and still growing. "The Spider Empire shall do as you ask, Marshall of the Haunt. What will we do about the Inquisition and their creations?"

"Lead them here after the civilians are safe. The Inquisition is looking for a fight, so let's give them one."

"Most excellent!" The Empress clicked her mandibles in approval, then turned to face her underlings. "Queen Cornelia, take command of Bumelia's cluster and evacuate the meat-sacks. Pirene, you are on standby. Reinforce the Marshall if need be. My own cluster shall take the most dangerous task and lure away the Inquisition," she announced proudly. The rest of the spiders clicked their approval and scattered into the night.

Kes watched them go for an instant. She'd never in her entire life seen as many horned spiders as the amount gathered tonight. Just the spiderlings were enough to cover the pavement in a shifting tide of chitin. It was as if a black sea had flooded the city. She could only thank whichever god was willing to listen that they were on the Haunt's side.

Next, boot! Ria urged her. The Marshall broke out of her reverie and turned to Klek and his Spider Riders.

"Klek, you're on life-saving duty," she explained. "Your team is nimble and excellent at infiltration. Get to those in need that our spiders cannot reach and do what you can for them."

Klek nodded, fearless. "We'll return when we're done, Kes. Lord Ed's gonna need some Adventurer Baning." He gestured at his batblins and his spiders, with Tulip by his side, trembling with the need to fight. "This way, Spider Riders!"

"See you on the other side," Kes said as they left. She couldn't help but marvel at the way Klek only seemed afraid when the danger was mundane—a wolf. Starvation, staying out in the rain... but when his people faced danger far beyond the norm for a batblin cloud, it was as if the little batblin turned to steel. As if somehow all his life had prepared him for this, even without realizing it.

Who were you before the Haunt? she wondered. Then, she turned to Kaga and his Monster Hunters. "You're with me. We'll need to bring Lavy's dish and Ed's drones to the highest point we can secure before Alder and Lavy enter the city." She nodded toward the drone team Ed had summoned—thirty of them, huddled near the gates, waiting for her signal to move forward. Ed had brought as many drones as he could create outside a dungeon's ley lines, putting him at capacity and leaving him at even more risk, since most of his fighting style involved droning his opponents in the dirtiest ways possible.

"It's going to get ugly," Kaga said quietly. The Monster Hunter's eyes were distant—he was thinking of his father and his clan, who were right now infiltrating Mullecias Heights along with Ed. "But we shall not fail you, Marshall. I stake my honor on my duty."

"I know," Kes said. Now she faced Costel, the leader of the Haunt's guard, who Kes had trained as best as she could, given the time-frame. "While Kaga and I move forward, you and your men will protect the drones. Ed is too far away to summon more for us, so this lot is the one we got. Protect them—and their cargo— with your lives."

The guardsmen exchanged nervous, terrified glances, as the drones moved forward at Kes' signal, dragging a cart with Lavy and Pholk's enchanted dish.

"Why?" asked Old Ivan nervously. "What's so important about some dirty glass?"

"That's our win condition," was all Kes said.

CHAPTER TWENTY-SEVEN

SUMMONED HERO

Scappi lost his footing and fell face first into a puddle, splashing murky water everywhere and screaming in surprise.

"Shut it, kid!" Oscor whispered angrily as he helped the gnome stand up. "You'll make every Hero in the neighborhood come after us!"

The rest of the smugglers fanned out to keep an eye on all exits. Wufroc, Sköm, and Cimeko remained near Oscor. They first two were his cousins, who had come with him all the way from the Manslan peaks. Cimeko was his on-and-off lover. Together, the four had braved countless danger and hardship. But nothing like this.

"What do we do, Boss?" Wufroc asked, as Scappi hurried along.

"There's a Thieves Guild safehouse three blocks from here," Oscor said. "If we reach it, maybe they'll hide us."

One of his smugglers hurried his way. "There are four Heroic parties spread throughout the area," the young dwarf said with a trembling voice. Only a few months ago, he'd been a heavy pixie dust user. Oscor had helped him get off the stuff, but the tremors remained. "They have magic-users slinging explosive spells. It's like they're trying to bring the slums down."

Perhaps the entirety of Undercity, Oscor thought bleakly. "We must sneak past," he said aloud.

"Heads up, over there!" another smuggler warned. Oscor followed the man's finger and saw the Heroic Wizard, floating in the middle of the air with a careless air to its blank face. The construct wasn't looking at them, thankfully, but it raised a hand somewhere in their general direction.

"What is he going to—" the *enhanced fireball* cut everyone's short. The impact was like a giant's hammer crashing against the building right next to the alley. The dying day shone bright for an instant, and then Oscor was lifted from the ground by an invisible force and thrown against the opposite wall like a rag-doll in a storm.

Seconds—or minutes—later, he stood up, rubble and dust falling from his body. His dwarven complexion, along with a couple Endurance talents, had eaten the brunt of the spell.

The pain in his ribcage, though, told him he had a couple broken bones to nurse. Later. If he survived.

"Who's still alive?" he breathed. The alley was in ruins, the smoke too thick to see, rock, glass, and rubble everywhere. A wall had collapsed.

"Over here!" Cimeko called. Oscor rushed that way, relief flooding through his body.

Cimeko was helping Sköm get up. The dwarf was badly wounded, with a nasty wooden spike protruding from his side, blood quickly soaking his shirt. He looked barely conscious, too shocked to react. Oscor grunted and threw Sköm's arm around his back.

"We need to reach the safehouse before we're buried along with the slums," Oscor said.

The three of them had barely had time to hobble to the end of the alley when the ruins of the building that had taken the *enhanced fireball* shook, and a shower of boulders rained down.

Oscor saw a burning iron beam approach. It all happened in less than a second. He pushed Sköm and Cimeko out of the way, and then disappeared under the impact.

ED WATCHED from the shadows behind the old mansion as the Militant soldiers paced atop their watchtowers, their eyes buffed by talents or spells to pierce the darkness like those of a cat. The array of *alarm* spells and magical defenses that formed the second line of defense would put the Inquisition on high alert that their main base in Undercity was under attack as soon as he made his move. Even with the element of surprise and the knowledge that most Inquisitors were out in the field, trying to keep a tight grasp on the city as his minions wrestled it from them, it was impossible for the Haunt to hold the mansion for long.

But then again, Ed only needed a few minutes. Enough for a chat, perhaps. He gripped his sword's handle. Outside, by the slum, innocent people were dying.

"Do it," he ordered, not taking his eyes from the watchtowers even for a second.

At once, Kagelshire gave the signal and one of his kaftar *messaged* the clan's Shaman, who was working his way through the Inquisition's defensive spells. Ed saw nothing to show that anything had changed—no show of light, no noise. It made sense. It was a kind of magical warfare designed for the user to remain as inconspicuous as possible.

Kagelshire turned to Ed. "It's done," the Chieftain told the Dungeon Lord. "We've got a breach right between those watchtowers. We climb the wall there, they won't know until we let them. Shaman Toremil is out of spells, though."

Ed nodded, taking the news into account. The Haga'Anashi

came from their hidden spots across the shadows of the parks that surrounded the mansion, almost as skilled as Thieves. A few rushed the walls, their feet wrapped in cloth to mask the noise of their steps, and others took aim with exotic blowpipes made of shiny wood. At a signal from Kagelshire's lieutenants, the blowpipes opened fire, and darts arced through the sky like a swarm of angry black bees, up above Mullecias Heights, and down with deadly aim into the unsuspecting Militant soldiers manning the towers.

The soldiers gasped, bent over, and collapsed in a few seconds. A couple had enough time to shout weak warnings, loud enough for Ed to hear, but likely not enough for the Inquisitors inside the mansion. Hopefully.

"Arrows would've been faster," Kagelshire said with just a hint of reproach.

"It's difficult to convince someone you're not evil after killing half their men," Ed pointed out. "This is a war. I know that. But that doesn't mean we need to take more lives than necessary."

Kagelshire said nothing. The Chieftain's eyes were hard and cold, and wouldn't leave the black mass of the mansion even a second.

The kaftar climbed the walls and disappeared inside along with a trickle of white spiderlings from Gloriosa's brood. The albino Queen waited for further orders close by, surrounded by her princesses and her guard.

After a while, Kagelshire nodded briefly. "The defenses are down. They don't expect a thing. Those cocky assholes didn't keep even a single griffin in reserve."

Ed glanced at the sky. He didn't share Kagelshire's confidence. The Inquisition had many tricks up their sleeve. They could summon reinforcements with magical circles, or simply *message* their griffins to come back. And if there were a team or two of Heroes nearby, the Haga'Anashi could suffer catastrophic losses.

"Let's go," Ed said. "Be quick, be silent, and try to take as many prisoners as possible. We won't have much time after they discover us." He strode over to Gloriosa. "My thanks, Queen Gloriosa, for allowing me to hitch a ride. I'm afraid I'm not as good a climber as our kaftar allies." Only a horned Queen was big enough to withstand the weight of a grown man wearing heavy armor, but as a rule of thumb, Queens of any species weren't in the habit of letting others ride them into battle.

Gloriosa clicked her thanks. "And you have my appreciation, Dungeon Lord, for asking instead of ordering."

Ed hopped on and clung to her as best as he could. It was harder than Klek made it look. The chitin was rough and serrated, and the stiff hair made the experience not exactly pleasant. Together, Dungeon Lord and Spider Queen headed into battle, surrounded by the albino cluster and the Haga'Anashi. They passed the walls to step down into a silent garden behind the mansion, thick with underbrush and exotic flowers.

There was no one around, but as the warriors headed deeper inside, Ed caught sight of a pair of feet sticking out of a bush—Kagelshire's infiltrators had done their job.

"Spread out," Ed told his forces. "Don't let them organize a resistance. If you see any Hero, report it and retreat. Any prisoner you get, web them to the trees." That would hopefully buy some time to retreat. He turned to Kagelshire. "Good luck."

"To you as well, Dungeon Lord." The Chieftain and his men fanned out toward the mansion and began their climb. They were here with a purpose—to find the captured Haga'Anashi and either free them or retrieve their bodies.

Ed's spiders had learned to keep a low profile thanks to his and Laurel's constant drilling. The spiderlings led the charge, spreading throughout the entire battlefield and locating every potential enemy combatant, as well as their weapon stashes and spellcasters. Then the spider warriors dealt with the weakest enemies first—those sleeping, or in the bathroom, or alone.

All over the mansion, Inquisitors and Militant soldiers fell to paralyzing venom. In this, the *resistance* that Inquisitors had worked against them, because the spiders had to use high doses to take them out of commission fast enough to stop them from yelling out. About one in four paralyzed Inquisitors died when their hearts gave out, and a few more would pass away from complications before the night was over. Ed knew this, and although he wasn't happy about it, it was harder and harder to feel empathy for the Inquisition with the fires of Undercity marring the night sky behind him.

Come on, Ed thought, clenching his jaw. The anticipation was killing him. For better or worse, he couldn't stand back while his minions did all the dirty work. But he needed to wait for the spiderlings to find the man with the description Ed had given them—someone somewhere in the mansion working with computer equipment. Describing *that* to the spiders had been a challenge, and he wasn't sure of the spiderlings' capacity to understand the command, but the only other option was to search the entire mansion.

A lone spider warrior skittered past a tree root and reached Ed and Gloriosa. Someone matching Ed's description was working by himself somewhere on the third floor.

About five seconds after hearing the good news, someone yelled out, hard. Lights spread out through the mansion from the windowsills, both magical and natural. The sounds of battle spread and grew like a small fire turning into an inferno.

It was incredible how quickly a good plan could go to hell. A *fireball* blazed out into the sky. Another one hit its mark, raising a cloud of smoke and debris. Someone cast a *thunderbolt* that reverberated across Ed's bones even in the distance—the Inquisition had a powerful spellcaster in tow.

"We better hurry," Gloriosa told Ed.

She didn't need to tell him twice. He hopped up again and together they climbed upward to the third floor, keeping away from the windows. As they passed the second floor, Ed saw frantic movement as Inquisitors, kaftar, and horned spider clashed.

"I'm too big to fit here," Gloriosa warned Ed as they reached the third floor's exterior passageway. "But I can have my guard escort you."

"Have them protect the stairs and the exits," Ed told her, hopping out onto the black-and-white floorboard. "I'll need privacy." He could feel his mouth drying and his body tremble with nervous energy. *Holy bolts* flew from the first floor and broke a nearby window. Ed ducked by instinct, but the shot had been a misfire—so far, no one knew he was there.

He jogged through the passageway, glad that his enchanted cloak muted the clanking of his armor as well as his footsteps. A small spiderling waited for him on the middle of the door of the room he was looking for.

Okay, Ed thought, reaching for the knob. *Here goes nothing.*

The Summoned Hero was older than he had expected. The man sat with his back facing Ed, bent over a desk with a metallic device that, for a second, Ed didn't recognize. It was a bulky box folded in half with a crystal screen on one end and a keyboard on the other—the same description he'd given to the spiderlings. An old laptop. It looked out of place in Ivalis, standing out in the worst way possible.

Like it didn't belong.

Outside, on the first floor, a spellcaster had created a magical circle in the middle of the main garden and was somehow holding it against Gloriosa's spiders, who kept pressing the attack. He defended with a never-ending flurry of area-denial spells and runes. One way or the other, if this bloodbath was to be stopped, Ed had to hurry.

He stepped forward, hands trembling and mouth dry. "Do not be afraid. My name is Edward Wright. Like you, I was summoned here from Earth. I don't know what they've told you about me, but you must believe me—they're lying. But I can explain. It's time for you and I to have a talk," he said.

He watched as the man squared his shoulders, set his hands on the desk, and slowly stood up. He turned to face the Dungeon Lord. He had a trimmed white beard and a long sharp nose, and looked like a private doctor more than a medic, except that his right arm was bent at an awkward angle, as if to offer Ed a handshake. He was holding some kind of black wand in his hand. Something so alien, so foreign to the world of Ivalis that the laptop vanished from Ed's mind as his eyes widened in recognition.

A revolver, he thought, as the Summoned Hero pulled back the hammer with his thumb.

"No," the old man said. "I've nothing to talk with you about. And I've never heard of Earth before. I was born in Heiliges." There was a crack like thunder and fire flowered out of the gun's barrel in Ed's direction.

THE FLAMES LICKED the Galleon's Folly structure with almost tender caresses, as its silhouette shone against the distant black shore like a star. Tonight, the shores of Undercity were full with stars like that one.

Berrick rubbed his long, thin hands with nervousness as bile rose through his throat. He could feel the lick of the flame on his face, despite the distance. Faint screams came through the smoke and were cut short, over and over. He couldn't breathe through the tightness in his throat.

This shouldn't be happening, the shoemaker thought as he ran through the narrow secondary streets of the harbor, trying to reach what, he hoped, was the safety of the slums. *They wouldn't let me out here to die. I served them as best I could. I'm useful!*

But the Heroes roaming the streets didn't seem to recognize him, nor care. They cut down anyone close enough to them and leveled any building that stood in their way. A few unorganized groups of resistance clashed against them in plazas and gardens—Akathunians assassins working in tandem with their old enemies, the Thieves Guild; a necromancer cabal allying with a rebel faction of the Watch; whores hurrying families into the secret basements they used to hide from the law.

Berrick didn't have many friends to help him hide. That was the sad reality of the informant's life. No one cared that he had only been doing his job, and that there was no opposing the Inquisition when it came for you.

He knelt behind a wet stack of trash, plugging his nose to protect it from the smell, and watched as the few remaining ships in the harbor disappeared further and further into the horizon. Smart men. The sailors had cut anchors as soon as they saw the way the wind was blowing, probably saving their lives in the process. A team of Heroes had sunk a few clumsy merchant ships too big or too undisciplined to react as fast as they could've, and now their remains littered the waters, cargo floating among dead men. Both would wash ashore come the morning.

Blue lightning flashed behind him, followed by a boom that raised all the hairs of Berrick's back. He saw the silhouette of four men walking rigidly behind a fountain of the park behind him. He realized with growing panic that he was facing the wrong way. He jumped over the trash, slipped and fell, cut his hand on something sharp, and hobbled away into a sidestreet as fast as he could.

Did they see me? He hoped against hope that they hadn't.

He never saw nor felt the ice bolt that pierced his skull from behind and nailed him to a nearby wall, legs twitching long after he was dead, blood trickling down into the cobblestone, mixing pink into a stream of rainwater, pouring down the sidewalk's drain.

THE SOUNDS of the battle raging outside came into Gallio's prison cell crystal clear, to the point that he could almost distinguish the individual skirmishes. Judging by all the cackling and excited war-cries, the attackers were kaftar. Probably the Haga'Anashi, come to pay the Inquisition back for what they'd done to the warriors' people.

Gallio sat in the middle of his cell, back straight and shoulders relaxed. It unnerved him how calm he was, even when his own people were fighting—and dying—only a few feet away from him.

Perhaps he'd always known the Haga'Anashi would come. It was like a kid launching his favorite marble into a pile and watching as all the marbles went rolling in all directions.

This was what the Inquisition did. They followed the tenets, they acted, they did the duty the Light expected of them. But when those duties involved inflicting pain and misery onto others, and when those others were left with no way out, it was no surprise that sometimes they struck back against the Inquisition.

It was a basic mercenary stratagem to always leave an opening for your opponent to retreat. A man fighting to the death will fight all the more fiercely than one who knows he can turn tail and run.

The Inquisition had left both the Haga'Anashi and Edward Wright nowhere to run. And now...

The marbles were rolling.

Metal struck metal right past the jail door. There was a flash of light and a *"Holy bolt!"* scream, and then the door opened to reveal six Haga'Anashi warriors, one of them decked in chain-mail, all wielding long, serrated spears, with curved scimitars hanging by their waists.

There was blood marring the floor outside and the walls and the wooden railing. As the kaftar strolled inside, the young Inquisitor who had beaten Gallio up slid down the wall and onto the floor, glassy eyes staring at nothing, hands still clenching his neck, trying futilely to hold shut the terrible wound, like a gaping smile.

The kaftar ignored Gallio at first as they searched the room while their leader waited. His men soon came back and announced something in their own particular language. The leader seemed disappointed, but he hid it well.

"You must be Kagelshire. The captives you're looking for are dead," Gallio told him. "It happened last night, during the interrogation. Or so I was told." He pointed a finger in the general direction of the interrogation cells. "The bodies may still be there, if you care to look."

For an instant, Kagelshire did nothing but stare down at Gallio, then made an almost imperceptible gesture. Two kaftar saluted him and rushed outside, weapons at the ready, following Gallio's directions.

"For what's worth, I regret it had to come to this," Gallio said.

Something like a black shadow crossed the old kaftar's eyes. He marched forward and was soon face to face with the Inquisitor. "I've heard of you," Kagelshire said. "You're Burrova's old Sheriff. Your old friends aren't so happy to have you, eh?" He cackled bleakly. "I believe Dungeon Lord Wraith would've rather we take you prisoner, but he's forgotten that I'm not bound by pact to him, and I'm not in the mood for mercy."

Kagelshire stepped back and headed out. As he left, he told his remaining four kaftar two words in their own language. Gallio could guess the meaning clear enough.

One kaftar closed the door, and the four of them regarded the Inquisitor wearily. One of them exchanged brief, heated words with another, who frowned and shushed him. Another shook his head. Gallio watched it all in silence.

The third one drew his scimitar and approached the cell. "My name is Abuya. In the name of our Chieftain and our clan, I offer my apologies. For the Haga'Anashi, it's a great dishonor to kill an unarmed prisoner. But Chieftain Kagelshire's judgment is clouded today. One of the men your Inquisition murdered was his late sister's only son." The kaftar shook his head sadly, and pointed his scimitar at Gallio. "I'd like to release you, offer you a weapon, and fight you honorably, man to man. But I have my duty to my clan, and my people's honor comes before my own." There was true pain in the warrior's eyes.

"Trust me, Abuya. I understand that better than anyone. I hold no grudges against you," Gallio said, clutching the metal bars.

The kaftar stiffened, then bowed. "Thank you, Inquisitor. You have my word this will be quick." He readied himself to strike.

For an instant, Gallio wanted to let it happen. But Abuya's words had rang true. "Likewise, my friend," he whispered. And then, diving forward against the bars, he summoned Alita's blessing with all the strength left in his body, because his honor wasn't as important as his duty to the Light.

"*SUNWAVE!*"

The kaftar, the cells, and the Inquisitor all disappeared under the roaring white light.

THE EXPLOSION RATTLED Karmich's teeth and the wave of heat singed his eyebrows. He watched through the bars of the second-floor railing as a pair of charred ogre bodies smashed through a brick wall, destroying a priceless bust and a bookcase in the process, then rolled on the floor until they came to a stop on the middle of the Ball Room. A tattered tapestry fluttered through the air and landed atop the broken ogre body, like a funeral veil.

The Ball Room was littered with the bodies of the defenders and the devastation the Heroes left in their wake. Karmich knew that scenes like these were happening all over the Guildhouse as the defenders rallied to protect the Thieves Guild headquarters. He wasn't willing to add to the bodies that littered the floors, so when the inhuman shadows of the Heroic team that had done the ogres in stepped through the rubble, he turned tail and ran farther upstairs, toward the third floor.

Few of the Guildhouse's defenders were Thieves. A Thief's job was to run and hide at the first sign of mortal danger, which was the reason Grand Master Bavus had outsourced the headquarter's security to martial professionals. It was mostly guarded by ogres smuggled into Undercity from the Netherworld, commanded by mercenaries and former Starevosi war veterans, but also enough traps and trained monsters scattered through the mass of the complex that it required any Thief apprentice to have a few years of training before daring the dangers of the Guildhouse—which was, in fact, the final exam into official membership.

With time, Karmich had grown to know every foot of the House better than he knew his own face. He knew which rugs hid a collapsible floor, what statues would summon the attack dogs if touched, which corners were the best for a quick fuck with a maid or a fellow Thief with an itch to scratch.

Each room he passed in his mad dash had dear memories attached to them. There was the table where Pris and he had planned their infamous Naked Heist; that was the broom closet where he'd hid from Alfred the Sly after Alfred found out Karmich had been cheating him out at cards for a year; and that was the carpet where Katalyn Locksmith had knocked him out cold the first—and last—time he had tried to get handsy with her.

All those dear moments, and as he left them behind, it was as if they faded into blankness. There was only the fear beating against his temples following his crazed heartbeat.

The wooden floor trembled like a stirring snake, and Karmich was thrown toward a wall headfirst. He used his *improved dodge* by reflex and dodged the incoming wall at the last second—an egregious abuse of Objectivity that could get him erased one day if he took it too far.

Karmich rounded a corner while the screams of the dying came from below. A distant part of his terrified mind wondered how many of his friends and family had made it out. He wished from the bottom of his heart that no one he particularly cared about had decided to stay and fight.

It all had happened so fast, though... First, the Guild had issued a red alert, *messaging* every Thief inside the city to *drop everything* and head to the House at once. At the time, Karmich had been in the middle of disabling the *alarms* of a rich merchant's house on the other side of town. As he headed for the House, all over the city he could see the signs that something was terribly wrong: Crowds piled in front of the barred city gates, with Inquisitorial teams keeping them away, ignoring the pleas and crying. Columns of smoke came from the slums and the pier, the Watch nowhere to be seen, as a few Dark cultists came out of their hiding holes in the catacombs and ran through the city half-naked in their black tunics, carrying as many secret spellbooks and scrolls as they could hold in their spindly arms.

Karmich had passed the first Heroic team on its way to the House, but at the time, he hadn't even dared consider they shared the same destination.

After arriving at the Guildhouse, he and an ever-growing crowd of green-caped Thieves had met with Grand Master Bavus himself in the Great Hall. Standing on top of the stairs, Bavus had faced the Thieves and laid out the situation for them. The Inquisition was coming for them. They weren't sure of the reason—had a few guesses, though, which didn't matter at the moment. They had prepared for this eventuality. This wasn't unexpected. The Guild knew what to do. They'd empty the coffers, evacuate into the slums and their safe houses spread through the city, and go dark until Bavus—or the highest-level surviving member—could come up with a follow-up plan.

Which would've been all fine and dandy if a Heroic Rogue hadn't jumped out of the shadows, dropping his *invisibility* as he did so, and gutted Bavus through the minotaur's enchanted armor right then and there.

Then someone had dropped a fireball, and after that, Karmich only remembered people running and fighting, and the chaos, and now here he was.

He rounded a corner and saw movement out of the corner of his eye, coming from the Guild Museum. He risked a quick peak. Pris was there, throwing glass displays to the ground and grabbing as many priceless Guild trophies as she could stick in the pockets of her armor and belt.

A wave of relief flooded through Karmich's body. She was alive. Also, she was an idiot. "Pris!" he called, rushing after her.

She turned and almost threw a knife his way, recognized him at the last second, and stopped. "Karmich! You dumb oaf, I almost—"

Karmich hugged her. "I'm so glad you're one of the cowards," he said.

Pris blinked. "Same," she said as Karmich stepped away.

"We need to get out of here," he told her. "No time to lose looting the room. The Heroes may arrive any second now."

Pris turned and threw another glass display at the floor, shattering it. "They're dying in droves against our traps." Another explosion punctuated her words as she bent down and picked up an emerald necklace.

"It doesn't matter!" Karmich said. Pris' crow-like attraction for shiny things had gotten them into trouble many times, but this was another thing entirely. "More will come—it's like a game to them! The more we kill them, the more the others want to take a bite out of us!"

He grabbed his friend by the neck of her cloak and pulled her back, dragging her toward the wall. "We can replace this stuff later, our lives are more important!"

"Where are you going?" she asked, trying to shake him off as they approached the open window. "We're three stories up above the river, you asshole!"

As a response, Karmich grabbed the butt of his dagger and

smashed a case with a steel gadget inside—a bulky cylinder, similar to a crossbow, with a hook at the end. It was the legendary grappling hook of Grand Master Armari, the famous gnome inventor. "I've got an idea," Karmich explained, grabbing Armari's hook.

Pris' eyes widened. "Karmich, that's a priceless Guild treasure," she said. "Don't you dare use it. There must be another way!"

At that moment, two Heroic Rogues jumped onto the balcony right outside the Museum, their cloaks floating after them like trails of shadow, their inhuman faces hidden in darkness, their scimitars glowing black and purple with enchantments and deadly buffs. They glided toward the Thieves without making a sound.

"Alita's fucking tits," Pris exclaimed. "What the fuck are you waiting for, use it, use it, use it—"

Karmich grabbed his friend by the waist and jumped out the window right before the Rogues reached them.

The world seemed to turn and freeze in place for an ever-lasting fraction of a second, the stars below and the black canal above, and then reality itself spun around Karmich. He'd have liked to say that he and Pris acted with bravery and dignity, but the fact was, both screamed like a pair of banshees.

He somehow took aim at the burning Guildhouse and pressed the hook's trigger. The weapon hissed and a small explosive charge triggered, propelling the hook into a nook of the stone. The steel cable attached to it tensed, and for a terrible moment, Karmich feared he'd dislocate his shoulder as he and Pris hung from the hook, holding tight to each other like a pair of lovers.

Half-way below them, dozens of shadowy figures jumped out of the building like fleas running off a dog's fur, escaping onto the city rooftops or scrambling into dark alleys, with Heroic teams hot in pursuit.

Pris and Karmich made eye contact as their screams slowly

faded. No one was paying any attention to them. "Fuck," said Pris. "I think we made it."

Then there was a loud screech as a griffin bolted out of nowhere through the fire and the smoke above them and the Inquisitor riding it aimed a rune Karmich's way.

The Thief felt a jolt of burning agony searing his arm, and his fingers lost their grip on the hook as the griffin rose upward for another pass.

The Thieves Guild burned, and all around it, the purge of Undercity was well underway. No one noticed the two silent figures hitting the cold waters of the canals.

AFTER SURVIVING many dangers thanks to *improved reflexes*, the talent had become part of Ed's instinctive response against incoming danger. When the fake Summoned Hero shot at him, Ed instantly activated the *reflexes*. Time slowed down to a trickle as he dove out of the way, which gave him enough time to realize that the bullet had already struck him in the chest long before his brain had even realized what was going on.

He saw in perfect, hyper-aware detail the aftershock of his armor's enchanted runes as they overloaded, and felt the strain of his body as his defensive talents fizzled out. An instant later, he gasped as air rushed out of his lungs and his ribs tried to hug his lungs. It felt as if a sumo wrestler had drop-kicked him in the chest. Still in slow motion, he slumped against the wall as his dive lost momentum and his legs gave way underneath him. He fell in a heap, gasping for air, as time resumed its normal flow.

"Interesting," said the man, smoking gun still in his hand. "Dungeon Lords are truly a pain to put down. What a waste of ammunition." He wasn't the Summoned Hero, after all—just another member of the Militant Church. He looked nothing like lanky young man in the Shadow Tarot card, and he spoke like a born Heiligian.

Ed placed his hand against the center of his chest where the bullet had struck. He lifted it, expecting to see it covered in blood. It was clean. He gazed down, and saw a round dent in his armor about the size of a Vyfara cent, with the charred remains of the bullet embedded in the center. The Dungeon Lord blinked, still too stunned to think. A small part of him wondered how a three-millimeter-wide piece of steel had stopped a modern bullet.

"Enchanted armor and defensive talents," said the fake, frowning in the focused way of someone reading a character sheet. "What an annoying combination. But I doubt your head is as protected as your heart." He took aim.

Clarity rushed at Ed like a storm. Many things happened, one after the other, as training took over Ed's stunned mind before he had time to think about his actions.

This time, he activated *improved reflexes* before the fake had time to shoot. Ed pushed himself to the side, hard, away from the man's aim just as his finger pressed the trigger in slow motion. The gun fired. The bullet struck the wall a couple inches away from Ed's head—he felt a sting in his temple right next to his helmet visor.

The fake cursed and took aim again, but Ed's hand was already clutching at his utility belt, the one he'd taken from the Thieves Guild a long time ago. He didn't go for his sword—it wouldn't do him much good in a cramped room against someone with a firearm. Instead, he went for a throwing knife kept in a sheath right next to the smoke bomb pouch.

"*Eldritch edge!*" The small blade caught in green fire right as it left Ed's arm in one smooth, practiced motion. The flaming projectile crossed the air like a ship sailing through smooth waters and embedded itself into the man's belly up to the hilt. The man slumped and his third shot went wide, breaking a window. Smoke and blood poured out of the terrible wound, soaking his linen white shirt in a crimson flower, small at first, but quickly blossoming.

Ed ended the *reflexes*. Both men stared at each other with wide eyes as if they couldn't believe what just had happened. The fake Summoned Hero opened his mouth as if trying to take a deep breath. With his free hand, he grasped the hilt of the knife.

"Don't," Ed gasped. "You'll only make it worse—"

The man, clearly in shock, tried to pull the knife out with one hard jerk. He almost succeeded. His face lost all color, his eyes rolled back, and he collapsed to the floor, dropping the gun and pulling the laptop down with him as he went. The machine bounced on the floor and slid away.

The trickle of blood feeding the crimson flower turned into an open faucet. *You struck an artery*, Ed thought absentmindedly. He could see the man's exposed guts, shredded and burned to a crisp. The smell filled the room. He'd done that to a person without even thinking about it.

Bile rose into his throat, and he fought down the need to heave. It was as if he was living a terrible nightmare from where he couldn't wake up.

No, no, no, no.

The man bleeding out onto the floor was the only person who could've helped him make sense of the Heroes. Even if he wasn't the person shown in the Shadow Tarot, he knew how to control the Heroes—Ed had seen him using the laptop. At the very least, Ed could have gotten him to make the Heroes to leave Undercity.

His win condition. He had killed his win condition.

He stumbled toward him and knelt beside him. He tried to staunch the blood-flow with his shaking hands, but it was like trying to plug a flood with a finger. "Where's the person who gave you that computer?" Ed asked.

To his surprise, the man opened his eyes slowly and met Ed's gaze. He could tell the wounded individual was in a dangerous state of shock. The kind that precluded only a few seconds left to live. "I've no idea... what you're talking about."

"He must've taught you how to use it. Come on! *Please!* We

could stop all of this—" he gestured with impotence at the battle raging outside the room "—right now!"

The old man frowned as if he could tell that something wasn't right. "We did it ourselves. Someone built the Heroes… Perhaps an Inquisitor…? Taught us how to use them at some point… Gave us the technology. He… Wanted…" He shrugged weakly.

"That makes no sense! That's a *laptop* from Earth, there was a Summoned Hero!" Ed could see the old man was about to die. The Evil Eye blazed with terrible anger born out of desperation. *"Tell me the truth!"* he bellowed, using a *minor order* spell. In his desperation, he ignored the fact that minor order definitely wasn't meant to be used this way, since demanding someone to speak truthfully wasn't minor in any measure.

And at once a sense of doom overcame him, passing him by as if the feathery wings of the angel of death had brushed against his heart. For one brief instant, he was colder than he'd ever been in his entire life. Like something huge and vast had reached out to crush him into nothingness and then had, at the last second, decided it wasn't worth the effort. *Yet.*

The dying man chuckled bleakly. "You know… if I hadn't been telling the truth… You would've broken… Objectivity's rules… Erased from history." He took one deep, ugly, throaty breath, and then something like clarity glinted in his eyes. "I should have lied. I could have done the world a favor."

The fake Summoned Hero died in Ed's arms, but his words awoke in Ed a terrible realization that overcame the Dungeon Lord and made all his plans and hopes for the future—a future that had been impossible since the beginning—collapse around him and vanish.

It was the first warning Kharon had given him about Ivalis. No one can break Objectivity's rules, not the gods, and certainly not bright-eyed men from Earth that thought they could change a world they barely understood. Today, he'd almost suffered the consequences of abusing Objectivity for one small mistake.

For long had the Summoned Hero been in Ivalis? According to Jarlen's story, the Heroes' creation had taken many years. In that time, a curious man from Earth may commit several minor mistakes. And luck didn't last forever.

The man in the Shadow Tarot must've been just like Ed. Proud, and playing with forces he didn't fully understand. Eventually those forces retaliated. The Summoned Hero wasn't in hiding. He had tried to fight the heavens and for that he'd paid the ultimate price.

There would be no peace. The card in Ed's pocket was the product of an unintended interaction between Objectivity and a legendary Artifact. It would never come to pass.

Dungeon Lord Edward Wright struck the floor with bloody fists and screamed at the sky until his voice gave out.

CHAPTER TWENTY-EIGHT

THE MAN FROM EARTH

A group of Inquisitors and Militant soldiers had managed to fight their way into the main garden in the middle of the mansion where a powerful spellcaster stood above a summoning circle. The spellcaster, a short, fat man with a feminine face, grunted with effort as he maintained a sort of bubble around the circle—a Heroic-ranked version of *circle of respite*—which kept Ed's forces away from the survivors inside.

The bubble was littered with the corpses of Haga'Anashi and spider warriors alike, including a few princesses. Gloriosa and the rest of her cluster surrounded the area, spread out to limit the effect of a *fireball* in case the spellcaster dropped the bubble and attacked. The Haga'Anashi did the same, their blowpipes and knives at the ready.

Ed regarded them all with cold eyes as he slowly walked down the stairs. The men and women inside the bubble saw him approach with a mixture of reactions—anger, fear, raw hatred.

One of the Inquisitors, a broad-shouldered man wielding a war-hammer and wearing a breastplate over an expensive tunic stained with blood, snarled at Ed and tried to shoulder his way past the spellcaster. "That's Wraith! Drop your spell, Hatter, so I can end him!"

Hatter shook his head while a pearl of sweat traveled down his double chin. "No. That's my last Heroic spell," he whispered.

"Then let us retreat already, before they figure out a way to get us!" exclaimed a woman dressed in the same tunic and silver mantle as the other two.

Again, Hatter shook his head. "No, Bartheny. Not without *him.*"

Ed ignored it all. He strolled forward until he was only a few feet away from the bubble.

"Lord Wraith," said one of Gloriosa's surviving princesses. "It's dangerous—"

"If Hatter drops the shield, kill them all," Ed said simply, without taking his gaze away from the circle. The Inquisitors seemed undeterred. But the circle stayed up.

"Yes, my Lord."

"You piece of—" began war-hammer man.

Ed raised the blood-stained laptop he was clutching with his right hand, up above his head for everyone to see. War-hammer man shut up, paling visibly when he recognized the machine. "You may not remember this. Not so many years ago, Alita—or whoever of her underlings you're in speaking terms with— brought you a man from Earth to help you fight the Dungeon Lords from Lotia. Back then, you were losing the war." Behind Ed, the fires of Undercity raged on. Black storm clouds hid the twin moons, and thunder roared in the distance. The air was so heavy with static that he could smell the incoming storm. It was going to be a big one—one to remember. "This person figured out a way to shatter the Dungeon Lords' advantage while killing as few people as possible—only you forgot to tell him the other side also has innocent people, didn't you? He automated the process of war. He created the Heroes using your kingdom's resources, then field tested and upgraded them until they were ready. When most of your Inquisitors failed to learn how to manipulate a keyboard, he decided to use people from our home-world instead." This was conjecture, but based on his experience, even people born in a world with computers oftentimes never bothered to learn the very basics. In a world without electricity, it was probably several orders of magnitude worse. "It probably helped that Objectivity is more lenient with people from a different world, to a point."

In fact, it was the key to the way the Heroes worked. Because, even if controlled at a distance, if someone from Ivalis was the one controlling the Hero as it earned, say, a hundred experience points—those would go to him. Swords didn't level up, and Heroes were little more than animated tools. But Ed knew that Objectivity rewarded risk. An Inquisitor sitting inside a castle a thousand miles away from any danger would earn pretty much none of those hundred points. Instead, by using people from Earth—which Objectivity couldn't reach—the Summoned Hero had found a way to let his creations, the Heroic constructs themselves, to absorb the points and use them to amplify their own ley lines instead.

In other words, the Summoned Hero had found a way to make the Heroes count as living creatures when it came to earning experience points.

But that very same stint that had gotten the Summoned Hero erased from history. After all, Objectivity often was flexible. But it had its limits, and the Summoned Hero had created thousands of Heroes, and changed the balance of history to one side.

And he'd paid the price.

Had he even known? Had the Inquisition even bothered to *warn* him about the risks?

"Creating the Heroic system destroyed your Summoned Hero. Not that you care," Ed said. "His creations stayed behind, and so did the training that he managed to impart on a few of you. Wetlands, you probably like it better like this—I know there are ways to figure out when Objectivity has annihilated someone

close to you, otherwise Ivalians wouldn't ever know it's a danger."
He could see something akin to shame, for an instant, showing its
ugly head in the spellcaster Hatter. It was all the confirmation Ed
needed. "You suspect what happened, but choose not to think
further about it. Because the Heroes are now yours to command
instead of belonging to someone who doesn't understand your
ways. Someone who may not have been as bloodthirsty as
you are."

"Don't you dare speak to us about blood-thirst, Dungeon Lord,
when your hands are slick with the blood of our people," the
woman named Bartheny told him.

"Fuck you—*you* did this," Ed said, pointing his finger at her
like he was aiming a sword at her heart. "I had nothing to do with
your war against the Dark. Had you asked me for my help back
when I arrived, I may have been on your side!"

"We would never ally with a spawn from Murmur," said the
war-hammer man through a scowl.

"And I would never help a mass-murdering bastard who razes
entire cities to the ground because a few men dare challenge his
rule." Ed pointed back and above him, at the columns of smoke
rising from the city and feeding the storm clouds. "YOU! DID!
THIS!" His arm was shaking with rage. He forced his Evil Eye off
and took a deep breath. "Whatever happens now is on you. Get
the fuck out of my city, you piece of shit. If any of you ever come
back, I *will* kill you. That's all the warning you get." Ed turned to
Gloriosa. "Get every prisoner you have and hand them to these
people. Do not attack if they drop the shield to get them inside,
but open fire if they take a single step out, or attempt to cast a
spell. According to their own rules, we could've infested their
friends with mindbrood larvae, so they must kill them to be safe.
Let's see if they have the stones to do to themselves what they so
freely do to others."

Bartheny scoffed. "Tall talk for someone with a few hours to
live. Enjoy Undercity while you can, Dungeon Lord. There's a

hundred Heroes out there, purging your evil from the land. The lives of all the good men you've killed today *will* be avenged by the end of the night."

"Only if I lose," Ed said. "If I win—and I intend to win—then your main advantage against me is gone. You know how to operate the Heroes, and you may even know how to create them, but you don't know how they work, or how to upgrade them. Whatever computing equipment you have in Heiliges is all you have left. Well... I doubt you know how to troubleshoot a computer. And you better pray to Alita I don't figure out this machine's password, or you may wake up one day being Ivalis Online's new villains." He handed the laptop to one of his Haga'Anashi. "Get this to the Haunt."

His minions hurried to follow his command, and the piles of webbed and paralyzed bodies slowly piled up as the horned spiders came and went in all directions. Meanwhile, the Haga'Anashi kept their blowpipes and bows aimed at the bubble, most of them at the spellcaster, who bit his lip and examined the scene, deep in thought. He seemed to reach a decision. He looked back over his shoulder. "When I drop the shield, get everyone you can inside. Don't put a foot outside the circle—if they attack us, I'll activate the circle and leave you stranded."

"You wouldn't dare!" bellowed war-hammer.

"Harmon, be reasonable. You cannot retake the city if you're dead," Bartheny pleaded. "The Heroes will handle it, as always. Let's use this chance to regroup and gather our strength."

Ed lacked the time to stand by and watch. Now that his chances at making peace with the Summoned Hero were gone forever, time was of the essence. He turned to leave.

At that moment, someone clapped behind his back. Everyone in the garden turned to see a mauled man painfully shuffle his way into the garden. His face was a mess of multi-colored bruises, and his torn shirt was bloody. Two kaftar darts protruded from his shoulders. His right leg had a slash above the knee, and he needed to use the Haga'Anashi spear he carried as a walking stick.

Despite all this, he moved with such confidence that he was half-way to Ed before his spider warriors realized the man was an Inquisitor, and began to close in on him. Ed raised a hand, gesturing at them to stop.

"I was wondering when you'd appear, Inquisitor," he told Gallio.

A CURTAIN of rain fell across the city, buffeted by a heavy wind. The Inquisitor and the Dungeon Lord faced each other, surrounded on one end by Ed's minions and on the other by the Inquisitors protected by Hatter's magic. Ed drew his sword, but kept it aimed down for the moment.

"So, you're killing Inquisitors now," Gallio shouted, as to be heard over the storm. "I figured the day would come. But it still pains me to see it."

"Isn't that Chieftain Kagelshire's spear?" Ed asked. "You are allowed to kill him, but we cannot defend ourselves?"

The Haga'Anashi jerked to attention at the news. A few of them had recognized the spear already. Some began to move toward Gallio, rage shining in their eyes. Ed showed them his open palm. *Stop. He's mine.*

Gallio shook his head. "I regret what I had to do. But I was fighting to save innocent lives."

"And I'm fighting to keep your dear Inquisitors from killing any more *innocent* people," Ed said. Other than them, the entire garden had gone quiet.

"And earning a city in the process is only a happy side-quest?"

"That's right. Are we going to talk all day? Because you're in the way of my conquering."

Gallio shook his head sadly. "I look at you and can barely see the young man I met in Burrova. You stand like a Dungeon Lord, friend Edward, and even talk like one. Proud. Powerful. *Dark*. The *sunwave* would tear you apart in a second."

"If you still had spells for the day, you'd have used them already," Ed said, chuckling mirthlessly, a sound that was lost in the storm. He raised his sword at the Inquisitor in challenge. "You can barely move, Inquisitor. Get out of my way."

Out of the corner of his eye, Ed could see that Hatter had dropped the shield while he thought Ed wasn't watching. The Inquisitors, this time, chose the rational approach and instead of jumping out of the circle to their deaths were hurrying quietly to drag the webbed prisoners inside. Gallio, who was facing the circle, had to be aware of this, so he was probably buying time in case Ed changed his mind.

"Will you kill me if I don't, Edward?" the Inquisitor asked.

Ed blinked. *I should,* he thought. He was perfectly aware that, if he let Gallio and the others go tonight, they'd come back to bite him in the ass later, when they'd recovered. They wouldn't care that he'd showed them mercy. If the places were switched, right now, he'd either be dead or subject to unthinkable torture.

A rational villain would have just killed the plucky adventurers and been done with it. Back on Earth, Ed, Mark, and Lisa, always made fun of the bad guys who had their heroes at their mercy early in the game's story, and then allowed them to leave either by pride or incompetence—usually both.

Ed only needed to give the order. These assholes weren't even plucky adventurers. By letting them leave, he'd be risking the lives of more innocent people. The Dungeon Lord opened his mouth.

Is that how I think of myself now? he thought suddenly. *As the villain?* Sure, the Inquisition insisted he was. The rest of the world insisted he was. But the Haunt thought otherwise. His friends thought otherwise. They were so sure in their conviction that right now they were out there, putting their lives at risk because they believed that what they were doing was worth it.

How would they feel if they could see him right now? He'd

seen Korghiran's futures. One of them was gone—erased by Objectivity—and the other two ended with him alone, one way or the other, having sacrificed or lost his everything along the way.

Korghiran had shown him his future, but not the Haunt's, because in her futures, the Haunt had none.

And that would not do.

Even if Gallio was right, even if he was more in tune to the Dark now than ever, Ed least could strive to be half the man Klek believed him to be.

With this decision, it was as if some heavy weight was lifted from his shoulders.

Korghiran's future had been only a possibility. It was on *Ed* to build the one he wanted, not some shady artifact owned by a princess of Hell. And the card in Ed's pocket showed three men, not two. The Summoned Hero was gone, but Gallio was still alive.

Even if Ed couldn't fathom a way for Gallio and himself to ever work together... Well. A practical villain would execute the Inquisitor because, after all the pain and death they'd inflicted on each other, it was a given that Gallio would fight him one day and possibly kill him. So executing the Inquisitor while he was weak and unable to cast the *sunwave* was the rational approach.

But sometimes heroes had to take a leap of faith. And between opting to be a rational villain or a hero, Ed knew what option the guy who arrived at Ivalis with clear eyes and a clean conscience would have chosen.

Ed smiled and raised his sword in challenge. "I'll kill you myself, Inquisitor, right where you stand, with all your friends watching." After all, he couldn't just let Gallio go. The Inquisitors would suspect that the man was allied with the Dungeon Lord. So Ed had to get creative. And he seemed to recall Gallio having a personal talent that allowed him to read people when they lied to him.

Gallio blinked, then paled. He grasped the spear with both

hands. "In that case, we don't have anything else to say to each other."

Then he launched Kagelshire's spear right at Ed's face with blinding speed.

"Gallio, no!" Hatter screamed.

Ed shifted his weight to the side and pivoted in place, throwing his left arm up and closing his hand into a fist. He caught the spear by the shaft and was driven backward a step by sheer momentum. And then Gallio was in front of him, brandishing a nicked short sword that had seemingly come out of thin air.

So you're not as wounded as you acted, after all, Ed thought as the Inquisitor launched a stab aimed at his neck.

Sparks flew as Ed drew a lazy arc with his sword and parried Gallio's blade with the flat of his, pushing it away only enough for both blades to miss his neck by millimeters. "*Stone pillar!*" Ed roared, aiming at a spot behind him and counting down in his head. Gallio tried to tackle him while at the same time wrestling to drive both swords against Ed's neck, but Ed was expecting it, and no matter how iron-clad Gallio's will, the Inquisitor was only running on fumes, while the Dungeon Lord was fresh and burning with energy.

Ed elbowed Gallio in the jaw with his sword arm, then stepped forward and into the Inquisitor's tackle, throwing his left shoulder under the Inquisitor's chest and shooting upward using his back, in a motion not unlike a bull launching a bullfighter into the air.

Gallio landed on his chest and rolled away trying to right himself, but the ground underneath him rose up as if the earth itself was trying to punch the Inquisitor out. He flew backward, hands uselessly reaching for the sky. At the same time, the pillar stood in the way of the couple of Inquisitors, including the warhammer man, forcing them to remain put for a brief second.

"That's for Kagelshire," Ed told Gallio as he landed on his ass…

...only a few feet away from Hatter's magical circle. "Now is our chance!" the spellcaster screamed. "Get him!"

The Inquisitors didn't waste a moment. Two of them jumped out of the circle and dragged Gallio in at about the same time the Haga'Anashi's darts struck them. Ed opened his mouth to order his men to stand down, but it was too late—a volley of arrows flew through the air just as Hatter's hand struck the circle's runes and a blinding flash engulfed the garden.

The arrows flew around the stone pillar, past the now-empty circle, then harmlessly bounced off of the wall behind. Ed and his minions stood in silence in the deserted mansion, rain sliding down their faces, thunder roaring in the distance.

"Damn it all," Ed said, covering his head with his cloak as to hide his grin as rain dropped down his hair. "Foiled again."

ED COULD FEEL his new dungeon grow through Undercity's entrails, bit by bit, tendril by tendril, avoiding certain areas and hurrying through others, always moving, always avoiding an unseen enemy. In a way, it was like watching the spread of a virus from afar.

Kes and the others were at the farthest point, leading the charge, risking their lives to save the city. As Ed stood at the highest point of the mansion's wall while his troops finished their retreat, he could guess where Kes was headed—a black tower like a needle rising up among the smaller guilds of the merchant district. That would make for a fine spot for the Jamming Tower.

It was also heavily defended. Since it was located near Undercity's downtown, most of the Heroes would be there, as well as the griffin riders not currently headed back to Mullecias. Ed knew that, all across his home-world, players everywhere would be waiting for the endgame of the World Event to show up—the final Boss, the one that a lucky party would face to finish the storyline.

Well. Better not to keep them waiting. If they wanted a Boss fight, then Ed would give them one to remember.

"I'm afraid I'll need your help once more, Queen Gloriosa," Ed told the albino Queen. He pointed at the black tower in the distance. "That's where I'm headed. That's where the Haunt rises or falls."

"Then it's an honor to be a part of our history," Gloriosa said, polite as always, like only royalty could be.

Ed climbed up the Spider Queen, and then turned to his troops, who were waiting outside the mansion's walls. "We're headed toward the city's center. There's no time to lose, so anyone not fast enough to follow should hide until it all blows over," he told them, his voice booming through the storm. "I'm not going to lie—most of us will be dead by the end of the night. Out there—" he raised his sword up into the air "—is a world that believes we're little more than pests to be rid of and forgotten about! Tonight, that changes. Tonight, we're not hiding anymore! Let's teach the Inquisition that it's them who should fear us!"

And with that, without turning to see if they were following, Ed and Gloriosa rode for the heart of Undercity, skittering through rain and thunder past the great parks of Mullecias, down the grassy hills and white paved paths that separated it from the rest of the city, and then into tight streets partially flooded. In the distance, Ed could see his dungeon still growing, the tunnels reaching for the ground beneath the tower like a drowning man reaching for the shore.

He rummaged through his belt, found a *vitality* potion, and downed it. At once, his body perked up as energy flooded into him. He was going to need it.

"We may get intercepted along the way," Gloriosa warned him. "My brood isn't exactly hard to spot from above."

Ed's eyes shone with the Evil Eye as he activated his *dungeon vision* as soon as he entered into contact with the dungeon below. "Don't worry about that," he said as his view rose and rose until they were but a small pale dot running through a labyrinth of streets and alleyways. "I'll tell you exactly where to go."

He could see Gloriosa's cluster following after them like a white tide, and the Haga'Anashi running among them, fast and nimble, eager for one last fight.

CHAPTER TWENTY-NINE

TOWER DEFENSE

"Three Necros on our tail," Lisa said, her fingers dancing across the keyboard with practiced agility. "They're comboing *rot cloud* with *weakness to disease*, zombie-enhancing auras are up. We're probably heading into an ambush. Omar, mind *fireballing* that open sewer over there? The last zombies came from under the city."

She countered the *weakness to disease* with a couple blessings, targeting Omar and Ryan and trusting Mark and herself to resist the curses on their own. Lisa used that extra time to blow the *rot cloud* away with a *stormwind*. Since Undercity registered rain and heavy winds, the spell was empowered enough to blow the sickly brown cloud back to the Necromancers, who coughed as tears of pixelated blood oozed down their cheeks.

Omar threw a blind *fireball* down the sewer, and parts of zombies flew out. Lisa grinned. Before the Necromancers had time to recover, Rylan Silverblade was among them, Lisa's *blessings* protecting him momentarily from the cloud. The Rogue disemboweled the Necromancers using *sneak attack*, scimitars shining a muted purple. All things considered, thin men running around in tunics were not that hard to kill, once you got up close and personal.

"This is the most fun I've had in months," Mark said. "They just keep coming!"

It was as if Pantheon had given up all semblance of realism, because the sheer variety of creatures they'd fought all over the city was staggering. Horned spiders, Thieves, elite kaftar, Assassins, cultists and Necromancers, lots of undead—she'd even seen a vampire flying nearby—an unlucky group of batblins, corrupted watchmen, ogres, Witch Doctors, pirates, smugglers, and many more.

Usually, a dungeon kept to a single group of creatures or one solid theme, but this was why World Events were so fun. The city was throwing so much shit at them that even high-leveled Heroes like them were running out of potions and daily powers. Lisa estimated that about a third of the original parties had been taken out as the Event started, but even old players that hadn't logged on in a while were now joining in as their friends called them up.

It wouldn't be long until the city was theirs. The only question on everyone's minds was, who would be the first to have a crack at the final Boss? After all, that was where the best loot was found. And, of course, the bragging rights, which were just as important.

The only thing marring her enjoyment was that not everyone in the group had fun under pressure. And Ryan was the kind of guy who made sure that, if he wasn't having fun, no one else would.

"Damn it, Lisa!" he squeaked over the chat. "That *cloud* shit ruined my damn Endurance, why didn't you use *Aucrath's Might* instead?"

Lisa rolled her eyes, feeling like a balloon had deflated inside her chest. "I spent it on Mark so he could keep aggro on the mutated crocodiles—I told you that three times!" If he'd waited only a bit longer for the cloud to disperse, he wouldn't have gotten the debuff, but he'd wanted to get the damn kills himself.

"Learn how to play! Mark's job is to tank—if he can't do it without your buffs then that's his problem!"

Rylan Silverblade advanced forward, closer to the city center, forcing the other three players to follow him before they had time to heal back up to full, because otherwise they'd split the party and Ryan would blame them. It had been like that since the beginning. "Come on!" he hollered. "The Boss is right after *this* corner, I just know it!"

Instead, they reached an area already scoured clean by other players. It was a merchant district, judging by the size of the houses and the markets. Lisa could see a few remaining Heroic parties hanging around, replenishing their HP and searching for loot or hidden enemies.

She checked her Quest-log and found a small alert that called all available Heroes to Mullecias District—an area whose access had been previously blocked so far. It made sense as a location for the final battle. "I think we went the wrong way," she pointed out, growing more frustrated by the second.

There was no way they'd reach Mullecias in time. She'd been looking forward to that Boss fight *so badly.*

After all the shit she had to deal with on a daily basis, the weird sensation of being watched at night, Ryan's bullshit, her inability to land another job, even things like Ed's disappearance... It was strange. A part of her seemed to believe that, if she could only have *one more* evening of honest fun, like the old times, when she was young and without a care in the world... one more night like that and she'd be able to deal with her shit. To finally do what needed to be done, the things she'd been postponing for so long.

But, of course, that chance was now gone. She'd have to spend the night listening to Ryan whine.

You know, you could've gone by yourself, a small part of her thought. *What are you waiting for, someone else to give you permission?*

It's been like this for years, Lisa. At some point, you need to start making your own decisions and living with them.

She bit her lip, hard enough to draw blood. Sure, going against Ryan's orders would make her lose her job, probably. But was that so terrible? Many people had periods of unemployment they couldn't afford and managed to power through them. She'd always known that. In a way, it had been her own fear keeping her at Lasershark.

"Damn it!" Ryan was saying. "You guys took too damn long to clear the city, and you should have read the log earlier! It's all your fault, you useless noobs!"

"Sorry, Ryan," Omar said sheepishly.

Her cursor hovered over Rylan Silverblade's character. A right click opened a small window. She paused over the "leave party" option.

"Let's go," Ryan said. "Maybe the Boss will defeat the first groups and we can take a shot at him still."

Hating herself, Lisa closed the small window and went after the Rogue, following Mark and Omar. Perhaps she'd handle her shit later. Right now, all she fucking wanted was a chance at one last fun evening, no matter how unlikely that was.

They were almost out of the district when the hell chickens arrived.

EVERYWHERE KES WENT, the drones dug underneath, stealing every uncontested inch of Undercity for the Haunt. Bit by bit, the tunnels of a new dungeon grew, like the roots of a tree spreading through the ground year after year. The new dungeon had its Seat in the middle of the undead-infested catacombs under the city. Kes even had the drones tunnel straight out of those catacombs into Heroic-controlled areas, to divert them away from the innocent citizens, buying time for Laurel and her cluster to get the civilians to safety—usually straight into the recently vacated catacombs.

Kaga and the Monster Hunters followed behind her, keeping to the shadows, blowpipes and *crow familiar* runes at the ready to keep the griffin riders at bay. It was clear by now that the flying Inquisitors were looking for Kes' group—the Haunt's presence hadn't gone unnoticed. With her avian vision, she could see the silhouettes of half the griffin riders encircling the slums head back toward Mullecias Heights, braving the growing storm as they did so. On the ground, many Heroic teams headed that way as well, leaving Ed's drones free to overtake the devastated territory they left behind.

Whatever Ed and the Haga'Anashi were doing in Mullecias Heights, Kes hoped they'd leave soon. Since the Heroes hadn't stopped their attack, she could guess the Dungeon Lord hadn't been successful on his personal quest.

At least, since she was still bound by minionship to him, it meant he was still alive. For now.

"Backs to the wall," she ordered, holding up a fist to stop her guards. Behind her, Costel barked her words at the rest of the squad, who hurried to obey. Not one second after Young Ivan had hidden himself under the shadow of a roof's overhang, five griffin riders flew in formation straight above them, circling the area.

Kes didn't move a muscle until the Inquisitors were out of sight, ignoring the cold that seeped into her bones. In this, the storm was a blessing in disguise. The rain and the darkness hid them better than most spells could have, and the winds forced the griffins to fly low, making them vulnerable to runic fire, as well as tiring them and their riders.

Rasvan coughed and cursed under his breath. "I cannot see my own hands in this rain!" he exclaimed. "Where are you taking us, Marshal?"

Kes realized that her guards could barely move under the rage of the wind. The Monster Hunters weren't faring much better—

for all their training, Brawn wasn't their strong suit. Hers either. But she knew that stopping meant certain death. "Over there." She pointed at a black structure in the distance, at least twice the size of any building nearby. "That's where we're headed."

"That's the Charcoal Tower," Kaga warned her. "It's the Akathunian headquarters. A den of villainy like no other. According to our spiderlings' reports, the entire district is overrun by Heroes wanting to take a shot at the Assassins. I doubt we can get anywhere close to it."

"Well, we'll need to figure something out," Kes said. "The dish needs to be high up for it to work properly, otherwise the city's buildings will interfere with it. No, Costel, we cannot have the drones build a new tower," she said, reading the question in the guard's eyes. "We don't have materials, and it'd take too long, anyway. It'll be better if we use the Charcoal Tower. Easier to defend." At least, that's what she hoped.

The main problem with building a new tower were the damned griffin riders. As soon as they saw the drones working on it, they'd realize something was up, and then they'd rain *fireballs* upon them. The Akathunian headquarters was an old structure meant to withstand a siege—from the Watch or from the King's officers, it didn't matter. Heroes or no Heroes, it was the best shot they had.

And they were running out of time. She threw a glance back, wondering if she'd be able to see Alder and Lavy approach. She'd left a couple drones behind to guide them on the right path, but in the confusion of combat, who knew if the drones would find her friends?

She hurried her pace, trusting her men to follow. They soon left the safety of the paved narrow streets and reached the luxurious merchant districts, the most affluent area in Undercity—not counting Mullecias Heights, where the ultra-rich and the royalty resided, but which was technically a different city in all but name. Kes arrived at the ample, well-lit streets and open parks with clear paths. They were fine for having a safe stroll at night during a normal day, but deathly dangerous tonight, when her best ally was darkness and stealth.

Her first instinct was to have the drones dig a tunnel straight to the tower so they could bypass the open ground, but the drones shook their heads when she gave them the order. One pointed its tiny finger at a few shadows who were standing in the middle of the main plaza without a care in the world.

Heroes, Kes thought. Not everyone had left for Mullecias, then. *Their presence is contesting the district.*

"We'll need to fight our way inside," Kaga said. Next to him, Yumiya nodded grimly. "A fitting end, to die fighting an impossible battle."

Costel and the other humans didn't look half as sure as the kaftar. For once, Kes agreed with them. She counted about five Heroic parties standing around, healing or breaking all crates and barrels in sight. "We've got Pirene on standby. Have the spiderlings tell her we may need some reinforcements in a few minutes."

Someone tugged at her arm. "Marshal?" asked Young Ivan. He had a worried look to his eyes. "Any chance that Pirene decided to charge on her own?"

Kes didn't like the kid's expression one bit. "Empress Laurel gave her strict orders to wait, so I doubt she'll take the initiative," she said. Then, frowning, she asked, "Why?"

Young Ivan turned back and pointed at the avenue from where they'd just come a few minutes ago. "Because a lot of somethings are coming our way, and they look pissed off."

At first, Kes didn't know what he was talking about. Her sight wasn't as good in the storm. But then she saw a red glint here and there, like shining blood droplets floating in the dark. Then she heard the distant *bawks*, almost entirely muffled by the rain, but growing stronger with each second—there was a lot of bawking, actually. And then lightning struck nearby, and the night became day for a flash, and Kes saw the army of hell chickens charging their way, steel beaks shining an evil blue. There was murder in their eyes.

She could swear she also saw a pair of terrified spell-casters riding their own hell chickens, leading the charge if only by a few feet.

"Oynnes' bountiful mercy," Costel whispered. "What in the Wetlands is that?"

Kes didn't bother with an answer. The hell chickens were getting closer *fast*. She turned to the nearby buildings that surrounded the plaza. The nearest one was about a hundred meters away, and the first Heroic parties were already heading to meet the hell chickens. "Get to that rooftop, everyone!" she bellowed, running as fast as her legs could go. "And don't you dare leave that dish behind!"

THE FEELING of oxygen rushing into his battered lungs was glorious, even as it seared his throat and filled his mouth with the taste of ash. Karmich coughed and spit cold water. His entire body ached, except his right arm below his shoulder, which he couldn't move at all. He waded through the canal's waters, grabbing on to a sort of wide, black log with many spindly branches coming out of it, and a long spike at one end. A silver thread was tied to the log, and it connected all the way to a group of inhuman figures waiting at the shore, partially hidden by the rainstorm. They seemed to be pulling the thread toward them, dragging Karmich to dry land.

Beside him, Pris was in a similar situation. She was unconscious—or that was what Karmich hoped. Her lips were blue and her skin deathly pale.

Then he saw the log that was carrying her and realized it was no log at all, but a horned spider. He tried to scream, and a wave of pain dragged him back into unconsciousness.

When he next awoke, he was lying on his back against the

stones of a causeway. He was shivering from cold and fear, and there was a giant horned spider staring him down with her multiple beady eyes, her mandibles half open to reveal slick fangs capable of tearing open a horse in a couple bites. Karmich whimpered.

"Fear not, meat-bag," the spider hissed. "For I am Laurel of the Haunt, first Empress among spider-kind. In the name of Dungeon Lord Wraith, I give you my word that you shall not be harmed, no matter how delicious you are." She seemed as confused by this as Karmich was. Something told the Thief that he was the Empress' first rescue attempt.

"Uh. M-my thanks, Empress," he stammered through clenched teeth. He was so cold. Glancing down, he realized the horned spiders had webbed the charred mess that was his arm. How thoughtful of them. It didn't hurt at all, somehow. Perhaps they'd given him a pain-numbing potion?

Pris, right next to him, came to. She opened her eyes, took stock of the situation, and began to scream.

"Quiet, meat-bag!" Laurel bellowed. "The Heroes will hear your screeching!"

Karmich dragged himself next to his friend, who was about to suffer a hysterical breakdown. "Pris! Listen, no, no, put the dagger down—they're on our side! I think they're working for Ed." That was enough to get her attention, but she kept the dagger aimed at the Empress. Not that it'd help. Karmich knew horned Queens were big, but Laurel was on a whole other level. Behind her, dozens of horned spiders of all sizes shifted nervously in place, their chitin glinting as the storm struck their bodies.

"What are you talking about?" Pris muttered. She couldn't stop shivering. Karmich hurried to put an arm across her back, ignoring the violent pangs of pain near his shoulder. Pris seemed to consider stabbing him instead of the Empress, but then thought better of it and huddled closer. A tiny sliver of body heat fostered between them like a spark trying to keep the darkness from engulfing it.

"Think about it," Karmich said. "It's not like we didn't have our suspicions. The ease with which he bypassed the walls—the tunnels, the kaftars. And the Inquisition has been searching the countryside for a Dungeon Lord. One who fought a Wraith. Makes sense, doesn't it?"

Pris grimaced. "No. That sounds like admitting we've been aiding a Dungeon Lord this entire time," she said. "And that's just not my style."

"Enough!" said Empress Laurel. "We must leave before it's too late. Can you walk on your own, or should I have you webbed?"

The Thieves didn't *feel* like walking, but they knew enough about horned spiders to instantly express, wordlessly, that they'd rather die than to allow themselves to be webbed. The two hobbled together, arms over the other's back, while Laurel's cluster skittered out of the causeway.

They headed south, parallel to the Western Gate, while doing their best to keep away from that direction. On their way, Karmich saw more horned spiders from different clusters, as well as kaftar and batblins. They were all working together, helping the survivors away from danger. Whoever couldn't stand was carried. Kaftars and batblins entered the houses, ushered out whoever was inside, and then the spiders webbed all entrances shut.

In fact, Undercity had begun to look dangerously like a spider den, with thick webs closing off narrow streets and hanging from trees and lamps. It was as if they were trying to keep *something* away from this general area, but Karmich knew the webbing would do little to stop the Heroes. What, then?

"Karmich," Pris whispered. "Look." She pointed at one side-street whose walls were enclosed by web. There was movement behind—a pair of creatures that looked vaguely like huge, murderous birds with beaks like cruel steel daggers.

"We better hurry," one horned spider of Laurel's cluster told them. "You don't want to be here when they figure out that our webbing doesn't stop their claws."

"What are those?" Karmich asked, dreading the answer.

"They are the Haunt's favorite meal," said the spider. "But they also have other uses."

In the distance, Karmich could see a lone Heroic Fighter being slowly devoured by a pack of those black birds, limb by limb. The Fighter killed many, but it only seemed to incense the birds. There was a flash of light when a beak struck the Hero's eye, and the construct disappeared as the runes of a summoning circle floated around him and teleported him away, leaving behind a very disappointed group of birds.

It would've been funny, except that they then turned Karmich's way. They had red eyes, with pupils like those of a cat. Predatory and hungry.

The Thief realized that he could walk much faster after all.

ALL THINGS CONSIDERED, Alder was having a pretty rough night. To start, his throat was sore from all the screaming, and he was pretty tired from keeping his *nimble feet* melody up for so long. As he and Lavy charged their way through Undercity, he didn't dare turn back to see what exactly was following behind. He kept his eyes focused forward, on the nearby future, and on the most important question in his mind.

How was he going to stop, exactly, once they reached their destination?

Having Blood Fiend simply stop running didn't seem like the best of ideas, given that the hell chickens chasing after them didn't intend to stop, which left him at his wit's end. All his life, he'd never before gotten himself into a situation that couldn't be solved by going the other way as fast as possible.

He grimaced. Being a hero definitely wasn't his thing. How did Kes, Ed, and Klek make it seem so easy?

At the very least, he wasn't alone in his suffering. The only remaining illusion was of Lavy, and it was running next to him, with the real Lavy riding on the opposite side, carrying one of Ed's drones in front of her like she would a small child. He was flanked by twin Witches, equally terrified. If he could only live long enough to write that down...

"Over there!" Lavy called, while her drone gestured in the general direction of a black tower in the distance. "That's where Kes is!"

"Fantastic, I hope she's up to stopping a few hundred hell chickens on her own!"

The Witch shook her head no, a motion that the illusionary version imitated a second later. "Don't worry about the chickens!" Lavy exclaimed.

"Why not? It seems like a huge deal to me!" Alder called back, pushing his throat to make his voice be heard over the storm.

"Because," Lavy yelled, "those assholes in front of us are probably going to kill us before the hell chickens can!"

Alder raised an eyebrow. He could barely see anything at all in front of him—salty, cold water kept stinging his eyes. "What assholes—" then he saw the Heroes strolling through an open plaza to meet them, magic crackling in the spellcasters' hands, enchanted weapons at the ready. He couldn't help but quote Ed: "Oh, shit!"

"Time to split!" Lavy roared, pushing Scar's reins to the side. The hell chicken followed, with Blood Fiend close behind, just as the first couple *fireballs* soared past their heads and vaporized a pair of hell chickens behind them. Almost as an afterthought, Alder willed Lavy's illusionary copy, which was heavily doused in pheromones, to charge straight at the nearest party of Heroes.

Alder looked over his shoulder in time to see a Knight with a broadsword hack off the heads of three chickens at once—and then be swarmed by their battle-lusted brethren. The Witch's illusionary copy disappeared under a barrage of *ice bolts* a second later.

"Over there!" Lavy said, gesturing to one end of the plaza, at a two-story building with broken windows and a partially caved-in entrance. There was the faint afterglow of a lantern shining on a balcony, and Alder could see Kes' figure frantically gesturing for them to come closer.

Ice bolts flew right over the Bard's head. He squeaked and hugged Blood Fiend to make himself a small target. His mount gave him a sharp, judgmental bawk and rushed after Scar, wading through a sea of angry hell chickens and wounded Heroes teleporting away.

Just as Lavy reached the walls of the building, she threw her hands above her head, and was snatched up by the furry arm of a kaftar hanging from the edge of the balcony. To Alder, it looked as if she was engulfed by darkness itself—it happened so fast.

"No, no, no!" With a supreme effort of will, the Bard shoved down his terror and let go of the reins. He straightened his back and raised his hands as high as possible. The kaftar's hand closed in on his. Alder's shoulders screamed in protest, and suddenly his legs left the hell chicken's back as the kaftar used Alder's own momentum to throw him upward using some sort of *acrobatic* talent. For an instant, Alder flew up a few inches through the air. He saw Kes' face right in front of him as the Marshal caught him by the waist and tossed him onto the wooden balcony.

More hands dragged him inside the safety of the building. The Bard caught a glimpse of Blood Fiend and Scar rushing away from the plaza, moving faster now that they'd lost their riders.

Alder spat rainwater onto the floorboards. He was soaked down to the bone. Around him, Costel and her guards covered the building's entrances, Kes squatted next to a broken window to watch the plaza, the surviving drones huddled around Lavy's dish, and Kaga and the Monster Hunters stood around Alder.

"Did the pheromones work?" Yumiya inquired.

"Too well, I'd say," Alder said. "I'd rather have them their usual angry selves than lusty *and* angry."

Outside in the plaza, the Heroes and the hell chickens fought a bloody, terrible battle. The spellcasters spammed crowd-control magic while keeping their tanks as buffed as possible, and the Haunt's black creatures fell in droves. But there were only four or five Heroic groups in total, and there were hundreds of hell chickens, and only so much a tank could do when his team was flooded by a storm of murderous feathers and sharp beaks looking for the soft spots underneath their armor.

Lavy hurried to Kes' side. "The chickens won't last long, and more Heroes are coming from Mullecias," she told the Marshal. "What's the plan?"

"Is that tower tall enough for your dish?" Kes asked simply.

"It'll have to be," Lavy said. "But I've no idea if it'll work, Kes. Pholk and I didn't have enough time to test it."

Kes nodded. "That's the usual story with new gear. Let's hope for the best, Lavy, but I swear if the thing explodes or fails to start I'm going to ground it back into sand."

"Well… you're welcome to try. It's sturdier than it looks," Lavy said with a small grin.

The Marshall stood and gestured at Alder and the others to group around her. Alder did so gladly, stepping closer to the kaftar as to steal a bit of their body heat for himself. He was shivering enough not to mind the kaftar's wet-dog smell.

"Here's what we'll do," Kes said. "We're going to reach that tower and bar it from inside while the drones hook up the dish to the city's ley lines. Since the dish and the drones are our win condition, we're going to form a circle around them and head to the tower by hugging the walls as much as we can. Then we're going to run and hope for the best. Lavy, Alder, you're our spellcasters. Do you have any juice left to help us out?"

Lavy nodded. "Specters should come in handy. I mean, they

always do… but hell chickens can't strike them, since their claws aren't magical. A zap or two from my specters should keep most of them away from us."

"I'm down to two incantations," Alder said. Keeping his illusions up all the way from the Haunt had eaten through most of his spells. "I could *nimble feet* when it's time to rush, and save a *dazzling display* in case the Heroes try to take a shot at us." He was so tired that he wasn't sure he wouldn't pass out while using *nimble feet* again, but he kept that to himself.

"Do it," Kes said. "Everyone, take your positions. We'll leave as soon as the flow of battle leaves us an opening." As the kaftar, the guards, and the drones hurried to follow her command, she headed for the stairs, then seemed to change her mind. She strolled back to Alder and Lavy. "I'm proud of you two," she told them. "Without the stint you pulled with the hell chickens, we'd all be dead by now. Whatever happens next, I'm glad to be your teacher." She left without waiting for a response.

Lavy and Alder exchanged glances. "What was that about?" Alder said quietly. "She went all sentimental all of a sudden. I mean, it's nice, but she never does that unless she's drunk."

The Witch smiled, but her lower lip was trembling a bit. "She thinks we're all going to die," she said.

"Oh," Alder said.

ONE FAMOUS DWARVEN philosopher had engraved a musing in stone that said when a brave dwarf drew his last breath, he'd see the silver gates of the Great Mountain slide open, and his ancestors and late family would storm out to greet him and shower him in cold ale and gemstone necklaces. They'd carry him inside the Mountain Palace, where he'd be bathed and his beard braided before a huge feast was served in his honor.

If the dwarf had been craven, though, the gates would never open. The Palace jester—an ugly creature that looked like a corrupted gnome—would appear to mock him, and the ground below the dwarf's feet would collapse and draw him all the way to the heart of the world, where his flesh would be stripped from his bones, and then his bones would melt and become part of the liquid steel heart of Ivalis itself, and the dwarf would burn until the world fire died out.

This is all to say that, when Oscor opened his eyes to see a weird amalgamation of a batblin and horned spider standing inches away from his face, he may have jumped to conclusions.

"Stay away from me, you damn jester!" he roared, trying to drag himself away and punch the aberration at the same time, yet managing neither. Something was holding his legs in place. "Sod off, you fuck, I'll fight you, I'll fight you and the entire damn Palace! Do you think I'm a coward, ancestors? Well, come at me, then, I never liked you much anyway, you bunch of stuck-up pricks!"

"What a loud little snack," said the spider half of the Palace Jester. "And it doesn't seem too happy about us saving his hide. Can I eat it now?"

"No, Tulip," said the batblin half. "We don't eat the people we rescue, remember?"

The horned spider seemed disappointed. Oscor blinked and did his best to clear the soot from his eyes with fists even dirtier than his face. He realized that the Palace Jester was, in fact, a batblin riding a horned spider princess.

Ah, so I'm only hallucinating, he realized. *Not dead yet... Ah. Sorry, ancestors.*

The batblin jumped off of the spider. "Don't be afraid," the critter told the dwarf. "My name's Klek, and my friend here is Tulip. I am the leader of the Haunt's Spider Riders. Lord Ed sent us to help. You'll be safe now."

"Lord Ed, eh?" the dwarf chuckled darkly to himself. "So that's why Ed is so weird. No wonder we're in this mess." He turned to look around at the ravaged alley. "Where are my friends?"

516

"Right behind you, Boss," Sköm said weakly. Oscor shifted painfully, still unable to move his legs—they were pinned down under a smoking beam. The fact that he wasn't in absolute agony at the moment worried him.

Sköm was surrounded by even more batblins riding spiders. There were about four more of them, all busy helping Oscor's smugglers get out of the debris or administering first aid. One spider webbed Cimeko's broken arm and bit her gently, using paralyzing venom to numb the pain. Oscor nodded in approval.

"We're ready," Klek said. The batblin had been busy somewhere outside of Oscor's field of view. When he reappeared, he was holding the end of several web-ropes, each connected to the beam crushing Oscor's legs. The batblin slid a wooden slab under the beam, next to Oscor, and stood back. "Riders, let's get this dwarf out!"

Batblins and spiders hurried to heed their leader's command, although Oscor could see they were worried—the explosions and the screams of the dying surrounded the alley, coming through the rain like the wailing of the damned. The battle for Undercity was far from over.

"We need to hurry," one nervous batblin told Klek, rubbing his hands and throwing furtive glances at the end of the alley. "The Heroes will arrive at any minute!"

"Then let's get him out fast, Vogkord," Klek said. He handed one rope to Vogkord and another one to his spider. "On my command, pull with all you've got, Rose."

The Spider Riders disappeared from Oscor's field of view again. A moment later, he could feel Cimeko's comforting hand brushing his hair. "You'll be fine," Cimeko told him. A kind of warmth traveled down Oscor's back, as if his body believed it quicker than his mind.

Oscor shook the hand away. "Of course I will be! Go help my smugglers, we don't have time for you to lie here!"

At Klek's command, the spiders and the batblins pulled with

all their might. At first, nothing happened. Then, Oscor could see the beam shifting. He could *feel* it. It moved a millimeter. Maybe another. *It's not going to be enough,* he thought, trying to pull himself out with all his strength.

Then Cimeko was there, helping the riders, with Sköm besides Vogkord, doing his best with only one arm. Every smuggler who could still move joined them. Slowly, inch by inch, the weight of the beam moved away from Oscor.

And then he was free. Relief flooded through him. He made the mistake of looking at his legs, and a dizziness overcame him. Even with his dwarven toughness, his legs had been turned into bloody pulp.

Klek's spider, Tulip, fashioned a sort of swing out of webbing for Oscor. She and another spider shared the weight between them. They used another swing for one unconscious gnome, and then the riders and the smugglers skittered out into the streets in absolute silence.

Oscor tried his best not to think of the bodies they'd left behind—Wufroc and Scappi and three other good, loyal men. He vowed to return, if he survived, and give them a proper burial.

And for a second, he really believed he'd make good on his promise. The streets the batblins had chosen were empty, except for the bodies in pools of pink water and the devastation left in the Heroes' wake.

Then a peal of thunder ruptured the darkness and Cimeko screamed and Oscor raised his head to see the silhouette of the levitating Wizard hovering a hundred feet in front of them. All hope left the dwarf. He was wet and tired. Best to get it over with.

"Oh, shit," Klek whispered next to him. The batblin clutched his spear. "Riders! Let's do what we do best! For the Haunt!"

The batblins and the spiders roared in unison. And as one, they all ran for their lives.

. . .

THE DRONES CARRIED the leather tarp with Lavy's dish inside while Alder and the Witch ushered them forward. As the spellcasters, they were inside Kes' circle formation, with the Marshal and the kaftar at the end covering the squishies and Lavy's specters floating a few feet away, trying their best to mesh with the darkness and the rain to not attract any unwanted attention from the Heroes.

A few hell chickens saw the group as they shuffled through the plaza while keeping close to the cover of the buildings. The specters flew down to meet them, zapping the creatures out of a couple points of Endurance. After a couple attempts, most hell chickens lost interest and headed back into the fray against the Heroes.

The Akathunians' tower was near the end and to the left of the plaza, next to the Brewers Guild headquarters—one of the most powerful "legit" Guilds in town, and technically the Haunt's competition. Alder noted with a slight pleasure that the Guildhouse's entrance had collapsed.

The pleasure vanished when he saw the bodies heaped among the rubble.

He clenched his jaw and marched on through the rain. In front of him, the kaftars kept their bows and blowpipes at the ready, in case a lucky hell chicken got through Lavy's specters.

He had no idea how long they walked. Time had no meaning with the carnage raging around him. It could've been seconds or minutes, but it felt like much more. Back in Elaitra, he'd read dozens, if not hundreds, of battle depictions written by Bards who had either been near the front lines or had interviewed soldiers who were.

This was different. Even though neither the Heroes nor the hell chickens were humans, seeing a living creature being torn open by a broadsword and its insides splattering into a puddle lacked the glory and honor that those Bards had claimed was found in combat.

Could it be that there was something wrong with him? If he survived, he didn't think he could find a way to describe the battle for Undercity as some sort of dance between glorious foes. His eyes could only see the blood and the guts and the very human-looking bodies that he and the others sometimes stepped past—they were the unlucky merchants that hadn't managed to evacuate in time.

Where was the honor in this? Where was the glory?

I'll show them, Alder vowed as he walked past the broken body of a half-elf wearing a yellow dress. *I'll show them the truth.*

For that, though, he needed to survive first.

Alder could swear he saw a cloud of purple mist soar through the battle and hover above them for an instant. Kes raised a fist and pointed a finger at the tower, and the mist shot in that direction. "It's open terrain from here to the tower," Kes told the group. "Get ready, Alder. On my mark!"

Around the Bard, everyone tensed, including the drones. Lavy gestured at her specters and they broke the circle, forming a wedge in front of the group as to force the surviving hell chickens in their way to move aside.

"Here goes nothing," Alder said.

Kes waited a few seconds, reading the ebb and flow of the battle in a way that escaped Alder. "NOW!" she exclaimed suddenly.

"*Nimble feet!*" Alder yelled as he ran. The effort almost floored him—his vision blurred, and he could only follow the shapes of his friends as he fought against cold and exhaustion. With a trembling hand, he procured the last *vitality* potion in his belt and downed it in a single gulp. It helped only a bit, since drinking several potions in close succession reduced their potency—and he'd needed to down a few just to keep the *nimble feet* up all the way from the Haunt.

Reaching the tower felt like wading through hell. Alder feared that if he slipped, he'd lack the strength to get up. Also, a few of the remaining Heroes saw them running and took potshots at them. Arrows and spells soared close enough that Alder could hear their screams and whistles as they tore through the air. In front of him, a kaftar stumbled and fell, an arrow protruding from his neck. A couple drones disappeared when an *ice bolt* struck them, and the dish wobbled precariously as the remaining drones tried to gather their balance.

Alder acted without thinking. He grabbed a corner of the tarp and steadied it. He ran along the drones, and ran, and ran, too tired and scared to even scream.

And then the doors to the Charcoal Tower were almost upon them, charred, splintered, and barely holding on to their hinges. Alder wondered numbly what would've happened had the doors been barred from the inside, and then the rain stopped smacking against his head as he rushed inside.

He stumbled and fell to his knees as soon as his *nimble feet* ended. Around him, everyone was steadying their breaths, even as they hurried away from the doors. The tower's interior was so trashed that it was impossible to tell what it had been previous to the Heroes' rampage inside. Akathunian bodies were strewn over broken furniture, bronze braziers lay on the cobblestone floor, hell chicken corpses, still smoking, fallen near the entrance, and a pair of naga spellcasters were nailed to the walls by *ice bolts*. All that could be broken was, and even a wall at the other end had collapsed to reveal the partially caved-in staircase to the upper floors.

"Well done, Alder," Lavy said, helping him up. She was panting and her cheeks were flushed red.

Behind them, the kaftar hurried to close the doors as best as they could, as the drones carried the dish farther into the tower.

"We need to hook the tower up to the dungeon's ley lines," Lavy told Kes. "Have half the drones start working on that and we'll help the others carry the dish. Otherwise, we'll waste too much time."

For a second, Kes didn't give signs of having heard her. The Marshal was frowning, her gaze focused on the shadowy corners of the tower. Then she nodded. "Do as she says," she told the drones.

The drones shook their heads, something akin to impotence showing in their ugly faces.

"That's weird," Lavy said. "They've never refused an order before."

Alder couldn't help but shake the feeling that something was off. His eyes rested on the hell chicken bodies.

It made no sense, he realized. The Heroes had ravaged the tower hours ago, then left. But the hell chickens had arrived with him and Lavy.

Who had killed those?

As realization struck him like thunder, and Kes' eyes were already widening in alarm. "They aren't refusing an order. The tower is contested!" the Marshal exclaimed. She raised her shield at the darkness just in time, because a flurry of arrows flew at them from the corners, whistling as they went. "AMBUSH!"

Around Alder, kaftar fell and drones disappeared.

Inquisitors poured from the shadows, weapons drawn, their silver armor turning gold as a Cleric cast his buffs on them.

LAVY'S REACTION SAVED KES' life.

Arrows bounced off the avian's shield, but the three Inquisitors were almost upon her, charging with shining white swords aimed her way. She knew she wouldn't be able to fight them off, not with the amount of buffs they had up.

Then all the specters flew past her without making a single sound, while Lavy spammed *witch spray* at the incoming Inquisitors, filling the air with colors. The white swords smote down the specters in seconds, and someone fired *ice bolts* straight at the Witch, but Kes stepped into the attack, deflecting the spells with her shield. Thanks to her improved *shield master* talent, the bolts broke against the shield instead of simply punching through.

As she rushed into battle followed by the surviving Monster Hunters, she'd realized there were three Inquisitors leading the ambush, armed to the teeth, as well as a Cleric in heavy plate flanking the side and preparing a spell. Five Militant soldiers, less armored than the Inquisitors, followed a few steps behind, carrying spears, although some held spent runes in their free hands. Lastly, three Militant archers hurried to nock new arrows.

She threw a stab at the Inquisitor that she guessed was the leader, a young man, powerfully built, who was barking orders even as he parried Kes' strike:

"Get the drones, Zeki! Archers, take out those casters!" With magically enhanced strength, he pushed Kes away with one mighty shove and his sword drew an arc aimed at her neck. She met it with her sword, and then stepped away from the Inquisitor's *real* attack—a kick aimed straight at her gut, which missed by inches.

The Monster Hunters reached the Marshal's side just as the Inquisitor's friends tried to get to her. Kaga threw a pair of throwing knives at the Cleric, but the man's magical armor deflected them. Then Yumiya snared him in a hunting net and pulled him down, dodging arrows as she did so, moving with unnatural grace. Scimitars clashed against longswords, and steel struck plate, leather, and flesh. All around her, people screamed.

From the corner of her eye, she saw the archers take aim at Lavy and Alder, who had stepped in front of the drones to protect the Jamming dish.

Kes figured it was as good a time as any to take a shot in the dark and hope for a miracle. "Now, Alder!" she ordered as she struggled to keep the Inquisitor at bay.

Alder took a step forward and activated his last incantation. "*Dazzling display!*" The supernatural music that followed drowned the sounds of battle. The notes were smooth like honey, and they came with their own light show, something that Kes had never seen, as if explosions of sound and music were going off around the Bard all at once.

The archers and the Militant soldiers stopped in their tracks, staring dumbfounded at the *bardic incantation* while the Inquisitors, who had higher resistance against Mind-altering effects, tried to push past Kes and the Monster Hunters to end the effect.

"I can0t hold it much longer!" Alder warned her. Kes knew that, when the Bard ended the effect, the archers would turn him into a pincushion.

"Jarlen!" she screamed, hoping against hope that she hadn't imagined the purple mist she had seen before entering the tower. "Archers!"

Kes' opponent was good. A talented duelist, judging by his stance. The Militant Church had probably trained him since birth, long before he passed the aptitude tests to become an Inquisitor. His sword danced and flourished around Kes' lunges and feints, which looked sluggish by comparison. He was good, stronger than her, and younger. He caught the side of Kes' blade and riposted so fast that only her shield already being in the right place to block saved her. His blade sprang forward and drew a slash that burned Kes' side. She could smell burning flesh where the *smite* enchantment had charred the skin. She bashed him with her shield and forced him to take a step back.

In a duel, Kes would've been in trouble. But this wasn't a duel. "*Cleave!*" she roared. Her sword soared through the air, and the man calmly prepared a parry—but instead of striking at him, she slashed at the Militant soldier a step away, a man who wasn't paying attention thanks to Alder's magic.

Kes' sword pierced his neck, and then the blade sprang, impossibly fast, right back toward the Inquisitor who was looking at the soldier and wasn't expecting it. He nevertheless managed a weak parry—a testament to his skill. Kes' blade bounced away.

"Power strike!" Her blade glowed red as she used the

momentum to fuel a side-slash aimed at the Inquisitor's temple. The beauty of *power strike* was that you only needed to hit *fast* and didn't need to worry about putting much weight behind the attack.

The Inquisitor caught the blunt of the hit with his sword's guard—saving his life—but the impact punched through it and mangled bone and tendon. He stumbled back, teeth clenched against the pain, and tried to switch his sword to his left hand.

Before he could, Kes darted forward and bashed him on the side of the head with her shield. His helmet's enchantments flared blue as he fell down, once again saving his life. She moved in for the kill-shot, but a second Inquisitor took his place, driving her back.

Then Alder's light-show ended, and the Bard fell to his knees.

"Archers!" the Inquisitor on the ground bellowed. "Take them out, now!"

Kes' heart skipped a bit when she realized the archers were still aiming, and Jarlen was nowhere to be seen. "Shit—" The arrows cut loose as she jumped in Alder and Lavy's general direction, raising her shield, but knowing she wouldn't make it in time.

Several muted thuds rang across the tower as the projectiles found their targets.

Kes blinked, and then cursed, as the two Inquisitors still standing collapsed with their backs filled with arrows. Without skipping a beat, her Monster Hunters pushed forward, making short work of the remaining Militant soldiers.

"What?" bellowed their wounded leader, trying to stand. "What have you done?" he yelled at the archers.

A shadow floated above him, half-mist and half-vampire, and coalesced into the shape of a little girl of about ten, dressed in a blood-stained dress. "Don't be angry at them," she said in a sing-song, her eyes glinting maliciously. "They only did what I asked them to do." Jarlen turned to Alder, who was panting on his knees and just as surprised as everyone else. "My thanks for pointing out those with weak Spirit, Bard. You made my job easier."

"No problem," Alder managed.

The last remaining Inquisitor fumbled to his knees, trying to enter a dueling stance again, but the shaking in his left hand didn't allow it. "Blood-sucker!" he exclaimed. "I knew Gallio should have destroyed you when we had the chance. It's a mistake I won't make. *Smite!*"

He attempted to strike down the vampire, but she dispersed into mist, which floated behind him before returning her to her normal shape. Kes saw with horror how Jarlen smiled as she hugged the Inquisitor from behind and drove her long, black nails into the man's eyes.

His screams only ended after she tore his neck open, putting him out of his misery.

"Some people don't know when to give up," Jarlen said as she fed.

Kes' stomach churned. She took a deep breath and looked around, because it gave her an excuse not to stare at the source of those slurping sounds. Kaga and Yumiya were alive, but wounded, although neither seemed to notice the blood staining their fur. Yumiya was busy sedating the Cleric and tying him up. Of the Monster Hunter's original ten, only six remained, and they were restraining the archers and the two surviving Militant soldiers. A little more than half the drones were still alive. Alder and Lavy...

Alder and Lavy were tired and battered, but they were alive.

The Marshal let out the breath she didn't know she had been holding. She allowed a second for relief to flood through her. They were alive.

That one was close, she thought. If it hadn't been for Jarlen... or for Lavy's specters... or for Alder's *dazzling display...* Things could've gone terribly wrong.

Enough commiserating, boot, Ria told her. *There's a war to be won, you cannot waste time having a small crisis every time you survive a skirmish.*

"What were they doing here?" Lavy asked weakly as she helped Alder up. "How did they know we'd come?"

Kes sighed and allowed her martial discipline to take over again, drowning all emotion. "This tower is a strategic position. When the Heroes and Inquisitors headed off to retake Mullecias, they left a few griffin riders to cover important zones. This man over here—" she pointed at one unconscious soldier "—is not a rider. My guess is that a few Militant soldiers stayed behind to secure the tower, and then you and Alder brought an army of blue-balled hell chickens to the plaza. The riders were probably in the middle of extracting their allies before we ran inside." Had the Inquisitors had a few more minutes to plan out their attack, it was doubtful that Kes or anyone else would've survived. If that Cleric had had a higher *combat casting…* she withheld a shudder.

"If you've finished chatting," Jarlen said, cleaning blood off her face. "I've missed half the fun already, so I'd like to kill as many people as I can before daylight comes. Pirene's spiders are climbing the tower as we speak, from the outside, trying to keep those pesky griffins away from us, but there's someone at the top who just keeps killing them with arrows. Anyone up for another round?"

"We are!" one Monster Hunter exclaimed.

Kes turned to Alder and Lavy. "You stay behind. No offense, but you're tired and out of spells. I don't want to have to babysit you while we clean up the tower. Stay safe and help the drones."

"That doesn't offend me at all," Alder said. "Be safe, Kes."

Kes grasped the Bard's forearm, and then went after Jarlen, trying her best to pretend she wasn't so tired she could barely swing her sword.

LAVY WATCHED as Kes and Jarlen disappeared up the trapdoor. The

Witch tried to listen to any sounds that might tell her what was going on up there, but the rain and the battle outside drowned it all. She hurried toward her dish and the surviving drones—about two dozen of them instead of the original thirty, but they were enough. They were digging a tunnel frantically under the tower, looking for the ley line, while others danced near every corner, "claiming" the building for the Haunt.

Alder hurried next to her. The Bard looked barely conscious, but apparently he was as stubborn as her. "I looked outside," he said. "Gloriosa's brood and the Haga'Anashi are kicking the ass of the couple Heroes remaining."

The news felt like a breath of fresh air in Lavy's battered lungs. "That means Ed's back," she said. With him and the rest of the Haunt buying them time while the drones set up the dish, they had a chance. "Alder, I think we're going to win!"

The Bard nodded. "Only if we hurry. Let's not leave Ed outside too long, or he'll get cocky and try to solo the rest of the Heroes, alright?"

Seconds after, the drones finished their little dance. Everything was coming together in such a way that Lavy almost found it hard to believe.

They were going to win. The words kept dancing around in her head, almost a foreign concept. She'd spent her life in one dungeon or another, always fearing when the day would come that the first team of Heroes arrived.

But this time would be different. All those people she'd lost over the years. Her parents, Warlock Chasan, Lord Kael. Not anymore. After tonight, it'd be the Inquisition that should be afraid.

And she'd helped make that happen. The thought made her weak in the knees. She wanted to weep from joy.

Instead, she took a deep breath and helped the drones carry the dish she'd built up the stairs. She was so happy she barely felt the weight. Her heart raced as fast as a hummingbird's.

They were halfway up when she heard a sharp crack and a puff of smoke, and the dish shifted precariously backward. *Dunghill!* She and the drones hurried to catch it, and managed it at the last moment before it fell down the stairs.

"What happened?" she asked, almost of the mind to blame the drones.

"I don't know," Alder said. He was at the back of the procession. "One of them just up and vanished."

"What?" Lavy asked. "That makes no sense." Was this one of the drones' tricks? But that couldn't be. They never acted up when the stakes were high. She gazed at the drones and froze. There was something in their eyes she'd never seen before.

Absolute horror.

Her blood turned to ice in her veins. "What's going on?" she whispered.

One by one, the drones began to vanish in puffs of smoke.

IT WAS NO BOSS FIGHT, but Lisa was starting to enjoy it. The creatures just kept coming, and unlike half the monsters she'd faced, they just didn't know when to quit. According to her screen, they were called hell chickens. They were some sort of black-feathered dinosaur, with powerful beaks and claws sharp enough to tear through her Cleric's armor.

Above, the griffins dove into the battle, claws at the ready, and came back up while carrying a hell chicken or one of the horned spiders skittering along the Assassins' tower. It was very cinematic watching the flying lions tear the creatures apart and shower the top-down camera with black feathers or blue ichor. Once in a while, a spider got lucky and managed to snare a griffin with their web, and then the critter and the rest of its nearby spiders would fall on the poor griffin and rend its flesh with their mandibles.

Yes, Lisa had to admit she was starting to have fun. Around her party, other Heroes fought fiercely—since they weren't going to make it to Mullecias anyway, there was no point in holding back.

The hell chickens were dying in droves. Their bodies littered the plaza in bloody heaps, Ivalis Online's graphic engine doing an incredible job at showcasing the causes of their deaths—they were charred, or torn, or vaporized, or frozen, or melted by acid, each with their own dying animations. The survivors were just as likely to go for the Heroes killing their brothers as they were for the fallen chickens themselves to feast on their flesh as the battle raged on.

Near a corner of the screen, a Heroic Knight was rushed by a dozen hell chickens just as his Priest used *restoration* on him. *Restoration* was a high-level spell meant to heal huge amounts of damage… And it was also completely useless in the Knight's situation. Lisa saw how the Knight went down in seconds. That was because *restoration* was an emergency spell, meant to take a character's HP out of the red. It was useless if the hell chickens kept the Knight pinned and just whittled away his HP over and over. Lisa, who had a bit more experience as a healer, always saved her single *restoration* for when it could actually make a difference.

Mark laughed merrily in the chat. His Fighter and Lisa's Cleric found themselves back to back, with the dwarf bashing his shield in wide arcs, pushing three or four creatures away with each arc, while she kept the buffs up and the circles of respite ongoing, as to force the hell chickens to fight them at a disadvantage. Even Ryan was quiet, too focused in the battle to be his annoying self as his Rogue darting in and out of stealth and *sneak attacked* everything in sight. Meanwhile, Omar emptied the Wizard's list of area-of-effect spells, launching *fireballs, blizzards, ice shards,* and everything else in his arsenal, without holding back anything for later.

Lisa wanted to advise him to save some juice up in case a mini-boss showed up. After all, Pantheon didn't usually care to create extra content for anyone not in the main area of the World Event, so it was clear the developers had something in mind. Perhaps she was right: Albino horned spiders arrived at the plaza, skittering atop the rooftops and the walls of the buildings surrounding them. Since they were a different color than the usual brown or black, Lisa was willing to bet shit was about to get real. *Perhaps we get to fight an elite Queen as a mini-boss,* she thought.

The horned critters rushed into the fray, doing their best to ignore the hell chickens. Lisa noted with pleasure that the hell chickens, whose numbers were thinning by now, attacked the albino spiders as well as the remaining groups of Heroes.

The event wasn't over, though. As Lisa's mace crushed a spider princess, a pair of elite kaftar rushed at her, brandishing long spears. Mark dealt with one, blocking the charge with his shield and his *taunt.* She handled the other one, casting a *stormwind* to push the hyena-man straight in the path of Rylan Silverblade, who chopped its head off with a well-timed critical hit.

"Hah!" Ryan laughed. "Take that!"

Around Lisa, more kaftar joined in, jumping at the remaining Heroes, most of whom were caught by surprise. Since few players had had the foresight to save their dailies up to this point, the elite kaftar began dropping Heroes like flies, either by spearing them themselves or by setting up a flank for the hell chickens and the horned spiders to abuse.

It was great. Lisa knew her group could mop up what was left of the monsters. All the glory would be theirs...

Then she saw the great white horned spider rising above the farthest rooftop. The albino Queen. Was that the mini-boss? She descended in a hurry and rushed toward the tower.

Someone in heavy plate armor was riding her. Lisa's eyes widened as she realized it was the final Boss. The Dungeon Lord. *Mullecias was a fake-out,* she thought. The real battle would be here. The other players would have to come all the way back from Mullecias if they wanted to take their shot.

Unless... unless she managed to take the Boss down first.

Her hands hovered over her keyboard. She'd finally read the tag above the Boss' head.

It said, "Dungeon Lord Edward Wright."

For a second, she froze, her brain not even recognizing the name. "Mark, are you seeing this?" she asked. She could even swear that the pixelated Dungeon Lord even looked slightly like her old friend. The hair was longer, and his face's features sharper and, perhaps, crueler, but the likeness was unmistakable. He and his Spider Queen rushed through the carnage, his sword and his eyes shining green as he led his minions into battle and his aura buffed them into a renewed ferocity.

Around him, the weakened Heroic parties fell left and right, teleporting out in flashes of light.

"Yes," Mark said quietly. "What the fuck?"

"Guys?" Omar asked. "What's going on?"

Lisa barely heard the kid. *Is Ed working at Pantheon now or something?*

She was so stunned that she only caught sight of Rylan Silverblade when he was almost upon the Dungeon Lord, creeping up on the Boss from behind with his *sneak* up. The Dungeon Lord and the spider were too busy fighting their way forward to realize the Rogue's presence. "Ryan, wait!" she called. Something was off about all this. Something was terribly, terribly wrong. She rushed at them.

But the Rogue and the Dungeon Lord were far enough from her that she could do nothing but stare in horror at what happened next.

"So you think you can make fun of me, Eddy, you little shit," Ryan muttered over his mic. His voice was trembling with anger. "Well. Let's see how you like *this.*"

And he *shadow stepped* above the Queen, double scimitars shining a bright purple as he unleashed the rest of his dailies in a flurry of deadly, magically enhanced steel. The Dungeon Lord reacted with incredible speed, managing to parry one scimitar with his flaming sword, holding it with both hands and screaming in anger.

Rylan Silverblade's second scimitar crackled as its enchantments punched through the Dungeon Lord's magical defenses and then buried itself within the Dungeon Lord's breastplate, tearing through it as if it were paper.

The Dungeon Lord and the Rogue seemed to stare at each other for a long time. The battle raging across the plaza seemed to come to a stop. Lisa could swear she heard a woman screaming.

And then Silverblade drew his blade out of the Dungeon Lord's chest, a spray of arterial blood marring the albino Queen's chitin. He kicked the Dungeon Lord off of his mount. Ed's flaming sword snuffed out as he struck the floor. Lisa screamed. The Dungeon Lord tried weakly to crawl away, leaving a trail of blood behind him. He didn't get far before his strength left him. The green light in his eyes faded by the second.

A group of four drones appeared around the Dungeon Lord, dressed in white tunics. They began to drag him away with desperate speed.

Rylan Silverblade stepped in front of the Dungeon Lord and disposed of the drones with quick strikes, then aimed its scimitars at Ed's neck, who feebly threw a green flaming knife at the Rogue. It did nothing.

"Was that all you had?" Ryan said, laughing.

CHAPTER THIRTY

THE LAST RAID

K es and Jarlen led the Monster Hunters up through the tower as fast as they could, securing as many nooks and crannies as possible without wasting too much time.

Hurrying was dangerous, and Kes knew it made them vulnerable to a second ambush, but it was a risk they needed to take—the longer they remained in the tower, the bigger the chance that more Inquisitors, or the Heroes, would arrive to finish them off.

Her legs burned with effort. The sword in her hand seemed as if it weighed twice as much as usual, and pearls of sweat added to the dampness of her hair.

Only a little longer, she promised herself. She was getting too old for this.

"Last floor," Jarlen called happily. In front of them, a luxurious staircase wide enough to accommodate an army rose up to two huge slabs of mahogany—the doors to the Akathunian inner sanctum. There were signs that the Heroes had already been around, of course. The rug was torn and tattered. The walls were missing most of their engraved silver panels, with trophies and rare pelts strewn about the floor like common trash. "The smell of blood is heavy past those doors."

That was expected. "Get ready, everyone," Kes said. If there were more Inquisitors past those doors, Kes' group would have no other option but to fight, no matter how tired they were.

"Allow me," Jarlen said. "I demand first bite out of whatever lies behind." Without waiting for Kes' command, she turned into mist and flowed past one of the doors' hinges and out of sight.

Kes steadied herself as the Monster Hunters fanned out around the doors. She made sure her shield was in place and that her sword hadn't grown dull during the fight with the Inquisitor. Then she nodded wordlessly at Kaga. The Monster Hunters pushed open the doors, and she advanced inside.

The chamber was wedge-shaped, with huge open windows that gave a beautiful view of the city below. A myriad tiny fires spread through the black shadows of Undercity's buildings, like orange stars in the night sky. The stone floor was littered with Akathunian bodies, their black tunics ripped and torn. A couple of explosions had gone off near the middle of the chamber, seemingly where Heroes had been too damaged to teleport away. One of those explosions had destroyed an anti-magic circle carved with silver in the stone. Jarlen stood above the remains, looking disappointed. She turned to face Kes.

"Empty," said the vampire. "Such a shame that no one's home. My thirst is not yet quenched."

"You've drunk plenty of blood," Kes told her, not even trying to hide her disgust.

"I wasn't speaking about blood," Jarlen said, laughing. "Death's in the air tonight, and I want to help spread it!"

The shining white arrow came through the open window, whistling as it went and drawing a graceful arc that left behind a trail of vapor and magical residue. The arrow pierced Jarlen's forehead right between her eyes, snapping her neck backward with the sheer force of the impact.

"What—?" the vampire began, crossing her eyes in an attempt

to look at the arrow's shaft protruding from her face. She raised an annoyed hand to pull it out.

Kes raised her shield just in time. The arrow, enhanced with *smite* and *explosive arrow*, went off an instant later in a burst of light, turning Jarlen's head into tiny black chunks that rained all over the chamber. Behind Kes, the Monster Hunters jumped for cover behind the doors. The headless vampire body turned around, blindly, and then exploded in a shower of mist that flew out the nearest window, heading back to the Haunt—and her coffin.

"If you want death, vampire, let me deliver it to you," said Alvedhra as a griffin approached the window, a wide shadow against the black sky, wings brushing against the tower, the wind from every motion buffeting Kes. The creature roared, and the ground shook as it tried to claw its way inside, but it was simply too big to fit. Instead, Alvedhra jumped off of her mount with a practiced, carefree motion and rolled inside. She sprang to her feet, holding her bow at the ready with another *explosive arrow*.

"Thanks," Kes said. "She was getting on my nerves." She readied her stance and planted her feet firmly on the ground.

Alvedhra grinned. "Any time." Then loosed her arrow at Kes.

THE SILHOUETTE of the Rogue loomed above Ed like the angel of death itself, twin scimitars glowing purple and readying an *eviscerate*.

Move! Do something! The part of his mind that was not yet consumed by the numbing agony spreading out from his chest screamed warnings at the rest of him. Plans flashed through his head at a dizzying pace. There had to be some way to get out of this. A way to survive. There was always one. It couldn't end like this. Maybe he could use *improved reflexes* and cauterize the wound with *eldritch edge*? But no, he couldn't even speak, much less cast a spell. His head spun, and his vision went white, and every time he tried to breathe he choked on some liquid pooling in his throat.

It was his blood, he realized numbly. He was drowning in his own blood.

He hadn't even seen Ryan coming.

One second he'd been atop Gloriosa, so close to victory he could taste it, the thrill of battle beating in his temples. And the next...

He could feel his awareness evaporating into a white canvas. His pulse was the only sound that reached his ears, and it was a rhythm that grew quieter by the beat.

Idly, he wondered how many experience points he was about to award Ryan. The Rogue readied a strike, and then a shadow passed over Ed as Gloriosa crashed against Rylan Silverblade in a storm of mandibles, steel, and horns. The both rolled away from Ed's view.

He felt a pang of gratitude for the Spider Queen. There was no way she would win that fight. But thanks to her sacrifice he could die in peace without annoyances. His mind wandered to his Haunt, and his friends, wherever they were—if they were even still alive.

If only I had done more, he thought wearily. In the end, he'd gone the way of the Summoned Hero. Both of them had tried to stand above the whims of fate, and reality itself had swatted them away like flies.

Three figures approached him and stood a few feet away. He recognized his own Wizard, and Lisa's Cleric, and Mark's Fighter between them, shield at the ready. The Dungeon Lord attempted a laugh, but all it came from his throat was a wet, gurgling sound. At least they still had the presence of mind to keep their guard up, even with him in this state. It made him proud—that's what he would have done in their place.

As the Cleric prepared a spell, his former Wizard stepped

forward, his golem hands already performing the motions of an *enhanced fireball.*

How fitting, was what he would've said if he had been able to. *Killed by my own character. At least, even if I failed at everything I set myself up to do, Murmur will still find this entertaining.*

He gritted his teeth and summoned strength out of a body that had none left. Then, pushing through agony, he managed to sit and stare straight at the Wizard's blank face, wondering what the person behind the character was seeing. It didn't matter. The only thing that mattered was going out on his own terms. He spat blood. "Let's get on with it," he mumbled. "I don't have all day."

The Wizard launched his *fireball.* Ed was surrounded by blinding white light.

LAVY RUSHED FOR THE DOOR, shaking off Alder's attempts at holding her. Something was wrong. Something was terribly wrong. She jumped past the disappearing drones, over her dish precariously resting against a wall, and down the stairs as fast as she could.

The scene outside in the plaza awoke a cold in her stronger than anything she'd ever felt until now. She saw, in terrible clarity —slowly, as if through *improved reflexes*—how the couple remaining Heroes fought against the desperate Haga'Anashi and what few hell chickens remained, mad in their attempt to finish off the fallen Dungeon Lord.

Ed's body was partially covered by his own cape, which was soaked in blood, as if he were already wearing his funerary mantle. He wasn't moving. Next to him, a Rogue fought against Gloriosa. The Queen was missing three legs, her horn was split, and half her gray guts were strewn across the plaza, but she was refusing to give ground. The Rogue's scimitars were slick with blue ichor.

It can't be, Lavy thought. *This can't be happening. We were winning!*

She tried to rush toward Ed and drag him to safety, but a pair of arms crossed around her from behind and pulled her back inside the tower instead. "NO!" she bellowed. "Alder, he needs us, let me go!"

"You're out of spells," Alder said. The Bard's face was so pale it was almost gray, and his voice was small and hollow. "If you go out there, you'll die. Do you think that's what Ed wants? For you to die senselessly?"

It was Kael's death all over again, Lavy realized. She and Alder would see the dungeon collapse around themselves, they'd have to run away once more—the only survivors—as their friends and family died around them and their screams pierced her ears as she ran. They would chase her like specters, the wailing of the dying drilling into her soul until, suddenly, they were cut short—and then the silence would be even worse...

How could she have thought this time around would be any different? How could she have been so proud... so stupid? This was the only way it could end for people like her. Ed was about to die in front of her, even though this time she was far more powerful than the scared little Witch with a single spell she'd been when Kael had fallen, yet it still wasn't enough!

"I can't do it," she whispered. "I can't do it all over again."

As the Rogue and the Queen fought, the other three nearby Heroes calmly strolled toward the fallen Dungeon Lord, not a single one of Ed's minions in position to stop them.

"We must," Alder said. "For the Haunt's sake! Its history cannot end tonight, no matter what, I *won't* let it—I'm not done with it yet!"

Without Ed's magic allowing her to connect her Jamming Towers to Ivalis' ley lines, though, Lavy knew perfectly well that the Heroes would never stop coming. Alder's strength of character showed her just how much the Bard had grown since Kael's fall. Perhaps he and Kes would be able to save part of the Haunt. Perhaps they may even be able to keep the dungeon going for a while, even without a minionship pact or drones. Maybe with Lavy's help they would hold it together a little longer before the horned spiders got hungry.

But she'd never be able to restart her research, and the very thought was like dying herself.

The Heroes reached the Dungeon Lord. The Cleric cast her spell, a buff of some kind, and the Wizard aimed a finger at Ed. The dwarven Fighter raised his shield and closed in.

The *fireball* shook Lavy to the core.

RYAN SMILED as the Spider Queen fell at his feet, at about the same time the new kid, Omar, unleashed his spell, the dust of the *fireball* engulfing the surrounding plaza. On a normal day, that would've pissed him the hell off—he had wanted to deliver the killing blow to the Dungeon Lord—but Ryan was in a good mood.

Whatever joke Eddy had tried to play on him, it had back-fired. Ryan had put a stop to that shit real quick. Even better, he now knew that Eddy had somehow found a job at Pantheon. Well, first thing in the morning Ryan was going to pull some strings. Pantheon better be ready to for a full-blown police inves-tigation.

Now, where were the experience points for almost soloing a Boss on his own?

Something strange out of the corner of his eye caught his attention. Omar's health bar had vanished. Ryan did a double-take, making sure it wasn't a mistake.

"Wait, what?" Omar asked, confused, over the mic. "Mark, why would you do that?"

The dust hiding Ryan's top-down view of the battle cleared to reveal a badly wounded dwarf Fighter standing with the molten remains of his tower shield hefted right in front of the spot where

Omar's Wizard had been. The Wizard was nowhere to be seen—either teleported or vaporized by the explosion.

"Sorry, new guy," Mark said, sounding like he wasn't sorry at all. "Ed's got seniority."

A chill ran through Ryan's spine, too confused to be angry. At first. Then he realized what spell Lisa's Cleric had used. Confusion quickly turned into anger. "What the fuck have you done, you assholes? What the fuck are you thinking—?"

"Well, you'd know if you had ever played with friends—people who actually like you, that is—at some point in your life, Boss," Lisa said. There was some strange kind of tension in her voice that Ryan had never heard before. He realized she was holding back laughter. She'd rarely laughed at all when he was around, and never like this—just pure genuine fun. It sounded to him like nails on a chalkboard. "See, for gamers all over the world, when your team leader switches sides, you switch sides too—no questions asked and screw the consequences."

Ryan punched his desk, making his keyboard jump and sending his cup of coffee smashing into the floorboard—he didn't care. "You motherfucker—"

The bitch laughed again, and both she and Mark cut communications with Ryan and Omar. A second later, they had left the party.

And, behind Rylan Silverblade, still covered in his own blood, the Dungeon Lord stood up.

DYING WAS SURPRISINGLY PAINLESS, considering the hole in his chest. Hell, he didn't even feel the wound anymore. Maybe the *fireball* had vaporized him.

"Perhaps I'm a wraith now," Ed wondered aloud, as he stood up, shaking his head to clear it. He didn't feel undead.

In fact, he felt pretty damn alive.

His Wizard had disappeared. In its place stood Mark's Fighter, a bit worse for the wear, with his shield gone and his armor blackened by the explosion. Lisa's Cleric was next to the dwarf, throwing small healing spells his way.

Slowly, Ed realized what had happened. "You kept your daily *restoration* saved the entire time?" he asked the Cleric. "Damn, Lisa. You always were one hell of a healer." With one trembling finger, he touched the naked flesh of his chest where the scimitar had punctured through his armor. There was no wound, only a white scar. That was the power of a high-level healing spell.

The Heroes stood immobile in front of him. They were probably having one very interesting—if short—conversation with Ryan through their mics back on Earth. Even Rylan Silverblade didn't move from his spot atop Gloriosa's corpse. At the sight of the fallen spider, who had brought precious seconds for him with her life, Ed could feel his heart racing in his chest, pumping recently regenerated blood through his veins. Gloriosa had fought against the Haunt during Clovis' rebellion. Ed had no idea what had compelled her to save him, and now he'd never now.

His sword was laying only a few steps away, almost as if waiting for him. He picked it up, and then turned to the Cleric and the Fighter. "What do you say, you two?" he asked them, grinning with bloody teeth as his Evil Eye flared bright. "One last raid, for old times' sake?"

Rylan Silverblade darted toward Ed, Rogue-fast. The Dungeon Lord rose to meet him. Mark and Lisa's Heroes charged alongside him.

"*Eldritch edge!*"

THE *EXPLOSIVE ARROW* BOUNCED OFF KES' shield and clattered on the floor. Kes stepped over it, as fast as she could, desperately hoping she'd remembered the *explosive arrow* talent description correctly and that it wasn't about to blow her legs off. She had to reach Alvedhra before she reloaded—at this distance, Kes' shield wouldn't save her forever.

The Ranger-turned-Inquisitor rolled away from a volley of darts that the kaftar shot her way. Kaga and his men streamed into the chamber, screaming bloody murder.

"Multi-shot!" Alvedhra darted behind an overturned table and shot four arrows at the kaftar. Most jumped out of the way, but one hooted in agony when the arrow pierced his shoulder.

Kes kicked the table away and struck the Ranger's bow with her sword, splitting it in two. Alvedhra stepped away, dropped the remains of her weapon, and drew a short sword.

Kaga and Yumiya were on her then, feinting with their scimitars like predatory wolves, slowly guiding the Inquisitor against the far wall. Kes followed. A part of her wanted to tell the kaftar to stand down. This was a matter between her and Al, after all. The Monster Hunters had no business interrupting something Kes had to do on her own.

She opened her mouth to give the order.

Boot, did you lose your brains along with your goddamn wings? You're fighting a battle, not playing a role in Alder's stories. I swear on all the gods, said Ria's voice in her head, *if you don't keep your damn mouth shut, I'll come back from the dead as a wraith and fuck you up.*

The thing about Kes' relationship with the voice of her old sergeant was that, although she was perfectly aware that Ria was only a figment of her imagination, she also didn't doubt even for a second that Ria *would* make good on her threat, somehow.

Sorry, Sarge. Just a moment of insanity, she told the voice in her head. *I've been through a lot of stress over the last few hours.*

Well, Ria said, *let's not make a habit out of it.*

Kes kept the pressure on the Inquisitor, using her shield and precise stabs with her sword to keep Alvedhra from counterattacking the kaftar. The Inquisitor snarled, perfectly aware of Kes' intentions, but also unable to do anything about it.

"What did you think was going to happen, Al?" Kes screamed over the clash of metal striking metal. "We outnumber you seven to one!" Sure, one of the Monster Hunters was down with an arrow in his shoulder, but Alvedhra wasn't in any position to count.

"My *plan* was to kill you quickly and then leave," said Alvedhra through gritted teeth. "But then I had an even better idea!" She feinted a dash at Yumiya and threw a sideways slash at Kes' neck. The Marshal tilted her neck to let the hit slide off her helmet and then bounce safely off her gambeson.

Kes tightened her fist around her blade and punched Alvedhra in the nose using the pommel of her sword. The Inquisitor recoiled, blood spewing everywhere. Behind Kes and Kaga, the other Monster Hunters shot darts at Alvedhra, but they were deflected by her armor.

It didn't matter. The Inquisitor's back was against the window, with only empty air behind her. She was done.

"Yes? From my vantage point, your idea doesn't seem that bright," Kes told her. *Now I'm taunting a defeated opponent,* she thought. *Is this how a Dungeon Lord feels all the time?* She had to admit… it was more than a bit cathartic. She'd *needed* this fight.

"It's very simple," Alvedhra said. She jumped back and hopped on the edge of the window, using her hands to steady herself. Kaga and Yumiya advanced, unsure if they should push her off or drag her inside. "My plan was to force that bloodsucker you brought with you to regenerate into mist, then track that mist as it flies straight into your Dungeon Lord's main dungeon." The Ranger gave Kes a nasty grin through her bloodied face. "See you soon, Kes."

And she jumped out, just before the kaftar could catch her.

Kes and the Monster Hunters looked out the window in time to see the griffin fly away in Hoia's direction, a battered Inquisitor on its back. A few kaftar shot *crow familiar* runes their way, but in an instant the griffin was well out of range.

"So," Kaga said, turning to Kes. He looked dejected. "They got away. What now?"

Kes let out a long exhalation. She couldn't admit it aloud, but she was glad she hadn't had to kill or capture Alvedhra. "We better cross our fingers and hope Lavy's invention works. Otherwise there's going to be a long line of Inquisitors and Heroes knocking at the Haunt's doors real soon."

THE RUNES ENGRAVED in Ed's sword flashed blue under the *eldritch edge* as the steel struck against Rylan Silverblade's scimitar. The Rogue faltered under the weight of the attack, but he slashed at Ed with his second blade, fearless and precise.

Ed slapped the slash away with his gauntlet as he stepped back, forcing the scimitar to strike his plate-covered shoulder. His armor's enchantments, enhanced by his *pledge of muted armor,* flared to life and the blade bounced off without doing any damage. The Dungeon Lord used that opening to hack at the Rogue, landing a hit that struck Silverblade's enchanted helmet. Arcane sparks erupted from the spot where the metals met, and both combatants pulled away to regain their stances. Ed's lungs burned with exertion, and the rain threatened to slip into his eyes at any second. He blinked furiously and bent his head at a downward angle.

Rylan's scimitars glowed purple as the Rogue crossed them in front of him—the telltale sign of a *shadow strike.* Ed gritted his teeth and prepared to defend, well aware that a shadow strike would make the Rogue disappear from sight and attack from whichever direction Ed *wasn't* facing, landing an instant critical hit. That had been the same attack that almost killed him minutes ago. A chill ran down the Dungeon Lord's spine—he wasn't eager to go through that all over again.

Before the Rogue could dart forward, though, Mark's Fighter

bull-rushed him with a tackle that sent the Rogue sprawling several feet away.

The Fighter ended his rush only a step away from Rylan, but for some reason, the dwarf didn't push the advantage and just stood there while Rylan jumped to his feet with a flourish. The Rogue didn't attack the Fighter either, choosing instead to activate a *shadow field* and disappear under a screen of gunpowder-black smoke.

Why aren't they targeting each other? Ed wondered. Next to him, Lisa's Cleric used *stormwind* to blow the *shadow field* away, but the Rogue had entered stealth while under the shelter of darkness and was nowhere to be seen.

Ed activated his Evil Eye, trusting its *veil-piercing* enhancement to reveal Rylan. The Rogue had gone invisible and was sneaking his way toward Ed. The Dungeon Lord rushed at the automaton and threw a downward slash with all his weight behind it. As he expected, the Rogue back-flipped away—a wasteful move that would surely give Kes a heart attack out of sheer anger if Ed ever tried it—and Ed went after him, trying to land a hit to end his *invisibility*.

During his time playing Ivalis Online, Ed had learned that Rogues excelled at dealing with elite enemies by delivering devastating amounts of damage in one single combo. No matter how skilled the opponent, he was sure to take some damage if the Rogue knew its job—the trick was in landing the first hit. Ryan had gotten his favorite strategy by reading the forums: he began with *shadow strike* to attack his enemy from a vulnerable spot, then transitioned into an *eviscerate*—which was easier to block, but ignored armor—and then finished his foe off with the rest of his powers.

Back there, when the Rogue jumped Ed atop Gloriosa, the Hero had only used a couple of skills because he'd been busy fighting the Haga'Anashi and the horned spiders, so most of his rotation was in cooldown. But Ryan was doing his best to set up another combo even as he fought the three of them—only using skills with short cooldowns while the others recovered.

To beat that strategy, Ed had to do two things. The first was to force the Rogue to use skills before it was the right time, and the second was to just fucking kill him as fast as possible.

The Dungeon Lord and the Rogue exchanged a flurry of strikes and counter-strikes, parries and dodges, arcane flashes sparking all around them as their armors ate the brunt of the damage. Blood poured from Ed's arms from long scratches wherever his enchantments had failed to protect him, but he barely noticed. It was as if his entire being only existed to deliver the next blow, to parry the next attack, to disrupt the next skill.

Rylan Silverblade stabbed forward with his scimitars. Ed managed to parry one, but the other struck his shoulder, next to his neck, and bit into his flesh in a spot unprotected by his armor. Burning pain spread across his body as rivulets of blood tinted red the bas-reliefs of his breastplate, and his mind snapped into a sharp focus. He punched Rylan's blank face with his black hand and wrenched a rank of Endurance out of the Hero in an almost-visible rip and tear of dark aura. It left a familiar taste in Ed's mouth, as if somehow he recognized it from somewhere.

There's something living inside that thing, Ed noticed as he pushed forward and slashed at the automaton's face, leaving a line of fractures across the Hero's skin.

Lisa used *holy carapace* to create a protective, sand-like layer of second armor around Ed, who could feel his *pledge* interacting with it and improving it even further—making him into a damn living tank. It would come in handy against Rylan's normal attacks, but he needed to be careful against his skills, which specialized in avoiding armor.

The Rogue darted to the side and tried to *eviscerate* Ed's guts, but Mark came out of nowhere and activated his *taunt,* forcing everyone in a small area around him to face him instead. That included both Ed and Rylan. At first, Ed tried to resist the compulsion, but he realized it was faster if he simply worked together with his friend. He faced the dwarf and rushed him while Ryan tried to dart away from the dwarf—which he couldn't attack. Ed jumped at the Fighter, planted both feet on the dwarf's chest, and pushed hard to propel himself like a Dungeon Lord bullet against the Rogue as he thrust his sword forward with all his strength. He aimed at Rylan's chest, hoping to pierce it enough for his sword's *anti-magic* enchantment to trigger.

At the last second, Rylan *shadow stepped*, only to reappear right next to Ed. Both scimitars struck at the Dungeon Lord mid-air, fracturing his golden carapace and sending him crashing against the ground. Ed rolled away and jumped to his feet, shaking his head and trying to clear his mind.

He and the Rogue circled each other, with Lisa's Cleric and Mark's Fighter to each side.

They can't directly attack each other, Ed realized, then. Ivalis Online didn't allow a Hero to target one another, they had been using skills that didn't *need* a target. *Bull-rush* was a movement skill, and *stormwind* was an area-of-effect spell.

Lisa and Mark weren't in a fight for their lives like he was they were playing a game under a specific set of conditions never intended by the developers—they needed to keep a Boss alive long enough for him to deliver a killing blow against a Hero, while at the same time not being allowed to attack said Hero themselves. The Militant Church would've forced them to log-out long ago, but thankfully, the laptop they would've used was now in the Haunt's possession, and the man trained for the job by the Summoned Hero was now dead.

Even then, if the fight dragged out, the risk that someone back in Heiliges or Galtia would figure out how to eject his friends from the game increased. Ed was aware the laptop wasn't the only computing equipment the Militant Church had, and the Summoned Hero had probably trained more than one person in its use.

We need to end this, Ed thought. But if he destroyed Rylan too soon, the Hero would just teleport away. If Ed waited for his friends to activate the Jamming Tower, Rylan would self-destruct. The only way to capture the Hero was for Ed to run him through with his anti-magic sword after as the Jamming Tower powered on. He could feel that his minions had finished capturing the Charcoal Tower in the distance. Alder, Lavy, and Kes had to be there, readying the Jamming dish. Would Ed and them be able to coordinate at exactly the right time?

Just like Mark and Lisa, he too was playing a game with a very specific handicap. Sure, he could destroy Rylan and try to capture some other Hero another time. But he *needed* to defeat the Rogue, the very core of his being demanded it. This fight was more than a battle to the death.

Ed had something to prove—to himself and to the rest of the world.

The card in his pocket showed a future that would never come to pass. The alternatives of the Shadow Tarot—the Wraith and the Tyrant—would *not* do. The only way forward was to challenge the odds and create a new path, like unlocking a secret ending in a videogame's storyline. The Dungeon Lord alone wasn't strong enough to achieve that ending—he'd gone down to Silverblade's attack just like so many others before him.

But Ed was alive, and not because of a hidden Dungeon Lord's power he'd unlocked all of a sudden, or a burst of determination, or the Dark's intervention. He was alive only because back on Earth, before the Mantle, and the dungeons, and the otherworldly powers, he'd spent many nights having a good time playing videogames with his friends. Friends who liked him enough that, when forced to choose between siding with him or their asshole boss, they'd gone with Ed—even with their jobs on the line.

It was humbling, and it went against everything Ed thought he'd learned so far. For a long time now, Ed had thought that as he increased in experience points and furthered his path as a

Dungeon Lord, he was becoming stronger than the helpless young man he'd been back on Earth.

Tonight was the first time he realized some part of him may have actually gotten *weaker*. Hadn't killing been coming easier to him, lately? Would Lisa and Mark have liked the man he was now, if they had they met him today for the first time?

Ed had needed to don the name of Lord Wraith just to survive in a cruel, unknown world. But surviving wasn't enough. All the other Dungeon Lords had survived, for a while, and then they'd lost, and Lord Wraith wasn't any different. Ed was playing to *win*. And now he wondered if the ace in his sleeve had been there, all along, waiting for him to claim it… Like a sort of heritage.

Perhaps, by aligning his two different personas—Dungeon Lord and nerdy IT guy—he'd find the strength to forge the path to his secret ending.

Both hands, black bone and human skin, closed tightly around the handle of his sword. He had a plan, but even though he had had a bit of practice before, it would be extremely risky. He could feel his body shivering at the memory of the scimitar piercing his chest, the animal part of his brain screaming against the possibility of experimenting that kind of pain again, begging for him to turn tail and run. Ed forced that sensation down, and steeled his will like a warrior honing his blade before battle, until there existed nothing else but that moment, the surrounding Heroes, with Rylan Silverblade squaring up against him. The trembling stopped. Since he'd taken running out as an option, his entire being prepared to fight.

"Hey, Ryan! Are you listening over there? Your combo is off cooldown already, so quit wasting my time," he taunted the Rogue, unaware if Ryan was reading his words through his computer monitor back on Earth. There was a small chance he was—Ryan loved to interrupt the final Bosses' speeches, but something told Ed that Ryan would listen to *him*, if only because of their mutual hatred. "You know, the problem with you is that you've always been a lazy player," Ed said as he lowered his guard on purpose, goading the Hero further. "That combo of yours? You stole it from other players as soon as you stumbled across the forums and have been using it ever since. The problem is… you're a one-trick pony. Back when we played together, if you used your combo and failed, Mark, Lisa, and I were stuck getting your ass out of trouble. No one's coming to save you this time. Have you thought about what's going to happen if you cycle through all your cooldowns and I'm still standing?" The Dungeon Lord grinned. "Well, that's when I get to teach you how to play this damn game at last!"

The Rogue's scimitars flashed purple, and he rushed at Ed, fast and silent. The Cleric and the Fighter charged after him, trying to interrupt Rylan's path, but Ed went after him, holding his sword in front of him as if offering the tip of the blade for Rylan to impale himself into.

Instead, the Rogue activated *shadow strike* and disappeared in a flash of purple light—in less than a second, he'd reappear exactly in the Dungeon Lord's blind spot.

So Ed activated his *dungeon vision,* using the Charcoal Tower that oversaw the plaza, and which was part of Undercity's new dungeon, as the focal point. In an instant, his field of view shot upward over the battlefield at dizzying speeds—but Ed was used to the sensation and expected it. He kept his footing as the blood and the bodies came into focus. His few remaining creatures and minions fought against last dredges of Heroic opposition in the plaza. He saw the griffin flying away, and the dozens—if not hundreds—of fresh Heroes eager for action coming from Mulle-cias Heights.

And then he focused the *vision,* so it showed the surrounding area, just in time for Rylan Silverblade to appear exactly behind Ed's back, scimitars already tearing through the air in a double horizontal slash meant to cut Ed's neck in a single strike.

Except that the Dungeon Lord saw it all, and using his

improved reflexes he arced his back and thrust his sword behind his head as if preparing for a heavy downward slash. Instead, he saw from his vantage point, high above, how the tip of his flaming blade struck against Rylan Silverblade's face right between the eyes. He felt a resistance like clay breaking and heard it shatter like glass as his sword pushed through.

The scimitar attack went wide and hacked at Ed's carapace, vaporizing it without damaging the Dungeon Lord. Still under the effects of *improved reflexes*, Ed turned to face the recoiling Rogue, drew his sword out, and punched hard at the crater that marred its charred and broken head—stealing another rank of Endurance as he struck.

The Hero recoiled, its movements less human and more mechanical by the second. He was about to counterattack when Mark *bull-rushed* him again and the both of them struck a dilapidated wall, collapsing it and showering the automatons in a rain of debris.

Ed adjusted his *dungeon vision*. Rylan stood, his body covered in superficial fractures. The Fighter, who had suffered an enormous amount of damage from that point-blank *enhanced fireball*, stayed down, trying to heal.

"That was lesson number one at how not to suck at the game," Ed told the Rogue. Now he was sure Ryan was listening. "After lesson two, you aren't getting back up."

LAVY HAD THOUGHT that her life in the Haunt had prepared her to be ready for anything, but the battle unfolding in front of her was on an entirely different level. The air was so thick with static that she could barely breathe, and the black clouds above had broken into a checkered pattern that revealed parts of the night sky. She was aware, theoretically, of what that specific phenomenon meant —only she had never, ever expected to see it happen with her own eyes.

But what Witch wakes up one morning knowing she's about to live through history in the making?

"Are we under some kind of Legendary-ranked illusion?" Alder wondered aloud next to her. The Bard and even Costel and her guards were next to Lavy, watching how a Dungeon Lord and two Heroes—who were under no mind-control or anything of the sort—teamed up against a third.

"If we are, don't dispel it," Lavy whispered.

For all her life, the world had operated under certain rules: if you killed a dangerous creature you got experience points. You could bend Objectivity's rules at your own risk, but never break them outright. A Hero is the natural enemy of a Dungeon Lord. Should they meet, one of them would be destroyed.

What Ed had done tonight had never happened—she didn't need to check with Alder to know that. Not only had the Cleric practically brought Ed back from the gates of death, he had gotten up as if he had expected it. As if the Cleric and the Fighter had set this up with him beforehand. She didn't know if that was true—hadn't Ed mentioned that those three were his old team? It was hard to tell. All Heroes looked alike—but she sure as hell knew what it would *seem like* to the people watching along with her.

The Cleric had stacked so many high-leveled spells on the Dungeon Lord that, for their duration, he was inhuman. The fight against the Rogue became a blur of movement and deadly clashes that would've killed a non-enhanced man several times over. Lavy could barely follow the seemingly uninterrupted flow of attacks and parries and counterattacks, but she could almost *feel* each strike rattling her body.

"This is impossible," Young Ivan said, his voice shaking. He gave the sky a frightened look. "What in the gods' name is going on? Is the world ending? Are Kharon and the old demons coming back to devour us?"

"Get a grip, kid," Costel said without taking her gaze from the fight. "And move back, you're obstructing my view."

"That's what the sky looks like when an area is saturated with Heroic-ranked—and above—scrying spells," Lavy said quietly. "In other words, *everyone* who can afford to hire a Diviner is watching this fight go down. King Varon, the Militant Church, most Dungeon Lords and Regents. Everyone who is someone, and a fair share of nobodies too. Probably even some gods—those who care about human affairs, at least." She placed a hand on Alder's shoulder.

"That checkered pattern is proof that we're witnessing history," the Bard said. "Every appearance goes straight into Bardic annals. It was visible during the final stand of Archlord Everbleed, and during Sephar's punishment, and the last battle between Numerios and Lord Khalfair. And now *we're* here to see it! Lavy, all Bards would *kill* for a chance like this—"

"Well, I don't get what has everyone so rattled," said Costel, frowning. "Dungeon Lords kill Heroes all the time—without help, even."

"But Ed's convinced two of them to switch sides!" Lavy exclaimed. "Don't you see what it means? The Heroes are no longer the unrelenting killing machines they were! Now the Inquisition won't know if they can trust the others!"

"Well," Costel said. "For killing machines, they are certainly struggling to bring down a lone Hero."

Lavy frowned and was about to tell the woman something biting when she realized Costel was actually right. In fact, Lavy saw how Ed clearly stepped back from a position from where he could have beheaded the Rogue.

What's going on? "Oh!" She turned to Alder and shook him. "He's trying to capture him!"

Alder turned and blinked. "What are you talking about?"

"He's waiting for us, you oaf! Quick, help me drag my stupid dish upstairs before the Cleric's buffs run out!" She pushed the Bard backward into the tower despite his protest—he was clearly too taken aback by the "history in the making" opportunity to think clearly—and then turned to the guards, who had remained in place. "Wetlands, I was talking to you people as well! MOVE ALREADY!"

We need a drone, she thought desperately as she rushed for the dish waiting in the middle of the staircase. *Without drones we can't connect the damn thing to a ley line...* But Ed's drones had vanished, hadn't they? If Lavy failed to activate the Jamming Tower, more Heroes would pour into the plaza and she doubted Ed would manage to convince half of them to join his side *this* time.

"Are there any drones left?!" Alder exclaimed as they climbed the last couple steps toward the tarp covering the dish.

"Fuck it, I'll do their stupid dance myself," Lavy said as she set her hands on the tarp. She let out a sharp yelp when she saw one single drone standing behind the dish, trying its best to fulfill the last order given to it by dragging the dish all by its lonesome.

The drone took one look at the Witch's expression and tried to run from her, but she caught him in a tight hug and held it against her chest as forcefully as she dared without risking unsummoning it.

"No one gets near this drone, you hear me?" she yelled at the guards behind.

Alder and the guards carried the dish up the stairs as fast as they could, grunting as they went, the weight of the glass threatening to unbalance them with every step they took.

Halfway up, they met with Kaga and his Monster Hunters, who had come down looking for them. "I can't believe you two are still alive! You ran out of spells a while ago," Kaga told them cheerfully as his men helped the overexerted humans carry the dish up the last floor. "If we survive the night, I'll have to ask my father to make you both into honorary Haga'Anashi!"

Kes was waiting for them in the middle of a chamber strewn with Akathunian corpses. Yumiya was tending to a wounded Monster Hunter at one side, and the Marshal had a distant look on her face that she quickly shook off when she saw Lavy's expression.

"What?" Kes asked her.

"Look out the window," Lavy told her. Then she turned to Costel. "Move those corpses out of the way! Hurry!"

In seconds, they had rested the dish on the floorboards. Lavy set the drone in front of it. "Dance, damn you!" she urged, inches away from the imp's face.

The drone gulped and nervously faced the dish. With tentative steps, like someone trying to perform for the first time without any rehearsal, it began to dance.

"Faster!" Lavy urged it. She was fully aware that everyone else was looking at her like she'd gone insane. She didn't care. "FASTER!"

The drone danced faster, its pink-and-purple tunic shaking madly with its frantic movements. Along the room, random debris and trashed furniture evaporated into smoky black tendrils that snaked their way through the air in synchrony with the drone's movements. Most of the smoke disappeared down the floor, but a small tendril surrounded the tarp and consumed it to reveal the carved glass below.

The dish stood, the smoke setting it in the correct position. A brass stand grew around the glass like vines, holding it in place. The brass kept growing until it was connected to both the floor and the ceiling. The remaining smoke flew into the glass, setting the engraved runes of its surface alight with raw energy.

The drone's dance reached a crescendo, and then the little creature stopped, looking tired. The smoke around the room vanished.

"Is that it?" Alder asked. "Is it done?"

The drone gave Lavy one worried glance and raised its shoulders while nodding over and over.

"But nothing is happening," Kaga pointed out.

Lavy shook her head, a sense of dread growing in her chest.

Her worse fear was coming true in front of her eyes. She had failed. "Something is wrong," she said. "The Jamming Device didn't activate. It should have done so by now..." She covered her mouth with her hands and took several frantic breaths. "Oh, gods. Someone needs to tell Ed!"

As ED and Lisa's Cleric squared against Rylan Silverblade for another round, the Dungeon Lord shifted his gaze to the inside of the tower, moving from one view to the other in constant flashes. He needed to coordinate his attack perfectly with the Jamming Tower's activation. At the moment, he spotted Lavy and Alder and a few others carrying the dish upstairs.

Rylan Silverblade dashed at him and attempted an *eviscerate*, but Ed stepped back just as Lisa got in the way of the Rogue. The blades stopped just an inch away from the elven Cleric's belly. At the same time, Ed circled around her and hacked at Rylan's helmet in a shower of arcane sparks.

Both Rogue and Dungeon Lord rained blows on each other, trying to do as much damage through their enchanted defenses and buffs as possible. Ed's body screamed with exertion as he overused *improved reflexes* just to keep up with the Rogue's speed. Every once in a while, he managed to steal another rank of Endurance from the Hero, but Ed burned through the extra energy just as fast, which only meant that both of them were slowing down at about the same time.

Except that Ed could feel Lisa's buffs on him starting to run out. With every strike and every parry, he grew weaker. The weight of his sword was growing to the point it felt like he was swinging a thick piece of wood, his shoulders, back, and arms screaming with the effort of every slash. Even his fingers were cramping up.

"*Eldritch edge*," he said, restarting the spell whose duration had just ended.

It was time to end the fight. Ed switched to a view of the tower —he saw his drone dancing atop, with Lavy shouting something at it, probably encouraging and cheering it on. The sky above had turned to an impossible checkered pattern, but Ed's mind shoved that detail away, all his focus pouring into the battle.

That's my cue, Ed thought, gritting his teeth. He locked blades with Rylan Silverblade, kneed the Rogue in the belly, and struck his broken face with his elbow. Rylan stepped back, otherwise undamaged, and renewed the attack, forcing Ed backward, pushing his sword away with sudden ease—Ed roared as a red line appeared on his leg right in the open space between his armor's plates. Rylan circled him like a bird of prey, but Lisa appeared to his side, canceling his attack and forcing him to reposition.

Ed shifted his weight to his good leg and, and rested his back against the Cleric's, defending against a flurry of blows so fast and savage that each successful parry threatened to tear his shoulder out of his socket. His sword was a nicked, dulled mess, and any second now Rylan would slap it out of his cramping hands.

"Now or never, Lisa!" he yelled as the Rogue's scimitars glowed purple. Ed and the Cleric circled each other and switched positions, with Ed facing the open plaza and Lisa facing the incoming Rogue. She rushed at the Rogue, preparing a spell as she did so. Right at that moment, Rylan Silverblade activated *shadow strike* again. The Rogue disappeared and then flashed back into existence in the space between Ed and Lisa, several inches off the ground, scimitars at the ready for a downward slash that Ed wouldn't be able to block this time—

Instead, the Dungeon Lord had already turned—he knew exactly where the Rogue would appear, after all—and had planted both feet firmly on the ground, ignoring the screams of agony of his wounded leg. He held his sword with both hands close to his body, tip aimed right at the Rogue's gut, more of a spear than a sword.

For an instant, it was as if the world had frozen in that

moment, with the Rogue soaring toward Ed, scimitars crackling with power, and the Dungeon Lord staring him down, mouth frozen in a roar to urge his body into one last surge of strength.

Then Lisa turned back and released her spell. The *stormwind* caught Rylan Silverblade from the back while he was still in the air and threw him forward with terrible violence like a leaf in a hurricane. Ed fought against the powerful wind to remain in position, back bent forward, sword at the ready, trusting in his own weight and the weight of his armor to keep him in place. Through his *improved reflexes,* he saw the Rogue fly toward him at impossible speed right as the Dungeon Lord's vision became an exhausted shade of red. Ed thrust his sword with all his strength, and for an instant felt a terrible resistance as Rylan Silverblade's enchanted leather armor tried to prevent the attack—and then a magical aftershock surrounded the Rogue and the Dungeon Lord when the armor gave and the flaming sword bit deep into the Hero's gut, piercing all the way to the back and then out. Ed buried the sword to the hilt, and then the Rogue was upon him, embracing him as if they were lovers. They clashed and Lisa's wind dragged them both through a confusing mess of steel, and Ed could sense how the Rogue's inner workings tried to teleport him away just as the *anti-magic* runes in his sword flared to life with cold, blue light—one more second and the self-destruct mechanism would trigger with Ed right next to it, and there was no healing magic that could bring him back from being blown to pieces...

"WE NEED TO LEAVE," Kes urged, grabbing at Lavy from behind and trying to drag her away from the dish.

Tears were streaming from the Witch's face. "No! You don't understand," she exclaimed. "I built this, everyone's counting on me!"

"It's not your fault!" Kes told her. Since when was Lavy so stalwart? Desperation seemed to have multiplied the woman's strength, because Kes was having trouble pulling her away. "You did your best, but now we need to evacuate the city before the rest of the Heroes arrive!" One more second and she'd just have to knock the Witch out.

"Damn it! I built it right, I know I did!"

"Lavy—"

The Witch elbowed Kes in the gut. Kes blinked, more surprised than hurt, and then Lavy wriggled free. She rushed the dish, her face contorted in a paroxysm of pure unbridled rage and agonizing despair. She began to kick at the glass so hard that the brass stand shook with each strike. "I. Built. You. RIGHT!"

Kes grimaced. Her hands were about to close on the Witch's shoulders when, back in the metaphysical realm where the drones had connected the energy of the ley line to the essence of the Jamming Device, something clicked loose and fell into place.

In a fraction of a second so small that it would've made the silence between a hummingbird's heartbeats seem like hours, the Jamming dish went from being inert glass to the glowing white eye of an angry god. The world turned to a white flash, and Kes wanted to scream in surprise, but before her brain could even signal for her mouth to open, a magical burst exploded in a growing sphere out of the glowing eye, traveled through Kes and past her with such speed that she felt it in her bone marrow, and then she was lifted off of her feet and thrown all the way across the room against the solid wall—only by some miracle missing the window—forcing all air out of her lungs and making her see stars.

It was only at that point that she managed to finish her surprised scream, but it came out more like a muffled groan. Then Lavy's slender form struck against her and then the Marshal was out cold.

. . .

JUST AS KES' feet were leaving the ground at the start of her inexorable path toward the wall, the burst had already surrounded the entirety of Undercity in a translucent sphere that saturated the air with the smell of ozone and blocked all incoming magical signals of a certain frequency. All over the world, Diviners shook their scrying devices as the sudden influx of static dulled their view.

Every glass window in the city exploded into glinting dust beneath the twin moons. Every summoned creature was vanished back to its realm, and all as one, every Hero in Undercity collapsed immobile, spasming as their rudimentary brains demanded input that wasn't arriving. They all either teleported out or self-destructed—all but one.

Empress Laurel glanced at the sky, feeling her insides churn with the influx of magic saturating the city. Underneath her, Karmich and Pris stopped as they entered the escape tunnel with the cart full of survivors waiting for them. The Thieves exchanged glances filled with wonder.

Klek and Tulip led a charge against the Wizard that had the Spider Riders and Oscor's smugglers in their sights, but Tulip stopped short as the Wizard threw its arms up and disappeared in a flash. Klek lowered his spear, his body trembling from terror and adrenaline, and glanced backward at the distant plaza with the black tower pointing up like a finger challenging the gods.

Bartender Max opened the cellar's trapdoor to the burnt, still-smoking ruin of the Galleon's Folly, and contemplated the checkered pattern of the sky above. A small, lingering flame licked the hairy man's leg, but it did no damage, and he seemed not to notice. The bartender smiled to himself and went back under his cellar.

After she'd circled the zone of the forest where she'd last seen the purple mist of the vampire, Alvedhra almost fell out of her griffin when she saw the city light up like a star for an instant. And she suddenly realized with growing dread that she'd made a terrible mistake by thinking that the Heroes and her fellow Inquisitors had the situation handled back there. Moments later, she'd sent Galtia a *message* with the Haunt's general location, and flown back to Undercity—but by then it was too late. Undercity had rallied—bloodied but very much alive and angry, against the Inquisition. Alvedhra returned to a routing unit of the Militant Church's survivors escaping from a suddenly hostile city and no Heroic support. She tried to reach the Charcoal Tower with her griffin again, on her own, but it was so heavily defended by then that the sky light up around her with runes and arrows, forcing her to retreat.

We gave him a city, she thought bleakly, hours later, as she stepped along with her defeated Inquisitors through Mullecias' magical circle. It was the first time in her lifetime that the Inquisition was forced to abandon a territory. *Oh, gods above, what have we done?*

All the way across the world, King Varon rose from his chair, which threw the court's scrying ball off the table and shattering it, much to his Diviner's chagrin. "Gather our armies," the King told the Knight General next to him.

And in Lotia and the Netherworld, both Demon Regents and Dungeon Lords alike rose with blazing eyes as their scrying devices showed Lord Edward Wright struggle to his feet, covered in wounds, armor so dented it was barely recognizable, cape torn to shreds and more brown than green, the last dredges of the Cleric's buffs fleeing from his body in trails of smoke. His expression turned inscrutable as he regarded the broken shape of the Rogue at his feet, the last remaining Hero in the city, and the first one in history to be in possession of the Dark-aligned. For a single instant, then, as his Evil Eye flared, Lord Wright seemed to gaze straight at the scrying device, but by then few Dungeon Lords were still paying attention. Most were already up and gathering their seconds-in-command with greedy grins flashing across their faces.

"Get me that Tower blueprint and that Hero," they told their minions. "No matter the cost."

- You have gained **235** experience points.
- Your attributes have increased. Brawn +1, Endurance +1, Spirit +1.
- Your skills have increased: Melee +2, Dungeon Engineering +2, Combat Casting +2, Leadership +5. Your aura's energy expenditure has been reduced.
- There are new talent advancement options for you.
- There are new Dungeon Upgrades available for research.
- The Haunt's level threat has grown enough for your enemies to know its approximate location.

31

CHAPTER THIRTY-ONE

ANCIENT TRADITIONS

*C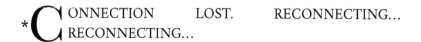ONNECTION LOST. RECONNECTING... RECONNECTING...

IVALIS ONLINE CRASHED. Lisa slowly took her hands away from the keyboard. That had been *intense*. Probably the hardest fight she'd ever faced. How many IO players could boast that they'd taken out another player by using a Boss to do the dirty work for them? *And as a healer!* Her forum account was already lighting up with notifications from hundreds of threads mentioning her username as players everywhere lost their minds because of her feat.

A flame-war started, with people split into sides calling Mark and Lisa either traitorous bitches or master team-killers worthy of admiration. There was even talk of getting her account banned. Lisa didn't care. After tonight, she suspected she'd milked Ivalis Online out of everything it had to offer her.

And that was fine. Games were meant to be finished. There was a pang of nostalgia in her chest, as if she was closing a chapter in her life. And, in a way, she was. At the very least, she wouldn't bother going back to Lasershark in the morning, and neither would Mark.

She had no savings and rent would soon be due, but she'd figure something out. Hell, she knew all there was to know about computer repair. Perhaps Mark and her could come up with something. Lasershark could use some competition.

They'd need a logo. Something with neon, of course. It was just her aesthetic.

Lisa grinned, feeling at peace and comfortably tired. The shadows in the corners of her home seemed to be just that, shadows. There was nothing threatening about them.

Before closing the web browser, she posted on the forums enough to fan the flame-war and make it last a couple more days. And as a final goodbye, she politely requested that the forum moderators go choke on a dick, then deleted her own account before they could.

Diana came home soon after, announced by her unsteady footsteps. Lisa's sister fumbled outside for her keys while rambling happily, then fought with the lock for a minute until she managed to get the door open and step inside, the reek of vodka inundating the apartment. Diana had her hair strewn with broken branches and dry leaves and was holding a stop sign in one arm and some random guy in the other. The random guy looked around the apartment in a haze and smiled like an idiot.

"Hey, Sis," Diana called. "We'll be right over there, alright? Alright." The two of them stumbled their way toward the couch, but then Diana stopped and turned to face Lisa, raising her eyebrows with curiosity.

"What?" Lisa asked her, grinning.

"Nothing," Diana said. "It's just... I haven't seen you smile like that in a while. What happened? Did your boss stick his head in a woodchipper?"

Lisa laughed and shrugged. "Just some dumb thing, really. I'll tell you in the morning, okay?"

Diana pointed the stop sign at her and smiled. "Sure. Just do it quietly, please. I suspect this hangover is going to be one to remember."

As she packed her stuff to give her sister some privacy, Lisa found the black calling card at the bottom of the desk drawer. She gave it a curious once-over. For a second, she wondered...

(Behind her, the darkness loomed, eager, waiting for a decision)

Lisa tossed the card in the trash. Whatever it was offering, she wasn't looking for. All she wanted was a quiet, happy life with her computers, her family, and her friends.

Wherever Ed was, she hoped he could find, one day, his own version of happiness.

Lisa's dreams went back to normal from then on.

A TALL GENTLEMAN dressed in a tailored black suit strolled into the Lasershark store. The place was chaotic, with a dozen customers standing angrily in front of the counter where a young blond manager frantically attempted to do the work of several employees at once.

Kharon smiled. It seemed that Mark and Lisa hadn't been the only ones to quit on Ryan. From what the Boatman knew of human affairs, this was nothing unusual—mortals were often emboldened by the meaningful actions of their peers, and once the first one was brave enough to act, others found it easy to follow in the individual's footsteps.

The Boatman whistled a happy tune while he walked around the store. In the end, Lisa had rejected the call of the Dark. That happened, sometimes. Contrary to popular belief, the Dark god Murmur did not force anyone to join his ranks.

He didn't need to.

In all realities, Ivalis and Earth and beyond, there would be mortals that—for one reason or another—weren't satisfied with their lot in life. Those who desired power did so for many reasons: ambition, revenge, despair, boredom, genuine good intentions. It was all the same to Kharon when he was summoned.

The Dark preyed on the men and women who desired more, who gazed at the starry sky above in challenge, or fell to their knees and despaired, and those who stared at the shadows of a dark corner in an empty house and wondered... And every time, Kharon would be there, with a lip-less smile full of teeth, and his hand extended with a silent offer.

Most would deny him. But enough would take the hand that was offered. That was the way it always been, and would always be.

Back behind the counter, Ryan's lips curled in a frown of disgust. He'd spent a sour night, alone in his big, cold house, plagued with anger and hatred and loneliness. The customers could sense his contempt and answered it tenfold, creating a feedback loop of hatred that Kharon could taste—it was delicious.

To him, the fact that Murmur's crazed plays always turned out to be, from the perspective of both the Dark one's enemies and allies, indistinguishable from mastermind plans that spanned generations or eons had taught Kharon much about how the world really worked. How *insane* everything was, and the importance of carving himself a little piece of the cake and enjoying the fireworks while reality itself collapsed around him. Because entropy always won in the end, but the end was still rather far away.

In other words, being a bit resentful against a mortal was fine, so long as it was fun. And Edward Wright could use being taken down a peg.

As Murmur's envoy, Kharon had some leeway in how he accomplished his tasks. The Dark one wanted a new Dungeon Lord to replace Jiraz. He also wanted more summoned Dungeon Lords from Earth, since the first one had been such a success. He'd decided that having a close friend submit to the same pact

Ed had would create an interesting situation while, at the same time, advancing the cause of the Dark by reinforcing its hold in Starevos. But Lisa had refused.

Well, Kharon could work with that. What possible choice could he make that would keep Murmur entertained, while at the same time pissing off Kharon's best friend—good old, moody Edward Wright?

The Boatman chuckled darkly to himself as he strolled toward the counter. He had just the right person in mind.

THE NIGHT in Hoia Forest was full of stars, with the air brimming with the noises of activity coming from the Haunt and its surroundings.

Ed sat alone on a tree stump, away from everyone else. He was dressed in a simple linen tunic to avoid attracting undue attention. Oftentimes, he found it refreshing to step out of the role of the Dungeon Lord and walk around the place he'd built along with his friends, simply watching the way people went about their lives.

Lately, there was much to be seen. Ed was finding it harder and harder to keep up with everyone's names, and sometimes people just... showed up. Like that peculiar halfling monk that was training a score of Haga'Anashi in his seemingly chaotic style of martial arts under the gaze of the moons. Ed had no idea where the hell the halfling had come from, but the kaftar seemed happy to have him around, and at this point it'd be awkward if Ed went up and asked him who the hell he was, so the Dungeon Lord just let them be. A bit of distraction from their mourning of the late Kagelshire would do them well.

Above Ed, Hoia's Jamming Tower rose like a black spire, the crown jewel of the surrounding circle of Scrambling Towers that hid the Haunt from prying eyes.

Next to the market outside the dungeon's entrance and closest to Ed's tree stump was the railway nexus, a zone where the tunnels all across the countryside, Hoia, and Undercity connected together. In a few years, the nexus would be the heart of a new city, and the dungeon would be its palace.

If they lived that long, of course.

People came and went out of the nexus at all hours. There where mercenaries from the Netherworld, Thieves, and smugglers, as well as emissaries from other Dungeon Lords trying to offer lavish gifts—or gruesome threats—in exchange for the Jamming Towers' blueprints or a look at the captured Hero hidden at the bottom of the Haunt.

Ed had minor demons manning the dungeons sprouting out in the countryside to keep the Inquisitors as far away from the Haunt as possible. Along with the demons were Wizards and Enchantresses, naga and kaftar, roving bands of werewolves, elves and gnomes and dwarves, and the list went on. Monster Hunters entered the nexus, dragging sturdy carriages loaded with iron cages that transported monsters—oozes, hell chickens, man-eating plants, zombies and skeletons.

Alongside them, the citizens of the Haunt—the Haunted, as they had taken to calling themselves of late—mingled and bartered, argued and joked and exchanged gossip. Andreena and her goat were talking with a gnome Witch Doctor about exotic herbal remedies, Heorghe and Ivona chatted with a traveling dwarven blacksmith about the carts and other machinery from the mountains, Zachary and a stern-looking elf argued—of course —about religion.

Most of those travelers had just... appeared one day, and their numbers kept growing even as some left and others stayed. Ed hadn't turned them away, he had simply had Kes come up with new security protocols in case someone was a spy. Now that the Haunt's location wasn't exactly a secret, he guessed word had traveled far, and there were always people in the world that were at home in a place like the Haunt more than in normal society. There were the petty criminals and the eccentric, yes, but also the dreamer and the rebel. Along with mercenaries came traveling troupes of fearless actors that performed in both Elaitra and the Netherworld, itinerant Bards and their shaggier cousins, the Skalds from the frozen north.

The secret was in the railway. There was always some sort of interaction between a dungeon and its neighbors, and Ed had made sure the interaction was mostly positive, or at least as not-negative as such a thing could be.

So far only three Inquisitors had managed to sneak inside the Haunt by pretending to be friendly travelers, but they had been easily discovered through Kes' safety measures.

Ed smiled as his Haunt bubbled with life around him. At that moment, despite the many dangers the future held for him and his friends, he was content.

Someone sat next to him on the tree stump.

"Do you mind having some company, Lord Ed?" Klek asked quietly, following Ed's gaze with the same look of wonder in the man's eyes. "You seemed a bit lonely from afar. But now I realize I got the wrong impression."

"Your company is always welcome, Klek," Ed told his friend. "To tell you the truth, I came here to take my mind off of tomorrow's meeting. I've been practicing with Alder and Lavy for a while—even Jarlen's going to play a part."

"What's so hard about a meeting?" Klek asked, his ears perking up with curiosity. "Compared to fighting the Heroes, talk must be easy for you."

Ed smiled and shrugged. "Well, I'm going to face most of Undercity's… influential men, and I'm going to try to convince them that I'll do whatever is necessary for everyone's survival… but for entirely the wrong reasons."

Klek cocked his head. "Why?"

"Because... see, they expect to meet a Dungeon Lord tonight. They have certain expectations." Ed thought of Gallio and Alvedhra, and all the Inquisitors Ed himself had killed during the battle for Undercity. "I've learned that when you challenge the way people view the world, they tend to react strongly." He paused and looked at the black Jamming Tower behind them. "And if I am to unite these people so we may stand together... then I need to give them what they need."

"So, you'll become the Dungeon Lord they expect you to be?"

"Oh, absolutely not," Ed said. "Not at all. More like, I hope to put on a very convincing act. Here's the thing, Klek. Dungeon Lords are much weaker than people think." He gestured at the nexus, the market, and the dungeon's entrance. "Ignoring all the flashy powers and the glowing eyes and the enchanted weapons... if someone takes a knife to my neck all I've built is gone. Just like that—" Ed snapped his fingers.

"That will never happen with me around!"

"I know," Ed said with a small grin. "But even then, someday we'll both get old, and then we'll die. And even if Lavy raises us as her undead servants, eventually the three of us will pass, anyway. It's life, and it happens to everyone," Ed said. "But I love the Haunt, and I'd do anything to have the certainty it will go on once I'm gone. The pacts and the Mantle magic will disappear when I do. That's why being just a Dungeon Lord is not enough. Really, the Mantle is nothing more than a disposable weapon of war for the Dark. I don't think the dungeons were ever meant to last. But men build families and kingdoms that outlast the most ancient dungeon and they do it without any magic—or at least, not the kind that's measured with experience points," Ed said. "I hope to harness a tiny bit of that magic one day. Lord Wraith may not be able to, but perhaps Ed of the Haunt may."

Klek sat in silence, his chin resting on his hands as he considered Ed's words. "So..." the batblin said. "You don't intend to leave us anytime soon?"

"Never," Ed said. "My dream is for the Haunt to keep the best parts of me, and that the worst parts are lost forever after I'm gone."

Very slowly, Klek nodded. Both man and batblin sat in silence for a long time, people-gazing.

After a while, Ed took out a small package from his pocket. "You know what?" he told his friend. "I realized that I've barely played any games at all since I arrived in Ivalis. Sure, I've had fun, but almost always the main purpose was to enhance my dungeon. I rarely play for the sake of playing anymore." He showed Klek the package—it was a deck of cards. "I had these made the way we play them on Earth. Would you like for me to teach you a couple of the games I played on my home world?"

The batblin's ears perked up. "Yes," he said. "I'd like that very much."

ALFRED THE SLY, the newly appointed Grand Master of Undercity's Thieves Guild, wearily climbed the steps of the Charcoal Tower while wondering to himself about the speed at which life could change without warning.

To start with, he'd never in his life expected to wear the Grand Master's overcoat—and he certainly hadn't expected to find himself stepping on the black and white floorboards of the former headquarters of the Assassins Guild.

A couple months after the Battle for Undercity, Alfred's wounds still hurt despite the Healers' best attempts at easing his many aches. He didn't complain—not aloud, at least. The fact that he had stayed in the burning Guildhouse instead of running like most Thieves, facing many Heroes on his own and *winning*, had earned the admiration of his peers and contributed greatly to his new position.

Alfred had simply forgotten to mention how he'd only stayed because he was too terrified to run, and those Heroes he'd fought were low-level survivors trying to hide and heal in the basement where *he* had already been hiding. He'd killed them right as they were drinking their potions. Small details like that were best kept out of the Bardic annals.

Although that asshole Karmich kept giving him funny looks every time they passed each other in the corridors of the new Guildhouse.

The Guild Master rested against a wall to catch his breath. Outside the window, the city was at once the same as always and utterly unrecognizable. People headed out on their way to work, priests, sailors, Witch Doctors, whores, bakers, shoemakers, ranchers, farmers, builders, dishonest merchants and hard-working Thieves, and so on and on. Some walked past the rubble of buildings that the drones hadn't yet gotten through to clearing, and others intentionally avoided the streets where they'd lost friends or family members.

New taverns sprouted up where others had burned down, and a new clientele heeded the call of the ale—fresh faces that would in time become known as "the same old regulars."

In the ports, the merchant ships had run away and never returned—the Heiligian Navy blocked all routes to Undercity. Instead of an empty harbor, though, the black flags of pirates and smugglers grew tall like a forest of sails swaying gently with the salty breeze.

Ask Barkeep Max, and he'd regale you with rumors of a Pirate Queen that had risen from the hidden islands of the East, claiming to have the blood of the royal family coursing through her veins and challenging the rule of both Dungeon Lord and Heiligians alike.

If you asked the newly risen Bandit King under the Galtian mountains he'd laugh in your face, telling you the Pirate Queen has as much royal blood in her veins as his horse. *He* was the true secret heir to the Starevosi throne. Then he'd rob you naked and beat you to a bloody pulp.

The coasts of Starevos brimmed with pirates and bandits like a disease sensing weakness in the defenses of the Militant Church's occupation. All over Starevos, rebellions brewed and flared as tales of a city surrounded by untamed dungeons reached and emboldened the ears of men and women that recalled the times when their country had been free.

Inquisitors marched all across the countryside, trying to halt the spread of the dungeons and their Jamming Towers. And in Heiliges, the Militant armies gathered...

Free. It was such a strange concept to Alfred. The sky was the same color as always—the people were the same. But a keen eye could pinpoint many differences in the way normal life was conducted. Necromancers walked freely down the streets, their reanimated skeletons carrying their scrolls around. Cults that had spent their lives hidden in the sewers or the catacombs now erected temples to their tentacled gods right next to altars to Oynnes and Hogbus. There was word of a vampire that hunted slavers. Batblins and kaftar patrolled the avenues, proudly wearing the colors of the Haunt.

And at night, if you paid attention, perhaps you could hear the bloodcurdling bawk of a hell chicken that had so far managed to avoid capture by the Monster Hunters.

It was the dawn of a new city, and it was also just another day. Life would never be the same, yet life went on, same as always.

Alfred sighed and hurried up the last set of stairs. The reason he was in such a pensive mood was because he was trying to distract himself from the statues that lined the halls of the Charcoal Tower—they had taught him far more about horned spider sexuality than he had had any desire to ever know.

He arrived at the doors of the palatial seat where the Dungeon Lord held court. This was not *the* Seat of Undercity, of course. The real one was said to lie under the undead-infested catacombs, surrounded by dangers and secrets that the Dungeon Lord and his minions and only just begun to crack.

The kaftar guards opened the doors for Alfred, and he stepped into a chamber just a floor below the Jamming Device. There was a magical circle drawn in silver lines across the floor, and the air was charged with anti-scrying spells and other enchantments. A richly carved table large enough for a feast filled the center of the room, with a curtain of water flowing down the wall behind the Dungeon Lord's chair opposite the entrance and disappearing inside a delicate model of Undercity itself, a small part of the fountain water becoming the city's canal.

"Grand Master Alfred," the Dungeon Lord greeted him cordially. "We were waiting for your arrival." He gave a wide, sweeping gesture to include the men and women sitting at the table with him.

There was a certain regal arrogance to the way Lord Edward Wright conducted himself, the kind present in men who had faced certain death and impossible odds and come up victorious. He was lean and spry with all the strength of youth still in his body, but his visage was grim and distant in a way that conveyed a degree of truth to certain rumors about his capacity to observe everything and everyone in his city at any time. His pupils shone with faint circles of eldritch green light—his Evil Eye deactivated less and less as time went by, and now it was rarely completely off. His black hair fell over the fur of his ebony cloak, and he wore a fitted crimson vest over a light, silky gray gambeson that was said to be made out of spiderweb. The silver rings on his charred black hand clinked together as he rapped distractedly on the table.

Much was said in Undercity about the mysterious man that had expelled the Inquisition and—depending on who you asked —either saved the city or condemned it in the first place. Rumors were, the insects and tiny critters of the city spoke directly to him, whispering unearthed secrets and naming those who opposed his rule. He could change bodies like a noble-woman changed gowns, and could walk through walls and make the livestock of his enemies fall ill with warts at the point of a finger. It was said that at midnight, the top of the Charcoal Tower would glow blood red as the Dungeon Lord held court with demons from the Netherworld and djinns from Plekth, and that if you listened carefully, you could hear the mad laughter of his Witches as they conducted seance in the catacombs of the city.

As a Thief, Alfred knew better than to heed most rumors. If he thought about it, Lord Wright looked... like he could use some sleep.

"My apologies for the delay," Alfred said. "A hell chicken snuck into the new Guildhouse last night and ate all our salted meat reserves. We managed to put it down, but it was... difficult." The Thief shuddered at the memory.

Lord Wright frowned. "Chief Kaga insists his Monster Hunters found all their nests already. I have no idea how they keep popping up."

"I swear the damn creatures are getting smarter and craftier the more we hunt them," said Grand Master Balgid of the Mercers Guild. "At least they don't know how to work door handles... yet."

Alfred took a look around the table. Everyone who was someone in Undercity had attended tonight's summons. Next to Wright were his most of his closest minions, except for the Marshal, who was rumored to be off on a diplomatic mission to a distant land. Around Alfred were the leaders or elected representatives of most of the city's associations, noble families, banks, guilds, trading companies, and leagues: the Mercers, the Brewers, the smugglers, even the pirates, the Watch, the church of Oynnes and the cult of Xethron the Many-Tentacled, the Necromancers, and a couple more. The Akathunian Assassins, though, were missing. They hadn't shown their faces much since they'd tried to increase their standing with the Dungeon Lord by gifting him a cadre of batblin slaves. Wright apparently favored humans slaves, however, because he'd reacted by feeding the Akathunian slavers to his pet vampire. In any case, Alfred had avoided offering lavish gifts to the Dungeon Lord until he became more certain of his preferences.

Grand Master Brewer, a man with a red, button-like nose, coughed politely. "Your Execrableness, every man of decency is here, as well as our less... savory guests." Brewer gave Alfred a nasty sideways glance. "Perhaps you may now shed some light on the reason behind our meeting. Why are we here?"

Most of the merchants and noble houses weren't friends with the Thieves Guild, for rather self-explanatory reasons. Except the Mercers, of course. Alfred had *once* bought a cashmere jacket from them. *Once.* To this day, he still wondered who the real professional Thieves were. "It certainly can't be because of your charming personality," Alfred told the Brewer. "When was the last time you took a bath, Hynek?"

Hynek's nose reddened a bit more, and he gestured as if to stand.

"Gentlemen," Lord Wright said, raising his voice just enough to be heard past the scraping of the chair. "Behave. Don't make me use the trapdoor."

A few laughed. Grand Master Hynek seemed dubious for a second, as if he was considering calling the bluff. Then he sat back down and ignored Alfred.

Wright nodded. "Good." Chronicler Alder handed him a long scroll that seemed decades old. "I summoned you here to talk about the future. But also to hear your answer about the offer I made you a week ago. That should have been more than enough time for you to read the Terms and Conditions of minionship. I'm sure you have found that they're quite reasonable."

Father Philip, the leader of the cult of the Many-Tentacled, shook a slithery appendage in Ed's direction. "What's not reasonable is the amount of pages in those terms, Lord Wright. My church lacks the funds to hire a clerk to make sense of them for us."

Alfred could see that most of the people around the table

seemed suddenly uncomfortable. Accepting minionship to a Dungeon Lord was a greater commitment than, say, paying taxes and tribute to a Heiligian conqueror. The Thief suspected that more than a few nobles and well-to-do merchants would've liked nothing more than to tell Wright to take his Terms and stuff them.

Of course, they couldn't insult the Dungeon Lord whose Jamming Towers protected Undercity and its surroundings from the Militant Church. Alfred wasn't a Diviner, but he was sure many of his peers were wondering just how true the rumors were regarding Lord Wright's overwatch of the city. The fact that some people at that very table hadn't yet tried to depose the Dungeon Lord spoke volumes about their unwillingness to meet in secret to conspire against him.

And there was also the vampire to consider. No one wanted to end up like the Akathunians, hunted like rats in their own city, wondering if the movement in the corner was a cockroach, or actually Wright's spy.

"Your Terms are most charitable, your Badness," Grand Master Brewer said, putting all his Charm ranks to use. "But given the... volatile situation of the city, I'm sure you understand we need more time before jumping to such an important—"

"Eighteen months," Wright said, speaking over him.

The Brewer began stammering, then shut up for a second. "Beg your pardon?" he managed, visibly confused.

"That's the window of time Heiliges needs to gather its armies and send them here to reinforce the Navy," the Dungeon Lord said calmly. "In other words, in eighteen months' time, Starevos will suffer a second invasion."

Whispers spread through the table. "A year and a half? That's impossible!" a nobleman exclaimed. His name was Theodor. His father had fought against Heiliges during the war, which gave Theodor great standing among his noble peers—as long as no Inquisitors were nearby. "Heiliges has relied on Heroes to do its dirty work for a generation—it can't just summon a new invading army out of thin air! They need to train their infantry, gather the commoners, forge weapons and armor, gather provisions, and deal with their noblemen... we're talking *three* years at least!"

Chronicler Alder raised a hand. "People! Our best Diviners and tacticians both confirmed it. When an entire country hates your guts and wants to travel half the world for a chance to kill you, they'll *make it happen.*"

Alfred turned to the Necromancer seated next to him. "I hear Plekth has a rather nice weather. And their new Adventurers Guild is hiring. Maybe it's time for a change of locale, eh? See the world?"

"Most adventurers aren't on friendly terms with Necromancers," the pale man said.

"Well, I can put in a good word for you," Alfred said with a wink.

Around them, people were losing their nerve. Alfred understood why. They were like rats in a bucket that was slowly filling with water. They couldn't abandon the city—the Inquisition still controlled the rest of Starevos, and the sea was under the dominion of the Heiligian Navy. That left only the Wetlands to the south, but that was as sure a death for a merchant.

"Can you stop them?" someone asked the Dungeon Lord. Alfred caught a glimpse of a smile dance across Wright's face.

Lavina, Head Witch of the Haunt, laughed in the face of the woman that had asked the question. "First you try to wriggle out of minionship and now you're asking us to save you? *Again?*"

"But you must!" someone else exclaimed.

Wright stood up, spreading the scroll he had been holding along the table. It was a map of Starevos. Alfred and the others stood as well, as to take a better look. The most important cities were marked on the map—Galtia, Basilia, Salda, Caranus, Mitena, Constantina, Raventa—along with trading routes, forts, rivers, mines, roads, mountain ranges, lakes, and so on. It was the sort of map a General may use to plan a campaign. "And I will," the Dungeon Lord said. "But the Haunt can't do it on its own."

He placed a finger over Constantina—it was the south-most holding of Starevos, which was how it originally got its nickname of Undercity—and traced a path to the northeast, past Raventa and Mitena and then farther beyond Galtia's mountaintops until stopping at the capital itself.

"As we speak, the Militant Church is leading a campaign based in Galtia to retake the lost territories around our city," Lord Wright said. "The Haunt's Towers deny access to their Heroes, so they must rely on Inquisitors and their Militant soldiers to destroy the Towers and allow the Heroes to move in. Meanwhile, we protect the Towers by creating dungeons around them, manned with mercenaries from the Netherworld hired with the taxes that the fine people in this room kindly share with us." He spoke smoothly, as if he'd rehearsed this meeting beforehand. Chronicler Alder seemed proud of himself, judging from the way he relaxed in his seat. "Day by day, the Militant Church summons more forces and high-level Inquisitors into Galtia. We've managed to keep the advantage by connecting every dungeon to our railway network, so we can move our forces back if they face unsurmountable odds. Nothing in our arsenal, though, is going to be enough once the Militant army arrives. An invading force meant to challenge a kingdom will crush a city's worth of resources like it was nothing." He stared at the grim visages in the room.

"*Unless*," Witch Lavina pointed out.

"Unless," Lord Wright agreed, "we welcome them with an army of our own, and a kingdom's resources at our back." He tapped on Galtia's position in the map. "The Militant Church is not attacking our dungeons in order to retake Undercity. That's what the army is meant for. The Inquisitors scouring the country-side are trying to keep the Haunt from spreading throughout the whole country. Well, sadly for them, that's exactly what I intend to do. Starevos has suffered under Heiligian rule for long enough, I say. With our combined might, we'll make a stand against the Heiligian host. We'll *break* them so they learn to never bother us again."

Silence spread through the room as, outside, Camcanna and its sister Ullira replaced the warm sunlight with their silvery blue glow.

"That's a mighty speech," Alfred said cheerfully. "Don't take this the wrong way, Lord Wright, but don't you need an army of your own to take a city? Some of our brethren are doing quite well under Heiligian occupation. They're sure to be rather... reticent to see the nobleness of your plan. They may need the kind of persuasion that a few thousand horned spiders and a kaftar clan won't be enough to deliver."

Wright nodded. "Thank you, Master Alfred. You're right. That's the reason why I desire all of you to accept my offer of minionship. In the Netherworld lies an abandoned facility that's capable of creating monsters, weapons, and spells for entire hosts of Dungeon Lords," he said. "This colossal complex, built during the old days, before Bastavar and Everbleed, has the resources to raise an army of monsters for me to face the Inquisition." An eldritch glint shone the pupils of his Evil Eye. "In the upcoming months, I'll enter a contest against the other Dungeon Lords for possession of this facility. I intend to win this Endeavor, but in the meantime, I must leave Undercity in your hands. The only way I can trust you to protect this city without you betraying me and one another is if you join the ranks of the Haunt as my minions."

"So it's real," Alfred whispered to himself, barely listening to the last part of the Dungeon Lord's words. "Saint Claire and Tillman. The Factory of Nightmares. I thought it was only a legend to entertain children before bed." He had been one such child, a long time ago.

And this man here, not a gray hair in his head, talked about becoming the owner of such a legendary place as if it was already a done deed.

Just what have we stumbled into? the Thief thought.

At an unseen signal from Wright or his seconds-in-command, the doors opened and two rows of drones marched into the room, each of them carrying a stack of papers. They set a stack in front of every representative, and then headed back out again. One of them looked over its shoulder at Alfred and raised its tunic— mooning the Grand Master right before leaving.

Alfred recognized the first page of the stack in front of him. It was a copy of Wright's Terms and Conditions. There was a small needle right next to the black line where the signature went. Carefully, the Thief held the pin between his thumbs.

The pirates' representative stood up, his gray whiskers trembling with indignation. "We knew this would happen! Your ambitions know no limit, Dungeon Lord. You intend to become a King, but you have no claim! Only the Pirate Queen is the true heir to the throne of Starevos, and she shall not abide by this!"

Lord Wright gave no sign of noticing—or being worried about —the way the pirate's hand rested on his sword handle. "I'd like for your Queen to be my ally in this fight. We all have the same enemy. Let's worry about royalty titles later. They're rather overvalued."

"Will you have me killed after I leave this room?" the pirate asked.

"Of course not. You're here in this city as my guest," Wright said.

As the pirate representative marched out, Chronicler Alder called after him, "The Queen hasn't answered my sonnets, by the way! Would you mind telling her to check her letters once in a while?" The blond sighed after the pirate was out of view. "Pirates, I swear. They've no manners. She'll come around, though. You'll see."

"*Alder*," Lavina whispered, elbowing him in the ribs. "Not now!"

Only Alfred noticed the exchange, however, because the others were too busy commiserating with each other. The Thief didn't need to listen in to know what they were talking about. The odds they had of profiting from accepting the pact, the risks, the pirate's importance for Undercity, Wright's own chances at surviving the Endeavor... in short, boring stuff. Alfred had made his decision long before arriving at the tower.

He made eye contact with the Dungeon Lord and with careful, deliberate motions, the Thief pinched his thumb with the needle until a drop of blood came out. He pressed his thumb against the contract, leaving a red fingerprint above the black line. Then he slid the stack of papers toward Lord Wright. "They *are* quite reasonable conditions," Alfred said.

Wright grinned happily. "Ah, so you read them?" he asked.

Alfred winced. "Well... there's a lot of pages," he said, watching as Wright's grin lost its luster. "I did skim them, though. In any case, we are already pretty much de facto allies with the Haunt, so we may as well make it official." And then he raised his voice to make sure the rest of the table would hear this part, "Also, the way I see it, we've really nothing to lose. If you manage to free Starevos, we're left in a much better spot than we're today. After all, we become a Guild backed directly by our new ruler. On the other hand if you get killed trying... then the pact is broken and we're back to square one."

"Thank you for being so reasonable, Grand Master," Wright said.

After Alfred, the Necromancer was next to accept the pact. It was a great show of faith because the Necromancer's terms greatly limited the sources of the bodies they could harvest to create their undead. "I figure there'll be more than enough corpses to get around anyway," was all the Necromancer said as he handed over the papers.

The Mercers, the church of Oynnes, and the cult of the Many-Tentacled followed.

Hours later, only the most respectable merchants and the nobility still had their doubts. "The pirate was right, you know," Theodore told the Dungeon Lord. "A Dungeon Lord as King? The idea is preposterous! Your kind is famous for hiding underground, raiding villages, and sacrificing innocents to your demonic masters. There's no way the people of Starevos will ever accept you. And without a claim? Impossible!"

Wright smiled, apparently impervious to Theodore's words. "Impossible, like the captured Hero the Haunt is studying right as we speak? Or impossible like expelling the Inquisition from a captured city and forcing their Heroes to stay away from us? Because people said both of those things were impossible, and yet here we are."

"Both achieved at a great cost of life, which, as I've heard, almost included yours," Theodore said heatedly. "To unite Starevos, you'll need the support of the commoners and the noble-born. The small folk will fear you, and the nobility will never accept you—there's no precedent for a Dungeon Lord's ascension—"

At this moment, all the candles in the room were snuffed, and a chill traveled across the backs of all presents. Alfred had been around enough to know what this meant—the Dungeon Lord's pet vampire had arrived. Around him, people reached for their silver amulets and their divine symbols. Theodore drew an elegant dagger infused with blessed silver. Mist poured from a window and coalesced into the laughing shape of a girl of about eleven years of age. She'd grown since the last time Alfred had seen her, if such a feat was possible for the undead.

"Precedent!" Jarlen snarled, advancing slowly toward Theodore with elegant movements like those of a cat stalking her prey. A veil covered her face to spare Lord Wright's guest the sight of her dead features. "How adorable. I was alive when the men you call ancestors were crying for their mothers and soiling their diapers. That's your precedent, mortal. Those who came before *me*, though... ah, they spoke of an age where what Lord Wraith proposes was the rule and not the exception. A time when the ancient Lords stood as kings among vast lands and whose armies of minions brought ruin and devastation to their enemies as rivers of blood drowned entire cities!" The Nightshade now turned to face the entire congregation, her voice rising in a terrible crescendo until it was as the wail of a banshee. "Have you heard the news the wind brings from distant places? The engines of war turn once more, and the ancient traditions are once again venerated! Forgotten evils stir in their tombs, the stars align across the vast night, and the portents speak of blood and fire, yet you dare attend this portentous meeting and speak to me about precedent?" She turned suddenly and swatted Theodore's dagger away. "Tell me, mortal, when the army that doomed your father marches upon your country once again, who would you rather have fighting by your side when it's time to protect your woman and your children? The men and women who faltered and ran when the Inquisition came knocking?" She pointed at the people huddled behind Theodore. "Or would you rather have *us*—the meanest, cruelest, most abominable creatures this side of the Netherworld?"

The shaking Theodore held the gaze of the vampire, and then he stumbled away. Jarlen hissed and walked past the congregation until she stood behind Lord Wraith. And in the end, despite the terror the vampire inspired in the living, most gazes fell on the Dungeon Lord himself. After all, he was the one who such creatures answered to. And Alfred found that, in the heavy darkness that had fallen upon the room, the only light visible was the otherworldly fire of the Dungeon Lord's eyes, giving his face the appearance of a ghostly skull, an image enhanced by the black skeletal hand that caressed his chin in a careless gesture.

Perhaps, thought Grand Master Alfred, *some rumors* are *indeed true.*

Theodore stood, his mustache trembling with unbridled rage. He marched as to leave the room, then stopped halfway, balled his hands into fists, and went back to the stack of papers in front of his seat. Dungeon Lord Wright watched as, all across the table, others did the same.

By the end of the night, Undercity was his.

EPILOGUE

Grand Master Gezved slid like a shadow across the dusty corridors of the Akathunian safehouse, his ears still ringing with the loss reports his men sent him all across the city. The slave dens had been raided by kaftar and those spider-and-batblin abominations, hunting Akathunians like a princeling chases after game. If that wasn't enough humiliation, the vampire kept killing his warriors, and the Netherworldly Diviners blocked his Guild's attempts at requesting help from the motherland.

Now that he was away from the prying eyes of his men— always on the lookout for signs of weakness—he allowed himself to rest his back against a wall and massage his temples.

Not long ago, the Assassins Guild would have simply killed Lord Wright for the trouble he brought. But that had been before the Heroes' rampage through the Charcoal Tower that had culled Gezved's forces. It was as if the Guild had suffered a terrible wound that night, and Wright's minions kept picking at the scab, forcing it to remain open and fester.

The Akathunian was of the mind that Wright had orchestrated the whole thing. The attack on the Charcoal Tower, the Heroic rampage, then Wright's convenient Tower popping out in the Akathunians' headquarters. Even his sudden alliance with two Heroes—if you believed the rumors—could be explained by an elaborate ruse that had been set up to destroy the Assassins Guild in one fell swoop.

But why? Had it been jealousy? Perhaps Lord Wright simply didn't like the competition. Perhaps he had some darker designs in mind.

Whatever the answer, he had to be stopped.

Gezved was not used to being hunted. Hiding like a common animal diminished him. His proud heritage demanded retribution.

Something inside his study clanked. The old Assassin clutched at the silver stake hanging by his neck, then relaxed his shoulders.

"Very well," he told the shadow sitting comfortably on the windowsill between the fluttering drapes. "Let us talk, Malikar."

The Lotian smiled. "I'm glad you've finally seen reason, Grand Master. Such a shame that it took the near-complete annihilation of your Guild."

"You and your master," Gezved said wearily, feeling like he was forging a pact not unlike the one Wright offered his minions, albeit without any of the benefits, "what do you want from us?"

"At last!" the Lotian exclaimed. "The right question. Was that so hard?" He raised his hands as he dropped down to the floor and strolled toward the Akathunian. "Peace, Master Gezved. We want peace. And all we ask from you in exchange..." the Lotian caressed Gezved's cheek with one cold hand half-closed, and the Akathunian saw the skin of the Lotian's face crawl as if a lurking creature stirred underneath, "...is your complete obedience."

Gezved stepped away from the man, cold fear spreading through his limbs. The Lotian laughed, and opened his hand to reveal a small, brown, worm-like creature wriggling on his palm.

· · ·

IN SOME DEEP, dark chamber at the heart of the Citadel, three figures straight out of the Bardic annals had one of their secret reunions. There were few among the Netherworld that possessed such knowledge of past, current, and future events as the three of them put together. They, who had once been active participants of history in the making, were now but lurking observers, watching from afar, and waiting—perhaps—for the day when they might rise once again.

Regent Korghiran, the Lady of Secrets, loved her little cabals. Today, though, she barely participated in the intrigues of the other two—most of her attention belonged to the Shadow Tarot whose cards were spread across the table in front of her with seemingly no rhyme nor reason. Her expression was and troubled.

Dungeon Lady Golsa, on the other hand, was ever the merrier. Her mood always seemed to brighten when the Endeavor approached—it was as if the prospect of Dungeon Lord blood being spilled enticed her. "Ah, my dear Regent, you oughtn't waste your time on daydreams. In truth, the Tarot has spoiled you. It barely shows anything of notice lately, only those boring black screens."

"Perhaps you're right, beloved," Korghiran said. Few would dare speak to the Regent with such familiarity as Golsa. Then again, none among Korghiran's mortals had lived in her domains as long as Golsa had. In truth, she'd come to see the geriatric Dungeon Lady as a sort of pet—like those small dogs yipping as they ran around the skirts of mortal Queens. "Although Lord Everbleed is as distracted with my little pastime as I am."

The two turned to the gigantic mass of muscle, horns, and black armor that was the third member of their cabal. Tonight, Archlord Everbleed inhabited the body of the Higher Devil Knight—the faithful servant of the Archlords, a creature so powerful it could snap a minotaur in two with a flick of its wrist.

Everbleed's real body wasn't as impressive, though. Many

years ago, his minions had brought him to his dungeon Seat—broken and barely clinging to life. There, his body had fused with the Seat, casting aside mortal needs such as hunger or sleep, and becoming a red jewel as eternal as the mountains, so long as no one destroyed it. Such creature was called a Dungeon Jewel, and it was one of the paths to immortality that powerful Dungeon Lords could aspire to.

"Forgive me, Lady Golsa," the Knight spoke with a booming voice, his eyes shining with a mystical black fire. "I am but an old man, with many fears and tribulations. If you will, distract me for a while." With a single fingernail, he sifted through some Tarot cards. "Tell me, what do you think of this year Endeavor's attendance?"

Korghiran smiled. Everbleed had brought up Golsa's favorite matter to get her to lay off their back. Now Golsa could speak at her heart's desire, and they could try to make sense of the mess that the Tarot showed. Korghiran had had her suspicions for a long time—as did Everbleed. None of them were good. Tonight they'd be forced to voice them. A perspective that neither looked forward to.

"Most excellent, Lord Alaric," Golsa said, clapping her hands. "So many powerful contenders! It makes me hopeful for the future of the Lordship. People from whom I hadn't heard in years are coming out of their hiding places to measure themselves against newly invested Dungeon Lords with luck and youthful passion on their side. Can you imagine the bloodbath? Ah, so exciting!" She gave a toothless grin. "Lady Vaines will win, of course. But I wonder if the rumors are true and the Boatman will bring his own Summoned Dungeon Lord to represent him."

Korghiran found one particularly worrisome card and handed it to Everbleed without a word. Like many cards, it showed that black screen so prevalent of late, but unlike most, this showed a possible future where the owner *won*. Everbleed met her gaze. The Devil Knight's visage lacked the facial flexibility to display

most emotions that weren't murderous anger or angry murderousness, but Korghiran knew the Archlord well enough to realize
he was as worried as she.

"Baseless rumors," the Regent told Golsa distractedly. "My
brother has no business in the Netherworld. His role is to serve
Murmur's will across the planes." Besides, the only Summoned
Dungeon Lord that Korghiran knew about was Wright, and he
was *hers*.

"Maybe," Golsa said. "Maybe not. In any case, that dreadful
Berserker shall be a huge annoyance, but Vaines has more combat
experience than anyone else. She takes the win, that's my
prediction."

"What about one of those young Lords?" asked Everbleed.
"Maybe the one whose Towers are giving the Heiligians such
trouble. Everyone in the Citadel is talking about *that*."

Golsa waved dismissively. "It was bound to happen that
someone would come up with a way to counter the Heroes. The
Wraith lacks the expertise, the allies, and the power to hold on to
his invention. Someone else shall come soon and take it from
him... or the Inquisition will figure out a way to bypass the
Towers and then they'll break him."

"If I didn't know you so well, beloved, I'd think you're a bit
jealous that some young upstart won where you failed," Korghiran
pointed out.

"Bah!" Golsa shook her head. "Not at all. Each generation has
its own challenges to overcome. I *won* mine, dear Regent. The first
iteration of Heroes were broken by my hands, and as long as my
rule lasted, it was great. My time passed as is the way of mortals.
The new Heroes are someone else's challenge, and that's alright
with me," she said in a tone that indicated she wasn't *entirely*
alright.

Korghiran had to smile. Sometimes, Golsa could be more than
she let on.

"You know," Golsa went on. "I once had such a strange dream.

In it, a man from another world had built the Heroes himself, instead of the Inquisition randomly coming up with them like it happened in the real world. This Summoned Hero and I were terrible enemies, and we faced each other in uncountable battles, his creations against my minions, and in this lethal rivalry, we were both extolled by the other's hatred. Facing him, in my dream, I was forced to be my best self. Terrible and brilliant as I've never been before or since. And there was this unspoken understanding between the two of us, that when the day of our final confrontation came, we'd be joined—in a way—when the loser's experience points were absorbed by the winner, and then our opposed ideals would finally find a common ground." The old woman bit her lip and shook her head, prey of a sudden, deep nostalgia. "But that fated confrontation never came. The man vanished before the dream was over. It was as if, since then, I am but a shadow of what I could have been. Not long after having that dream, the new iteration of Heroes replaced the old, and the rest is history. Sounds silly, doesn't it? It was only just a fantasy..." Golsa trailed off, her gaze distant. For some unfathomable reason, she was crying. Maybe she had finally gone senile.

The Lady of Secrets turned to the Dungeon Lady. The silly daydreams of the old crone had gotten the Demon's attention. *A man only remembered in a dream.*

When Objectivity erased a person from history, it wasn't a complete erasure—otherwise no one would know it had happened at all in the first place. One of the places where Objectivity's interference could be revealed was in the Shadow Tarot. Another was in the dreams of those closest to the erased. And none were as close to a man of destiny as its forsworn enemy...

Could it be?

"Korghiran," Everbleed called, breaking her out of her revelry. The Lady of Secrets dismissed her train of thought as a silly idea. Why, Golsa the Gossip, this old pet of hers, a Summoned Hero's nemesis? The idea was contemptible. Sometimes dreams were only dreams. "Can the Shadow Tarot show the possible futures of a dead man?"

For an instant, Korghiran thought Everbleed meant the person in Golsa's dream. Then she realized he was handing out the card back to her. "Never," she said. "The dead have no future."

"And yet the owner of that card has been dead for decades," Everbleed said quietly.

Like that, Everbleed and Korghiran faced the truth neither wanted to confront. "What does that tell us?" she asked the Archlord.

"Wait a second," said Golsa, blinking and becoming good, old Gossip Golsa again. "A dead man's future? Who are you talking about?"

Both ignored her. "I did not want to believe it," Everbleed admitted. "But it's harder every day to keep ignoring the facts. My men have found evidence—nothing more than suspicions and conjectures, really—of a hidden hand guiding mortal affairs toward chaos and war to an unknown purpose. Something that goes beyond the means of a normal Dungeon Lord—in fact, it's said that Dungeon Lords are being as manipulated as kings and generals alike."

"I have found the same," Korghiran told him. "It has *his* mark all over it."

Korghiran gazed at the black expanse displayed in the card. For an instant, she'd thought the darkness had *crawled*. As if the black screen wasn't a malfunction of the Tarot at all, but a real possible future where the world was consumed by untold millions of crawling, hungering creatures, bloating the sky, devouring all life.

A heavy silence fell across the chamber. Korghiran thought it fitting. If it was the time for the old traditions to return, it was also the time for the ancient monsters to walk the earth once more.

"It's time to consider the nightmare scenario. That he fooled us

since the beginning," Everbleed said. "That somehow, somewhere… Dungeon Lord Sephar is alive."

EDWARD WRIGHT

S **pecies:** Human
  Total Exp: 750
  Unused Exp: 245
  Claims: Lordship, Undercity's Ruler.

ATTRIBUTES
  Brawn: 13
  Agility: 11
  Endurance: 14
  Mind: 13
  Spirit: 16 (+1 Dungeon Lord mantle)=17
  Charm: 13 (+1 Dungeon Lord mantle)=14

SKILLS

ATHLETICS: Basic (IX) - The owner has trained his body to perform continuous physical activity without penalties to their Endurance. For a while.

-Basic ranks allows them to realize mild energy-consuming tasks (non-combat) such as running or swimming without tiring. Unlocks stamina related talents.

MELEE: Basic (IX) - Measures the user's progress in physical combat. It opens up melee-related talents as well as advanced martial skill specializations.

DUNGEON ENGINEERING: Improved (IX) - This skill represents the user's knowledge of magical constructs pertaining to dungeon-craft. As it improves, it opens new rooms and traps, as well as adds to the Dungeon Lord Mantle capacity of storing the user's own blueprints.

COMBAT CASTING: Basic (VIII) - Pertains to the speed and efficiency of spells casted during combat or life-threatening situations.

-Basic status allows the caster to use spells every 20 seconds - 1 second per extra rank. The caster must say their names aloud and perform the appropriate hand gestures.

LEADERSHIP: Improved (VI) - Reflects the owner's capacity of inspiring and managing his troops and minions. For a Dungeon Lord, improving this skill adds to the bonus he and his minions receive.

Talents

EVIL EYE - ALLOWS THE DUNGEON LORD TO see the Objectivity of any creature or item. If the target of his gaze possesses a strong Spirit (or related Attribute or Skill) they may hide their information if the Lord's own Spirit is not strong enough.

- *Veil Piercing Evil Eye* - The Dungeon Lord's Evil Eye is upgraded with a constant effect. The Evil Eye can now detect invisibility and similar forms of concealment and has an advantage at piercing illusions and magical misdirection. Veil Piercing cannot affect Legendary-ranked magic or higher.

ENERGY DRAIN: Active. Very Low.

DUNGEON LORD MANTLE - The mantle is the heart of the Dungeon Lord and represents the dark pact made in exchange for power.

-It allows the Dungeon Lord access to the Dungeon Lord status and powers, as defined by the Dungeon Screen.

-It allows the Dungeon Lord to create and control dungeons, as per the limitations of his Dungeon Screen.

ENERGY DRAIN: None.

IMPROVED Reflexes - Allows the owner to experience increased reaction time for a small burst of time.

-Basic status elevates his reaction speed to a degree dictated by the owner's Agility, for a duration of 3 seconds per use.

. . .

IMPROVED METABOLISM - REDUCES the energy costs of all talents by 25% - the caloric requirements of the user are increased by the same amount.

ENERGY DRAIN: Activated. High.

RESIST SICKNESS: Basic - Allows it's owner to resist disease and sickness.

-Basic status allows the owner to resist non-magical sickness as if they had Endurance of 15 and were in optimal conditions (clean, well-fed, rested).

SPELLCASTING: Basic (IV) - Domains: general. Forbidden: Healing - Represents the owner's magical ability.

-Basic status allows the caster to use and learn all basic related spells of their domain. Extra ranks improve each individual spell's characteristics, such as range or damage.

-Efficient status grants the owner 1 extra basic spell.

-Allowed spells: 1 basic per day + 1 basic spell due to Dungeon Lordship

ENERGY DRAIN: Active. Varies per Spell.

ANCIENT LORD AURA - The owner creates an aura around him that enhances allied beings inside its area of effect. Affected beings can use the Dungeon Lord's Spirit as their own while this aura is active. Their physical attributes are also bolstered +1 while this aura is active. If the creature is a minion of the Dungeon Lord, they are immune to fear while affected by this aura.

Duration: 1 minute.

Energy Drain: Activated. Moderate.

Pledge of Armor - Any armor that the Dungeon Lord wears is considered magical, as if it had a minor *protection* enchantment. This bonus stacks with any *protection* enchantment the armor may have, or any other similar defensive enchantment. Magical armor can deflect spells of similar power-category, as well as normal weaponry.

Restriction: Selecting this talent locks out the Pledge of Bloodshed advancement option.

- *Pledge of Muted Armor* - The Dungeon Lord's Pledge of Armor is upgraded with new effects. Upon falling unconscious or being otherwise impaired, a team of four rescue drones is generated around his person. The rescue drones will stop at nothing to drag the Dungeon Lord to the nearest safe place, but they lack defensive capabilities. In addition, the Dungeon Lord can hide his armor's magical output at no extra energy cost.

Energy Drain: Passive.

Spell List

Minor Order - Command. The caster forces a target creature to follow a simple order, as long as said order is not immediately against the creature's moral code or presents a threat to its life.

· · ·

Eldritch Edge - ENCHANTMENT. The caster adds a magical flame to the edge of a weapon. This flame makes the weapon magical for the duration, allowing it to bypass weak magical defenses and mundane ones.

Duration: 1 minute per Spellcraft rank.

Murmur's Reach - COMMAND (Mantle) - The caster possesses a minion located in the same dungeon as the caster. The caster's body is left defenseless during this time.

Duration: Ten minutes per Spellcraft rank.

Dungeon's Message — Divination — This spell allows you to send a 140—character message to any minion of the caster located anywhere on the same plane as the casting Dungeon Lord. The message is sent through the link between minion and Dungeon Lord, and as such, cannot be replicated by others. (Warning: this does not stop a minion with a very low Mind score from being tricked by non-magical means.)

Stone Pillar - The Dungeon Lord targets an area of solid ground of 5 feet radius which, after 3 seconds, bursts upwards in the shape of a stone column, rising to 20 feet or until it reaches a ceiling. This effect is limited by the availability of material in the chosen area and cannot be used to create matter out of nothing.

If the Dungeon Lord has an Improved Combat casting above 5, the channeling time is reduced to 2 seconds.

ACKNOWLEDGMENTS

If you're reading this, you've reached the end of Dungeon Lord: Abominable Creatures. Thank you for sticking with Ed and me for three entire books! The Dungeon Lord's adventure is far from over, though, and I hope we meet again in Dungeon Lord: Ancient Traditions, which should come out, hopefully, early in the first half of 2019. (If you're reading this in late 2019 and there is no Ancient Traditions anywhere in sight, feel free to hurry me along at hugohuesca.writer@gmail.com ! You can also join my Facebook group, Hugo Huesca, and leave a comment there.)

Writing this book was a special kind of challenge. It's the longest one I've ever written (so far) and the history of the tribulations I went through while writing it could make for their own tale. At one point, the *entire* manuscript was lost when my hard-drive got corrupted so hard it also—somehow—managed to delete all my cloud backups. Thankfully the data was recovered in its entirety by the heroic actions of a Lasershark's team, and I learned a valuable lesson in keeping off-site backups.

In the end, I'm glad to have faced the challenge of Abominable

Creatures, and I'm eager to begin the next chapter in Ed's adventure.

See you there!

—Hugo Huesca.

PD: Feel free to contact me at hugohuesca.writer@gmail.com or leave a comment in my Facebook group. That's where I usually post the updates regarding the next books' launch dates, but if you prefer email I you can join my newsletter.

Reading your words of encouragement means a lot to me and genuinely inspires me to do my best. More than a couple times I've managed to power through a particularly nasty bout of writer's block after reading a letter from a reader. In a way, this makes the Wraith Haunt's tale a group effort between us all. Let's see where our path leads us.

Edward Wright will return in Dungeon Lord IV: Ancient Traditions

ABOUT THE AUTHOR

If you want to find out about Dungeon Lord's next installments before anyone else, you can do so here:

www.subscribepage.com/dungeonlord

Printed in Great Britain
by Amazon